Harriet Hudson was born in Kent. After taking a degree in English literature, she was a director of a London publishing company and is now a freelance writer and editor. She is married to an American, and they live in a Kentish village on the North Downs. She is the author of four previous sagas, and also writes crime novels under her real name, Amy Myers.

Praise for Harriet Hudson's novels:

'Has captured all the beauty of nineteenth-century Kent but missed none of the gritty realities. Her heroine is impulsive, determined and hot-headed, and all the more likeable for her weaknesses'
Kent Evening Post

'Refreshing' *Woman's World*

'Very readable love story' *The Star*, Sheffield

The Girl from Gadsby's

Harriet Hudson

KNIGHT

First published in 1993
by HEADLINE BOOK PUBLISHING

First published in paperback 1994
by HEADLINE BOOK PUBLISHING

This edition published 2002 by
Knight an imprint of The Caxton Publishing Group

10 9 8 7 6 5 4 3 2 1

ISBN 1 84067 519 5

Typeset by
Letterpart Limited, Reigate, Surrey

Printed and bound in Great Britain by
Mackays of Chatham plc, Chatham, Kent

Caxton Publishing Group
20 Bloomsbury Street
London WC1B 3JH

ACKNOWLEDGEMENTS

I owe an enormous debt of gratitude to my mother, Grace Howlett, who was a 'girl' at a Regent Street fashion store in the 1920s and whose recollections have enabled me to create Gadsby's. I am also grateful to Peter Gent, Henry Green, Jean-Marie Quitard de Liocourt and my uncle, Len Hudson, and once again to my agent Dorothy Lumley and editor Jane Morpeth, who have gently and expertly guided the text to publication.

Chapter One

'Not even Queen Mary gets in 'ere, miss, not before a performance.' And especially not someone as humble as Nell Watkins, the doorman's voice seemed to suggest, goodnaturedly enough. There was no need for more. Alfred Hughes, ex-sergeant major, the Buffs, had spoken. The way to the inner mysteries of the Albion Theatre was inviolate to those who did not receive his blessing. He knew his job, and he knew that the cloche hat that had seen at least two seasons and the home-made costume with large hems, denoting that they had been turned up to meet the calls for ever-rising hemlines, were unlikely to figure in clothes worn by Miss Hargreaves' social circle. So that, Hughes assumed, was that.

But he had reckoned without Nell.

'She's going to see *me*,' she announced pugnaciously.

Hughes blinked, unwillingly impressed by the lively, determined brown eyes; even the bouncy unfashionable curls escaping from under the hat seemed to suggest that Nell was no ordinary star-struck lass. Nevertheless, 'Not even Queen Mary—' he began. Then, ''Ere, where d'yer think you're going?'

Nell had had enough. Taking advantage of the fact that the doorkeeper for all his majestic height and build was laying down his law from behind the window in his cubbyhole office, and that it would take him at least a few seconds to get into the corridor, she hurried straight past

1

him, breaking into a run. She had not the slightest idea where she would find the dressing room of Melissa Hargreaves, beautiful star of the London musical comedy stage and at present in the hit *London Lady*, but it should be simple enough, provided she eluded the retribution thundering after her.

''Ere! Come back 'ere!' he yelled furiously. A vain hope.

'I'm going to see her,' she hurled back, as she shot round a corner to the right.

'She won't see the likes of you!' Hughes panted round after her, by no means as fit as he had been on parade.

Nothing here, no dressing rooms, and he was gaining on her. Seeing a small staircase to the left, Nell ran up two steps at a time, hoping that her quick young legs would outstrip his. She was going to find Melissa Hargreaves and confront her, no matter what. Hughes made a grab at her jacket and missed, causing him to stumble then swear with all his old fluency.

At the top of the stairs Nell almost collided with a young man. Surprised to see Hughes who never normally left his post he stood stock still, causing the doorman to pull up momentarily.

'Miss Hargreaves?' Nell shouted at the young man. 'Where?'

Automatically he jerked a thumb. 'Along there, miss,' sidestepping the wrong way and cannoning into Hughes. He was pushed unceremoniously aside as the doorman hurled himself after Nell.

This was it. From the large sign on the door, there was no doubting it. Nell thumped hard as Hughes arrived. He pushed her aside and stood with arms outstretched across the threshold facing her, a Horatio defending his bridge against all marauders – to the great surprise of the dresser who opened the door. Hughes' great bulk almost filled the space.

'Miss Hargreaves,' Nell shouted, making an attempt to duck under his arm.

'Hoh, no you don't, miss.' An enormous arm restrained her. Behind him, she could hear the bewitchingly beautiful, hated voice saying languidly, 'Whatever is it, Hughes? I hadn't realised you were such an admirer of mine.'

'It's one of those Bolsheviks, miss,' Hughes replied savagely, as Nell was forced to bob up and down in front of him trying to see inside.

'I'm not,' she shouted.

'Oh, what a pity. I've never met a real Red,' Melissa replied with amusement. Anything to while away this tense time before curtain up. 'Who are you then?'

'Who are you?' repeated Hughes, as if Nell, barred from sight of the goddess, was also deaf.

'Nell Watkins.'

'She says she's Nell Watkins, miss,' roared Hughes grimly, keeping his eyes firmly on Nell.

'Who on earth is Nell Watkins?' Melissa asked lightly.

Nell's patience snapped as Hughes began ponderously: 'Who—?'

'Tell her,' she yelled, 'I'm the girl from Gadsby's.'

The day had begun ordinarily enough. The train had been five minutes late arriving at Charing Cross, but Nell had run most of the way to Regent Street so that she could still walk, albeit breathless, through the staff entrance at Gadsby's two minutes before the prescribed hour of nine o'clock.

'Good morning, Mr Perkins.'

'Morning, miss.' Perkins, doorkeeper of the staff entrance to Gadsby's, gravely marked down her exact time of arrival. Another ex-soldier, though not as grand as Harbottle, Gadsby's commissionaire, another ex-sergeant major. Even now, early in 1925, there were many ex-soldiers of the Great War who had found no jobs, a few

3

still reduced to selling matches in the streets. Those more fortunate took their duties very seriously.

Nell made the usual face, unseen by Perkins, and sped on her way down to the basement cloakroom. It was full as usual, but at this tense hour with locker doors slamming shut and arms flailing as the junior staff changed their clothes for the Gadsby 'blacks', there was little time or energy for conversation. Their 'blacks' were neither fashionable nor unfashionable. With their long sleeves, hemlines neatly between the dowdy and the outré several inches below the knees, and their neat white Peter Pan collars, Gadsby's junior staff, sales assistants and understudies, though at least spared the indignity of wearing overalls like the humble trotters and matchers, were as indistinguishable one from another as the six uniformed page boys.

This morning, daringly, instead of the staff stairs Nell used the customers' grand staircase while the floorwalker's gaze was fixed on the front entrance, awaiting their arrival. It amused her to pretend she was one of the elect, A Customer, as she minced, nose in the air, up the ornate curved staircase to the first floor. Every inch of gold paint on the banisters proclaimed how unique, how special Gadsby's was, and how fortunate the customer had been in choosing to be dressed there. Retribution awaited her, however, as the immaculate guardian of the first floor spotted her arrival.

'I'm sorry, Mr Mather,' she said brightly. 'Miss Danzy wanted something from Umbrellas in a hurry. They hadn't got it,' she remembered to add belatedly. Catch him checking with the Dragon, she thought with satisfaction. Even Mr Mather avoided confrontation with old Danzy.

Every one of her five foot five inches held regally upright, she sailed graciously through the palatial spaciousness of Gadsby's first floor. Welcoming soft pink-patterned carpets, Louis XV-style chairs covered in rose

4

red plush and gold paint, and comfortable ottomans awaited their customers. To her left were the coat and costume showrooms, rejoicing in the departmental name of Mantles. To the right was the magic world of which she was such an insignificant part. First came Teagowns, where a few stands showed ready-made floating dreams of georgette and chiffon, the models bought from Paris this spring. Discreetly displayed were a few silk and crêpe de Chine nightdresses and pink camiknickers; the latter were the only modest concession to modernity. Even more discreetly displayed were old-style heavy boned corsets, bust bodices and garment shields, flanked by a once daring pair of tango knickers. In another alcove blossomed a row of ready-made blouses. This, and the goods of the Sporting Wear department on the ground floor, represented the limit to which Gadsby's was prepared to pander to modern taste. For beyond Teagowns was the Fashion Department, centring on the showroom, spearhead to the core of Gadsby's business. Here there were no models displayed, merely chairs, side tables and ottomans. Here was the setting for a daily ritual attended by some of the richest women in England and representing the acme of haute couture.

Taking a deep breath and winking at Cissie and Winnie, the other two understudies in the department, Nell said meekly: 'Good morning, Miss Danzy.'

The saleswoman's legs, so angular they seemed to be protesting at an exposure that had been none of their making as hemlines inexorably rose, turned their owner round from her discussions with her two counterparts, Mrs Amble ('Old Ample' as she was fondly known) and Miss Beeson ('The Beesknees') to the girls. Miss Danzy was unquestionably the most formidable of the three.

'Good morning, Miss Watkins,' her thin voice acknowledged. 'No doubt now you have joined us you'll be good enough to inform the model room that Lady Lenham is coming in this morning, and will wish to see the entire range of day dresses.' Her beads almost clacked in their owner's indignation at being deprived of the opportunity to accuse her understudy of being late.

Nell's heart sank. Lady Lenham was one of their most exacting customers. Unfortunately she was also one of the richest. Why did she have to come to the Dragon and not Old Ample or the Beesknees? Life was very unfair. Nell had been understudy to Miss Danzy now for three years. Sometimes she wondered how she had managed to endure it for so long. Before that the Dragon had terrified a succession of girls into leaving after only a few weeks. Nell had come to Gadsby's five years ago, in 1920, as a humble eighteen-year-old matcher, rushing round London stores to match such things as lining fabrics when Gadsby's own Fabric Department could not oblige. After a few months she was promoted to trotter, go-between between the showroom and the workroom, and since she was assigned to the sleeves' workroom, grew heartily sick of all such appendages, from raglans to dolmans, caps to bells. She had seized the promotion which had been offered when, bored beyond belief, she gave in her notice, and thus came to the heart of Gadsby's. The only flaw was the Dragon that guarded this castle.

Here, so far as Nell could see, she would stay. One did not become a saleswoman at Gadsby's until at least thirty-five. Thirty-five, another twelve years. She might be dead by then, she thought despairingly. Not that she particularly wanted to be a saleswoman, but it was at least promotion, and some of those ideas bubbling inside her head might get a chance to emerge. After all, Gadsby's was the summit of the dreams of most girls of her age, a fashion house frequented by the richest in society. With its huge façade on London's Regent Street, sufficiently far down to be removed from the hurly-burly of Oxford Street, it remained superior in its uncompetitiveness.

Even Harvey Nichols and Harrods were selling a few ready-made fashion dresses now, but not Gadsby's.

Gadsby's would go on just as it was for ever, until like the dinosaur it just faded out. That's what Nell was beginning to think, after the first stars had faded from her eyes in the Fashion Department. Surely there could not be money enough in the world to keep Gadsby's alive for ever? Though at the moment, in April 1925, one might be forgiven for thinking so. The prices of these dresses made her blink. Thirty guineas for an evening dress? That was nearly a year's wages for Nell.

Today Lady Lenham was at her worst. Nell returned from a disgruntled model room, having ordered at the Dragon's request all the day dresses to be ready – only to find her ladyship duly installed but demanding to see evening dresses. The Dragon however was equal to the occasion. 'Certainly, Lady Lenham. Miss Watkins,' a sharper note to her voice, 'the Book if you please.' Snap of the fingers.

Woof, woof, was always Nell's muted reply as she rushed for the sacred Book giving details of all models with their respective numbers.

'Numbers 8, 22, 32 and 40,' the Dragon commanded of Nell, who resisted the temptation to touch her forelock as she rushed back to the model room.

'Is that all?' Lady Lenham's deep voice enquired icily, after the last mannequin had paraded to silence despite the Dragon's best oiliness. Her ladyship was cultivating the Queen Mary look today, Nell noted, with her upright back, almost ankle-length skirt and old-fashioned high-necked blouse.

The Dragon did not hesitate. '*All* that might be acceptable to madam. There is 21 of course, but perhaps not quite—'

Nell's eyes opened wide. *Twenty-one?*

'I'll see it,' Lady Lenham ordered contrarily.

'Miss Watkins?' Snap of the fingers.

Woof, woof.

Even the austere woman who ran the model room could hardly repress a smile when Number 21 had come in after the Paris spring parades. Everyone knew The Buyer was on the point of retirement, but this was proof she should have gone long since. The Buyer was the elderly personage in the neat black suit in overall command of the Fashion Department. She seemed to Nell ten foot tall, though reason told her she was only a few inches more than Nell herself. If The Buyer had a name, it was rarely used. Somehow The Buyer, like God, was above all that. The Buyer rarely made mistakes when she went to Paris on her twice, sometimes thrice yearly visits. Her taste was like Gadsby's itself, on the conservative side, following a cautious distance behind the extremes of fashion, but sufficiently attuned to keep Gadsby's of interest to the fashion journalists. While haute couture magazines like *Vogue* might not cover their shows, journals and newspapers for the general reader, such as the *Daily Telegraph, Illustrated London News* and *The Lady* did. But every so often, and increasingly now, Nell noted, she made mistakes. Normally these were glossed over in the general profitability of the Fashion Department. Number 21 was the exception. Since their own spring show two weeks ago, at the beginning of April, not only had no orders been received for it, but a distinct titter had been heard from some customers at its appearance. What was Paris thinking of? seemed the unspoken verdict. Full-skirted, full-bosomed and full-length, Number 21 stood out from mid-twenties' fashion like a carthorse among thoroughbreds. Worse than its lack of adherence to modern lines was that it suggested pre-war days in its fussy ornamentation. Instead of one subtle use of feather, fur or ribbon, it poked them in at every opportunity, detracting even from the young mannequin's beauty.

8

'So unusual, Lady Lenham,' was all the Dragon could find to say, in contrast to her usual eloquent pleadings.

'I'll take it.'

'But—'

'Exclusively, mind.'

'Ah.' This usually required delicate negotiation. Not today. 'I think that could be arranged, Lady Lenham.' Miss Danzy snapped her fingers. 'Miss Watkins.'

'Yes, Miss Danzy?' Nell murmured deferentially as the fitter was summoned for measuring, and Nell noted down details of fabric and decoration. Miss Danzy was going to be pleased. The day was going well, Nell thought, relieved, as she hurried back from the Fabric Department having reserved a length of unfashionable moiré taffeta. Mr Polgarth, the buyer, had been only too eager to reserve it, especially when he heard whom it was for. She went back to the department in high good humour.

'Good morning, Nelly Watkins,' came a cheery shout, then long legs streamed past her in a most unGadsbylike way up the stairs, leaving her to answer weakly, 'Good morning, Mr Gadsby,' to the back of his immaculate sports jacket and incredibly wide, to her amazed eyes, flannel trousers flopping round the agile legs.

Her day was complete. Tom Gadsby, with his fair hair, blue eyes and happy laugh, had spoken to her. The heir to Gadsby's itself and, in theory at least, general overseer of the store. But the latter didn't seem to take up too much of his time. There was always plenty left, she deduced from the society pages, for his motor-racing and aviation projects. She had been in love from afar with him ever since she arrived as a starry-eyed eighteen-year-old to his then mature twenty. She told herself firmly that Tom Gadsby was a daydream, and had nothing to do with Real Life. Real Life was Joe Simpkins in Fabrics with whom she'd been 'walking out' – as it was still termed at Gadsby's – for eighteen

9

months. And, she was unpleasantly reminded as she reached the Fashion Department again, Real Life consisted of Dragons not fairy princes.

Whatever Tom Gadsby was saying to Miss Danzy was apparently pleasing her. He and Lady Lenham had managed the impossible. The Dragon was looking positively cheerful. Sometimes Nell dreamed that she would faint in Tom Gadsby's path so that he would scoop her up and lay her gently on an ottoman where, unconscious, she would blurt out all her ideas for store management and the improvement of Gadsby's. When she awoke, she would see his blue eyes, frank in admiration – and something else. Could it be the dawn of love? 'By Gad, Nelly Watkins, you're a wonder,' he'd say, looking at her in quite a new way. Then Nell would laugh at herself. Firstly, she wasn't the fainting sort. And, to be honest, so far as she could see Tom Gadsby had less interest in ideas for running Gadsby's than in his motor-car magazines. Yet you could forget Rudolph Valentino and Douglas Fairbanks, in Nell's view. Beside Tom Gadsby they were nothing.

Miss Danzy's pleasure did not seem to extend to Nell, and her voice was as tart as ever as she commanded, 'Miss Watkins, kindly escort Lady Lenham to the fitting room.' Snap.

Woof, woof. 'Yes, Miss Danzy. Would you come this way, Lady Lenham?'

By the time she returned there was no doubt that something was up. Everyone was running around like scalded cats, and the one customer still present, a new one, seemed to be receiving less than even old Ample's full attention. There was no sign of the Dragon.

'She's in the model room,' hissed Winnie, whisking by on her way to the internal telephone.

Wonders would never cease! 'How did she know where it was?' Nell whispered, daringly following her as unobtrusively as she could, lest her disappearance from her post be noted and reported.

'The *London*—' began Winnie, then broke off hurriedly as the Dragon swept through the doorway, firmly scooping up Nell in her wake.

'Your place, Miss Watkins, is at my side, not engaged in idle chatter. I have been forced, in your absence, to carry out your work Myself!'

'But—'

'But is not a word we use in Gadsby's, Miss Watkins.'

'No, Miss Danzy,' murmured Nell mechanically, her mind still racing about what could be in the air.

'Miss Melissa Hargreaves is arriving shortly.'

'Yes, Miss D—*Oh*!'

Everyone under the age of seventy and most people over it had heard of Melissa Hargreaves, the beautiful talented star of *London Lady*. Nell rarely went to the theatre, but even she had queued up for the gods and seen this play, with its lively music and catchy songs. And the dresses! Shimmering silvers and golds, and a stage alight with colour and life in these new and exciting times. Melissa Hargreaves was known for her roles in romantic musical comedy, and opinions differed as to whether her singing, dancing or comedy acting technique were best. Women, just as men, took her to their hearts, her innocent blonde beauty stirring protectiveness in both, as she danced her way on stage from adversity to true love and marriage in plot after plot.

And this paragon was about to descend on Gadsby's! Every time the bell went to alert the floorwalker that a new customer was coming up the stairs, or in the elevator, they jumped to attention like the gardeners for the arrival of the Queen of Hearts. There were five false alarms before Melissa Hargreaves eventually floated in. There was no doubt it was she, for that lovely face had been photographed in every magazine in England. Today, Nell saw, it wore a petulant frown. So she was not pleased to be here – unless she always looked like that of course. It contrasted oddly with her otherwise ethereal fairy-tale image: a slim sky blue coat trimmed with a narrow strip of white fur at the bottom, on the cuffs and the collar, and matching hat. Tiny delicate bar shoes in the same colour, white clutch bag and gloves . . . Nell's eyes drank in the picture with the same admiration and look of envy that she had for the Royal Family or Mary Pickford.

Miss Danzy bustled forward. 'Miss Hargreaves, such a pleasure. Do sit down. May we bring you some tea?' She snapped her fingers.

'Coffee,' contradicted Melissa Hargreaves, slipping her coat from her shoulders into Nell's eagerly waiting hands with one dexterous movement, revealing an incredibly short tunic dress in the same blue with a white trim. Snap of Dragon's fingers. Woof woof. Nell ran to hang up the precious coat, and to order the coffee.

'What can we have the pleasure of showing you, Miss Hargreaves?' the Dragon was purring on her return.

'Dresses, I suppose,' the beautiful but sulky voice replied, crossing one leg over the other in bored fashion. How on earth did she judge it so precisely so as not to reveal her stocking tops? thought Nell, lost in admiration. It was a major preoccupation with most of her friends, though less with her since her mother kept a strict eye on the length of her skirts which shot up and down like yo-yos according to whether she was at home or not. Lucky she had learnt to sew so quickly.

'Evening dresses, madam?'

'Good heavens, no.' The voice intimated that she would not entrust anything so vital to Gadsby's. 'Ascot, Henley, garden parties, that sort of thing.'

'Ah, yes, we have a particularly fine range. And how many, madam?'

'Oh, I don't know. About twenty, I suppose.'

'Twenty?' Danzy shrieked almost uncontrollably, as Nell stifled a gasp. *Twenty?* Three or four was usually the maximum.

Melissa languidly raised her eyebrows. 'Do you not have as many as that?'

'Naturally, naturally,' Miss Danzy murmured weakly, then rallied. Snap of fingers, and Nell removed the coffee cup as Melissa bestowed a brilliant smile upon her. But she's not *seeing* me, Nell realised instantly. Why should she? She must meet hundreds and thousands of Nells.

'Perhaps you might prefer to order them in groups of four or five at a time?' the Dragon suggested helpfully.

Nell bit back a laugh. The helpful note was for the benefit of their workrooms already rushed off their feet by orders for the social season.

'No, thank you. I will order *now*. And have them fitted altogether. Delivery by the middle of May.' The charming smile that accompanied this astounding statement was implacable.

She'll tell her to push off, she'll have to, thought Nell, amused. Not even Danzy could get the workroom to agree to this outrageous proposal. But astoundingly the Dragon seemed to be submitting after a few words about consulting the fitters.

Nell was busy in the model room for the next twenty minutes as it was galvanised into activity. She rushed from department to department on behalf of the models borrowing shoes, hats, umbrellas that no one had expected to be showing today. Not to mention the surreptitious borrowing of a few ready-made tennis and motoring dresses to gloss over gaps.

Melissa Hargreaves regarded the parading mannequins in silence, puffing occasionally at a cigarette, to old Ample's visible horror. Half an hour later she announced she liked none of them.

'Perhaps in a different material,' Miss Danzy

announced in a steady voice. Snap, woof woof, and Nell was off, racing down to the Fabric Department to fetch the pattern book. Melissa Hargreaves flicked through it in silence, despite the Dragon's increasingly desperate suggestions. Then she looked up, bestowing her brilliant smile once more on Nell. 'I'm afraid,' she said, sighing, 'I still don't like them.'

'Perhaps in the piece,' said Miss Danzy firmly. She admitted no failure.

Resignedly Nell rushed down to Fabrics yet again.

'Miss Danzy wants the lemon shantung, peach georgette, ivory silk.' She reeled off a string of requirements, daringly adding one of her own which she thought might suit Melissa. Fortunately she got on well with Mr Polgarth – indeed she was popular with the whole department, especially Joe, whom it was widely assumed she would marry. This morning she wasn't popular with any of them, however, as they obscurely seemed to blame her. Almost the entire departmental staff had to form a procession to carry the heavy rolls up to the showroom.

One after the other the young men threw the rolls of fabric on the carpeted floor, unrolling them with practised ease, to display their virtues at Melissa's feet. The golden-haired goddess sat surrounded by her tribute of colour from palest ivory to bright greens and reds.

'No,' she said simply. A shudder ran almost visibly round the room, the word 'time-waster' in everyone's mind if not on their lips. Every one of those rolls now had to be painstakingly rolled up again and carried down to the Fabric Department again. Perhaps something of their feelings communicated itself to Melissa. 'Wait,' she commanded and looked again.

'That one,' she pointed at a rose-pink georgette, 'has possibilities for Ascot.' It was Nell's choice, a fact that most rapidly communicated itself to the Dragon and boded no good for Nell. But for the moment, sales came first.

Having yielded ground, Melissa then went all the way. Nell was kept busy as the Dragon snapped instructions at her for writing down in the Book. Number 26, as model, citron shantung. Number 51, no cuffs on sleeves. Otherwise as model. Allow ½ yd extra. Number 72, collar facings to be in contrasting material. Number 34 – no sleeves.

'Oh, *no*,' said Nell involuntarily.

Two pairs of astounded eyes were turned on her.

'It wouldn't suit you,' Nell blurted out, conscious of her mistake yet blundering further in. 'It would make your arms look fat.'

Melissa's mouth fell open in astonishment. Tears welled up in her eyes. 'I have *not* got fat arms,' she cried pettishly. 'Did you hear what she said to me?' she shouted at the Dragon who did not disappoint her. A smile of triumph on her lips, she turned to her victim.

'Kindly leave the room, Miss Watkins. You will report to the Fourth Floor in an hour's time.'

So there was to be no reprieve. Fourth Floor was a fate reserved for the worst offenders. Minor misdemeanours were dealt with in the directors' office on the ground floor, where two directors, ostensibly named Counting House director and Supplies director, in fact did the work of the usually absent Store director, Tom Gadsby. Head held high Nell left the showroom, watched in pity by her friends, to take refuge in the cloakroom for an hour, too much in shock to cry or even ponder on the rebuke that would lie ahead. It was so *unfair*.

At one minute to twelve she was on the Fourth Floor, the holy of holies. She walked past the board room, past the directors' dining room, diving past Tom Gadsby's own personal room. Heart sinking she knocked at the door which *was* the Fourth Floor.

'Come in.' A bark from within. Bracing herself, she opened the door and walked in. For only the third time in her career, she was face to face with Jonathan Gadsby.

Jonathan Gadsby would be seventy-five years old in August and had every intention of living another seventy-five to ensure Gadsby's survival until at least the twenty-first century. He looked rather like Methuselah too, with his long white beard, old-fashioned side-burns and gleaming bright eyes. Age could not wither the governing director of Gadsby's. Jonathan's word was law. He might have directors, but he took care they owned no more than one share each. Power was firmly in the hands of Jonathan Gadsby, and in due course would pass (in the twenty-first century) to his grandson Tom. Tom's father Nevil, destined for this mantle, had been killed in the Great War and since then Tom had been the lodestone towards which Jonathan's plans were directed. Tom could do no wrong for he was a Gadsby. Indeed, since he was now the only (male) Gadsby save Jonathan himself, he had to be the heir, whether he showed aptitude or not. That he had not, and would not, was an unfortunate fact that Jonathan, astute as he was in every other way, succeeded in ignoring.

In 1870 Jonathan had come to help his uncle William Bush to run the thriving draper's shop he owned in North Kent, not far from where Nell now lived. Within five years young Jonathan had added a thriving outfitting department, and within fifteen, leaving his uncle's modest expectations far behind him, had expanded Bush and Nephew into a chain of such stores all over Kent.

In 1890 his uncle died and in grudging recognition of the role played by his nephew, left the empire to him. Ungratefully, Jonathan promptly sold it. With the proceeds he formed a company, appointed himself governing director for life in order to retain maximum control, and took a lease on two shops in London's increasingly fashionable Regent Street. He realised that changing times brought new opportunities, and that while ladies' bloomers and stockinette vests would sell steadily for ever, they were unlikely to bring the name of Gadsby the fame and fortune he craved. The new craze for cycling, however, brought a new need. Women were getting more adventurous, and their everyday clothes were not merely no longer suitable, but were positively dangerous. Fashionable women required a fashionable store to set this matter right.

So Gadsby's opened up in a modest way to sell ready-made bicycling and golfing clothes and accessories; the idea appealed, the advent of motoring brought a new and younger clientele to Gadsby's as it leapt whole-heartedly to meet the challenge and became a store for go-ahead young ladies. It seemed a natural progression to meet all their fashion needs. Jonathan promptly took a lease on as many buildings fronting Regent Street and adjoining Gadsby's as he could; the future of the store was assured.

Jonathan was then fifty, and as full of fight and enthusiasm as ever. Gadsby's became a fashion house, buying Maison la Ferté models from Paris and copying them for its customers with its own expert workrooms on the third floor, in which now buzzed and hummed nearly two hundred busy bees. The giddy young things of 1900 were now sober matrons, but equally fashion conscious, and remained faithful to Gadsby's. The more conservative of them had emerged from the war with impaired finances that were speedily improved, the Gibson and Gaiety girls of Edwardian days married prosperously into the aristocracy, and in addition a whole new class of nouveaux riches was emerging. All conspired to ensure Gadsby's prosperity in the giddy days of the early- and mid-twenties. Its wealthy customers were unaffected by the industrial slump of 1921, but shared fully in the reckless spending and gaiety that followed it in a country that, having survived the deprivations of the Great War, was fully convinced that it could never be threatened again. If Jonathan ever sniffed a hint of changing times he firmly ignored it. Gadsby's would prosper no matter what; it had always done so and would continue to do so.

Sometimes now his eagle eye observed on his daily perambulation of the store, however staff tried to hide the fact, that customers on the premises were not quite so numerous as before; he saw from the books that increasing numbers of regular customers were too infirm to leave their homes or arrived in bath chairs, and that of the new customers, the younger ones tended to be the daughters of the older. He ignored the implications and so had not been pleased when three years ago a junior member of staff had brightly pointed this out to him, together with a few wild ideas from her Olympian height of saleswoman's understudy as to how the situation could be improved. He had been on the point of reneging on the promotion he was about to offer her when he remembered that she was the protégée of Emmeline Parks, the sweetheart of his youth. Nevertheless, he decided to keep an eye on her. He didn't want revolutionaries in Gadsby's.

'Come in,' barked Methuselah.

The door opened. He never forgot a face, even if names sometimes eluded him.

'It's you again,' he roared at her.

'Yessir,' Nell managed to admit.

'You were the one bleating to me about encouraging younger customers?' he informed her grimly. 'This how you propose to treat them? Insult them?'

'Yes, no, sir!' She stumbled on the words.

'Not at Gadsby's, young woman. Dismissed. Get your wages from the Counting House and go.'

'But—' She stood her ground, stung with shock and injustice.

'Go'.

'But' was not a word to be used at Gadsby's.

'I just wanted you to know, that's all,' Nell finished after her tirade to Melissa. How dare she so lightly play with the lives of others with no thought for the consequences? For it hadn't been just the Dragon's doing, much as she'd welcomed the chance no doubt of ridding herself of her turbulent understudy. Gadsby's was fair, if strict. There would have to be a direct complaint from the customer before dismissal would be contemplated.

Melissa's hand was poised in the air, still waving an eye-brush, as she absorbed the consequences of her visit. 'You were sacked. Oh dear.' Her eyes were full of tears, Nell saw with amazement. She surely could not be faking that. She was really distressed. 'All the same you shouldn't have said my arms were fat,' Melissa added firmly.

'I didn't,' Nell stated flatly, cheeks flushed. 'I said if you had that dress sleeveless, they would *look* fat.'

'It's the same thing.'

'It's not,' said Nell exasperatedly. 'Look, this dress you're wearing has cap sleeves, and your arms look slender and pretty. Now look.' Somewhat nervously she pushed the flimsy silk back over the shoulder, with the shoulder bone showing. 'Your slender neck, and the bone structure here, make the bare shoulders look—'

'Like a hunk of beef,' said Melissa entranced, turning from her mirror to laugh up at Nell, eyes sparkling.

'I was going to say, "larger than they need",' said Nell primly, catching Melissa's eye and bursting into laughter with her.

As they subsided, Melissa stared at Nell with troubled eyes. 'Oh, but what can I *do*?'

'You can't do anything,' she said defiantly, 'and I don't want you to.' That wasn't what she had come for. 'I just

19

wanted you to know what your bad temper resulted in.'

She held her breath as Melissa scowled. Would she explode? No. Suddenly the famous smile that had bewitched London shone out.

'You're quite right,' she agreed. 'I *was* bad-tempered. I didn't want to go to Gadsby's for my frocks.' She made a face. 'I wanted to go to Drécoll in Paris.'

'Then why change your mind?' Nell asked, puzzled.

'To please my fiancé,' said Melissa disarmingly. 'and *now* see what I've done. Oh, *Nell*,' she burst out suddenly, 'I've had a splendid idea.'

'I don't want—' she began alarmed, beginning to back out.

'Stop,' commanded Melissa fiercely. 'Come here.' She patted the seat next to her. 'Wait while I get this make-up plastered on. Ugh. Bother beastly old greasepaint.'

Nell watched curiously, uneasily aware that she had no place in this room full of ordered racks of dresses and accessories, as much a working room as any at Gadsby's.

'You must stay to the performance,' Melissa informed her. 'I'll arrange a seat. And afterwards I shall ask my fiancé to get you your job back.'

'I don't want my job—' Nell began automatically, but stopped. Of course, she did. She couldn't lie, however much pride urged her to. She needed her job and she wouldn't get another easily after dismissal for insolence. 'I can't,' she improvised. 'I might miss the last train to Bexleyheath.'

'Don't worry,' said Melissa airily, waving this aside. 'We'll drive you home and on the way we'll discuss what to do about the silly old job. Won't that be top-hole?'

'But what can your fiancé do about my job?' Nell asked, bewildered.

'Quite a lot,' said Melissa offhandedly. 'He's Tom Gadsby.'

★ ★ ★

Nell had the box to herself, torn by conflicting emotions at the events of the day. Overriding them was firstly a sense of excitement and anticipation that she, Nell Watkins, should be sitting in grand style in a box at the Albion in her home-made checked costume, the guest of the famous Melissa Hargreaves. Secondly, the numbness of loss.

Melissa had struck her yet another blow, albeit this time not her fault, when she told her of her engagement to Tom Gadsby. The trouble with daydreams, Nell thought rue-fully, was that like bubbles they punctured all too easily. Of course Tom Gadsby would be in love with someone like Melissa Hargreaves. Especially Melissa. He had fallen under her spell, just as she had herself by now. How was she going to bear seeing them together?

The rise of the curtain took her mind off Tom Gadsby temporarily. Although she had seen it before, it seemed entirely new to her. Melissa played the chauffeur's daugh-ter who is forced to stand in for her father when he is taken ill and drives Binksie Fullilock, the son of the household, with whom she is hopelessly in love, to see his fiancée, the Honourable Winifred Hunt. Naturally all comes well in the end, with Binksie realising that true happiness lay with his lady chauffeur, not with the Hon-ourable Winifred. The plot was slight, the effect was not when the songs, music and dancing were added together. 'Raising the bonnet', the daring 'Love-all, deuce it' and the wistful 'You were but a dream' had the audience humming as they left. Nell grinned ruefully as she watched Melissa singing plaintively of her love. Tom was real enough for Melissa. Well, surely now she knew he was engaged, Nell would be able to forget him? Perhaps she'd even marry Joe . . . Perhaps together they'd be able to impress old Gadsby with their ideas. With a jerk, she realised that at the moment there was every likelihood she would never see Tom, Joe or Gadsby's again. Neverthe-less Melissa had said . . . Pulling herself together she

21

imperiously demanded entrance at the stage door afterwards, grinning at her triumph as with barely concealed rage Hughes admitted her. Not personally though. He scored his revenge by putting her in charge of a bell-boy.

'By Jove, if it isn't our Nelly Watkins,' announced Tom, astounded, opening the door to her.

'Not yours any longer, Tommy darling,' Melissa called, still changing behind a screen. She popped her head up over the top to shout a joyous hello and shortly emerged wearing a flimsy copper and green tissue dress, its metallic threads sparkling and highlighting the gold of her hair. 'I have done *the* most terrible thing, and you're going to put it right for me.'

Tom's eagerness changed to slight wariness.

'I got her sacked but she needs her job back. You see, Tommy,' a break in her voice, 'her family depend on her. You have a starving, weakly mother, don't you, Nell? And a baby sister dying of consumption?'

'By Jove, I'm sorry to hear that,' said Tom uneasily. 'Er, where's your pater these days?'

'Very much alive and maintaining the household, which is entirely healthy,' said Nell firmly. 'But I do want my job back, Mr Gadsby.'

'Leave it to me,' he said grandly, looking at Melissa devotedly.

'That's all right, then,' Melissa said happily. 'Now we're motoring to Bexleyheath, Tommy.'

'Bexleyheath?' he bleated. 'But we were going to the 43 Club. Dash it, Melissa, I haven't had supper yet.'

'I don't need—' Nell began.

'Nonsense,' said Melissa happily. 'It's nothing in the darling Fanny-Lea, is it, Tom? Not to my dear old Tommy Atkins.'

'Nothing at all,' Tom agreed fervently, as she brushed her lips against his cheek.

★ ★ ★

The night was April enchantment. Even from the dicky seat of the Lea-Francis, even suffering from the pangs of lost love. Nell held her face up to the cool breeze, savouring every moment. In front of her two blond heads were close together, singing lustily and alternately 'Always' and 'The Robbers' March'. At the moment they were the two beings she loved best in all the world, bent towards each other in adoration yet including her in their enchantment, engulfing her in their own happiness. South London seemed almost beautiful as the Lea-Francis sports car glided through it; the Old Kent Road was imbued with a special magic all its own; New Cross, seen only from the crowded train in the mornings, suddenly seemed romantic, and up on to Blackheath.

'Hope we don't meet any highwaymen,' shouted Nell ridiculously, holding on to her hat. 'That's what it's known for.'

'I'd *love* to meet a huge, dark highwayman,' shouted Melissa happily. 'He'd sweep me off just like Valentino in *The Sheik*. You wouldn't mind, would you, Tommy?'

'Yes, I would.'

'Silly old pooh-bear. I'd come back to you, after he'd had his wicked way. You'd look after him while I'm away, won't you, Nell?'

'Yes,' she yelled happily, her role somehow now delineated. She took her hat off and let the wind blow her unruly curls as it would. She did her best with kirby grips and bandeaux to make them conform to current sleek hairstyles, but when they refused she gave in to them, acknowledging that sleek shingles and bingles were not for her. All the same, she admired the back of Melissa's wavy but sleekly shingled hair a little wistfully.

'I say, I recognise this,' said Tom suddenly.

'It's Shooter's Hill,' Nell told him.

'Thought so,' he said, pleased. 'Isn't there a big park near here?'

23

'Yes,' she told him. 'Danson Park. It's being opened to the public by the council this year.'

'I used to stay there before the old girl who owned it died. Landed the old Avro in the park, hauled out the old bag and into the mansion. Nice little pile. Grandfather knew the family. Did you ever meet the old girl?'

'Not socially,' Nell said a little drily.

'You'd have liked her,' Tom assured her over his shoulder.

Ten minutes later they drew up outside Watkins' Draper and Outfitters next to the Crook Log Post Office, and Nell jumped out, painfully aware of the difference in the window display compared with Gadsby's. Where Gadsby's displayed a single garment in stately splendour, Watkins' stuffed every nook and cranny with its wares.

'Jolly little shop,' pronounced Tom approvingly of her mother's lovingly ordered selection of cambric handkerchiefs, dishcloths and curtain nets, and her father's bolder display of long-johns and vests.

Nell caught Melissa's eye. Melissa looked innocent, and Nell laughed.

'Come in on Monday,' said Tom casually. 'Elevenish. I'll have sorted something out for you.'

She stood and watched as he cranked up the Lea-Francis and off they roared into a magic world of their own, a world that she had briefly shared. She was still in love, this time with them both, as Melissa's voice singing 'If you were the only boy in the world' floated back in the night air. Later, she was to remember. Remember how true, how false.

Miss Emmeline was the tall one, Miss Gertrude the short one. They were both in their early seventies, but Nell never thought of age in connection with them. To her they had always looked the same, ever since as a child of about ten her mother had taken her on the tram to Welling to

24

have her first dress made for her. Parks' Dressmakers was infinitely more respectable than ready-made cheap stores elsewhere. They lived then above the store. In the windows only a few stuffed canvas models with a sad-looking frock or two were displayed. One had to know about the Misses Parks, who disdained cheap publicity. Their work, painstaking, respectable, reliable and thorough, was done in the fitting and workrooms beyond, a business involving infinite tact and integrity where in a village such as theirs trade mostly depended on the wives of rival shopkeepers and traders.

'Nell, you have been sitting in that chair for fifteen minutes without speaking,' Miss Emmeline informed her.

'I've got to tell Father I've got the sack.'

'The sack?' said Miss Gertrude, shocked at this colloquialism more than the news. 'Dear Jonathan dismissed you?'

'I suppose he couldn't really do much else,' said Nell fairly.

Miss Emmeline looked severe. 'Did you deserve it?'

'No, but—'

'Then I shall have words with Jonathan,' she announced. She looked as if she were about to don her old wide-brimmed flowery hat straight away. The two Miss Parks still wore full-length skirts and high-necked blouses, and the demise of their shop had undoubtedly been hastened since in modesty they could not bring themselves to adapt to rapidly shortening hemlines. They were getting on in years and their day was over, they concluded. They closed the shop at Easter 1920 and with it went the old-fashioned mid-Victorian dress-stands with their modest lack of shape, over which lengths of fabric were displayed for decency's sake when not in use; the smell of damp woollens being pressed into shape; the rows of pincushions, the button-boxes and pieces box. All of these Nell had loved.

It was to Miss Emmeline and Miss Gertrude she had come to 'learn her trade'. Her father had assumed she would help her mother serve in the shop when she left school at fourteen, as she had done all her life. Her mother was called down from their upstairs rooms when ladies required to purchase intimate garments, and from her earliest years Nell would follow curiously to see the matrons of Bexleyheath and Welling sitting in the straight upright wooden chairs in line, waiting to be served. How she had loved as a child sorting out cottons and pins, braids and ribbons and above all buttons. Buttons of all shapes and sizes – bachelor buttons for men, buttons for ladies with butterflies.

As she grew up she became interested in other aspects, however: how the shop worked, its profit, its weak lines. Was it not uneconomic to stock those huge bloomers for Mrs Waites when she was the only one who ever bought them? And, yes, she realised that it was a service to please a customer, but there was only a certain amount of room in the shop and could they not start stocking brassières for instance, to attract a wider trade? But her father wasn't interested. He had a son to whom to leave the shop, Nell's older brother Alfred. She could serve under him if she liked, but as for running things, no. Women, he explained kindly enough, did not understand business. That Nell patently did while her brother did not, much preferring to fiddle with the excitements of electricity, passed him by.

When she left school, Nell refused point-blank to work in the shop. Perplexed at this ugly duckling in their nest, they asked what she proposed to do. She would go to work in London, she told them. At Gadsby's, she added with pride. Her father had laughed her to scorn. Without training? Impossible. This was something she had not considered. Her mother had then had a brilliant notion and apprenticed her awkward daughter to the Misses Parks in Welling High Street, who had taken a fancy to her. They were growing old, possibly even – her imagination ran riot – Nell might *run* the business for them in due course. She did not communicate this brainwave to Nell's new employers, which was just as well since the Misses Parks, proud as they were of their fledgling, were as intransigent in their way as old Gadsby himself. They would make up dresses for the more affluent of their customers from sketches in ladies' magazines, and that was as far as fashion would go for them. Nell had four years' hard apprenticeship; sewing, learning to make toiles and patterns, making-up, fitting – and less successfully in tactful negotiations with customers.

'You will never make a fitter, dear,' Miss Emmeline informed her after she had stuck pins into Mrs Pilker's large bottom.

'You will never make a needlewoman, dear,' Miss Gertrude clucked over her fingers blooded in the fray of making a toile on the dress stand, forcing needles through the stiff mull.

But they kept her on for they knew what Nell *could* do, which was far more important. She had an eye. She knew instinctively what would suit and what would not. With her endless poring over fashion pages, she knew what went with what, what current trends were, and where they might lead; she became adept at persuading customers into buying what suited them, and not what didn't. She learned to sew and fit well enough to pass. She learned about materials; what they could achieve, how they could enhance or detract, where and if they would give.

But even Nell could not keep the Misses Parks in business. The more affluent of the ladies of Welling now went to London to buy their dresses by the railway which had come to Welling in 1895, and as soon as the war ended travelled up to 'town' far more freely than hitherto. A small faithful core remained with the Misses Parks and grew old along with them, until their energy came to a standstill. They shut up their shutters for good, leased the shop to a draper and moved to a house in the Bellegrove Road. First, however, they thought of Nell. Miss Emmeline put on her hat one day and paid a venturous trip to London to see her old suitor, Jonathan Gadsby. Gadsby summoned Nell, looked her up and down, assessed her as a potential troublemaker, but unable to refuse Miss Emmeline anything, took her on as the lowliest of the low, a matcher.

'You can tell Mr Jonathan Gadsby,' announced Miss Emmeline now, 'that I shall visit him *myself* if he does not reinstate you immediately.' She paused and went pink. 'If all else fails, you may mention The Hat.'

'The Hat?' repeated Nell blankly.

'The Hat.' Miss Emmeline pressed her lips together firmly.

Nell dressed with care, vigorously trying to sleek down her hair with a little brilliantine in the hope of keeping it subdued. She must be ready for whatever might face her at Gadsby's. Of course Mr Tom Gadsby might have forgotten. So might Melissa, she thought without rancour. Or perhaps his father would just refuse to reinstate her? No, probably not, for Jonathan's blind adherence to Tom's decisions was a byword in the store.

When his father was killed, Tom, then seventeen, had been rapidly deflected from his chosen career of pilot and ordered to train to be the heir to Gadsby's. He was given a whirlwind tour, working a month in each department, beginning in the Fashion Department (not a success), Teagowns and Lingerie (even less), Mantles (moderate success), the Counting House (he survived), the workrooms (blank incomprehension), Fabrics, Men's Department (only slightly less of a disaster than Fashion), Hats (surprisingly, he took to this), Umbrellas and Scarves, Sporting Wear (his favourite, for Gadsby's had always kept a strong line here and augmented it keeping a careful eye on new fashions in sports), Shoe Department, Gloves and Hosiery, Haberdashery and Jewellery.

After all this, the directors knew, the staff knew and Tom knew that he would never make a manager. The only person who did not was Jonathan Gadsby and he was the only one that mattered. Tom's every hesitant suggestion was put into instant effect, to the despair of his fellow directors who took comfort in the fact that he made very few. Tom's roving brief of Store Manager meant nothing, except when he chose to exert his influence, which was virtually never – save on this Monday morning.

Nell found herself automatically walking to Gadsby's though it seemed odd to be arriving at eleven o'clock. She had not dared tell her parents, comforting herself that if she was lucky they need never know, but was she customer or staff? she puzzled. Which door should she use? In the end she elected boldly for customer and brazenly walked past the head commissionaire, an act which in itself could ensure dismissal for junior staff.

'Good morning, Miss Watkins.'

Nell almost stumbled on her new high heels in shock at the unexpected greeting. This was very strange. She hurried to the main staircase and with head held high marched up the stairs, aware that the ground floor walker who had never hitherto given her a second look was staring at her. News of her dismissal had obviously travelled quickly. She hurried along to the next flight lest her old friends from Teagowns notice. They did, amid a curious and sudden hush.

And up to the workroom floor; through a glass panel she saw Mr Bolton staring at her, second only to directors in authority. Mr Bolton's Room, as it was always known, was the clearing house for every transaction between showroom and workroom in theory, and in practice, it seemed, everything that was anything at Gadsby's. All

29

events and all persons were known to Mr Bolton. Including the fact that Nell Watkins had been sacked, she thought wrily, and now had the temerity to be walking past his office. She almost ran now up the last flight to the hallowed sanctum of the Fourth Floor, and nervously knocked on Tom Gadsby's door. He opened it himself.

Beyond him she could see the formidable figure of Jonathan Gadsby, standing with his back to her, staring out of the window. She gulped.

'Ah, Miss Watkins, come in,' Tom said cheerfully. 'We were just talking about you.' Judging by the look on Jonathan's face it was not an enjoyable talk, but Tom looked happy enough, she thought cautiously.

Jonathan swung round. 'My grandson, Mr Tom, tells me you want your job back,' he boomed without preamble.

'I would be most grateful, sir. I can promise you—'

'You aren't getting it,' he cut in.

Her heart plummeted and she flushed with shock.

'Dash it, sir, you've frightened the girl,' Tom said reproachfully.

'Nonsense, you couldn't frighten Miss Watkins if you tied her to a dozen wild horses,' Jonathan replied testily.

'What Mr Gadsby means, Miss Watkins,' Tom hastened to say, 'is that we've given you another job instead.'

A trotter? A pin-picker-upper? Tea girl? Her imagination roamed wildly.

'We want you to be the Buyer in the Fashion Department. The old girl's retiring,' Tom continued matter-of-factly.

The Buyer? Nell goggled at him. The Buyer was God. You had to be at least sixty to be God. The Buyer was law, The Buyer was *it*. The Buyer *was* the fashion. She couldn't have heard properly. She, Nell Watkins, twenty-three, of only five years' experience, plus four in the Misses Parks' workroom in Welling, to be buyer for

Gadsby's Fashion Department? The store's plum job in buying and in prestige? She *was* dreaming. She must be.

Tom seemed to be suggesting she wasn't. 'Got a hunch about you,' he said complacently. 'Besides, Melissa thought I ought to do something. She was very upset,' he told her almost reproachfully. 'Told me I must do something big. So I *did*.' He looked like a puppy dog wagging his tail for a biscuit, thought Nell disloyally to her fairy prince.

'I can't,' she stuttered.

Tom looked anxious. 'Why not?' he asked cheerily. 'Only a matter of buying a few frocks, ain't it? You can choose. Young blood.'

'But I'm too young,' she heard herself bleating. Was this her saying this she wondered?

'Doll yourself up a little,' he told her offhandedly. 'That will make you feel better. Look,' he had a sudden idea, 'take the rest of the day off and come in again tomorrow. You'll feel better.'

Did buyers take buses? she asked herself. Or taxis? Unable to answer, she decided to walk, despite the heavy new shoes. She felt uncomfortable and ill at ease, for the first time wondering if she had been entirely right to rely on Miss Emmeline's and Miss Gertrude's advice. True, she wanted to look older, more 'respectable' and conventional, and so they had ransacked the remains of their stock and added a *postiche* of hair in a chignon. She had surveyed herself in the mirror doubtfully at home. She certainly looked older, but somehow the effect was not Nell Watkins. Yet that was the point, wasn't it? She advanced cautiously on the new Lily Langtry shoes. Could these really be this year's fashion? And this high-waisted dark black dress, nearly down to her ankles, with the long rows of diamante beads out of Miss Gertrude's collection – they might pass as real or at least look good, she told

31

herself firmly. Did they really make her look authoritative?

Mr Perkins frankly stared (he's impressed, she tried to convince herself) as he recognised her and automatically took out his notebook, then remembered that buyers did not expect to have their time of arrival noted. When the news had come round from Mr Tom's secretary yesterday morning, eager to break the gossip even before Nell had arrived, it had seemed frankly incredible. Now it was not only incredible but downright disastrous. Where was Gadsby's going? The old man had gone mad, that was for sure.

Nell advanced. In for a penny, in for a pound. No staff staircase this morning. Never had it seemed so far from the cloakroom to the staircase. Without looking left or right she knew that all eyes were on her, that as soon as she had embarked on the staircase the secret bell had been pressed to announce to the next floor that someone of importance was on the way. Well, so she was important, wasn't she? She was The Buyer.

Teagowns let her pass through in silence, their faces either blank or flabbergasted. And so she moved into her new kingdom, risen from the ashes of her old. Fashion. There waiting for her were Miss Danzy, Old Ample and Beesknees, and their understudies, plus a new girl hastily promoted in her place from the workroom. They stood in two rows almost as if drawn up in military order to be inspected. As she came through the archway Nell drew herself up to her full five feet five inches.

'Good morning,' she greeted them.

Startled silence as they took in their new boss's appearance from head to foot.

Then it began. Began as an uncontrollable snort of laughter from an understudy, a titter from Beesknees, a smirk from Miss Danzy, then a joint uncontrollable hysterical laughter as, with tears streaming down their faces, they welcomed The New Buyer.

Chapter Two

Were these lumps of bread pudding *her* legs? If she did not act now, it would be too late, the moment gone for ever, and with it her only chance to succeed in this job. Well, she might look like a clown, but by golly, she wasn't going to act like one. There they were, all smirking and tittering. Even Old Ample, whom she had thought quite liked her. Nell drew herself up on the uncomfortable Lily Langtry shoes and stared at them, obliterating with great force of will everything but a certain disdain from her expression.

'Is this how you intend to behave to new customers?' she asked them haughtily. 'Not in my department, you don't.' A sudden hush as surprise temporarily quelled laughter. A moment's breathing space to marshal her strength, to take control of the situation.

'I thought,' she steadied her voice, sensing a slight quaver, 'by dressing this way I'd be able to judge how far your standards of politeness reach. A test,' she informed them loftily, 'and you've all failed it.'

An astounded silence now. It was a gamble, for surely they would not really believe her? But if she could inject enough confidence in her voice to make them doubt their assessment just for a moment, she might win. If she could hold their attention . . .

'I intend to make this department the best in London – not just *one* of the best, but *the* best – and that means beginning with the staff. I could have the best ideas in the world,' she rushed on, lest astonishment at her own gall overcame her, 'buy the best dresses in the world, and it's no use if you all have preconceived ideas about customers just from what they're wearing. You've got to want to help *everyone*, so that *anyone* can come in here, no matter how they look, and be treated like a duchess and go out looking like Melissa Hargreaves. Then I know when I go to Paris . . .'

The Dragon at last found her voice, albeit a strangled one, almost yelping with venom and shock. 'Go to Paris?' she ridiculed. 'You think you'll still be here? You won't last five minutes.'

Nell held her eye. 'I can dismiss a lot of people in five minutes,' she told her matter-of-factly.

'You wouldn't dare,' sneered the Dragon. 'Only the directors can do that.' The others shifted uneasily.

'On my recommendation,' Nell said flatly. 'And dare? Oh, I would *dare*, Miss Danzy. You needn't doubt that. It's just a question of whether it's in the interests of Gadsby's to sack you. You're a good saleswoman –' she informed her, as the Dragon's eyes flashed at this new impertinence '– and I want my department to have lots of good saleswomen. *Polite* saleswomen!' She looked round at the six faces watching her expressionlessly. They were cowed but not won, instinct told her. Oh no. They were just being cautious at the moment. The battle was merely under starter's orders, waiting for her to fall at the next fence.

A few minutes later Nell closed the door of the small office that was each buyer's own domain; each senior buyer had their own cubby-hole for which she was thankful. It would be lunchtime before she had to face them all. She drew breath, looked at herself in the mirror and made a face at the pale image looking back at her under its picture style hat with the artificial violets which she had told herself looked so smart only this morning. Smart on a matron of fifty perhaps. But on her? Nell Watkins? What should Nell Watkins wear now she was buyer for Gadsby's Fashion Department? She couldn't wear her old understudy's dress, couldn't wear her own clothes, for they had to be black and black was not a colour that featured highly in her private wardrobe.

Why had old Mr Gadsby agreed to his grandson's suggestion? she wondered. It must be because he had thought a lot of her ideas when she expressed them. True, he had not appeared to be impressed at the time. She was right though. They must have younger customers to survive. How to keep the old but attract the new?

She thought of that cover from the French edition of *Vogue* last November, which she had pinned up at home . . . Just a woman and a car, but what a woman, what a car – and what a dress. The fluid lines of all three seemed to merge into one another, all softness and straight flow, emphasising the new age by the zigzag pattern on the dress, suggesting speed, progress, cool acceptance of the future. And now she was the buyer of Gadsby's fashion, she could take the department in the direction she chose. *That* direction.

Of course she'd be earning more – this happy thought struck her for the first time. How much? Some of the buyers were rumoured to get £10 a week but she couldn't believe she would be so lucky. Perhaps £8. The enormity of this beside her previous 18s 0d suddenly became real. She grinned at the reflection in the mirror.

'You can look like Frankenstein's monster for all I care,' she told it perkily. 'You're going to be *rich*!' She stuck the bunch of artificial violets between her teeth, held her arms up at right angles, turned her face askew and executed a neat Valentino-like tango with the chair – just as Miss Danzy, hardly bothering to knock, entered.

'I wonder,' Miss Danzy asked blandly, apparently

35

deferentially, 'if you could spare a moment to advise a customer . . .'

'Mrs Willoughby would like to know, Miss Watkins, what line you expect the current trends to be following in Paris this autumn?' The Dragon had waited until they reached the customer before springing this on her.

Nell's heart sank. She might have known it would be a trap, and could hardly say she'd never been further from England than the end of Margate pier. But no dragons were going to beat her. She didn't need a St George. She put on her brightest expression for the 40-year-old fashionable woman with the oh-so-bored look – at least it *had* been bored. Now that she had taken in Nell's youth, horror was replacing it. 'I thought . . .' She turned crossly to the Dragon.

'Motor-cars,' said Nell quickly. Anything to get her attention.

'*Motor*-cars?' echoed Mrs Willoughby blankly.

'Aeroplanes,' Nell rushed on firmly. 'This is the age of technology. We're forging ahead. New boundaries – new horizons.'

'And what does this have to do with haute couture?'

'Everything,' Nell said desperately. 'Like Tutankhamen's tomb and the Egyptian look two years ago. Now it's fluid clean lines. Everything functional, easy to wear, like a tube.'

'I'm afraid I don't quite see myself as a water sewer,' Mrs Willoughby announced haughtily and dismissively, rising to her feet.

Round One to the Dragon, thought Nell savagely.

'Darling!' The sweet high voice projected over the showroom. Thank heavens! Round one was not quite over, she was saved by the bell, Nell realised gratefully as Mrs Willoughby sank unobtrusively back into her seat with a renewed interest in Gadsby's models.

'Melissa!' Grandly Nell excused herself from Mrs

Willoughby and went to meet her as she floated in in a grey face-cloth coat trimmed with the new and fashionable chinchilla with a chinchilla hat to match.

'I just wanted to say how absolutely right you were, darling Nell, about the sleeves on the yellow foulard, with the heavenly handkerchief points on the skirt. I want them changed. You'll do that for me, won't you?' She turned to Miss Danzy, flourishing the famous smile like a weapon.

'Oh, what a perfectly ducky little dance dress,' she cried, whirling round and seeing the model parading before Mrs Willoughby in a full-skirted royal blue satin dress, completely backless and doing its best to repeat this achievement on the front of the bodice too. 'Now why didn't I order that?'

'You did, Miss Hargreaves,' Miss Danzy told her eagerly. 'But in green silk.' Then looked aghast as she realised she had flouted the strict rule of the showroom, that each lady should believe (though not be promised) that the dress she was ordering was exclusive to her. Such was the diversity of figure and of materials that this had rarely been proved an embarrassment. Gadsby's economics were after all at stake. There had, of course, been the unfortunate occurrence when the wives of the two most prominent political leaders of the day had appeared at the State Opening of Parliament in the same gown, and Gadsby's clientele had taken some time to settle down thereafter.

'Did I?' Melissa looked vague. 'If you say so, *dear* Miss Danzy.' The smile flashed again, and Danzy looked quite human. 'Nell darling, I really called, apart from seeing dear Miss Danzy again, and all of you –' she said, throwing her arms wide '– to sweep you out to lunch. Would the Ivy suit you?'

Nell stared, flabbergasted. 'But I can't . . .' She became aware of listening ears.

'Oh, *Nell*!' Real disappointment in Melissa's voice.

37

'I only have three-quarters of an hour for lunch,' she explained.

'Even for an important client?' Melissa reminded her innocently.

Nell took a deep breath. 'I would like to, Miss Hargreaves, but I ought to see my fellow buyers at lunch. It is the first occasion that I can discuss rather important matters. I would have loved to come though,' she added wistfully.

'Then come to Old Ma Meyrick's with us tonight,' said Melissa warmly, 'or I shall be hurt. Come to the theatre after the show. And if you're worried about that silly old train, you stay with me in Charles Street. There's plenty of room in my flat. You'll love it.'

'Thank you,' Nell stuttered.

'And have you a beau to bring?' Melissa added offhandedly. 'That nice young man who showed me the rolls of cloth. I saw him winking at you.'

'Joe,' said Nell dazedly. 'Yes, I'll bring Joe.'

It was like going down the helter-skelter at the Blackheath funfair, she thought as she hurried to catch the Bexleyheath train to go home to change. You got on your little mat at the top and away you went, whizzing round corner after corner, with nothing to do but imagine you were flying through the air. Until you hit bottom, she thought soberly. And the bottom so far had been the buyers' dining room.

More by instinct than reason she had decided to try to subdue her usual impulse to grasp a problem by its horns and to appear meek and anxious to learn. Having removed the false tonsade from her curls and subdued them with a plum-coloured bandeau and a few kirby grips, she felt more able to cope with the forthcoming ordeal. She fixed an expression on her face which she told herself was confident but humble, and sallied into

38

the room. She was the last. Eleven pairs of eyes greeted her. Miss Copsy from Teagowns (rumoured to be living with an ageing White Russian prince), Mr Langer from Mantles (every other department store in London called this department Coats by now; Mr Langer clung obstinately to the term of his youth), Mr Johnson, Men's Made-to-Measure Suits, Mr Polgarth (Fabrics), Mr Dickens (Umbrellas and Scarves), Miss Hogarth (Hats), Mr Santos (Sporting Wear), Miss Routledge (Gloves and Hosiery), Mr Jacks (Shoes), Mr Paxton (Haberdashery) and Miss Marchant (Jewellery). They were the twelve Gadsby buyers, some ranking higher in the hierarchy than others; each knew his place and jealously guarded it. Just how jealously she did not then appreciate. She only knew that her allotted place seemed to be between Mr Dickens and Mr Johnson, whom she hardly knew, squashed up against the far wall under the draughty window.

'Good morning,' she said brightly, determined not to be intimidated.

'Good afternoon, Miss Watkins,' returned Mr Langer gravely and resumed his conversation with Fabrics. The men seemed undecided whether to rise to their feet or not, and compromised with scrabbling their feet and bowing over the soup plates. Nell looked at the unattractive lump of meat pudding in front of her and wondered if the angry tears she was holding back would do anything for the unappetising congealing gravy.

'I see Miss Hargreaves was in again,' said Miss Copsy kindly at last, taking pity on her, woman to woman.

'Yes,' Nell replied gratefully, on safe ground here. 'I hope she will become a regular customer when she marries Mr Gadsby.'

What on earth had she said wrong? Something, that was quite obvious. Miss Copsy went red, and the men studied their meat puddings with great interest, and there was a

distinct titter from the other women. Did they not know of
the engagement?

'I wonder whether Gadsby's will make her wedding
dress?' she ventured.

Another silence.

'Hardly likely, is it, Miss Watkins, in the circumstances,' said Umbrellas and Scarves, smirking.

Nell looked at him, puzzled, for she could make nothing
of this remark, and as both her neighbours appeared
preoccupied with tales of budgets and projections far
above her head, she chewed her way through the meat
pudding in silence.

Thank goodness Joe was there waiting as promised under
the clock, she thought gratefully, running towards him at
Charing Cross, now transformed in her one evening dress
of cream satin with a (for her) daring V-neck. Joe had
been unexpectedly hard to persuade into coming with her.
'It isn't right now,' he had said. 'You're a buyer, Nell,' he
said awkwardly.

She had been astounded. 'But Miss Hargreaves has
asked you to come, and *what's* not right now I'm a buyer?'

'It's different,' he'd said mutinously. Nevertheless he
had come. He too was looking transformed in an evening
suit borrowed from his father and consequently somewhat
on the large side. But Joe was so good-looking that no one
would notice that, she thought fondly. Night clubs were
not their usual haunt. They seemed to have been going
out for ever, and she supposed one day she'd marry him,
as everyone expected. Joe seemed to be dropping rather a
lot of heavy hints about when he could expect promotion.
He was twenty-five now, but his salary of £1 a week wasn't
enough to wed on, he told her. A faint relief had been her
first reaction – not because she didn't love him, she told
herself, but because there was no need to make a decision
yet. Besides, she liked working; she wasn't going to give it

all up and settle down before she had to. She certainly didn't love Joe in the way she loved Tom Gadsby, and sometimes when he was kissing her goodnight she had a treacherous fantasy of what it would be like to be in Tom's arms.

Joe was a very correct young man, and never tried to go further than a goodnight kiss. There had been a tacit agreement that there was 'time enough' for that. Sometimes she would awake unable to sleep, wondering what came next. Not all her beaux had been as reticent as Joe, but as the morals of Bexleyheath were not those of the Bright Young Things, they were easily deflected from their explorations. Often, however, she tossed restlessly, imagining how it might be if Tom were with her, but failing, for his image was as elusive as the dream she had.

Normally she and Joe would meet at weekends, to go rambling, play tennis, and cycle into the countryside. He lived in North London and it was a fair trek down to Bexleyheath by train, but he never seemed to mind, even when it meant escorting her home late at night if they went to a theatre. Once you were on a train, he told her, you were as good as there. That her promotion might make a difference to their relationship was a new and unwelcome thought. Marriage had seemed a long way off, but nevertheless had provided a milepost towards which she gently ambled. Now it was threatened, and not by her wish.

Melissa's blonde head was hard to spot in the crush in her dressing room at the Albion, and they hovered, daunted, on the threshold. Then with a sudden quickening of her heartbeat, Nell saw Tom pushing his way through.

'Evening, Nelly,' he waved a glass at her, and turned to Joe. 'I say, haven't we met?'

Joe gulped. 'In the Fabric Department, sir,' he muttered.

'Oh.' Tom looked relieved that the problem was so

41

easily solved. 'At Gadsby's then?'

'Yessir,' Joe replied woodenly. Nell could see he was hating it and squeezed his hand comfortingly.

Melissa suddenly emerged like a daffodil amid the crocuses. 'Darling!' flinging her arms round Nell, and her eyes sliding to Joe. 'What a handsome beau you have, hasn't she, Tom?'

Tom surveyed him. 'Lucky dog,' he informed him carelessly. 'Our Nelly's a corker, isn't she?'

'Darling.' Melissa looked worriedly at Nell's cream satin. 'I don't think that dress will quite do.' Her simplicity robbed the words of offence as Nell glanced at Miss Emmeline's best efforts in concern. 'Now what can we find?' She slipped her arm confidingly through Nell's. 'First, Tom, we can get rid of all these people.' She waved her hand at the gathering now into their second case of champagne. 'You're even skinnier than me,' she told Nell matter-of-factly, 'but we're much the same height though my legs are longer . . . yes!' She dived at the rail of dresses, hurling the protective sheet off it. 'Now, *this* one should fit.'

'But that's your dress from the play,' Nell stuttered, recognising the wispy silver tissue dress.

'So what? It'll be back for tomorrow. Now, there's a screen there if you're modest.' And she pushed Nell towards it, turning back to pour Joe a drink despite the fact he already had one.

'It won't fit,' cried Nell, in an agony of embarrassment, struggling with buttons and hooks.

'Nonsense,' called Melissa gaily, not moving.

'It *really* won't.'

Melissa, shrugging, went behind the screen and burst out laughing. 'Not over that brassière, darling. Not nearly flat enough. And so visible. Now that *would* be a new fashion. Take it off.'

'I haven't another,' hissed Nell, wretchedly aware how

embarrassed Joe must be listening to this now that the hubbub had died down.

'What does that matter? You just need this. Look.' She taped Nell's breasts as tight as she could with a piece of sturdy ribbon, held in place with strips of sticking plaster.

'There,' said Melissa. 'Off you go.'

Feeling almost naked, Nell walked out defiantly, avoiding Joe's eye, catching sight of a new Nell in the mirror – certainly a lot more of Nell both in front and behind, not to mention her legs, than had ever appeared in public before. The silver tissue threw a sparkle into her face, set off her brown hair and heart-shaped face, so that for a moment she forgot her awkwardness.

'Doesn't she look pretty, Tom?' Melissa said, delighted at her efforts.

'A stunner,' he replied obediently. Joe remained silent, just staring at her. He could say *something*, Nell thought crossly, as he squeezed in beside her in the Lea-Francis and Tom roared off on the way through to Gerrard Street.

So this was the famous 43 Club. She had passed the entrance often enough for Gerrard Street was near the heart of the fashion world. Not the fashion world seen by the public but the behind the scenes industry in which hundreds of small firms made accessories or wholesaled goods to keep the fashion houses supplied, not to mention an even wider network of home workers. In front of her at the doorway Melissa had slipped her arm through Joe's – who had, Nell noted, leapt out of the dicky seat to hand her out of the car, leaving Nell to clamber inelegantly out alone. She couldn't blame him, she supposed ruefully. Melissa's fragile beauty positively demanded it, though fragility was not a quality associated in other ways with Melissa, she was beginning to realise.

Having yielded her coat Nell felt vulnerable in the low dress – until she saw the crowd inside. In the haze of tobacco smoke, women flocked like glittering, twinkling lights around the black-suited men; long cigarette holders, bandeaux, close-shingled hair, ropes of beads adorning skimpy frocks, whirling out from the hips as they danced. Not a waist in sight – but plenty of knees visible as the short skirts flared, Nell noticed instantly; she would indeed have looked out of place in the cream satin and was grateful now to Melissa for her forethought. Even if her breasts were bobbing up and down despite the tape.

Although there seemed not a square inch of space, one sight of Melissa (or was it Tom?) and an empty table was miraculously found, followed one minute later by drinks. 'White Ladies,' Melissa informed them. 'We'll get champagne if you prefer.'

Cocktails! Nell chose excitedly. Bexleyheath was not known for its cocktails.

The small dance floor was packed with jigging figures, shrieks of pleasure occasionally drowning the orchestra's jazz rhythms.

'You're very quiet, Joe,' Nell said at last, taking a gulp of this extraordinary drink as they watched Melissa whirling on the dance floor, her twirling feet bobbing up and down to the syncopated rhythm, the fringe of her dress and beads flying wildly.

'Not your sort of place, this,' he replied simply. 'Nor mine. Nor her.' He glanced at Melissa.

'You haven't been able to take your eyes off her,' laughed Nell, 'you old hypocrite.'

'She's a beauty, that's why,' he said, flushing, 'but she's not our sort. We're both seeing her with stars in our eyes, or rather you are.'

'I'm not. *You're* seeing her all wrong. I'm just seeing a kind, generous and beautiful girl.'

'She's not of our world.'

'Our world is what we make it,' she retorted, suddenly angry that he was not as swept away by the excitement of the evening as she.

'No. Look at the dress. It's all right on her, but on you it's disgusting.'

'It is *not*,' she glared at him. 'It's *fashion*.'

'Come on, you two, why aren't you shimmying? Joe, come here and do the Gadsby Gallop with me,' Melissa commanded imperiously.

'What's that?' Nell laughed, as Tom sank back in his chair.

'Darling, I don't know. Joe and I will make it up, won't we?' She started a wonderful imitation of old Jonathan, hands behind back, slowly marching to the floor, then leapt around her stolid partner bowing unctuously on her points before whirling into action. 'Now you, Joe,' she shouted. 'You do the Gadsby Gallop too . . . Throw me those rolls of fabric.' She imitated his actions, looking rather like a picador. But Joe could not be bullied and after a while she came close to him, dancing cheek to cheek, her arms inexorably round his neck.

'She's a good dancer, isn't she, Nelly?' Tom remarked suddenly, snapping his fingers at the waiter to order more champagne.

'Wonderful,' agreed Nell fervently, for he seemed anxious for reassurance. Perhaps he would ask her to shimmy. Perhaps they too could dance like that. And at last he did.

Nell firmly put out of her mind all thought of Melissa and Joe – just to enjoy the sensation of being in Tom's arms. Very well, he'd rather be with Melissa, but tonight in this dress she *felt* like Melissa. Unfortunately very little of the dance *was* in his arms. He was a superb dancer, if not so outrageous as Melissa, and trying to follow his complicated manoeuvres kept her fully occupied. She enjoyed being whirled high in the air, exhilarated, not thinking it a bit strange to have Tom's arms clasped firmly round her thighs, and among the forest of females hoisted aloft she waved happily at Melissa. However had she

45

prevailed on Joe to lift her up so? she wondered hazily.

This was indeed a new age. Recovered now from war, the country looked to the Flappers for the future. The world was theirs to do what they liked with – provided it did not include war.

At last Tom brought her down, shouting something at her.

'What?' she yelled above the noise.

'Like being buyer, do you?' He brought her close so he could shout in her ear.

'Yes,' she replied, anxious to please but wondering if he had any idea of the problems, petty and major, that faced her. 'It's a wonderful opportunity,' she added, irrationally deflated. But he did not notice anything, only beamed happily. 'Good,' he said, jerking her back into the dance, his eyes straying to Melissa, her fair head against Joe's shoulder now. Joe looks as if he's enjoying it, Nell thought suddenly, pleased for his sake. So much for his 'this is not our world' stuff. This *was* her world. The Edwardian days had passed forever. Women could do anything now, even become a buyer at Gadsby's at twenty-three, and tonight she would be sleeping in Mayfair, at Melissa's house.

'Look at me, look at me,' Melissa called joyously to them. Her fringe was whirling so fast her stocking tops and suspenders were on full display as her flying feet twinkled their way round her maypole partner. Though even Joe was getting into the way of it now, Nell saw amazed, as he executed a few movements of his own. 'What's this, Nell? What am I doing?'

'I give up,' she shouted back, watching Melissa's extraordinary movements.

'The Danzy Dipso . . . Do you think she drinks, Nell?'

'Not now,' shouted Nell full of exhilaration. 'Not now I'm buyer.' Then she glanced at Tom nervously, remembering who he was, and wondering if he would disapprove of this disloyalty to his staff.

'Tommy darling, Nell looks tired,' remarked Melissa as she returned at last to the table. Joe's eyes were fixed on her in adoration now.

'No, I—'

'It's past one o'clock,' said Melissa firmly. 'And you have a job to do. It was selfish of me to want you to stay tonight, when I don't have to get up till midday. So Tommy will take you home to Bexleyheath in the Fanny-Lea and Joe can take me home by taxi when we're ready.' She smiled brightly.

'But—' Nell stared aghast, torn between the rival delights of a journey home alone with Tom and disappointment at not staying in Mayfair with Melissa.

'Of course,' said Tom quietly. 'Good night, darling.'

'But the dress—' Nell began, remembering it had to be back at the Albion for tomorrow.

Melissa considered, then smiled brilliantly. 'Your bag's in the car. You can change in the cloakroom here.' It was an order.

Fifteen minutes later Nell climbed into the front seat of the Lea-Francis, clad in her old cream satin.

'If it wasn't for this,' she gestured at the car, 'I'd feel I was Cinderella,' she joked. 'But this is still a wonderful coach. You won't turn into a mouse, will you?' She laughed.

'Sometimes I think I have,' he began savagely, and then stopped, clearly remembering who Nell was. 'Not me,' he amended cheerily. But he fell silent again despite her best efforts, until she turned the subject to cars. 'Do you race this motor-car?' she asked awkwardly.

He looked at her as if in surprise that anyone should be interested.

'No, not this old lady. First I had an Alvis, a 10/30, lapped Brooklands at 93 in '20.' This was double-dutch to Nell. 'Know Brooklands, do you? Have to take you sometime,' Tom assured her. 'I've got the new 12/50 now.

47

Racing version of course. Guarantee of 90.'

'Oh,' said Nell, resolutely determined to keep her end up without betraying her ignorance. 'Only 90 are to be made, you mean?'

He shot a look at her, grinning. 'You're a nice little thing, Nelly. I've been bad company this evening. Things on my mind.'

'Gadsby's?' she asked sympathetically.

'No,' he replied sharply, 'not Gadsby's,' leaping from the car outside Watkins' Outfitters. 'And it's ninety miles an hour to those who know about motor cars, Nelly Watkins,' he added laughing, as if to make up for his curtness. Then, perhaps seeing he had disconcerted her, he bent down from his lofty six foot and planted a quick kiss on her cheek. 'We won't forget Brooklands, Nelly,' he called, tooting the horn as he drove off into the silent night.

Was Joe avoiding her? Nell had visited the Fabric Department twice to make an arrangement to see him that evening and on each occasion he had apparently been fully occupied with a customer who seemed to be doing quite well on her own. At lunchtime Melissa swept in, insisting that she must take Nell out for 'a quick delicious bite', only for Nell to find that the 'bite' was a visit to Stagg and Mantle in Leicester Square to buy her a new black dress suitable for the buyer of Gadsby's Fashion Department.

'But why?' she asked when Melissa insisted on paying the, to Nell, incredibly expensive 69s 6d for a dress of black marocain. She hadn't got used to the fact that her buyer's salary of £8 made more possible than her previous wages of 18s a week. This dress, with its front skirt draped up to the hip-line join with the bodice, was simple yet wonderfully elegant. Melissa replied seriously, 'Because you're my friend, Nell.'

48

'Am I?' she asked, bewildered.

'Oh yes, darling, my one true friend. Now how about this delicious little hat?' Melissa rammed it down over her own golden curls and made a face.

'You look rather like a snail,' Nell informed her, laughing.

'Now that's a good idea,' said Melissa, tossing the defamed hat aside. 'Let's go to the Café Royal.'

So it was not until six o'clock that Nell finally managed to accost Joe. He was supposed to finish at 5.30, but had clearly manufactured an excuse to be late leaving.

'You're avoiding me, aren't you?' she accused him.

'No,' he said, shutting his mouth obstinately. 'And it's not right for you to be hanging round waiting for me, like a—'

'Like a what?' she retorted angrily.

'Like a shop-girl,' he snapped, lengthening his stride to get away.

'I *am* a shop-girl,' she retorted fiercely. 'I'm a girl and I work in a shop.'

'No, you're not. You're different now. *And* you're bewitched by that woman. I heard – out to lunch with her ladyship today. Your breath smells.'

Nell stiffened. She couldn't deny there'd been some strange taste with those snails. Garlic, Melissa had said. 'And what about you? You danced with her long enough. Couldn't have got a piece of gauze between you, you were so close.'

He flushed. 'Maybe. But she's not your sort.' And stopped suddenly.

'Why not?' she said angrily. 'She's been kind to me, says I'm her friend.'

'And you believe her?' he said scornfully. 'You're simple, Nell Watkins. You'd believe the Prince of Wales if he said he wanted to marry you.'

'Why not, if he loved me?' she replied. 'What's Melissa

49

done that you're so rude about her?'

He stared at her, drawing her into a doorway of Swan and Edgar's as they approached Piccadilly Circus.

'She's marrying Mr Gadsby in the summer,' he said in a rush, 'but she made me go back to her home with her last night and go in with her – said she could never sleep till she knew there weren't any burglars in there.'

'What's so terrible about that, you nincompoop? You are an old prude, Joe.' She laughed unwisely, relieved that was all.

He flushed angrily. 'I'll tell you what's wrong. She wanted me to – kiss her.'

'Actresses are like that, Joe. It means nothing,' she told him impatiently. 'She told me I was her one true friend, but that's just an exaggeration.'

'You don't understand,' he muttered angrily. But he was beyond explaining now, so switched back. 'Do you know what they're saying about you, Nell?' he demanded. 'About how you got the job?'

'No.' She looked at him suspiciously, suddenly alarmed.

'Well, I'll tell you. They say you got the job because you were Tom Gadsby's fancy woman and it was a way of paying you off before he marries Melissa Hargreaves.'

'What?' The blood drained from her face as she looked at him, standing in judgment over her, his jaw stuck out truculently. Then the humour of the situation conquered outrage. 'Me? A fancy woman. Oh, Joe, who'd want to fancy me? Where are the diamonds? Where is my chinchilla coat? Where's the Mayfair flat?'

But Joe was not laughing. 'You got the job, didn't you?' he said slowly. 'Why, if not that way?'

'I told you,' she began, then stopped. Why should she have to explain herself to Joe? Why should he assume she didn't deserve it? He was as bad as the rest of them. Worse, because he'd been her friend for eighteen months now. He should *know* her. *Believe* her. But he didn't.

50

Sharply, Nell drew in her breath. 'Anyone who has to ask whether that rumour's true doesn't know me. You're right, Joe, you're not of their world. You belong to the curtain-twitching brigade. I'd rather have Melissa' (and Tom she would have added) 'even if she forgets me tomorrow, than you and all your sort. Goodbye, Joe.' And she marched across Piccadilly Circus bound for Charing Cross.

'You fool, Nell, you fool!' he shouted after her. But she chose not to hear.

'Of course, Miss Watkins, you are young—' Mr Lorrimer, the kindlier of the two directors and the one in charge of supplies, informed her at the buyers' fortnightly meeting, 'and thus perhaps do not fully appreciate the extent of the division between the generations at present – quite unprecedented in my experience. Gadsby's clientèle is often, I am afraid, rather shocked at this so-called modern age, or rather at the way it demonstrates itself in shorter hemlines, backless frocks and –' he cleared his throat '– freer figures. Were we to follow your suggestions and follow these giddy fashions, we would soon have no clientèle at all.'

'You soon won't anyway,' said Nell, ignoring her fellow buyers' shocked looks, 'because Gadsby's clientèle will be dying off.'

'Come, come.' Mr Lorrimer was determined to keep his temper in the face of the most trying circumstances. 'Not quite yet. And slowly, slowly catchee monkee.' He waggled his finger. 'Change certainly, but little by little. The tortoise and the hare, you know.'

'Tortoises live a lot longer than Gadsby's clients,' she rejoined. 'Hares have fun, and *everyone* wants to have fun, whatever age they are. It isn't just hemlines,' she rushed on, ignoring the expressions that suggested fun was not top priority for the Lorrimers and Langers of this

51

world. 'Everything needs to be streamlined now. Elegant but comfortable. Corsets will go for good soon, as old-fashioned as tea-gowns. Gadsby's must fall in with that, as with everything demanded by a new generation.'

'*Must*, Miss Watkins?' retorted Miss Copsy tartly for her, as Nell belatedly realised how tactless she had been. It was an open secret that sales of her full-length flowing gowns were falling rapidly, and her old-fashioned lingerie following the same trend. Hardly surprising, thought Nell ruefully, but she was upset at having hurt Miss Copsy, particularly as she was her one ally among the buyers.

And how she needed allies there. Their pettiness still amazed her. The first area of contention was the table arrangement, as she came to realise they regarded the placement as a matter of strict hierarchy and complacently thought themselves clever to have reduced Nell to well below the salt instead of at the head of the table. As soon as she realised, she knew with sinking heart she too must play the game or she would never have their respect. Nothing so crude as arriving first and sitting in the honoured seat would do. She thought about it, arrived first one day, and when the others assembled they found her sitting in her accustomed place by the draughty window.

'Oh,' she then cried in vexation, 'I see your napkin ring has been laid here by mistake, Mr Langer. We shall have to change places.' She held his eye. The gold napkin ring was his alone. Silently, unwillingly, he did so, and she was not challenged thereafter. The minor annoyances of which peg to use in the cloakroom, the correct order of precedence when entering and leaving and speaking at the buyers' meetings she left them to work out as they would. Her point had been made.

'Gadsby's leads fashion, it does not follow it,' Miss Copsy continued tonelessly.

'But *where*'s it leading?' asked Nell desperately. 'You

run a wonderful department, Miss Copsy, but we are all bound by what we buy from Paris. Are we buying the wrong things? Is it our choice what we buy or is the house we buy from – I think we now have an exclusive contract? Not providing a wide enough range?'

'What do you intend to buy, Miss Watkins, when the time comes for you to go to Paris in September?' the other director, Mr Charles, asked smoothly, avoiding the question.

'I don't know till I see it,' replied Nell, in so far now she might as well go on. 'But I shall know then.'

'I do beg you, Miss Watkins –' real anxiety in his voice '– to take care. Fortunately you cannot go far wrong with Maison la Ferté,' he added with some relief. 'They understand exactly what Gadsby's requires. We have always been in accord.'

'*We'll* look after Miss Watkins when the time comes, Mr Charles,' Mr Langer cut in firmly. Miss Copsy nodded vigorously. 'Naturally she can't make decisions alone at this stage. We will—'

'If I'm to bear the responsibility,' said Nell firmly, 'I must make the decisions alone.'

They looked at one another. 'Fortunately,' said Mr Charles, retreating to base position, 'you will have an excellent teacher in the count.'

'Count?' asked Nell, bewildered.

Miss Copsy smiled in response. 'The Count Guy de la Ferté, my dear. You mustn't be nervous. I'll look after you.'

The summer became a kaleidoscope in which Nell was tossed between the excitement of life with Melissa and Tom, and the depths of despair as she wrestled with one ordeal after another, battling not only with the job itself but with the hostility of those ranged against her. They were like crocodiles waiting for her to spill blood before

53

they leapt to crunch her between them. There was nothing they could do until she had shown her hand, and that would not be until early September.

She visited current exhibitions hoping she might gain ideas from it much as she gathered people were from the Art Deco exhibition in Paris. But she came away totally bewildered, for once unable to spot trends in anything, let alone what might take place in the fashion world. Wasn't there some old Greek god who spent his time suspended between heaven and earth? Well, that was just how she felt, she reflected dizzily: shot out of heaven, and unable to come down to earth again. Her parents, unable to appreciate her change of status, had politely congratulated her and turned to matters more within their ken – the new underclothes she would now need from their stock, for instance. She had hugged them, accepted their gift – and resolved tactfully to replace it at the earliest opportunity.

Occasionally Melissa would descend, a veritable goddess ex machina, to sweep her off on a shopping expedition, sometimes for advice on her own clothes, but generally to teach Nell about choosing her own. She had no illusions on this. What she could see so easily for others, she could not apply to herself.

'Now, look at your hair, Nell,' forcing her to stand in front of a mirror. 'Really, look at it!' Melissa stood behind her, sweeping it off the face. 'See how this suits you? How the shape of your face emerges? Why cover it up? And you've a high forehead. Why not a ducky little fringe? I shall send you to Maison Nicol in New Bond Street.' She waved aside Nell's protestations at this still novel idea of attending an establishment merely to have one's hair cut. 'Nonsense,' she told her firmly, 'Marcel will look after you.'

And look after her he did. Instead of fighting the rebellious curls, he induced them to flick off the face. 'It is not the shingle, it is not the bingle, it is not the Eton crop. But it *ees* Miss Nell.'

And the same with dresses. What had been a chore before now became a pleasure as she trotted in Melissa's wake through Harvey Nichols, Woollands and Dickens & Jones in search of a new Nell.

After much thought, she moved up to London into a 'small but ducky' little flat in Chesterfield Street to the dismay of her parents, plus a certain relief that unconventional though this might be, they would no longer bear the anxiety of her return in the small hours, only to rise again at seven day after day.

The run of *London Lady* was at last to end in July and Melissa laughingly parried all questions as to what she would do then. Now was always more important. What to do this evening? They would go to dinners after the show, to clubs, gatecrash private bottle parties, to debutante dances. Usually Tom was there, sometimes just a haze of unfamiliar faces. On Sundays they would drive out in the Lea-Francis to the countryside, boating or picnicking. Nell loved it best when there were just the three of them, but Melissa grew bored all too quickly without a crowd and usually therefore several motor cars would set off in cavalcade in fine style, their occupants singing their way through Kent or Hertfordshire or Surrey, like gods freed from Olympus to rove the mortal world. It was exquisite agony to be brightly chatting to Tom, while his eyes and thoughts were fixed on Melissa. Her laughter would soar over to them as Nell valiantly tried to talk of the race at Le Mans or the Chitty-Bang-Bang series, until Melissa should decide to come to reclaim her own. Sometimes she tried to reproach her, but Melissa would just laugh and say goodnaturedly, 'You don't understand, Nell. I love Tommy. After all, I'm going to marry him.'

'When?' Nell steeled herself once to ask.

Melissa shrugged her elegant shoulders. 'Soon.'

Yet despite the agony these times were paradise before she was flung back into the maelstrom of the showroom, and the implacable hostility of the Dragon and Beesknees. Only Old Ample showed her any sympathy and that was dependent on whether or not the other two were around. Gradually she began to recognise Miss Danzy's new tricks, however, and turn them against her.

'I have just been telling modom that the blue suits her just as much as the brown, and if she cannot decide between them, they both look so charming that she should consider both.'

Both of them looked equally hideous, Nell raged, and Miss Danzy knew it. Both shades were too indeterminate to suit this customer.

'Charming,' she agreed brightly. 'You are quite right, Miss Danzy. Compare for instance this green . . .' She held the piece up against the customer in front of the mirror as she delivered this judgment of Solomon.

'Oh, I like that,' exclaimed the customer.

'Really? Ah, yes, I do believe you're right,' Nell said demurely.

She hated it when saleswomen sold customers colours that were wrong for them, no matter the fashion of the moment, and it frequently led to clashes. She observed the results in the workrooms and fitting rooms and raged about it. Then it came to a head, as for the fourth time that day Danzy requested her 'assistance'. It was a new customer and a highly difficult one, judging by the icy expression and exasperated finger tapping on the arm of the chair.

'Modom cannot find anything to suit, Miss Watkins. I've shown her—' and she reeled off nearly all the evening dress models. 'I thought you might have some in reserve. For special customers.'

Nell had, as Danzy well knew, but they were models already promised on a strictly exclusive basis. All save one in a mustard shade that had definitely been a mistake on the part of the last buyer. So horrible was it that like the infamous Number 21 no one had requested it, even in a different colour. Nell studied the client carefully. It just might work.

The model appeared to the usual snort of disgust from the customer. 'Charming, madam,' Danzy said automatically.

'Nonsense, woman, it's hideous and you know it,' beginning to rise to depart.

'Is that a Transformation?' Nell butted in almost without thinking, looking at the customer's hair.

'How dare you?' the astounded woman replied. 'Who is this impertinent girl?'

'Miss Watkins is our buyer,' the Dragon informed her happily.

'If you'll come with me, somewhere private, I'll show you what I mean,' Nell said desperately. Instructing the model to send the dress to the fitting rooms, she led a highly reluctant customer there too.

'Now, ma'am, let me just show you. *If* you could take the wig off . . .'

Unwillingly the woman did so and Nell sighed with relief. She was right. The woman's natural hair colour had a reddish tint. 'You've such lovely hair, ma'am, such a pity to hide it. If you'll permit me.' She patted the hair quickly into shape and held the dress against her. 'You see,' she said quietly, 'it just didn't look right with blonde hair.'

'But my hairdresser tells me I need it. He's the best,' she told Nell unconvinced.

'It was the best butter', Nell was tempted to echo, but kept a straight face. 'I know they're fashionable, ma'am, but this is making your skin look dull. The best colour to bring out a lovely skin tone like yours is that of your own hair. Greying or not,' she added boldly.

'Young woman,' the client said after a pause, 'you'll go far.'

Not if Danzy has anything to do with it, thought Nell tiredly.

'Nell, darling, look after my Tom while I talk to Adrian, will you?' Nell had no objection at all, but it occurred to her that Adrian seemed to be creeping into Melissa's conversation rather frequently.

'He's a kinema film director,' Melissa finally told her one day. 'He's going to star me in a series of films to be shot at Walton-on-Thames. Think of that, Nell!' She danced round the dressing room. 'I'll be in Valentino's arms yet.'

'Walton-on-Thames is a long way from Hollywood,' Nell said dubiously. 'I thought the film industry here was going bankrupt.'

'Not with me in it, it won't,' said Melissa complacently. 'We thought we'd start with *Romeo and Juliet*.'

'*What*? But Melissa – you can't play Juliet!'

'How do you know?' she retorted, hurt. 'I've not tried yet. Of course I can. I'm an actress.'

There seemed to be a lot of looking after Tom. For nearly a month (save for Ascot of course) Melissa rushed down to Walton-on-Thames during the afternoons and was back for the evening performance; then she would dance the night away. Concerned at the signs of strain on her face, Nell taxed her with overdoing things, but Melissa merely laughed – and informed her she was fussing. When she and Tom saw her after the show, she was her usual gay, insouciant self, but her talk now was always of the film world. Of Adrian, of takes and camera shots and angles, of the meaning of Shakespeare, of the vital importance of kinema in the future of artistic life in Britain, of how only British film directors understood quality films.

But no one wanted to see British films, Nell knew. Last November she had read that not one British film was showing anywhere in Britain. Everyone wanted to see American films, full-length Douglas Fairbanks or Mary Pickford films, not the shorts being rushed off the cameras in Britain. Even when the British did make a good film few could show it because of the block booking system pressured on exhibitors by American companies.

In early July, full of importance, Melissa announced she was going to Walton to see the first screening of the film. Unable to accompany her, Nell waited anxiously in her dressing room at the Albion as the minutes ticked by to curtain up – and still no Melissa. The understudy was already in costume when Melissa arrived – in tears.

'Oh, Nell,' she shrieked, throwing herself into her arms, 'I'll never work again. Never.'

'What's happened? Tell me,' Nell asked frantically.

'He said Felix the Cat acted better than me,' moaned Melissa.

'Who said?'

'*Him*,' wailed Melissa. 'Adrian. I could see,' she admitted, 'that I wasn't quite as good on the screen as on stage – it's all so different. But he needn't have been so rude. Not after . . .' She broke off and hugged Nell. 'You won't desert me, will you?' She sobbed. 'He's cancelled this film, and the others. He doesn't want me any more.'

'Probably run out of money,' said Nell practically.

Melissa stopped wailing. 'Do you think so?' she asked cautiously.

'Certain of it,' said Nell robustly. 'Have you had anything to eat?'

'I couldn't eat a thing,' Melissa wailed again. 'Oh, the awfulness of it. Seeing me up there, looking so – so – funny!' she said, peeping at Nell. 'I'll never work again.'

'Nonsense,' said Nell firmly. 'Now listen—'

But there was no need for Melissa to listen. Tom had

arrived. 'Oh, Tommy.' She burst into tears and flung herself into his arms. 'Let's get married quickly. Quickly!'

Quickly meant August apparently. Some giant hand seemed to be rushing Nell along, only for her to remain exactly where she was, as the season scurried around her in full swing. With Ascot behind them, Wimbledon, Henley and Goodwood loomed. As Nell's work at Gadsby's slackened, as customers were temporarily satiated with new clothes, so Melissa's demands on her time increased. In truth, her time was free enough. She saw Joe occasionally and exchanged a few stilted words in the course of daily business, and was relieved when she heard from Mr Polgarth in Fabrics that Joe was 'stepping out' with young Polly Hobbs, the pretty fair-haired assistant in Umbrellas and Scarves. She told herself firmly that she had moved into a new life, and she wished Joe well.

Whether her new life was an improvement on her old one, Nell did not stop to ask herself. She was too busy. Living alone had its disadvantages, she had discovered. There never seemed time to do the washing and ironing; scarcely time to eat, caught up as she was between Melissa and Tom. She had told herself that seeing them together would cure her of her love for Tom, but it didn't. It increased it. Each time she saw his handsome face, puzzled at some extravagant gesture or disconcerting action of Melissa's, she wanted to hold him close, tell him she alone understood him. No, she must not think that way, she told herself. It was a betrayal of Melissa, who loved Tom and must know best how to treat him.

Late in July, after *London Lady* had closed, Melissa grew increasingly restless. 'Pre-wedding nerves,' said Tom knowledgeably to Nell, as one Sunday having summoned them to dinner she decided that she wanted to 'slum it in the country'. 'Richmond,' she cried. 'We'll go to Richmond. *Now*.'

'But it's dark,' Nell pointed out, surprised.

'You're always making difficulties, Nell,' Melissa snapped. 'Tommy darling, we can go to Richmond, can't we? I *must* go to Richmond.'

Goodness knows how much money changed hands to persuade a boatman to row them on the river at midnight, Nell thought dazedly, but of course it was accomplished. And somehow, since Melissa was Melissa, no one questioned the rightness of her decision. It was indeed the perfect end to a perfect evening.

Ahead of Nell in the boat, Melissa sighed with happiness, her head on Tom's shoulder. Above them the velvet night air was soft and watching his arm steal round Melissa's shoulders, Nell knew she was of as little account to Tom as the stolid boatman pulling rhythmically between them.

Melissa demanded Nell's help in every detail of the wedding which was to take place at St George's Hanover Square, with Nell as her sole bridesmaid to her amazement. Rather to her surprise, the wedding dress was being made at Gadsby's, albeit to Melissa's design. It was, to say the least, dramatic, being on the knee at the front, sweeping lower at the back, and with a silver lace train from the shoulders to the floor. The workrooms were agog as it passed from Bodices to Sleeves to Skirts, all handling the heavy white silk with reverence.

'Don't your family want you to get married from home?' asked Nell curiously, for Melissa never mentioned her background.

'I don't have any,' replied Melissa quickly. 'I'm A Norphan,' she told her, mock-mournfully. 'Oh, *Nell*, I've *such* an idea. Suppose I get married from *your* home? A country wedding, and we could have the reception at that ducky house in Danson Park? There, that's settled!'

'Melissa,' Nell spluttered, 'it's a public park now.'

'Oh, lovely, lots of people. Tom will arrange it. And there must be a church somewhere too, isn't there?'

'At Bexleyheath. Christchurch,' said Nell weakly.

'Tommy can get one of those special licence things so I won't have to camp in the park for three weeks, and there we are. You see, darling, how easy it is when you try. Now when are you bringing the dress round for the final fitting?'

When Nell arrived at the Charles Street house for the fitting, two weeks before the wedding, she saw the Gadsby delivery van outside, obviously delivering the wedding dress and part at least of the trousseau. The door to the house was ajar so she knocked and entered, expecting to find the delivery man handing over his wares to Gwen, Melissa's housekeeper. There was no one there. Odd. Nell closed the door and went in search of Melissa or Gwen. She could find neither downstairs and ran up to the first-floor drawing room. It too was empty. It must be Gwen's day off, but where was Melissa? Nell called out but there was still no reply. There was definitely somebody upstairs, however, for there were creaking noises as of someone moving about. Melissa must be in the bedroom unpacking and not have heard her.

She ran upstairs where the door to Melissa's bedroom was open – and stopped transfixed. On the floor, scattered around, were boxes, some spilling their contents. From one, the wedding dress lay half exposed in a crumpled heap. Melissa was indeed in the bedroom. She was in bed, but not alone. And not asleep. Her naked body was writhing on top of another one – a man's, whose face she could not see, as she stood unbelievingly, numbly at the doorway. What she could see of Melissa's lovely face from this angle was red, distorted, unrecognisable as she cried out unintelligibly. Then Nell must have made a movement, for the man – Tom? Nell thought stabbingly – moved his head and saw her, jerking with horror. Melissa

62

peered round; she said not a word, her expression did not change as she turned back to smother the man below her with kisses. The man was not Tom.

Nell turned blindly, fleeing down the stairs. At the front door she made herself stop. *What* was she running from? Melissa. Why? She, Nell, was not at fault, she told herself. Melissa had been expecting her. Outside was freedom of a sort. A world without Melissa, a world she could reckon with and understand, a world she could cope with. Here? Here were dark depths, where she was being manipulated by another's whim. Yet that other person had called her friend and she had accepted it. Didn't that mean she must at least see it out? Speak to Melissa before cutting the bonds? Surely she owed her that much. For whatever motive, Melissa had been generous to her, her warmth and gaiety had lit her life as a beacon, and she could not snuff it out without at least trying to understand.

With unsteady legs she walked into the morning room, took a cigarette from the obscene Manekin Pis cigarette box that Melissa was so proud of, and sat down to wait, too stunned to think clearly, fighting nausea. She watched her trembling fingers detachedly, as though they were no part of her. Who was that man upstairs? And did Tom know?

The door opened and Melissa came in, dressed in an old satin wrap, hair still tousled, bright-eyed, defiant, wary. Her eyebrows shot up coolly as she saw Nell waiting. Outside, the sound of a van engine being cranked could be heard.

'He's your delivery man – that's what you wanted to know, isn't it? He's only a boy really. A *sweet* boy.'

'Gadsby's delivery man?' Not understanding yet.

'Yes, darling.' No warmth in the endearment.

'But are you in love with him?' Nell faltered, aghast.

Amazed, Melissa regarded her, then burst out laughing. 'My poor Nell, of course I'm not in love with him!'

'Then *why*? And what about Tom?' Nell's voice rose angrily.

'He has nothing to do with this,' Melissa said in a detached voice.

'He has everything to do with it.'

'No! And you're going to tell him nothing.'

'Why not?' Nell replied dully.

'Because you wouldn't want to hurt him. You love him too much,' said the suddenly hateful voice. 'I can always tell,' Melissa added complacently, seeing guilt written all over Nell's face.

She swallowed. 'So that's why you wanted me with you such a lot? So that I could engage Tom's attention while you went to bed with the delivery man.'

'Oh, not just the delivery man, darling,' said Melissa offhandedly. 'I only met him today. Anyone really. My leading man, naturally. Michael. Anyone amusing and handsome enough. And if there's no one amusing,' she added with a note of bravado in her voice, 'why not the milkman? Or the theatre cleaner?'

'Or Joe,' said Nell bitterly.

'Or Joe,' agreed Melissa. 'Poor Joe. He was almost reluctant – at first.'

'You think we're all just marionettes to dance to your bidding,' said Nell in disgust. 'And heaven help us, we *do*. But no more. Not now I know how rotten the puppeteer is.' She got to her feet. The door was but a few paces away. Soon she would be free. But she did not reach it.

'No.' Fear in Melissa's voice, the sharp smell of it in the air as she ran to Nell, throwing her arms round her. Nell stood like a statue.

'I love you, Nell, you're my friend. You really are. I need you, Nell. I need you more than anything.'

'More than the delivery man?' she asked, still not moving.

'That's not fair. It's not the same,' cried Melissa. Tears began to roll down her cheeks. Not her usual tears blinked up in clear blue eyes, but ugly tears coming in gasping sobs. 'I can't *help* it. Truly I can't. You *must* believe me. I do love Tommy. I want to marry him – but he's so good, so simple, he could never understand how much I need. I *have* to have other men. Do you understand at all?' She broke off in despair.

'No,' said Nell simply. 'If you love him—'

Melissa gave an impatient sigh. 'It's just not like that. You're a virgin, aren't you, Nell?' And sensing her stiffen, rushed on before she need reply. 'I first let a boy do it to me twelve years ago when I was thirteen. And they never stopped. I lied to you, Nell. I'm not an orphan. My parents threw me out when I was fifteen because they couldn't control me. I don't even know where they live now. I dressed up, changed my name, went round the provincial theatres, and here I am in London several changes of stage name later. And I got here more on my back than on my stage legs. That's the bit they don't tell you in the theatre magazines,' she added bitterly. 'Anyway, it wasn't just for my career. I *have* to have men.' The simplicity of the words robbed them of their enormity. 'It doesn't have anything to do with love, Nell. It's more like an illness. An addiction. Like opium. Only no doctor knows how to treat it, or even recognises it. I tried telling one once and he told me I was a slut. Maybe I am, but anyway it's fun,' she tried to say with bravado.

'Please, Nell,' she changed tack, 'you won't tell Tommy, will you? I do truly need you as my friend. You're one of the few really good things that has happened to me. I've got thousands of so-called friends and not one of them really knows me or cares about me. You cared about me and now you *know* me too. Don't leave me, Nell. You're honest. I can rely on you, trust you—' She was beginning to babble, clutching at Nell, the tears making her face ugly now. 'Please always be my friend. I need you so.'

'Just because you don't want me to tell Tom?' said Nell implacably, not yet betraying her instinct to throw her arms round Melissa in forgiveness. 'That's the real reason. You don't need me, you don't need any *real* person. Only yourself, and your men.'

'That's not true,' said Melissa quietly. 'If you knew, Nell, if only you knew the dreams, the torments I have. I'm so afraid – afraid of everything. Of walking on to the stage, of drying up on stage, of failing on stage like I have on film, afraid of age, of losing my looks, of having nobody and nothing. Afraid of loneliness—'

'Except in bed.'

Melissa flushed and Nell was ashamed.

'Most of all then,' Melissa said in a low voice. 'It's terrible, Nell, to be hunting, hunting for something and think you've found it, and you cry out to yourself, "Here it is, I've got it this time." And the next second, you know it's worthless, you've missed it again. But the next time it happens just the same. It's always so convincing, so real – and then it's empty as air. You see something in someone's eye and you follow it, only to find too late you were deceived all along. Like a hall of mirrors, distorting. You know what will happen but you can't find the way out. You'll lead me out, Nell, won't you. You'll lead me . . .' She broke off, unable to continue, reaching out.

Nell looked at her, battling with herself. In that moment she saw quite clearly that Melissa would not change for all her friendship. She would give what she could in return, but was it enough? But how could she measure it in such terms? She could go back, she could go forward. And Melissa was part and parcel of the challenge of forward. 'Yes,' she promised at last, 'I will,' taking Melissa's hand.

'And you'll always be my friend?' The grip was like iron.

'I'll try.'

'When you try, Nell, you win. I don't. You are fortunate.' Melissa paused. 'When Tom and I are married, you'll be *both* our friends, won't you, Nell?' she asked anxiously. 'You won't desert me?'

'No, but—' She hesitated, wondering how to put it.

Melissa gave her a look. 'Will I go on in this way after we're married? Oh no, because I'll be safe then. Tommy will keep me safe. I won't need to go looking, you'll see. Not with both of you to look after me.'

It rained on the wedding day, but Melissa's beauty shone over it all. She walked from Christchurch on the arm of her proud new husband like a queen. Behind her followed Nell, the beige-coloured satin of her dress reflecting the stone that was her heart. Behind her the Gadsbys, led by old Jonathan, back where he'd started his career fifty-five years ago. On his arm was Miss Emmeline Parks. Behind them, Nell's own parents with Miss Gertrude, and Tom's sister Rose, and then all the hundreds of friends of bride and groom, followed by it seemed the entire population of Kent as the procession made its way to the waiting motor-cars to drive to the Palladian mansion of Danson Park. As Nell watched Melissa's white satin shoes skipping up the grand flight of steps into the house, and Tom's broad back beside her, it seemed to her that symbolically they were walking out of her life and she following into theirs. Should she follow or stay, she thought crazily, as Jonathan Gadsby caught her up.

'What are you waiting for, Miss Watkins?' he roared genially. What indeed?

'Come along, Nell,' beamed Miss Emmeline. 'Mrs Gadsby will be needing you.'

Nell smiled at her. 'So she will,' she answered quietly,

and ran quickly up the steps after the happy couple.

Four hours later she was descending them again, as Melissa and Tom departed in the Lea-Francis for their honeymoon. Melissa glanced up after she jumped into the motor-car. 'Here,' she shouted, tossing her bouquet of red roses at Nell with such force that it thudded against her as she automatically put out her hands to catch it.

'You'll be next, darling,' Melissa called. 'Darling, *darling* Nell.'

Maison la Ferté had now been established for exactly the length of Jonathan Gadsby's life, and like him it had sprung from small beginnings. It began with a woman – a girl to be precise – Marguerite Massenet, who in 1850 left her farmer parents' home in the Auvergne and travelled to a luxurious apartment in Paris as the mistress of the Comte de la Ferté. Having a *comtesse* and a thriving family, not to mention vast and struggling estates, the count was naturally unable to spend as much time as he could wish with the delightful Mademoiselle Massenet, who amused herself in his absence not by buying from couturières but by designing for them. When the count discovered that several of his wife's friends, among the most elegant women in Paris, were wearing designs emanating from his mistress, he was at first amused, then intrigued, and finally contemplative. Instead of selling designs to others, why did she not, he suggested, set up her own business, financed by himself? Anxious to oblige, Mademoiselle Massenet did just that, and when she died twenty-five years later the de la Ferté estates were once again thriving and the count again a rich man, thanks to the royal patronage of the Empress Eugénie who, while she might take her evening gowns from Monsieur Worth, patronised Madame Massenet for her day dresses – which after all reached a wider public than her evening gowns.

So firmly established was Madame Massenet that the

fall of the Empire made not a whit of difference; at her death, the count promoted her chief lieutenant, his eldest son who had no ambitions towards running estates, to be chief designer, which when Paris had accepted this change of sex, had ensured that the house of Massenet la Ferté became simply Maison la Ferté. Since then an ample supply of sons had kept both design and control of the business, despite its rapid expansion to a point where it rivalled the House of Worth, in the hands of the de la Ferté family. By 1925 not only did one not need to specify at which number of the Avenue Montaigne in Paris the Maison la Ferté might be found, one scarcely needed to specify the arrondissement. Control and design were both now in the province of Guy, Comte de la Ferté, a man in his early-fifties, and 'charming, oh so positively charming', Miss Copsy informed Nell ecstatically.

'You have only to put yourself in his hands, with us to guide you and you have nothing to fear,' Mr Langer reassured her kindly.

Fear? Nell had enough to do coping with a strange country, for it was the first time she had ever been abroad; moreover a country where everyone spoke French, of which she could remember very little from her schooldays. Never had she seen such supercilious-looking women, or such elegant men. Everyone seemed to be rich and distinguished. Gadsby's customers looked positively angelic, even the Lady Lenhams and Mrs Willoughbys, compared with these hard-faced immaculately dressed women with their black poodles and rich clothes. After coping with the streets of Paris, the autumn opening, as they called it here, at Maison la Ferté was hardly something to fear. Or so she had thought. Today was the third day of the opening; the first was reserved for the press, the second for important private clients, and today for the hoi polloi – the foreign professional buyers.

Nell had employed her time well, escaping from her

watchdogs' strict eye and touring the shops and smaller fashion houses who were not so chary of strangers attending their shows, to get her own idea of what the current trends were. The smell of the wind, her father used to say knowledgeably when preparing his orders for the next season. And the wind blew the same in Paris as Bexleyheath.

Now within the august precincts of the Maison la Ferté her nerve suddenly deserted her and she wished she had not eluded Miss Copsy's eye this morning on the pretext of visiting the powder room. Wandering through these stately high rooms, with marble floors and elegant furniture, she felt as if she were at Versailles rather than a showroom. Surely showrooms, however elegant, should look welcoming? And these did not, merely intimidating.

She wandered through a side arch into yet another room, again empty since everyone was probably gathering in the main showroom now for the opening, and found herself in the lingerie room. Of that there was no doubt she thought in amusement. Miss Copsy would have a fit if she saw this compared with her own discreet arrangements at Gadsby's. Here a pink carpet set off creamy pink walls covered by a white trelliswork about ten foot high, along which lingerie was displayed in its full glory. Deep cyclamen camiknickers, sky-blue shifts, daring black crêpe de Chine nightgowns. And the corsets! Small, light, brightly coloured with red suspenders and bones attached . . .

'*Est-ce que je peux vous aider, mademoiselle?*' a cool voice enquired. Caught in the act of fingering the cyclamen camiknickers she jumped guiltily and turned round to face the speaker, a slim young man, taller than many Frenchmen, wearing a harassed expression and the best cut grey suit she had ever seen. No Oxford bags here, she noticed. How very strange to have a young

70

man in the lingerie department! Paris *was* an odd place. An exciting one too. How Melissa would . . . A stab of jealousy at the thought of Melissa and Tom in each other's arms made her voice sharp.

'No, thank you, I was just looking.' No, he was French. She began again. '*Je seulement cherche*—'

The mobile eyebrows shot up. '*Alors, la chasse est finie, mademoiselle*. These are perfect, just for you.' He reached up and twitched down the camiknickers, displaying them like a bullfighter's cape over one elegantly sleeved arm.

Nell stared coldly into his amused brown eyes. She would not give in and speak in English, as he clearly expected.

'*Je ne suis pas une acheteur de camiknickers*,' she told him firmly. '*Je cherche les mannequins.*'

'*Quoi*?' The amusement disappeared from his face. '*C'est vous? Merde*! English as well as late. And you are too short, *mademoiselle*.'

'There's not a lot I can do about that,' she retorted curtly, taken aback.

It happened so fast she hardly had time to realise what was happening as he unceremoniously grabbed her by the hand and pulled her after him, rushing out of the salon, then through a series of equally palatial salons, finally arriving via a short corridor at a room full of racks of clothes and plaster models. Here at last he released her and she rubbed her wrist ruefully.

'*Qui êtes-vous*?' she managed to gasp. Had she fallen down her own personal rabbit hole like Alice in Wonderland?

He took no notice, rummaging through one of the racks. 'No chic,' he muttered to himself. 'But we have no option.' He turned round at last. 'Take your clothes off,' he commanded wearily.

That settled it. Nell clutched her coat defensively round

71

her and swiftly debated which door to make a dash for. But her move was forestalled by his moving behind her, snapping, 'There is no time for modesty, mademoiselle. I will help you,' already tearing off her coat.

'Just a minute,' she panted, tangled up with her handbag and the coat sleeves, but the zip of her green repp dress was already being wrenched down and the frock slipped over her shoulders, falling to her feet as soon as she released herself from the last coat sleeve.

'Never again do you model for the Maison la Ferté.' He yanked impatiently at her wrist as clad in her sky-blue shift, she bent over to pull up her dress again.

'Model?' she yelled, tears of mingled embarrassment and fury pricking at her eyes. 'I'm here to *buy*.'

'*Quoi*?' That stopped him at last.

'I'm the buyer from Gadsby's in Regent Street,' she told him unsteadily, slipping her frock back over her shoulders with trembling hands.

A deep red flush flooded his face. 'But you are—' He stopped helplessly.

'So if you wouldn't mind telling me where I should go?' she began as haughtily as she could while carrying out the contortionist manoeuvres demanded when the zip jammed.

'Permit me,' he murmured, deft fingers rapidly dealing with the problem. 'Mademoiselle, we are missing one mannequin – a replacement for one who is ill. I was searching – how can I apologise? Fashion houses do not often have buyers so young and beautiful. Forgive me, please. Miss Watkins, is it not?' He bowed over her hand, kissing it lightly on the palm.

Something snapped inside Nell. Whatever sympathy she might have had for him vanished, and she snatched her hand away with a burst of angry laughter.

He straightened up instantly. 'Something amuses you?' he asked coldly.

'You. So young, so beautiful,' she repeated furiously. 'All you young assistants think you're Rudolph Valentinos. You only have to kiss our hands and we're your slaves for life. That's his trick, kissing the palm. It doesn't mean a thing.'

He stiffened. 'I beg your pardon,' he replied stiffly. 'I was attempting to apologise. I was unaware that I was making myself ridiculous.'

She was instantly contrite, but before she could put matters right, he had snatched up the cyclamen camiknickers, which in his headlong rush through the building he had brought with him by mistake, and presented them to her. 'Pray accept these as a token of my respect, mademoiselle,' he said vengefully.

Furious with herself for being so ungracious, much as he deserved it, Nell hurried to the showroom in the charge of a young page he had summoned and took her seat with Miss Copsy and Mr Langer, who greeted her with relief. At least Miss Watkins was deigning to grace the opening with her presence.

Nell slid into her place at their small table in the packed room, just as a distinguished grey-haired man arrived, circled by a small entourage. Obviously this was the Comte de la Ferté himself. Mr Langer introduced Nell to him in tones that suggested Nell should drop to the floor in obeisance. She very nearly did for his gracious politeness impressed her greatly as without a flicker of an eyelid at this surprising change in Gadsby's policy he welcomed her.

'We too have changes this season, mademoiselle. It is high time we older hands acknowledge the advance of time.' He glanced over his shoulder and beckoned. 'May I present my son Lucien who will be looking after export buyers from now on.'

Unsmilingly the young man advanced, took her hand

and shook it with no sign of recognition.

'*Enchanté, mademoiselle.*'

NEXT CHAPTER
PAGE 114

Chapter Three

A grand opening at Maison la Ferté was a very different occasion to the spring and autumn shows at Gadsby's, to which Nell had been used. Still smarting from her unfortunate encounter with Lucien de la Ferté, she began to think furiously of possible improvements which she could make to her own first dress parade in two weeks' time, and excitement crept over her again. A few bunches of flowers had been the only concession to ceremony at Gadsby's.

Here, everything suggested an affair of immense importance, which the spectators were privileged indeed to attend. As indeed they were. Each guest was carefully selected to avoid the possibility of pirating – the greatest curse of the trade, Miss Copsy would inform Nell solemnly, her dangling pearl earrings bobbing vigorously. Here, the subtle angle of chairs and tables, the imposing carpet specially laid down in the centre, the raised platform on which the mannequins would first appear, swathes of delicately coloured fabrics to decorate and complement the subtle colouring of the salon, all added to the anticipation. Ah yes, Lucile, or rather as she was now, Lady Duff Gordon, might have advanced the art of the fashion parade (and indeed begun it in London) by her use of tall mannequins and by choosing them for their looks, but Paris, Nell was reluctantly forced to admit, could still outclass London for sheer sense of occasion.

Nervously she clutched her fountain pen and pad, noting that an ink blob already adorned her middle finger and surreptitiously trying to wipe it off on her handkerchief. Miss Copsy and Mr Langer had no time to spare for her now, thank goodness; eager expectancy rippled through the hall as Lucien de la Ferté appeared on the platform. Still shaken by their unorthodox meeting, Nell tried to study him dispassionately as he began his introductory speech. He didn't *look* like a dress designer, she decided, or did his father do the designing? What *did* he look like? Not like Tom, with his fair good looks and open frank warmth. Light brown hair, obviously with an inclination to curl like her own, thin face, not as tall as Tom, five foot ten inches maybe, and not nearly as well-built. He had nice brown eyes, she decided, that animated his face, but it was not a face you'd remember. Almost nondescript. Or was it? That jawline looked extremely firm. How would she deal with him when it came to buying the dresses? Carefully, she decided instantly. Unpredictable, that's what that face said. She thought back to what Miss Emmeline had once said of the local ironmonger's son: 'Young Tommy Thompson may look like a sparrow but he's the instincts of a buzzard.' Nevertheless she would be a match for Lucien de la Ferté, Nell thought complacently.

Horrorstruck she realised she had missed the first two models and had hastily to note down their characteristics from their disappearing backs. How should she judge which to buy, which would adapt best, perhaps in alternative materials, for Gadsby's customers? She quickly decided on a points out of ten system. But would she remember them all clearly enough afterwards? After all, as Miss Emmeline was forever reminding her, she was no dress designer, no appreciator of fine detail, of whether revers or roll collar might be more fashionable this year. Her strong point was the general trend of fashion, so she should centre her planning on that.

She concentrated hard on the mannequins. Surely no

real women existed like this? Impassive faces, beautiful and ice-cold, stared haughtily at their audience, their garments speaking for them. Velvet. So the rumour was right. Velvet was returning to decorate dresses and coats. Here was a dress and coat in *velour de laine*, the cedarwood colour coat with new Highwayman collar in velvet, the frock in repp with a russet nuance and trimmed with a chevron on the front bodice of the same velvet. Frocks of marocain, streamlined to the hip, had apron skirts flaring out. Everything had velvet in the form of bows and on the cuffs to the long closely fitting sleeves. The latter was something new – it could catch on, Nell thought. Or would it? Yes.

Bemused she let them vanish without noting numbers and had to hasten to catch up with her notes. Yes, that one was right for Lady Lenham – perhaps in green? And that for Mrs Willoughby though in silk not wool marocain. A rustle of renewed excitement as the evening dresses came on. Only one now full-length, she noticed, the others were calf-length or sometimes just below the knee, and occasionally petalled to make them seem longer. Even the floating georgette dresses with fluted skirts boasted velvet somewhere: velvet bands, velvet bows, velvet flower motifs. Satins gleamed above white silk stockings, something Nell had of course never been able to afford; how different they looked to the new artificial silk. With what grace these girls moved – save for one, whom she realised with some amusement must be the replacement for whom His Imperial Highness had mistaken her. She wondered, regretfully, what would have happened if she *had* gone on to model. That would have been one in the eye for Mr Langer.

As well as having natural flair the mannequins had obviously been rehearsed time and time again. Perhaps more training could be given at Gadsby's? It would mean yet another row – her heart sank – in persuading the

Gorgon of the model room, but it would be worth it. At last it was over, as an ostrich feather-trimmed gleaming ivory satin dance dress with matching mantle vanished behind the curtains. Every model had been an artistic triumph. And yet she realised with surprise that she was left with an irrational sense of disappointment. Why? She could not pin the answer down, but before tomorrow morning, when all three of them bargained with Lucien de la Ferté, she would have to do so.

'It is the custom of our maison that we take to dinner important new buyers – "a small bow to her" – in order that we may become accustomed to one another before we do business. My son would be honoured to entertain you this evening,' the Comte de la Ferté told her smoothly. His son did not look honoured. She glanced at him, seeing the dislike in his eyes, a dislike surely mirrored in her own.

'I would be equally honoured,' she informed them in as haughty a voice as she could manage.

'I thought perhaps Voisin,' Lucien informed her off-handedly, 'if you care for French cuisine, Mademoiselle? Otherwise we could of course visit the English Tavern in the Rue d'Amsterdam. I hear they produce excellent Irish stew.'

The count glanced at his son, surprised, and smoothly intervened. 'Mademoiselle Watkins as an international buyer deserves the best of *our* cuisine.'

If the count had been English, Nell would definitely have interpreted the look he gave her as a wink.

She might deserve it, but could she eat it? Nell stared doubtfully at the oysters on her plate, waved aside the sauces, and plunging into the array of cutlery picked up the first knife and fork she came to to attack the first one as to the manner born.

'I see you are not in the habit of eating oysters,' Lucien remarked conversationally, poker-faced. 'Pray allow me the honour of instructing you.'

Pray do, thought Nell through gritted teeth, having been deprived of the right of selecting her own menu. She watched while he dexterously added sauce, twirled a small two-pronged fork and popped the result into his mouth, followed by an interesting manoeuvre that would never have been tolerated at Bexleyheath of tipping the remaining liquid straight from the shell into his mouth.

'This is your first visit to Paris, Mademoiselle?' he asked formally, ostentatiously watching as a drop of what tasted to Nell like sea water managed to avoid the square yard of gleaming white napkin positioned in her lap by some superior being in the form of a waiter, and landed on the jade-green georgette evening dress 'passed on' by Melissa (in fact had Nell but known it, specially chosen for her – albeit unconsciously with Melissa's own tastes in mind, rather than Nell's).

Her heart sank. There was to be no reprieve. So much for getting to know one another before business commenced. She took a large gulp of the excellent champagne and plunged into conversation.

'Monsieur de la Ferté, could we not forget about this morning and start again as though we had never met? After all, you can hardly blame me for what happened. Why did you stop to talk to me in the lingerie department anyway? You'd hardly expect to find a missing mannequin there,' she pointed out.

'I thought you might be a spy,' he informed her blandly.

'A spy?' she repeated mystified, then burst out laughing. 'Like Mata Hari?'

Lucien de la Ferté evidently considered her levity out of place in a smart restaurant devoted to haute cuisine. 'When you have spent longer in the fashion business, Mademoiselle, you will realise that illicit copying is the biggest threat to haute couture.'

There was a silence, then Nell burst out bluntly, 'There's no need to be so pompous!' In so far, she might as well dive to the bottom.

'Pompous? You call *me* pompous?' A muscle twitched angrily in his cheek.

'Yes,' she went on defiantly. 'Not just you,' she added hastily, remembering she was supposed to be getting on better terms with him, 'but all you French with your air of superiority about the famous French style.'

'And you think you English are better?' he remarked. 'I have to give a commentary to you in English in my own country because you cannot be bothered to learn French.'

'I—' She could think of no rational answer to this. 'There were other buyers there from other countries,' she told him weakly.

'But tomorrow it will be you, me, Madame Copsy, Monsieur Langer, and we will speak *English*. It is you who are arrogant, Mademoiselle Watkins, for you never question your right to do so. To you, every nation is your colony. Don't worry,' he added coldly, seeing her glance doubtfully at the dish that had just arrived. 'It is their speciality, *pommes de terre Anna*. It will not poison you. We have some experience of cooking in this country.'

'If not of putting guests at their ease,' she replied tartly, just as a woman dramatically dressed in ivory satin seemingly scalloped entirely in oyster shells, with a similarly flounced short red jacket, glided across the room towards him. With an apology to Nell, Lucien rose, kissing the woman on both cheeks and had a short conversation with her before she glided back to her table.

'Your wife?' she asked uncertainly.

His eyebrows rose in ironic astonishment. 'You have much to learn, Mademoiselle Watkins. A fashion journalist. That dress and jacket are Poiret of course.'

'Past his prime,' she informed him knowledgeably.

'That is so,' he agreed, 'but Marie-Claire Rosier has one quality that many fashion journalists lack. She is loyal. Moreover, from *un grand maître comme Poiret* there is still much to learn, even if the days of the hobble skirt are over.'

She felt reproved, which made her angry since after all it was her dignity that had suffered at his hands, rather than the other way about. So she concentrated in silence on the delicious food, wondering how long this Ordeal by Dinner would continue. Could she escape after pudding? She looked longingly towards the door, as though it represented the freedom she would never attain.

'And what, mademoiselle, did you think of our collection?' the cool voice continued.

Two poached eggs were placed in front of her. Poached eggs? After steak and potatoes. This was a strange country indeed. Politeness told her she should stall on the question of the collection. Integrity told her to go right on. She grated pepper on to the poached eggs, his eyes upon her. 'I liked it,' she informed him, picking up the only knife that seemed left to her, as he politely handed her a fork, seeing her predicament.

He bowed his head slightly in acknowledgement. 'Maison la Ferté is honoured. I look forward to discussing your purchase order tomorrow morning.' The corners of his mouth seemed to be twitching.

'But I think it lacks something.'

He grew very still. Even about to eat a poached egg he looks elegant and aloof, she thought savagely, disliking everything about him, and feeling awkward and ill-dressed before him. But she was determined to master Paris and her job, even if it meant having to master him too.

'Pepper, perhaps?' He smiled, as she took a mouthful and choked. It was not a poached egg; it was an apricot, surrounded by milky-white cream custard.

Fury battled within her to burst forth but lost. She was going to be *subtle*.

'Exactly, Mr de la Ferté,' she told him sweetly. 'How perceptive you are. Your collection lacked pepper, spice.' She took another mouthful.

For the first time he looked her straight in the face, appreciatively and a little curiously.

'Each one of your dresses was wonderful,' she continued, pressing her advantage, 'but added together they should suggest a direction, a style.'

'*Naturellement*.' His voice was neutral.

'Your style was neither one thing nor the other. It wasn't a romantic style like Jeanne Lanvin's but it wasn't a new direction either. It did not provide a taste of the future.'

The champagne and wine were making her head swim, and she refused abruptly when he attempted to refill her glass.

'And what, in your opinion, is this taste, this new direction?'

There was no telling from his expression or voice what devastating retort he was preparing, but there was nothing she could do about that now.

'Take your hemlines, first. Fashion has demanded rising hemlines, so you follow it, but you do not go all the way; you still reach the calves by fringes, frills, uneven hemlines, anything to avoid committing yourself to the future. Your whole collection is following fashion, not leading it. Not making a new departure.'

'Miss Watkins, perhaps you do not realise that most of our customers are mature; they need to advance gradually in fashion, not bound from rock to rock like mountain goats.'

'You are wrong,' she said firmly. 'Paris leads fashion – or it has no future.'

At that he actually laughed, albeit somewhat ironically.

'The Maison la Ferté is grateful for your advice. I will tell my brother, Philippe, who assists my father with design, that Miss Watkins of London, at least twenty years old—'

'Twenty-*three*,' she told him stiffly. 'I'm sorry if you think it's an impertinence, but –' emboldened again '– I *am* a buyer. And I'll be a buyer for many years.'

'And the customer *is* always right, as are you,' he said gravely, retreating. Perhaps he was not such a fighter after all, she thought, relieved.

'This afternoon,' she told him, as she greeted coffee gratefully, 'I went to the Art Deco Exhibition.' And then broke off as he sighed heavily.

'Miss Watkins, I expected more of you. The whole *world* has been to the Exhibition. They say this is the new age. This is the way that fashion should go. But we in Paris are cautious when people order us to go this way or that. We work on our instinct, on our knowledge of women.'

'But this *is* a new age,' Nell said vehemently. 'Women see themselves differently, not merely as slightly more modern versions of their parents as has always happened up to now. The modern technological age is bringing a new role for women.'

'You think women have changed?' he said, clearly bored now, as he glanced over her shoulder and acknowledged another woman passing by. 'Miss Watkins, let me tell you something. Neither women nor men change. They remain deep down the same, even if from time to time the façade alters.'

'Thank you,' she murmured crossly. 'I am a woman. That entitles me to an opinion, I suppose.'

'You do not believe me?' he said suddenly. 'Very well, I will prove it to you.' He whirled into action; the bill, her wrap and his motor-car appeared in quick succession, the latter waiting at the entrance when they reached it. He held the door open for her, his eyes on her legs, she noted as she swung them in, irrationally glad that this was one

83

feature of which she could be proud.

'Where are we going?'

'Montmartre. Then you will see, mademoiselle, whether men and women change.'

She glanced at the sharp profile beside her and he turned his head as if to meet her challenge. She had been on the point of saying she preferred to go to the hotel to prepare for the morrow, but changed her mind. He might interpret it as a victory for himself.

In the next few hours she was subjected to an intensive sight-seeing tour beginning with the Moulin Rouge. It was nothing like English music-hall, she thought, stunned. The costumes, the sets, would leave even Melissa gasping. 'We have Mistinguett, Maurice Chevalier – *they* understand, Miss Watkins, what men and women are.' From there he swept her up to the hill itself.

'Le Moulin de la Galette.' He waved his hand, rushing by at top speed after he had parked the car. 'A dance-hall now for *midinettes*. You think things change since Toulouse-Lautrec, since Renoir? *Non*. Not at the Moulin Rouge.'

Whatever midinettes were, they seemed to be having fun, Nell thought enviously. She was led from one extreme to another. Sacré Coeur to a *cabaret artistique*.

It wasn't like the 43 Club, she thought immediately. No crazy dancing here, no men balancing drinks on their noses, no women in extravagant exotic dresses enjoying the sheer fun of life. The atmosphere here was almost decadent, she decided. She'd never realised what that word meant till now. There was an age-old atmosphere of world-weariness as male and female singers sang with husky voices; she didn't understand the words, but the mood she did. And it bore no relation to *London Lady* and the kind of love songs that were the rage in England. Exotic liqueurs appeared in succession before her, all too easy to drink in her bemused state.

'Now, Miss Watkins . . .' Surely he would let her escape? It was past two o'clock. She had had far too much to drink, and she longed only for death or sleep, whichever came first. Pride would not let her give in, however, when before he allowed her to enter the Hôtel du Louvre he insisted on walking her down to the banks of the Seine where a few young lovers were still at this late hour clasped in each other's arms. She was rapidly changing her mind about Lucien de la Ferté. Nondescript he was not, and she looked forward less and less to facing him across a desk tomorrow.

'Do you still think men and women change so quickly, Miss Watkins?' His voice came out of the cool night air, startling her, lost in contemplation as she was of the sight of Paris's river and Notre Dame in the distance. Then, changing his tone, 'You are shivering, Miss Watkins. I will take off my jacket and place it round your shoulders.' The black jacket engulfed her, cocooning her like a prison, as for a moment he appeared more human. Then she realised too late this too was a trap as he whispered in her ear, 'And so you see men and women do not change. You accept my protection, and I am proud. *Voilà!*' He stepped back like a magician flourishing his cloak. 'I have proved my point,' laying a restraining hand on her arm as she immediately struggled to be free of the jacket.

'Perhaps France will be surprised one day,' she told him, defiantly, pushed on to the defensive. 'Women are doing so many different things in England. They're working, they're in Parliament, playing sports, challenging men in everything. The place of women in society is changing. We're all equal now, companions, without the old restricting barriers of sex.'

'Sex – ah yes, sex,' he said, the hint of a laugh in his voice, now victory of a sort was his.

The cool night breeze was blowing his hair, as it was

hers, but she doubted she still looked as elegant as he. Elegant . . . how ridiculous in a man, she told herself. As if Tom, a real man, needs to be *elegant*.

'And now,' he continued, 'sex is finished in England you tell me. How sad. Women want only to be regarded as men's companions.' His voice was serious as if he followed her argument with due consideration, but there was a mocking smile on his lips she noticed.

'Yes, in England. Perhaps not in Paris.'

'Ah, yes, in England and America, those advanced countries where the rage of the cinema was *The Sheik*, with the oh so sporty and companionable Rudolph Valentino. Is this not the film where the poor Lady Betty is swept off in the desert by Valentino on to his Arab steed and thrown down like a bundle of rags in his tent? What is to happen to me? this poor abducted lady cries. Are you not woman enough to know? Monsieur Rudolph enquires, and then he has his horrible way with her. And are not the so popular novels of your Miss Elinor Glyn similar – the sister of Lucile whom I see designed that dress that is so entirely unsuitable for you. And you still tell me, Miss Watkins, that English women want to be, as you would put it, good *chums*?'

'Films and books are not real life,' she tried to say, stumbling over the words in her annoyance at being out-manoeuvred.

'They are our dreams, what we would have in a perfect world, and you think they are not important?'

She was about to come back at him by reminding him of Michael Arlen's *The Green Hat* which had swept London, the story of a girl, a Bright Young Thing, Iris Storm. Then she remembered Iris Storm hid her broken heart in one affair after another. One man after another, no matter who. Like Melissa, now married to Tom.

When she did not reply, caught by the pangs of loss, he took her silence for submission and continued as victor:

'But you, Mademoiselle Watkins, you have an *ami*, a lover?'

Melissa throwing at her: 'You're a virgin, aren't you?' The memory stung her. 'Yes, and why not?' she had wanted to cry then. Now, she wanted to fling the defiant truth at Lucien de la Ferté too. But this man, this game, needed another answer, despite her outrage.

'Yes, I have,' she told him carelessly.

'And does this lover of yours treat you like a good chum?' he asked relentlessly, coolly.

'No,' she cried, defensive of a shadow. 'No, he's romantic.' Tom walked proudly into her heart, taking his place at her side as bulwark between her and this terrible man.

'And when you lie side by side, his arms are round you, and only the pillow hears what you have to say to each other, what does he call you then, our prim Miss Watkins?' His voice was openly mocking now.

She could not let him win, she would not, as she battled with honesty. She summoned Tom to her, he took her in his arms –

'What does he call you then?' the sardonic voice went on inexorably, 'as in love he calls out your name?'

Nell shut her eyes and gave her heart, her thoughts, her love to Tom. 'Nelly,' she blurted out. 'He calls me Nelly Watkins.'

A startled pause, then, '*Nelly Watkins*?' Lucien almost choked with laughter, having to hold on to the wall for support.

Later that night his mocking jeers still rang miserably in her ears, as the oyster, steak and *pommes de terre Anna*, diluted later by unknown and unsuitable liqueurs, left her in sordid and miserable circumstances. Liqueurs were not for her. And nor was Paris.

For once grateful for the bitter black coffee and plain

bread and croissants that faced her at breakfast, Nell staggered into the meeting, pale of face, feeling like a naughty child sandwiched between Mr Langer and Miss Copsy. Needless to say, Lucien de la Ferté looked as if he had retired to bed immediately after a light supper of boiled eggs, Nell thought savagely, as he formally kissed her hand as if they had not parted a mere seven hours previously.

'Permit me to introduce my brother, Comte Philippe de la Ferté. The designer for La Maison la Ferté,' Lucien added a trifle maliciously. Comte? And this one looked younger than Lucien, who must be about twenty-seven, she had decided – so Lucien would be a Count too, if it was the French practice that sons were thus addressed as well as the holder of the title. Nell's heart sank. She'd been addressing him as a plain mister. So what? she told herself: no one told me. *He* should have, she instantly decided, prepared to loathe his brother too on sight as if by association.

'*Enchanté, madame.*' Comte Philippe greeted Miss Copsy, bending over her hand while she almost visibly preened herself. 'Mademoiselle?' A curious look at Nell as he bent over her hand before moving on to Mr Langer. He was nothing like his brother, save in build. He was dark, Latin-looking, classically featured – but just as assured as his brother.

It was clear that Lucien intended to control the meeting. 'I intend, as I have told the other buyers, to expand the exports of Maison la Ferté, for it is an increasingly important part of the couture business.' He glanced at his notes. 'I see our business with Gadsby's was worth in sterling £7,450 in 1924, and the half-year figures to June this year are proportionally somewhat down on this, £3,620. Can you tell me why?

He looked at Mr Langer, Nell noted. Not her. She could tell him though.

'Merely general trade conditions,' Mr Langer informed him ponderously. 'For the winter, trade will improve. It always has and always will.'

Will it indeed? thought Nell. Not unless Gadsby's changes its ways, it won't.

'In that case, if you care to give me a list of which models you wish to see, we can commence.' Lucien held out his hand, looking at Nell for the first time. But it was Miss Copsy and Mr Langer whose orders he took and discussed first. It took an hour and a half while Nell fidgeted restlessly, as her fellow buyers twittered in ecstasy, Miss Copsy at the new knee-length lounge coats in lace and georgette for entertaining at home, Mr Langer extolling optimistically the chances of the double-breasted high-waisted coats in fancy coating trimmed with beaver. Catch her wearing that! thought Nell. And at last it was her turn. She took the bull by the horns.

'I'm concerned that you have little for our younger clientèle. Our contract is for a minimum of seventy-five, but I had difficulty in finding sufficient models in your collection to cover the whole range of Gadsby's clients.'

Philippe, after a quick look at his brother, began to speak but Lucien smoothly interrupted him. 'I think you will find, Miss Watkins, that your younger clientele will be suitably impressed with the pastel georgette and satin evening gowns, and among the day dresses it seems to me the styles for this season are equally suitable for mature and youthful figures alike.'

'Of course they will be,' said Nell, meaning it, 'but nevertheless, like you, at Gadsby's we seek a style – ' she saw Mr Langer and Miss Copsy looking at her in astonishment for this was news to them '– and if our customers are to become regular, our young customers that is, they will need the security of knowing that they can rely on us to provide a style that will carry them in the forefront of fashion. That if they come to Gadsby's, they will find what expresses their personalities without having to invent their own fashion to superimpose on what they buy.' Where had that come from? she wondered. It was true, but she hadn't consciously thought it out before. 'I rather miss that here. Perhaps you have some ideas for next spring?' she asked innocently.

Again Philippe began to speak and Lucien cut him off sharply. 'I believe you may rely on us, Miss Watkins,' he said firmly. 'After all, we do have an exclusive contract with you. We understand your English tastes, and our interests are mutual.'

'Of course,' Nell said warmly. 'Nevertheless Gadsby's might one day have different interests. If our styles should diverge, that is.'

'And then, Miss Watkins?' Lucien asked drily.

'I'll withdraw the exclusive contract.'

Lucien smiled. 'I'm terrified, Miss Watkins,' he replied politely in tones that told her quite clearly that they were twenty times more important to Gadsby's than Gadsby's was to the august and unassailable Maison la Ferté. If she was to be a David threatening to break every bone in Goliath's body, she'd start by strangling *him*, thought Nell viciously.

'Oh, darling, I've missed you so much.' Melissa flew lightly out of the newly decorated drawing room of Tom's Eaton Square home and hurled herself into Nell's arms.

'Melissa, you humbug. You've been on honeymoon in Greece and Italy, while I've been slaving away in London, crossing horrible Channels, fighting sharks in Paris, and you tell me you've missed me!'

'So hot in Greece,' said Melissa vaguely, 'but divine men,' she added. 'Tommy was quite jealous, weren't you, Tommy?' she called gaily, leading Nell in. 'Come and look at this. I've redecorated three times now. I think I'll get Syrie Maugham to do the rest of the house.'

The effect was quite breath-taking, like a piece of the Art Deco exhibition plomped down in Belgravia. Silver-mounted triangular mirrors adorned two orange walls, Cubist paintings were scattered on the other peach-coloured walls, while leather armchairs sat on a white carpet with brilliant designs on it, picking out the shape of the mirrors. Stark white velvet curtains hung at the windows. Tiny glass tables would have been invisible without the tortoiseshell ashtray carefully positioned on each one. The effect was stunning, but in the midst of it Tom stood awkwardly like a fish out of water in his fair isle pullover and flannels, his face sunburnt from the Mediterranean.

He came to her and gave her a hug. 'How are things at Gadsby's, Nelly?' he asked almost wistfully.

'Splendid,' she answered firmly. It wasn't true. Business in all departments was still distinctly slack.

'How did Paris go?' he asked with interest. 'The la Fertés eat you alive for breakfast, did they?'

'They couldn't. Not without spoiling the line of their dinner jackets,' she joked back, a memory of Lucien de la Ferté at Voisin's coming back to her.

'Good for you, Nelly. You showed them, did you?' He was genuinely interested she told herself with some surprise.

'There wasn't much I could show with the exclusive contract in force,' she pointed out.

'They know what they're doing at Dirty Firty's.'

'*What*?'

Tom looked embarrassed. 'Sorry. That's what the Governor calls 'em – all in the way of joking, that is,' he added hastily. 'Going back to some deal he had with Guy's father. Keep it to yourself, won't you?' he added hastily.

'Of course,' said Nell, charmed, and suddenly feeling part of a family again.

'Better get back to work tomorrow,' he added brightly. 'I expect you've missed me.'

'Of course,' she said loyally.

Melissa pouted. 'What am I to do while you're at work?'

Tom looked worried, considering this earnestly. 'Shopping? Theatre trips? Teas? Or redecorating the dining room. You'll find lots to do, darling.' He kissed her lovingly. 'Bye Nell,' giving her a peck on the cheek. 'Due at the RAC. Better get going.'

Did he ever realise how much he meant to her? Nell thought sadly, until she saw Melissa watching her in amusement, clearly reading her thoughts.

'I'm sorry, darling,' she said genuinely. 'But you see, he loves me. He really does.'

'I know,' said Nell. 'And who wouldn't?' she said in a rush of fondness, only belatedly thinking of the ambiguity of this statement.

Melissa giggled. 'Now, Nell, I've given all that up. I'm so happy. I'm just going to run the house and entertain. And we'll go out lots. It will be such fun. Won't it?'

Nell did not answer. Somehow she could not see Melissa being content with playing Happy Housewife for long.

Nell stood back and surveyed her handiwork. Well, the showroom was ready. And it was different – as the parade was going to be. The la Ferté frocks were wonderful to look at even if not startlingly eye-catching. Perhaps even *Vogue* might come this year, she thought hopefully. While three saleswomen under Danzy's leadership looked scornfully on, their understudies had scurried about at Nell's direction, fixing remnants begged from the Fabric Department in imitation of the swathes at Maison la Ferté. Nell had decorated these herself with the motifs of the coming season: velvet bows, crystal embroidery, rainshades with rubber flowers adorning them, and chain after chain of Ciro pearls. Mr Langer and Miss Copsy, who shared the show with her, made no comment, obviously choosing to let her fall by her own hand.

Jonathan Gadsby, however, did comment. 'Looks like something out of my draper's shop in the seventies,' he informed her brusquely.

'But look how successful your shops were, sir,' she replied firmly.

Jonathan Gadsby regarded her with eyes that were bright under his bushy eyebrows, for all his seventy-five years. 'New ideas, all been tried before. Too much attention paid to you young people. Just the same as the old, you'll see. Remember, I've got my eye on you, missy.'

Lady Lenham took the same view of the innovations, as she arrived for the parade. 'Am I on a kinematograph set?' she enquired acidly, on viewing the decor.

Miss Danzy rushed forward unctuously. 'Just an experiment, Lady Lenham. I'm sure you'll find the dresses quite charming. Our new buyer had the benefit of Miss Copsy's experience in Paris.'

Nell was meant to overhear and did, steeling herself to silence.

'Darling Grandpapa-in-law!' Melissa swept in with Tom and a group of friends, who trotted in her Shalimar-perfumed wake.

'By Jove, this is jolly,' Tom said with sudden interest, looking at Nell's decorations.

She flushed with pleasure at the compliment, her confidence returning as she showed Melissa and her friends to their places in the front row. Melissa would not disappoint her, she knew. Nor did she. She exclaimed in delight over the blue nappa coat with its moleskin lining, causing Mr Langer's chest to puff, and was ecstatic over Miss Copsy's lounge coats. The ground was thus prepared.

'Oh!' she clapped her hands at the petalled drapery skirt of the crêpe-de-Chine evening dresses, leaned forward entranced at the ribbed velour in what was already dubbed disrespectfully 'pickled cabbage' colour. 'So clever,' she said loudly to Nell, as if she had personally dyed it. 'The Bois de Rose summer colour deepened. How *exquisite*.'

Jonathan shot her a baleful look. There was armed hostility between himself and his granddaughter-in-law, with Tom unconsciously keeping the two sides apart. Jonathan distrusted her, and had noted with disapproval Nell's attachment to her.

As a result of Melissa's championship, Lady Lenham was charmed into giving the Dragon her biggest order for years, and Mrs Willoughby was impatiently awaiting her turn. Nell decided it might be politic to engage her in conversation. It was thus some while afterwards that she came to talk to Melissa and her friends.

'So lovely, darling', 'so clever', 'the dearest little petals', 'positively bubbly little bows' fell like music on her ears. But a word of warning, a sinister note to Nell's perhaps over-sensitive ears: 'So romantic, so safe. I feel I could wear it anywhere.'

Today's young people did not want to feel safe. Today was a time for experiment. Next spring, Nell thought dismally, they would not return to Gadsby's, for all their kind words now.

Melissa glanced at Nell, reading her thoughts. She slipped an arm through hers. 'Darling, I've had the loveliest idea. Why shouldn't Gadsby's dress my new show?'

'New show?' asked Tom quietly. He'd been so quiet, Nell had almost forgotten his presence.

'Yes, darling. That's if it comes to anything.' Melissa smiled brilliantly at him. 'Didn't I mention that Vincent Wright was writing one for me?'

'No,' he said slowly. 'No, you didn't mention it.'

'What's this about a new play, Melissa?' Nell demanded on the first occasion they were alone.

'I doubt if it will come to anything,' she answered carelessly.

'Nonsense, Melissa. You know very well that if you want it to, it will. *Do* you want it to?'

'Married life can be the teensiest bit boring, darling.' Melissa lit a cigarette to avoid Nell's direct gaze.

'Oh, Melissa, she said in despair. 'Tom—'

'I know. You've told me. Tommy loves me so much,' Melissa replied crossly. 'But that doesn't mean I have to be chained to his side forever, does it?'

Nell could imagine no greater bliss, but tried to see Melissa's viewpoint. She had been used to the constant stimulus of an audience and having a career. Now she was the wife of Tom Gadsby. Nell could not conceive of circumstances where this would not be sufficient for her, but for Melissa – she did not even dare contemplate the other possibility; that one man alone might not be sufficient for Melissa.

'The play will be based on this new dance, the Charleston,' she was explaining. 'Vincent wants to take a gamble. He thinks the dance could really catch on, particularly as the Prince of Wales apparently likes it. I think Vincent's right. Anyway, we've a long way to go yet. I'm sure it won't happen,' she said again, avoiding Nell's eye.

No more was said and Nell thought the play was forgotten, an idea that had come to nothing. Then, a month later, the doorbell rang late at night. Peering from the window, she saw Tom on the doorstep. Flinging a wrap over her pyjamas, she ran downstairs, alarmed, to let him in.

'Is Melissa here?' he demanded unceremoniously.

'No,' she said in surprise. 'I was in bed.'

'Sorry, Nell,' he muttered awkwardly, seeing her night clothes. 'She said she'd be home when I got back from Brooklands. It's my birthday, you see,' he added simply.

'She must have forgotten,' said Nell defensively, realising too late she was making matters worse. 'Oh, Tom, I'm so sorry. Something must have happened. The hospitals—'

'I'll try the clubs first,' he said sadly. 'More likely. Would you come with me?'

She looked at him with amazement but he was serious, and half flattered, half reluctant, since she had to get up early, she hurried to change.

Melissa was in none of her usual haunts. Eventually they found her at Elsa Lanchester's Cave of Harmony club. 'Darlings,' she said, waving at them happily from a sofa where she reclined in the arms of a complacent-looking young man with sleeked-down black hair. 'Vincent's had his play accepted. Isn't it marvellous? It will come on at the Princess Beatrice in January. Have a drink, darling. Drink to *Charleston Lady*.'

'Melissa—' Tom began.

'Now don't be a crosspatch, darling,' she told him happily. 'You run along and I'll be home soon.'

Tom stood undecided, then suddenly reaching a decision, gripped Nell by the arm and marched her back to the motor car. He drove her home in silence, recklessly.

'Steady, Tom, this isn't Brooklands,' she tried to say lightly, her arm still smarting from his grip.

He slowed down but still did not speak. He drew up outside Nell's flat, took her key and opened the flat door for her. Only then did he speak. He pulled her roughly to him, held her against him for a moment and then released her. 'What would I do without you, Nelly?' he said thickly.

Not we but I, she realised, as dizzy with mixed happiness and foreboding, she leaned from her window to watch him drive off towards Eaton Square.

Nell was so used to being asked to play a third in their relationship that she was taken by surprise when Melissa announced she and Tom were going to the Gadsby family home in Kent for Christmas. '*Kent*! Such a bore, darling. Nothing but sheep and hops. All that *beer*!'

Somehow Nell had stupidly taken it for granted that their plans would as usual include her. How ridiculous, she told herself firmly. She *wasn't* part of their world, only a visitor to it. Yet at Bexleyheath she was treated with a politeness and deference that made her feel like a cuckoo in the nest. Her family's interests were no longer hers. Her parents were wrapped up in the shop, and her brother had now married a local girl (who had persuaded him of the merits of a secure future in drapery), moved in next-door and would next year produce what was firmly expected to be another male Watkins. Their pride in their daughter was obvious, but now she had sloughed off the chrysalis of home she could no longer slink back in. She was an honoured visitor there. Only Miss Emmeline and Miss Gertrude remained unperturbed by this new fashionable and confident Nell. They had always predicted a brilliant future for her, and now she had in their view achieved it. But even so she was not above reproach.

'Nell, your talk seems unusually full of references to Mrs Gadsby –' how strange to hear Melissa termed this '– *and* Mr Gadsby.'

'We are close friends.'

'I trust not too close,' Miss Emmeline remarked grimly. 'The Gadsbys are a strange family. Fortunately I—' She broke off, slightly red in the face.

'Strange?' said Nell defensively.

'Single-minded,' amended Miss Emmeline. 'Capable,' she grew even pinker, 'of great devotion to *one* person.

Gertrude, another cup of tea, if you please.' The conversation was at an end.

Returning to Charing Cross after Boxing Day, Nell felt despondent rather than refreshed by the holiday. She was neither flesh nor fowl but a kind of vegetable of unknown species, she decided glumly. She no longer belonged to Bexleyheath, was merely an outsider allowed peeps into Melissa and Tom's world, and was definitely not part of the Parisian scene. Only at Gadsby's, despite her slow progress, did she stand a chance of belonging. Slowly but surely she was gaining ground – even Jonathan Gadsby would admit that – and the coming spring would give her a chance to test her own ideas on the world. She, Nell Watkins, fashion prophet. She laughed aloud, to the amazement of her fellow passengers who shifted uneasily in their seats. But what more could she ask? Tom Gadsby needed her, albeit in so humble a way, and so the world was hers.

London was beginning to move to the Charleston's rhythm now after its slow beginning the previous summer. Dancing entered a new hectic phase as it became a consuming passion first for the flappers, then for the middle-aged. The Charleston was beginning to *be* London. And straight to the centre of the burgeoning craze came the first night of *Charleston Lady*. Dressed by Gadsby's, twenty beautiful chorus girls Charlestoned over the Princess Beatrice's stage. At their head flashed the flying feet of Melissa Hargreaves, bewitchingly beautiful, sparkling in tissue and lamé and the new luminous lace, discovered and bought in by Joe as a favour to Nell specially for Melissa's show. No Eton crop for Melissa. Her blonde hair was shingled to just the right amount to complement her *gamin* features, her quick sharp movements perfectly symbolising dance and the new modernism. The story was slight: an earl's daughter who refuses to marry the man of her parents' choice and instead falls in love with a professional dancer, an American who has come to London to teach the Charleston. But slight or not, the audience took it to their feet as well as their hearts on that first night, Charlestoning madly in the aisles at the curtain calls.

Tom seemed to have got over his former disapproval of Melissa's participation and beamed with pride as he led Nell round afterwards to the dressing room. Or party room, as it seemed to be tonight.

She's happy again, that's why he doesn't mind, Nell realised with sudden prescience, and wondered why this should make her fleetingly so downcast.

'Darlings!' Melissa embraced them both together, as they fought their way through the mob. 'I think it went all right, didn't it?' she asked innocently, and laughed delightedly with them. 'Now, Nell, this is Robert Stock-bridge. He's my leading man – well, you know that. We'll all go out to dinner to celebrate. And maybe, Tom, we'll all go on somewhere and *dance*. Oh, isn't this wonderful? I don't want tonight to end, ever.' Melissa was back on form, revived by the lights of theatre, and Nell too found herself the happier for it.

'Why me?' Nell had demanded suspiciously. 'Why not Miss Copsy or Mr Langer?' This invitation to the de la Fertés' country château was the last thing she had expected after the spring show in Paris.

Lucien shrugged. 'Miss Copsy and Mr Langer do not share your problems of principle, Miss Watkins. Their orders are quickly given. My father thought you might care to have the weekend to reflect on your policy.'

So that I feel bound to you for your hospitality, she thought instantly. As if reading her thoughts he continued: 'Naturally so far as the Maison La Ferté is concerned, it is entirely a weekend for our mutual pleasure.

Les affaires can be resumed on Monday. Furthermore,' he added casually, 'my brother Philippe wishes to talk with you to gain your views on the style of the collection from the British point of view. I too feel I can learn from your opinions on what the British want.'

She eyed him even more suspiciously. Flattery from Lucien de la Ferté? What possible interest could he have in the views of Nell Watkins from Gadsby's? Perhaps, however, on reflection, she *had* impressed Philippe last autumn.

'After all,' Lucien continued, 'I understand you have employed your time in Paris well, viewing many other collections.'

The final and deadly rapier-thrust. Well, she was ready for that. 'I would not consider I had done my job if I was unable to give my employers an overall view of the Paris trends,' she told him demurely.

A pause. '*Touché*, Miss Watkins. You will pardon me if we stop here. I need to buy petrol. You would like a drink while you wait?' He pulled up at a village bar/tabac.

Nell followed him into the smoke-filled bar, with a dozen or so blue overalled workmen crowding at the counter and other groups involved in card-playing or newspaper reading. They eyed the new arrivals curiously, the elegant Parisian (*sans doute*) and a foreigner, smartly dressed in a blue coat with fur collar. Silence fell.

'Coffee?'

'Tea, please,' said Nell, striking a blow for England.

That settled it. Murmurs broke out to the effect that the young mademoiselle was obviously English. As Lucien disappeared to buy petrol, Nell peered dubiously at the concoction referred to as tea, uncomfortably aware she was the centre of attention.

'*Ah, des beaux yeux*,' an appreciative murmur went round. Then one more forthright asked, 'You are English, mademoiselle?'

'Yes,' she replied, smiling at them.

'*Les Tommies! Votre père était un Tommy dans la Grande Guerre, mademoiselle?*'

She gathered the gist of what he was asking.

'Too old. But my uncle, he was in the army over here. At the Somme.'

'Ah. *Moi aussi, moi aussi*,' two shouted in reply. This clearly constituted an introduction and by the time Lucien returned it was to find Nell supported by a stalwart Frenchman either side and part of a circle of intertwined arms, lustily singing '*Au près de ma blonde*'.

'*Alors, mon brave, vous êtes un homme heureux*,' shouted one burly man, clapping Lucien on the shoulder and sweeping him willy-nilly into the circle. It was twenty minutes and several songs later before he managed to extricate himself and Nell, looking far from the happy man he was deemed to be. Silence reigned in the motor-car for the next half-an-hour.

'Welcome to Petit Andely and Château Gaillard,' Lucien said at last. So they at last appeared to be nearing the end of the journey, she thought with relief, as they entered a village dominated by a ruined castle on a hill top, stark in the greyness of bleak February.

'Gaillard?' she repeated.

'The castle built by your King Richard I.'

'The one where he heard his troubadour Blondel singing outside and managed to escape?' she asked with interest.

'No, but I am delighted you are a romantic after all,' he murmured smoothly. 'How fortunate for Maison la Ferté!'

Not romantic enough. She had been dismayed by la Ferté's dress parade viewed this morning, for there was nothing *new*. True, this was also so of other collections she had seen, but Maison la Ferté's had lacked the relief even of the dance frocks applauded elsewhere and specifically aimed at young people, the short taffeta picture frock with

101

its bouffant skirts, and the bustle bow frock which was even shorter with drapery sweeping up behind into a huge chenille velvet bow. La Ferté produced dramatically beautiful frocks of gold lace over straight scalloped skirts, ornamented, excitingly decorated – and ageless in their appeal. Where were the stark lines, the simplicity and lack of ornamentation she had seen in other houses? Only their chiffon afternoon dresses with jazz design patterns suggested that the Art Deco movement even existed.

The Château de la Ferté on the banks of the Seine, a little way from the village, was an imposing building of grey stone unrelieved by colour of any kind, she instantly noted, and was taken aback, wondering whether its cold appearance would prove indicative of her welcome there. There were no signs of flowers in the gardens, only formal trees.

'I will not be intimidated,' Nell told herself firmly as she braced herself to meet her host, his wife and Philippe, assembled to greet her formally on the front steps. Philippe, it was now clear, took after his mother, whose olive complexion, dark looks and slender figure made her a perfect model for la Ferté gowns. She proved to be the perfect hostess too – over-perfect perhaps. A little genuine warmth instead of quite such exquisite manners would not have come amiss, thought Nell, sitting at the huge formal dinner table. She was becoming accustomed now to the long duration of French meals, but it was her first one in a French home. If 'home' were a permissible term for such grandeur. Lucien was the quietest member of the family, an odd contrast to his assured self in Paris society. Here he sat silently, almost overtly distancing himself from his lively brother and mother.

'My sons tell me you have interesting views on the future of fashion, Miss Watkins?' the count addressed her.

Was he serious, or mocking, like Lucien? Nell decided she had to treat it as the former. 'I can only judge from

Gadsby's point of view,' she replied. 'And Gadsby's is not Maison la Ferté.'

'*Entendu*,' murmured Lucien, cutting some Brie from the cheese tray held by a servant at his side.

Philippe shot a sharp look at him. 'I am most interested to hear,' he told her attentively, waving aside the cheese.

One in the eye for you, Nell thought happily as Lucien rearranged his supercilious expression into one of polite interest.

'I can't see that a fashion house like Gadsby's can continue without broadening its range,' she said flatly. 'Things move so fast nowadays, there is not the time to devote to fashion there once was. Women do not have the time to attend parades, pick styles, and attend fitting after fitting. Not young people anyway. I think fashions will change so quickly that more and more young people will not only demand their own styles, but will want them quickly.'

A look passed between the men.

'You refer, of course, to the ready-made market,' the count said eventually.

'Yes,' she said bluntly, knowing this was the subject of much contention in Paris as well as London. 'Not mass production necessarily, but instead of copying the designs you send us individually for each customer, we would make up limited numbers in stock sizes ready for them.' She looked at the stony faces and quailed. 'Of course, the old system would continue side by side, at least for a while.' In for a penny, in for a pound. 'And eventually I want to have a ready-made department as well with cheaper dresses aimed specifically at young people.'

'Do Jonathan and *mon cher* Tom know of these revolutionary ideas of yours, mademoiselle?' the countess enquired, no hint in her well-bred tones of approval or disapproval.

Nell's heart sank. How could she have forgotten that

the Gadsbys and de la Fertés were friends?

'You realise these ideas are hardly new, Miss Watkins?' The count's tone robbed his words of rebuke. 'Ready-made clothing has been a matter of constant discussion among Paris couturiers since the end of the war. We feel at Maison la Ferté that it is important to keep to our principles if we are to survive as the world's leading fashion city. Already we countenance limited licensed copying abroad, as we do to Gadsby's.' He inclined his head. 'I believe your contract stipulates not more than twenty-five copies of each model. Further than that we would not go.'

The demarcation lines had been set, Nell realised. What was she going to do on Monday? Although they received a favourable price for exclusive British copying rights because of the large number of models they bought, the margins were not wide once forty per cent of Gadsby's sale price was allotted to materials, and another twenty per cent to workroom charges. Of the remaining departmental credit of forty per cent, salaries and commissions and model prices accounted for nearly thirty per cent. If that remaining ten per cent were to be whittled away through declining orders, the hub of Gadsby's would soon come to a halt.

The countess rose in a shimmer of silver. 'Shall we adjourn to the *salon*?' she murmured rhetorically to both Nell and her family. The French appeared to have no rules for leaving the men to their port, and Nell felt the countess had scored a point as she herself was forced to retire temporarily for the traditional reason. By the time Nell returned, Philippe was putting dance music on the gramophone and the countess was moving into her husband's arms. Philippe whirled round to ask her to dance – Lucien made no such effort, she noticed – and was soon holding her uncomfortably close, or perhaps not so uncomfortably close she realised after a moment. He was a superb dancer, and she found to her surprise that she was enjoying herself immensely.

Only once in the evening did Lucien come to claim her. 'This *is* my dance, Miss Watkins,' he said casually. 'The tango. All Valentinos are excellent at the tango, are they not?'

He certainly was, much better than she, making her feel self-conscious, aware she was only a moderate dancer. Perhaps realising this, he toned down his movements, holding her closer so that he could guide her. Dancing was a strange thing, she thought dizzily, when for a few moments you were locked in intimate embrace with someone you disliked. They were so close his face was touching hers as he leaned over her, so close that she was aware of the light freckles on his cheek, the small mole on his neck and the lines of his lips. The lips that on Monday would be challenging her every statement in a battle neither would be prepared to lose.

At midnight the countess rose and bade them good-night, the count and Lucien followed, and Nell rose to leave too. Philippe restrained her.

'A flapper cannot be tired,' he mocked. 'You never tire. Now, Mademoiselle Nell, I wish to learn this Charleston.'

It was another two hours before she finally insisted, laughing, that she must go to bed. His arm round her, merely to steady himself, he insisted, he walked her to her room, where his arms stole quickly right round her and his lips met hers. So this was how Frenchmen kissed, she thought dazedly, laughing as he pushed in to her room after her and had to be rather forcefully ejected. It all seemed enormously funny – until she saw Lucien, attired in a red silk wrap, watching them with disdain on his face.

'*Je m'excuse, Philippe,*' he said stiffly. 'I heard a noise and thought perhaps our guest required something.'

She saw the look of scorn he bestowed on his brother as

Philippe passed him, but not the gesture of triumph Philippe gave him in return.

'You do not like our new collection, Miss Watkins?' She stared at Lucien's remote, almost disdainful, expression on Monday morning across the desk in what she supposed could be termed his office. It bore no relation to a Gadsby's office; this was more like a drawing room with its elegant chairs and even a sofa. The one table was clearly so antique that the telephone on it looked almost apologetic, Nell thought idly. Then with dismay she realised suddenly why he had been so cool to her yesterday and was looking quite so askance at her now. He must, she uneasily reflected, have thought his brother and she had been making love on Saturday evening, as he had only seen his brother emerging from her room, not entering a mere two minutes earlier. Well, who cares *what* he thinks? she told herself defiantly. But said to him: 'It's beautiful, it's flattering, it's romantic, yet it's only a main line.'

'*Pardon*?' His voice was cold.

'It's not adding anything. I think fashion is like a railway with lots of branches. You need a main line as backbone, but without the branch lines, which are each season's fashions, no one would get what they really want, where they really want to arrive on a particular journey. Your fashions are the main line. Wonderful though they are, they don't lead where a great many travellers want to go.'

'They lead to many satisfied customers,' Lucien countered immediately. 'In Italy, Germany, the United States, Japan.' He managed to indicate courteously a warning that Gadsby's was hardly the only client of the Maison la Ferté, and that though the British market might be the most important of his export markets, Gadsby's was not synonymous with England. 'And I should point out that the main line railway trains run to large cities, and that

106

most people live in cities, not villages.' He paused, clearly wondering whether she was worth discussing the matter with further. Evidently she passed muster, for he continued: 'At Maison la Ferté, Miss Watkins, we keep graphs of fashion changes. You understand?'

'No,' she was forced to admit.

'It is simple. Since the house was founded we keep track of developments in all branches of fashion in percentages: width of skirt to total height of figure, distance of the edge of the skirt from the ground in relation to height, the décolletage to total height, length of waist, width of waist, width of décolletage, types of dresses, types of coat silhouette, types of coat sleeve, shoes, style of hats . . .' He stopped. 'I impress you, Miss Watkins?'

'Yes,' she said simply. 'I had no idea. But of course it must help.'

'Enormously. For example,' he seemed to forget to whom he was talking in his own interest in the subject, 'you would agree that whereas a fashion trend in small accessory items such as flowers or jewellery, will only last a season, and that in materials or colour may last a year, the general trends in silhouettes will last several years?'

'Yes,' she said valiantly. In truth, she had never reasoned it out before, and unwillingly was fascinated by the rationale.

'The sharper the fad, I believe you call it, such as for boat necklines, the swifter it will pass. *And* the longer it will take to come back. With V necklines the graph line is less extreme, and they will return to popularity the sooner for it.'

'And this is what you base your designs on?' she asked.

'*Non*. This is *my* part of it, Miss Watkins. I am a businessman. I use reason, sense, and what my flair tells me should happen as a result. But no *maison de couture* could exist like that. There is design that interprets and leads. In this house at the moment . . .' He swallowed and began again. 'In this house, my father is both *un homme d'affaires* and an *artiste*. I inherit the first from him, my brother Philippe the second. He is a good designer, but even the best designer needs a railway system, Miss Watkins.'

He hesitated, clearly wishing he had not said as much, and reverted with aplomb to her analogy. 'This railway line of yours, Miss Watkins, must therefore continue on its way, undeterred by demands that we turn ladies into triangles and pipes. However loudly Art Deco shouts, the corners must be rubbed off from the triangles and curves added to pipes before they can enhance a woman's beauty, not detract from it. You will no doubt think our views old-fashioned, Miss Watkins. They are not. We are far, far too experienced to lag behind in our views. We would no longer be in business if we did. We see the true point of fashion, to bring out the best of women in the age in which they live.'

'But what of the future?' she said, impressed but unconvinced. 'There is nothing to excite younger people.'

'And nothing to drive them away,' Lucien interrupted. 'No doubt you discussed your ideas with my brother,' he said, glancing away from her. 'He too wishes to have crinolines and bustles back again for today's branch line. You have much in common it seems. And not merely in haute couture.'

She gasped with outrage. 'I thought,' she said icily, 'that this was a business discussion.'

'My apologies, mademoiselle.' But he did not sound apologetic. 'To revert: I cannot believe this craze will last.'

'Paris thought that about short hemlines a few years ago and here they are shorter than ever,' she reminded him, determined to counter him, though in fact she suspected he was right over the bustle effect.

He stared at her in dislike. 'Paris makes mistakes. But

108

you prove my point. We tried to lengthen skirts again three years ago and it did not work, any more than it did when we tried to help the fabric industry by imposing pannier backs on hobble skirts before the war. But both these were mistakes born of panic, the last one because of the industrial slump of 1921–2. If we had followed the fashion trends shown on our graph, then we would have avoided those errors. I maintain fashion is a gentle progression, not a matter of fits and starts, like an English motor car, Miss Watkins.'

She smouldered, unwilling to admit the force of his argument, while he did not admit hers. 'What does it matter if fashion moves in jumps? All the better for the couturier. Everyone is complaining there is so little change this season. And that's *despite* the Art Deco exhibition.'

'*Eh bien.*' He lost patience. 'Do you wish to buy or not?'

'Yes,' she said, holding his gaze firmly. Odd to think she was dancing in his arms less than two days ago. 'But not exclusively from you.'

He smiled. It was not a pleasant smile. 'Gadsby's has always been on an exclusive contract with us. You realise what will happen if we withdraw from that?'

He was eager for battle, she saw with some surprise.

'Yes, the price goes up by twenty per cent per model. It means, I'm afraid, my department could afford to buy very, very few. Perhaps five a season and only if we have exclusive rights to those five of course.'

'For five, it is not worth our giving exclusive rights to produce up to twenty-five copies, when the preferred policy of la Ferté is a maximum of five copies per country.'

'If so, then I must look elsewhere,' she said more steadily than she felt, hoping to call his bluff. He couldn't afford to lose seventy-five assured sales a season without thought, surely?

'So,' he said softly, leaning back in his chair, as if perfectly relaxed, 'you are declaring war, Perfidious Albion.'

'Not perfidious,' she answered swiftly. 'You and your father have as good as told me that Gadsby's isn't that important to you, so why should we pretend there is loyalty concerned?'

'All this for the sake of a few lines, a few triangles?' he asked derisively.

'Have you ever seen a line drawing by Picasso or Laura Knight? That's just a few lines too. But see how much they can say with them.'

He paused, considering this. 'You're wrong,' he said at last. 'Paris may have made mistakes, but surely you too are wrong, for you English now wear your frocks on the knee and it is predicted,' he shrugged, 'the hemline will continue to rise. Without constant care we men see your stocking tops and suspenders or garters.' His eye fell deliberately to her knees, and she had to fight the temptation to smooth down her undoubtedly short skirt. 'Erotic, perhaps, mademoiselle, but it is not romantic. Perhaps in England,' his eyes glinted, 'this is intentional, for there you do not understand romance. But here in Paris ladies know the true meaning of sexual love, and also know that mystery is part of it. The age-old Eve.'

Nell could no longer resist it. She burst out laughing. 'Don't you think the legend of the French being all-knowing about love is rather passée now?'

'You did not appear to think so on Saturday night, Miss Watkins. I trust my brother was an excellent *chum*.'

'What do you mean by breaking the exclusivity contract?' roared Jonathan Gadsby.

Nell gulped. 'I had to, Mr Gadsby. We're losing custom which is decreasing our profit per model to a point where

110

it will soon be non-existent. We'd be bankrupt in a few years.'

'We'll be bankrupt long before then if we go on paying these prices.' He flipped a finger through the pile of invoices from the new suppliers Nell had hurriedly tracked down to replace Maison la Ferté, all but the ten models she had agreed as a compromise for this season – but at a price. She still smarted from his having taken advantage of her frankness.

'But I've some wonderful new models from Patou and Coco Chanel.'

'Wonderful!' Jonathan snorted. 'Well, it's the last time. I'm going on my hands and knees to the count and asking him to restore the contract.'

'In that case, I have to resign,' said Nell through stiff lips. Never, never had she expected this. Not even to be given a chance.

'Don't think I wouldn't jump at the chance of sacking you, missy,' Jonathan roared. 'But I can't. My son and that wife of his think you're worth keeping in Fashion. Melissa says quite flatly she'll take her and her friends' custom elsewhere. I'm not going to be blackmailed in my own store,' he shot at her. 'So you'll go where you can do no harm.' He paused malevolently. 'Deputy in Teagowns.'

So much for her dreams. So much for her grand ideas of leading Gadsby's fashion future. Now she would be working under Miss Copsy in a department dying on its feet with no future. Next door in Fashion, the Dragon, promoted in her place, Jonathan informed her with satisfaction, would reign supreme, and, worst of all, her ignominy would be known to Paris as well as London. If it wasn't for Melissa, she'd leave, but Melissa had pleaded with her not to.

'Gadsby's needs you,' she told her. 'I need you there, if I'm going on getting most of my clothes from there – and

Tom likes having you around,' she added discerningly.

Gradually Nell realised that going elsewhere might only compound her humiliation, now this was generally known. Far better to make a success of Teagowns. But how?

Nell shivered in the cool breeze at Brooklands, wishing she'd had the sense to bring a coat like Melissa. Watching motor races was a static and lengthy business. Melissa was clearly bored, though she had been animated enough when they arrived with Tom and were chatting with the other drivers.

'I'm so glad you came, Nell,' she told her. 'I just don't understand what men see is so fascinating about whizzing round and round in little cars.'

As they watched the sports cars flashing past, Nell felt in entire agreement with her. Even love of Tom could not interest her in motor-car racing. She loved tennis, walking, even golf, but the excitement of speed left her uninspired. She had asked Tom once what enthralled him so much about racing. He had looked at her in some surprise, and answered vaguely: 'I'm good at it.'

'You're good at flying too.'

He glanced at her. 'Yes. Both the same, I suppose, Nelly. You forget the rest of the world.'

'Gadsby's?'

He had chuckled at that. 'No.'

'What's wrong?' she'd wanted to cry. But she couldn't because he and Melissa were married now. If he were to answer her, 'Melissa', what could she do? It would seem a betrayal. There was the old Alvis now streaming round the corner; Tom must be third she thought, but it was difficult to tell because of the sports cars lapping each other. The Bugatti was definitely leading, with an Alfa-Romeo close behind.

'Come on, Tommy.' Melissa had decided to get interested and had climbed on a bench cheering, waving her scarf. 'Buck up!' But as she climbed down again, taking her eyes from the track, Nell saw a wheel spinning high in the air, hardly daring to look in case she saw what she feared. She watched it, fascinated, as though it alone ruled the rest of her life. Then she had to, *had* to look further. The Alvis had crashed into the guardrail, its rear axle shaft broken. It did not look badly buckled, but its driver did not get out.

And then it was all running, screaming, rushing, a stretcher being hoisted into an ambulance and Melissa still screaming: 'He's dead, I know he is. I won't go. I can't.'

'Then I must,' said Nell, sick at heart, climbing into the ambulance as it started off. Jolting up and down over rough lanes, then roads. And finally, there were uniformed nurses, doctors.

He was unconscious, white. Perhaps dead? How would she know? He didn't *look* badly hurt. Then he was swept away from her. Three hours later she was still sitting outside. 'Mrs Gadsby, your husband's recovered consciousness.' A nurse appeared before her. 'He's not badly hurt. We'll keep him in overnight and then—'

'I'm not Mrs Gadsby.'

'Oh.' A frown of disapproval. 'In that case—'

'Mrs Gadsby sent me instead,' she managed to explain through her relief.

An even deeper frown of disapproval as reluctantly she was ushered in.

Tom turned his head. 'Hallo, young Nelly,' he said with an effort. 'Some race, huh?' A frown. 'Where's Melissa?'

'She was too upset,' Nell told him gently. 'She loves you so much, she couldn't bear to see you hurt.' Even to her own ears it sounded inadequate. Yet it was the truth, wasn't it?

'Yes,' Tom replied weakly after a moment, turning his head away. 'Of course. That's the reason.'

★ ★ ★

They sprang apart as she entered the dressing room, Melissa and Robert Stockbridge. Nell's stomach churned. She wasn't even surprised. Her subconscious had told her all along that Melissa had not changed, and she'd hardly needed this proof.

'It's all right,' Nell said wearily into the silence. 'He'll be home tomorrow.' Then she burst out: 'Why didn't you go, Melissa? Don't you love him?'

'Of course.' It was said in a high brittle voice. Then seeing Nell's face: 'I know you think I was awful letting you go to the hospital instead of me, but suppose Tommy had died? Just suppose. I'd have had no one.' Dark blue eyes staring into an unpredictable future. 'I couldn't face it. Do you understand, Nell?'

'No,' she said shortly. 'I don't. All I know is that he needed you and you weren't there. He adores you, Melissa.'

'Odd way of showing it,' Robert observed, not bothering even to glance at Nell as he ostentatiously replaced his arm round Melissa's shoulders. 'Dashing around motor tracks when he could be with beautiful Kitten here.'

The beautiful Kitten said nothing, and, sickened, Nell turned to leave. Then Melissa said, 'Come home with me tonight, Nell. Please. I can't bear to be alone. And Robert's got—' She broke off, large tears forming in her eyes. 'Please, Nell, please.'

'Very well,' she said dully. As she closed the door, Melissa was already moving into Robert's embrace.

Chapter Four

'Mercedes-Benz have got a new beauty coming out this year. Engine designed by a chap called Porsche. Like to get my hands on one of those. Won't see it over here, I don't suppose,' Tom said ruefully, as he drove the Alvis away from Brooklands a few weeks later. It hadn't been a good start to the racing year.

'Why not?' asked Nell curiously.

Tom shrugged. 'Don't ask me. Something to do with keeping Germany in its place, no doubt.'

'That doesn't seem to make much sense,' she observed.

He glanced at her. 'Better not let the Old Man hear you say that,' he said seriously. 'He's convinced we haven't heard the last of Germany.'

'And what do you think?' Nell demanded.

'Me?' He seemed first flattered that anyone should want to know his opinion, then confused as to what precisely he *did* think. 'Sport's the thing. Countries joining together to conquer the elements, that sort of thing. Shackleton trying for the South Pole, Mallory having a go at Everest, now Cobham's trying to fly to Cape Town, Alcock and Brown buzzing over the Atlantic by aeroplane.' Tom sounded wistful. 'That's what I think anyway. Pulling together to show the world.'

'And what about the General Strike?' asked Nell quietly. 'Not much pulling together there, was there?'

The long-awaited, long-feared strike in support of the miners had taken place and been over in nine days.

Guiltily, she had found it exciting. When all public transport ceased, volunteers had driven buses, trains and trams to keep London moving. Gadsby's staff had struggled in each with their own tale of how they did it. When it finished (for everyone save the poor miners) normal life had returned surprisingly quickly, and the monsters whom press and government had represented as Threats to Democracy resumed their everyday cheerful faces as bus conductors and tram drivers. Britain breathed a sigh of relief and was settling down to resume its contented enjoyment of the new age.

Tom frowned. 'You *are* a New Woman and no mistake, Nelly. They caved in, didn't they? Saw sense. They are British, after all.'

She laughed.

'What are you laughing at?' he asked in bewilderment.

'Just at the fun of being here,' she answered quickly.

'It was good of you to come, Nelly,' Tom said awkwardly, as though for once he realised there might be something odd about his being accompanied not by his wife, but by her friend. He drew up with a flourish at a roadhouse. 'Melissa—'

Nell cut in quickly. 'She loves you too much to watch you race, Tom.' Was it true? she wondered traitorously. If so, why was Tom spending more and more time flying or racing or even at Gadsby's? Or even with her? She desperately looked forward to the times when Melissa would fling at her carelessly, 'Darling, go and keep Tom company, will you? I simply haven't the time to watch those silly motor cars yet again.'

Time? For Robert Stockbridge, perhaps? Certainly he seemed to be around more than his co-starring role justified – and perhaps that was fortunate, Nell thought, remembering Melissa's usual choice of bed partner. But the bored and petulant look she feared so much was appearing more and more often on Melissa's face. She was being used, Nell recognised ruefully. Melissa could trust her to keep Tom quiet, without fear of her encroaching on her territory.

'Does she?' asked Tom quietly.

Nell was shocked at the open unhappiness on his face.

'Of course,' she said firmly, banishing her own doubts. 'She loves you. She needs you.'

'Perhaps the latter,' Tom amended, summoning the waiter to order a second bottle of Château Margaux to Nell's amusement, as she wondered not for the first time if he had any idea of the value of money. 'But I—'

Tom hesitated, then rushed on: 'It's like being married to Tinker Bell in that Barrie fellow's play. *Peter Pan* isn't it? She's only there when she wants to be, then just a laugh and she's gone again. You can't grasp her, somehow. I thought when she married she'd settle down. A baby would be fun, but it's been nearly a year now and she's in this play and won't hear of it.'

Nell felt awkward, disloyal to Melissa, wondering whether it was entirely wise to be with him so much. But she realised how much she'd come to rely on these outings when Tom was removed from the sphere of her daydreams into a real-life companion, if not lover. She had tried to go out with other men, but beside Tom they were pale indeed, and unaware of the Viking hero with whom they were compared they soon fell away. So far she'd never minded; better her half loaf in Tom than an unappetising pile of crumbs elsewhere, she put it to herself. When she tried to point out her invidious position and suggest she should not be with them so much, he was shocked.

'Only thing that keeps the peace between us, having you around, Nelly. You're a good sport.' He reached out his hand and squeezed hers in gratitude. A memory of Lucien de la Ferté kissing it floated quickly through her mind. How much better was the equality of the sexes in

117

England than his outmoded attitude to women.

Melissa too when faced with the same question dismissed her worries. 'Tom understands,' she said vaguely. 'After all, I have to be in this play, and afterwards I have to unwind – plus the fact that as my public expects to see me offstage as well, I have to be seen at clubs and restaurants. Publicity is so important,' she informed Nell. 'I'd love Tommy to come too, but he won't. He's such a dull old stick-in-the-mud, you can't imagine,' she burst out in a fit of confidence.

'Dull? *Tom*?' Nell stared at her in amazement. 'Perhaps to you,' she said unguardedly.

'There you are then.' Melissa pounced happily. 'So you won't complain if I leave you with Tommy. After all, you're hardly likely to seduce him, are you? And even if you did, I wouldn't have much to worry about.'

Nell's temper boiled over, as it rarely did with Melissa, who generally got away with most things through genuine charm. 'How do you know I won't seduce him?' she snapped. 'And why wouldn't you worry? I'm not that plain. How do you *know* he won't seduce me?'

Melissa stopped in the middle of applying her mascara and looked at her in some surprise. 'He wouldn't seduce you,' she said simply, 'firstly because he's so devoted to me, and secondly, he's more interested in engines than sex and—'

'Stop,' choked Nell, unable to bear it.

'And thirdly, you won't seduce *him* because you're too honourable,' Melissa finished matter-of-factly.

'How can you trust me?' demanded Nell. 'How do you *know*?' with visions of leaping on Tom the very next time she found him alone.

'Oh, Nell,' murmured Melissa, as if exasperated. 'Because I do. And what's more I'm going to need you even more now.' She shot a sidelong look at Nell, then studied herself assiduously in the mirror. 'I think I'm going into films again.'

'*What*? Surely not after last time. Oh, *Melissa*!' Nell cried despairingly.

'This time it's all different. This director says—'

'I thought there'd be a man in it,' said Nell resignedly.

Melissa laughed, unoffended. 'Of course,' she said. 'He's divine. He's a mixture of Rudolph Valentino, that adorable Ivor Novello and darling Noël Coward.'

'I'm really impressed,' remarked Nell drily.

'He tells me that British cinema is going to change. There's been a lot of discussion and a bill is going through Parliament next year which will make everything all right for the British film industry. Something to do with quotas,' she said vaguely. 'Anyway, it will be marvellous and everyone will be wanting British films, even in America. Isn't that wonderful?'

'Wonderful,' agreed Nell hollowly, 'except for your marriage,' she added, but Melissa ignored her.

'He's going to start shooting the first one in the New Year. It's the story of Lady Arabella Stuart. He wants it to be ready for when the big demand comes.'

'If it does,' muttered Nell, trying hard to remember what she had read about film. The American distributors had been forcing kinemas in Britain into block bookings, so that they had to take bad and indifferent films to be sure of getting the good ones, thus leaving little free time for showing British films. The new bill would stipulate that every kinema had to show a certain percentage of British films to give the home industry a chance. The percentage would gradually increase. Naturally, Melissa intended to be right there in the forefront.

'Jack is perfectly sweet,' Melissa informed her. 'He's not interested in my body at all,' she told her friend innocently. 'It's all in the cause of art.

★ ★ ★

119

Life in Teagowns was a life of purgatory. A dying department indeed despite the new lounge coats, which had not really caught on with Gadsby's thinning ranks of customers. Nell had little to do except to 'supervise' the understudy, and supervise rapidly became a euphemism for 'dogsbody'. Every idea she put forward was firmly quashed by Miss Copsy, who instructed her to learn by her example. Like Mr Asquith, her policy was 'Wait and See'. Wait and see whether new fashions last. So they continued to stock the old heavily restricting boned corsets of old, and though they stocked one or two in the new lighter materials, with (great daring) flat form front busks (in fashion for the past four years), these were kept very discreetly in the rear. As for the new brassières said to divide one breast from another, these were an innovation that would not last, she told Nell firmly when she suggested it, and in any case there would be no demand. Instead, she announced proudly, she intended to stock a wide range of the new aertex underwear for all the family.

'This is the way to appeal to your young people you want to cater for, Nell,' she added indulgently, for she liked the girl.

No belts or girdles, no suspender belts for the young and firm of body, and no pretty peach, ivory, eau de nil, rose, cyclamen crêpe-de-Chine underwear. Plain white or pale pink and that was it. Miss Copsy had almost fainted on the spot when Nell suggested black. Nell had laughed, remembering Melissa once prancing around drinking champagne in her dressing room in black underwear and nothing else, oblivious of the gentlemen crowding in to congratulate her. Or perhaps not so oblivious, she now thought wrily.

But Miss Copsy's days were numbered. Half-way through August, Nell found her crying in her small office. 'What is it?' she asked, alarmed.

'I'm leaving,' Miss Copsy told her between sobs. 'I've resigned.'

'But why? You're not due to retire for another five years,' Nell cried.

'It's that woman,' she gasped. Gradually the story emerged. Miss Copsy was no longer to travel to Paris to buy for her department. Her presence was not considered necessary.

'They're closing the department?' Nell asked in trepidation.

'No. Miss Danzy is going to combine this department with hers.'

'*What*?' Nell stared at her in horror.

Miss Copsy nodded. 'I'm afraid you'll be working for her again, Nell.'

'What's this, missy? Complaining about my decisions again?' Jonathan rumbled.

He was beginning to look his age, Nell thought suddenly, diverted from her own problems.

'You get to know your place,' he roared at her. 'You're lucky to be on the staff at all.'

'Then you can have my notice too,' said Nell quietly.

Jonathan Gadsby stared at her. 'Aha,' he trumpeted. 'Just as I thought. No backbone, see? Give up at the first hint of opposition, eh? I summed you up right from the first, my girl.'

'I am not *giving up*,' she flashed. 'I just won't work under these conditions.'

'And where do you think I'd be today if I'd told Uncle Bush that back in '70? I tell you where I'd be, missy. Sitting on my backside in some hovel having done nothing but sold pins and needles for other people all my life. That's where I'd be. You wait your opportunity, girl, you'll know it when it comes. *If* it comes,' he concluded with scorn.

121

Nell considered. 'I'll give it till Christmas,' she told him grandly. After all, her record wasn't going to get her much of a job elsewhere. Her reduced wages in Teagowns had made life in London difficult. Melissa had insisted on helping her to keep the Mayfair flat. ('After all, I may want a bolt-hole one of these days, and you'll soon be earning more money again.') If she went elsewhere with this record, she'd get even less money. So, smarting, once again, she was forced to submit. Until Christmas.

'You will run this department under my direction, Miss Watkins.' Triumph glowed on the Dragon's face as she took vengeance on Nell who had committed the unforgivable sin of being right.

Among the models that Nell had bought from houses other than Maison la Ferté, the bustle-bow dresses and the taffeta picture frocks had proved very popular despite Miss Danzy's never recommending them save as a last resort to save her commission. Nell waited in trepidation to see what horrors the Dragon might bring back from Paris from the autumn parades in late August, but even she could not have foreseen what was to happen. And it hardly improved relations between herself and the Dragon. She was summoned to a meeting, not in the ground floor directors' room but on the Fourth Floor. Her heart sank, though she could not for the life of her think of any crimes she had committed recently. Recently, it appeared, was not the operative word.

'Well, missy, see what you've done?' Jonathan Gadsby roared from his governing director's seat at the head of the table. Miss Danzy and Mr Langer smirked, Mr Lorrimer and Mr Charles looked suitably disapproving and Tom, dear Tom, nervous. 'Maison la Ferté have told us they won't reinstate the exclusive contract. And who put that idea in their minds, I'd like to ask?'

'I wasn't there, sir,' stammered Nell.

'It's the consequence of your actions in the spring, Miss Watkins, so I'm told. Can't be bothered with us, no doubt, now they think we've shown a lack of confidence. You realise what this means?'

'It means that Gadsby's will have a far wider choice to reach a far wider range of customers,' Nell tried to say firmly and almost succeeding.

'Like last time, Miss Watkins?' came the Dragon's dulcet tones. 'With all those ridiculous picture frocks and bustle bows?'

'I thought they sold well,' said Tom innocently, surprised into speaking.

'Of course, Mr Gadsby,' the Dragon said smoothly. 'But only, if I may say so, through my own powers of persuasion. We haven't seen any of those customers since, I may say, proving it was merely a passing trade and not the regular clientele Gadsby's wishes to encourage.'

'To do that,' said Nell steadily, 'you must have a wider selection to follow the lines that have sold well. And unless Maison la Ferté has changed, you will not achieve that there.' She looked round her adversaries. There was something more, she realised from Miss Danzy's lack of desire to pounce on this provocative carrot. More bad news.

'Indeed yes, missy,' Jonathan informed her with gusto. 'Maison la Ferté have clearly decided that if they can't join us, they'll beat us. They're opening up in London, right near us in Conduit Street, in the New Year. What do you think of that, missy, eh? Thanks to your brilliant strategy, we can't buy any models at all from la Ferté.' He sat back after his tirade almost with satisfaction.

'You mean they're going to sell straight to the British market and not allow any British copying rights?' Nell asked in dismay.

'Yes,' said Miss Danzy coldly. 'They've decided to design a new line especially for Britain, which is why the

123

count's son himself is coming, And the only reason,' she burst out vehemently, 'that you aren't looking for another job, Miss Watkins, is that he has a higher opinion of your powers than I hold, and has also endeavoured to help us find replacement suppliers for the new season.'

Design especially for Britain? So Philippe was coming to work in Conduit Street? An immediate rush of pleasure swept over her at the thought of meeting him again. Perhaps he'd ask her out? It would be pleasant to have fun. Much as she loved Tom, it would undoubtedly be exciting to be with Philippe de la Ferté. A glow of pleasure seized her at the thought that he had been so impressed by what she said at dinner at the Château that night.

'I think it's excellent news,' Nell maintained stoutly. 'It will shake our thoughts up. Make us consider our future.'

All save Tom looked at her bleakly.

'I'm grateful for your views,' Miss Danzy informed her icily. 'Nevertheless we will not require a shake-up, as you put it. I have found another couturier who understands our needs perfectly, Monsieur Mennais.'

Nell stared at her aghast. The House of Mennais was a famous one, but its great years had been at the turn of the century. Its style had remained locked there, producing beautifully made clothes for wealthy clients. Now that a new age was upon them, Guillaume Mennais had lost direction, in her view, seeking to replace style with ornamentation. Much, much worse than Maison la Ferté for Gadsby's.

'I hope you had a successful visit,' she managed to say stiffly.

'Indeed I did. I bought some delightful ankle-length teagowns for you, Miss Watkins,' the Dragon informed her spitefully.

Delightful they would indeed have been twenty years ago,

124

thought Nell despairingly when the models arrived from Paris. Who on earth would want to buy these now? The middle-aged matrons were now past the age of floating chiffons and the need for them, she thought irreverently, remembering the talk that floated round the salesroom of fashionable ladies entertaining their lovers unencumbered by the need for corsets. The younger ladies of 1906 were still fashionable enough in 1926 to wish to keep up with the times, and with skirts even shorter this autumn, the old-fashioned type of full length teagown was no longer part of them. Nor, she thought crossly, was this awful lingerie.

It added to her chagrin to open the fashion pages of the English magazines and read about the new Paris taffeta *robes de style* imitation period-style dresses which were both fashionable and suited the older ladies. Miss Danzy had not ordered even one, although Nell knew despairingly she could have sold many in the pre-Christmas period. By next spring they'd be out of fashion again no doubt, even if she had managed to improve her position by then and escape the Dragon's clutches. Or else left.

There was no one she could talk to at the store about her problems, with her former friends there no longer considering her as one of themselves and her peers and superiors hostile. Even had it been fair to worry Tom about it, he had little time for internal problems at Gadsby's. He seemed lost in a perpetual maze, his usually cheerful face wearing an abstractedly lugubrious look, as of a lost spaniel. What preoccupied him was fairly obvious.

'Were you ever in love with anyone, Nell?' he asked her gloomily one day.

'Yes,' she replied guardedly.

'Nice sort of chap?'

'Very,' she answered dully.

'Why didn't you marry him?'

'He preferred someone else.'

'Oh.' A pause. 'So does Melissa.' He shot a look at her.

Nell was silent. Should she prevaricate? No, she hated doing that. She just wouldn't get too far in. 'Are you sure?' she ventured cautiously.

'Quite,' he said.

What on earth had happened? Nell wondered wildly. Was he just assuming this was the case from the number of occasions Melissa was absent, or had he seen her with other men? Surely he could not have interrupted a scene as she had witnessed, or found out about Robert Stockbridge?

'This sex thing,' Tom continued.

'What about it?' she asked non-committally, wondering what on earth was coming.

'Do you think it's that important?'

Nell opened her mouth and shut it again, feeling she was getting into deep waters. 'To some,' she said cautiously, remembering Lucien de la Ferté's mocking comments. 'And how would I know, anyway?' a little crossly.

'All-important?' Tom ploughed on doggedly, ignoring this.

'To some,' she repeated shortly.

'To Melissa?' he ploughed on relentlessly.

'I can't answer that, Tom,' she answered, aghast.

'No. Unfair of me to ask you,' he said hastily. Then burst out: 'Why can't husbands and wives be chums, friends? Like you and me, Nelly. Sex gets in the way.' He took a gulp of whisky and changed the subject. But that night he kissed her, not as before but full on the lips. She did not, could not, resist, and went home in a glow of happiness.

From then on she seemed to spend more and more time with Tom. Melissa was either at the show or engaged in private business of her own, returning in the small hours, or sometimes not till morning, and disappearing by lunchtime. If this was gossiped about at the store, Nell neither knew nor cared.

As autumn wore on, Tom sprang a surprise invitation on her. 'Come and spend Christmas with us in Kent, Nell. I'd like to have you there, down at Merryfield. It might be quite jolly. Melissa's bringing that film director bloke,' he added nonchalantly. 'They've got to discuss work, she says.'

'So you know about the film?' she said with relief. One less secret to keep.

'I can't stand in her way, can I?' he said defiantly. 'Any more than she could stop me motor racing or flying.'

Did she want to go to Kent with them? It meant facing Jonathan Gadsby. Could she stand in the middle of a human triangle trying not to make it look like a square? Could she bear it? But where else to go? Her parents had made it clear they would be at her brother's new house, and the prospect of Christmas alone was no fun at all. One way and another, her private life left a lot to be desired, she decided ruefully.

'The de la Ferté chap will be there,' Tom added.

So she'd meet Philippe again, she thought, with a leap of interest. At least she could have fun dancing with him, to stop the pain of watching Tom and Melissa, tearing their marriage to pieces. 'Yes, Tom, I'd like that. Thank you.'

By the autumn there was little doubt but that Gadsby's trade was slipping, and not only in Teagowns. Even Sporting Wear showed a decrease in turnover. True, it too showed a tendency to cater for the traditional approach to sports, those who watched rather than those that took part, as well as not acknowledging new sports such as flying. This could account for some of the decline. But whatever the reason, the directors set a date for the January sale with more alacrity than was usual at

127

Gadsby's, whose sales were half-hearted affairs to say the least in Nell's opinion. All she could offer was a slightly sad array of Miss Danzy's choice of ready-made and model teagowns and a discreet display of old-fashioned chemises and corsets. Miss Danzy grew more and more bad-tempered as the autumn progressed, but it was not all Nell's doing. The Dragon had good taste but this was modelled on what her customers usually bought. She lacked flair and sense of direction, and would never contemplate leading her customers' taste.

Thus every suggestion Nell made was quashed. It was hard to endure customers' disappointment, to see elegant monied backs disappearing from the department, knowing they would not return. The last straw was the Christmas season which normally in the lingerie department was a busy one as husbands bought gifts for wives. This Christmas, however, they had clearly decided Gadsby's nightdresses and camiknickers were hardly likely to cause them the erotic thrill that changing times were encouraging them to expect. Though they looked, they rarely bought.

Nell could stand it no longer. After Christmas she decided she would leave. And go . . . where *would* she go? Work her way up in some other store? Even if she did feel like a rat leaving the sinking ship, she now had no choice.

Merrifield House, a large eighteenth-century mansion of red brick just outside Ashford, looked warm and welcoming despite its formal circular drive and winter-bleak gardens. Nell was glad of it for she had to face Jonathan Gadsby, to which despite Tom's solid presence she was not looking forward.

The Lea-Francis drew up outside with a casual honk on the horn. Despite Tom's mutterings that he was going to replace it, he seemed merely to have added to his collection, retaining 'Fanny-Lea' for Melissa's sake he said. The latest addition was an awe-inspiring Arab Super Sportscar, low and lean, which he had 'picked up at Brooklands' in the summer. For a few weeks it had been his pride and joy, but as autumn had approached he'd lost interest and it remained at Merryfield, polished every day by Jonathan's chauffeur and driven only by request. In fact, ever since Alan Cobham had successfully flown to Australia in October, Tom's talk was less and less of motor races in which he had participated, and more and more of aeroplanes and what still remained to be achieved.

'I'd like to do something,' he once told Nell wistfully. 'Before it's too late.'

As well as facing Jonathan, Nell was not looking forward to seeing Tom and Melissa together again. There was an increasing tendency for her to see Melissa and see Tom but not together, a fact that eventually struck her as ominous when he picked her up to drive her down to Kent. She had assumed she would be in the dicky seat, and asked with some surprise where Melissa was when Tom had drawn up outside Gadsby's to collect her on Christmas Eve.

'She's driving down with the film chappie,' he told her briefly.

One glance at his face and she asked no more.

Jonathan Gadsby might be a formidable employer but he was a genial host, coming through the front door and down the steps to greet them. His wife, Tom's grandmother, had died ten years earlier.

'Delighted you could join us, Nell,' he greeted her informally, with only the slightest gleam in his eye that the tenor of their previous encounters was recollected. 'I've put you next to Melissa,' he told her. 'Thought you'd like that. Mrs Hopkins here –' indicating the housekeeper '– will show you where. Come downstairs when you're ready.' A note in his voice suggested this should be soon as it was already eight o'clock.

An army of liveried footmen was already marching past in column with baggage, not that Nell had a great deal. Tom disappeared, leaving her to Mrs Hopkins, making it clear, if his father had not already implied it, that he and Melissa weren't sharing a room, or even adjoining rooms. In fact, she herself seemed to be sharing a bathroom with Melissa, from the array of beauty articles laid out in it. Odd to make their disharmony so obvious, thought Nell, then dismissed the thought as she began to look forward to her forthcoming Christmas of luxury. She changed into a silver lamé knee-length evening dress, with a head-dress to match, conscious that its waistline was in slightly the wrong place since it dated from last spring, and that although Tom would not notice, Philippe definitely would. So what? she thought defiantly. She wasn't the buyer of Gadsby's fashion any more, and silver suited her.

'You're a stunner, Nelly Watkins,' she informed her reflection in the mirror in case there should be any doubt on the matter. Then, taking a deep breath, she marched down to the drawing room. Melissa, clad in the latest Paris craze for black lace over shell pink taffeta, came to her immediately, breaking off from instructing the butler on how to improve his cocktail expertise.

'Oh, darling, how lovely to see you. Now I want you to meet Jack Fisher.'

A usual enough name for a very unusual person. His hair was incredibly long by present standards and unrestrained by oils and cream floated haphazardly around his head. She was taken aback by the piercing dark eyes that seemed to bore right through her like a screwdriver (and not the sort the poor butler was failing to get right, thought Nell, watching his efforts with amusement as Melissa made her liquid requirements known to him). She took a second look and decided Jack Fisher's expression was the carefully cultivated look of bored indifference combined with all-seeing percipience that she was used to seeing in the Chelsea artistic set, whom she ran into on occasional forays with Melissa to parties. The bright pink shirt he chose to wear with his black tailcoat settled the matter.

'Isn't he the sweetest thing, Nell?' enthused Melissa, throwing her arms round his neck.

Jack Fisher didn't look at all the sweetest thing, in Nell's view as he limply took her hand, immediately dropping it again. Nor in Jonathan Gadsby's, she noticed. He was glaring at them from the far side of the room where he was engaged in conversation with a group of people Nell did not recognise.

'Hello, Melissa,' said Tom genially, as he came in. He might have been greeting a casual friend. His fresh complexion glowed healthily above the severe black and white of his evening clothes. 'Jack.' He bowed slightly to the film director, receiving a slight nod in exchange, and came over to Nell.

'You haven't met Sis, Nelly,' he declared. 'Rose, come here!'

A slightly younger and chubbier version of Tom obediently detached herself from Jonathan's group and hastened to her brother's side.

Dressed by Gadsby, and badly, was Nell's reaction, though she must be a new customer for Nell herself had not served her in her understudy days; but the warm friendliness that exuded from Rose's face instantly attracted her.

'Tom's told me about you,' she told Nell. 'I hope you'll come here lots. It's so dull here. I wish Grandpapa would let me work in the store,' she said wistfully.

'Your job's to marry,' declared Jonathan, overhearing as he walked up to them. 'Nell, two friends of yours.'

'Of mine?' she queried, puzzled.

'Thought you'd like a few friends around,' he said

affably. 'Drove 'em down myself.'

'Now, Jonathan, that's not strictly accurate,' said a familiar voice, its owner turning around. 'It was your chauffeur who drove, when you kindly called for us.'

'What do you think Welling made of a Rolls-Royce calling for *us*?' her sister joined in excitedly.

Nell flung her arms round them. Miss Emmeline and Miss Gertrude were the last people she'd expected to see here, and yet why not? They were old friends of Mr Gadsby's. More than that, if rumour were true. Their black and purple satin respectively, with high-necked collars and old lace, added an oddly exotic rather than an old-fashioned look to the gathering. Suddenly Nell knew she was going to enjoy herself after all, despite the strained situation between Tom and Melissa, especially with Philippe coming too.

'Ah. There's young Ferté now.' Gadsby looked towards the door.

Would he even remember her? Nell wondered as she looked up to greet him.

'Phil—' The name died on her lips.

'My apologies for disappointing you, Miss Watkins.'

It was not Philippe but Lucien who joined them, mockery in his voice, his bright eyes watching her.

Dismayed, Nell pulled herself together and automatically held out her hand, wondering whether he would kiss it or shake it. As if accepting some kind of challenge she hadn't meant, he chose the former, but it was very deliberately the palm he kissed. '*Enchanté*,' he murmured distantly, and turned away to talk to Jonathan.

'Oh,' Nell cried without thinking, 'this doesn't mean it's you opening the new store, does it? I thought it was Philippe—' Her voice faltered as his frosty glare was turned on her once again. 'After all,' she finished weakly, 'he is the designer.' She was conscious of her own rudeness. Why did it always happen with this man?

132

'I regret it is myself, mademoiselle. However, it need not disturb you, since we are no longer business associates,' he said softly.

That settled it, thought Nell, furious. Why feel ashamed of rudeness to *this* man?

'Darling, who is your perfectly gorgeous friend?' Melissa wafted over to them and Nell introduced her to Lucien, watching with some interest both their reactions. Melissa slipped into her usual demeanour on meeting a new man – on the whole unassumed, Nell decided. Somehow Melissa's features seemed to melt, her whole body regressing into an impression of great fragility. She only needs a Lanvin frock to walk straight into Victorian vapours and simpers, thought Nell with a sudden rush of fondness for her. But Lucien, she noticed with scorn, was responding with another sickening French display of admiration. Ah well, another trout on the line. Nell's fondness suddenly turned to irritation, even on behalf of Jack Fisher, let alone Tom.

'My husband Tommy,' breathed Melissa, managing both to gaze adoringly up at her spouse and to convey an impression of 'If only . . .' to Lucien. Or any attractive man, Nell amended to herself. How does she do it?

'*Naturellement*, madame. I have known Tom for many years.' Lucien turned to greet Tom, and chatted casually to him.

Aghast, Nell remembered her conversation with Lucien by the Seine. Thank heavens she hadn't told Lucien who her 'lover' was, or even described him.

The evening seemed to turn into a keen competition between Lucien and Jack as to who could be of most service to Melissa, who was sitting between them at dinner. Nell, seated by Tom, tried valiantly to disengage his attention from this enthralling scene but failed. He too had eyes only for Melissa. Why shouldn't he? He's her husband, Nell tried to tell herself. If Melissa weren't there; if only there'd never been a Melissa . . . No, she would not think that way, she told herself firmly, looking up suddenly to see Lucien staring at her contemplatively, a slight smile on his lips.

When dancing commenced though, Lucien turned not to Melissa but to Rose, until Melissa, bored with Tom's choice of records, marched across to put on the Charleston. Here Lucien was clearly at a loss, noticed Nell with amusement, as she herself embarked on a spirited exercise in dance with Tom. Rose endeavoured to teach Lucien, but thirty seconds later Melissa intervened to take over the new pupil's instruction.

'Darling, *I'll* show him. After all, our guest deserves the best, the Charleston Lady herself,' she announced grandly.

Nell groaned inwardly at Lucien's naivety as Melissa devoted herself to her task. He would be more puppet than pupil. Nevertheless, by the time she said goodnight to the company, Lucien was back with Rose. 'As you see,' he remarked casually, as he swept by her, 'I too can be a good chum.'

Chapter 5 157

Melissa was not alone when she returned to her room that night. The familiar giggles were mixed with a distinct masculine undertone. So much for good chums, Nell thought savagely. Of course, it might be Tom. This thought caused her to toss restlessly for some time, despite its unlikeliness. Yet after all, would Melissa be foolish enough to entertain lovers under her father-in-law's roof, and with her husband in the same house? Yes, thought Nell. Oh, yes. Quite foolish enough. It was probably His Haughtiness Comte Lucien with her, testing his theories of True Womanhood. And she dived under her blankets as if by so doing she could obliterate her thoughts as well as the chill December air.

It wasn't Lucien with Melissa, she discovered in the

morning in the most indisputable way. She walked into the bathroom, whose occupant had foolishly left her communicating door unbolted – to find a skinny, naked Jack Fisher in the bath. With Melissa.

Christmas Day, despite its inauspicious start, proved remarkably enjoyable, and chatting to Rose and the Misses Parks, Nell was almost able to forget the less happy side of this holiday – until the evening, when Melissa decreed that hide and seek, at least for the more energetic, would be an excellent plan. Of the dozen or so projected participants, several were distinctly unwilling.

'You look annoyed, Lucien,' Nell observed sweetly. It sounded strange to address him thus but she was definitely not going to call him 'comte'.

Unexpectedly he smiled. 'It is not the custom, save for les enfants, to play such games in France.'

'It's all part of being chums,' she assured him innocently. 'After all, Melissa is the hare in hiding. Aren't you eager to find her?'

'Not so eager as her husband,' he murmured.

'I don't know what you mean,' she said feebly, taken aback.

'Very well, Nell, let us seek this foolish, frightened, innocent hare, shall we?' he said suddenly. 'Before even more eager hounds do so, yes?'

It took some time, however, to find Melissa, as she had clearly intended it should, especially in the dark. Then a shrill scream came from further along the corridor. Startled, Nell turned the wrong way in the darkness, bumping into Lucien, hearing his quick breathing, almost his heartbeat before firm hands came out of the blackness and steadied her.

'Come.' He took her hand and they hurried towards a bedroom where the sounds of altercation could be heard. An illicit torch, displaying Tom's unmistakable large figure behind it, was pointing into the huge old wardrobe.

'What is it? What's wrong?' hissed Nell, trying to get past Lucien's restraining arm, and unable to see what was happening – or what the torch might be illuminating.

'I think,' he told her drily, 'that Tom has found the hare, but someone else has found her first. In the good English sporting tradition, the hound is ready to tear them both to pieces.'

'I must go to help.' She tried to push past him.

'You will not,' he told her firmly. 'You can do nothing.' And gripping her arm tightly, he escorted her away.

Whatever happened after they left, the atmosphere was even more strained next day. Even Miss Emmeline and Miss Gertrude noticed it, but attributed it (in Miss Gertrude's case at least) to an excess of Christmas Day fare. Rose announced a party would be leaving to attend the meet of the Tickham Hunt, and in the end everyone went – save for Melissa and Jack who had disappeared.

Tom imbibed freely of the stirrup cup, helped down by several of the landlord's own cups, and drove back recklessly until Nell squawked with fear and he slowed down fractionally. The rest of the party was behind them, and thus when Tom and Nell walked in, they were the only ones to find Melissa and Jack lying full-length on the sofa in the drawing room entwined in each other's arms – and, to Nell's horrified realisation, clothing. It was the last straw. Regardless of his father whose voice could be heard entering the house with the rest of the party, Tom's temper boiled over.

'What the blazes are you doing?' he demanded, intemperately for him.

'Kissing, Tommy darling. Just a friendly Christmas kiss,' Melissa said, albeit a shade nervously, as her head popped up above the back of the sofa.

'Kind of kissing you were doing last night?' he shouted.

'What do you mean?'

'In that wardrobe,' he roared, exasperated at her pre-varication, 'and later too, I've no doubt. You weren't in your room. You didn't answer, anyway. I can guess where you were though.'

'Looking at the moon, old chap. We took a stroll down to the lake,' Jack informed him, getting up and strolling over to pour a drink.

'I'll damn well throw you in it.' Tom charged forward and seized hold of him, shaking him to and fro.

'Tom!' roared Jonathan, coming through the doorway. 'Enough.' Lucien, on his heels, took in what was happen-ing and flung himself forward to intervene, colliding with Nell on the same mission. He pushed her roughly aside and went to rescue Jack. He was too late. Tom had floored him with a straight punch to the jaw.

'I will not have fisticuffs in my house, sir,' shouted an enraged Jonathan, not used to being disregarded.

'Jonathan, I feel—'

But whatever Miss Emmeline felt was drowned by the noise of Melissa's sobs as she threw herself down upon her beloved, now trying to struggle to his feet, an attempt thwarted by Melissa's violent assault.

'I won't stay in this feudal prison,' he yelled.

'You won't have to, darling,' she sobbed. 'We'll leave right away.'

'You'll stay here, Melissa. It's Christmas, dammit,' snarled Tom, totally unrecognisable from the man Nell thought she knew.

'She will not,' roared Jonathan. 'No adulteresses sleep under my roof, sir.'

'Gad, sir, she's my wife,' flared Tom, suddenly chang-ing sides.

'I don't care if she's Queen Marie of Roumania. She leaves.'

'Then I leave too.'

The sound of a gong, firmly struck by Miss Emmeline, silenced everyone. 'I always think,' she said calmly, 'that luncheon is a good idea at such times. If you will escort me, Jonathan?'

Meekly, to Nell's utter amazement, the great Jonathan Gadsby took her arm and marched out, casting one word as an order behind him: 'Luncheon!'

Armed neutrality reigned for forty-five minutes, chiefly since the talk was uninterruptedly of the old days of Welling, of the quirks and foibles of village life, and anecdotes of its past worthies. Even Lucien seemed diverted, especially at the anecdotes involving Nell.

'I'm afraid dear Nell will never make a dressmaker,' Miss Emmeline beamed. 'Do you remember, dear, the day you sewed the underarm seam in the sleeve to the shoulder seam in Mrs Postlethwaite's blue brocade, so that the sleeve stuck straight up in the air?'

Nell scowled, feeling sixteen again.

Oblivious, Miss Emmeline continued: 'And then the day dear Nell mistook our new cleaner for the Honourable Mrs Higgins and gave her tea and scones in my private office. Though,' she added fairly, 'it is true that Mrs Smith had much more flair for apparel than Mrs Higgins.'

'Where the blazes is Melissa?' Tom suddenly demanded, after the party adjourned for coffee, Miss Emmeline still happily reminiscing.

'Powdering her nose,' Miss Gertrude informed him, quivering with fright at this unusual situation and rather wishing she were enjoying Boxing Day listening to the Salvation Army singing carols on Welling Corner.

'With that fellow?' demanded Tom grimly, realising belatedly that Jack too had disappeared. Tom hurtled outside, and his roar as he discovered Jack's motor car had been summoned and had now departed brought Nell rushing to his side. 'I'll thrash the bounder all the way from here to Timbuctoo,' he declared, rushing to the garages.

'Where are you going?' she shouted, panting after him.

'After them, of course. Back to London. Stand out of my way like a good girl,' he said, cranking furiously.

'But—'

He leapt in and the Lea-Francis roared into life. Nell desolately watched the cloud of smoke from the exhaust as it raced down the drive.

'Why this unhappy expression, Nelly Watkins?' murmured Lucien, coming up silently by her side and making her jump.

She gulped and tried to be nonchalant. 'I have to get back to London tonight to be at the store tomorrow,' she said a trifle forlornly. 'I expect he's forgotten.'

Lucien sighed heavily and audibly. 'Pray allow me to offer you a lift back to London, Miss Watkins. I too must leave. In any case, I feel perhaps that the Christmas festivities are now over, *n'est ce pas?*'

He drove up the London road in silence to her relief. She had enough to think about. He didn't appear to have the same addiction to motor cars as Tom, she reflected. She knew enough about them now, thanks to Tom, to recognise this one as an old Talbot-Darracq. It was strange to be sitting on the wrong side of the car, but he seemed to be safely on the left side of the road. Not that there was much traffic on these country roads. Especially in the middle of Boxing Day when most sensible people were in front of a roaring fire.

'Do not fear, Miss Watkins.' At last Lucien spoke. 'Your lover will not succeed in catching Melissa. Or if he does, then in holding her. Butterflies must flutter.'

'My lover?' she gasped, outraged. 'How *dare* you? Tom's *not* my lover.'

'My apologies, perhaps I phrased it badly. The man you love. Your good chum. On consideration, I do not think it

139

would occur to him to be physically unfaithful to his wife. The worst kind of English gentleman: to keep a mistress and not make love to her, save in the mind.'

'Stop the car,' she ordered ridiculously.

He sighed. 'If you wish me to stop so that you can attack me for my interference in matters that are none of my concern – unless of course you still hanker after my brother also – then I will do so. If you merely wish to make a foolish gesture by walking back to London, I do not propose to stop.'

'I do not hanker after your brother,' she shouted.

'I am relieved. Though it is scarcely flattering to him that you prefer someone with so little to offer as a lover as Tom.'

'You're wrong!' she cried vehemently, horrified at this interpretation. 'He's warm and generous.'

'That is not what I said,' he replied mildly.

'It's the same thing,' she said impatiently. 'For heaven's sake, *look* at me, Lucien. Do you really think I'm Mata Hari, Iris Storm and Madame de Pompadour all rolled into one?'

He glanced unwillingly at the brown curls that defied submission, hazel eyes that looked at him so brightly, cheeks pink from winter cold, innocent of make-up, the upturned nose, the freckles on her temples, and the mouth that wore a bright red lipstick far too harsh for it.

'No,' he said reluctantly, 'but—'

'There you are then,' she said crossly. 'You – oh look, be *careful*!'

In front of them a rabbit, scared by the approaching wheels, was bobbing blindly straight ahead of them down the road instead of into the hedgerow.

He tooted the horn, but the rabbit merely galvanised himself into faster action in the same direction until suddenly the white rump skidded to a stop, and its owner turned and faced them, stock still. Whether it was Nell's

140

scream or the rabbit or a combination of both, Lucien applied the brakes too sharply and the sports car slithered to the far side of the road, landing up half-way into the ditch. Flung sideways, Nell was deposited on top of Lucien lying half-way in and half-way out of the motor-car, their hats in the mud.

She wriggled cautiously, wondering for an instant whether Lucien had been thrown out, until a muffled voice came from somewhere underneath her.

'Nell? Ça va?'

She wiggled a leg which was wedged uncomfortably under something and realised it was trapped by his body. 'Lift up your left side,' she panted.

A muffled curse and she was free, rolling forward and half somersaulting, tumbling into the ditch.

'Are you all right?' she asked doubtfully, as he still did not move.

'Now I am disentangled from your delightful person, I will find out!' He began cautiously to shift his body.

Nell scrambled to her feet, slithering on the mud, and gave him her hand. He did not take it, preferring to manoeuvre himself sideways, free of the crazily angled motor-car, into the ditch. By this time she had clambered to the road and he took her proffered hand, landing beside her with a half-smothered yelp.

'What is it?' she asked anxiously.

'A slight twist of my foot. It is nothing.'

'Good. Well, what do we do now?' she said, looking ruefully at the mud on her clothes, legs and shoes. She began to laugh.

'I am glad you are amused,' he said sourly. 'You may continue laughing here while I walk to find help.'

'I'm not going to stay here alone,' Nell declared, teeth chattering with cold and shock. 'I'm coming with you.'

'If you wish. I do not care.'

Lucien set off grimly along the road, limping slightly,

141

without another glance to see if she was going to follow suit. Distinctly unamused now, she did so. At least walking would be warmer than waiting. It was a road that seemed to stretch a very long way ahead without sign of habitation.

'Why is it,' he burst out after a while, 'that whenever I am with you, Miss Watkins, crazy things happen?'

'They don't,' she said defensively, stopping to scrape off the caking mud on her shoes. 'Anyway, it's never my fault.'

'Is it *my* fault you do not speak French well enough to make yourself sufficiently understood to avoid having your clothes removed in perfectly understandable error? Is it my fault you establish an *entente cordiale* with every group of workmen you come across? Is it my fault you insist on following rabbits down the road? You are crazy, Nell Watkins. Crazy.'

'Crazy?' she yelled, tears forming in her eyes as she stomped angrily along. 'If you think I'm crazy, you should get to know Melissa.'

'I'm terrified,' he said ironically. 'At least Melissa is all woman.'

If you only knew, thought Nell savagely, furious at the comparison. 'And you think I'm not? Hell and tommy, at one moment you call me a Mata Hari, the next I'm some kind of Fat Lady at the Circus.'

'You do not look like a Fat Lady, this I concede,' he told her curtly.

'And you,' glancing at him and bursting into a sudden laughter that surprised her, 'don't look very much like the heir to Maison la Ferté. Look.' She fished in her handbag and produced her lipstick mirror. He looked briefly at the mud and grass stains adorning his temple, and the mud on his hat, and then down at the muddy torn overcoat.

'I see nothing wrong,' he told her coldly.

'They say love is blind,' she told him grandly, unable to resist.

'I am not vain,' he shouted, his composure going.

'Said the peacock,' she jeered.

'I'd rather be a peacock than a peahen,' he threw back at her, yelping as in anger he leaned too hard on his injured leg.

It took her a second or two to remember the dull unassuming nature of the peahen's plumage. Then: 'Oh!' She swung her handbag at him in fury, catching him on the side of the face before he gripped her wrists and made her drop them.

'Call me irresistible,' carolled a raucous voice advancing in a squeal of brakes. They had not even heard a motor car; both looked round together and dived for the hedge-row as the motor appeared to be taking no notice of its brakes and was coming straight for them with an extraordinarily dressed driver crouched grimly over the wheel. Its sex was indeterminate so smothered was it in goggles, hat and scarf. Why someone should wish to drive with the top down on a day like this was beyond Nell.

'Can I be of help?' the driver bawled at full voice, at last stopping, as they scrambled on to the road. 'Or are you enjoying the walk?' It proved to be a woman, though for a time only the voice identified her as such. She was swathed in such an extraordinary combination of bright shawls and scarves that with her close-fitting gold hat she looked rather like one of the finds from Tutankhamen's tomb that had appeared in the newspapers that year and re-lit public excitement in it.

'Saw your old bus back there,' she bawled. She must be about sixty, Nell decided, though she'd never seen a sixty-year-old dressed like this before.

'If we might have a lift to the nearest village to telephone to a garage?' Lucien requested politely.

A burst of laughter. 'You won't wake old Jenks up till

143

New Year, man. Get in and I'll get Roper to pick up the motor and bring it back for you. Straighten out the bumps. He's a marvel, ready for you tomorrow morning.'

'But—' Alarm was written all over his face.

'Nonsense, no trouble,' she waved aside his protestations. 'We'll pick up your bags and whizz right off. Topping.'

'You're very kind,' said Nell meekly.

'You'll both have to sit in the back. I've got the parrot here in front. That's why I'm out. Chasing him all over Kent. Tracked him down in Chilham church, waiting for the next service.'

Lucien wore the expression of one to whom fate could do no more as he held the door open for Nell to climb up.

'It's an adventure,' she whispered hopefully, trying not to laugh. 'Don't you like adventures?'

'Not with crazy women.'

'I'm not crazy,' yelled the driver cheerfully, misinterpreting and failing to take offence. 'Bobsy Bertrand, at your service.' A pause.

'Lady Bertrand?' asked Lucien, taken aback. 'The wife of General Sir Cyril Bertrand?'

'The same. Widow,' she bawled. 'Took the last salute two years ago, poor old chap. How d'yer do?' She turned round to them, taking her hands off the wheel.

'Miss Nell Watkins, and Lucien de la Ferté,' Lucien said quickly, only too eager for her to return them.

'Hold on to your hats, here we go,' she cried. 'Wheeeeeeeh!' whizzing round a corner and down one of the steepest hills Nell had ever driven down right into the valley of the Weald of Kent. Suddenly she shot off right along a rough lane, the car bouncing up and down, turning into tall, iron gates. 'Welcome to the old homestead, pals,' she told them gaily, as she drove up to Missinden House honking continuously. By the time they reached it, three liveried men awaited their arrival.

'What do you think of my bloomers, young man?' she roared as she climbed down from the car, revealing her lower half for the first time. It was covered in bright checked tweed plus-fours.

The lips of the heir to the Maison la Ferté twitched. 'They are inimitable, madame. As are you.'

'Now there's what I call politeness,' declared Bobsy, gratified. She strode towards the house, already scattering scarves and shawls to her following retainers. 'Make yourselves at home. I'll find a bedroom or two. Are you married? Well, Roper's other half will know about that,' she said vaguely, speaking over their united 'No'. 'Wait in there.' She strode off as soon as they entered and they followed the direction of her pointed finger into a huge room.

'Is this a museum?' asked Nell faintly, the first to speak.

'More of a temple, I'd call it,' shouted their hostess, already returning.

To what? thought Nell, not daring to look at Lucien. This was surely Art Deco gone mad. One wall was black, one white, the other two graded shades of red, from bright red to even brighter red, relieved only by angled mirrors of the length and width of pipes hung in groups of six, thus reflecting not apparently the occupants of the room, but a kaleidoscope of colours and elongated vertical stick insects. One or two modern surrealist paintings vied with them for attention and the furniture was piles of cushions the same colours as the wall. These replaced chairs and tables, though one glass table with drinks was a concession to tradition. Their hostess climbed on to one pile, sitting cross-legged. Lucien followed suit, looking quite at home. Only Nell in her short skirt failed the cross-legged test and had to tuck her legs to one side. Lucien was suddenly looking the other way, she noted with fury, as if to make a point.

'Mrs Roper's bringing tea.' Bobsy brought down the

tone of the room with this mundane pronouncement. Nell had expected nectar at the very least. 'And I've asked her to lay out a few dresses.'

'That's very kind,' said Nell, slightly dazed, 'but we have our baggage with us.'

'For tonight,' Bobsy said, surprised at such obtuseness. 'Sheikhs and Shulamites.'

'*Je m'excuse, madame*?' Lucien said, his face a study. 'I do not understand.'

'My party,' Bobsy beamed. 'Fancy dress. The lads are sheikhs and the lassies Shulamites.'

Nell began to grin as Lucien fought like a trapped tiger. 'We cannot possibly intrude. We will go—'

'Nonsense,' said Bobsy, seeing to the heart of the problem. 'You'll love it.'

Nell knocked cautiously on Lucien's door some hours later, but when he opened it, he showed no signs of looking forward to loving it. She tried to restrain herself from laughter, seeing him clad in white burnous with furious indignant eyes glaring at her under the hood. 'This is not a house for adults,' he declared. 'It is for *children*. What—' he took in her costume for the first time, 'are *you*?'

'I'm a Fair Shulamite,' said Nell complacently. 'You know, Solomon's beloved. I am "fair as the moon, clear as the sun, and terrible as an army with banners".'

His eyes gleamed. 'Ah, yes. The fair Shulamite. Now I recollect. Are not your two breasts like two young roedeer that are twins which feed among the lilies?' His eyes travelled over her very brief costume, consisting of a fringe over the two young roedeer and a somewhat longer one as a skirt.

'I can't really judge that,' said Nell with dignity, and turned to go down to the party.

Lucien clearly decided there was safety in numbers, as he stayed by her side, but once the dancing began

Nell soon managed to lose him, and enjoyed it immensely, Charlestoning with partners young and old for hours on end. Amid the flock of white burnous, she forgot to look for Lucien. Bobsy entertained them from time to time with remarkable solo dances she had picked up on her travels around the world or else recounted anecdotes. It was three o'clock when Nell remembered with horror that she was due at work in six hours' time, and ran up the stairs to her bedroom. In the corridor she found Lucien standing silently. He was the only person who was. Inside both their bedrooms a pillow fight was in full flood of feathers. Moreover, several bodies recumbent in sleep, despite the racket raging round them, had already taken up position for the night. Should they join them? Dispose of them? She looked doubtfully at Lucien.

'*Non,*' he said simply. '*Non.*' He looked at her equally appalled face. 'Bring your suitcase, and *come*!'

Obediently she dodged feathers and pillows, grabbed her small suitcase and followed him quietly down the stairs and outside where he put her coat round her bare shoulders. 'Now,' he said, taking her hand, and leading her to the old stables, where motor cars now mingled with horses. Half asleep, she was pulled up a ladder and found in front of her a pile of hay.

'Do not think I have designs on your body, Miss Watkins,' Lucien assured her coldly.

'I wouldn't care if you had, provided I can sleep,' she said dozily.

'It is merely that to come here alone might occasion comment and offend our hostess,' he explained, taken aback at this lack of opposition. 'Together, it might be assumed we wished to seek a discreet place for love.'

'Quite,' she agreed, snuggling down. Then sat bolt upright. 'What about my reputation?' she asked indignantly.

A pause. 'You may return to the pillow fight with your chums if you choose.'

She stared at him as he removed his head-dress, looking more like Lucien and less like T.E. Lawrence of Arabia. Or Valentino.

'I'll stay here,' decided his Lady Betty crossly, secure in the knowledge that she was the last person he would choose to prove a true woman.

The journey to the Fourth Floor was getting quite familiar, Nell thought wrily, half-way through January. She had deliberately held back from giving in her notice to avoid seeing him for a week or two after the Christmas fiasco, and so it was doubly annoying to receive a summons from Jonathan Gadsby rather than the other way about. She had not seen Jonathan since Christmas and wondered if he would refer to the unfortunate happenings. He did not. Jonathan Gadsby believed in keeping his home life separate from work. It was hard to see in the dour frock-coated figure in front of her the genial host of Christmas Day as he'd carved the huge turkey – a task he'd never, he informed them, entrusted to the footmen.

'I'm putting you in sole charge of Teagowns, Miss Watkins,' he told her without beating about the bush, and as astounded she tried to thank him, added, 'Provisionally. If sales go up, you stay. If they don't, you go altogether. Agreed?'

She managed to pull her thoughts together coherently. 'I have a proviso too,' she told him.

He glared at her belligerently. 'I'd be surprised if you didn't, missy.'

'I'll accept, provided I can do my own buying in Paris and not have to accept what the Drag— Miss Danzy chooses.'

He frowned. 'Agreed,' he said quickly enough.

'And I'd like to expand into—'

'Not agreed,' he barked. 'One proviso only, that's what you stipulated. A contract's a contract. Agreed?'

'Agreed,' said Nell sadly.

Tom came round that evening, the first time she had seen him since Christmas. He flung himself down on the carpet in front of the fire, and announced he'd be glad when the motor racing season started again, and that he didn't like winter. Next year he'd fly off somewhere maybe, if he could get a good kite.

'I don't think it's winter to blame, is it, Tom?' she asked gently.

'No!' Then, 'I'm going to divorce her, Nell,' he blurted out.

'Oh, Tom, no! She loves you.'

'Hah!' he said. 'Odd way she has of showing it. Look at the evidence I've got.'

'Jack Fisher?'

'Jack, Robert, Marmaduke, Archibald, anyone you care to name, and dear old Uncle Tom Gadsby her husband and all – only I'm the last in the line to crawl into her bed.'

So he knew now at least. Nell felt a shiver run down her back despite the warmth of the room. Should she have spoken before they married? No. How could she have known for sure that Melissa would not change once she had the security of marriage? 'Have you talked to her?' she asked wretchedly.

'I've talked, shouted, pleaded, threatened, coaxed, till I'm blue in the face and all she'll say is: "You know how I love you, Tommy." Her eyes light up and she smiles the way she does. You know?'

'Yes, I know.' How much did Melissa mean it and how much was the emotion of a moment, a self-serving moment? Surely not all of it? Surely she did love Tom?

149

How could she fail to? He was so generous and good to her.

'I don't care any longer, Nell. Love isn't worth it, not on these terms. I won't put up with it any longer.'

'Does she know?'

'I'm going to tell her this weekend.'

'Be careful, Tom. She's not so tough as she appears,' said Nell. 'She really is as fragile as she sometimes appears.'

He stared at her, unheeding. 'I've got the Gadsby name to think about,' he said obstinately. 'I'm not going to let it be a laughing stock. That's what Grandpops told me,' he added ingenuously. 'I thought about it – and he's right.'

Nell came back from the 1927 February Paris shows with little to boast of. Advance talk in the press of what she would find there had not led her to expect very much for her department. Teagowns had disappeared from their consideration; everything was sports, sports, sports – yet Mr Santos, Gadsby's buyer, wasn't even there, because he was only allowed to buy from Britain. She tried to buy the delightful afternoon chiffon dresses under the guise of teagowns but was firmly ordered off her territory by Miss Danzy. No sign here of the exciting new rest suits with their chiffon velvet trousers. True, skirts were fractionally longer in all the collections this spring, but once again she felt Paris was wrong. It was not yet time for long skirts to return.

But there was no breaking the new exclusive contract with the Maison Mennais. Nell groaned inwardly as she saw what the Dragon was ordering. Calf-length evening dresses. And fussy lace and bows, when fringes and feathers called the tune? True again more graceful lines seemed to be suggested for this summer, but not a return to Victorian femininity. The lines could be graceful per-haps, but designs should be geometric, stark, interesting, not florals. All she could do so far as dresses were concerned would be to choose the least disastrous. She had one card left in her hand. Limited only by her small budget, she could buy lingerie from whomever she chose. No exclusive contract bound her here.

Flushed with success she returned to London having placed orders for coloured camibockers, the new night-dresses that in their design could have been worn to Ascot (if it weren't for the transparency of large care-fully chosen areas), silk chemises and georgette cami-knickers. Ever since she had rather hesitantly worn the cyclamen camiknickers Lucien had flung at her, she had been aware of the luxurious difference between Paris lingerie and Gamages', and was determined her custom-ers should too.

Her spirits bounced back even more after a chance meeting with Joe Simpkins, somewhat more friendly since her fall from grace, obviously feeling that he could talk on equal terms now. He was married to Polly now, had a baby son, and had recently been made deputy buyer. Family life and promotion clearly agreed with him.

'So here am I, running a Teagown department with no teagowns,' she said ruefully, telling him about Paris.

'Make your own,' he said idly. 'We have some lovely georgette in.'

'Have you *seen* my efforts at pattern-making, let alone toiles?' she asked him. 'Not to mention the mere matter of design.'

'Polly could do that,' he said diffidently.

'Who?' she asked blankly, her mind running rapidly round London's fashion trade and unable to recollect anyone by that name.

'My wife,' he said proudly.

'Of course. I'm so sorry,' she said, recovering quickly. Then embarrassment took over. 'But—'

'She's good,' he told her stiffly, picking up her

hesitation. 'You come and see if you like. I'll pretend you just dropped in for a chat.'

So Nell went and saw.

'I need him, Nell. Oh, Nell, I need someone. I did love him, I did! I shall marry Jack as soon as this divorce is over. In the summer.'

'But it won't go through as quickly as that, Melissa. It has to come to court, you have to get the evidence of Tom's adultery –' what a farce that would be '– then you have to get a decree nisi, then wait six months for the decree absolute.'

'Well,' Melissa flashed a quick, nervous smile, 'it seems there's just the teensiest doubt about the validity of my marriage to Tom, darling, so it may be nullified or voided or something.'

'Why? What on earth are you talking about?' Nell demanded, stunned.

'I was married before you see, when I went to the States on a tour.' Melissa studied scarlet fingernails. 'It was all over *ages* ago – well, it only lasted three months – and I got divorced, really and truly I did. I thought, as that was all right, no one need know. But now it turns out we shouldn't have got married in church and lots of people are upset, and now they're being really stuffy because my divorce was in the United States, and I wasn't living here at the time which makes a difference for some reason. They're talking about bigamy. How ridiculous! It's non-sense, of course, but it means we may have to go to America to sort it out. Perhaps get divorced there. It's so much quicker. They understand marriage there.'

'But *who* were you married to?' said Nell, totally bewildered.

'Oh, he was lovely, darling. He was some kind of farmer, I think. All those muscles. But those cows, day after day. So *boring*.'

'Are you sure you can't love just Tom as he wants?' asked Nell, hurting, hurting, but bound to try.

'No, darling. You'll look after him, won't you?'

The opening press show at Maison la Ferté in Conduit Street held in early March, to which somewhat surprisingly Nell, the Dragon and Mr Langer were invited, was a great success – to Miss Danzy's obvious dismay. Nell too was a little shaken. This was not the same style she had seen in Paris. Many designs showed a distinct bias towards the younger market, and those that did not were very much to English taste. These georgettes with their Magritte designs – how right for Ascot. And the evening dresses – a décolletage more daring than would be tolerated in Paris, surely? Philippe's work, no doubt. And here he was, coming towards her, kissing her hand, clearly delighted to see her again, withdrawing her to one side, which flattered as well as somewhat annoyed her, aware that Lucien's mocking eye was on them.

'So you like my dresses, *hein*?' Philippe asked beguilingly. 'You will wear them? Order them?'

Smilingly she told him that Maison la Ferté's models were somewhat beyond her budget.

'Ah, but for you yourself, Nell, so you no longer dress à la Gadsby's, we make a special price. But then, what does it matter, all this fashion, for when a beautiful rose blooms it does not matter if the leaves are green or blue? One sees only the rose. Only you, dearest Nell.'

'Dearest Philippe, I fear you are a flatterer,' she informed him. 'Either that or your brother, who considers me a peahen, is vastly mistaken.'

'A peahen?' He looked astounded. 'Lucien said that?' His lips twitched. 'In that case, dearest Nell, we must undoubtedly acquaint ourselves more deeply with one another on every occasion I am in London, and I will show my brother how wrong he is. Me, I create on the body,

153

you know, not on the page, and what pleasure to create on yours.' His eyes sparkled mischievously. For a moment, she forgot Tom, and thought only of the fun it would be to be courted by Philippe. Even the other secret she nursed was forgotten for the moment. After all, surely for once Gadsby's could take second place?

Miss Danzy's mouth fell open. It was not a pretty sight. Her eyes bulged at the sight of the row of leisure gowns in the newly named Lingerie and Leisure department (so named after much dispute with Mr Santos in Sporting Wear). Simple linen dresses with appliquéd triangles and squares for morning wear, ranging to flowing georgettes and chiffon printed with geometric designs for afternoon wear. None came lower than the knee and the linen dresses were slightly above it, in defiance of Paris.

'Where did you get them?' she demanded.

Nell swallowed. 'A British designer,' she informed her casually.

'Name?'

'It carries the Gadsby label.'

'Made here?' sharply.

Nell shut her eyes and plunged. This was the biggest fence. 'Yes.'

'The Fourth Floor shall hear of this. *Now*.'

This time the Fourth Floor did not summon Nell. It descended to her. Jove had come down in person, bearing few signs of the genial host of Christmas.

'Fired!' he shot at her triumphantly. 'For misuse of workroom time.'

'If you wish, Mr Gadsby. But I have sold six already, and it's only ten-thirty.'

Jonathan Gadsby's eyes shot to the rack of dresses which two young women were examining with obvious pleasure. 'Teagowns, are they?'

154

'Leisure gowns,' she amended. 'No expansion. Replacement.'

'Very well. Another week,' he barked.

She had almost expected him to say Case Dismissed. Miss Danzy went red, then white. 'Another week *only*,' she said vindictively.

But in another week . . .

'I've sold the lot, Polly,' Nell told her jubilantly. 'I'll need more. Lots more for next season.'

Polly's blue eyes glowed with pleasure and excitement.

'Darling, it's wonderful to be a free woman,' Melissa told Nell in late-June. 'Tommy's been a sweetheart and sorted out that wretched American divorce of mine. I can't remember whether I've been voided or divorced from Tommy now, but anyway he's divorced me from that first husband of mine, so that I can marry whom I like in six months. Arthur B. Hopkins III is his name.'

'Who?' asked Nell blankly. 'Surely you're going to marry Jack?'

'Arthur was my first husband, Nell. Aren't you listening?' asked Melissa crossly. 'And do you know, darling, I'm not sure if I am going to marry Jack any longer. Isn't it a bore? The film's finished and I thought he'd want to shoot me in another one. Such a silly word, shoot, isn't it? It makes one sound like a pheasant. Anyway, he's cast this other girl as Flora MacDonald. Some nonsense about the public not accepting me as both Lady Arabella Stuart *and* Flora. And as he always makes a rule of sleeping only with his leading ladies – for the sake of his art – that's that.' She smiled brightly, but Nell thought she saw a tear blinked away by her long lashes.

'Oh, Melissa, I'm so sorry.'

'What for, darling?' she asked, surprised. 'I thought I'd marry Robert instead. You'll come, won't you?'

★   ★   ★

155

'What is it, Tom?' asked Nell, laying her hand on his arm. 'I've been making bright conversation all evening and you aren't listening. Is it Melissa?' she asked sympathetically.

'Good Lord, no,' he said, surprised. 'I've been trying to pluck up courage to ask you to marry me, Nelly.'

Chapter Five

Nell Gadsby, she was Nell Gadsby she kept reminding herself firmly. But it was very easy to forget it in the Eaton Square house. She was surrounded by Melissa at every turn: her decorations, her pictures, her bed. 'Do anything you want, darling,' Tom had told her generously, but where could she start when the real problem was in her mind, not plastered on the walls? She did not resent Melissa, far from it, but she had been a guest far too often in this house to slip quickly into possession of it.

They had married almost immediately, since it turned out from what Tom told her that Melissa's marriage to him had been shown to be invalid, and it was only by the skin of her teeth and quite a lot of combined Gadsby and theatre management pressure that Melissa avoided a criminal charge. The honeymoon had been a dazed blur of foreign lands, impressive sights, hot, hot, sun, and the wonder of a Tom for her alone, *her* husband. A husband who loved *her*, and no longer Melissa. That had been a mad passion, he told her, that had passed. He'd been a fool to have thought the marriage could ever have worked. He needed a wife like Nell, whom he'd come to love gradually, and with whom he could live happily and contentedly. And that, Nell vowed, he should do.

Now she felt as she had after school holidays had ended. September had come and with it the real world. London was reawakening and Paris collections were beckoning.

Outside it was raining, and she stood by the huge

window looking down into the street below, waiting for Tom to join her for breakfast. There was a Harrods delivery van passing, a woman stopping to talk to the milkman, two boys running past with a dog . . . Oddly she suddenly felt trapped. How ridiculous, she told herself; she was merely coming down to earth again after a honeymoon, something all brides had to adapt to. Tom had been a wonderful companion, attentive and loving, and she must remember the sun of Italy in the rain of London. Places she had never seen and thought never to see, Tom had taken in his stride as familiar landmarks. They had spent a week in Venice, a week in Rome, searingly hot, coming back for two weeks on the French Riviera at Menton and Cannes. There they stayed at the Carlton where Tom was greeted by the liveried staff as an old and regular customer. Dazed, she felt a Cinderella privileged to remain within the castle, and not to have to flee when the clock struck twelve.

The Carlton looked like a castle, its twin cupolas modelled after the breasts of the courtesan La Belle Otero, or so Tom had informed her. Nell looked at them critically, imagining them squashed by Gadsby's latest lingerie. 'She wouldn't like today's fashions,' she commented. 'We'd soon get rid of those at Gadsby's.' Tom had laughed at that. He was beginning to laugh spontaneously again, she noticed with pleasure, proud that she had achieved this small triumph in their marriage.

Honeymoons weren't always easy, she'd been warned. She couldn't imagine Melissa finding it hard, but then Melissa was not in the ordinary run of mortals. She herself found a faint dissatisfaction. Was this all there was to it? she asked herself in bewilderment. She couldn't see why Melissa got so excited about it if so. She banished the disloyal thought. Tom's hands explored her body gently and tenderly. She hadn't been sure quite what was happening, as he breathed so heavily above her, nor indeed quite sure what should happen, but he kissed her lovingly and long. No, she wouldn't remember that afterwards on that first night treacherously the thought of Lucien de la Ferté's mocking came back to haunt her. 'And when . . . only the pillow hears what you have to say to each other, what does he call you then?' What in fact had Tom said? He'd uttered just one word, a sleepy 'Melissa'. It was natural, she told herself fiercely, and next morning he was happily teasing her, laughing with her. Life was fun again, and what was past was past.

They were getting to know one another better and better. She was lucky beyond measure to have married the man of her dreams. She glanced round as a maid came in the room with coffee. It seemed there was an army of servants in the house, most of whom treated her with a cool politeness as though she were merely a guest. She wondered uneasily if she was being compared unfavourably to Melissa, and decided she did not care. Tom had not been happy with Melissa. He *was* happy with her, Nell. It wasn't the same kind of love that he had had for Melissa, and thank goodness for that. It was based on warmth and affection, a modern marriage. The days of her hero worship were past. She was married to the real man now and thank goodness, she loved him even more than the hero. Theirs was a deeper married love, based on mutual regard. How much better than the breathless headiness with which Melissa so disastrously treated life.

Tom ambled in, making straight for the breakfast table and *The Times*, calling out a happy, 'Good morning, darling.' Then his expression changed: 'Where are you off to?' he asked frowning. 'And why are you dressed like that?'

'Work,' she replied gaily, coming across to kiss his cheek. 'Remember? It's only a few days before the autumn parades. I must go to Paris even if I'm not buying because it will give me a better idea of the trends than the

English magazines and I need to discuss them with Polly.'

'What on earth do you mean?' Tom's brow was furrowed as he looked distastefully at the egg in front of him. 'You don't mean you're going to Gadsby's, do you?'

'Of course,' she answered, surprised. 'I'm not able to walk in at all hours like you. I have to be there at nine.' Her voice trailed off as she saw his indignant face.

'But my wife can't work in the store.'

'Why not?' she asked, bewildered.

'You're my wife,' he said firmly. 'And I'm Store director. You can't be a saleswoman . . .'

'Buyer,' she corrected mutinously.

He shrugged impatiently. 'And anyway, you'll have enough to do here as my wife.'

She stared at him, pink and angry that she had not thought earlier that he could possibly object. 'But I need to, Tom,' she told him firmly. 'And Gadsby's needs me.' Even as she said it, this struck her as odd. Yet she was suddenly sure it was so. 'You *can't* stop me working there. I love it. Oh, Tom, you can't honestly see me as a society wife, can you, trotting in and ordering clothes from the old Dragon – wouldn't she love that? Not that I'd be seen dead in any of her models! I can't exist just going to Ascot and Henley.' For the first time she began to think. Of course he'd want her to go to Ascot with him, Henley, Goodwood, not to mention all his races. How could she have been so stupid as not to have insisted on discussing it tactfully earlier? Because she'd had stars in her eyes, she supposed. Now what to do?

Then she realised. She ran to him and put her arms round her neck. 'It's Melissa, isn't it?' she cried. 'Melissa wanted to go back to the stage and was bored at home. You're afraid I'll do the same thing if I go to work, and forget you. Oh Tom, you needn't worry. I love you, I really do. I'll look after you always.'

He hugged her. 'I know. I know you do, Nelly,' he said

huskily. 'But I *need* you, I don't want to share you with Gadsby's.'

'Then we'll compromise,' she told him brightly. 'I'll go on working at Gadsby's till I have a baby and we start our real home life.'

There was a pause. 'Very well,' he said lifelessly. 'If it means so much to you.'

'After all,' she tried to joke, 'I've got my one share. I've got to make sure the firm stays in business.'

Jonathan's wedding gift to her was one 10s 0d ordinary share in Gadsby's. The shares and their voting rights in Gadsby Limited were firmly under his control. Over half were Founders' shares, entitling him to forty per cent of Gadsby's profits, after payment of a dividend on the remaining shares. From this his vast personal fortune had grown. The remaining capital of £350,000 was split between 40,000 preference shares of £5 and 10s ordinary shares. Of the latter 200,000 belonged to Jonathan, 98,000 to Tom, and 1,997 to Rose, one each to Mr Lorrimer and Mr Charles – and now one to Nell. It had been, Tom had told her, Melissa's and had been promptly demanded back as part of the price of sorting out her matrimonial adventures. No one outside the Gadsby family was going to hold a share, save for the token one each to serving directors. Nell had been highly amused to be asked to sign a confirmation that if she and Tom were to divorce, she too would hand back her share.

Jonathan had for once been badly caught out; he would not let it happen again. Particularly where Nell Watkins was concerned.

From now on, she vowed, she would redouble her efforts to show Tom how much she loved him. It did not always prove easy, however. Sometimes she would return from work tired out to find Tom eagerly awaiting her return in order to go out and dance the night away. At other times she would return looking forward to an

161

evening at the theatre only to find he had forgotten about it and was staring abstractedly into the fire with large whisky and soda in hand.

Her household duties could scarcely be said to be onerous. Meals appeared as if by magic. She descended to the kitchens on several occasions, where she was treated politely, but it was made clear that the first Mrs Gadsby had left everything to them, and they fully expected the second to do the same. Nell made a face to herself and retired with as much dignity as she could muster. She told Tom diffidently she could check the accounts each week, but he replied, surprised, that this was his task; it was one he was good at, for he had a sharply observant eye where his personal money at least was concerned, and so she acquiesced. As for the decor, it seemed pointless to change it for the sake of change. If Tom could live with it, so could she. Angela, her deputy in Lingerie and Leisure, was very reliable and she found she was able to take the odd afternoon to accompany Tom to Brooklands or Hendon which pleased him, though it usually ended in her standing around shivering while he chattered endlessly to mechanics.

Nevertheless, he came back happy on such days, talking animatedly of Malcolm Campbell and Henry Segrave, of their race to reach 200 mph first. Or of Cobham and his record-breaking flights. Or of Lindbergh, whose recent solo flight across the Atlantic to Paris had been the most highly publicised exploit yet. 'If I don't hurry,' Tom joked, 'there'll be nowhere left for me to fly to.' Nevertheless, she saw with relief that little by little the strain was leaving his face. Perhaps now he would need her more in other ways, she thought wistfully, for though they shared a bed, he seemed to need her far less than she'd been led to expect. Men were all different, she told herself. When they made love he was happy, and therefore so was she. Though at Gadsby's it had not all been plain-sailing.

★ ★ ★

'Tom tells me you're carrying on working here,' Jonathan had begun without preamble, as Nell obeyed the now familiar summons to the Fourth Floor just before she left for Paris in September. Jonathan had been affable enough to her at the wedding, going out of his way to be pleasant to her parents. 'We shopkeepers—' she had overheard him say to them at one point, to their great pride. If Tom had faced opposition to their wedding at home, he did not tell her, nor did Jonathan reveal anything other than courteous pleasure on each occasion he met her in a family context – fortunately few so far. Yet it was the affability of armed neutrality rather than genuine warmth. And at Gadsby's his army held the machine-guns.

'Yes, in the same capacity and on the same terms naturally,' Nell told him nervously. 'I wouldn't expect—'

'And what if I object, eh?' he cut in. 'A woman's place is at her husband's side.'

'But Tom works here too,' she said innocently. 'It means we will be together more, not less.'

He glared at her. 'And what about my grandchildren, eh? Last one showed no signs of rushing to do her duty. Don't tell me you've got the same ideas, missy?'

'No,' she said, surprised. 'I'd love to have children. And I've told Tom I'll work just until we do.' And then we'll see, she added mentally to herself.

'Humph,' was Jonathan's non-committal reaction to this obliging statement. 'And just what do you find so exciting about working here?' His bright eyes stared at her intently from under bushy eyebrows.

Something told her to answer carefully, that she was being tested. 'Tom has his motor racing and flying,' she pointed out. 'I have Gadsby's. I want to—' She stopped. How could she explain in this half-hearted way? Jonathan said nothing, the silence between them almost daring her to speak. And so she did. She took a deep breath. 'I

163

believe that the way the world is going, there won't be room for fashion houses like Gadsby's any more,' she told him bluntly. 'For the top couturiers of Paris and London there will be, but we're not in that class because we don't produce originals. We're part of a chain, however near the top. And trade is falling off everywhere, not just in Gadsby's. People don't have the money to buy clothes such as Gadsby's offers any more. Nor the occasion to wear them.'

A complacent smile was on the old man's lips. 'You're going to tell me we ought to be going into ready-mades?' he said almost gently for him, luring the victim into his den.

'Yes. Not entirely, of course, but we must become competitive.'

'Poppycock!'

'And develop our other departments,' Nell went on recklessly, so far in now she might as well continue. 'We should develop our accessories departments, our men's wear, shoes and millinery. At the moment the public trade of most of our departments is rated second to the necessity of complementing the Fashion Department.' A department still run by the Dragon, she was tempted to add.

'Do you know how many stores in London we'd be competing with, if I followed your tomfool ideas?' said Jonathan matter-of-factly.

'No, but quite a lot,' she said stoutly, 'so we would have to ensure that Gadsby's stands out in some way. And I propose—'

'Propose!' he thundered, picking up on her unfortunate choice of words and coming down like a wolf on the fold. 'What you propose is neither here nor there, missy. You keep to your teagowns and lingerie, and keep your hands off everything else. Or you'll be out on your ear, granddaughter-in-law or not. Understand?'

'Yes,' Nell muttered unwillingly. She understood all

right. Whether she could obey was a different matter.

'You're not my granddaughter-in-law here, you know,' he said, mellowing slightly. 'Though come to that, I'd rather have you than young Melissa. I know where I am with you.'

'On opposite sides of the fence,' she said flatly.

'With me on the winning side,' he told her, regarded her for a moment and said almost kindly: 'We're two of a kind, Nell, but there's only room for one of us running Gadsby's, and it's going to be me, as long as there's breath in my body. And *that* will be for a good long time yet.'

She could not deny, however, there was a certain ignoble pleasure in being Mrs Gadsby. At first merely to see the Dragon's face was a delight. Fortunately Nell was blissfully unaware of the rumours and gossip the sensational news of their hasty marriage had caused in the hierarchical ranks of Gadsby's staff, though she was curious.

'What are they saying about me now, Joe?' she asked apparently casually. She had gone out to their Lewisham home to see Polly principally, who was at home with their baby son, Ben. Nell had plopped down a pile of fashion magazines together with her own notes made in Paris a few days earlier.

Polly fell on the magazines greedily. Joe watched her for a moment before replying to Nell.

'That you're a lucky one,' he told her noncommittally.

'Is that all?' she asked suspiciously.

It wasn't, but Joe had no intention of telling Nell that. So far as he was concerned, she'd lifted herself out of his walk of life the day she became buyer, then just as he got used to being friendly again, she married Tom Gadsby. And that was that. He simply forgot the girl he'd shared those bike rides with. This one in front of him was someone new to be treated with caution. Then he relented a little. Perhaps he owed her this.

'It's not going to be easy, Nell,' he warned her. 'Whatever you do in the job, you won't get credit for it. It'll be because you're Mrs Gadsby.' He paused. 'The Mrs Gadsby who was clever enough to seduce Tom Gadsby away from Melissa Hargreaves.'

Seduce? She laughed in sheer amazement, unable to take it too seriously. 'If only you knew how unfair that is, Joe.'

'Maybe,' he said stoutly, 'but that's what they're saying, and nothing you can do will change it.' He looked fondly at Polly, buried in the Autumn Fashion forecast number of *Vogue*.

'Oh, Mrs Gadsby, You've brought me the American edition too!' Polly flipped from one to another in excitement. 'I think Benito's style just a bit too strong for Gadsby's, don't you? Too stark. But Lepape – oh, look!' She pointed to a flaring red and russet cover design of a model – head only – about to eat a grape. 'Simple, straight and still *soft*. Mrs Gadsby, I think strong but not harsh forms and colours for day; I could design some simple soft wool afternoon dresses.'

'Splendid. But I've got an even better idea now,' Nell told her excitedly. 'And this concerns you too, Joe, so you can take that "this is nothing to do with me" look off your face. I think that Leisure could be extended to cover dance frocks for young women, don't you?' she asked innocently.

Polly's eyes gleamed. 'Oh, *yes*, miss – Mrs Gadsby. Oh!' Her hands were already reaching for the pad. 'No strong colours though. Not those reds, but—'

'Wait a minute,' laughed Nell, 'there's more. When I was in Paris I met a textile designer and manufacturer called Dessanges from Lyon who has invented the most marvellous new material. Wait till you see it. I've managed to buy six months' exclusive British rights in it.'

'*What*? But that's old Polgarth's job,' cried Joe indignantly. '*And* mine!'

'I know,' admitted Nell, realising belatedly that what Nell Watkins could get away with, might run Nell Gadsby into unexpected difficulties. 'You don't have to stock it in your department if you don't want to. But I hope you do,' she said in a burst of honesty, 'because otherwise my entire budget for the year is gone,' she said ruefully. 'I had to pay a premium and guarantee minimum orders.'

'Of course, Mrs Gadsby,' Joe said stiffly. 'I'm sure if you speak to Mr Polgarth—'

'Now, Joe, *please*. I don't want that. I want you to believe in it. As I do. *Look*.' She took a small roll about a foot long from her bag and spread it out on the table, waiting on tenterhooks for his reaction.

It came. 'That's not new, Nell,' said Joe scornfully. 'If you'd asked me I'd—'

'Look again, Joe,' she told him. 'Metallic thread isn't new, but just look at this one. Shake the material, hold it at an angle. The thread is woven in.'

'Lots of tissues have that,' he began as he did as she suggested, but stopped. He saw woven into the heavy blue crêpe-de-Chine that the metallic thread he had thought pink was blue, the blue of the crêpe. Or was it silver?

'It's a metallic thread,' she explained excitedly, as he grew interested, 'but with strands of several different colours which pick up the colour of its setting as you look one way, and glint with different colours at other angles. And it's woven right into the crêpe-de-Chine so that the stripes could easily carry on downwards into a fringe.'

Joe fingered it, unwilling to betray too much excitement. 'This heavy crêpe-de-Chine is a bit like Chatillon Mouly-Roussel's *petite reine*, isn't it?'

'Yes, and since that became all the rage at the end of last year and the beginning of this, all their competitors are vying to rival it. This is something new – a cross between that and a tissue really. It's called *jeune princesse*, and although it hasn't the range of *petite reine*, it's absolutely ideal for dance dresses. If we have a range in different colours, and say three different styles, I'm sure girls will flock round like moths.'

'I'll have a word with Mr Polgarth,' said Joe at last. 'Mind you, he won't like it. Not one bit.'

'Then let's wait until Polly's dresses are on our racks. *Then* there'll be a demand, you'll see,' she told him confidently.

'I'd better warn him,' Joe replied, somewhat ungraciously.

Nell heaved a sigh of relief. Tact, tact, tact, always tact. It was almost as bad as dealing with Lady Lenham. Dear Joe, so typical of the best of Gadsby's staff – loyal, hardworking, good at their jobs, but blinkered. Fine for the palmy days of 1923 and '24 but what if at the end of the road they plodded so patiently along lay another industrial slump like that of 1921-2 which this time might affect Gadsby's more than the previous one, coupled with the already slackening trade caused by changing ways of life and wealth? The lanes and byways that they had so consistently been blind to might then prove their salvation. Though which lanes? The sunshine glimmered down so many side-turnings. And moreover the entrance to each was guarded by a many-headed hydra: Jonathan Gadsby.

Melissa developed the habit of bouncing into Eaton Square, tossing down her hat and erupting into the drawing room without the formality of announcement. 'Hornton's used to my ways, aren't you, Hornton?' Melissa informed her happily.

Nell was amazed to see that, though his face tried to remain impassive, the dour butler looked almost human.

'Darling, what are you doing in that dreadful old black

dress? Go and change at once. It isn't at all suitable for dancing.'

'I've just come home from work, Melissa,' Nell said wearily, 'and I wasn't planning on dancing anywhere.'

'Work? Oh, *Gadsby's*,' said Melissa vaguely. 'Now, where's Tom – oh, Tom, *there* you are!' She rushed out and buttonholed him in the entrance hall as he came in. 'Darling, how are you?' She embraced him, kissing him twice. 'It's such an age since I've seen you. Now run away and change because I'm taking you both to the Ivy.'

Nell's heart sank. She really didn't feel she could cope with Melissa tonight. Melissa was still hurt that she had been excluded from their wedding. Jonathan had flatly refused to invite her, and despite all her blandishments to Nell's parents, they were too much in awe of Jonathan to yield to them. She was very cross. 'Poor Robert wanted to come so much,' she informed Nell. 'After all, I'm best friends with you both, aren't I?'

'With me,' Nell corrected her bluntly.

'Oh, *and* Tom. You'll see,' Melissa replied happily. She had compromised by sending them as a wedding present a huge Art Deco-style six-foot-long elephant with a triangular trunk. Apart from hanging a hat on it, it had no apparent purpose. In despair, Nell consigned it to the garden studio. Melissa had not so far noticed.

Best friends? thought Nell. Yes, she supposed she still was for oddly enough nothing seemed to have changed between herself and Melissa. Melissa seemed to have taken it as the most natural thing in the world that Tom should marry Nell. Nevertheless she noticed that he was always very silent after Melissa had left, and wondered what he was thinking of. Was he missing her? Regretting marrying her, Nell? Yet he was always very loving to her after one of Melissa's visits, so gradually it ceased to worry her and she took Melissa's eruptions into their lives rather like those of an over-friendly neighbour.

169

This evening it appeared Melissa was bored. 'My play finished last week,' she complained, 'and there's nothing, but *nothing* to do.'

'Isn't there another one coming up?'

'Yes,' Melissa said lightly, in a tone that told Nell this wasn't the problem. 'A ducky little musical comedy called *Cloche Hats and Cowbells*. It's fun, but it isn't *art*, darling. My acting's so good, I should be creating artistic master-pieces, Jack says.'

'Jack?' Nell picked up sharply. 'I thought you didn't see him any more?'

'Did I say that?' Melissa bestowed her sweetest smile on her. 'I just bump into him now and then. While Robert's at the theatre in that boring old play. Not a song in it.'

All Nell's forebodings rose to the surface again. 'You're happy, aren't you, Melissa?' she asked doubtfully. For if she wasn't . . .

'Happy?' Melissa made a moue. 'What kind of word's that? There's life which has to be lived, that's all, darling. That's all there ever is, Jack says.'

'But what about Robert?' Anxiety sharpened Nell's voice.

'Don't sound so disapproving about Jack, darling. Robert doesn't mind. He really doesn't.'

'*What*?' Nell's voice rose to a shriek. 'But Melissa, you're going to marry Robert in December. He can't "not mind", if he knows about it, that you're seeing Jack again. And, knowing you, I suppose seeing isn't all that happens,' she added grimly.

'Oh, darling,' replied Melissa sadly, 'you don't understand. You really don't.'

There was another aspect to life with Tom that Nell found it hard to accustom herself to. The house was frequently crowded at all hours of the day with his friends from motor racing or flying circles: a bewildering array of

170

young men talking either ailerons, air speeds and throttles, or chassis, cylinders and crankshafts. Or both. Sometimes one or two women ventured into the masculine purlieus but Nell had little in common with them, and preferred to talk to the men who accepted her as a kind of necessary adjunct to Tom rather than seeing her as a person. She often wondered what their reaction would be if she reciprocated with the latest developments in corsetry. Even with Tom, talk of Gadsby's seemed to be a taboo subject. He would listen patiently if she talked of the store – though she kept the excitement of *jeune princesse* to herself – but never offered comments or guidance. At first she thought this his policy in view of his position as Store director, and appreciated it, but soon she reluctantly came to the conclusion that he simply was not interested. Neither in her department nor any other. This had always been the case but now it seemed more important. Perhaps because of her one little share, she laughed to herself. It seemed ironic that Gadsby's was more important to her than to Tom who was the heir, but when she tried to talk about the future, which could not be far off surely in view of Jonathan's age, he firmly changed the subject. No entry proclaimed the barricade.

She struggled to enjoy the few dinner parties Tom told her were essential, though fortunately he was not keen on this form of entertainment and in any case with a staff so eager to prove their independence of her she had little to do but issue invitations. One, however, late in October, was different.

'Philippe?' Nell's interest quickened. 'Splendid.'

'And his brother, of course,' Tom told her.

Ah, well, there had to be drawbacks, she told herself resignedly. And she'd enjoy seeing Philippe again. She found herself looking forward to the evening, despite the unwelcome thought of having to make polite conversation to Lucien de la Ferté, and dressed carefully. Even if I can't beat Melissa, I'll join her, she vowed. Clothes were beginning to be one of her greatest problems. She had flatly refused to be dressed from the Dragon's department, but Tom had refused to allow her to buy models from anywhere else. They compromised cheerfully enough with her buying ready made dresses out of her salary, save for occasions when she was a 'Gadsby wife' for which she ordered from Gadsby's models. Tom never realised fortunately that by the time they reached Nell they had been altered out of all recognition with Polly and Joe's help and the workroom's blind eye to the excessive changes. Since the Dragon never saw the finished dresses, she was none the wiser, and remained smugly believing that Nell was obliged to wear her models.

One person recognised straight away: Lucien de la Ferté.

'Madame,' he greeted her formally, 'how delightful to meet you again.' Nothing save the words to suggest he found anything delightful about it. His eye flicked over her dress, eyeing Mennais' crushed strawberry silk that now had a two-tiered skirt and no ornamentation whatsoever save for a large oval cameo on one shoulder. It was an automatic movement, but she saw a muscle twisting in his face that could be indicating suppressed amusement.

'Your frock is quite exquisite, madame. Have I not seen something similar in the Mennais collection, though yours is infinitely preferable? Not to mention that most attractive pink charmelaine, so distinctively different from Mennais' lavender brocade.'

'You're very observant, Comte Lucien,' she announced coolly and formally.

'It is my business.' He shrugged offhandedly, lest she mistake it for interest in her, she realised. 'Yet,' he added thoughtfully, 'there is something about the cut of that skirt . . .'

'*Ma jolie* Nell,' Philippe came across, cocktail in hand.

'Ah, madame, you have deserted me. I hear of your marriage. I am devastated. Shall I kill myself? No, I decided after much anguish. I have too much to offer the world.' He too glanced approvingly at her dress, but did not comment. Indeed he had no chance for Melissa advanced, a vision in grey lace over taffeta, creating as usual an image of fragile beauty not long for this world, thought Nell with a sudden rush of amused affection for her friend.

'You are so right, *monsieur le comte*.' She smiled winningly at Philippe. 'So very right.'

Here we go, thought Nell a trifle crossly. Philippe was *her* friend, not Melissa's.

Melissa was determined to be everyone's friend, however, dominating the conversation at dinner, enrapturing all three men. This left Nell to talk to Rose, whom Tom had invited up from the country specially, and who was about to marry a businessman called Gordon Holdsby. He wasn't the sort of man Nell instantly took to, and she couldn't see his attraction in Rose's eyes.

Perhaps indeed he didn't have a great deal, for Rose was clearly peeved at the fact Lucien had not come near her. She had always been fascinated by him, Nell remembered, but for the life of her she couldn't understand why. Beside Philippe, with his dark good looks, Lucien faded into insignificance – save when he spoke, and animation lit his face. He had an interesting way of using his hands to express a point; not with Philippe's quick gestures of Latin impatience, but slowly, almost gracefully, a movement at odds with his prominently sharp chin and nose that betrayed a firmness of purpose his otherwise unremarkable face did not.

Lucien looked up suddenly and saw Nell's eye on him. The colour rose slightly in her cheeks. Annoyed at being caught studying him, she turned her head hastily to talk to Rose again. One elegant eyebrow might have been raised in sardonic query before Lucien turned slightly away to speak to Melissa.

There was something wrong there, Nell realised. Melissa was too brittle, too febrile. Her face looked thinner, and the famous laughing beauty seemed just a little strained now. She was twenty-seven years old. Was it just age? Nell wondered. No. More than that. Perhaps problems between her and Robert or Jack.

'Nell darling,' she announced while they were waiting for the men to join them after dinner, 'you do lay on the nicest parties. However do you get Hornton to organise them? He never would for me,' she said carelessly.

'Melissa, that's not true,' Rose informed her, amazed. 'He would do anything for you, you know that. He always did, despite his disapproving air.'

Melissa looked disconcerted, then laughed dismissively. 'Perhaps. You're such a blunt old thing, aren't you, Rose?'

Rose stared at her bewildered and hurt.

'Melissa,' said Nell gently, 'it doesn't *matter*.'

'But—' Melissa pouted, then grinned. 'What would I do without you, Nell?' She lit up a cigarette, and Nell could see her hands trembling slightly as she did so.

'You're exhausted, Melissa,' she said, concerned.

She turned, suddenly showing lines of age and strain; she seemed about to say something as the door opened and the men returned. Immediately her face was transformed. The eyes lit up, the smile played once more on her lips and the pink cheeks once more betrayed nothing other than girlish innocence. She at once monopolised Philippe and Tom, leaving Lucien to join Nell and Rose, with evident reluctance, Nell noticed. She was suddenly determined to enjoy herself.

'I congratulate you,' he said neutrally, 'on the improvement in your department. An interesting range of—'

'Particularly of leisure gowns,' she interrupted

demurely. 'I was flattered indeed that the Maison la Ferté took up my idea.'

'Your idea?' he said sharply. 'You believe *we*, the Maison la Ferté, have stolen an idea from you?'

'*Robes de loisir*, I believe you call them,' she said lightly. 'Please do not think I object. I am honoured.'

'Miss Wat— Mrs Gadsby, you may be assured that the Maison la Ferté does not spend its time walking round Gadsby's in search of inspiration,' he answered curtly.

'Merely of customers,' she continued sweetly. 'I hear Lady Lenham and Mrs Willoughby are now clients of yours. Not to mention Melissa—'

'Is there some law against competition in England?' he enquired, furious. 'And in any case, Mrs Gadsby, can you blame them?'

She stared at him, caught in a trap.

'Gadsby's has—'

'Can you blame them, madame?' Lucien repeated relentlessly.

'No,' she flung at him, almost shouting so that Tom and Philippe looked round in surprise. How could she in honesty? Trade was falling fast among the top fashion houses, now that changing times were completing what the war had begun. No longer did leisured, wealthy women change their dress five or six times a day, and no longer was it such a sin to be seen in the same dress more than once. And with neither wealth nor leisure quite so prevalent, no longer was the word ready-made quite so socially abhorrent. Except, of course, at Gadsby's. Moreover Nell was forced to admit that the London house of Maison la Ferté had always had a policy of keeping a select ready-made stock of many of its models. Was it such a big step to carrying a special range of leisure dresses?

'Moreover,' Lucien continued, seeing her quiet and glorying in his triumph, 'our *robes de loisir* are for the older woman. I gather your speciality line of leisure robes

175

is for a more transitory market, girls between about eighteen and twenty-four. *Not* the la Ferté market at all. You need have no fear.'

'Fear?' Nell echoed, bridling.

'Ah, you two always discuss work. Lucien, how can you insult our lovely Nell?' Philippe joined them. 'You must forgive my brother, Nell. He is more interested in wooing trade than ladies.'

Lucien said nothing, but his lips were compressed, and for a moment she sensed the same charged atmosphere between the two brothers as she had at the Château. But she must have been mistaken, for Lucien said easily enough, 'I leave romance to you, Philippe. I merely learn. And from Mrs Gadsby there is much to learn.'

She looked at him suspiciously but he seemed quite serious.

'This is true, Nell?' Philippe asked, intrigued. 'You have been telling Lucien of your plans for the future of Gadsby's? You have plans, I trust?'

'Yes, of course I do. Lots of plans.' As she spoke, her excitement, kept so carefully restrained nowadays, began to well up inside her. Soon the *jeune princesse* range would be ready. Something must have shown in her face for Philippe looked at her inquisitively, but he said no more on the subject. Instead: 'Do you not mind, Nell, that your husband is on such splendid terms with his former wife? Our valued client,' he said deliberately, provocatively, but smiling at her to rob the question of offence.

She followed his glance to see Melissa laying her hand on Tom's shoulder, his arm round her protectively. 'Why not?' she said slowly, a little shaken. 'She's a friend of us both.'

Philippe took her hand and kissed it slightly. 'Friends? Ah, Nell, perhaps you and I could also be friends like Tom and Melissa? Would that not be enjoyable?' His eyes danced.

Aware of Lucien, who although he was now listening to Rose could undoubtedly also overhear their conversation, she laughed delightedly. 'We can be more than friends, Philippe,' she told him. 'We can be chums.'

Nell was hard put to it to keep the secret of *jeune princesse* and marvelled that the whole of Gadsby's did not already know. Delivery men, workroom girls, accessory departments, dear old Mr Bolton through whose hands every requisition for every item down to the last button must pass, all knew about the dresses. Nell's own excitement grew. In mid-November she was at last able to put them on sale. Realising the rumpus that would erupt, she got to the store especially early to have everything ready by the time customers (and staff) arrived.

She handled each dress lovingly. *Jeune princesse* had made up just as she had seen it in her imagination. There were three designs, each in two colours, and as they swung on the rail the metallic threads gently flashed with colour, enhanced by the crêpe-de-Chine in which they were set. Her deputy, Angela Field, was struggling to dress a plaster model with one while Nell stole down to the window, trying to evade notice, and certain that guilty excitement must show in every movement.

'Just re-dressing the window, Mr Jones,' she informed the ground floorwalker gaily and misleadingly. The displays were taken out at night, as in all the exclusive fashion houses, and the windows re-dressed in the morning. Re-dressed was the operative word, however. They were not intended to alter dramatically without prior consultation with the other buyers. She shared a window with Umbrellas and Scarves, and had ensured that a plaster model should take its place in the window some days earlier, ostensibly to show a leisure dress. Now the latter disappeared in favour of a *jeune princesse* dance dress, Nell having taken care the night before that the surrounding scarves and umbrellas would enhance its colour.

By the time she returned to her department, the storm was brewing and about to burst. A relieved Angela turned despairingly to her.

'What might those be, Mrs Gadsby?' said a grim-faced Dragon, pointing disdainfully to the shimmering dresses.

'Leisure dresses, Miss Danzy,' Nell informed her, as if surprised.

'They are not. They are *dance* dresses.' Every syllable was clipped.

'Is not dancing considered leisure?' enquired Nell innocently.

'You are quite determined to undermine the prestige of my department, Mrs Gadsby. That is obvious.' The Dragon was pink-cheeked with glittering fury.

'No. You are achieving that yourself, Miss Danzy,' Nell retaliated and, suddenly tired of prevarication, added mischievously as Miss Danzy turned on her heel to depart, 'the Fourth Floor will hear of this.'

'Naturally. You are Mr Gadsby's wife,' Miss Danzy said, whirling round viciously on her.

'That has nothing to do with this, as you well know. All that matters is whether these designs will sell.'

'Designed by Gadsby's,' sneered the Dragon, reading the label inside one of the dresses. 'We shall see, Mrs Gadsby. We shall see,' she murmured darkly.

By lunchtime fifteen dance frocks had been sold at £10 each. Nell wasn't present to see the next sale, for she had received the familiar summons to the Fourth Floor. This time, however, she was looking forward to it, and had her arguments ready. Miss Danzy was already sitting smugly installed when she arrived.

'Of course I realise I ought not to be so outspoken, Mr

Gadsby, about Mrs Gadsby,' the Dragon murmured hypocritically. 'If you desire Gadsby's to sell ready-made clothes—'

She made them sound like rags at Ascot, thought Nell.

'Ready-made,' barked Jonathan suspiciously, seizing on the controversial word. 'Nell?'

'The Teagown department has always sold ready-made dresses, Mr Gadsby,' Nell addressed him formally. 'Now we are renamed the Leisure and Lingerie department, they are naturally called Leisure Dresses.'

'These are *dance* dresses, Mr Gadsby. Evening dresses are my best trade.'

'And how many short evening dresses for younger people do you stock?' enquired Nell. 'I think none, according to your Buyer's Book!'

Miss Danzy turned purple at this outrage, spluttering. 'How dare you look at my confidential records!'

'Well, missy? What do you say to that?' Jonathan barked at Nell. 'Fight fair. Your turn.'

Nell tried to repress a grin as the humour of the situation threatened to overcome her. 'The main thing is that I've sold fifteen at £10 each this morning, and we took orders for others—'

'Flooding the workrooms with cheap work that should be making up *my* customers' orders.'

'Saving at least thirty jobs that would otherwise go through lack of trade,' Nell pointed out quietly.

Jonathan looked at her sharply, as Miss Danzy endeavoured to rally from this shock. 'I deny that. But you are bringing down the good name of Gadsby's to a mere *dime* store,' she announced distastefully. 'Is that what you want Gadsby's to become?'

'It won't,' Jonathan assured her blithely, cutting across the tirade. 'Your turn,' he said to Nell.

She could have sworn he was enjoying himself. 'We have this new material exclusively for six months – it could

179

bring extra revenue to Fabrics, for people to make up their own dresses.'

'Thus ruining the bespoke trade,' said Miss Danzy icily.

'Which is in its last days,' said Nell, earning herself a glare from her grandfather-in-law.

'How can I carry out my duties here when Mrs Gadsby rides rough-shod over the rules? If Mr Polgarth in Fabrics has this cheap flashy material thrust upon him—'

'Which is clearly already selling well—'

'That's enough, missy,' Jonathan stopped Nell short. Solomon had reached a judgement. 'Go on making and selling these dresses till the end of the year. Then do me a report. I'll compare it with the loss of sales in the evening dresses in the Fashion Department and any drop in revenue. And that's enough, Nell. No more of these little expansions of yours, hoping they won't be noticed.'

'Sir, if only we could—'

'That's enough.'

A look of triumph from the Dragon as they descended the staircase. 'So, Miss Watkins, how much for your cheap lines now?'

'Look,' said Nell, stopping in her tracks, 'this is so ridiculous. We both know our trade is slackening. We should be working together, not pulling apart. Why don't we try?'

The Dragon stared at her then said smoothly, 'Certainly Mrs Gadsby, perhaps that would be best. As you say, times are not what they were.'

She's submitted too easily, thought Nell, uneasy at this sudden volte face. But she was too busy revelling in the expanding opportunities for her department to remember this for long.

Melissa's new play seemed to keep her unusually occupied thought Nell with some surprise, realising it was at least three weeks since she had seen her. Not since the first night in fact. She called at her home in St John's Wood one Saturday morning, normally a good time to find Melissa in – usually still in bed in fact, but she never seemed to mind being awakened. On this occasion Robert answered the door, which took Nell aback since they were not yet married and Melissa was a stickler for public if not private appearances.

'It's Saturday morning, Robert,' Nell pointed out, looking at him critically. Unshaven, bleary eyes with sagging pouches under them. Not the handsome boyish-looking man she remembered. What on earth had happened? Surely even Melissa couldn't be responsible for this degeneration?

'Matinée,' he grunted. 'She's left already.'

'There's no matinée today,' Nell said without thinking.

'No? She told me there was,' he said indifferently as Nell's heart sank. He didn't seem to care. That didn't augur well for the marriage. Perhaps it was all falling through? She felt a sudden ray of hope until he said: 'Perhaps it's the film. With Jack, you know. You do know Jack Fisher?'

'Yes,' said Nell dispiritedly. 'I know Jack.'

She heard no more of Melissa till early in December, when somewhat to her surprise the marriage to Robert went ahead as planned. It was a discreet affair, held in Derby, since Melissa had no intention of flaunting her marital affairs before her adoring public who still saw her as the innocent heroine of *London Lady*. Nell and Tom and Robert's parents were the only guests, and the wedding itself was a hurried affair in the Register Office. The dinner afterwards was muted too, and it was with some relief that they waved the happy couple off as they departed once more for London. Commitments prevented a honeymoon, explained Melissa, clinging to her new and adoring husband's arm. But when Nell and Tom went to the first showing of Melissa's film, Melissa arrived swathed in white fur, not on Robert's but on Jack's arm, and greeted them as if this was entirely normal. As indeed perhaps it was, since Robert had a matinée and was unable to attend, Nell tried to convince herself.

The film which Nell had been rather dreading, such was the standard of most British films at the moment, was surprisingly good. Melissa was, Nell acknowledged, an accomplished actress, well able to deal with a screenplay based on the life of Lady Arabella Stuart, and the merest improvement on history provided a happy ending. More than that, she was adapting to screen technique, Nell realised. Whereas most films still displayed stage actors and actresses reproducing overblown stage gestures and effects, Melissa had developed a way of acting straight into the camera's eye as if it, not an invisible audience, was her only love. It was clearly altogether different from her first disastrous appearance on screen.

The audience was clearly impressed, and Nell saw Jack looking thoughtful as Melissa was surrounded by people eager to express their congratulations. Nell knew that British cinemas were now bound to use five per cent British-produced films. There hadn't been many good ones this year, but the situation at least seemed hopeful. Jack was the sort to be at the head of any such movement, and now that Melissa had done so well in *Arabella*, it seemed she too might have a new career. Melissa and Jack. Was it just her innate caution that told her the road to a new kind of stardom for Melissa might well contain pitfalls?

Melissa's offhanded 'I'm going back into films, darling, isn't that nice?' in January convinced Nell it wasn't over-caution on her part. She sighed. So it had come. 'I thought Jack didn't want you any more – for films, that is?'

'He had a nice surprise with the reception of *Arabella*,' Melissa told her ingenuously. 'Did you see that

182

ducky review in *Kinematograph Weekly*? Jack was so pleased. A lot of other directors are after me now, so Jack decided I wasn't so bad after all.' She giggled, and Nell marvelled that for all her faults personal vanity was not among them.

'But how can you bear to go back to him professionally,' Nell demanded, 'after what happened?' She tried to put out of her mind any question of private motivation. After all, Melissa was newly married once more and even she wouldn't – would she?

Melissa puffed on her cigarette and considered Nell's question seriously.

'I *need* to work with him. I think I still love him,' she finally announced.

'Oh, *Melissa*,' groaned Nell. 'What about Robert?'

'What about him?' said Melissa, almost viciously for her, stubbing out the cigarette.

'You've been married six weeks,' yelped Nell.

'And I wish I'd never left Tom,' Melissa burst out. 'Oh, I'm sorry, Nell. I don't mean to upset *you* but Robert, honestly! Just think, darling,' she smiled brightly, 'he prefers *men* to me. I actually have to beg him to – to have sex with me. *Me* – the great exponent of *It*. The Clara Bow of England. Elinor Glyn's typical romantic sexy heroine. Having to *beg*. At least I don't have to *beg* with Jack. He wants me,' she cried, tears pouring down her cheeks.

'Oh, Melissa, *don't*!' Nell ran to her chair, cradling her in her arms. 'What do you mean, Robert prefers men to you? You mean he goes drinking—'

'Oh, Nell, you *can't* be as naive as that,' said Melissa, half-laughing, half-impatient. 'He goes out hunting for men, just as I do. It used to be fun – which one of us could seduce someone first. It was a game. First back to the house won. But after a while, I found he was winning all the time. I thought if we married it would be different.'

She collapsed into sobs. 'There, now I've told you. You'll be so shocked you'll never speak to me again. My only friend and I've lost you.'

'Nonsense, Melissa,' said Nell firmly, too preoccupied with her writhing body and hysterical sobs to think through what she was saying. 'You know you'll never lose me. I promised you that, didn't I?'

'Yes.' Melissa sniffed, drying her eyes. 'And now I'm married to a nancy, I need you more than ever.'

'You must have known he was a – a homosexual,' Nell stumbled on the word, 'before you married him.' A fleeting thought of how her parents would have reacted if they could have overheard this conversation crossed her mind, and for a moment also regret for the simpler world of Bexleyheath and Watkins' Outfitters – a world into which she could no longer fit, even if she wished to.

'Yes,' Melissa said mournfully. 'But he was so handsome, and he made love to me as well so beautifully, so gallantly, just like Tom really. I thought Robert would change after we married, that he really wanted just me. Why else did he want to marry me, after all? And he was so loving. It was all such a change to be treated as a lady after Jack. Jack's an animal,' she said complacently, sidetracked. 'A great big roaring tiger.'

'What fun,' commented Nell drily.

'Now, Nell, don't be so old-fashioned. This is the twenties. Anyway, Robert made love to me, so it never entered my head he wasn't enjoying it as much as me. And now he says he only married me to avoid scandal, because the police were getting uncomfortably close to arresting him. How could anyone do this to *me*? Oh, Nell,' she wailed, 'I'll have to divorce him, of course. I've got to.'

'On what grounds?' she asked curiously, hardly surprised. 'You've only been married a few weeks and so no judge is going to be favourably impressed by your powers of endurance and tolerance. Is homosexuality grounds for divorce?'

A pause. 'Well, actually we've agreed I'll divorce for adultery coupled with cruelty, perhaps later this year.' She giggled, and at once her face was miraculously clear of tear-blotches. 'He'll go to Brighton for the day with one of those women who oblige at a price. He'll hate being found in bed with her, poor love.'

'Poor love, indeed,' said Nell, exasperated. 'Oh Melissa, *really*!'

'Can I have a word with you, Mrs Gadsby?' Joe was twisting his hat nervously, at five-thirty, just as the store closed for the day.

'Oh, Joe, I'm *Nell*,' she told him impatiently. 'I do wish—' She stopped, reluctantly conceding he was right within the confines of Gadsby's. 'Is it about ordering more material?'

'No,' he told her shortly. 'More private-like.'

They went to the Fuller's teashop opposite, and she ordered two teas and slices of walnut cake. 'There,' she announced diplomatically, so that she could pay, 'now I can ask you about the spring designs.'

'Blow the spring designs,' he told her, suddenly angry. 'I want to know what's going on, Nell!'

'With what?' she asked blankly.

'You and Polly, that's what.'

'I haven't seen Polly for weeks, not since before Christmas. Now the magazines are beginning to leak news from France about the spring trends I was coming to discuss new designs with her before I go to Paris, to give some preliminary time for thinking.' She broke off alarmed as she saw his white face. 'What's the matter, Joe?'

He swallowed. 'Polly told me she was with you. She's been going out of an evening, leaving the baby with me. Says she was round at Eaton Square.'

185

'*What*? But she hasn't been near us. Not unless it's to see Tom,' she added doubtfully. He had certainly been acting strangely recently.

'It ain't Mr Gadsby I'm worried about,' he said darkly. 'He's a gentleman.'

'What?' Then she laughed. 'Oh, *Joe*, surely you don't think Polly's being unfaithful to you?'

He turned red. 'She's young, Nell. She can have her head turned. 'Specially by big fashion folk flattering her.'

Nell stared at him, feeling slightly dizzy as she picked up what Joe was hinting at.

'You think someone's trying to bribe her away from Gadsby's?' she asked slowly.

'Or worse than bribe,' he said. 'I just don't know. But she's been doing a lot of designing lately, and if it's not for you, who's it for?'

'It might be preliminary ideas and sketches for me,' she suggested hopefully.

'She hides it away when I come in. I thought nothing of it, assuming it was for you. Now you says it isn't.' Joe stared forlornly at his walnut cake.

'And you're worried she might be designing for someone else?'

'I don't care who she designs for,' he replied vehemently, 'though I'd prefer it to be you, Nell. I do care when she comes home all flushed, and too tired to pay due respect to me, her husband.' He blushed and she tactfully looked away. 'And I think that de la Ferté bloke is behind it. And you know why? I saw your Miss Danzy going in his private door one evening. See what I mean?'

'Yes.' Nell went white with shock. 'But how could she have known about Polly? I always carefully guarded her identity,' she cried, appalled. Then she reflected. Of course, the Dragon could have found out if she was determined to do so. If not through deduction, since Polly was Joe's wife, then through the Counting House records.

'I don't care what you do,' said Joe, 'now I've told you. But I want it stopped.'

Whom to tackle first? Danzy, Polly or even Jonathan? she thought dazedly. Much as he disliked Nell, Jonathan was hardly likely to condone treachery to his beloved Gadsby's. But she needed proof.

It came all too quickly. Maison la Ferté announced a brilliant new line in a new material, *belle fille*. Two days later she detailed one of her staff to buy one. She hardly needed to look at the label, 'Polly at La Ferté', to confirm her suspicions. They had offered what Nell could not yet promise. Her name on the label. That and more intimate inducements. She felt sick at their duplicity and Polly's naivety. Nor was this all. *Belle fille* sounded suspicious, and by the next post came a letter from France, from Dessanges. They had decided not to renew the exclusive contract.

'Mrs Gadsby! I am honoured.'

Lucien, clearly taken aback, stood before her in the doorway to his private rooms at the side of the Maison la Ferté premises.

Nell had seen a light still burning above and could wait no longer. 'You won't be when you know why I've come,' she informed him belligerently.

With a look of astonishment, then amusement, he stood aside to let her come inside. 'Please do inform me,' he murmured, glancing curiously at what she carried. 'Shall I lead the way?'

She marched up the narrow staircase, hating every inch of the rear view of the beautifully tailored back before her. Such arrogance, such patronising condescension. Wait till she'd finished with him!

He showed her into a small study-cum-waiting room, obviously where business was transacted. He hesitated. 'Perhaps,' he said politely, 'you would care to join me in an apéritif here before we begin to discuss business?'

'I don't care what I join you in, provided it's not as crooked as the rest of your dealings.' She stomped past him into a sitting room elegantly decorated in traditional French style, noticing with satisfaction that at last she had shaken him.

'Crooked?' he said, as if puzzled. 'You mean dishonest?' Red spots of anger suddenly appeared on his cheekbones.

'What about this?' She flung the red dress scornfully at his feet.

Deliberately controlled, he stooped to pick it up. 'One of our frocks,' he said. 'How good of you to buy one. Are you not satisfied with it? If it—'

'You *pirate*,' she raged. 'You have no originality of your own so you steal my ideas *and* my designer. You can't fight fairly. You talk about competition, but you don't *compete*. You undermine.'

He looked startled, handing her a strange-looking concoction with the same aplomb as if they talked of the weather. 'Would you please explain what you mean, Madame Gadsby? It is true that Polly Simpkins now works exclusively for Maison la Ferté, but this is surely fair competition? You should guard such valuable assets more carefully,' he told her coolly.

'I can't offer her what you can.' She set down her drink lest her trembling hands let it fall.

'Money?' he said. 'Why not?'

'Not money, as you well know. *It*.'

'*It*?' he repeated blankly.

'Sex appeal,' she blurted out impatiently. 'You seduced her.'

'I did what?' His voice went very flat, a note of deadly anger in it of which she failed to take warning.

'You *seduced* her. Her husband warned me about you, and now she's admitted it to me herself.'

188

He said nothing, fighting to control himself. Then: 'And you believed it, *naturellement*?' Polite enquiry.

'Joe wouldn't lie. Nor would Polly, once she'd decided to tell me. Do you realise just what you've done to their marriage?'

'I must speak to Madame Polly,' he said absently.

'Very good of you,' she shouted. 'You seduce her, tire of her, and now you'll throw her out because it's inconvenient.'

'No. She is an excellent designer,' he told her coolly.

'That's just what I'd expect from you. She's served her purpose as a mistress, but you might as well go on enjoying the fruits of your theft in other directions.'

'You have a very low opinion of me,' he said coldly, fighting now to control his temper. 'But I assure you Maison la Ferté does not do business this way.'

'Apparently it does,' she retorted. 'You haven't denied it.'

'I do not use women in business.'

'Naturally not,' she said ironically. 'For you business is a man's world. "And so you see men and women do not change," ' she mimicked savagely.

He clenched his hands on the back of a chair as if to keep himself in check. 'A lesson you do not seem to have taken to heart,' he threw at her savagely. 'Yet I must point out that as you believe men and women are equal, Polly did not have to *submit* to my evil desires. She had a choice.'

'No. She's young and inexperienced. You're—'

'Old and a roué?' he enquired drily.

'You know what I mean. She doesn't know about men like you. And I do.' She was hardly hearing what she was saying, swept along by anger. 'I'm a woman of the world.' She'd intended, she thought, to continue 'compared with Polly' but had no chance.

He burst out in derisive laughter.

'You?' he spluttered in angry mirth. 'You are no more a *femme du monde* than Charlie Chaplin.'

'At least I'm *demi-monde* then,' she cried, confused and outraged at being humiliated.

At this unconscious gaffe he hung on to the chair for support while he shook with mirth, entirely out of control now.

'How dare you laugh at me?' she shouted. 'I *am* a true woman. I'm married.'

'A woman?' He looked up and in two strides was face to face with her, pushing off her coat then ripping it from her arms and hands and tossing it on one side. He gripped her by one shoulder, putting his other hand flat across her breast. 'A woman?' he said contemptuously. 'You try to look like a boy, behave like a boy. You have no breasts, no mystique – you are no woman.' He broke off as she stiffened in his grasp, alarmed at the sudden pallor of her face. 'Nell, what is it?' he asked in quite a different tone. '*Tu vas mal*? What is wrong?'

'It's nothing,' she managed to gasp out. No mystique, no sex appeal? Was that why Tom wanted her so rarely? That Melissa had been lover while she was chum? *Had* been lover? Suppose she still was?

'Nell, tell me,' Lucien was shaking her vigorously. '*Mon dieu*, you *must* tell me.'

'I'm sorry,' she said through trembling lips, sitting down on the sofa. 'I'm all right, really.'

'You are not all right, Nell,' he contradicted her gravely. 'Here.' He seized her drink and made her sip it.

'This is ridiculous,' she said, choking as the strong liquid went down her throat. 'I just took what you said a little personally, that's all.'

'I think that is not all,' he frowned. 'But nevertheless, you must forgive me please for what I said. It was unpardonable.'

'And untrue?' she said unforgivingly.

'I would think untrue. But I do not know you as a woman,' he said. 'Only as—'

'A chum?' she said wrily.

'A rival chum,' he amended gently. 'Now will you not tell this rival chum what ails you as a woman?' Then as she flinched, withdrawing her hands from his, 'It is Tom, is it not?'

'No,' she cried fearfully, standing up. 'I'm sorry – I'll go.'

'Nell, come here.' He caught her hand and pulled her down again. 'You must tell me. He no longer loves you? He loves Melissa still?'

'No, *no*!' she shouted, unable to block out this terrible thought. 'Of course he doesn't. He loves *me*.'

'And how does he love you, Nell? Does he take you in his arms every night, whisper of his love to you, stroke your breasts with his lips, take your body in love to his own, and afterwards lie awake with you in paradise?'

'No,' she shouted, struggling to get up. 'I mean, yes, yes he does.' Tears were streaming down her face, as he refused to let her go. Then as she saw genuine concern in his face, her defiance crumpled. 'He won't – only rarely.' Seeing first comprehension, then horror dawn in his eyes, she grew angrily defensive, tearing herself away and making for the door, hurling at him, 'He says he loves *me*.'

'That's not enough.' He was coming after her.

'It is, it is!'

'If you were mine, I'd—'

'Oh, yes?' she hurled at him, suddenly turning in anger to face him. 'What would *you* do?' she blazed. The grip on her wrists tightened and the look on his face changed. He let go abruptly, staring at her.

'I'd—' Then he swore under his breath in French, long and softly.

'Lucien?' she said uncertainly, watching the muscles of

his face working, hearing the ticking of the clock, seeing an out of focus picture slowly clarifying.

He moved. Or did she? She only knew she was in his arms, feeling his body against hers, and he was kissing her. Was he? Or was he pouring out sweet words of passion and love that seemed a kiss? His lips began a flame that his hands kindled till her whole body seemed alight. Her hands and lips seemed to be acting independently of her, clinging to him, forcing her ever closer to the flame. Then she was hazily aware that she was lying down on the sofa again, with him above her, feeling his hair against her cheek, then his lips seeking hers once more. And further down – she cried out.

'Nell?' His hands were on her. 'Nell? Must I stop?' he managed to ask her hoarsely.

Stop? When all she wanted was to be closer still? She raised her legs slightly, gripping him lest he leave her. 'Nell,' she heard, half as her name, half a long cry of love, and felt him removing her clothes. She struggled up to help that she might be with him the sooner. She glanced bewildered at his face, at this stranger she had known and not known. Lucien leaned forward, taking her in his arms slowly, deliberately, putting his lips on hers, claiming her for his own. The flame burst into fire and she distinguished nothing more until suddenly she gave a cry of pain and he stopped abruptly, trembled, then a muttered curse and he was with her again, and this time together.

Had she really thought his face nondescript? it occurred to her to wonder as she held him in her arms. Each freckle, each tiny line, seemed an extension of herself, something so prized, so precious that she could never let it go.

'Lucien?' she enquired anxiously. 'You look so sad. Aren't you happy?'

He kissed her eyes, he kissed her nose, he kissed first her left breast, then the right.

192

'I am partly sad,' he admitted.

'Why?' Alarm sprang through her.

'Because I have lost a chum.' His hand closed lovingly between her legs. 'But found my heart.'

Chapter Six

A last flame flickered red-yellow then died into a crimson glow, lighting up his face. Nell was aware of the touch of his arm round her shoulders, that she had but to turn her head to see his face, and perversely chose the sensuous pleasure of delay. Lucien moved forward on to one knee, throwing another shovelful of coal on to the fire, which paused defeated, black, until new flames leapt from it in triumph. He glanced over his shoulder at her, huddled on the carpet behind him, swathed in one of his bathrobes. There were dragons on the red silk, but it was a serpent that suddenly began to uncoil itself deep inside her. She stretched out her arms to him.

'Nell.' He was with her in an instant, with such force that she fell backwards on the rug and he with her, and the serpent died and disappeared.

'So,' he said softly, drawn out until it was a sigh of love, 'is this a way for a buyer of Gadsby's to behave?' as she wriggled luxuriously beneath him.

'Only with Comte Lucien of the ancient and respected family of la Ferté.'

'What shall two such sober and respectable persons do on a rug before a fire on a cold March night?'

'What they did not so very long ago?' she suggested.

'Sometimes,' Lucien said, kissing her ear, 'Gadsby's produces, if not original then highly delightful ideas.' He slipped his hand beneath the robe to ease it off and the coals were glowing red once more by the time she was again conscious of them.

It occurred to her, as she lay sprawled on the carpet, with Lucien lying in her arms, his head on her breast, that there was something she should be thinking of, many things, yet she could not. She wanted only to stay here, like this, with him.

'Nell . . . what a ridiculous name this is. Do you not have another?' he asked her lazily, as at last he sat upright and put his arm round her shoulders again.

'I do, but you won't like it.'

'What is it please?'

'Ermyntrude.'

'*Quoi*? *Impossible*! What kind of name is this?'

'A great-aunt's,' Nell told him ruefully.

'I do not wish to make love to a great-aunt,' he told her firmly. 'I will call you Ellen, that is your full name, is it not?'

'No, I'm just Nell,' she told him.

He looked at her. 'You are right. And now,' he added quietly, 'you must tell me, if you please, Just Nell, why you were still a virgin?'

Half-formed suppressed questions and doubts hammered in her mind. She stiffened, pushing them away, then fearfully recalled them, confronting them now that they were answered. But how to speak? Only one way. The truth. 'I – did not know.' She looked away, reddening, unable to bear the look of amazement at such ignorance that must surely be in his face. How incredible it must sound, in this, the 1920s. And she had boasted of being a modern woman!

'I thought that was all there was to it,' she added weakly, confusingly.

'But now you know it isn't,' was all he said, after a pause, 'what now?'

She turned to him fiercely. 'Don't let's spoil tonight by

196

questions like that. Let's pretend that outside doesn't exist.'

'*Non*,' he replied sharply. 'Let's enjoy it because it *does* exist. You,' he said with an effort, 'have a home you must return to. And – I will not say husband – an obligation.'

'More than that,' she said dully, shivering.

'I have made you sad, my Nell. We will not talk any more of outside. We will talk of your beautiful face and beautiful body, of your—'

She laughed. 'You make me sound like a Fair Shulamite. You know very well I'm not beautiful.'

'Ah, but you are wrong. Though,' he added, 'that truly terrible frock you wear tonight makes you appear not so. Tan indeed.'

'Melissa chose it.'

'Ah. It's an abomination.'

'Nonsense.'

'*Pardon*?'

'I said nonsense.'

'No one says nonsense to a de la Ferté,' he informed her, stroking her cheek with the back of his hand.

'I do.'

'That merely confirms my point. A de la Ferté is *always* right about everything.'

She considered. 'Nearly always,' she amended.

'I am always right about you. Your face tells clearly what you are thinking, like a summer sky, and I see what ails you.'

'What?' she said sharply, drawing a little way apart and unconsciously pulling the robe tighter around her.

'You are beginning to think of Tom,' he told her matter-of-factly, 'that you should be returning lest he worries, but not wanting to. You want to stay here with me. You would like to go back to yesterday when all was safe and Nell was Nell. Now you wonder who she is. And whose. Am I not right?'

'Wrong,' she announced.

'What then, *ma rose*?'

'I'm hungry.'

Full of mortification at this dereliction of a Frenchman's first duty, to enquire after a companion's gastronomic requirements, Lucien hurried her to a small restaurant in Soho. 'It is true,' he explained with twinkling eyes, 'that it is Italian not French, but nevertheless *le patron* is a friend of mine. He will do his best for us.' He hesitated. 'And you need not fear that our presence together will be noted—' He stopped, seeing Nell's initial bewilderment, then comprehension, and cursed himself for putting the idea in her head. But now he must continue. 'After all, if a buyer from Gadsby's and the manager of Maison la Ferté dine together, what of it?'

'We're rival houses,' she managed to laugh. 'Like in *Romeo and Juliet*.' It was a bad choice to speak of star-crossed lovers and they fell silent, pretending to pay due attention to the last mouthful of tagliatelle with truffles.

Lucien looked up as the waiter removed their plates, to find Nell staring at him.

'I thought you were turning into a director of the Maison la Ferté,' she told him frankly, seeing his look of enquiry. 'And I was afraid I might turn into the Girl from Gadsby's. Especially in this dress,' she added disarmingly.

His mouth twitched. 'And has either of those terrible things occurred?'

She studied him carefully, wondering how ever she could have regarded his face as nondescript, how she could have so disliked him, how regarded him as a cold opinionated businessman. 'No,' she pronounced gravely. All she had to do was put out her hand towards him in love . . . She glanced at her hands which were obediently serving some unconscious order from her brain to manip-

198

ulate knife and fork in the process of tackling sautéed kidneys, which had somehow arrived unnoticed before her. In her mind those hands were doing something far different, and seeing his eyes on her, she blushed.

He smiled, as if following her thoughts exactly. 'I am relieved, *ma chérie*.'

'I don't think I like being called your *chérie*,' she told him.

He looked puzzled. 'But no one can overhear.'

'No. But it makes me feel like all those other women in your life. The ones who float across Paris restaurants in wonderful clothes, wearing painted masks of faces.'

One eyebrow rose as he considered this carefully.

'There must be a word somewhere just for us,' she said anxiously. 'Mustn't there?'

'There is. And I will find it.' He paused for a moment, then smiled. '*Ma truffe noire*, my pearl of great price, who will flavour my life with her presence as does *la truffe* the humble omelette.'

'Truffles?' asked Nell, somewhat indignantly.

'If you knew how Frenchmen prize them, you would not so disdain my word of love.' Another pause. 'Nell, for one moment I must turn into that so-terrible director of the Maison la Ferté, and you into Madame Buyer. I wish to talk of Polly.'

'Polly?' For a moment she could not think what relevance Polly had. Then she remembered, and was astounded that she could have forgotten, flushing in indignation. 'You said—'

'Nell, will you *listen*?' he interrupted. 'It was not me, if indeed it is true at all. You have only Polly's word that anything happened. But I fear –' he hesitated '– I fear it was Philippe. He is proud of his success with women.'

She flushed, conscious of her past instant attraction to Philippe, how she'd looked forward to his coming to London. Him, not Lucien.

199

'Forgive me, Nell, I know you like him. Indeed, I thought . . .' He broke off.

'You thought,' she interrupted crossly, 'that we had made love together that night at your house?'

'Yes, I am ashamed. But I did not know you then. I saw only Philippe coming from your room making the sign he always makes when he has a "conquest".'

'You don't like him?' she asked curiously.

He hesitated. 'He is my brother, Nell. I like him, who would not? I do not trust him though. Philippe is ambitious, and never forgets he is the younger brother.'

'I think you're wrong,' she said, puzzled. 'He speaks with great admiration of you.'

He shrugged. 'Perhaps. He does not deny that he wooed Polly away from Gadsby's – by paying more money. If it was with his body also, I did not realise. But with money alone there can be nothing wrong, surely? It is good progress for Polly, and is just a matter of business between you and me.'

She bit her lip. 'And of treachery.'

'What treachery?' he retorted fiercely. 'None of mine.'

'No,' she said quickly, 'but it was one of Gadsby's staff who discovered about Polly and betrayed the secret to Philippe.'

'This I did not know.' Lucien frowned. 'And I do not approve. Nevertheless, now it has happened it is for Polly to decide her future after her contract to us for a year is fulfilled.'

'Then you will win again,' Nell said matter-of-factly. 'I can't afford without official backing to pay her what she deserves. Especially if Philippe and she still—'

'He is back in France. I will ensure that no liaison continues, and I will go to see Joe. Does that make you happy?'

She smiled wanly at the idea of Joe and Lucien engaged

in a man to man talk. 'Better,' she conceded, 'but I still don't have a designer.'

He relaxed, smiling at her in challenge. 'And you would have me sacrifice the interests of Maison la Ferté for Gadsby's? Would you give up yours for us?'

'No,' she said unwillingly, 'but—'

'Then it is war, perfidious Albion, just as before. Save,' he added, 'in love.'

Nell returned to Eaton Square at midnight, dazed, sure that the change in her must be visible in her face, and that such had been the momentous events of the evening that everything at home must also be different. But all seemed the same. She let herself in quietly, and was shaken to find Tom still up. He was in the drawing room, dark save for a single light above him. The fire had long since gone out. He was engrossed in several maps spread out before him, but looked up eagerly as she entered. 'Come and look at this, Nelly.'

Isn't he going to ask me where I've been? she thought, amazed, as she crossed to the table. Apparently not, for he plunged straight into the middle of Africa with his finger.

'It's time I had a stab at this. Motor racing is all very well, but flying is the way to the future. Everyone at the club is buzzing off all over the world, breaking records, opening up air routes. Why shouldn't I? What do you think, eh?' He looked up at her expectantly as she leaned over him. She had not seen him so excited for months. 'Now look, old thing,' he went on, 'Cobham's just reached Cape Town again in his flying-boat *Singapore*. Next he plans to come back along the West Coast – this way, see? Thought I might toddle out to the Cape in the old Moth and follow him back. I could be there and back in a month,' he said optimistically. 'A chap managed it solo in a Moth last autumn in twenty-six days. I could knock spots off that. Good for Gadsby's, eh? Tell you what, I'll call the old kite *Gadsby Girl*. You'd like that, wouldn't you?'

'But Tom,' she said faintly, anxious all the time that one part of her was thinking, Lucien, I would be able to see Lucien, 'you haven't the experience. It's dangerous. It's—'

He gave her an odd look. 'Don't worry about me,' he said firmly. 'I can look after myself. So long as you don't mind, that's the thing.'

She shook her head. 'If you feel you really want to.'

'I do.'

'Then I don't mind.'

'What would I do without you, Nelly?' He leapt up and hugged her. 'Best thing I ever did, marrying you. Knew you'd stand by me.'

Stand by him? Was that what she was going to do? Tom felt more like a dearly loved brother than her husband, she thought detachedly, despite the dizziness of her emotions. True, husband he had never been, she now knew, neither physically, nor emotionally. One part of her cried out to her to deny it, that if only she could reach him, cross that barrier, all would be well and Lucien would dissolve into the madness of a moment, that what had happened had happened merely out of her need. The other part of her looked at Tom, engrossed again in his maps, running his hand occasionally through his thick fair hair in excitement, and admitted the truth. A truth that would not vanish. Her love for Tom when she married him had been part of her daydream, one that had now been shattered for ever.

Next there was a battle she could put off no longer. Nell faced her quarry leaving the buyers' dining room. 'I understand,' she began, 'that you have made it your business to inform the Maison la Ferté of my designer's identity?'

The Dragon's face went red, but she maintained control of herself. 'Indeed? Have you proof?' she enquired.

'Enough,' Nell replied.

'I don't believe you,' Miss Danzy answered disdainfully. 'I shall deny it. I shall say it is mere spite because you resent my running the Fashion Department so well, and that you are jealous of my experience and flair.'

'Say to whom, Miss Danzy?' Nell enquired icily.

'Why,' the Dragon lost a little of her composure, 'to the Fourth Floor. Mr Jonathan. I assume—'

'I don't intend to go to Mr Gadsby,' interrupted Nell. 'I intend merely to warn our fellow buyers of your treachery, and if you—'

She was interrupted by a shriek of laughter. 'You think they'll believe you? They only tolerate you because you're the Old Man's granddaughter-in-law, and stole Mr Tom.'

Let her think she's won, thought Nell, biting back her instinctive reply, realising that this time she held the upper hand, despite the Dragon's bravado – an upper hand she would use at a time of her own choosing.

But Fourth Floor found out anyway. Nell was summoned a few days later, apparently to discuss the monthly figures. They were good, so perhaps this was merely going to be a pat on the back, she thought without much hope. It wasn't given to the Fourth Floor to issue summonses merely to praise.

Jonathan looked up as she came in, a rare honour.

'You look healthy, Nell,' he remarked genially. 'Having a baby, are you? About time. Get you out from under my feet,' he informed her genially.

'No, sir,' she told him stoically, while a sudden spasm of alarm shot through her. Suppose . . . Anyway, she could hardly tell him she stood little chance of having a baby by Tom.

'You've been married some time now. Haven't been going to see that cranky woman Marie Stopes, have you?'

Nell did not answer. 'Was there something you wanted to see me about, sir?' she asked pointedly.

Jonathan chuckled. 'Yes. Two things. Sit down.'

Sit down? It couldn't be too bad then. She cautiously obeyed, but sat on the very edge of the chair in order not to relax too much.

'Number one: I'm sacking Miss Danzy.'

'What?' Nell yelled, half leaping up again and subsiding.

'Thought you'd be pleased,' he said complacently. 'Had a visit from young Lucien de la Ferté. Remember him?' He shot her a look. 'I gather there's been skulduggery.'

Lucien? Her heart lurched at the mention of his name.

'I won't have treachery. Not in my store. I told her that. She's gone.'

'And what—' Nell broke off, careful not to display too much interest.

'I suppose you think I'm going to put you back on frocks, don't you? Well, you're wrong, missy,' he crowed triumphantly. 'Mrs Amble is going to take over.' He grinned maliciously while Nell battled to keep disappointment from her face. 'Few other changes, though,' he added offhandedly. 'I'm giving you Sporting Wear too. Old Santos is past it,' he explained scornfully of a man merely in his fifties. 'It's important. Mind you don't let me down, young woman. That's how Gadsby's started, you know, with sporting wear. People still notice what we're doing. Or did,' he added more truthfully.

'Sporting Wear's on the ground floor, sir,' said Nell, her mind racing, already buzzing with ideas. After all, there were such things this season known as sports evening gowns. Perhaps she could . . .

'Very observant, young lady. You can move Teagowns or whatever you call 'em and leave Lingerie upstairs. How's that?'

She drew a deep breath. 'Thank you, Mr Gadsby. I'm

sure I can do well in Sporting Wear. But I'm still worried about the overall direction of the firm.'

'*I* do the worrying about Gadsby's direction,' he barked warningly. 'Not you, young woman.'

'But the heart of Gadsby's is its Fashion Department, sir,' she continued bravely. 'Everything else depends on it.'

'That's right,' he said grimly. 'Just remember that. Especially,' he added gleefully, 'since you don't have a designer any more. Going to give up your tomfool ideas for ready-mades, are you?'

'No, sir,' she replied steadily.

'I gather young Polly is staying on at la Ferté. What are you doing for the summer?'

'I thought I'd have some of Polly's earlier designs made up in printed chiffon, sir. And bring back *jeune princesse* next year when I've found a new designer, even though we don't have it exclusively.'

'You're not thinking straight, Nell,' he told her.

She might have known Jonathan Gadsby was too canny to believe that, she thought ruefully. It would never work and he knew it.

'You need a designer *now* if you're going to carry on.'

'I've someone in mind,' she began loftily, exaggerating the true position.

'I've got one for you,' he told her.

Her heart sank. More problems. 'Oh?' she said guardedly.

'My fiancée's sister.'

'Your *what*?' wondering if she'd misheard. 'Tom didn't tell me—'

'He doesn't know yet. Going to get hitched next week before that idiot grandson of mine breaks his neck flying.'

'Er – who—?' Nell had visions of a nubile young twenty year old. She'd heard of such things. Surely Jonathan wouldn't be so foolish?

'Think I'm past it, do you? I'm only seventy-seven. That's not old, and she's two years younger.'

'But who—'

'Miss Emmeline, of course,' he said surprised. 'Who else did you think it was?' he added testily, waving aside Nell's delighted cries of pleasure. 'I wanted her to live down at Merrifield with Gertrude, but she won't have it. Insists on travelling around with me. Well, I told her, Gertie can work for her living while she's here. It's all blackmail,' he added gloomily.

'Miss Emmeline *blackmailed* you into marrying her? I don't believe it!' Nell said indignantly, grappling both with the idea of Emmeline as temptress blackmailer and of Gertrude as designer of modern dance dresses.

'Says she'll tell the world about The Hat if I don't,' he explained. 'No choice. Women!' He glared at Nell. 'Whyever did they let you out of the kitchen?'

Tom left in mid-April, three days after Jonathan Gadsby took Miss Emmeline Parks, spinster of this parish, for his wife at the new St John's Church, Welling. A procession of motor cars then proceeded with a large assortment of guests, plus an even larger assortment of luggage, to Merrifield for a reception. A nice week at Folkestone was all the bride requested as a honeymoon, while Miss Gertrude, in her element, reigned supreme as acting mistress of Merrifield. For Nell it was an occasion of mixed pleasure. Tom was talking endlessly of his forthcoming flight to anyone who would listen, she was trying to calm Miss Gertrude and act as matron of honour to Miss Emmeline who was the calmest of them all. As she walked up the aisle behind a lavender satin-clad Miss Emmeline, she was conscious of only one thing: Lucien de la Ferté standing next to his brother, Philippe, was amongst the guests – looking straight ahead. No mistaking that chin, that nose. No mistaking that he was as aware of

206

her presence as she was of his. No forgetting that since that night they had not seen each other.

'Sure you'll be all right, Nelly?' Tom asked anxiously as she steeled herself to see him off on his flight at Croydon.

'Quite sure,' she said levelly. 'And please, Tom, take care.'

They both knew the dangers, and neither mentioned them. Dangers not only from mechanical failure but from what might happen if he were forced to land. She was well aware that he had packed a gun, and several clips of ammunition.

'Goodbye, old thing. Goodbye, Nelly.' He half choked, then clambered quickly into the Moth. There were an unusual number of photographers. Solo fliers were two a penny nowadays but not ones as newsworthy as Tom Gadsby. She watched as the heavily laden Moth climbed steadily into the air, torn with guilt because it was not of Tom that she was thinking.

'So you have come,' Lucien said simply, standing aside to let her in.

'It was simpler to wait,' was all she could say. How could she explain? That other Nell, the Nell who had married a man she thought she loved, had put up a fight before she could acknowledge, even to herself, that a new Nell had been born. A Nell who knew true love, who knew passion, and having crossed their threshold was changed forever.

'For you perhaps,' he said politely, ushering her into the drawing room. That was all he said, waiting for her to speak.

'Lucien—' she began, then changed her mind. 'Don't you think I wanted to come?' she said huskily.

'I did not *know*.' Each word was clipped.

'Then you should have known,' she burst out, and was in his arms. He covered her face with kisses, muttered

207

endearments as she clung to him, smothering her efforts to free herself, her muttered protests, till she ceased them, clinging to him, and all conscious thought was lost.

'So what did you come to tell me, Nell?' Lucien said casually, his back to her, apparently occupied with pouring drinks.

She started to say something, then stopped, thrown by the distance between them, by the elegant, robe-clad back. 'I came to tell you,' she began again loudly, 'that I love you.' It wasn't what she'd meant to say at all.

He spun round, the drink splashing unregarded as he came towards her, a flame in his eyes: of relief, of unguarded love.

'And that's why I can't see you again,' she blurted out.

His face twisted but he said nothing.

'Do you understand why?' she asked uncertainly.

'But yes. You are naturally scared.'

'*Scared*?' she repeated, dumbfounded.

'Of course. It is a big step for you and you have not the courage.' Was that scorn in his voice? 'It is always easier to do nothing than to do something. It takes courage to love. So you convince yourself you are betraying Tom. Why, I cannot see because—'

'Stop!' she cried, but he continued remorselessly:

'He has deceived you. He has not behaved like a husband to you.'

'Tom needs me,' she cried. Had she not been over and over the arguments endlessly in her mind during the last two weeks? Traced her former hero-worship of Tom through to her current affection for him? After all, that too was a kind of love. And had she not promised 'for better for worse'? Even if she decided to break her vows, there remained the insurmountable problem: how could she behave to Tom just as Melissa had? No human being had the right knowingly to inflict such hurt, such humiliation. Changed in herself she might be, but that did not, could not, make her immune from her obligations to Tom.

Yet now with Lucien this cool stranger again, who only half an hour ago had lain with her, twisting and turning in passion in her arms, the arguments that seemed so straightforward at home seemed to crumble and dissolve before the fire of his scorn.

'And do you not think that I need you?' he enquired. 'That because you love me – you say – that gives me too some claim? I am thirty. Do you not realise I have searched for love for many years? My parents constantly urge me to marry to have an heir. My father does not wish –' he flushed slightly '– the title to pass to Philippe. So one fertile lady of suitable rank and beauty after another is suggested. It never ceases. I say that if I am to have a child, it will be born of a woman I love. I have searched for such a woman through many *amours*, but never found her. Now that I have done so at last, she is married to someone else. *But could be free*,' he ground out. 'Do you not realise that I too need you?'

She stared at him, appalled, sickened almost at this spelling out of what seemed now a public duty rather than a private love. 'But you are a Catholic,' she stammered.

'Of course I am a Catholic,' he replied coldly.

'Then we couldn't marry anyway.'

His hand trembled slightly on the glass, the only sign that this was other than a purely business discussion. 'Forgive me for being blunt, Nell, but since you seem intent on making both of us unhappy, there is no need for reticence. There is no question of a divorce. There was no consummation. An annulment would be the correct procedure. Unfortunately, as there is now no physical evidence,' he said wryly, 'you would have to obtain Tom's co-operation.'

'No! *No!*' she whispered, backing away. 'I can't do that to him, I won't. I can't.'

His face went white. 'No,' he said at last. 'Of course. I cannot ask it of you. You must forgive me if you can, Nell.'

They stared at one another in silence, appalled and unable to reach to each other.

'Go,' he burst out violently. 'Please go.'

There was only work. But Gadsby's, which once offered such challenges, such far horizons towards which she strove with endless enthusiasm, now presented only a series of hurdles – and what lay at the end? Jonathan Gadsby, who showed no sign of flagging in his determination to run the store as undisputed captain of the ship, albeit a leaky ship. A series of telegrams arrived from Tom from exotic places, which eked out by newspaper reports, enabled her to chart his progress. Anxiety for him was always present, not for a lover, or even a husband, but more as a child – the child she'd never have, she supposed bleakly. Cairo, Khartoum, Tanganyika, and finally Table Mountain. He had arrived at Cape Town in eleven days' actual flying. Not non-stop. He wasn't up to that yet, he'd told her rather wistfully. But one of these days. Coming back on the western route would take rather longer, but he'd be back in time for the Derby he assured her blithely.

Miss Emmeline (as Nell still thought of her) and Miss Gertrude looked as at home in Jonathan's Park Lane home as they did in Welling High Street; Emmeline took staff and wealth in her stride, to Nell's bemused acceptance. 'But after all, Nell,' Emmeline told her primly, 'I have *some* experience of keeping staff in order, do I not?'

'Yes, Miss Emmeline,' said Nell meekly, remembering her early days at Parks' where a fierce, exacting, if kindly employer had gimlet eyes everywhere for the least departure from prescribed rules. 'Oh, and what *do* I call you? I can't call you Grandmama-in-law.'

Miss Emmeline considered. 'What do you call Mr Jonathan?'

'Terrifying,' replied Nell promptly.

The gimlet eye had lost none of its force and she felt abashed.

'I think Mrs Emmeline would do nicely.'

Nell had summoned up all her courage for this meeting. What on earth was she to do? Excellent designers though they were, Mrs Emmeline and Miss Gertrude were well into their seventies and even in their heyday had designed for Welling gentry and not to compete with the greatest fashion houses of London. Surely Jonathan Gadsby would understand this? Yet how could she hurt her oldest friends?

Every table in the morning room seemed to be covered with magazines and sketch pads, a scene Nell remembered vividly from Welling days, for it was a constant matter of regret to Mrs Emmeline that genius (in the form of Gertrude) must not be stifled by insisting on the usual rules of order and tidiness.

'The problem is,' Nell began tactfully, 'I need designs rather outside your experience.'

Miss Gertrude's face fell, Mrs Emmeline's remained impassive.

'Modern party frocks. And in the Sporting Wear department too. Besides equipping women for sporting activities, I want to try a line of evening dresses suitable for sports gatherings that continue into the evening. I could even branch out—' She stopped as caution overcame enthusiasm, remembering Emmeline was now Mrs Jonathan Gadsby.

'What do you consider sports, my dear?' Mrs Emmeline enquired briskly.

'Shooting, tennis and golf,' began Nell, feeling she was losing control.

'You are a little behind the times, Nell.' Her voice was

reproving. 'There's motoring, flying—'

'Bridge, croquet,' put in Miss Gertrude brightly.

'Oh, *no*,' Nell cried without thinking, visions of Edwardian ladies in S-bend corsets dancing before her eyes.

'My dear Nell,' Emmeline informed her severely, 'the trouble with you young people is that you never *think*. Or if you do, you believe everything is new, invented by you young folks. In fashion *everything* has been done before. You seem to believe you have to discover Tutankhamen's tomb in order to start a new fashion. Take these wretched little Mexican beads, so popular this year. Here today, gone tomorrow. Fashion, my dear, as I tried – apparently without success – to impress upon you, is one continuous though waving line; these fads are merely blind alleys.'

Lucien, that was what he had said.

'We must be inspired by the past,' Mrs Emmeline concluded.

'And adapt it for the present,' Nell said excitedly, beginning to see croquet frocks in an entirely different light – or rather in chiffons printed with modern designs.

'Within bounds,' said Mrs Emmeline.

'No, not within bounds,' cried Nell, gambling. 'Let's give Miss Gertrude her head. You always love fairy stories, romances, don't you, Miss Gertrude? I think romance is going to come back into fashion, so why, as well as the practical for sports, can't we have romance as well in the evening frocks?'

Miss Gertrude clucked excitedly. 'I do have one or two ideas already.' She burrowed amidst the papers.

Nell stared at a drawing in silence.

'It's one of those sports evening gowns,' said Miss Gertrude, her face falling.

'It's lovely but . . .' Nell struggled for words. It was a monstrosity. It hung like a cleaner's overall – long, loose

212

and enveloping. 'Sports gowns are for young people, and when you see what they wear at night clubs—'

'Oh, you mean something like this,' interrupted Miss Gertrude almost crossly, sketching quickly on an old envelope. Before Nell's eyes, in a few lines, a low-necked dress, clinging in at the hips and flowing out in flounces to the knees, sprang into being, was already on the rails in Nell's eyes.

'Shantung,' she breathed.

'And satin,' amplified Mrs Emmeline smugly.

'You mean you actually like this?' said Miss Gertrude, surprised. 'But what about my sports gown?'

Nell took the sketch of the monstrosity. She smiled. 'Here,' she said, rubbing out the last six inches of skirt. 'Knee-length and –' she sketched in some more '– fish-tail train at the back. Long sleeves. Printed georgette, not satin. Hey presto. A bridge coat.'

Miss Gertrude and Mrs Emmeline stared at her handiwork suspiciously, then Mrs Emmeline raised her head.

'What are you waiting for, Gertrude?' she said crisply. 'The buyer has commissioned you.'

It was almost a shock to see Melissa, who had not been to Eaton Square for some time. So preoccupied had Nell been with her own affairs that she had not found the time to call on her friend, and felt almost guilty as a reproachful Melissa arrived one Saturday morning. The theatre seemed to have recovered from its disasters of the previous year, *Cloche Hats* had been succeeded by *Dancing in the Dew* which seemed only to be rivalled by *Showboat* at Drury Lane. Melissa sang and skipped her way to London's heart, and Nell had therefore assumed her problems were at least temporarily resolved. She was wrong. Nothing about Melissa was ever resolved.

'Where's Tommy, darling?' she asked in surprise, seeing no sign of him in the house.

213

'Away. Flying back from Cape Town,' said Nell drily. 'I believe a newspaper or two mentioned it!'

'Oh. I never read newspapers. Except reviews of course.' Melissa was disappointed and Nell wondered why. She'd never evinced much interest in seeing Tom before. So little in fact that it had occurred to her that perhaps Melissa's sexual relations with Tom had been as inadequate as her own. But she dismissed the thought. It was far more likely that her new found enthusiasm for him was caused by a lack of other male attention in her life. Tom and Melissa – no, she *would* not think about it. Whatever the truth, it was irrelevant now.

Melissa soon forgot about Tom, however, and proceeded to chat gaily about the play, the divine new composer and even more divine leading man, the heavenly designer at Maison la Ferté, and last night at the Ivy.

Nell waited stoically. Sooner or later the reason that the mountain had decided to call on Mahomet on this particularly occasion would become apparent.

'And how have you been, Nell?' she asked carelessly. 'You look rather peaky. Love, I suppose. I'm glad you still love old Tommy.'

Nell compressed her lips.

'You're missing him, aren't you, you romantic old thing you. Either that or – I say, you aren't taking a leaf out of my book, are you?' Melissa was apparently intent on the chocolate biscuits, but didn't miss the slight flush on Nell's cheeks. 'I do worry about you, you know, Nell. Fancy still working at dull old Gadsby's. Why, for heaven's sake? You could be having such fun. Not to mention a little baby,' she added innocently. 'I can see you as a fat old mum.'

'I'm at Gadsby's because I want to be,' snapped Nell. Trust Melissa to stir things up. Why *did* she continue at Gadsby's? Nell wondered. The store was going nowhere –

just like her marriage. 'Because it's a challenge,' she finished defiantly.

Melissa laughed delightedly, knowing she had hit home. 'I'm not a prospective employer, darling, or Grandpa Gadsby. You can tell me the truth.'

The truth? What was it? That if there were no Tom and no marriage, only Lucien, Gadsby's would disappear in the twinkling of an eye. Lucien's eye. A Gadsby's that was hers to run as she chose would be different. But this Gadsby's was a dinosaur lumbering to extinction, and all the ready-made bridge coats in the world wouldn't change that while Jonathan Gadsby remained in charge.

'Come down to the studios with me, darling. I've got to fly.' So this was it. For some reason Melissa wanted her to see the studios. Interested despite herself, and despite the thought that she'd probably meet Jack again, Nell agreed. At least it would prevent yet another day of trying to restrain herself from contacting Lucien.

The studios of Fisher Enterprises were hardly Hollywood and Nell was surprised when Melissa drew sharply up outside the old warehouse on the Thames.

'Here we are, darling,' she cried.

Inside, all was businesslike enough. Wires, canvas, sets, men wandering everywhere. Jack perched in his chair like a buddha, with men rushing up every few minutes to consult him. Melissa's 'dressing-room' was a cubby-hole she shared with several spare cameras.

'What do you see in this?' Nell asked, bewildered, as Melissa quickly changed into a long flowing silk gown, totally impractical thought Nell, amused, for traversing Sherwood Forest as Maid Marian. Now a new Gadsby sports gown –

'It's exciting. It's the future, Jack says,' Melissa repeated obediently. 'It's illusion. It's finding perfection. It's shooting all day, just for one perfect moment. Not like theatre,' she announced scornfully.

'When talking pictures come perhaps it will be better.'

'Oh, they won't last,' said Melissa simply. 'That's what Jack says. He's seen them already. True art is this.' She waved her hand at a tacky-looking plywood set and painted backdrop as they walked outside into the gloomy, chilly warehouse with about twenty people standing around disconsolately. All began to move fast enough, however, once Fisher saw Melissa and snapped into action. Melodramatic gestures that would never be tolerated on stage, artless simpering far from Melissa's usual acting, and quite ridiculous plot – even for *Robin Hood*. Was this true art?

It didn't look like it, thought Nell, horribly fascinated, huddling down in an unobtrusive corner while shot after shot was taken, and strange commands rapped out. To her eye, Melissa had never looked less enchanting. She looked cold, miserable, unappealing and was acting abominably. And *still* she didn't know why Melissa had wanted her there. It wasn't long, however, before she found out. It was her old role. Buffer-in-chief.

'Darling, I must go,' Melissa told Jack brightly immediately shooting finished. 'Nell's insisting I take her back to town straightaway and feed her. Poor love. Stranded here all day without a bite.'

Nell mentally counted to ten. 'I'm sure—'

'You can come back,' Jack flung at her, scowling.

'Not tonight darling. Nell wants a real old chin-wag. Girls' talk.' Melissa smiled brightly and whisked Nell off.

'You might have warned me,' she grumbled as the Austin-Healey hurtled its way back to London.

'What about?' asked Melissa blankly.

'Jack,' said Nell. 'Come on, you're not getting away with it. What's wrong? Is your divorce from Robert going through?'

'There *is* the teensiest little problem, actually.'

216

'You don't mean Robert's changed his mind?' asked Nell in horror.

'Yes. He thinks being married to me is a better cover for him.'

'Can't you divorce him for being a homosexual, or something?'

'I've got my reputation as a sex goddess to think of!' Melissa sounded shocked.

Nell laughed aloud. 'You're only playing Maid Marian,' she pointed out.

Melissa looked hurt, then dismissed this as irrelevant. 'Anyway, I don't want to send poor Robert to gaol,' she said virtuously.

'What you mean is, he's threatened to Reveal All about you,' said Nell bluntly.

Melissa giggled, 'I prefer to think he *likes* being married to me.'

'And Jack?'

'I—' She changed gear viciously. 'He's turned very odd,' she explained. 'Once he didn't want me at all – now he's gone the other way. He won't let me out of his sight.'

'You must be flattered.' Nell did not give an inch.

'No. I'm frightened, Nell. Really frightened. He's an odd man. He stares at me so, I sometimes think—' she broke off.

'What?'

'Nothing.' She smiled brightly. 'Now what shall I do about Robert?'

'Stay married,' suggested Nell practically.

'But that would mean committing adultery all my life, Nell,' she said indignantly. 'What an odd creature you are. I never thought you'd approve of that. Still, I suppose it *is* a good idea, isn't it?' she said doubtfully. 'Jack couldn't complain. He knows I'm safe with Robert. It would solve everything.'

'I doubt that, with you, Melissa,' said Nell drily.

★ ★ ★

'No,' roared Jonathan Gadsby, inspecting his new Sporting Wear department. 'Rubbish.'

'But if ladies are to buy their tennis frocks here, surely it makes sense to sell rackets for those that play and picnic boxes for those who watch. And cushions, and shooting sticks – they'd all sell,' Nell pointed out.

'We could sell bundles of firewood if we piled them on the pavement outside,' Jonathan retorted rudely. 'That doesn't mean it would be good for Gadsby's. No.'

'But we're in a trap now,' she said. 'We're neither able to compete with the top fashion houses nor broad enough to compete with the new department stores. We're Grand old Duke of Yorks – neither up nor down.'

'I'll be the judge of that, young woman,' he roared. 'And what's *that*?' pointing with his stick at the row of gaily coloured gauze dresses edged with marabou.

'Bridge dresses,' replied Nell.

'Are they, by God!'

'By Miss Gertrude, in fact,' replied Nell demurely.

He eyed her and then the dresses. 'They'd better sell,' he said darkly, stomping off.

They did, and so did the sports evening dresses, for the summer of 1928 was a hot one. Not that that hindered the sale of Miss Gertrude's outfits for shooting – short skirts with plus fours underneath. Nell had tried hard to persuade her into experimenting with divided skirts like Paris, but she remained adamant. 'Not for England, Nell dear. We cater for *ladies* here.' Though turnover increased, the heart of the problem remained. Gadsby's reputation rose and fell by its Fashion Department and that was still catering essentially for a bygone age.

Tom returned well in time for the Derby, highly pleased with himself. It had taken much longer on the return journey up the West Coast, but nevertheless he had what he considered a feather in his cap, since Sir Alan Cobham's flight on the same route had ended in his being forced to land on the French Ivory Coast, where his huge flying boat and crew, including his wife, still remained. He himself might not have broken any records, Tom pointed out, but at least he brought 'Gadsby Girl' back in one piece. Or nearly. It transpired that he'd flown a large part of the journey back with a cracked tank. Nell shuddered, but he brushed this aside.

'It's worth all the danger in the world, Nelly,' he told her, eyes bright, as they drove out of London in his new Alfa Romeo coupé. She'd wanted him to relax at home their first weekend back, but he wouldn't hear of it. 'They're expecting us,' he pointed out. 'Big party. You'll enjoy it; bit of country air. Melissa's going, she's between plays. Did you know?'

'No,' she said crossly, 'but I'm not between jobs. I can't take Saturday morning and Monday off, just like that.'

'Dash it, Nell,' he'd said almost angrily, 'you're my wife and I'm the heir to the whole bally shop. I have to get something out of it. It's always Gadsby's with you, isn't it? I want you there. How'd it look if I'm down there with Melissa without you, eh?'

'Oh, very well,' she muttered ungraciously at the time, but now they were actually leaving London, she felt better. Leaving London, if only for two or three days, meant leaving the ever-present ache of Lucien behind.

'Up there, Nell,' Tom was talking almost non-stop about flying, 'you can feel you're really achieving something. This makes up for missing the war. It's even better because it's for the future. Helping to link up the world. Up there, you feel as old and as young as the stars themselves.' He laughed self-consciously. 'I sound like that fellow T.S. Eliot, don't I?'

'A little easier to understand,' Nell said. 'But just as poetic.'

219

He glanced at her, revving up the coupé, as if to reinforce the sudden holiday spirit. 'Looking down from the sky, you wouldn't believe how beautiful it is – mountains, rivers, small towns. And the desert. There's something about it . . .'

'The ruins, you mean? Temples?'

'No. The desert itself. The emptiness. Just a sea of golden sand with only the occasional outcrop of rock or a dune breaking the horizon. And yet it's alive. And the colours – they seem to be calling to you somehow. It does something to a chap. I had to land one night – nothing serious, but there was nothing to be done till daybreak. Nothing but sleep under the stars. Those stars—' He broke off sheepishly. 'There I go again. And, by Jupiter, I'd like to,' he added enthusastically. 'You wouldn't mind, would you Nelly?'

'No,' she said guiltily. She tried to convince herself she did not object because it had already done so much for him, but she knew it had nothing to do with that. 'We're not going to Merrifield, are we?' she asked suddenly recognising Wrotham Hill and realising they were on the Ashford Road.

'Good Lord, no,' he said cheerily. 'This is supposed to be a jolly weekend.'

She recognised it straightaway, despite the riot of rhododendrons, lining a driveway that had been barren, despite the profusion of roses climbing over the front of the red brick house. She did not need the sight of the familiar figure rushing down the front steps to tell her she was back at Missinden. Bobsy was no longer clad in Eastern or motoring garb, however. Instead she seemed to have adopted some kind of Pre-Raphaelite dress. 'It's one of my Aesthetic days,' she proudly informed them.

'My wife, Nell,' Tom said. 'Lady Bertrand. Bobsy to her friends.'

'As Nell is, aren't you?' Bobsy said brightly, winking at her.

'Yes please,' said Nell warmly, trying to ignore the wink. 'It's wonderful to be – to see you again, Bobsy. You don't have any Sheikhs around, do you?' she tried to joke.

'Oh, *no*,' said Bobsy, shocked. 'This is an artistic weekend. Just a few close friends. We're all going to be very, very sensible, my darlings. Just you wait and see.'

Nell looked suspiciously in the wardrobe of her bedroom but there was no sign of any Shulamite costumes or any others to her relief. She was apparently free to be Nell Gadsby with all her lack of fashion flair. How very Edwardian, she thought, amused, to have Tom placed in an adjoining room. He still slept in the same bed as her usually, even though . . . She would not think any more of that, she told herself firmly. She dared not. Quickly she changed into her new dress, one of Miss Gertrude's, a crimson georgette with a full gathered skirt – what a change after the skimpiness of recent years. She flung some beads round her neck, remembering too late Tom liked her to wear the Gadsby jewels when she was with him, and was ready when he knocked.

Everything had changed. Where was the Art Deco decor? Where the piles of cushions and stark grey walls? Nell blinked. Everything now spoke of Sex; languorous sofas and tiger-skin rugs complemented deep red curtains and soft shaded lights. Straight out of Elinor Glyn, she thought, trying not to laugh.

'Like it?' yelled Bobsy, appearing with two glasses of a lethal-looking blue concoction she called the Picasso because of its colour.

'Love it,' Nell yelled back in the din of chatter. There must be forty people here at least. Just a few close friends indeed!

Bobsy was sporting a feathered hat of which Josephine Baker would have been proud, and this obscured much of

221

the room from Nell. Only when she moved did she see Melissa. A Melissa emanating frailty and femininity in chiffon gold lace, its folds sensuously hugging her hips and then flowing around her as she twirled and twisted in the light, turning to smile tremulously at the man she was with. It was Philippe de la Ferté. Then he was coming towards them, with Melissa following, to greet, it seemed, his dearest friend.

'Do you two know each other?' asked Melissa sweetly, giving Nell a meaningful look which puzzled her greatly.

'You know very well we do, Melissa. We're business acquaintances,' said Nell, trying to keep irritation from her voice. Where Philippe was, could—?

'Surely more than that?' Philippe bowed over her hand. 'One evening we spent in each other's arms, did we not? Dancing, naturally,' he added to Tom, laughing.

He was not listening, Nell noticed. He was staring at Melissa.

'Run along, you two,' said Melissa happily. 'I've so much I want to say to my darling Tommy.'

Philippe shrugged, and put an arm round Nell's waist. 'He is foolish to trust you to me, Nell,' he said darkly. 'Come, shall we run away together, you and I? Shall we wander by the lake so that you can tell me the designer of this most interesting dress?' He was steering her to the terrace doors. 'And then I can declare my love for you – ah, *mon frère*.' He broke off, not a whit disconcerted.

'Hallo, Lucien.' Nell tried to smile brightly.

'*Bonsoir*, Nell,' said his cool voice. '*Comment allez-vous*?' Without waiting for an answer he turned straight to Philippe. 'If you please, there are matters to discuss.'

'Indeed, Lucien,' agreed Philippe, tightening his hold on Nell. 'Between Madame Nell and myself. *C'est des affaires, je t'assure.*'

Nell managed to get through the evening somehow by

desperately pretending Lucien was not present. After all, it was to be expected she would bump into him sometime, and it was no worse here than in London, she told herself. In vain. It was worse. This was a trap from which she could not escape, where every room brought back memories of the Christmas before last. A time when she had been free and had not the sense to realise where she was heading. She was thankful now for Philippe's presence. Tom spent the evening locked in talk with Melissa, and Philippe was at least some sort of barrier between herself and Lucien. She tried to reflect that he had no morals, either in business or outside, but told herself that she was dancing with him, not making him a life partner. And so she would enjoy herself.

She did not manage it. Tiring of her, Philippe went to find another partner, leaving her alone. Lucien did not come near her.

'Darling, why did you abandon Philippe last night?' Melissa came rushing across the lawn on the Saturday morning clad in the flimsiest tennis frock Nell had ever seen. 'Aren't you pleased I brought him down?' she went on. 'You *are* having an affair with him, aren't you? That's why I took Tom off your hands,' she informed Nell, pleased with herself.

'Oh, *Melissa*, why do you always interfere?' Nell groaned.

'Darling, I thought you'd be pleased. I told Philippe I knew all about it—'

'You *what*? Melissa, how could you? Of course I'm not having an affair with Philippe.' Melissa merely looked worldly wise and Nell was in despair. Philippe was far from slow-witted. Suppose he suspected? Come to that, suppose in his vanity he assumed she was indeed attracted to him?

'Sometimes, Melissa, I just wish you'd try to help

223

yourself and *not me*,' Nell flung at her, just as the butler came out with a message for Melissa.

'The police?' Melissa repeated in bewilderment. 'Whatever can they want?' She ran back into the house, cannoning into Tom in the doorway. He promptly changed his mind about coming out and went in with her. Curious, Nell waited, watching the tennis for a while – then unable to bear the suspense when neither Melissa nor Tom re-appeared, she decided to follow them in. But as she walked across the lawn, Lucien, clad in white for tennis, came running towards her from the house.

'There is bad news, Nell,' he said abruptly, taking her by the arm. 'Robert Stockbridge has been found dead.'

'*Dead*?' repeated Nell, horrified. 'How? An accident? Heart disease?'

'No. Apparently he was murdered.' Lucien hesitated, seeing her shocked expression. 'I hope he was not a close friend of yours?'

'No,' she said numbly, running through all the ramifications. Murdered? Could Jack be implicated somehow? was her instant thought.

'Melissa will need you,' Lucien said quietly.

She went to pass him to run into the house, but he stopped her with his arm in front of her. 'No, I mean she *will* need you in the days to come. But she has left Missinden already,' he said. 'And Tom with her.'

'Tom? Without even telling me?' she cried, without thinking. 'No, he wouldn't—'

'Without telling you, Nell,' Lucien agreed coolly. 'Shall we play?' And, as she stood numbly, 'There is nothing for you to do. They have gone.'

Dazed, she let him take her arm and escort her on to an empty court. She stood waiting, trying to concentrate, Melissa, Tom – and Lucien, in the sunshine, fully stretched, racket high as he served to her. She didn't even see the ball coming. Heard only the ping as it hit the fence behind her.

'My point,' he shouted.

'Agreed,' she replied dully, as she bent to pick up the ball.

Robert had been found stabbed at his home, so she found out later. He had died some time on Friday, rumour went. And rumour went a lot further too. Melissa had wanted a divorce . . . he'd refused to give it to her. No one voiced the obvious link but it hung unspoken in the air. The name of Jack Fisher was also apparently well known to most of the company here. Why not? Melissa was never the soul of discretion, thought Nell wrily. The heat had not lessened although the afternoon was nearly over, and Nell felt oppressed in the heavy air. She had the whole evening to get through, and, worse, it would be a party where at all costs she must avoid Lucien.

'You'll find your dresses in your rooms. No stockings, girls,' yelled Bobsy. 'Much too hot.'

That was all very well, thought Nell grimly, but with the costumes, or rather lack of them, that Bobsy favoured, she might welcome their presence. Trust Bobsy. Artistic, she had said. An opera? she had heard Lucien enquiring. No, it was a sort of dance, Bobsy answered vaguely.

Nell rushed back to her room to find her worst suspicions confirmed. Laid on the bed with a neat note from Bobsy explaining that Kinema was the theme of the evening was her costume – not that there was really enough of it to make a costume. Resignedly, wishing only that she had the looks of the Tarzan girl, Clara Kimball Young, she donned the tigerskin. Perhaps she thought, as she regarded the result in the mirror, she could make an appearance in this and then escape to don something more substantial on the grounds of being cold.

She was not the only person unhappy with their

225

costume. She opened her door to walk straight into Philippe, obviously on his way to her, and splendidly attired as Chang, the famous Siamese trader.

'My brother requires your admiration, Nell,' he said, eyes glinting. '*Voilà*.' He took her hand and threw open the door to his own room dramatically. Within there was a furious and most unamused Charlie Chaplin.

'The prospective head of the Maison la Ferté does not approve of these "baggy trousers",' said Philippe mournfully. 'Nor of this delightful moustache, nor of these elegant shoes. Nor—'

'*Ça suffit*, Philippe,' snapped Lucien as Nell battled to keep from laughing.

'I think your brother looks delightful as Charlie Chaplin,' she said to Philippe with a straight face. 'But I'll see if they left one for Tom,' she said, eager to escape, and thankful when she went into Tom's room that it was not a Felix the Cat costume lying on the bed but one from *Black Pirate*.

'My brother will be grateful,' said Philippe behind her, uncomfortably close. 'Though I doubt that Douglas Fairbanks is any more his style than Charlie Chaplin,' he added offhandedly. 'Nevertheless it is more *comme il faut* and that will please my so-correct brother.' His hand had crept round her tigerskin-clad waist, and was definitely slipping lower. She removed it promptly. He laughed delightedly. 'And an oh-so-correct English married lady. What a pity.'

He may be bowing over my hand, but his eyes are on my legs she noted crossly as she retreated.

The evening was superb – or should have been, had Nell's thoughts been less chaotic, torn as they were between Melissa's problems and her own. Dinner was taken outside on the terrace, the walls of the old house trapping the evening scent of the roses. There stars of the screen ate by candlelight. After dinner there was rowing

226

on the lake, floating in the dusk across the lily-strewn water. She did not join in, content to watch from the bank, glad she had not succumbed to an almost overwhelming temptation to join Lucien in a boat. But as the sounds of music began to float across from the terrace, Philippe found her once more.

'Dearest Nell,' he said, 'how fortunate the handsome Tom is not here. Now I can have you all to myself.'

'Philippe, go away and find someone who is not an elderly married lady like me,' she told him, exasperated.

'In that tigerskin?' he asked, pained. 'You expect me to leave when I can dance with my hand on that—'

'Philippe!'

He laughed, and giving in she went back to the terrace to dance with him, both relieved and jealous to see Lucien dancing with someone else. Philippe refused to let Nell go and she was glad of it, for it helped her avoid temptation.

'Philippe,' cried Bobsy, rushing up in a farthingale, 'I know I'm an old woman compared with Nell, but I'm your hostess, you handsome boy, and it's high time you danced with me. If you can get near enough to me in this thing.' She kicked at the farthingale disgustedly.

Instant panic struck Nell, but Lucien did not even turn his head. Relieved – was it really relief? – she hurried into the gardens, glad of the chance to be by herself, to think over what had happened on this terrible day. But she did not find herself thinking of Robert, nor even of Melissa and Tom. Instead she smelled the flowers, heady in the walled gardens, saw the rising moon overhead, felt the warmth of the evening air on her bare legs and arms, and knew only that this was a night made for lovers and she was alone.

'Nell!'

Startled, she looked up to see him at the far end of the long narrow walled garden she was in, standing perhaps thirty yards away, a dark figure but unmistakable in his pirate's costume even if his voice, not cold now, but full of longing, had not been as familiar to her as her own. Quickly she looked for an escape. How could she speak to him on a night like this and not want to love him? She took a cross path into the next garden, then the next, and doubled back, then walked further on, anywhere – to be free, not of him, but of herself. She ran blindly towards the next archway only to find him facing her by the sundial, only a few feet away, his arms held wide open allowing no possibility of escape.

'No,' she cried incoherently, running to him.

'No what?' he asked gently, folding her into his arms, any doubts he may have had answered now.

'No. I'm fighting—'

'No one fights on a night like this. Even the birds have stopped singing now to make love to their chosen mates. We too, Nell, we too.'

Her body ached as his lips closed on hers. She must fight, a voice somewhere inside was insisting. But she could not, and feeling her relax, he held her the more tightly.

'After today you cannot say you owe Tom anything.'

'I can, I can!' Why did he have to mention Tom?

'No, you cannot. This time, Nell, you shall not escape me.'

His hands were moving over her, lovingly, undemandingly, until suddenly his kiss grew hard, one hand clasped tightly at the top of her bare thighs under the tigerskin, holding her against him. 'I shall come to you tonight, Nell.'

'No.'

'Only if you can tell me honestly you do not want me, do not love me, *ma truffe, ma truffe noire*.'

'I—' She could not. 'I'll lock my door,' she managed to say at last.

His lips and hands continued their caressing, undeterred, until she could bear it no longer. 'No,' she managed to say. With that last denial she tore herself away, and he did not follow her.

She bolted the door to her room and leaned back against it, exhausted. There, it was done. The decision made for ever. She would not look back. She took off the tigerskin and slipped on her nightdress. Soon sleep would come. But it did not. She heard the door handle moving, watched it, fascinated, knowing all she had to do was leap out and open it and she would be in Lucien's arms. Somehow she managed to resist temptation, and outside Philippe, unused to failure, returned thoughtfully to his room.

Nell tossed restlessly. Too late now to run after Lucien, call him back. She had made her choice. The moonlit night, still warm, mocked her, as the curtains stirred faintly in the breeze. How could she sleep on a night like this, with her body still restless from desire?

And then she heard it. An insidious sighing – no, a tune. A whistling from the garden, faint, growing louder. *Au près de ma blonde* . . .

It *was* nearer. Right underneath her window. She tried to bury the sound in the pillow, but it insidiously fought its way on through her head, carried on the June night air. She got out of bed, ran to the open window, a magic casement opening on faery seas forlorn. Laughing up at her, still whistling, Lucien, a black pirate etched in the moonlight, was climbing up through the roses, on the wall supports, thorns tearing at him and ripping his clothes. *Au près de ma blonde* . . . Only a rose and a heartbeat away before he laughed at her triumphantly and swung one leg over the sill.

'Tell me to go,' he mocked, still astride, and when she did not, quickly jumped down into the room.

She hated him for his arrogant confidence; she hated

him for the smile that taunted her as he threw off the jerkin, clad now only in shirt and tights; she hated him for the way he held out his arms and waited; she hated him even as she threw herself into them, feeling his hard body against hers through the thin satin of the nightdress, hated him because she did not have the strength or the desire to resist him any longer, hated him because she forgot all else save the need to be with him, hated him because he had made her love him when she did not want to – and knew she lied in all of these. She did not hate him. She knew only love as he tore off the nightdress, swept her off her feet and carried her triumphantly to bed.

Chapter Seven

Back in London on Monday morning the reality of Robert's murder became inescapable. The weekend newspapers had carried a brief paragraph that the popular star of last year's musical comedy *Mountain Ranger* had been found dead; foul play, it managed to convey, was suspected. Monday's newspaper showed no such reticence. 'Melissa Hargreaves' husband murdered.' 'Melissa Hargreaves too distraught to be interviewed.' 'Melissa Hargreaves under doctor's care.' And suspicion? wondered Nell fearfully, as she hurried late into Gadsby's.

Fortunately Angela had not been expecting her that day, but even so she felt guilty. Buyers – especially the wife of the Store director – should set an example, was Gadsby's creed. Lucien had driven her back to Eaton Square, where she had been half perplexed and half relieved to find Tom had not returned. It postponed the moment of having to face him, but also raised unwelcome questions. Questions she would deal with later, she told herself, as she flung the newspapers aside. At lunchtime she would go to see Melissa, and find out for herself what was happening. So far at least there was no hint of that other life of Robert's, or even of any rift between the 'happy' couple. How long would it take?

She found no escape in the routine of work, however. The whole store was talking of the murder, from the trotters to the buyers, taking a vicarious pleasure in their erstwhile connection with Melissa Hargreaves. The trotters speculated wildly, so far as Nell could overhear from their whispers, on Melissa's jealous lovers; the buyers on the increasing seriousness of robbery in London by cat burglars prepared to stop at nothing.

Never had Nell been less enthusiastic over the rival merits of pink piping or lace trimming for lingerie, or gauze or georgette for bridge coats, or whether a husband might prefer to see his wife clad in absinthe green or skyblue camiknickers. Had she only parted from Lucien two hours ago? It already seemed a lifetime, and responsibilities weighed down on her from all directions. Gadsby's, Tom – and above all, Melissa. She could imagine her panic – there was no knowing what she might say, and Tom would be no help. As soon as she could decently leave for lunch, she hurried to get a taxi to Melissa and Robert's St John's Wood home. Her heart sank as she saw a policeman guarding the door. Summoning her brightest, most confident air she strode up to him.

'I'd like to see Mrs Stockbridge, please,' she told him.

'So would the inspector, miss,' the police constable told her woodenly. 'Are you a friend of hers?'

No point in denying it. 'Yes,' she said.

'She's done a bunk,' was his unexpectedly open comment. 'Any idea where she might have gone?'

Nell groaned inwardly. Trust Melissa.

'No. I'll think about it,' she told him, uneasiness growing, and leaving her name and address, returned to Gadsby's.

The mystery of where Melissa had vanished to was easily solved when she returned to Eaton Square that evening. Tom met her at the door, half apprehensive at seeing her, half proud of what he had to relate: 'We've got Melissa in the blue room,' he told her. 'She's asleep, poor little thing.'

'How is she?' Nell asked, genuinely concerned, though a part of her was wrily contemplating some well-chosen words to the 'poor little thing'.

'Very cut up, naturally. I'm very worried about her. Glad you've come home, Nelly,' he added.

He did not look worried, she noted. In fact, he looked rather well. That treacherous thought returned. He'd been away two nights – and Melissa was Melissa. She dismissed the thought impatiently; after all, she was in no position to cast stones. Her heart gave a painful thud, thus reminded so sharply of Lucien.

'Tell me about it,' Nell demanded, and he followed her into the morning room. 'I've only read what's in the newspapers, and that's precious little.'

He poured a whisky and soda, and handed it to her. She looked at it with distaste. 'Take it,' he said. 'It will perk you up.' She grimaced but obeyed.

'He was stabbed with a kitchen knife, found on the floor of the bedroom.'

'At least they can't think Melissa did it,' said Nell thankfully. She glanced at his face. 'Can they?' sharply.

'It's not so simple as that,' he mumbled. 'They think she may have been present, or known something about it. It's that Jack Fisher fellow,' he said vehemently. 'Melissa's such a trusting outspoken little thing, everyone knew Robert was refusing to divorce her and that she wanted to marry that fellow. Apparently he was piling on the pressure. The bounder! Telling her if she didn't get free of Robert, she'd seen the end not only of him, Jack, but her film career too. And –' he looked studiedly into his glass '– there were other threats he made, too, that I can't go into. Why didn't she come to *me*! I'd have seen him off all right. It's him did it, of course, not her. You know Melissa – she's so friendly and trusting she gets into all sorts of scrapes.'

Perhaps he knew a different Melissa to her, thought Nell, listening to him, even though she worried about her herself. '*Was* Fisher there?'

233

'Yes. She doesn't deny it. They were both there earlier trying to persuade Robert to change his mind about the divorce, but she says nothing happened and they'd both left before he died. That was about four o'clock the police think. She thinks it was a burglar who did it.' He looked at Nell hopefully as if she might confirm this extraordinary theory.

'That sounds pretty unlikely to me,' declared Nell. 'In fact, so does her whole story,' she added, to his obvious disapproval.

'The place stunk to high heaven of booze. I think it was blasted Fisher himself stabbed him. Probably drunk, and terrified her into saying nothing.'

'They could be innocent,' Nell pointed out, her mind racing through endless dark possibilities, none of them good for Melissa, as she walked upstairs to visit the lady herself.

Melissa opened her forget-me-not blue eyes wide. Her golden-haired head was on the pillow, the rest tucked beneath the lavender-coloured sheets. 'Nell,' she whispered tremulously, 'can you ever forgive me?'

Nell sat at her bedside. 'For what?' she asked cautiously.

'Coming here, burdening you like this. I asked Tommy to bring me here just so that I could be with *you*. You're the one person who's always sane in the middle of a whirlwind. How do you manage to be so sensible and controlled, Nell?'

If only she knew, thought Nell wrily, a memory of last Saturday night leaping unbidden into her mind, of Lucien laughing at her as she performed a nude and solo tango with a rose between her teeth, and then it was no longer solo – and then—

'I'm just naturally dull,' she said lightly, telling her body to quench its unwelcome flame.

'Yes,' agreed Melissa seriously, 'I suppose so. And

234

that's why you're so good for me.'

'Sometimes, Melissa, you—' Nell broke off in despair. What was the use? Melissa was Melissa, and that was that.

'What am I going to do now, Nell?' Melissa asked plaintively, but there was a note of real desperation in her voice.

'That depends on what you've already done,' replied Nell flatly. 'Tom told me Jack and you were together at the flat earlier in the afternoon. Do the police think he could have been killed then? Or that you left Jack there and he did it himself? And, oh, Melissa, do they know about Robert's double life? And yours, come to that,' she declared roundly.

A pause. Then, 'I don't think so.'

'But suppose it was one of his lovers? Or even one of yours?' Nell was appalled. 'Do *you* think Jack went berserk and did it after you'd left?'

'He could have done,' Melissa said with what seemed eagerness in her voice. 'He has the temper – and the motive. How do I know?'

'But where is Jack? What does he say?'

'He denies it. But then he would,' Melissa said quickly.

'And I take it you didn't do it yourself?' Nell watched her carefully.

Melissa's eyes flew open in what seemed to be genuine indignation. 'Of course not! Nell, how *could* you think that. It *must* have been Jack.'

'You want it to be him, don't you?' said Nell, dumb-founded. 'I thought you loved him. Why—' She broke off, swallowing hard, trying to put her thoughts in order. 'Melissa, you've got to tell the police about Robert and yourself. Suppose it was one of your—'

'No,' she said, her face turning ugly. 'No, I can't. I can't. It was Jack, Jack, *Jack*!' she began to shout hysterically.

'The police will find out anyway,' said Nell soothingly,

'as soon as they really investigate.'

'But surely they won't investigate too far?' muttered Melissa, alarmed. 'Jack's the obvious suspect.'

'Yes,' admitted Nell. 'But suppose he's innocent?'

'Oh!' wailed Melissa. 'I thought you loved me.' Hysterical sobs then: 'Don't you see? Suppose it *was* one of those people Robert brought home. Sometimes he . . .' She added in a small voice, 'We weren't very particular. Oh, Nell, don't desert me. I can't bear everyone knowing. I'll be notorious. I want everyone to go on loving me.'

'A murder charge won't incline people to go on loving you,' said Nell, exasperated. So that was the reason she was so eager to blame Jack. 'And that's entirely possible either for both of you or Jack alone, when it comes out you were lovers.'

'You're right.' Melissa stared at her thoughtfully. 'But there's no proof. The knife had been wiped clean of fingerprints,' she added querulously, her voice rising. 'And anyway, we didn't do it.' Her sobs began to increase in volume, bringing Tom racing into the bedroom.

'What are you saying to upset her, Nelly?' he asked indignantly.

'Go away, Tommy, there's a dear,' said Melissa brightly through her tears. 'I need to talk to Nell. She's so much more sensible than you.'

His face stiffened in hurt resentment and he left without a backward glance.

'Dear Tommy,' said Melissa inconsequentially, smiling innocently at Nell.

Nell knew that smile of old, and knew what it meant. Melissa was just the slightest bit ashamed of something she had done, something she could not or would not discuss with Nell. And on this occasion it confirmed Nell's suspicions. Going to bed with Tom would mean nothing to Melissa, if she needed him temporarily as she had done this weekend – but what would it do to Tom? Only remind him that what obviously worked only too well on Melissa failed with his wife.

'Melissa, for Jack's sake *and* yours, you must tell them about Robert before they find out for themselves.'

'How can I?' said Melissa sulkily, plucking at the bedclothes. 'You don't know what it's like. Suppose I tell them about the clubs Robert went to? They'd show Robert's photograph around – and sometimes we went to the same ones, you see. So it's impossible. You must realise that.'

'Then what are you going to do?' said Nell bleakly. 'If you don't tell them, I will. I'm not going to have you arrested—'

'They wouldn't dare!' Melissa sat bolt upright in panic. 'I forbid you to tell them, Nell. Promise, promise, *promise* me you won't?'

'But—'

'It's my life. You'll ruin me. You will, you will!'

'Then you must do it,' said Nell intransigently.

'Go away, Nell.' Real weariness in her voice, no acting now. Melissa slipped down under the sheets again and in seconds was asleep, the ugly flush and worry lines ironed out to give her the beauty of a sleeping child. Nell tucked in the sheets, bending over her and kissing her cheek.

'I'll have to do it, darling. You know that, don't you?' she whispered as Melissa slept peacefully on.

To her amazement, Melissa appeared at breakfast before Nell left for the store. She was brighter than Nell herself, and thankfully seemed to have taken her homily to heart.

'I'm going back home after I've been to the studios today. I've been thinking it over. I will go to the police, Nell. You're quite right. It's best to tackle things head on. What perfectly delightful coffee this is, darling. No wonder Tommy married you.'

★ ★ ★

237

'You drove her away,' Tom accused her when Nell returned that night.

'Of course I didn't,' she said, hurt at his attitude. 'If you'd been up earlier you'd have heard her tell me she was due at the studios today and then wanted to go home after seeing the police.'

'I went to the studios,' he shouted. 'She wasn't there, and hadn't been. Or at home.'

'Then she was with the police,' said Nell, firing up. It was unlike Tom to be so unfair.

'Inspector Johns to see you, Mr Gadsby, Mrs Gadsby,' Hornton annouced disdainfully. His whole bearing seemed to imply that it had been bad enough to have to endure unexpected guests, even if it was the first Mrs Gadsby, but with murder now touching the household so unmistakably in the form of detectives, his personal dignity was impugned.

Johns was a small man – why had she always thought detectives would look like Sexton Blake? Nell wondered. This one looked like that ferret-faced counting house clerk at Gadsby's.

'I understand Mrs Stockbridge stayed here,' he began in a monotonous voice, just like the clerk's. 'But that you were enquiring after her today at her home, Mr Gadsby?'

'Nothing's happened to her, has it, Inspector?' Nell asked in alarm.

'Not in the sense you mean, Mrs Gadsby.' He sounded almost bored. 'She's left the country.'

'*What*?' Tom bounded out of his chair. 'She didn't tell me. I'd have gone with her.'

The inspector blinked at this surprising statement and Nell hastily intervened, furious though she was.

'My husband and I are close friends of Mrs Stockbridge, Inspector. Naturally we want to do all we can for her. My husband means he would have accompanied her to the police. She was scared of approaching you on her own.'

No choice now. The fool, oh, the fool! Nell was thinking. Now the police would be sure of her guilt. *Could* Melissa have done it? Could she at least have egged Jack on?

'Went with that fellow Fisher, I suppose,' Tom asked suddenly, as if picking up her thought.

'No.'

'Looks bad for Fisher, then,' said Tom with some satisfaction.

'I don't think Jack Fisher would murder anyone,' said Nell bluntly. 'He's too fond of his own skin, for all his jealousy.'

'The heat of passion, Mrs Gadsby,' murmured Johns lugubriously. Passion? Did he know what passion was? Nell wondered irrelevantly, perhaps to postpone the shock of thinking about Melissa. Did he mutter words of passion and love to a Mrs Johns each night . . . She was being stupid. She must think of Melissa.

'Where has she gone? Do you know?'

'They, Mrs Gadsby, not she. Mrs Stockbridge wasn't alone.'

'But I thought you said—'

'She was accompanied by a gentleman by the name of André Messines, another film director I gather.'

'I've never heard of him,' said Nell, astounded, wondering wildly whether Melissa had merely picked him up by chance on the railway train. No, of course not. She'd just planned an escape route. Melissa always had a fall-back position – in every sense, she thought bitterly. In case she tired of Jack, she would have her next choice already selected. And how convenient that had been this weekend. To have run away with Jack would have doubly confirmed their guilt. Melissa must know he was guilty was Nell's conclusion. Either that or she was guilty herself. But suppose neither of them were? Perhaps Melissa wanted her to believe them guilty, so that she would not tell the police about Robert's sexual life. Yes. Her heart sank. That was probably it.

'They've boarded the Blue Train for the Riviera, Mrs Gadsby. We're keeping an eye on them.' He watched her face impassively.

How typical of Melissa, thought Nell wearily. No travelling quietly or hiding in remote villages in far-off countries for her. She was probably staying at the Carlton or the Negresco. At least they obviously weren't going to arrest her. Not yet anyway.

'Are you arresting Jack Fisher?' She licked her lips nervously.

'Questioning him, Mrs Gadsby.'

'Then there's something you should know,' she began awkwardly. Avoiding Tom's horrified expression, she explained about Robert's life, as circumspectly as she could, and omitting the sexual competition between Melissa and Robert.

'Aren't you overlooking something, Mrs Gadsby?' Johns enquired impassively when she'd finished. 'It doesn't have to be one of Stockbridge's male – companions. Suppose Mrs Stockbridge had other gentlemen friends of her own? This film director – or even less savoury ones.'

'If you knew about all this, why did you let me go on?' Nell burst out angrily.

'One can always learn more, Mrs Gadsby, by listening. The Pink and Blue Club for instance, I hadn't heard of that one. I'll pay them a visit.'

When Johns had left, Tom's anger exploded. Anger not at Melissa but at Nell. 'Why didn't you tell me?' he demanded.

'She made me promise not to tell anyone about her needs—'

'No,' he said grimly, 'I knew about them. I mean about Robert.'

'Robert?' she repeated, astounded he was more upset about Robert's homosexuality than about Melissa.

'Poor little girl, what she's had to put up with.'

Nell's jaw dropped open. Poor little girl indeed. 'And just how sorry are you for her, Tom? Did she invite you to her bed this weekend so you could cheer her up?'

He flushed bright pink. 'That's between her and me. We were married, you know.'

'And now you're married to me,' Nell said bitterly, seeing the wasted years past, the terrible prospect of empty years ahead. Unless . . .

'You don't do so badly, Nell,' he said awkwardly. 'Melissa told me about you and that fellow—'

She froze. Melissa, her friend. Her betrayer.

'You've been seeing Philippe—'

'*Philippe*?' She didn't know whether to cry with outrage or relief. Lucien was her other life, the life of the real Nell Watkins. The one who existed here was a shell, and she fought against the whole idea of the two overlapping. This was her method of survival, and she must, *must* maintain it. 'Do you mind?' she managed to say inanely, not denying his charge.

'Of course I mind,' he said, staring at her. 'What the hell do you think?'

'I don't see how you can reproach me, Tom. You married me under false pretences – and look what's happened.' She meant Melissa but he took it more personally as a reflection on his failure.

He flushed bright red. 'I'm sorry, Nelly – I haven't been much of a husband to you, one way and another, and especially one way,' he said jerkily. 'I can't blame you. I suppose it's too late now? If I went to see the quacks . . .' He broke off for there was no enthusiasm in his voice.

'How could it help? It's in your mind not your body, Tom,' she said gently. 'You can love Melissa, but not me. Why don't we – couldn't we? – oh, Tom.' She could not restrain herself. 'Melissa needs you. She really does. This new man won't last. Why don't we divorce or get a decree of nullity?' (Lucien! Lucien!) 'We could, you know. Then you could return to Melissa where you belong. And I could—'

'No,' he shouted, red in the face. '*No!*'

Her hopes punctured like a balloon. 'Why not? It's the rational thing to do,' she persevered. 'Think about it at least. It will mean a lot of bad publicity, but we can survive that.'

'No. *She* suggested that too,' he yelled at her. 'It would suit you both. It won't work. I won't marry her again. I can't—'

'Why not?' said Nell, bewildered. 'I don't understand.'

'No,' he said savagely. 'How can you? You don't know what it was like to be married to Melissa. Well, I'll tell you. I loved her, and I still do. Always will. She dances through my mind like a plague of ants. She's always there. The only time she goes away is when I'm with you, Nelly. Being married to her is like roaring round Brooklands at 105 mph day in day out. You can't do it – it wears the old engine out. But Melissa wants to. Oh, yes. And if it isn't your motor it's someone else's. No matter whose. Just as you said. It doesn't stop when you marry.

'It wasn't too bad at first. At least they were decent chaps. But when you come home and find a damned navvy in your bed, or a prize fighter, always a different one – I protested, you know. She said she'd reformed. I thought she had. Then I found out she had a flat of her own. Pinched the key one day. Went to see. It was horrible, Nelly, horrible. Photographs, place full of photographs – that sort of photograph. And other things. I put my foot down. Said I'd leave her. But she laughed in my face. She thought I wouldn't.

'Then that Christmas. Her and that fellow Fisher in the wardrobe. What you probably never saw, Nelly, was that they weren't the only two in there, they'd got a footman too. Wedged in like blasted sardines. Under Grandpop's roof! That was the end. Yet she still knows if she lifts her little finger and says she'll give me five minutes of her marvellous body, I'll come running,' he said bitterly. 'Maybe I will. But I won't marry her again.' He looked at her. 'You still want to send me back?'

'No,' she managed to say through trembling lips, 'but we can't go on as we are. I still want an annulment—'

'An annulment?' he repeated, amazed. 'What the hell do you think I am? You think I can stand *that*?' He began to shake, then to cry. Appalled, she stood frozen for a moment, then ran to him and he clung to her. 'You're all that stops me going out of my mind, Nelly. You and the desert,' he said oddly. 'You deserve better than me. But how can I let you go? Do anything you want, but I'm not letting you go.'

In the midst of summer, glorious, glorious summer, how to think of autumn? Even of winter? The fashion trade was like that, Nell told herself firmly. But this year it was different, for there was Lucien. Lucien who made the summer dance away and whirled her into ecstasy. Lucien whom she saw formally sometimes by day in his fashion house if she walked, oh so casually, down Conduit Street, or he strolled through Gadsby's, or else glimpsed at a fashion function, at Goodwood, Henley, even once at Brooklands. And it did not trouble her, for this was some other Lucien; hers was the one she knew when he was hers alone, late into the summer's night, wandering on a river towpath or motoring slowly back along the English lanes after a weekend in France.

But now August was here, and already fashion eyes were turning to Paris, dropping mysterious hints. Paris was something that beckoned enticingly again, for this year she had won Jonathan Gadsby's reluctant approval to her going there as buyer for the Sporting Wear Department. (To his pleasure – which he would never reveal to her – its turnover had risen to make it a prominent feature of Gadsby's once again, now rivalling the Fashion Department.) Lucien too was to find it necessary to visit Paris for the autumn dress parades.

First there was work . . .

'The uneven hemline reigns supreme,' read out Miss Gertrude from a magazine, clearly disapproving of such untidiness.

'Please remember what Nell told you. Don't think of what we'd wear, but of what she'd wear. And after all, Gertrude, our Nell is developing into a comely young woman,' Mrs Emmeline added thoughtfully, looking at her glowing face and bright eyes.

'And people younger than me,' said Nell quickly, remembering all too vividly Mrs Emmeline's powers of logical thought. 'It's the Sporting Wear Department, after all. Our customers can be anything from sixteen to sixty – eighty even,' she hastily amended in view of her company. 'They watch as well as participate. It's a whole new fashion market.'

'I keep wishing dear Jonathan would put you in charge of the Fashion Department, Nell dear,' said Miss Gertrude wistfully. 'Such fun I'd have with godets. And young people nowadays simply do not appreciate how much can be achieved with a nice dart.'

Mrs Emmeline remained diplomatically silent.

'Well, why not?' said Nell. 'What more practical for afternoon sports dresses than godets and darts?' She giggled, for the distinction between true frocks and those in what was now the Leisure and Sporting Department was getting narrower by the day. A fact of which Mrs Emmeline, she was sure, was quite aware and chose to ignore.

'Not lace, of course, but how about using a godet of

wool in tweed golfing skirts? That would give slim hips –
just like the pleated draping effect in the '80s, do you
remember, Emmeline? – and plenty of room for the lower
limbs,' Gertrude said primly. 'Quite revolutionary, I
think,' she added, highly pleased with herself.

'Very,' said Nell enthusiastically. Wait till Miss Gertrude saw the chrome leather flying suits for ladies she'd
ordered, with their suede linings and breeches reaching
right down to the ankle, moulded nearly to the shape of
the leg. She could hardly wait for their arrival. She'd got
the exclusive market, and hugged the knowledge happily to herself, thinking of Lucien's face when he
realised Maison la Ferté hadn't thought of flying suits
first.

Such discussions took time, occupied much of her
working day. But that still left time for pleasure . . .

'Madame Gadsby should naturally have an apartment
of her own, and not share the hotel with the other more
common buyers of Gadsby, *n'est-ce pas*?'

'*Certainement*,' Nell agreed happily, entering the small
pink-washed house set back in a courtyard in Vincennes.

'I, myself, have much urgent work to do, and have
therefore taken an apartment in Paris in order to be on
hand for the maximum amount of time, rather than
travelling in from my father's house in St Germain or the
chateau. You understand that for this purpose Vincennes
counts as close at hand.' He took the key from her hand
and opened the front door.

'*Je comprends parfaitement, Comte Lucien*,' she replied
gravely, seeing his luggage already installed.

'And you have no objection?' as he closed the door
behind them.

'For once the buyer for Gadsby's is entirely satisfied
with the la Ferté suggestion,' she pronounced gravely.

A battle of love, a battle of work. She was due to attend
two parades at Lelong and at Chanel, for these were

where she had bought in the past. She had no excuse to request a ticket for Maison la Ferté – that was solely Mr Langer's privilege now, for she had broken with them even for teagowns and old Ample still doggedly went to Mennais. She longed to see the la Ferté collection, but her pride would not let her beg. Until the very last moment as, looking critically in the mirror, Lucien adjusted his tie, smoothed down the last wrinkle from his formal suit and disciplined an exceptionally daring lock of hair back into place.

'I am free this evening,' Nell announced calmly, knowing the parade at Maison la Ferté was timed for six o'clock. 'We could meet for dinner, so perhaps you could get me a ticket to see the collection? It would be more convenient.'

'*Non*,' he said, continuing to make the minutest adjustments to his tie.

'Why not?' she said indignantly.

'You do not wish to buy models. That is not your job. You wish to spy,' he informed her firmly. 'This I know.'

'Mrs Amble especially asked me to see the la Ferté collection so that she could consider transferring our business back to you.' Let him get out of that.

'Mrs Amble did no such thing. I spoke to the good lady before I left London.'

'Oh,' said Nell, deflated.

'It is war, perfidious Albion. You remember? I will, however—'

'Yes?' she said eagerly.

'Tell you about it when I return.'

She looked crossly at the baguette and cheese which the kitchen offered, and decided against them. She too would dine out. She sallied forth to the main street of Vincennes where a small local restaurant, charmed with an English milady, plied her with food, courtesy and compliments enough to give balm to her wounded pride. Lucien did not return until after twelve.

'I have dined with a beautiful Italian buyer,' he informed her.

'I'm very glad.' She yawned ostentatiously, not looking up from her book.

'You too are beautiful,' he told her placatingly, kneeling at her side and laughing at her.

She glared at him. 'I'm not.'

'Ah, but you are.' He pulled her up and frogmarched her into the bedroom, standing behind her in front of a full-length mirror. 'I have made you a beautiful woman, Nell,' he told her complacently. 'See. Have I not?'

'You are so arrogant,' she complained, laughing at last. 'It's nothing to do with you, even if you're right,' she amended hastily.

'Love has made you beautiful,' he conceded. 'But then I made love, did I not?'

'Invented it,' she agreed politely.

He laughed. 'And now, my Nell, I shall make you more than beautiful. I will give you *chic*. I will give you style. I will give you Maison la Ferté, the line you so much disdain, and I will make Nell Watkins the most admired woman in society.'

'I don't want to be the most admired woman in society,' she said crossly. 'I want to be me. Anyway,' belligerently, 'what's wrong with my clothes?'

He sighed. 'You recognise style on others, but you do not yet apply it on yourself. You wear now nice clothes that suit you, and think that is enough. But you follow Melissa's style – what she says suits you. And because she is jealous, she misleads you.'

'*Jealous*? Of me?'

'*Naturellement*. You are happy, she is not.'

Nell considered this. 'Perhaps,' she conceded. 'But you are wrong about the reason she may mislead me over

247

clothes. She isn't petty. If she does it, it's because they're colours that would suit her.'

'*Peut-être*,' he said grudgingly. 'But nevertheless, this *thing* –' he picked up a corner of her dress and dropped it again, sighing heavily '– it is enough for Gadsby's no doubt, but it is not enough for Maison la Ferté.'

'What are you going to do about it?' she said, twisting free of his grasp and challenging him, arms akimbo.

'This.' And like lightning he was behind her, unbuttoning the frock – one of Miss Gertrude's sports evening frocks, which she'd donned since she wasn't to be called upon to appear *en grande tenue* at Maison la Ferté. As she struggled, he held her firmly with one hand, tickling her till she doubled up with laughter and he could remove her dress with ease.

'*Eh bien*,' he declared, freeing her and holding up the frock. 'What have we here? The material . . . it is good but of entirely the wrong shade of blue for Miss Watkins. As is also the shade of contrasting blue on collar and waistband. It makes the other blue look dull and washed out. The style is very good—'

'She's Gadsby's own designer,' Nell told him proudly.

'Then I must ask Philippe to seduce your new designer also.'

Nell burst out laughing. 'I'd like to see him try. She's—' She stopped quickly before saying 'seventy-four'. She'd kept the secret of Miss Gertrude's identity so far and she'd go on doing so. 'I think you'll find her impervious to Philippe's charm,' she finished demurely.

'Then I shall try myself,' Lucien said dismissively, while she giggled. 'Now, the cut – it is terrible. That too is Gadsby's, yes? And cut is all-important. I shall dress you myself from now on.'

'You seem to be more efficient at undressing me,' she said crossly, suddenly annoyed at having a business discussion in flimsy chemise, brassière and knickers.

'Ah, this you must not mind. I am not a man at the moment. I am head of the Maison la Ferté's English branch, anxious only to perfect my customer's toilette. You recall Monsieur Worth ordered the Princess Metternich and all his other customers to attend at his Maison before entering a grand ball so that he might check the final details of their toilette in order that his reputation might not be disgraced? So I do the same—' He swooped on her, holding her down on the bed. 'Now how *dull* this chemise. For what purpose? It has no strength, no body. No, this we can do without. This brassière and knickers? *Oh, la, la! Demodées*. This season's lingerie is so much more feminine, like the la Ferté frocks. Fuller dresses, tulle, net – no more of these satin rags. Women are to be women again, Miss Watkins. And my professional eye tells me those stockings are not of the finest Lyon silk, nor the suspender belt of any distinction whatsoever.'

'Leave my underwear alone,' she shouted, struggling in vain. 'If you're a professional you shouldn't be tearing off my underclothes. I can't imagine Monsieur Worth doing that.'

'A true professional will make any sacrifice for his art,' he told her, sighing. 'And these – must go. Tomorrow we create you anew.' His hands mercilessly ripped her remaining clothes off. 'And now,' he said, pleased, having completed his handiwork and keeping her firmly in place, 'you are naked, my Nell, the professional has finished his work. And the man may begin.'

Though she would not admit it to Lucien, Nell was rather pleased with the effect in the mirror the following day after the contents of several boxes had been spilled out and donned. Facing her was a svelte lady in a low waistlined sheathlike dress with pleated skirt and blue trimmings, a tiny blue hat to match. Simple, yet it made Nell Gadsby look suddenly a different person. She considered this for a while, wondering whether she wished it to be so. Yes, she decided. *Yes*. After all, the old Nell had not exactly been a brilliant success in achieving her ambitions. Perhaps this one might do better?

She spent the next two days going from one collection to another. From some she was turned away, at others, from whom she had bought in the past, she was welcomed. Some seemingly had open doors. Frocks, jumper suits, sports clothes . . . all she seemed to remember afterwards was an endless procession of legs. She even dreamed about them, had nightmares of armies and armies of legs, each with a different coloured hem above it, some dipping, some straight – and never anything above them, just the relentless army of legs threatening to swamp her. She even woke up screaming and drenched in sweat one night to find Lucien at her side, comforting her. 'I'm sorry.' She shook the nightmare free of her. 'I am dreaming of legs,' she managed to say.

'*Moi, aussi*,' he murmured lovingly, drawing her down beside him.

One thing still eluded her – knitwear. She had no designer in England, and no supplier here that she could afford. Yet she was sure if she could find the right supplier – a Coco Chanel of her very own – then she could extend the boundaries of leisure wear just a little further.

It was in the market, that she saw it. The ordinary twice a week vegetable market in Vincennes. She could not face another day in Paris, and was wandering aimlessly around Vincennes itself – the park, the château, the zoo – when on her way back she stopped to buy cheese and vegetables for a picnic lunch. She was halfway through struggling to explain just how much Tôme de Savoie she required, when she saw it. It flashed by on the back of a young dark-skinned girl pushing her way out from the charcuterie stall in the next row of stalls. With a quick apology to the stallholder, Nell ran, diving in and out of huddles of gossiping women and determined shoppers, until at last she caught her. It was beautiful. Red – no, cherry coloured – and such soft knitted wool, but cut as if it were tailored, as if it were tweed. And the design – it was like a Matisse, she thought, dazed. Yet this girl was no Paris society woman. How could she afford it? Was it stolen perhaps? She summoned up her best French.

Nell looked doubtfully at the slip of paper in her hand and continued to climb round and round the never ending staircase. The *ninth* floor? In an old crumbling block of flats in Vincennes? Such a designer came from here? The name on the door was correct: Maniosta. She knocked. Nothing. Knocked again. This time the door flew open.

She must be over six foot, thought Nell when she'd recovered her breath. But height was not what one looked at. It was her blazing dark eyes and the mane of dark frizzy hair that stuck out almost horizontally from her head in two huge wings. And what was she wearing?

Nell sighed in pure happiness. 'May I come in?' she asked.

Saying nothing, though clearly suspicious, the girl held the door open for her to pass. She walked into a small room, crowded with wools and fabrics, knitwear lying casually on chairs and sofa, a small cutting table.

'Do you speak English?' she asked the girl.

'*Inglese, non.*'

'French?'

A shrug. '*Peu.*'

Then I'm going to have to learn Italian, thought Nell resignedly.

'So how do you amuse yourself today?' asked Lucien that morning.

'I've been designing in the Vincennes market,' said Nell innocently, trying not to reveal her excitement.

251

Lucien looked at her sharply. 'You design dresses of bananas, perhaps, like Josephine Baker's?'

'Not quite,' she said lightly. 'You'll have to wait and see. And so will Philippe.'

His face clouded. 'Have you seen him while you have been in Paris?'

'No,' she said, surprised. 'Of course not.'

'I believe he knows – or has guessed – about us.'

'Does it matter so very much?' she asked. 'Are you worried about your father knowing?'

'*Non*. It is Philippe I am worried about. He is not one to let valuable information go unused – and he will not use it lightly. If he sees a chance to do me real harm, then he will use it. Not otherwise.'

'Then let there be no such chance,' she said stoutly.

'Perhaps the matter may answer itself,' he said quietly, and when she looked at him, uncertain what he meant, continued: 'I do not think, Nell, that I can continue always unable to claim you as my own, whatever the situation between you and Tom.'

'But we've discussed this. I've explained—'

'Yes, you've explained. But I do not fully understand. You say you love me and not Tom. You say Tom says he still loves Melissa, but that he will not go back to her. Melissa has not been faithful to him; she is a *femme du monde*, that is true. But men have survived more. And she needs looking after, that one. Tom is excellent at that. *Why* does he not go back to her?'

But that was the one question Nell could not answer. Had promised not to answer.

There had been silence from Melissa apart from one postcard sent, as Nell had foreseen, from the Carlton in Cannes. It announced she was having a perfectly splendid time. Every day Nell expected to read of Jack's arrest, but it never happened. After many dark hints, the newspapers

252

fell silent on the subject of the Stockbridge murder until one weekend news broke of Robert's double life. There was not a word about Melissa's adventures. Whether it was the libel laws or genuine sympathy for a wronged wife, no word but praise was forthcoming for her. At least in print. Then at last a letter arrived. Nell read it aloud to Tom.

Darling Nell,
   Oh, the wonderfulness of life here. Every day is like a sunny paradise – you can't imagine. Except that I miss my Nell of course. André and I are bliss together. The film is pure art, and André says I'm as good as Lilian Gish and that together we will take the French film industry by storm, then Hollywood. You can't imagine how happy I am.

There was a silence as she put the letter down. 'I think,' she observed, 'life sounds just a little bit too wonderful to be true, don't you? After all, talking films will be here any moment. How will that affect her?'

Tom did not answer. He had picked up the letter and was re-reading it.

Three days later, right at the end of September, Nell read in the newspapers that Daniel Ross, a young film extra, had been arrested for the murder of Robert Stockbridge.

'Film extra?' she queried to Tom, a hollow pit in her stomach.

'It's not what you're thinking,' he replied instantly, defensively. 'He was an habitué of the Pink and Blue Club. That's where Stockbridge picked him up. Nothing to do with Melissa at all.'

Relief flooded through her. 'Thank heavens for that. Are you sure, though?'

'Absolutely, Nelly. Melissa's in the clear.'

253

'These are most interesting garments, Nell,' Mrs Emmeline remarked on a rare visit to the store. Nell whirled round. They were still under covers, but trust Mrs Emmeline to ferret them out.

'Yes,' she replied nonchalantly.

A pause. 'I take it you do not wish me to draw Jonathan's attention to them, my dear?'

Nell took a deep breath. 'They are Sporting Wear,' she said evenly. 'As you can see from the motifs.'

'I do see that this modern young lady swinging a club woven into this most elegantly knitted two-piece has some relevance to sport. But sporting *wear*?'

'Certainly,' said Nell, reddening. 'Where else to wear it but a golfing function? There are spectators as well as players, you know.'

'And this delightful blue dress with aeroplanes taking off at intervals around it?'

'You've no idea the number of people who watch the displays at Hendon,' Nell said firmly, meeting her eye to eye.

'And,' Emmeline rummaged further, 'the pink with the most attractive walnut cake displayed on it?'

'Teagowns,' said Nell weakly. Then burst into laughter. 'Oh, Mrs Emmeline, don't you think they're *fun*? Just look – fun in fashion, along with elegant cut that shouts Paris.'

'I rather think there will be more than Paris shouting,' said Mrs Emmeline resignedly, eyeing the new soft leather flying suit for ladies displayed on a papier mâché model. 'Is this some sort of suit of armour, I wonder?'

'I don't think Lady Lenham would like it,' said Nell. 'But then I doubt if she is going to fly round the world.'

For once Nell had over-estimated London's fashion taste, however. Maria Maniosta's designs stayed firmly on the racks. Each night Jonathan emerged and ordered their removal. Each morning Nell replaced them.

'Come in, come in,' she prayed to oblivious crowds of shoppers.

They did. They giggled, but they did not buy. At last she hit upon the solution. She gave several away free to friends who frequented social events – and she wore them herself. She wore them to Hendon, to all Tom's aviation gatherings, and any other sporting events held in London. Tom never noticed. She wore them, greatly daring, to non-sporting events such as walks in the park or by the river. And Lucien did notice.

'What,' he demanded, fingering a lurid red jacket with a rowing boat across the back, its oars descending the sleeves, 'is this? It is a joke?'

'Not really a joke,' she said. 'Fun.'

'Fun,' he said scornfully, then took a closer look. 'That is from Paris,' he said, surprised. 'This line is not provided by your Miss Gertrude.'

'How did you know about her?' she demanded.

Lucien shrugged. 'It is my business to know,' he said. 'And do not fear. I shall not seduce her.'

She glared at him.

'But this,' he said, 'is a different matter. I wonder. I wonder very much.'

At the end of April Tom flew off once more. He had talked of little else since Christmas, and guiltily she felt nothing but relief when he finally departed. He spoke of attempting to beat the 1927 RAF flight from Khartoum to Nigeria by flying to Cairo and on to the Gold Coast. But somehow she knew that it was not the Gold Coast that beckoned with its enchantment but the Sahara itself. On the return trip he would fly back to Tunis, an even greater part of the Sahara to be crossed. She tried hard to understand its allure, but he failed to convey what called to him so strongly. All she knew was that the desert offered something that she could not.

Three days later she received the phone call. Melissa was incoherent, crying hysterically, and it took some patience on Nell's part to work out what the problem was. It couldn't be the film, surely. She'd read even in the English press about the success of La Folle and its star, Melissa Hargreaves. So it must be a problem with André.

'He's left me, darling. Can you imagine?'

'Why?' Nell demanded. 'And where are you?'

A pause. 'He gave some stupid reason about his not being able to cope with his own success. I didn't believe him, so I badgered him for the real reason. And, oh Nell, I was faithful to him, I really was. He likes helping people, he says, and I don't need help any more. And he says I'm too old. Old, me! I'm only twenty-eight. You've got to come!'

'What do you mean – come?' said Nell. 'I can't, you know that.'

'I'm going to kill myself,' said Melissa. 'I shall, I shall—'

'No, you won't, Melissa,' said Nell wearily.

'I haven't any money,' she sobbed. 'And no work. None of the other directors want to take me.'

'Why not – after the success of La Folle?' Nell asked, startled.

'They say although talking pictures have been held up in France, because of some copyright problem, sooner or later they'll be here. And, oh Nell, I can't speak French! Suppose they're as successful here as they are in England? I'll be ruined. I am ruined. They've turned me out of the hotel.'

'Can't you find a cheaper one?'

A storm of sobbing alarmed her. 'Melissa, where are you?'

But she had hung up.

'I'll have to go, Lucien. What else can I do? I'll take a

week and go and find her. I'd never forgive myself if anything was really wrong with her.'

Melissa adrift penniless on the Riviera was too awful a prospect to contemplate.

'What madness is this, Nell? You cannot go alone.'

'You can't stop me.'

'*Non*, but I can come with you.'

The hillside of La Californie with its huge villas and luscious gardens gleamed in the spring sunshine as the motor-car climbed slowly up the steep winding lanes. Spread out beneath them was the bay of Cannes, with the Pointe de la Croisette on the one side, representing the new Cannes, Palm Beach with its yachts and the summer casino, and on the other Mont Chevalier, the core of old Cannes, the fishing village that had endured ravages by Romans, Barbarians, Saracens and Italians until there came the final subtle invasion they could not resist: the English, spearheaded by Lord Brougham who came here by chance in 1834.

Nell was bewitched. The drive down from Paris on the long straight road through Lyons and Avignon had shown her wonders enough, but nothing prepared her for the beauty of the Riviera coastline itself. Lucien had driven slowly along the winding roads cut through wooded perfumed hillsides, overlooking the spectacular blue Mediterranean; as far as the eye could see, bay after bay was fringed with golden sands and small colourful villages or towns.

Now at last, high up on La Californie, he stopped before huge iron gates. 'Here,' he said, holding the door for her to get out. 'You unlock the gate.' He pushed a huge key into her hand. She stared at it uncertainly for a moment, as though it were the symbol of something far more important than a mere gate to unlock, then planted a quick kiss on his lips and slowly turned the key in the lock, pushing the gate open. He drove inside as she stood gazing at the huge palm trees and cypresses before them.

'Come,' he said, taking her hand and walking up the sloping path and round a corner. And there was the house. Senses were assailed as one as the warm air brought perfumes so heady they were almost stifling. Before her stood a pink-washed stone villa with white columns and windows, green shutters and exotic flowers she did not recognise climbing over the front. Geraniums, for all it was only May, adorned each tiny window balcony and sprawled from terracotta urns on the ground before the house.

'This is your family house?' she asked, amazed. 'How can you even bear to leave it?'

'It is mine. Philippe prefers St Tropez. *Mon père* the Château at Petit Andely. It is called "Villa Fleurie".'

'Is it these flowers I can smell?'

'More than these. The hillsides round Cannes are covered with flowers, especially at its back, for there the *parfumiers* of Grasse grew their flowers. Jasmine, roses, violets, hyacinths. So many.'

Inside the house was cool, with shutters closed against the sun, and a middle-aged man and woman were standing ready to greet them. 'Monsieur and Madame Dufy, Nell.'

She greeted them warmly as they frankly and uncritically appraised her. Their devotion to Lucien was in no doubt from their beaming expressions on seeing him, and she supposed it was natural they should be curious about her. She wondered idly how many other women Lucien had brought here and dismissed the thought firmly as immaterial. That there had been some she had no doubt, but after all, she had never talked to him of her times with Joe – how far away those seemed now. The past was just that – past.

Madame Dufy indicated Nell should follow her, and with a glance at Lucien she followed the housekeeper upstairs and was shown into a bedroom overlooking the front gardens and hillside, down to the blue bay beyond and the small islands lying off the coast. It was a bedroom, she noted, without any sign of masculine possessions, a dismal thought confirmed when only her luggage arrived, courtesy of Monsieur Dufy. A few minutes later, a light tap and Lucien entered.

'You are pleased?'

'I feel like a princess in a castle,' she said sincerely, looking out into the paradise of the Riviera. 'Without a prince,' she added casually.

He laughed and kissed her hand. 'Why, Nell, you English ladies are truly vamps now, all Clara Bows. Now you have *It*, you want only to be with me. It is very flattering.'

'I thought you said women never changed?'

'This is true,' he conceded. 'So, yes, I agree they always want only to be with me. Fortunately,' he added, ducking the indignant push she turned to give him, 'my room is next door.' He paused, then added soberly: 'If only you would marry me, Nell, there would be no need of this – pantomime.' He went out and the door banged behind him.

So easily it happened. All a sea of blue until the underlying rocks revealed their jagged edges. Didn't he realise how much she wanted to marry him? she thought miserably. Did he think she enjoyed being parted from him? Perhaps some day Tom would relent, she thought optimistically. Perhaps this trip to the desert would give him the confidence to face life without her. Perhaps . . .

Lucien seemed himself once more as they sat in front of the villa, enjoying the last of the evening sunshine and waiting for dinner.

'Tomorrow,' he told her, 'I will drive you to Antibes. You shall seek your friend while I return to do business here.'

Stupid of her to think she could monopolise him. 'Business?' she repeated, surprised. 'Here?'

He laughed. 'Where rich holidaymakers flock, couturiers follow. There are several in the town, and it is necessary to ensure one is not left behind. But once your friend is found, and you are happy, then we have some time to ourselves, *hein*? And I will show you Cannes. Not those beaches down there. That is business too, for one must think there of ladies' bodies and what is on them. I will show you instead the real Cannes, and then Provence itself.'

Antibes was hot and dusty, and the studios were nowhere near the sea. Nell had decided these were obviously her first port of call. André might know where Melissa was, even if he was no longer working or living with her. As the day wore on, and no studio claimed knowledge of her, and no hotel either, visions of Melissa starving, prostituting herself or lying drunk in a gutter, grew more lurid. She must have covered every blessed hotel from the top to the bottom in category, and every rooming house in Antibes, Nell thought despairingly. Perhaps Melissa was back in Cannes? No, she'd have gone to Nice rather than Cannes, for there the biggest studios were situated. Tomorrow she'd try there.

The next day boded little better than Antibes. Nice was bigger, noisier, and seemingly just as empty of Melissa. Tired, Nell walked along the Promenade des Anglais, jealously regarding the holidaymakers. At the same time, anxiety for Melissa was sharpening. She glanced up at the palatial Hotel Negresco. Relief, mixed with instant irritation, flooded over her. Melissa was coming out, attired in a frock that Nell recognised as Lucien Lelong and clasping the arm of an elderly gentleman on one side, with a younger, moody and handsome man on the other. She was quite clearly not in the gutter, nor did her beaming smile denote a broken heart. The familiar laugh trilled towards her.

'Melissa!' Nell cried in a strangled voice. She felt hot, sweaty and distinctly unlike the Nell Lucien supposed he had turned her into.

'Darling!' Melissa stood still in astonishment. 'Nell!' A shriek of delight, and she hurled forward to clasp her in her arms. A few words and the men went back into the hotel with an air of resignation on their faces.

'What are you doing here? Is Philippe with you?'

'No,' shouted Nell, goaded. 'I was worried about *you* after your telephone call. That's why I came.'

'Oh, goodness,' Melissa looked concerned. 'It was naughty of me not to write, but everything in London seems so far away. Jack was angry with me for leaving, so was the theatre. It seemed better to forget it on the whole,' she explained.

'Even me?' demanded Nell unbelievingly.

'Oh no,' said Melissa, shocked, 'but I sent you a postcard and I telephoned. After that, I felt better – and, see, you haven't forgotten me, have you?'

'However could I?' cried Nell affectionately, relieved and laughing. 'Do you know, I actually thought you might be in the gutter?'

'Oh, I nearly was,' Melissa assured her happily. 'You wouldn't believe the number of hotels that insisted on my paying their bills. And André was absolutely horrid to me.'

'And who,' asked Nell resignedly, 'were those two men I saw you with?'

'Ah,' said Melissa mysteriously, 'you won't have to ask that much longer. Raoul is a *superb* director. He really is. And he's persuaded that charming gentleman to finance the most wonderful film. It's about Lucrezia Borgia. Apparently she's much misunderstood. And Raoul *believes* in me, you see.'

261

'But talking pictures are coming in,' said Nell, bewildered, trying to cope with the idea of Lucrezia Borgia as a twentieth-century heroine. 'And you can't speak French well enough, that's what you told me.' Memories of the excitement of *The Singing Fool* at the Regal and of people everlastingly singing 'Sonny Boy' since, flooded through her mind.

Melissa impatiently dismissed her fears. 'Raoul says this fad for talking pictures won't last, and even if they come to France, they'll soon disappear. Just like Jack, Raoul believes the real art lies in silent pictures. It's all to do with the loudspeakers. Because they're stationary, you can't move about on talking pictures, so you have to stand still and wait for the camera to fix on your face to show you are the one speaking. How ridiculous. Think of the fluid movement of silent pictures; you can really act in those. Oh, you should see me in the murder scene, Nell. *Lucrezia* is going to be my best film yet. I'm dedicated to my art now, you know.'

'And to Raoul?' Nell cut across this affecting diatribe drily.

A short silence. Then Melissa's famous laugh rang out over the Promenade des Anglais. 'Oh, darling, you of *all* people know what Frenchmen are like. It does make my poor old Tommy rather *dull*, don't you think?'

'So I needn't have bothered,' Nell finished ruefully. 'I feel rather foolish.'

Lucien took her hand. 'I am most glad you bothered,' he said firmly. 'And even more delighted that Melissa has no need of you. For now we have three whole days to ourselves. And for la belle Provence.'

And beautiful it was: tiny Provençal villages, sleepy streets and orange brown roofs clustered together, clinging to their precipitous hillsides with nothing but the barking of the occasional dog to disturb the peace, for holidaymakers rarely infiltrated beyond the coast line. Inland, Provence was theirs. Long, lazy dinners in the villa garden, and warm nights, the shutters creaking occasionally in the slight night breeze. The days were spent wandering the villages – save for the day they took the boat for the Iles de Lérins.

'What's that there?' Nell pointed to the grey fortress that dominated one end of the small island of Ste Marguérite.

'A prison.'

'Sounds *very* exciting.'

'It is no longer a prison. It was the home of the Man in the Iron Mask.'

'As in the Douglas Fairbanks film?' she asked with interest.

'The very same. Only I think a little less dashing, and alas no musketeer came to rescue him. History is duller – or perhaps more exciting, for still no one knows for sure who he was or why he was imprisoned, though there are many theories.'

'And what else?'

'Nothing but a few houses, including one given to Napoleon III's cast-off mistress, when he married Eugénie. A remarkable Englishwoman in fact.' A shadow crossed his face, and he continued hastily: 'There is a restaurant.'

'*Naturellement*,' she said gravely. 'Nowhere in France seems complete without its little restaurant.'

'And woods, where we can wander under the eucalyptus trees and feel ourselves a million miles from Cannes. And small beaches – not good, but where we may be alone, away from the sounds of the Côte d'Azur.'

'All this and the seaside too,' she exclaimed with pleasure. Her visits to the sea had previously been confined to short visits to Whitstable and Margate. They did not resemble Cannes in the slightest. Nor the tiny cove on

263

the far side of the small island, to which they forced a way through undergrowth.

'It is not warm enough to swim, I think,' Lucien said judiciously. 'But to eat, yes.' The sun obediently became warmer, and after finishing the bread and cheese and wine they had brought with them, he took her hand as they looked out on the sea, lapping not far from their feet. 'Tomorrow we return to London, Nell. Will you enjoy that?'

'No,' she said bluntly. 'No—' She turned to him and he took her in his arms. 'You must be brave, Nell,' he said. 'There are times when decisions must be made, leaps taken, no matter what the cost. You know what I'm asking you.'

She was very still. Of course she knew. She raised her face to his. 'I'll leave him, Lucien. I'll tell him as soon as he gets home. I'll come to you.'

He said nothing, but his fingers tightened on her shoulders as he kissed her. The kisses grew stronger, harder, until she felt herself gently pushed back against the rough grass, and there was nothing but the lapping of the waves, the breeze stirring in the tall trees above them, and Lucien above her.

They arrived in London four days later. The first thing they saw was the newspaper placards: 'Missing airman seven days overdue in Tunis.'

Her face blanched. It was Tom, she knew it was. It was hardly necessary even to rush inside the house to confirm the truth.

'Nell, can I do anything?' Lucien asked. 'Let me stay with you while you wait.'

'No,' she said dully. 'I'm better on my own.'

He looked at her face, said, 'Of course,' somewhat bitterly, and left. Locked in guilt and worry, she did not take note of his tone.

264

Tom was found the same night by Bedouins, and was back home ten days later, minus the Moth and two hundred pounds in ransom money, but rather proud of his adventure. 'The desert's the place, Nelly. Odd things happen there. Great fellows, the Bedouins. You should see their tents, and the carpets. And their treasure chests they cart around with them.'

Filled with your money, she longed to point out, but had not the heart to do so. To tell him now? She tried to conceal her impatience and let him talk about the desert, about the silence and the mirages, the colour and the glory, for several days before she broached the subject of the future.

From amicable affection his face changed to obstinacy. 'No, Nell.'

'I mean it this time, Tom, I'm sorry. I'm so sorry, but—'

He thrust his hands in his pockets. 'I won't divorce you, and you can't divorce me – you've no evidence. And you can forget about that other thing,' he said darkly. 'Annulment. You'd need me to agree and I won't do it. I'd counter sue. You'd lose.'

'Then I shall go and live with him.'

'The Dirty Firty family will love that, won't they, Nelly?'

She went white at this uncharacteristic cut. It hadn't occurred to her to consider Lucien's family. Of course he was Catholic and expected to carry on the line. If she loved him, how could she do this to him? Alienate him from his family, and bar him from having legitimate children?

'Tom, please,' she said through dry lips. The dream was slipping away . . . away . . .

'I'm sorry, Nelly.' He looked at her pleadingly, but implacably. 'I really am.' He forced a laugh. 'I don't know who needs you more, me or Melissa, eh?'

And what about me? a small voice clamoured inside her; a flame of rebellion that flickered and died in the knowledge of defeat.

He opened the door. He did not smile, did not kiss her, merely stood aside to let her pass inside.

'I've come to tell you—' she began, and stopped, unable to believe she had to say these words.

'There is no need. What you have come to tell me is written on your face, Nell,' he said quietly. 'If your absence had not already told me.' Then he burst out, 'How could you not come? It is a whole week. Have you no feelings?'

'Oh yes,' she said bitterly. 'I have those all right. He won't let me go, Lucien,' she said flatly. 'I've tried every argument.'

'Then leave him and come to me,' he said, amazed.

'No.'

A pause. 'You have not the courage?' A tone of polite enquiry.

'I don't have the courage to destroy your life by coming to you.'

'You think by leaving me you are not destroying me?'

'I don't know, I don't *know*!' she cried. 'I only know if I come, then I stop you from having the family you want, you need. If I stay away then—'

'Then what?' he said coldly.

'Then,' she forced herself to say, 'there is a chance you will find the nice French girl your family wants. You'll marry and have children, and even if it is not the same,' her voice quavered, 'much of the time you will be content enough. Life's like that.'

He stared at her. 'Nell, there's still something I don't understand.' He banged his fist on the top of a bookcase. 'We have Tom who loves Melissa. We have you who love me – you say. And yet you stay together. You give me reasons, but they do not make sense. Tell me, Nell, *tell me. Why?*'

She looked at him wretchedly. How could she tell him when the secret was not hers but Melissa's? 'It is as I have said,' she stammered. 'I have told you all.'

He paused and then said icily, 'Very well, so I find my oh so beautiful French wife, who will never notice that I do not love her. And if she does, will not mind. We will be happy on Mondays, Wednesdays and Fridays perhaps. But what of you? You will find another lover,' he said bitterly, 'to replace me, to make up for your lack of a husband?'

'No!'

'You will endure without love?'

'If I have to. Yes.'

'Without children?'

'Yes.'

'For what will you live? What else is there?'

'Gadsby's,' she said without thinking, without hope. 'I can live through Gadsby's.'

Chapter Eight

Nell closed the front door behind her. She was home, but it seemed like a prison gate clanging behind her. Before her were the familiar trappings of everyday life: Hornton's back as he entered the breakfast room, the ridiculous china dog that Melissa had fallen in love with and bought, and which Nell had never had the heart to consign to a less prominent place, the blue vase that Mrs Emmeline had bought them as a wedding present. Yet the light had gone from them as surely as from her life.

Why? Lucien's word seemed seared on her heart, such was the pain. And she hadn't even been able to answer. Did she even know the answer? She'd promised to love Tom when she married him, and love him in a way she still did. But not as she loved Lucien, never that. How could she have been such a fool as to mistake her adolescent crush on Tom for love? They had separate bedrooms now, to her relief, since it saved the nightly anguish of frustration over her own stupidity. It was like living in amiable companionship with a brother. Or rather it had been, until now. Now the tearing pain, the constant questioning of whether she was throwing away happiness for nothing, would begin. She must ignore it, never examine that, for that way lay madness – and what use would she be to Tom or Gadsby's then? Lucien must be in the past now. Whether she had made the right or wrong decision, it had seemed to her the only one, and it had been made.

As if mocking her, when she stood hesitating in the doorway of the drawing room, the first thing she saw was the huge photograph of Melissa in *Charleston Lady*, the wedding scene. Marriage wasn't like that, Nell thought bitterly. Smiles and bouquets. They were merely a trap in which if you were unlucky you were imprisoned. And yet they called it love. Too late, too late now for that. Feeling nausea creeping up on her, she fled upstairs. She could not face Tom yet.

Fortunately with the approach of summer he was more and more absorbed with motor racing – and flying. Between them they left him little time for her or for Gadsby's, and he seemed to notice nothing amiss with her, particularly since she found it relatively easy to maintain conversation on these objective subjects for it kept tension at bay. She managed to talk of Brooklands, of Bugattis, of Amelia Earhart, of Amy Johnson, of Lindbergh, with an enthusiasm that was almost genuine, throwing herself into it to such an extent that she almost forgot how real was Tom's involvement. Until one day she returned from work to find him reading *The Seven Pillars of Wisdom*. He put it aside almost reluctantly as she came in.

'You don't fancy yourself as Lawrence of Arabia, do you?' she joked unthinkingly.

Tom didn't laugh. 'I might surprise you yet,' he said. A pause. 'Contrary place, the desert,' he commented, but as she was about to ask more, he fell to studying the book once more.

Relieved to see him happily absorbed and thankful there was no word from Melissa to complicate life, she turned to her own plight again. Not the main cause of pain – there had been no word, no glimpse – but Gadsby's. She had said it could be her life, and now she must make it so. Perversely, for the first time, the prospect terrified her, as of another prison that sought to claim her, another

270

mountain to be climbed, when the summit seemed not worth attaining.

Firmly she told herself that when she set her sights on that summit once more, then her old enthusiasm would return. After all, she was buying for an ever expanding Leisure and Sporting Wear Department as well as for Lingerie. The buying for the latter she was beginning to delegate to Angela through sheer pressure of work. Miss Gertrude had produced some delightful sports dresses of subtly combined dress and jacket; they looked like morning frocks but the yoke was in fact a tight jacket that when removed revealed a strapless short evening dress. There were great possibilities for this style, she was sure. If only Old Ample would expand her range. Nell knew she herself was too near the boundaries of leisure wear to take her frocks much further, but she chafed at the restrictions.

She was too proud to ask Tom's assistance. Indeed, he would have been perplexed had she done so. His responsibilities at Gadsby's still consisted of walking round each department once a day, unless he were engaged elsewhere, a brief chat with the buyers, a glance at the Sporting Wear department and Men's Wear, two minutes in the counting house, and a five-minute chat with Jonathan Gadsby. Once a month he attended a directors' meeting. Of the heaving hive of activity, of the hopes and fears that went on underneath the superficial life of the store, Tom had not the slightest idea, nor would he have cared even if he had. The problems of its future were not his concern. Nell often tried to talk to him about where Gadsby's was going, and what would happen when Jonathan died, only to be told that she underrated him. Whether or not this meant that Tom was convinced Jonathan was immortal, she never discovered, for after a time he would grow impatient and pick up a book or newspaper.

Nell looked wistfully at Paris models displayed in

London stores, afternoon frocks just a little longer now, chiffons and georgettes with a new subtlety. One fabric she particularly liked was printed with designs after Watteau. If only Old Ample had gone back to Maison la Ferté. At least that would have been a good compromise. But no. With Mennais Gadsby's was still locked in old-fashioned charmeuse and heavy silks – where the new age demanded lightness and delicacy, a butterfly effervescence. Yet as the Callot Soeurs had once done in Paris, Old Ample harked back essentially to a bygone era though, alas, far more out of tune with current modes than the Callot sisters. They at least had still operated in a world where time, money and way of life had remained constant for many years. Old Ample looked back across the gulf of war to an age that was dead, not merely changing. Today's customers had not the time, or the money, or the kind of lives that would lend themselves to backward glances.

In Nell's depressed state, pressures seemed to increase everywhere. The buyers' dining room, instead of being an exciting challenge as it had been since the Dragon left, was once again a hotbed of hostility and petty bickering – or so it seemed to her. Nit-picking irrelevancies, and inter-departmental disputes dominated every day.

Three months now and no word of Lucien, let alone *from* him. So many times her footsteps had almost taken her automatically along Conduit Street to gaze in at the windows of Maison la Ferté, but she'd always resisted. Gadsby's and Eaton Square, these were her life, and nothing else. Nowhere else either lest she meet Lucien accidentally and not have the courage to resist him again. If he said 'come' once more, she would go.

The heat seemed overpowering today, almost as hot as last year. Inside the store it was stuffy, a never-ending sea of faces. A never-ending stream of questions. Nell's legs felt heavy, her eyes smarted and she longed only to return to Eaton Square.

And it had to be today that Lady Lenham returned to Gadsby's for the first time since her defection to la Ferté. She might have been en route to the Fashion Department – Nell did not know – but whether she was or not, she had decided to walk through the Leisure and Sporting Wear Department where her eye was caught by Miss Gertrude's golfing dresses which sailed perilously near the borderline of Old Ample's department. Simple woollen frocks flared from the hip, loose-sleeved, allowing room for the swing, with matching waterproof jacket, both trimmed in the same contrasting trimming. Well pleased, Lady Lenham purchased one, and stayed to add another purchase of a tennis frock – strictly for spectators – in cream linen. She then left, but news had already travelled by the time Nell, hot and weary, arrived in the buyers' dining room. Mrs Amble's cheeks were more than usually flushed and her feathers distinctly ruffled.

'I understand, Mrs Gadsby –' no Nell today '– that Lady Lenham was intending to return to my department but that she was persuaded to purchase two ready-made garments and then left. I must say, I think this is a most short-sighted policy for Gadsby's.'

'I did not—' Nell stopped. What was the use? Why didn't someone open a window? She looked again, and saw that they had. It was just hot, and the fatty meat in front of her did nothing to help. 'I'm sorry if you're offended, Mrs Amble. I'm sure Lady Lenham will return.'

'I doubt it,' remarked Miss Hogarth of Hats (as Nell always thought of her) smugly, 'she purchases models at Maison la Ferté now.'

'Not since Comte Lucien left,' said Mrs Amble sharply.

'Left?' said Nell weakly, waves of nausea flooding over her.

'Returned to France, Mrs Gadsby,' Mr Langer

273

informed her. 'It's a new fellow, Monsieur Maurice Don-neur, I hear.'

But Nell heard nothing. The group of buyers' faces rose, swelled and receded before her, as she slumped in her chair and then slipped to the floor.

'I'm perfectly all right,' she told Tom wearily as he fussed over her, having been speedily summoned to take her home. It had happened to be one of the rare days when he was lunching with Jonathan in the directors' dining room.

'The doctor told me to keep you quiet here,' Tom had said unexpectedly firmly the next day, anxiety all over his good-looking face.

'There's no need.'

'Then you can tell him that. He's coming again today, and I'm going to be here to hear what he says. Brooklands can do without me.'

'I'm perfectly well,' Nell shouted as soon as the doctor arrived and Tom left them alone. 'Can I go back to work now please?' She mechanically answered all the questions he asked her, ashamed of her own childishness.

'If you take things carefully,' he beamed. 'The baby won't be here for another six months. Beginning of February.'

'Baby?' Nell stared at him blankly. *Baby*? Then it dawned on her. So that was why he'd asked her all those questions. She was the biggest simpleton out. A fool. *Why* hadn't she thought? She'd just put down her missed periods to depression and low state of health. She could say nothing, feel nothing, merely stared at him.

'You're pregnant, Mrs Gadsby. Isn't that splendid? Mr Gadsby will be thrilled.'

'Don't tell him,' she managed to say. 'I will.'

'Of course, Mrs Gadsby,' the doctor said somewhat huffily. 'Naturally I would leave it to you.'

She tried to listen to the stream of advice and instructions and did not hear them. She only wanted him to go. When at last he did so, the full import of what this meant began to flood over her. How could it have happened? She and Lucien had always been so careful, after that first occasion. Then she remembered an island, an afternoon, years ago it seemed, another age when she was in the sunshine of love, with no premonition of the eclipse so soon to come. Her stomach began to churn again. Lucien, far away in France. The son he needed, and she was tied to another. The child would grow up fatherless. No, she painfully remembered. There was Tom. And how to tell him?

You've made a fair old mess of things, Nelly Watkins, she told herself ruefully. For the first time self-pity overwhelmed her and she sobbed helplessly, torn between pleasure at the thought of Lucien's child, and despair. Also, for the first time, she had not the slightest idea what she should do.

It became an obsession. She had to tell Lucien before she told Tom. He had a right to know, she told herself. She would not think beyond the telling, yet sometimes as she tossed and turned at night, or vomited in the morning, she clung to the wild hope that all might be well. Tom would realise that she must leave him, and irrespective of his family, or anything else, she would never be parted again from Lucien.

Tom didn't appear to notice, nor wonder why her frocks were looser. He had accepted her explanation that she had been overdoing things because of the summer season, and since he did not hear her morning nausea, eyed approvingly the slight fullness to her cheeks and figure as the result of his 'fattening her up'.

She made her plans carefully. She would go to the autumn dress parades in Paris, and would go to the la Ferté parade. This time she appealed to Jonathan

Gadsby. Where tickets were barred to the buyers of Gadsby's now, for old times' sake Jonathan could appeal to the count himself. It was a passport to Lucien. Jonathan had been surprisingly easy to persuade, perhaps because in his heart of hearts he still hoped the old exclusive contract might be restored. He questioned her keenly, but she explained – truthfully – that she needed to see the Paris competition in order to guide Mrs Emmeline and Miss Gertrude for the new season.

So little had changed since her first unfortunate entry through these august doors; she even recognised the porter. At least her French was a little better now, she thought, laughing to herself. She was buoyed up with excitement. Soon she would see Lucien again, albeit merely on a platform. Then she would have to wait until at least four hundred dresses had been viewed. Nevertheless, today she would see him, talk to him, tell him. The sickness bouts that had bedevilled her mornings had eased slightly in the last few days, but today qualms of anticipation had overcome her. She was glad that this was an afternoon parade so that her loose printed chiffon dress did not look out of place. Anyway, she thought with bravado, what does it matter it I look *enceinte*?

Somehow Miss Gertrude's best design did not look quite so chic here as it did in London, but it *was* fashionable, with the emphasis on the back and the simple front. It was hard to remember that she was here to see a winter collection in the midst of the cool-looking summery audience.

'Madame Nell.' Philippe was suddenly before her, clearly delighted to see her. 'I heard you were coming, and how beautiful you look.' His eyes flicked approvingly over her. 'You are coming to buy, yes?'

She nodded. 'I hope so. Sportswear, of course.'

'My brother will be delighted,' he said, kissing her hand and passing on.

My brother will be delighted. She was dizzy with excitement. On came *les mannequins*, tall, stately, haughty; so fascinating in their own right that she almost forgot she was here to look at designs, ostensibly at sports dresses and leisure wear of course. So skirts were longer – and still dipping, though not so markedly. She joined in the general gasp of surprise. Jersey dresses, of course. Nothing but Jersey – something for Maria here? – cape coats, three-piece ensembles, and yes the picture frocks again. She almost giggled to see the deep V necks and bouffant skirts. Had Philippe *no* new ideas? The cut was magnificent, but the designs! She glanced at the programme. No mention of Polly's name here, yet Lucien had told her she was designing for Paris also. Did she do nothing – or was Philippe jealous of his preserve? Perhaps he kept Polly's name firmly in London if not her designs?

And another puzzling thing. Why was it the count who introduced the show, and a stranger who introduced the models? Where was Lucien? She could not see him afterwards. She searched in vain in the milling congratulatary crowds. She would ask the count, he would tell her. He liked her. Fighting a sudden panic she began to make her way towards him, only to find Philippe at her side again. She uttered polite words of congratulation, then, unable to restrain herself, burst out: 'I thought Lucien would be here.'

Philippe kissed her hand again, thanking her at length for her compliments. He paused. 'Ah, Lucien, *mon frère*,' he murmured gently. 'I think, Nell, perhaps he will be here to take your orders on Monday. *Oui*. Or perhaps not. You must forgive him. We men are weak. I think perhaps he could not face you.'

'But I— ' Nell stopped. She wasn't going to tell Philippe that she brought good news. That was for Lucien's ears alone. 'Tell him I would like to see him, please, Philippe,' she said firmly.

'I will. But, Nell, remember he will be embarrassed. Michelle does not like him to—'

'Michelle?' Nell said sharply.

'Mademoiselle de Compreys. They are much together, Nell,' he said gently, 'and I think they will marry.' Then, seeing the look on her face, 'Come, let me get you *un verre de champagne*. You were fond of Lucien, yes? Yet you are fortunate, Nell. You have a husband *sympathique*. Such things happen. And they pass. For my brother and for you.'

'I don't believe it,' she wanted to shout. She didn't trust Philippe. She had told Lucien to find someone else. But so soon? And not want to see her now? No, that she couldn't believe. Honour at least would send him to her. Philippe was lying, he was jealous of his brother. She would ask the count. No, she could not involve him. Pride would not let her. There was one person, she remembered, who would have no reason to lie: the commissionaire. Fighting panic, she collected her wrap and went to the main door. She would know the truth. Nothing else mattered.

'Monsieur,' she greeted him hesitantly.

'Ah, madame.' A grin spread over his face as he recognised the gauche girl of four years earlier.

'*Monsieur le comte Lucien – il est ici?*'

A look of surprise. '*Ah non, Madame. Il est déjà parti.*'

Already left? He had seen her and gone. No, he might not mean that. He must mean left the Maison la Ferté.

'But he still works for the Maison la Ferté?'

'*Mais naturellement. Il—*' But Nell had heard enough. Thanking him, she walked out on unsteady legs. He had no intention of facing her, whether because of Michelle or for any other reason. He did not want to see her. Philippe for once had been telling the truth.

'*Maria! Magnifico!*' It was heartfelt. For an instant her old enthusiasm swept back to blot out the pain.

'You like, eh, Nell?'

Maria Maniosta, arms akimbo, dressed in a skimpy jersey frock of her own creation, proudly surveyed her new premises. They weren't a Maison la Ferté, but they were in the Avenue Montaigne, albeit high above it. And most of all, they were in Paris, not Vincennes.

Three rooms, an office, a showroom and a workroom. All round the modest showroom were samples of her work. Blazing coloured jersey frocks with outrageous bold designs on them – designs from modern artists, like Léger and Matisse, and one or two delicate Monet water lilies, the designs not a small ornamentation but huge, and dominating the dresses.

'What you think of this, Nell?' Maria demanded, tossing back her dark mane of hair that made her look like a fierce-eyed Amazon. 'This' wasn't knitwear. At first sight it looked a sombre three-piece woollen suit, beautifully cut. Plain navy blue. And another in deep purple. Then she flung open the jacket, to reveal bright pink linings, printed with fierce tigers, lions and pumas. Flicked open a godet to reveal a bright yellow crêpe-de-Chine panel with a dark brown monkey apparently about to leap out. All so exquisitely worked that they pleased rather than shocked. A small bear dangled from huge earrings, a polar bear clung to the end of a gilt belt, a giraffe's head appeared on the reverse of the revers of a collar, its long thin legs running as delicate trimming down the front of a bodice.

'Is nothing,' Maria shrugged, though clearly delighted at Nell's praise. 'Now I do Indians.'

'The Taj Mahal?'

'*Non*. Squaws, feathers, wigwams. It will be fun. You'll see.' Then, seeing Nell's anxious face, let out a bellow of laughter. 'For you, Nell, I do you more. Gadsby Games, yes?'

'Yes please,' she said fervently. 'Jumpers, skirts, jersey dresses,' she added, greatly daring, seeing Maria frown, then Maria grin. 'You do not find enough at la Ferté, eh?'

'No,' said Nell ruefully.

'Pah!' said Maria. 'He holds his nose so high, he falls in the *merde* that one.'

'Philippe?' asked Nell quickly. Surely not Lucien.

'*Si*. He is not a designer, that one,' Maria dismissed him scornfully. 'He is a couturier. He cuts, he cuts oh so well, but he does not have ideas. *Eh bien*. That is good if you recognise it. But that one he does not. He thinks he's couturier *and* designer. And milord too,' she added.

'That's what I'm beginning to realise,' Nell said. 'He had picture frocks in the collection again.'

Maria flung back her head with another bellow of laughter as her mane of hair swung to and fro. 'Picture frocks? We go back to your Queen Victoria. Yes? This too I can do, but I do picture frocks differently. See?' She quickly sketched a few lines and showed it to Nell. 'Bouffant, yes. So romantic, yes?'

'Yes,' agreed Nell, 'but too short.'

'And under here,' said Maria, 'we put a straight skirt with a big Indian, yes? With a tomahawk? And every time our young lady dance, the bouffant swirls and we see a Red Indian. Ayyyy!' She let out a screech so loud Nell clapped her hands over her ears. 'War-cry, yes?'

'I don't think Gadsby's is ready for that quite yet,' Nell said drily.

'Then I sell it to la Ferté perhaps,' said Maria, chuckling.

'So that's why you went to Paris,' said Tom, face blank. 'To see that fellow.'

'Yes, Tom,' she said gently. 'He is the father.'

'And what did high and mighty Mr Philippe have to say about it?' said Tom grimly.

Philippe? She almost laughed at the irony. She'd forgotten Tom still thought it was Philippe. And what matter now? 'It isn't Philippe,' she said flatly. 'It never was. It's Lucien.'

'Lucien?' Tom's face went quite blank, and she thought he was going to explode with anger. But he didn't. 'Why didn't you tell me, Nell?' He sounded puzzled.

A searing pain. 'Would it – would it have made any difference?' she whispered through dry lips.

He considered for a long time. Too long. 'Tell me, Tom.'

'No,' he said at last. 'It wouldn't. Now it does though.'

'Why?' Hope battled with fear.

'Rather liked Lucien,' he said simply.

'So now, when it's too late, you'd let me go to him, is that it?' she said bitterly. 'Because you like him. Now that he—' She stopped. Pride wouldn't let her speak.

'No,' he said, apparently surprised she should think so. 'I meant, I won't mind having Lucien's kid around.'

She stared at him, unable to believe her ears. 'Tom, I'm having another man's child. Don't you mind at all?'

He swallowed. 'I can't very well, can I?' he muttered. 'Besides, it will be jolly having a baby in the house. Think how pleased Grandpops will be.'

Jonathan – this was a dimension she hadn't even considered, and she began to laugh weakly at the unexpectedness of life. So Tom would overlook the fact he wasn't the father for the sake of his pride? Men were strange creatures.

'Glad you're pleased,' Tom said, brightening up. 'After all, we can make the best of it. Er – I take it Lucien won't be claiming it?'

'I didn't see him – and he won't know,' she said firmly. She expected him to ask questions but he did not.

'One thing the desert teaches you,' he said unexpectedly, 'is how to come to terms with things, accept them as they are. When's it coming?' he asked.

281

'The beginning of February. I'll have to tell Grandfather.'

Tom stared at her aghast. 'No!' he said violently.
'You're not going to do that to him, Nell. *Or* to me.
What's happened remains between us.'

'But he'll think it's a Gadsby,' Nell pointed out, stupe-
fied. 'Suppose—' she broke off. She could hardly point
out, if Tom did not see it himself, that with him the heir to
Gadsby, any son she might have, or even daughter, might
affect the store's future. Worse was her realisation of
another reason that Tom wanted to keep the baby. It was
proof to the outside world of his manhood – which he had
doubted since Melissa left. Not love for her. Need perhaps, but not love.

The first Nell heard was Melissa's telephone call. Naturally she was staying at the Ritz. The familiar laugh, as
though they had seen each other yesterday, instead of
breaking a silence of over six months.

'What are you in London for?' asked Nell.

'That horrid trial, darling. Have you forgotten?'

She almost had. Robert's murder seemed of another
age. Now in a rush all Melissa's fears came back to her.
She sounded cheerful enough, however. No hint that she
might be about to face an ordeal. All the same: 'Do you
want to stay with us?' Nell asked cautiously.

'Sweet of you, but I think I'll stay here. So much more
public. I can put a brave and beautiful face on things.'
Melissa giggled, and somewhat relieved, Nell arranged to
meet her for cocktails after work. Her cocktails tended to
be mixtures of orange and lemon juice nowadays, with
only three months before the baby was due, and she eyed
Melissa's White Lady enviously. She was looking drawn,
Nell thought worriedly, despite her apparent gaiety.

'Oh, this is nice,' said Melissa, sighing and surreptitiously wriggling off her shoes. 'Just like the old days. And

you are going to advise me, Nell. I am just the teensiest bit worried.'

'About the trial?'

Melissa pulled a face. 'About my career with Raoul. Paris is talking about nothing but those stupid talking pictures now. *The Jazz Singer* opened last week, and several others, and naturally while everyone is talking about them – silly things – Raoul is finding it just a little bit difficult to find a backer for a new silent film. It's superb. About Attila the Hun. He'll find one, of course.' She smiled lightly. 'He's sure to. But he's beginning to think of directing a talking picture first. *Phèdre*.'

'That's a good part, isn't it?' said Nell, unthinking.

'For a French actress, yes,' said Melissa crossly.

'Oh.' Nell was annoyed with herself. 'Of course.' Melissa couldn't speak French well enough. 'Couldn't you come back to England to work?' she asked.

'Yes.' Melissa sounded doubtful, then added airily, 'Actually it rather depends on the trial.'

'What are you afraid of?' asked Nell bluntly. 'That your name will be dragged in in other ways than that of grieving widow?'

Melissa avoided her eye. 'Something like that,' she muttered.

'Like what?' demanded Nell inexorably.

'I know Danny Ross,' Melissa announced at last.

Nell groaned. 'How well? No, don't tell me. I'll just guess. You're afraid it will come out in court in his defence.' A ghastly thought struck her. 'You mean, he might say you incited him to do it?' trying desperately to keep her tones light and conversational in view of their public setting, and finding it harder and harder.

Melissa nodded miserably and a large tear plopped on cue into the White Lady. 'Isn't it a bore?' she said brightly.

'Rather more than that,' Nell told her grimly. She

hesitated. 'You didn't, I suppose?'

'What?'

'Incite him.'

Melissa was indignant. 'Of *course* not. Why should I? I didn't want to have to marry Jack, after all. So I didn't need a divorce. Danny is –' She considered, the blonde head tilted becomingly to one side to display her best profile to the rest of the room (quite unconsciously, Nell decided) '– rather impetuous. He did so love me, the sweet thing.'

'Very sweet,' agreed Nell hollowly. 'Let's hope his sweet nature hasn't been soured.'

'I was rather afraid he'd done it because of me,' said Melissa, a distinct note of complacency creeping in, 'but I think Robert must just have annoyed him. He was very fond of him too.' She looked hopefully at Nell as if she might provide some kind of answer, now that she had told all.

Nell could not. Even if Melissa avoided implication in the murder, the trial was probably going to reveal unpleasant truths about her – and if so, Melissa's future in British theatres could be doubtful in the extreme, even if she restored relations with her former theatre management.

'What about that film *Atlantic* they've just made at Elstree in three languages? Couldn't you get your director friends to do the same sort of thing in France? So you don't have to come back here to work?'

'Perhaps,' Melissa said, suddenly anxious to change the subject. 'Do tell me about yourself, darling. Any news?'

'I'm having a baby,' Nell told her somewhat tartly. Only Melissa could have failed to notice.

'Oh. I wondered why you were wearing that awful dress. Full waistless dresses aren't really *you*, are they? You look better in fitted styles.'

'*Bonsoir, mesdames.*'

Nell turned. What an evening this was turning out to be. It was Philippe de la Ferté.

Melissa apparently did not share her annoyance. 'Oh, Nell, how naughty of you. You didn't tell me Philippe was here.'

'I didn't know,' retorted Nell, disconcerted, while Philippe looked at her benignly.

'That's nice. You can take us to dinner, Philippe.'

'I should be enchanted,' he said politely, sitting down and flicking his fingers at a waiter, his sharp dark eyes flicking over both of them.

'I'm in London for the murder trial,' Melissa announced loudly and publicly to Nell's amusement. 'And Nell's a lady in waiting.'

'As I see,' he murmured. 'Felicitations, dearest Nell – to you *and* Tom. Pray do congratulate him for me.' Was it her imagination or was there the slightest hesitation before the 'Tom'? It must be her, for he was chatting away quite naturally.

'Tommy will love being a father. I do envy you, Nell,' Melissa said artlessly. 'I can't have any sprogs.'

Nell was startled. This was something she'd never known. 'I'm sorry,' she murmured, uneasily conscious of Philippe's presence.

'I'm not. I had one once,' Melissa pulled a face. 'Or at least, part of one.'

'Part of one?' echoed Nell blankly.

Philippe, controlling his face, murmured his apologies and tactfully disappeared towards the bar. Melissa said carelessly, 'I had an abortion. Only it went wrong and mucked things up, so I can't have any more. I was only sixteen,' she added, something that might have been a shadow crossing her face. 'I was touring somewhere – Glasgow I think – and the manager found out I was pregnant, and said he'd have to sack me. So I found this man – anyway, it went wrong.'

'I'm so sorry, Melissa.'

'I'm not,' she said, cheering up. 'Think how much easier it makes things.' Then she met Nell's eye. 'Well, I'm just the teensiest bit sorry,' she conceded. 'Nell, I—' She leaned forward, suddenly serious. 'When I have those dreams, you know, and my face gets all wrinkled and ugly and no one wants me any more, then I wish I was plain like you. Just think, Nell – all those years ahead, forty to fifty, then sixty – what will it be like? That's why I really want to go on acting, on and on, but it's not easy for actresses as they get older.'

'Melissa.' Impulsively Nell took her hands. 'I'll always be here, you know that.'

'I know,' she said, drying her eyes. 'Thank goodness. I know I'm not a good friend. I don't keep in touch, but when things are awful, I just think – there's Nell, and I know everything will be all right.'

And for her? Unbidden, fear rose and swelled inside her – all those years, forty to fifty, sixty, all of them without Lucien, the vast barren desert of life to be walked alone – save for his child.

Melissa's gift for survival triumphed again. The charge against Danny Ross was reduced to manslaughter because of provocation (Danny had been defending his honour, Melissa told Nell unblinkingly) and this promptly diminished press interest despite the appearance of Melissa Hargreaves as witness. No hint that there was a rift between husband and wife emerged, and Jack Fisher's evidence was confined to Robert's state of mind when they parted on that afternoon. Melissa looked so lovely and fragile as the widow, forced to give evidence that Robert's sexual tastes had rarely included her, that sympathy welled over for her. When Danny's counsel attempted to suggest that Danny's services could have been fought over by them, the court failed to pick up the full implication, and the prosecution's helpful suggestion to her that such services were in respect of odd jobs around the house had her full support. With little jury deliberation Danny was sentenced to ten years in prison, and the case was at an end. Thus far Melissa's luck extended, but then it began to trickle out.

Nothing appeared in the press, but the intermittent whispers that had always existed in social circles about Melissa Hargreaves but which had been quiescent while she was abroad now joined the gossip from London's less respectable clubs, fed on themselves, and gradually swelled.

It was typical of Melissa to want to 'celebrate' as if she, not Danny Ross, had been on trial. 'Just to cheer us up,' she cried gaily to Nell and Tom as they left the court. 'We'll go to The Cockatoo, and then on to Ma Meyrick's or The Kit Kat Club, just like we used to. Do you remember, darlings?'

Would she ever forget? Nell thought with a familiar lurch of irritation coloured with affection. She didn't feel like 'celebrating' anywhere. Her body felt cumbrous and heavy and so were her spirits. She was even crosser when Melissa appeared, swathed in white fur and flanked by two familiar figures – Jack Fisher and Philippe de la Ferté. Her heart sank at the thought of Philippe's sharp inquisitive company for a whole evening, and what on earth was Jack doing back on the scene?

'Now I know it's just the teensiest bit naughty of me to invite Philippe along,' Melissa said innocently.

What's she talking about? thought Nell wildly, thrown off-track, until she remembered that Melissa still believed Philippe her ex, if not current lover, and she shivered at the very idea, good company though he was. And he needed to be – Clubland was a depressing scene of too much drink and too much money, people crammed in for the privilege of late night drinking.

'I might have brought Lucien too. I am so naughty, aren't I, Tommy?' Melissa finished outrageously, as she sat herself complacently at a table reserved for someone else. 'My dearest friends,' she said fondly, spreading her arms as if to embrace all four of them.

'Why?' Tom asked absent-mindedly, studying the wine list. Melissa smiled sweetly and Tom did not pursue it. Nell breathed a sigh of relief since now the moment would pass. It was the last thing she needed to have Tom reminded so publicly, and by Melissa of all people, of the true father of her baby. It was just Melissa's usual chatter and she was reading too much into it. Melissa couldn't possibly know that Tom had not been able to consummate their marriage, for he would never have told her, of all people, and even if she suspected Nell had a lover, she still thought it was Philippe. Nell looked up to find his eyes resting on her in amusement.

'My devotion to beautiful women is always steadfast,' he said hand on heart. 'If, alas, sometimes unrequited,' he added lightly.

Melissa giggled. 'Philippe has the most lovely house in St Tropez. We're great friends, aren't we, darling? Not as great friends as with you, Jack,' she patted his arm consolingly, 'but I mean real friends. We have such lovely chats about Nell. And Tommy, of course,' she finished brightly.

'I'm delighted,' said Nell drily, wondering just how often Melissa frequented Philippe's bed.

Philippe stared at Nell sardonically, as though he knew just what she was thinking, but when he spoke it was not of Melissa. 'Tom, I have not yet congratulated you on the delightful news that you are to be a father.'

Was he being genuine? Nell wondered uneasily, remembering Lucien's distrust of Philippe, but she dismissed the thought.

'I think our Nell will be the most splendid roly-poly,

apple pie and rice pudding mother, don't you, Philippe?'
Melissa chattered inanely, and as so often entirely without
regard for the effect of her words. '*And*, since I can't have
children of my own, I'm going to be the best aunt there
ever was to Nell and Tommy's child.'

'And for myself, I shall be uncle,' declared Philippe,
equally warmly.

Nell looked at him sharply, instant guilt making her
assume the worst. She forced herself to relax. It was a
perfectly innocent remark, that was all. Even if Lucien
had been right and Philippe had guessed about them, he
could not possibly *know* that the baby was not Tom's.

'And, dearest Nell,' he continued, 'you have as usual
inspired me. We have paid but little attention to the
requirements of pregnant ladies at Maison la Ferté. I must
find some pregnant ladies in Paris, and create designs on
the body.'

'Knowing you, you'll be the one who makes them
pregnant,' observed Melissa lightly.

'How well you understand me,' he said smoothly.

He didn't like that remark, Nell noted, in jest or not.
Why had she not noticed that his eyes could look so
malevolent, almost hooded like a snake's? Yet at once
that look was gone again as he laughed, his easy self once
more.

'And how,' Philippe remarked casually to Nell, as one
fashion expert to another, 'are your new Jungle lines
selling?'

'Very well,' she said non-committally.

'Dear Maria,' said Philippe, 'so very talented.' His
smile could have been a gauntlet laid down.

Nell stopped daily attendance at Gadsby's at the end of
November, but still paid visits twice a week. Much as she
tried to concentrate on future motherhood, her steps
seemed constantly to lead her to the store.

'You're giving up Gadsby's for good now,' Tom reminded her in astonishment. 'Why are you still so interested in every damn' thing that goes on there?'

Nell had completely forgotten that Tom might still be under the impression that she was stopping work for ever. It was her fault for not taking more care. Now she had to tread lightly.

'That was agreed a long time ago, Tom. Much has happened since then.'

'I want you at home. You said you'd give up.'

Sulkily he gave in, however, provided she could get Jonathan's permission, which was not easy. 'No,' he roared flatly. 'You're leaving, and that's final.'

'Then I shall get a job at another store when the baby's able to be left,' Nell countered, throwing down her ace at the beginning of play.

'No one would have you.'

'Oh, yes. Reville have approached me, and Jay's. Maskell's, too,' she tossed her ace in nonchalantly, by naming their direct and nearest competitors.

Jonathan too could play poker. 'Take up Maskell's offer,' he told her cordially. 'Or any of the others, if you like. But you're not coming back here, missy.'

'If you wish.' Nell shrugged. 'It's a wonderful offer. After five years, if all works well, they'll offer me a partnership. Maskell and Gadsby it will be.'

A gleam came into Jonathan's eye. 'You're lying, girl. They're slipping, they won't be here in five years. And even if they are, they wouldn't offer *you* a partnership without money.

'They *will* be here in five years if I work for them,' said Nell coolly.

'Bluff,' roared Jonathan.

Nell shrugged, and said nothing.

'Who's going to look after my grandson, eh, if you go gadding about working?' he roared suddenly.

'We are getting a nanny to look after him – or her,' she added deliberately. 'Or I could bring the baby to work with me if you're worried.'

'I don't want yowling babies here, even if it is a Gadsby,' said Jonathan testily. 'I'm too old.'

A Gadsby. Nell swallowed. Rose and Gordon Holdsby had produced a son, but he of course did not carry the Gadsby name. How ironic to have a true Gadsby not recognised and an untrue one, who because Tom would not let her tell Jonathan, would bear the famous name – and be the heir after Tom.

'Then I'll take it to Maskell's with me,' said Nell.

'How are you going to feed him properly?' Jonathan shot at her, ignoring this.

'I'll manage,' said Nell.

'I don't doubt it,' said he feelingly. 'Have him strapped to you like a papoose no doubt. Not going to bottle-feed him, are you?'

'I'll manage,' repeated Nell, in tones which indicated the discussion was over.

'Sometimes I think I'm getting old,' muttered Jonathan, relaxing and looking his age. 'That's what Emmeline tells me, but it's hard to realise it. How are we going to manage while you're away, eh?' Change of tack and admission of defeat.

'My deputy Miss Field will take on another assistant, and I shall be taking a keen interest in design and budget. I'll miss the February shows, of course, but I can organise that through Miss Field and direct with my suppliers. Maria Maniosta is coming here to see me and—'

'Got it all worked out, haven't you?' he grunted, but there was no heart in his disapproval now.

Nell sat down again, slightly perturbed at the greyness of his face. 'Is something wrong?' she asked gently.

'None of your business, miss. You're not a director. Tom is, but that's nothing to do with you.'

'No. We never talk about Gadsby's,' she said wrily. Tom still showed no interest in the store, and as for board meetings, she doubted if he even heard much of what went on.

'Very proper of him,' Jonathan said approvingly, perking up. 'That's the one good thing you've done for us, Nell,' he threw at her provocatively. 'The future's taken care of. Make sure you produce a boy.' It sounded surprisingly like an appeal.

'The store's in trouble, isn't it?' Nell said worriedly, going to the heart of the matter. From the look on his face she knew she was right.

'It's not serious,' Jonathan glared. 'We might have to take out a loan, that's all. Everyone does it. Prided myself *I'd* never have to do it though. But it's just to tide us over.'

'But if the crash on Wall Street last month has repercussions here,' she said, concerned, 'trade might not pick up enough to cover it. It would go down, if anything. Just as—'

'Oh, would it, missy? Big business lady now, are you?'

'It's obvious. What would the interest rates—'

'None of your business,' he shouted. 'I won't discuss business with a woman. And especially not you.'

'But you discuss the buying side with the buyers,' she pointed out, 'and that is the kernel of the business. I think trade will continue going down. The Fashion Department is still sliding – you can almost *see* it day by day. But sales of dresses designed by Mrs Emmeline and Miss Gertrude are increasing,' she put in cunningly, 'partly because of their good design but also because of their comparative cheapness and convenience.'

'No,' Jonathan roared.

'I haven't asked you anything yet,' she retorted. 'We must stop concentrating on Fashion Department bespoke orders as the hub of trade and broaden our horizons further.'

'Trade doesn't change that much.'

'But times do,' she said sadly. 'Oh, they do. We're so different now to before the war.'

'If we become like all the other stores, we go under.'

'We compete,' she said firmly, 'and that's what's going to be important. We compete by standing out for excellence among our competitors, not by ignoring them. At the moment Umbrellas and Scarves, Fabrics, Millinery and so on are all there first and foremost to service the Fashion Department. We've got to make them departments in their own right, of equal importance to Fashion. And then we should have a ready-made fashion department of good quality—'

'Like a dime store.'

'*No*! High class, even expensive if you like, but *convenient*. And a young people's department where cheaper clothes can be bought, to appeal to all the working girls. They haven't the money to spend on Paris models, but want to look fashionable. Oh, and we should have a pattern department next to Fabrics for those who want to make their own dresses.'

Jonathan growled in disgust. 'When this slump—'

'So you admit it will affect us?'

'Not at all. We're over the worst,' he said defiantly.

'Oh no, it's only just coming,' said Nell slowly. 'And we've got to be ready to fight it.'

Jonathan stared at her.

'No,' he said at last. 'I know you mean well,' he hurried over this surprising admission, 'but I've spent my whole life waiting for, planning for, building up Gadsby's. I *know* it, I love it, and I know what's right for it. It's bad trading to panic and go into reverse, or turn to right or left in bad times. You face them head on with what you *know*. Like in the war.'

Perhaps once, but now he was wrong and Nell knew it.

'I'll concede one thing,' Jonathan said slowly. 'Your

Leisure Wear turnover is going up. *If* you come back, and *if* I consider my grandson is properly cared for, I'll give you back the Fashion Department.'

Nell bore Lucien's son after sixteen painful hours late in the afternoon of 2 February 1930. When she awoke, Tom was bending proudly over the cradle at her side. Lucien . . . it should be Lucien there. In her weakness a trickle of tears escaped, rolling down her cheeks.

'Don't cry, Nelly,' said Tom cheerfully. 'He's a dear little chap. He weighs nearly nine and a half pounds. He's going to be a big 'un.' He paused. 'Just like me.'

Looking after the baby took all her time and energy. Her mother, maternal instincts overcoming reluctance at entering the alien world of Eaton Square, had insisted on staying with her for two weeks, to Nell's great relief. Now she had gone, and maternity was smothering her. She managed only hurried discussions with Angela and with Maria, Mrs Emmeline and Miss Gertrude. All the while the baby lay in his cradle, gurgling up at her with contentment, interspersed with screams. She tried to tell herself that he looked like her, but when she looked at him she could see only Lucien. And what to name him?

'Could we call him Luke?' Nell asked hesitantly.

'What's wrong with Tom?' he said mutinously, picking up the baby from the cradle and holding him against his broad shoulder, till he gurgled with delight. 'Or Jonathan,' he added in a rare moment of perception.

'No.' She grinned wanly. 'Let's stick to neutral ground. Let's do what everyone else does, and call him David after the Prince of Wales.'

'David. David Gadsby.' Tom tried it out. 'Do you hear that, old chap?' He swung the baby down. 'You're royalty now. Gadsby's by royal warrant, by Jove. Won't your

Aunt Melissa be pleased. She always wanted to meet the Prince of Wales.'

Meet wasn't quite the word she'd used to her, Nell recalled, amused. She wondered idly where Melissa was. Apart from a telegram and a large box of French baby clothes, there had been silence. So she must be all right, mustn't she?

If in need, Melissa would have telephoned her, so she must have found another film or another lover, or both. But still Nell was worried. When she heard about the revolution that talking pictures had caused on the continent, despite Melissa's confident assertion that they were a passing phase, she expected her daily to return to England. But she did not – perhaps could not. The name of Melissa Hargreaves was still circulating in London gossip, but not for her charm and acting abilities. Scandal had now crept from clubland to theatreland, so Nell had discovered. What had before been mere delicious rumours now became 'fact' and passed from fellow actors to theatre management. And management, Nell guessed, would avoid trouble if it could, however talented and famous the star.

There were no new films starring Melissa Hargreaves now showing to persuade them to change their attitude, and in the British film world, Jack Fisher was adding confirmation to the gossip. And, worse, the scandal was spreading wider in London society. When it reached Gadsby's sales assistants, reported by Angela, Nell feared Melissa was truly doomed so far as any return to work in London was concerned. What one did behind the scenes was one thing, but once it became public knowledge, more than horses were frightened.

Late in May Nell left on the Golden Arrow for Paris, on a quick trip, leaving David with Tom and the nurse. She'd wanted to bring him – oh, how much she'd wanted to – but he was too young. Yet she had to go. If Tom guessed part of her reason for going, he made no comment, secure in the knowledge that legally David was his. Indeed, she thought often he had obliterated all thoughts to the contrary from his mind. He adored the baby, often taking him with him to Brooklands or Hendon, giving him earnest instruction in the arts of driving and piloting as the baby gurgled back knowledgeably. The screams he kept for her, Nell noticed wrily.

Taking a deep breath she walked through the portals of Maison la Ferté once again. From the collection – which she viewed with dazed eyes, always hoping, waiting to see Lucien – a part of her mind knew she could find enough dresses to tide her over until the autumn. Her eye needed time to adjust again to fashion trends. She noted an evening dress with diagonal neckline that pleased her, afternoon dresses with pouched bodices, close-fitting dresses flaring out at the hemlines. Tea-dance georgette frocks which were attractive – but still ankle-length – though there were some afternoon dresses of matching but separate bodice and skirts which were a novelty. The collection contained no trend-setters but was designed to appeal to most ages. It would do – for now. It wasn't Lucien, however, whom she faced across the desk when it came to bargaining. Schooling herself to business first, she worked her way through her requirements.

'And *le comte Lucien*?' she enquired eventually. '*Il va bien*?' Not a tremble in her voice for this man was a stranger.

'*Oui, madame.*'

'*Il est ici*?'

Surprise. '*Non*. He is in Cannes, *naturellement*.'

'At his home?' Was this voice hers, so apprehensive, so tremulous?

'Perhaps. He has run the Cannes branch of Maison la

Ferté, madame, since he opened it over a year ago. Did you not know?'

No, she didn't. The heavy weight that was her heart almost choked her as she returned to her hotel. Philippe had let her think he was still in Paris. Or had she just assumed that? She couldn't remember. Her head was throbbing and a dull fear seemed to have taken possession of her. Her fantasy that once he knew he had a son he would claim both him and her, and sweep away all obstacles, shattered into fragments. But for what cause? she asked herself, desperately trying to be rational. Nothing had changed, save that nearly six hundred miles still lay between them. Six hundred miles that were so easily covered. And how fitting that she should tell him of his son in the place where he was conceived, she told herself firmly.

Nell stepped out of the Blue Train into the brilliant afternoon sunshine of the Riviera, and hesitated. Would Lucien be home from the fashion house yet? If she walked, then surely he would. The thought of the villa brought rising excitement. Only a year ago – yet it seemed a lifetime. David's lifetime. She tried to stop herself from hurrying, hurrying to tell Lucien about his son. It seemed but a few steps to happiness. She walked down to the Croisette, and watched the sun shining on the fishing boats in the harbour for a few minutes. On the far side of the bay she could see the yachts at Palm Beach across the twinkling water. A playground. An unreal paradise, but a paradise that held Lucien.

Filled with excitement, she walked along the Croisette towards the hillside of La Californie, then up the narrow paths she remembered so well. Nothing seemed changed, save that the gates stood open. She walked steadily up the path towards the house.

'*Madame*!' It was Madame Dufy, her face wreathed in

297

smiles, who came hurrying towards her. Nell shook hands warmly, her heart beat so loud it sounded like a hammer.

'*Monsieur le comte est ici*?'

'*Oui, madame, et la comtesse.*'

The hammer crashed down upon her. So he had married that Frenchwoman? Philippe had not lied about his closeness to her. The flowers bloomed as before. Madame Dufy had not changed, the house still stood before her. Only her heart had been torn from its reason for living.

'Darling. How clever of you to find me. How did you hear? Oh Nell, *darling*.' It was not an unknown Frenchwoman hurrying down the steps. It was Melissa. And behind her, in the doorway, attracted by her voice, stood her husband. Nell just had time to register the dearly beloved features of a stranger that was Lucien, before she turned and ran. Ran from the nightmare.

Chapter Nine

In August 1930 Jonathan Gadsby was eighty years old, and determined the world should know it. With some reluctance he abandoned his original plan of throwing open the ground floor of Gadsby's one evening for a huge celebratory party. With the rise in unemployment following the Wall Street crash of '29 leading many now to fear a slump comparable to that across the Atlantic, Jonathan's instincts, finely tuned to popular reaction, told him that any apparently ostentatious display of wealth would invite more criticism than admiration. His plans were therefore amended to a business acquaintances' reception at the Savoy, and a huge party for family and friends at his beloved Merrifield.

One large marquee on the lawns catered for the inner well-being of the hundred and fifty-odd guests, and another encircled a dance floor for those young enough to have the stamina for evening dancing after the daytime party. Every hostelry in the neighbourhood had its rooms booked for overnight guests, and when this proved insufficient nearby villagers had dusted, polished and tidied spare rooms with alacrity at this unexpected source of generous income. Mrs Emmeline was in her element, clad in Miss Gertrude's creation of flowing lavender georgette, as composed as if hostessing parties for one hundred and fifty guests had been commonplace in Welling High Street. She alone was unsurprised when against all the odds the sun shone that day at Merrifield, since she had unlimited faith in Jonathan's organisational abilities.

'You're as skinny as a filleted fishbone,' remarked Bobsy, critically and cheerfully to Nell by way of greeting. Her own bony figure was swathed in a voluminous pyjama suit in bright orange topped by a flowing headdress that would not have disgraced Lawrence of Arabia. 'Haven't seen you for ages. Not broody, are you? You can't be compounding the son and heir with that figure.'

Nell bestowed on her that polite smile she reserved now for such questions, even from friends as close as Bobsy. *Especially* from Bobsy. She looked down at her second automatic route of escape from direct questions, but David was for once peacefully asleep amid the social hubbub. She twitched at the blankets, fussing over the exact amount of coverlet over him. Better that than face Bobsy's concerned gaze. With other people she could maintain a cool distance – pretend that other world inside her did not exist. She could continue with her life with Tom, her work, her plans for the future of Gadsby's, the ever-running battle of wits between herself and Jonathan, as she inched her way towards progress, until constantly brought up short by his challenging sharp eye on accounts and stock. She was relieved that Tom was happily discussing with a group of men the merits and demerits of the Standard Wolseley he had just bought – somewhat to her surprise, for Tom's taste was usually more exotic. Naturally Bobsy would know that Melissa had married Lucien. Bobsy always knew everything, by some miraculous means considering she lived in the middle of the countryside. Any moment now she would raise the forbidden subject. Murmuring polite excuses, Nell made her escape, as Bobsy called after her cryptically: 'She's no Penelope, you know.'

Nell paid no attention, concentrating on reaching Tom and safety. Walking up behind him, all she could see was Tom's broad back, and only when it was too late did she see that the earlier group had shrunk to one listener, and that one was the one person who would take her back inevitably to that morning of horror three months earlier. It was Philippe . . .

In a blur of disbelief Nell retreated, running down the lanes of La Californie, past high gates protecting cool palatial mansions, as though the more she distanced herself physically, the more unlikely it was to be true. The sailing boats and yachts out in the Bay of Cannes seemed to mock her, disassociating themselves from the horrors of land. Surely, *surely* she must have been mistaken? It couldn't have happened. Melissa must have been merely visiting. After all, she lived nearby, didn't she? A wild hope seized her, then fell away. Madame Dufy had referred to Madame la Comtesse. And she had turned to look towards Melissa. And standing behind her had been Lucien, looking straight at Nell, his face a mask, the expression in his eyes that of the strangely remote man she had first met nearly five years ago. All that had passed between them had gone, forgotten for ever in his new life.

Lucien and Melissa—Why? How? Questions hammered at her brain without respite as she took the train back to Paris, and on to the Channel. And so she had reached England once more and comparative safety, for *that* was in another country and far away. Like the love that had existed between them. As the weeks passed she tried to think dispassionately about what might have happened. True, he was bitterly angry with her, Nell, for as he saw it preferring Tom to himself. But why Melissa, when he wanted children and Melissa could not give them to him? Did he know that? she wondered suddenly. Surely she would have told him? And did he know the truth of Melissa's life? Whether he did or not, it was too late now.

As to why Melissa should want to marry Lucien, the answer was only too obvious, Nell thought with pain throbbing like a toothache inside her. With Lucien Melissa believed she would find the precious security she sought; his name would be a barrier between herself and scandal. She would find a new life . . . or would she? Perhaps it would be the old life once more when the excitement of her new position had worn off. Nell ached for Melissa the innocent whom she had first known, not that woman who had come to greet her, hypocritically welcoming, unrepentant and challenging, fully aware of the situation. Melissa the ruthless . . . No, she was being unfair. Melissa believed Nell to be in love with Philippe, not Lucien, didn't she? And in his bitterness Lucien would not have disillusioned her. Why should he? Their love had been over long since, so far as he was concerned . . .

When Nell returned to Eaton Square, she had to face a resentful Tom, who had guessed where she had been.

'Lucien had a right to know,' Nell had replied dully. 'David is his son, remember.'

Tom flushed, irrational and rare anger bursting from him. 'He's ours!' he shouted. 'Ours! Do you hear me?'

'Nothing can alter facts, Tom.'

'You have to prove them first,' he shouted at her. 'Can you?'

She stared at him, nonplussed, and a smile of satisfaction crossed his face, almost sly in its smugness, sending a shiver of apprehension through her. 'Why should I need to?' she countered quietly.

'You won't. Provided you don't try to take him away from me again. He's mine. The heir to Gadsby's after me.' He was almost ugly, a stranger.

'No,' she said dully, 'I won't let that happen. I've decided. Not unless Jonathan knows.'

'Tell him anything of the sort and I'll have every lawyer in London proving you've been deranged since the baby was born,' Tom replied, unemotionally now. It was almost as if he'd prepared this argument in advance, thought Nell wildly. This couldn't be *Tom*, surely? 'And the Dirty Fertés aren't going to support you, not now His Snooty Lordship Lucien has married Melissa.'

Dazed, Nell looked at him. 'You knew!' she cried disbelievingly. 'You *knew*. All the time. And you let me *go*.' Anger, horror, passion, sent her flying at him, using fists, legs, anything to pummel him, and such was the force of her attack that it was some moments before he could grasp her hands to control her. Her passion restored him to something like his usual self.

'Easy, old girl, easy.' And when she could struggle no more, he said belligerently, 'Why not? How do you think I felt when *I* heard what she'd done?'

'She's your *ex*-wife, Tom,' Nell said unbelievingly. 'I'm your wife *now*. In name,' she added bitterly, miserably. 'Don't you think that entitles me to more consideration?'

His face grew purple again. 'All right,' he said thickly. 'You want to be my wife like Melissa. Let's try, shall we?' And ignoring her alarmed protests, he dragged her up the stairs to his bedroom, bearing down upon her on the bed with all his huge weight, one hand across her mouth to prevent protests or screams, the other tearing at her clothes, then his. A nightmare of sordid ugliness enveloped her, and as she felt her legs being forced apart she gave herself up for lost, losing track of the passing minutes. Then suddenly she was free, the vice-like grip relaxed and the only sound muffled angry sobs. Not hers, she realised now. His. It had been no different from all those early occasions when, she now realised, he tried so hard, and failed. 'Can't – can't! I'm no use, Nell; no use to you. Not without Melissa.'

Still shuddering with shock, Nell heard David crying out in his sleep. The baby needed her. He would need Tom. Slowly, painfully, she turned to the destroyed man huddled at her side.

'It doesn't matter, Tom,' she forced herself to say. 'It

303

will never matter. Not to us.'

When Nell had recovered from the immediate shock of what had happened in Cannes, she marvelled bitterly at her naivety. How could she have set off so expectant of a fairy-tale happy ending? Had she supposed that faced with the knowledge that he had a son, Lucien would storm over to England and succeed where she could not in persuading Tom to end their marriage, and that somehow or other they would then be together for ever and ever? Yes – and why not? Had it not been for Melissa it might well have been so. Jealousy gnawed at her like ravenous pangs of hunger. Her only way of quenching them, she came to realise, was by blotting out everything save her child and Gadsby's.

It was fortunate that there was much to occupy her at the store this summer. With a slump indisputably taking hold, the Fashion Department was taking fewer and fewer orders, and it was starkly obvious to her, and she suspected to many of her colleagues, that Gadsby's desperately needed reorganisation if it was to survive. And the one person who stood in the way was celebrating his eightieth birthday today, as obstinate and obdurate as ever.

'We rode out the last slump,' he told her complacently, time after time. 'And we'll do the same now. Quality, not quantity, missy.'

'This time it's different,' she told him flatly, ignoring the 'missy' which she suspected he used deliberately to remind her of her place. 'Last time it did not affect our customers. Now it's beginning to touch everyone. We've noticeably fewer regular clients and those who remain only order one or two outfits a season instead of half a dozen.'

Still Jonathan waved aside her arguments. 'It's those damnfool sacks and dishcloths you order from that Italian woman. I told you our customers don't want to look like something out of Sanger's circus. They want quiet elegance – as they've always done.'

'They don't seem to want anything at the moment,' she answered wrily. 'Even demand for my ready-made leisure dresses is falling off,' she added incautiously.

Jonathan shot a triumphant look at her.

'So how much for your answer to everything, missy?' he said triumphantly. 'Go into ready-mades, lower the price and back will come the customers. Now you see it doesn't work.'

'We need total reorganisation, as I first told you ages ago,' she retorted steadily. 'The departments should not be spokes circulating round the hub of the Fashion Department, but each one independent and working to the same profit margins as Fashion. The major part of each department's income should come from outside custom and not, as at present, from its supplies to Fashion to fulfil bespoke orders. That way, you build up a wider customer range. At the moment each department stocks just what the season's models are likely to demand. With people coming off the street not to order dresses but to buy a scarf or shoes, or a hat, we can stock a much wider range and attract—'

'The bailiffs,' cut in Jonathan with relish. 'This wider stock – how long's it going to stay on the shelves, eh? Thought of that? And who's to pay for it? Thought of *that*? We'd have to raise extra capital, and I'd hoped—' He broke off and glared at her. 'No, missy, *no!*'

There was no budging him. Like Maison la Ferté, Jonathan Gadsby believed in letting the times adapt to the store, rather than the other way about. Invincible in its ivory towers Gadsby's would remain, until its fabric crumbled as fungus ate its deadly path upwards.

First Jonathan – and now, when she felt least able to cope with him, Philippe.

★ ★ ★

'How charming you look, Nell. So slender, so *soignée*.'
Philippe greeted her so pleasantly that Nell wondered if
she imagined the mockery in his eye. She shook herself
impatiently for seeing betrayal everywhere, seeing Philippe through Lucien's eyes.

'I see –' Philippe considered '– you are wearing one of
chère Maria's frocks.' Only Maria could have thought of a
border of embroidered lions at the hemline, to emphasise
the new longer length. And anyone else would have added
a matching border on the magyar sleeves. Not Maria. Just
one solitary lion snarled halfway across the top right arm
seam so that at every movement the lion's muscles seemed
to ripple.

'How is Maria?'

Philippe raised an amused eyebrow. 'Everyone in Paris
haute couture knows how Maria is. So original in her
ideas, yes? No idea of cut. She and dear Elsa Schiaparelli
are making quite a name for themselves in Paris. Fortunately at the Maison la Ferté—'

'I know,' she interrupted, smiling. 'Maison la Ferté, like
Worth, goes on for ever.'

'Precisely.' He smiled. 'Ideas are ephemeral, la Ferté *is*
couture and couture is without end.'

'Like the Third Empire,' Nell murmured.

He smiled, not a whit put out by her mockery. 'You
have a song, do you not, about a Vicar of Bray who
adapted his cloth to changing times? As with us. When the
Empire ends, *vive la république*. After all, women do not
change – only politics.'

A shadow flitted across Nell's face, at a memory of
Lucien standing by the Seine using just such words.

'So this is the Gadsby heir,' Philippe continued, looking
down into the pram. Was there a trace of mocking
emphasis on the Gadsby? Nell dismissed the thought
impatiently. 'He lacks Tom's fair hair and blue eyes, I
see.'

'He takes after me,' said Nell shortly.

'*Entendu*,' he murmured. 'And how did Tom take the news of Melissa's new marriage?' And then swiftly, like a snake: 'And you, Nell, how happy you must be to see two of your dearest friends married to each other. Was it your doing? But no, that cannot be, of course, for when Melissa invited me to the wedding, she explained it was to be a quiet affair since they were both concerned not to upset you in view of your former close friendship with my brother.'

Nell stared at him, waves of sickness almost overcoming her. 'What do you mean?' she said weakly, licking dry lips. Inadequate, ingenuous words, but something to say, grappling with the implication of his words.

Philippe shrugged. '*La belle* Melissa was so amused when she told me, for she had thought, before my brother explained his own relationship with you, that you and I were lovers, Nell. I was flattered indeed. I denied it, I trust vigorously enough to make her believe that you had not taken the entire Maison la Ferté staff to your bed. After all, I have my reputation too, you understand. I must marry and marry soon. To be thought to have had a liaison, however tempting, with the wife of *mon ami* Tom Gadsby, would not look well. Fortunately I do think Melissa believed me—'

But Nell had ceased to listen. Melissa had not only *known* about her and Lucien, but Lucien himself had told her. Perhaps he had only confirmed her own suspicions – she remembered Melissa's strange reference at the club. Knowing Melissa, she would also speedily have guessed David's true parentage.

The August afternoon sun seemed just as treacherous as that on the Riviera all those months ago. Of course Melissa had known. She had instinctively recognised, then discounted, that look on Melissa's face of half-triumph, half-shame that she knew so well, when she had done

307

something of which she was ashamed yet was glorying in her naughtiness, like a child. Melissa had gone ahead without a word to her friend, without confronting the issue by telling Nell face to face, her lack of security driving her on. She could not believe Melissa was really in love with Lucien, so how could she do it, leaving her in ignorance? Friendship indeed Melissa had to offer, but a friendship that went only so far. Where her own interests and self-preservation were at stake nothing would stand in her way. She would persuade herself that Nell no longer cared for him, that she was doing an embittered rejected Lucien a favour by marrying him. Jealousy seared through Nell at the thought of them in each other's arms. First Tom, now Lucien.

Philippe watched the shadows flit across her face. He took her hand gently. 'After all, Tom needs you, Nell.' He kissed it. A pause. 'So does the baby,' he added politely.

'I'm dashed well going.' Nell heard Tom's voice raised in anger, as she hurried through the house in search of somewhere she could be alone to sort out her chaotic thoughts, having left the baby in Rose's care.

'You are not, sir. You have a responsibility to the store.' Jonathan's special roar, seldom heard outside the store. So it was serious. What on earth was happening now? Unwillingly Nell stopped. It was almost unknown for Jonathan and Tom to quarrel and this was clearly something to do with Gadsby's. Reluctantly she entered the library to find both men red-faced, still shouting at each other. Jonathan didn't bother to take his eyes off his recalcitrant grandson as she entered.

'There you are, missy. Kindly tell this husband of yours he has a duty to see to his inheritance, if only because of his son.' Nell stiffened, as he continued: 'He thinks he's gadding off all over the place just as we're entering a slump.' Despite his fury, there was real concern in

Jonathan's voice. 'What's it going to look like, eh? What am I going to tell the board?' Matters were serious if Jonathan had to resort to summoning 'the board' as an argument.

'Going off, Tom?' Nell looked at him anxiously. He had said nothing to her and at this of all times!

'Yes,' he said defiantly. 'I know I hadn't told you yet, but I would have done this week. So much on my mind, I forgot. Well, I'm driving to Kabul and maybe on to India.'

Forgot? Forgot to tell her he was going to drive to Afghanistan and that he'd be away goodness knows how long? she thought despairingly. 'Is this really a good time to go?' she asked desperately.

Tom was slightly taken aback. 'We've thought the scheme up and we are all free to go now, so why not? Four of us in two cars. That way if we lose one car we're all right. Cut down on the luggage. Bit of an adventure driving all that way in an ordinary car. Breaking new ground. Some desert driving too. Be good to see the desert from the ground.'

'And what about Gadsby's while you're gallivanting round the world?' enquired Jonathan grimly.

'You don't need me to run it, sir. You know that. And Nell will be here.'

Despite herself, Nell bit back a wry smile as Jonathan turned a scathing look on her. He had little time to waste on side issues, however. He was intent on his main target, unaccustomed to Tom's not obeying his every word. 'If you go on this preposterous trip,' he informed his grandson, 'there'll be no job for you when you get back. I've been thinking of bringing Gordon in for some time and, by Gad, I'll do it.'

Nell froze. Gordon Holdsby, Rose's husband? She shuddered at the idea. A smooth-talking, self-possessed man, pleasant enough on social occasions, she instinctively felt he was all wrong for Gadsby's. Tom looked first puzzled, then as realisation sank in, belligerent. 'You must do as you like,' he informed his grandfather coldly.

Gordon, Nell remembered with sinking heart, had recently lost his job in the City on account of the slump. But as Gadsby's Store director? Worse, on the board? Surely this was just a move to spite Tom? He at least left things at the store alone – which was preferable to a meddling interloper anxious for power. Rose doted on her husband, but Nell distrusted the bland pleasant manner. His charm was a barrier behind which lurked an unknown quantity. It might be benign, but she feared it could well be the opposite. It was true that she did not know him well. The joint family occasions tended to be few and far between. Gordon and Rose lived in Sussex, and rarely visited Merrifield at the same time as Tom and herself. Only at Christmas and on Jonathan's birthday did the Holdsbys with their two young children, a boy and a girl, come in force. Rose looked pregnant again, in fact, Nell realised. Now Jonathan was talking of bringing Gordon in to manage the store, with no experience. But if Jonathan was merely using this as a threat to Tom, it wasn't succeeding.

'I won't be blackmailed,' he shouted angrily.

'You can do as you damn well please, sir,' retorted Jonathan. 'And if you don't come back in a better frame of mind, I'll change my will too.'

If only he would, thought Nell longingly. Then there would be no question of the shares coming to David afterwards. Surely even Jonathan wouldn't go so far as disinheriting his grandson though? Tom flushed and said nothing as Jonathan stamped out in high ill-humour.

'Do you have to go on this trip?' Nell asked when he'd gone.

'Yes,' Tom said obstinately.

'But he's right. You shouldn't leave the store.'

'Don't you start, Nell,' Tom retorted. 'I've made it clear

310

time and time again that I work at Gadsby's because he wants me to, and in return I do what I want, when I want. Now he's got David to satisfy him too. What more does he want?'

'Some interest on your part,' exploded Nell. 'Some understanding. And he *hasn't* got David, as you put it, and one day your grandfather will know it.'

'We've been over this before,' Tom said angrily. 'He's our son. He *is* a Gadsby.'

'In name only,' countered Nell quietly.

'And that's what counts. I'm bringing him up, aren't I? Now forget it, Nell. I know my grandfather better than you. He'll come round, you'll see, and he'll never change his will.'

'If you won't tell him about David, I will,' she said steadily. 'This deception has gone on long enough.'

'You'll break his heart,' said Tom complacently. 'You won't risk that. I know you.'

Tom was threatening her! To what a pass had they come that they couldn't even talk things over any more? Seeing Nell fall silent, Tom knew he'd won his point.

'David is the only Gadsby there is of the next generation. Grandfather doesn't want Holdsbys on the board. It's the name he wants, Nell. That's all he's concerned with. And we've given it to him.'

'We?' she thought dully, defeated. David was Lucien's but who would ever know it.

Two days later she left to view the Paris collections. She had set herself this hurdle to leap, to face the possibility that in Paris she might meet Lucien by chance, although she resolved she would go nowhere near Maison la Ferté. He was almost certain to be there at some point, and Paris was not so large as London. It was a smaller, more intimate society. In sprawling London broken hearts could lose themselves, but in Paris it was different. On the Champs Elysées might she see him by chance, sipping coffee and watching the world go by at Fouquet's? Might she see him hurrying along under the trees towards the Avenue Montaigne? At any moment she might look up and there he would be. It was possible, always possible, in Paris.

There were other challenges there too. A quarter of the city's economy was based on the fashion business, and Nell had hardly been there a day before she began to notice tell-tale signs, not obvious but suggestive, that Paris too was affected by slump. She had paid to come here on this occasion out of her own pocket, for Jonathan had bluntly told her that there wasn't the cash for the buyers to attend Paris collections. Buying was to be done by correspondence. Or Maria must come to London. Sketches could be sent. Dismayed, Nell decided to go anyway. How could one gain the true feel of what was happening by sketches? Now she saw the odd lace shop here, a fabric shop there, an artificial flower maker's shop, all with shutters closed with an air of finality about them that a decision to follow the majority of Parisians to the seaside in August could not explain.

Maria, however, appeared to be flourishing. Her establishment was still in the Avenue Montaigne, but she had moved from her previous attic rooms. Now she had the first two floors of a large house and was negotiating for a third. Or rather her manager, Jacques Peyrier, was. His advent was no surprise to Nell, since she had seen his signature on letters, but his obvious familiarity with Maria was. She took an instant dislike to him.

'I want to design, Nell,' Maria told her casually. 'I can't be bothered with details of paperwork and Jacques is perfectly splendid.'

So he obviously was for the house of Maniosta was running faultlessly, and improving its position all the time. Nell was glad of it, for Maria was no businesswoman. Intuition and flair were her forte, not money.

312

'Jacques wants me to marry him.' Maria flung back her head and laughed. 'I shall not do so, naturally.'

'Don't you want to get married?' asked Nell curious, relieved that Jacques was not destined to play a larger part in the fashion house.

Maria was surprised. 'Of course, Nell. And to have *bambini*. But not before—' she broke off.

'Before what?'

'Before I paint my Sistine chapel, create my *look*. I must design something so beautiful that years after I am dead, women will look at pictures of it and say that was not just fashion. That was art.'

'What will it be?' asked Nell, curiously, fascinated.

'I don't know, but when it comes then I shall,' Maria answered simply. 'Then I shall say, I have done my beautiful thing and it is time to marry. But not now, and *not* to Jacques.' She laughed again. 'We women are free now, are we not, Nell?'

'Sexually perhaps – but not in other ways,' she replied soberly. Free? Bound by love for her child, bound by loyalty to Tom, bound by the past. Freedom?

'What is freedom to you, Nell?' Maria asked idly.

She considered. 'Gadsby's,' she said at last. Every other path was blocked. Gadsby's alone held a way to independence. 'If I could run it as I want. Unless I do, it will be swallowed up in a year or two, a victim of this slump. But I *won't* let it happen,' she added fiercely.

Maria shrugged. 'If you want that enough, it may happen that way. Sometimes things do.' She flashed her wide smile at Nell. 'And now, Nell, you see my show. You buy them *all*, yes?'

'I buy them all, *no*, I'm afraid,' said Nell ruefully. 'I'd love to, but I don't have the money for more than thirty. It's the slump.'

'I hear of that,' said Maria sympathetically. 'I am lucky, but others not so. I have *ideas* and those intrigue the grand

313

signoras of Paris. They say they must have a Schiaparelli this season; and they must have a Maria Maniosta this season. This is good for me, but for houses like la Ferté,' she shrugged, 'not so good.'

'Maison la Ferté is not doing well?' asked Nell, apparently casually. Not casually enough, for Maria looked at her in curiosity.

'The de la Fertés are friends of the Gadsbys I have heard.'

'Yes,' said Nell, trying to sound unconcerned. 'We all know the count and his two sons. And of course I know Melissa.' A slight tremble in her voice.

'Ah,' said Maria. 'You have known Lucien—'

'And Philippe,' said Nell quickly. She didn't want Maria to dwell on Lucien.

'The so-charming Comte Philippe,' said Maria, frowning. 'He is under much pressure, that one. Their trade falls off, and he must design with imagination to attract custom. Cut is not enough. But I was right what I told you once. He has no new ideas; he can only create on the lines of the old adapted to meet the new fashions – *after* someone else has had the idea that takes fashion leaping forward. These old couturiers that live on tradition are the ones that now suffer. See how they are bought up by other companies. One by one they fall. And those that remain must woo their customers. La Ferté designs specifically for the average woman; they flatter, they do not lead. This year Philippe hopes to make women look slimmer by his designs. And he is clever. A straight panel at the back to the hips, a half-belt fastened in front coming from the side seam, both for day and evening wear. He uses his charm in this collection and it works. But next time? And the time after?'

Maria's new collection was as breathtakingly original as her earlier ones, with no concession to the past. Full-length evening gowns with three tiers, in plain colours,

314

with just one splash of Maniosta inventiveness: a tiger, prowling at a waistline, a giraffe extending under one arm, a koala bear hugging one shoulder in stark contrast. Quilting – as in the collections of other houses – but here used far more effectively in matching ensembles of dress, coat and hat. Only these no longer matched in colour, but contrasted. Only the trimmings drew the ensemble together. Raised waistlines brought grace and height to the models. For evening Maria had made brilliant use of the new chiffon gold lamé in bolder and narrower skirts than her competitors, which clung to figures and shimmered in the artificial light. For afternoon, she had created a range of dramatically patterned dresses, in contrast to the plain colours of morning and evening. Patterns as bold as the new women themselves. Taken from modern artists or Cretan friezes, they all were effective, if startling. When at last the parade was over Nell turned to Maria, saying ruefully: 'I wish I could order them all.'

Maria was pleased. 'Good, eh? Now, for you, Nell, I show you this. No one else sees it.' She beckoned her into her private office and pressed a bell. Through the curtains appeared a model. Nell was stunned, as the willowy girl stood like a statue, allowing the full effect of the gown to be seen. The line of the long skirt, almost but not quite straight, clinging to the curves of the figure. Nothing new, this. What was, was the balance given to it by the emphasis on the shoulders, which were built up at the seam and ruched in chiffon. The whole silhouette thus made the previous year's fashions immediately outdated and even threatened Maria's present collection.

'This is your beautiful thing?' asked Nell in awe.

'No,' said Maria slowly. 'I think not. But it is a *look*, is it not? I work on this now. It is not yet ready. But next spring then we shall see – and then, pouf! to all the other fashion houses. I have other ideas too,' she said happily.

'How will I afford you soon, Maria?' asked Nell in despair, seeing Gadsby's future slip away from her for lack of money and power.

'For you, Nell, there is no problem,' said Maria, surprised she could think so. 'Nothing can come between you and me.'

Tom left in January in Nelly I. Nelly II was a Ford, Nelly I the old Alvis. He had had a last-minute change of heart, switching from his Standard Wolseley to the faithful old Alvis. For the last six weeks he had been engrossed in maps of almost every country she had ever heard of, it seemed, and quite a few she hadn't. Hornton had been engaged in packing and re-packing continuously as Tom fussed over every item, checking for weight. The Alvis seemed to require more baggage for its own needs than those of its driver, until it resembled a portable garage, combined with a housemaid's kit: 'Dust – you've no idea what problems a little bit of dust can cause, Nelly.' Finally, however, Tom was ready, the two motor-cars leaving Eaton Square to a toy trumpet fanfare from a neighbour's child and a bevy of press photographers. Affection returned to Nell as she watched the Alvis turn the corner, giving her a last glimpse of a fair head held eager and proud. She would not see him again for at least eight months, unless the trip was abandoned.

She had expected to feel loneliness as she walked back into the huge and empty drawing room, but unexpectedly she realised guiltily that it was relief that flooded through her, an exhilaration that for all the months ahead she could plan her own life – and David's.

'Anything more you require, Madam?' Hornton's voice from the doorway.

'Nothing, thank you.'

Nothing more.

Tom had been morose ever since August, save when

preoccupied with plans for his journey. He had not repaired the rift with Jonathan, and true to his word, although Jonathan still kept him on the board, he had brought in Gordon Holdsby as Store director. Already this had led to trouble. So far Gordon had avoided conflict with her, but the other buyers were already complaining of his overzealous interest in books and accounts, culminating in the abrupt departure of an offended Mr Polgarth from Fabrics. This was good news for Joe who despite Gordon's nomination of an outsider was promoted to buyer. But it did not bode well for the future. Gordon's pleasant social charm did not extend to staff, it seemed. The next to offer to resign, early in February, was one of the two directors, Mr Charles. Almost in tears, he informed Jonathan Gadsby that he was too old to change his thirty-year-old system for coordinating departmental accounts. This time Jonathan intervened. Perceiving acquiescence to be the logical course, Gordon retreated. Mr Bolton was not so lucky two weeks later. His all-important office for the smooth running of the whole of Gadsby's was filled by a lady of Gordon's acquaintance, Miss Ankering. Miss Edith Ankering, in her late-thirties, knew little about the smooth running of fashion stores but much about pleasing Gordon Holdsby.

This brought about Nell's first head-on clash with Holdsby two months later. Checking the arrival of made-up orders from the workrooms, she found to her stupefaction that the trimming on one of the gowns was of machine-made lace, not hand-made. Storming into the workrooms she was directed with some smugness to Miss Ankering, who had refused to pass the correct order through to the Haberdashery Department on grounds of cost. A short sharp battle ended in the defeat of Miss Ankering, the reversal of the order and an admission that Mr Holdsby had set a ceiling on cost for trimmings and accessories in relation to selling price.

317

'Why was I not informed of this, Mr Holdsby?' Nell icily enquired, emphasising the *Mr*.

'My dear Nell,' emphasising the *Nell*, 'I regret this has caused you so much concern. Your part after all is done by the time the order is taken. Mine begins.'

'My part, as you term it, is *partly* done when I have delivered the finished product to a satisfied customer,' she rounded on him. 'And not over until I have returned satisfactory turnover figures and accounts to Mr Charles.'

'And the latter are hardly likely to be satisfactory using hand-made Brussels lace.'

'Nor if I lose my regular clients by cheating them,' she replied steadily. 'Gadsby's cannot afford to lose clients.'

'Or to pander to them,' he picked up equably.

'I believe Mr Gadsby understands the importance of quality.' She thrust down her gauntlet.

He picked it up unhesitatingly. 'Unfortunately bankers do not always follow suit. There is the question of financial commitments to consider.'

'Bankers,' she repeated blankly. 'But Mr Gadsby has no loans. I know he considered it but—'

'I don't believe you're a director, Nell,' he informed her pleasantly. 'I, on the other hand, am. Perhaps you do not understand the mechanics of capital investment by debenture, and how much stores need it if they are to survive.'

A director? She had had no idea that Gordon was now on the board. Jonathan had meant what he said then, and no word of it had reached her. No reason that it should – and yet she was stung that Jonathan could keep her in so much ignorance. But how to reply? Carefully? Why bother to be careful? She'd say what she meant.

'I understand enough to recognise the difference between loans from banks to capitalise expansion and loan-raising revenue just to tide one over difficult periods. And that, presumably, is what you have persuaded him to do. What Gadsby's needs, Mr Holdsby, is to increase turnover and profit, not pay interest charges on debentures.'

He sighed. 'As you are my sister-in-law, I can hardly behave to you as to the other buyers. I trust you will not take advantage of our relationship, Nell?'

'Nor you of yours.' There was no need for her to spell out it was his influence on Jonathan Gadsby she had in mind. Jonathan must indeed be bitter against Tom to have appointed Holdsby. Gordon could hardly fail to resent the fact that Tom was still – presumably – the sole heir and his own son barred from succession because he did not bear the Gadsby name. Could he do anything about it? that was the question. For the first time she wished Tom were here, but it would be September at the earliest before he was back and much could happen in the firm's politics before then. After all, Jonathan was eighty years old, and even his strong nose for business must start to twitch less keenly soon.

In any case, she'd always understood from Tom that the company could not raise extra capital without changing the Memorandum of Agreement – and that could only be done by a Special Resolution. Surely Tom would have told her? But he had been away and could not have left a proxy vote because he had not known about it, she remembered uneasily. What about her one meagre share? Surely a resolution of that magnitude had to be voted on by all shareholders? She couldn't have influenced the decision, true, but there should have been a meeting. And there had not been one called. Her uneasiness grew. What was going on?

Despite this looming question mark over the future, her pleasure in Gadsby's continued, as the great store hummed into life in the mornings, then throbbed through the day, its wheels turned by the ever changing momentum of its customers. Jonathan, for all his obstinacy and distrust of her, was straightforward – she could

319

talk to him although she failed to convince him. She had tried diffidently talking to Mrs Emmeline of her worries, but she had immediately made it clear that business was business, and darling Jonathan understood what he was doing.

Maybe he did, but he understood it on the principles of a bygone age, not in this climate of uncertainty that had so suddenly descended. Times had changed after 1918. The war to end wars had seemed at first to bring greater security, but now this had faded and an uneasy feeling reigned.

Early in May she went upstairs one evening to say goodnight to David and to read him a story, endeavouring to make her voice its usual bright self. She came downstairs exhausted, sitting in the drawing room before dinner, disloyally grateful to have it to herself, and enjoying the peace. Until the telephone rang.

She left it for Hornton to answer, hoping against hope it would be for Tom, so that she would be left in peace. Tom had reached Persia now. She had received a letter from the Riva Palace Hotel via the British ambassador in Teheran, ecstatically recounting their journey across the caravan trails of the Iraqi desert, and the perils of the route to Kasr-i-Shirin, where it was hard to tell whether they faced greater danger from bandits or from the road itself.

The call wasn't for Tom, however.

'For you, Mrs Gadsby,' Hornton announced, a peculiar shade of reverence in his voice that she half recognised.

Then she did recognise it, just as he gave the name: 'The Comtesse de la Ferté.' For a moment she hoped wildly that he meant the Comtesse Guy, but of course it wouldn't be. It could only be Melissa. Nell went slowly towards the telephone, as though her body had suddenly been pumped full of lead. Perhaps she could just hang up without speaking? No, that would be Melissa's victory.

She picked up the handset, unable to frame any words besides a croaky, 'Hello?'

'Darling,' said Melissa cheerfully, in the old well-remembered tone, just as if six years had dropped away and she was about to invite Nell to old Ma Meyrick's. A younger naive Nell. A Nell without caution, for then she had never been betrayed. Now she was wary. Not for her the whirlpool, but the calm ripples of an ebbing tide.

'I'm in London,' the familiar voice announced happily. 'Wouldn't it be fun to meet? I thought you might like to come over for drinkies and dinner.'

Nell fought for control. Come over? What the blazes did Melissa think they were going to chat about? The weather?

'Is—' She stopped to frame the question.

'Lucien's not here,' said Melissa brightly, interpreting correctly. 'Why don't we have a jolly evening, like we used to? Just the two of us, quietly. I'm at the Dorchester.'

In spite of herself Nell laughed. Only Melissa would choose to have a quiet tête-à-tête in full view of everyone at the Dorchester. She wanted to refuse. She wanted to avoid remembering nightmare. Yet if she refused, she did so for ever. If she went forward, she risked – what would she risk? Nothing. She was stronger now, fully armed. And curiosity linked hands with past affection to drive her on.

'Very well,' she said guardedly. 'But just for a cocktail.'

'Oh no, *do* let's have dinner. I'm *starving*,' Melissa wheedled.

Why not? The waiters would provide a buffer between them. She could pretend – no, not pretend. She never had done so and she never would. She dressed with care in one of Maria's startling new evening dresses, with a dramatic cowl collar. She wanted to distance herself as far as possible from that Nell of six years ago. For once, instead

321

of taking a bus or taxi, she decided to summon the Rolls-Royce, to the surprise of its chauffeur, since he was rarely called upon by Mrs G. Nell intended to arrive in style. She too was somebody now. Thanks, originally, to Melissa, her innate honesty reminded her painfully. Always thanks to Melissa. The debt was paid, it was true, but not forgotten. Somewhere the old Melissa might lay buried beneath the web of betrayal and come forward smiling with hope. A rush of affection for that naive girl and bright star Melissa returned. Then vanished as she braced herself for what was to come – meeting Lucien's wife.

She sailed in through the main entrance in fine style, nodding at the doorman to whom she and Tom were known. She left her wrap and headed for the cocktail lounge. No Melissa. Even as she searched in vain, a page boy came up to her. 'Miss Hargreaves would like you to join her in the dining room, Mrs Gadsby.'

How like Melissa. So hungry she couldn't wait for her guests to have a cocktail. And yet she kept her fantastic figure. Almost laughing now, Nell went into the dining room. She followed the maître d'hôtel, torn between her eagerness to see Melissa again and a desire to get the ordeal over with.

Melissa hadn't changed. Beneath a huge potted palm she sat at a table, the golden hair marcelled into glowing beauty, her slim shoulders encased in shimmering chiffon lamé. By her side was a man. Almost unrecognisable at first, until he looked up and saw her. It was Lucien. No, Melissa hadn't changed. This had been planned. The shock Lucien obviously felt had the effect of steadying Nell. So he hadn't expected her? Melissa the spider had entrapped them both into her bewitching web.

Somehow she reached the table, sat on the chair that the maître d'hôtel pulled out for her, nodded at Lucien as he resumed his place opposite. Then Melissa – leaping up a little too late for the best theatrical effect, noted Nell dispassionately – threw her arms round her and kissed her.

Judas, Judas, *Judas*!

'There,' she said, pleased, 'isn't this nice?' as she sat down again.

'*Comment allez-vous*, Nell?' enquired Lucien through stiff lips.

Comment allez-vous? Tears and an insane desire to laugh seized Nell together. Both repressed. This was going to be easier than she'd thought. This was a stranger. This was not the man she had known, who had . . . No, she would not think of that.

'It is, I believe, the first time we have seen you since our marriage,' he continued. 'I have of course heard much of Gadsby's and what you are achieving. Maria Maniosta is going to be one of our great designers – I myself think this raised shoulder effect she introduced this spring will stay with us. Slimmer skirts, balanced by width above.' He went into a detailed analysis of style, but she ceased to take in the words. The same voice, but not the same man. He was giving her time to relax, she realised suddenly, with surprise. How controlled he was. So it *was* all past. Dead. So much easier. She could pretend that it had never happened. She would give no sign that she still felt otherwise. After all, this was the 1930s; love affairs were common, but what had passed was irrevocable, and friendship must replace love.

Her eyes fastened on Lucien's hand gripped round the stem of his glass, as the waiter poured wine into her own. It was gripping very tightly. She watched him raise it to his lips, as Melissa chattered.

'It's a splendid offer. Don't you agree, Lucien darling?'

'I—' He choked over his wine, spluttering into the napkin. 'You must excuse me.' He pushed back his chair violently, and hurried away, pausing only to speak briefly to the maître d'hôtel. So he would not return. Of course he wasn't a stranger. He was Lucien, married to Melissa. Neither of them had forgotten, any more than she had. The dull ache inside her sharpened into a knife-edge.

Melissa was looking at her in something like apology. 'I'm sorry, darling,' she said unaffectedly for once, 'but I had to know, didn't I?'

'Know?'

'Whether he still felt the same about you,' Melissa supplied matter-of-factly. 'And now I do. And you still feel the same about him, though I didn't have much doubt about that, you loyal old thing. Still, you thought you loved Tommy once and then found out you didn't. You might have found out the same thing about Lucien.'

'Why did you marry him without telling me?' Nell was quite calm now, almost detached, with a curious interest as to why it should have been so.

'I didn't know,' said Melissa quickly, looking guilelessly straight at her. 'I thought you loved Philippe. You never told me I was wrong, did you?'

Nell stared at her. 'You never could lie convincingly,' she informed her. 'Lucien told you before you got married, so Philippe said. I wouldn't have believed what he said if I hadn't seen it written all over your face. Or if he was lying about Lucien telling you, then Philippe told you himself. Either way, you knew.'

'No!' Fear in Melissa's eyes. 'No, you can't believe that.'

'Oh, but I do,' said Nell, trying to be matter-of-fact. 'It's so like you. Do it first, and wheedle forgiveness later.'

'You're my friend, Nell. You know that,' Melissa babbled. 'You *know* I wouldn't do anything as bad as that. Not to you.'

'If it was sufficiently in your interest, you would,' said Nell flatly. 'And this was. You wouldn't let anything come between you and security. Not even me.'

'How can you say that?' moaned Melissa. 'I never wanted to hurt you really. Anyway, you were married,' she added, a note of defiance entering her voice.

'Yes,' said Nell bitterly. 'I was married to a man who still loved you.'

'Tommy would have stayed with me if there hadn't been you,' said Melissa startlingly. 'See how he came to me when I needed help? It could be said you took him from me, Nell.'

'Me?' she said, stunned, confused at this topsy-turvy analysis.

'Yes,' said Melissa defiantly. 'And now,' she looked at Nell coolly, 'I've got Lucien. So we're quits in a way.' She saw Nell's face and began to cry, to the great interest of the next table. Nell passed her a handkerchief unsympathetically. Melissa could even look pretty blowing her nose. Sure enough, one tiny blow and all signs of tears obediently vanished.

'Nell,' she said suddenly, in a quite different voice, 'let's start again. I still need you. You don't understand—' And clearly she could not this time speak of it. 'I didn't know about you and Lucien until you came to the villa. Truly I didn't. You can ask him.'

Nell flinched. Ask Lucien? Of course. Melissa would bank on her not doing so. But Philippe? Lucien said he was not to be trusted, that he used information to cause maximum trouble at the right moment. Had he done so in this case to drive a further wedge between her and Melissa? Why should he? Which of them to believe: Philippe or Melissa? Only one answer. 'It doesn't matter now, Melissa,' she said, strength flowing into her again. 'Nothing matters. Let's start from here.'

'But where is here?' said Melissa. 'Help me find it, Nell. Help me.' She stared bleakly down at the dessert. Then she looked up brightly. 'These French strawberries are *delicious*, aren't they?'

325

Chapter Ten

That image of Melissa, the last forgotten teardrop falling on to the bright red of the strawberries, stayed with Nell, a symbol of the disasters that threatened to engulf not only Britain but the whole world as autumn came on, she thought fancifully, a requiem for the bright hopes of the twenties, and of all that followed the war to end war. And with Britain, Gadsby's too would be engulfed. For this time it was not an imperialistic Kaiser that threatened safety, but economic disaster. All over Europe, save for France, banks and financiers hiccupped, faltered and succumbed.

Preoccupied with the daily minutiae at Gadsby's, Nell did not fully appreciate the implications of what was happening. But the formation of a National Government in August followed by the unthinkable, a strike of naval ratings at Invergordon, over the reduction of their pay by a shilling, caused all her forebodings about Gadsby's to return. The dole was cut, Means Tests introduced and Hunger Marches belied the cheerful face presented by most newspapers.

The receipts of the Fashion Department, however, were telling a different story to that presented on the ladies' pages of the magazine and newspaper world. Velvet tea frocks, white printed chiffon afternoon dresses, exciting new shifts in millinery to small tip-tilted hats, ermine wraps – none of these spoke of hardship and deprivation, or even of the drastic reduction of expenditure on clothes amongst regular Gadsby's clients that was playing havoc with their turnover.

It wasn't a problem confined to Gadsby's. Gamages were forced to sell their newly opened Oxford Street store, many department stores were either going out of business or drastically reducing prices to attract custom. Others, like Gadsby's, hung on grimly in the hope of better times, defiantly flying a flag in which Nell had ceased to believe. There was even talk of the new Government imposing crippling import duties to encourage home trade, something that worried her greatly. If she could no longer afford to buy from Paris, especially from Maria Maniosta, she would be forced to start again to rebuild the Fashion Department, using British designers, at the worst possible time. Miss Gertrude, now seventy-seven, was still happily designing half of the sports dresses required per season and a few leisure wear dresses. For her to take on the entire Fashion Department, however, was quite out of the question. And to look elsewhere for a competent designer would undoubtedly bring her into conflict once more with Gordon Holdsby.

She rarely had head-on collisions with him but she was uneasily aware that he merely bided his time. She tried to tell herself she was imagining it. He was, after all, doing a good job in one way. Waste was being ruthlessly abolished, everyone was more cost-conscious. What worried her was that his methods of attaining savings clashed with what Gadsby's stood for. The weekly discussion of her accounts with him developed into a hitherto subdued running battle which was gaining in intensity. He had begun with buttons.

'Why so many, Nell?' he enquired, frowning, holding up one of Maria's stylish dinner dresses on which the offending item was deliberately the only ornamentation, a focal point to attract attention and help emphasise the long bias line of the dress – an essential in Paris autumn fashion. 'They seem highly expensive items to employ sixty-four on the one gown.'

'The model requires it. They are the vital feature,' she explained.

'Use less on further orders,' he commanded.

'The model requires it,' she repeated steadily. 'If we use less, we are guilty of false pretences, open to complaint from Paris and from the customer.'

'They'll never notice a few less,' replied Holdsby pleasantly.

'You underrate our customers,' Nell told him sharply. 'I won't take the responsibility.'

'I will.'

'Then I shall take this to the Fourth Floor,' Nell informed him, standing her ground.

Holdsby had backed down on that occasion, but similar battles cropped up over the use of cheaper linings and trimmings, even plain loops instead of frog loops to save workroom time, until Nell realised that inevitably she could not hold out much longer. Zealously he delved into the workroom practices, constantly suggesting new economies. In some cases she was forced to admit he was right, but the way he imposed them created ill will, resulting in many of the best workers leaving, to be replaced by juniors at a third of the cost. The workroom manager, with twenty years' experience, gave in her notice. He took this as a triumph.

Then he turned to costs, insisting that workroom costs charged to the showroom should be cut. It helped Nell's accounts splendidly, but the results for the workroom were devastating since it resulted in the necessity for reduction of workroom wages. Holdsby bowed out of this aspect, leaving a new inexperienced manageress and a demoralised and lower standard of working force.

Did Jonathan ever notice? Nell wondered despairingly.

Did it occur to him that the high rate of staff loss was due to Gordon Holdsby? She once tried to speak to him about it, but he refused to listen.

'You're always saying that younger folks should have their say, missy. Now I'm agreeing with you. So that's enough.'

'Not this way,' Nell said stoutly. 'You—'

'Your way, eh? We'd be a sixpenny store before you knew it. Holdsby understands my methods all right.'

There Nell agreed with him wholeheartedly. Gordon Holdsby had the measure of Jonathan Gadsby and would not rest until he'd conquered him by one means or another. Conquered Jonathan – and won Gadsby's.

Then Holdsby turned his attention to the ready-made sports dresses. 'You could make them cheaper,' was his claim.

'Of course, if I made them in rayon not silk,' Nell retorted. 'And then they'd *look* cheaper.'

'But they would be bought,' said Holdsby, smilingly, smoothly, reasonably.

'Not necessarily,' said Nell coolly. She tried once more. 'If we go into the cheap ready-made market, we are competing where we have no experience and where we would have powerful rivals. At the moment we have a niche of our own.' How strange to think she was echoing broadly what Jonathan and Lucien had maintained, that a reputation for quality had to be adhered to at all costs. 'Our customers—'

'What there are of them,' Holdsby interrupted casually.

'Expect quality,' Nell continued. 'And quality we must give them or we go under. My plan would include—'

'*Your* plan, Nell?' said Gordon, eyebrows raised.

She cursed herself for her stupidity. Holdsby would never brook competition, and so far she had bought time by making him think she had no desire for power. Indeed she had not. But she did have a great desire to save Gadsby's.

Early in October Tom returned, highly pleased with his achievements and to a fanfare of publicity. The other car had had to be abandoned, leaving the old Alvis to take all four of them. The 'old lady' had accompanied them home by ship and was finally put into retirement at Merrifield.

Tom spoke of new cities, new worlds – Persia, Iraq, Afghanistan, India – of having to improve or even build bridges before they could cross rivers, of the lack of roads, of the native populations – but most of all he spoke of achievement, of six months crowned with fruition, instead of monotony. Nell came to realise that places and people were only incidentals to the quest itself, the need to arrive. Save only for the desert, to which he returned in conversation time after time. The glaring, merciless heat, the harsh blue sky, the havens of the stockades, the dragonflies sometimes many miles from water, the miraculous effect of even the slightest fall of rain, when desert dwellers would ride a hundred miles or more to reach the suddenly green blossoming desert; the stately much-prized camels, the cold of the nights, and above all, the wonder of the stars.

'And the roads! I can tell you, Nelly, Porlock Hill will seem like Watling Street compared with some of those tracks. And not even tracks in some places. You just follow the sun. A thousand miles without water. More sometimes.'

Sunburnt and skin-roughened, he strode around the house as though it were his newly conquered kingdom. Eagerly he showed her the photographs he had taken – buildings, strange people, faces – in an experience whose value he could not properly communicate. Always he would come back to the desert:

'Nothing beats it, Nelly. It's beautiful enough the way

331

we saw it. But coming to it from the air – now, that's the true way. You see yourself face to face then.' He broke off as if unwilling now to attempt to explain what it was like.

His first thought when he arrived home, however, had been for David.

'How's the little chap?' he asked her anxiously, dumping canvas and haversack unceremoniously in the hall for Hornton to attend to.

'Asleep,' said Nell ruefully. 'He tried to keep his eyes open as long as he could, knowing you'd be back, but—'

'Not for long, he won't be,' shouted Tom happily, bounding up the stairs more like a boy of fifteen than a man in his thirties.

He had been back three weeks before he even mentioned Gadsby's. He was never at home, but he was never at Gadsby's either, always off on one mysterious mission or another. Even then she had to prise news out of him, seeing the frown on his face one evening.

'Been to a board meeting,' he admitted at last. He had adamantly refused to approach Jonathan on the question of resuming his former job, despite Nell's worried persuasive words.

'Gadsby's *needs* you back, Tom. It's no wonder you feel you don't know what's going on.'

'But I don't need Gadsby's. Jonathan won't cut me off without a penny, you'll see,' he said reassuringly. 'Young David will still get it in the end.'

She fell silent, battling once more with the problem of David and Gadsby's. Then: 'So what worries you, Tom?'

'There's something odd going on,' he replied slowly. 'There's a couple of new fellows on the board, Jones and Palgrove. As well as our chum Holdsby. Know anything about that?'

'No,' Nell answered with foreboding. 'I don't.'

'Friends of Holdsby's, I think,' said Tom. 'Financial chaps from a bank. Something seems to have happened

332

while I've been away, and it's something to do with money.'

'You've got to find out, Tom. Urgently,' she said, all her fears rising to the surface. 'I'm sure Gordon's up to no good. There should be a general meeting to appoint new directors, shouldn't there? There hasn't been one. Or to authorise new capital.'

Tom's brow furrowed. 'I'd better talk to the old codger, I suppose.'

'Let me come,' said Nell worriedly, but he refused to let her.

He returned, reassuringly. 'You were wrong,' he told her. 'A governing director can appoint new directors himself. And the money is for expansion,' he explained. 'Gordon arranged it,' he added gloomily.

'And what about the meeting for that?' Nell demanded.

'All taken care of, Grandpops said.'

'But—'

'Now, don't make a fuss, old girl. The debentures are held by a highly respectable merchant bank, Tolwell's, and you of all people should be glad of the chance of expansion. We don't have any restrictions in our articles on how much we can borrow and don't have to hold a general meeting. It is Grandpops' company, you know,' he told her somewhat reprovingly.

'But the interest,' she said. 'How's that to be found, and how much new capital?'

'Another three-quarters of a million at 10 per cent.'

'How can we afford it? And what's it *for*?' she demanded. 'When our profits are falling?'

'Apparently not,' said Tom defiantly now. 'We made a profit this last six months, and Holdsby needs more capital.'

'Does Jonathan think this extra capital is a good idea?' asked Nell unbelievingly.

'The profit's impressed him,' said Tom. 'It's a good

show, Nelly, whatever you think about Holdsby.'

But Nell knew precisely what she thought about Holdsby – and was deeply concerned. Jonathan's head was so firmly in the sand, convinced that Gadsby's would survive as it always had, that he was failing to account for the fact that to others Gadsby's itself might be less important than power. Fine, provided Holdsby's and Gadsby's interests were the same, but what if, soon, they were not? And that niggle still at the back of her mind. Surely the company's Memorandum had to specify a right to borrow, and brief though her own look at it had been when she was handed her one share, she could remember no such right. She tried to talk to Tom about it, but he lost first interest, then patience. Instead he turned to aeroplanes.

'I'd like to have a crack at the Cape record,' he muttered. 'Amy Johnson's taken care of Australia. Can't beat nineteen and a half hours. But the Cape – there are still possibilities. I'd come back the same way, and maybe land in the desert on purpose this time. Swoop down like a god into my kingdom. Fanciful, eh?' He laughed.

'Gods are immortal, Tom. You're not. For every one who survives there are a couple who are never found.'

He laughed. 'Never fear, old thing. I'm jolly well immortal too. While David needs me.'

Maria's bright face had borne no signs of worry this autumn in Paris. Magnificent as ever in one of her own creations, she looked even taller than she was in a deceptively narrow skirt to mid-calf. The bodice and skirt were made in one with no joining seam, Nell noted. Tall, tall, the dress seemed to flow on for ever. But envy was no use. She was Nell Gadsby and that was that. Despite Lucien's valiant attempts to create a Parisienne of her, she seemed to have reverted to just Nell again. She noticed Maria's glance at her serviceable light tweed costume, but her friend avoided comment. After all, she was here in pursuit of others' beauty, not her own.

'You have no problems at Maison Maniosta?' Nell asked, aware of the rumours that even Paris *haute couture* was hit by the slump.

'I don't understand money,' Maria told her ruefully, running a hand through the mane of hair like a black halo round her head. 'But I am lucky. Jacques is clever and sales are good. So why worry, huh?'

'There's good reason,' Nell told her tartly at this short-sightedness. 'By next spring we might have import controls. It would mean I can't buy any more from you. It may not mean much to you, but it could to haute couture in Paris generally. If not Maniosta,' she added.

Maria was not so insouciant as she'd thought. 'You think I think only of myself, eh? I do not. I think of others, and I do not do what *they* do, like Maison la Ferté.' Her eyes glimmered. 'They live on their old customers. There is *always* wealth in France somewhere, you know. Despite war, despite slump, despite revolution. And la Ferté knows where it is. But how much longer can they live this way.'

'If controls come in?'

'Yes, that will hurt them. But they have deeper problems.'

'What?' Nell asked abruptly.

Maria twinkled at her. 'Oh, Nell, you are British. You think I give all Paris's secrets away? No. Me, I am loyal. You want to know, you find out yourself. But for me, because we are friends, Nell, I show you how *I* will live through this slump.' She seized Nell by the wrist and marched her into her inner office. 'No one comes in here. Only me. Now you. *And* I keep it locked.'

'So you've learned that not all Paris couturiers are loyal?' asked Nell innocently.

Maria looked disconcerted, then laughed. 'I am careful.'

she conceded. 'So Mr Fairbanks, he is the only kind of pirate who gets in here. Now, *ecco!*'

She took out a pad from a locked drawer and flipped it open. Nell drew in her breath. 'See? See?' Maria flipped over the pages.

'But—' Nell was bewildered. 'In a *slump*, Maria? These?' Challenging but wearable, glamorous and attractive.

'In these bad times, people go more and more to the cinema, yes? And they all want to look like Greta Garbo, Marlene Dietrich. If we looked like them these wonderful things would happen to us too, they reason. John Gilbert, Fairbanks – he would love *me*. So this is my idea, Nell. Film dresses for everyone. Hollywood Maniosta. Bravo for me. Yes?'

'Bravo.' Nell thought about it. 'But how can you *copy* film dresses? What about copyright, and even if there were no question of that, surely you would not want merely to copy other people's designs? Pirate them?'

'No,' said Maria impatiently. 'You do not understand. Me, I design for the stars. Then afterwards I copy the dresses.'

'You're going to Hollywood?' Nell asked astounded.

'No. Hollywood will come here to me. But at the moment it is London. These designs are for Falconwood Films. You have heard of them?'

'Yes.' Of course she had. Falconwood was not far from Welling and Bexleyheath and the opening of the studios two years ago was a source of great local excitement, her parents had told her.

'They are doing a series of musical films. A romance naturally and lots of singing and dancing. I dress the ladies. Mainly the star.'

Even as Nell asked automatically, 'And who's that?' a sudden feeling of horror told her the answer.

'Melissa Hargreaves,' Maria told her proudly.

336

Forewarned was not forearmed. Nell tried to put it out of her mind, arguing that even if Melissa were working in England, that was no reason to suppose Lucien would accompany her. Melissa on her own would be tolerable, since Nell could simply wipe the thought of Lucien from her mind. So she thought. Until the day she opened *The Illustrated London News* to find a photograph of Tom and Melissa taken at dinner at Grosvenor House. She was still staring at it disbelievingly when Tom came into the room. She held it out to him. 'You didn't mention this,' she said crossly.

'Didn't I?' he answered carelessly. 'I thought Melissa would have been round to see you by now to tell you herself. Let's invite her to dinner.'

Nell hesitated. She had no objection to seeing Melissa but . . .

'She's on her own,' added Tom with a rare percipience. 'Lucien is in Cannes.'

Much to her surprise, Nell enjoyed the evening enormously, though fully aware Melissa was out to make sure she did just that. Nevertheless she'd forgotten just how much fun Melissa could be and for a time the years vanished as they reminisced about the London of 1925.

'How long are you in London for?' Nell enquired.

'I don't know. A long time though,' Melissa announced airily. 'I've bought Charles Street back, you know. It depends how long the play runs.'

'Play? But I thought it was a film you were here for,' Nell said, taken aback. A play would run for a long time and that meant—

'Oh, you heard about that? Isn't it fun? I thought my career in films was over. In fact, I thought it over in theatre too, come to that,' she added ruefully. 'All that fuss about Robert and so forth. And then those wretched talkies coming in in France. Now it seems their lordships at the Princess Beatrice are prepared to give me another chance. I'm on probation.' She pulled a mocking face.

Tom stared down at his plate, as though the housekeeper's Pond Pudding were the most fascinating dish in the world.

'I shall be good,' Melissa informed them. '*Very* good. And as soon as I've finished this delightful dessert, I want to see litle David.'

Nell had dreaded this moment. She had ensured that he was safely in bed before Melissa arrived, and thereafter had given her guest no time for visits to nurseries.

'He's asleep,' she informed Melissa quickly.

'I shan't make a sound,' Melissa assured her.

'We'll all go and have a look at the little chap,' said Tom, casting a reproachful look at Nell.

Unwillingly she led them up to the nursery, where David, thumb in mouth, was soundly asleep. She felt a rush of pride as she looked at his rosy skin, the lock of brown hair that had fallen over his forehead.

'What a dear little boy,' Melissa said perfunctorily, after a casual glance. 'Now you run along, Tom, I want to talk to Nell.'

Her heart sank, but Melissa did not raise the subject she dreaded.

'Now we are going to be friends here again, aren't we, Nell?' Melissa beseeched. 'You needn't worry about Lucien,' she added offhandedly. 'He really is in Cannes. I'll tell you if he's coming over – but I don't think he will.'

'Because of me?' Nell blurted out through stiff lips.

'Oh no. I don't think he cares about that,' Melissa informed her brightly. 'But he's not very pleased with me. He found out I can't have children.'

'You mean to say he didn't know?' Nell said, appalled.

'No.' Melissa looked sulky. 'I don't know how he found out. You didn't tell him, did you?'

'Me?' said Nell, outraged. 'No, I did not.'

'Oh, well.' Melissa shrugged. 'It doesn't matter now, I

suppose.' She glanced down at David again. 'So like Tommy,' she said almost fearfully. 'Isn't he?' She raised her eyes, questioningly, to Nell's.

'Yes,' said Nell slowly, 'he is.'

Bright genuine tears in Melissa's eyes. She gave Nell a quick hug. 'You lucky old thing you. Having David. And Tommy.'

'Yes,' said Nell dully, thinking of the long nights of sexual frustration, which she overcame by exhausting herself with work at Gadsby's, and at weekends by playing with David. Anything rather than think of Melissa and Lucien together. 'Have you parted from Lucien?' she asked.

'No,' said Melissa quickly. 'Of course not. But I thought I'd escape for a while.' The old disarming smile.

Lucien and Melissa. How could she have been deceived into thinking the marriage was a success? Nell thought, wondering what agony Lucien might be going through. Did he see it as betrayal? As bad luck? Then she dragged her thoughts away. Whatever Lucien felt, he was married and for him there could be no divorce.

Melissa's play *Morning Glory* opened at the Princess Beatrice in the New Year of 1932. The rumours that had swept round London at the time of the trial did not appear to have reached the general public and absence had obliterated any grey areas of memory, leaving only the image of the Melissa Hargreaves they had originally adored. Full houses proved there was no slump in theatre attendance, and the theatre management breathed a sigh of relief that they had taken the gamble. A gamble that would continue to pay handsome dividends if the Falconwood Film series were also a success. They sent for William Cartwright who had written *Morning Glory* and commissioned another musical.

'Darling, you should see him,' Melissa enthused. 'He's

quite divine.' She caught Nell's eye. 'Not that I would, of course,' she said in a shocked voice. 'I am a married woman.' But she could not sustain the act, and relapsed into giggles. 'Of *course* I won't, you old puritan. But it is nice to be admired.'

Nell froze. Melissa's intentions were all too clear.

'He is a little younger than me.' She looked rueful. 'And with all that wine in France, I have to diet.' Her slim figure didn't look as if she had to. 'Especially for the films. They are so particular at Falconwood. They've given me a newcomer as leading man. Perhaps it's as well. I can exercise my charm on him, can't I?'

'Melissa, take care,' said Nell warningly. 'You've got this chance. Don't lose it, please.'

'Do you mean the film, darling – or Lucien?' Melissa said, disconcertingly straight to the point. 'Because if it's the latter—'

'I mean the play and the films!' said Nell firmly.

'I'll be discreet as a church mouse,' Melissa answered.

'That's not what I meant,' said Nell angrily.

'You mean I should be faithful to beloved Lucien,' asked Melissa airily, taking out her third cigarette in half an hour.

'No – yes,' said Nell, confused.

Melissa glanced at her. 'I do seem to have a habit of picking on men you're in love with, Nell, don't I? I'm so sorry.'

Nell drew herself up proudly, wishing she had a devastating retort. As usual where Melissa was concerned, she did not. Even if she had, she might not have delivered it. For all her apparent *joie de vivre*, Melissa's face was thinner, slightly strained. Nell couldn't help noticing the number of drinks that Melissa managed to dispose of.

'Don't worry so much about me, Nell,' Melissa assured her blithely. 'It's like old times. Just you and me. As if nothing had happened.'

As if nothing had happened! With Nell married to a man who still adored Melissa, and Melissa married to a man whom apparently she did not love. And Nell did.

Now that the excitement of his trip to Afghanistan and India had died down, Tom became moody, and the only person who could stir him into animation seemed to be David. Nell was aware he still saw Melissa, though this increased rather than improved his moodiness. In desperation she took to accompanying him and after a while they slipped back into a habit of long ago, going to the theatre to meet Melissa after the show, and taking her to supper or a night club, as her whim dictated.

Tom enjoyed it immensely, but Nell found it a strain after a day's work, managing to disguise this with great difficulty. Sometimes William Cartwright would make up a fourth. He was quiet, devoted to Melissa, seemingly unaware of his extreme good looks that cast him more in the role of leading man than playwright. The romantic music in his plays was composed by himself, together with the lyrics, and Melissa, apparently, was their inspiration. So far as Nell could tell, however, she lived alone. If William spent time in Charles Street she never spoke of it, and somehow Nell suspected this was not the case. Melissa wouldn't be able to keep it secret for long, and when they went out together at least William punctiliously returned to his Bayswater home.

But Nell had little time to ponder Melissa's problems, however, for she had enough of her own. Clashes with Holdsby were increasing. As February approached and the Import Duties Bill was passed and became law, just at the time she would have to consider summer fashion requirements, Holdsby chose to spring his new, oh, so sensible sounding plan for Gadsby's economics on her. Hitherto Gadsby's had exercised a policy of trusting its buyers; their accounts had to fall within defined percentages of costs to

341

turnover, with monthly checks, but allowed for some flexi-
bility of pricing by the buyers, according to whether they
judged an item a swift or slower seller. Now, Holdsby
proposed to introduce cost budgets and target turnovers.

Nell stared at hers in amazement. 'I can't possibly run
the Fashion Department on forty per cent for workroom
charges and materials. *And* design included. That's slash-
ing it by half,' she told him.

'I am afraid you will have to, Nell,' he informed her
pleasantly.

'How on earth can I buy top class models on this?'

He shrugged. 'Buy cheaper models, cut your costs – or
put your prices up.'

'No,' she said quietly. 'Not without permission to
expand as I wish. And that's not possible on this.' She
gestured at the contemptuous maximum cost figure of
£22,000 pa. 'So, no.'

'What choice do you have?' he asked. 'This is an order,
Nell.'

'Of course I have a choice,' she told him steadily. 'One
always has choice if one's prepared to make it.'

In all her years at Gadsby's, she thought wrily, as
she marched up the familiar staircase, this was the first
time she had willingly walked up to the Fourth Floor.
And it had to be for such a reason! Life was very
strange.

Jonathan Gadsby's bark seemed as fierce as ever,
despite his eighty-one years. Or was it? Was there not a
note of tiredness in his voice, as he demanded: 'What do
you want, Nell?'

No 'missy', she noticed. 'I've come to talk about
budgets.'

'Ah,' he said. 'That should please you. Cut down,
save costs. Do it cheap. Isn't that what you've always
wanted?'

'No,' she told him, aware of being goaded. 'Quality is

342

important, not cheapness. We're not Gamages. We're Gadsby's.'

'We're in a slump.'

'So you admit it.'

'Certainly. We'll come out of it.'

'Not we,' she told him sadly. 'I've come to give you my notice.'

For the first time ever, she had shaken him. 'Giving in?' he asked her, with only a hint of his old vigour, and for once clearly seeking time to think out his reactions.

'No. Giving up,' she told him bluntly. 'I'll leave just as soon as Gordon Holdsby can find a replacement.'

Had it been a conscious challenge on her part to suggest Holdsby and not Jonathan Gadsby was responsible for something so important as choice of a new buyer for Fashion? Whether it was or not, it worked. His eyes flickered, he seemed to gain strength, become once more the Jonathan Gadsby she'd always known.

'Reconsider,' he told her, not a hint of pleading in his voice. It was an order.

'No,' she said firmly. 'I want to. But I can't work under that man any longer and see him ruin Gadsby's.'

He glared. 'He's a good manager,' he told her belligerently.

'No doubt,' she said politely. 'But I don't think he's right for Gadsby's and he's certainly not right for me. I've decided to leave. Now, for preference.'

'Stay,' he said surprisingly. And before she could refuse again, 'Stay on, and I'll put you on the board.'

'But you don't like me!' she blurted out fatuously, taken by surprise.

'Stuff and nonsense,' he said testily. 'What's liking got to do with it? I told you once before, we're two of a kind, enjoy a good fight. What do you say, eh?'

Nell thought quickly. On the board she could accomplish much, but she would still be up against Gordon

Holdsby and she had no illusions. It would be him against her. And as Store director, he would still have day to day power over her department.

'I'd still keep Fashion and Leisure and Sporting Wear?'

'Yes.'

'I need autonomy. If I'm to have a budget imposed, it must be agreed at board level, not dictated by Holdsby alone.'

'You think I was wrong, don't you, missy, to appoint Holdsby? Had to do something though, you said so yourself.'

'Yes, but you went the wrong way.'

'You think so, eh?' He chuckled. 'Just you try arguing that with me at board meetings, missy. See how far you get.'

Tom hardly reacted when, full of excitement, she told him the news. Depressed at his reaction she went to whisper it to a sleeping David. 'It's something, isn't it, my lovely?' And the gurgle he gave in his sleep seemed confirmation enough. Smiling, she tucked him up, put his teddybear back within his grasp, and went down to face another evening of maps of Africa. However, it was Tom who two weeks later brought home news of her official appointment. Jonathan, whatever his autonomous powers as Governing Director, always made a point, theoretically at least, of obtaining board approval.

'It was touch and go,' Tom told her, slightly reprovingly, as if this were her fault. 'The two Poker-faces' (his name for Jones and Palgrove) and Holdsby were dead against it. Lorrimer was away ill, and Charles didn't fancy having a woman on the board. So Grandpops had to override the board decision in the end. You'll have trouble there, you'll see,' he warned her.

'I'm ready for them,' said Nell lightly, though in truth she was not so sure. Was this what she really wanted –

344

constant boardroom battles over the future of Gadsby's? She comforted herself that at least it was a step up to a vantage point from which she could see the thorny path ahead.

David jumped down from the motor-car, tugging Nell after him excitedly. He adored Melissa, clinging to her perversely despite her patent lack of interest after the first formal hug and kiss. A visit to Auntie Melissa's was already an afternoon to be looked forward to. This Saturday afternoon vague promises of model boats and Kensington Gardens had been held out by Melissa, exciting him so much that he had been awake much of the night in preparation for this great event.

'I hope she hasn't forgotten,' muttered Nell to herself as she knocked at the Charles Street door. It was neither Melissa nor Gwen who answered but Lucien. A tired, thin-faced Lucien.

'She said she'd warn me when you were coming,' Nell stuttered out without thinking.

'*Je n'ai pas*—' he began and stopped, staring at her without moving, glancing down at David, then back at her. 'She'll be down soon. Come in.'

She moved backwards on the step. Something was wrong. She knew that expression. 'No.'

'You must.' Angrily he took her arm and pulled her inside, closing the door. 'You can wait in here.' He threw open the door to the morning room, and David toddled inside eagerly. She followed him, not looking behind her, fearing, hoping, he had closed the door and left. But he hadn't. 'You would like a drink?' He moved towards the cocktail cabinet. That broke the spell, returned her to normality.

She laughed shakily. 'It's half-past two, Lucien.'

'So it is.' He turned to look at her and made an effort to speak normally as David continued to bounce on the velvet cushions of Melissa's favourite sofa. 'Do I see Maria's hand in your dress?'

Nell glanced at the slender-fitted grey linen under her jacket. 'You see a Gadsby copy,' she acknowledged.

'You should have come to . . .' He broke off, unable to keep up the effort. Then a tiny movement, a well-remembered twist of the lips, and she was in his arms. 'Nell—'

Fire leapt within her – as the door opened and Melissa came in with Tom. Tom, why Tom? was Nell's instant thought, regardless of her own compromising position.

'David,' Melissa said lightly, 'why do you think your mummy is kissing my husband?'

David, oblivious, ran to her, chuckling with pleasure.

Lucien released Nell slowly, saying nothing, merely shrugging, greeting Tom as if nothing had happened.

Tom, red-faced, grasped David by the hand, avoiding looking at Nell.

He's yours, Nell wanted to shout, to shout at Lucien. *Yours*. But she didn't, though tension crackled in the air. 'Melissa, David's all ready for the great adventure.'

'Aren't we all, darling?' she said brightly. 'Who with though, that's the problem? What a pity there's no choice.' She put her arm through Tom's. 'Come along, Tommykins, time for the Round Pond.'

Strangely, Tom said nothing more about what had happened, and relieved, it never occurred to Nell to wonder why. The afternoon had proceeded so normally after its disastrous beginning that she almost wanted to laugh. Only afterwards did the shock hit her. Those few seconds in Lucien's arms – did they really happen? or was what followed the reality, two couples, a child, a boat and an unexpectedly sunny afternoon in early February?

Determined not to think about Lucien, she concentrated all her energy on Gadsby's. Indeed, this was almost

346

essential now, for the Import Duties Act required complete reorganisation of her departments. First of all, she could buy little from Paris now and was determined to tell Maria herself on a visit.

The city was bleak, cold and as unwelcoming as only Paris can be when she does not set out to woo. Nell shivered, pulling her thin coat round her as she walked from the Champs Elysées down the Avenue Montaigne. Quickly she strode past the Maison la Ferté, for she did not want to be reminded of Lucien more than the very pain of being in Paris without him automatically inflicted. Had he stayed in London? Returned to Cannes? Might he be here at this very moment? There were no answers to these questions, for they were part of the greyness.

The bleakness extended to the House of Maniosta too for something was different here, even about Maria herself. Worry dimmed her bright eyes and pervaded the whole house.

'Ah, Nell, you come, eh?' An attempt at the old Maria.

'What's wrong, Maria?'

She shrugged. 'The slump, Nell. It is hard here in Paris.'

'It's more than that.'

'Money then.'

'You said that was all being taken care of, Maria. Isn't Jacques doing well?'

'He does very well,' Maria answered defiantly. 'But even Jacques cannot make orders.' There was a weakness in her voice that spoke of lack of conviction.

'And the spring collection?' Nell asked quietly.

'It is good, but there are few buyers. But the film dresses – they will save me. When Melissa's films start coming. Then we will see.'

'Will the films be shown here, though?' Nell asked doubtfully. 'If not, then you'll run into the new import taxes.'

'No. They will be shown here *and* I license them to be

347

made in England. To you, Nell.'

'Me? But – oh, Maria, if only I could. But copying rights for twenty-five copies isn't going to be enough for you, is it? You need mass reproductions and I can't—'

This time it wouldn't be Holdsby, she thought ruefully. On this, she would be up against Jonathan Gadsby himself. The old argument, and the old result. Jonathan Gadsby would never allow the ready-made market to encroach too far on Gadsby's, whatever the quality. How odd to think that in this battle Holdsby might be her ally. 'I can't.'

'We shall see – when the films are released,' Maria said wistfully.

'And till then?'

'I have work to do.' Maria looked evasive.

'What?' asked Nell curiously, even as her eye fell on a letter with a familiar heading, a familiar crest. Maria followed her gaze.

'You're doing work for la Ferté?' Nell asked, horror-struck.

'A little,' said Maria defensively. 'And not under my name, Nell. But I must live.'

'Why?' asked Nell heavily.

'The count no longer designs – he is not well. Philippe cannot manage it all, so I design for them. It is good of them.'

'There's nothing *good* in it,' said Nell angrily. 'They're the ones to benefit. What of you and your ideas? No wonder your spring collection isn't your best.' It was true. Nell had been disappointed for it showed the usual flair for style but without the added originality that a Maniosta collection should have. It even lacked the youthful emphasis which other Paris collections showed, despite a noticeable trend to economy.

Maria flushed angrily. 'It is no business of yours, Nell. My friends should understand.'

348

'All I understand, Maria, is that you're heading for trouble. Do you remember you told me of your great dream of something beautiful you would design, to transcend fashion fads and be eternal? Where is it now?'

'When ugly times are over, Nell, then we turn to beauty.'

'No. Beauty is needed *now* and so are dreams to get us through. Where is yours?'

Maria did not answer.

Miss Gertrude tried valiantly, but the breach left by lack of designs from Maria was too wide to fill. 'I fear, Nell, I have just a little less energy than I used to have,' she said apologetically. Fifteen designs were all she could manage, she estimated, in addition to her sporting wear. Established British designers were too expensive in the sudden flush of business that the new import duties brought to them, and day after day Nell interviewed aspiring young designers without seeing anything that immediately said 'Gadsby's' to her. Too outrageous, too conventional, too expensive – nobody fitted her requirements.

She was beginning to think that the Fashion Department might have no models at all this season when the problem answered itself. A knock on the office door and, slightly flushed in the face, Polly Simpkins came in. Nell had not seen her since she left to work for la Ferté's London house and Joe said little about her. She stared in amazement. This was a new Polly. Gone was the mop of fair curls, the unsophisticated round eager face. Here was a slimmer, elegantly dressed Polly, with an unmistakable air of Paris about her. A new confidence too, save that her face showed signs of strain and uncertainty.

'I'm coming back to London, Mrs Gadsby,' she announced. 'To Joe – if he'll have me.' She saw Nell's expression. 'Didn't you know I'd left him? I went to work in France and took the baby with me, two years ago. Well,

'I'm back now it's time for Ben to go to school.'

'No, he didn't say anything.' How like Joe, Nell thought sadly. She'd talked to him on countless occasions in the store and he'd never said a word. Not to her or anyone else, or she'd have heard about it. But now Polly was back. Then light dawned. 'It isn't just your son, is it? You've left la Ferté because Maria Maniosta has started designing there?' She promptly regretted being so blunt as she saw Polly's face.

But Polly shook her head. 'No. Maria was a help if anything,' she said defiantly. 'Took the pressure off me. But now Joe's lost his job.'

'Lost his—' Nell echoed faintly, wondering why she had to be told what was going on in Gadsby's. Had she been so preoccupied?

'Last week. Asked for a raise and that Holdsby sacked him instead.'

'But that's outrageous! I'll get him—'

Polly shook her head. 'He wouldn't come back even if you could do something. That's not why I've come. I'm here –' she hesitated '– to ask if you'd give me another chance,' she said in a rush. 'I wouldn't let you down this time. I don't deserve it after what I did to you, Mrs Gadsby, but I'd make it up to you.'

Nell was silent. Polly was older now, wiser, but had she changed that much? Or would she leave again at the drop of an attractive offer – by an attractive man? Then she reminded herself she was in no position to be choosy.

'Do you know, Polly, I think it might serve very well. Can you start—'

'Today, Mrs Gadsby,' Polly grinned. 'With all the latest Paris trends.'

'You were right, Tom, I think there's trouble coming at the next board meeting. I have a feeling Holdsby's planning something. Bit by bit, he's taking more and more

350

of the decisions in the store.'

'You'll sort it out,' Tom said reassuringly.

'Me?' said Nell, puzzled.

'I won't be there, Nelly,' he told her soberly.

'Why not?' she asked, astounded.

'I told you what I wanted. I'm off in the new Puss Moth – attempt to beat Mollison's new record to Cape Town. I should have done it before him, and I can't let Amy Johnson beat me to it, can I? Now her husband's done it, she won't be long in trying to have a go herself.'

'Oh, Tom, not *now*, please.' She was so sure something major was afoot. For one thing Holdsby had been suspiciously nice to her. He had not quibbled about her budget – or indeed anything for several months. She didn't trust him an inch. True, Polly's designs were undoubtedly cheaper to acquire than Maria's, if not so dramatically original. She could price them competitively while still maintaining top quality. Holdsby praised her highly for pursuing such a sensible policy. And yet, and yet—

'When is it?' Tom grumbled.

'Next week.'

'All right, I'll come. But then I'm off,' he said firmly.

At first, all seemed routine. The usual budget discussions ranged from heated to amicable. Everything was resolved until it came to Nell's turn to discuss the problems of the Fashion Department. She quickly sketched in the position over her switch of designers and then came to the matter uppermost on her mind.

Melissa's first film for Falconwood, of her old hit *Dancing in the Dew*, was showing now in London and was soon to be released to provincial cinemas. 'And when it is,' Nell announced to blank faces, 'there's going to be an enormous resurgence of interest in British musical films. Just as great as in America. I want Gadsby's to benefit.' She glanced at Tom, hoping he would support her in agreeing that Melissa Hargreaves was set for an enormous revival of popularity once the film was widely seen. Oddly, he said nothing.

'Just how do you propose we benefit from that woman's cavortings and caterwaulings?' Jonathan demanded, bringing a reaction at last from Tom.

'Melissa,' he muttered, 'that's her name, not "that woman".'

Nell cut over him quickly, anxious not to deflect Jonathan's attention from business. 'I can buy licensing rights to make copies of her dresses.'

'Well? Sounds sensible to me,' Jonathan barked.

'Licensing rights for unlimited copies,' said Nell steadily.

A pause, then everyone spoke together, but Jonathan's voice was loudest. 'Another of your ventures to make Gadsby's into a dime store, eh? No. And that's final.'

'Is it, though, Mr Gadsby?' Holdsby of all people coming to her aid. 'I believe we should hear further what Mrs Gadsby has to say.'

Cautious, since he of all people must guess how much the rights would cost, Nell went on to explain fully. 'Six thousand pounds?' Jonathan roared when she'd finished. 'You're busting your budget on a couple of dresses?'

'But with unlimited potential for sales,' said Nell. 'And it won't bust the budget, because I hope to economise in other directions.' This was optimistic to say the least, but the important thing was to get it agreed in principle.

Jonathan snorted. 'This is a slump. You're off your head, missy.'

'Is she, Mr Gadsby? I wonder. Perhaps not.'

'And if you agree with her, Holdsby, you're as off it as she is.'

'We must move with the times, Mr Gadsby,' Holdsby said.

Nell blinked. Holdsby still agreeing? She was missing a trick here.

Mr Lorrimer looked confused, Mr Charles lost, Tom uninterested – and the Pokerfaces, as she too now called them, very keenly interested. Almost before she realised it, the discussion adroitly moved from the necessity to increase Nell's budget – if the motion were approved – to overall budget, and how the latter was jeopardised by interest payments on loans.

'Especially,' said Jones (alias Pokerface 1, thought Nell wearily, wondering how to turn discussion back to the budget), 'since the interest has not been paid for three months. I'm sure you realise the difficult situation this puts Mr Palgrove and myself in, since the bank could sue for negligence. We would of course resign.'

'Negligence?' roared Jonathan. 'You told me yourself the bank would ride it, Palgrove.'

'I must deny that,' he said promptly. 'I am secretary, after all.'

'Then it was you.' Jonathan turned to Holdsby.

Holdsby looked startled. 'It may be you misinterpreted something I said, Mr Gadsby. Certainly I would never advise non-payment of interest. Why, I recall the cheque—'

'What's going on here?' said Jonathan slowly.

'What's going on, Mr Gadsby,' Jones took up the cudgel, 'is that the bank is seriously worried about its investment. It can of course withdraw its debentures with two weeks' notice as interest payments are in default.'

Jonathan said nothing but every hackle was raised, Nell saw, her own worst suspicions fully confirmed.

'There are also other matters that concern the bank. Irregularities.'

'What?' Jonathan barked out the word.

'The Company Memorandum gives no provision for raising extra capital. A Special Resolution should have been passed by all the shareholders to alter the Memorandum. Mr Palgrove can find no evidence that it was. Furthermore, no statement of increased capital was lodged with the registrar.'

Nell's heart sank. She should have pursued her suspicions at the time.

'Fiddling details,' roared Jonathan. 'I own this company, and every damned thing in it. And there's no getting round *that*.'

'Precisely. And you are therefore legally responsible. I have to say that in view of the serious penalties that face the company, our bank no longer has confidence in your leadership, Mr Gadsby.'

Nell sat very still. She would not speak, not till she knew the worst. Even Tom was looking aghast now.

'And what do you propose to do about it?'

'Request your resignation as governing director, sir.'

Jonathan's face bulged with anger. 'You nincompoop. I refuse, sir.'

'In that case, we will notify the registrar of serious – perhaps fraudulent – activities and call in our debentures.'

'You can't do it without a general meeting, and I control the voting there. I've well over three-quarters of the voting rights,' Jonathan declared triumphantly.

'You need three weeks for that, sir. The bank is only prepared to wait two. In any case, controlling voting rights does not defend you from a prosecution – or bankruptcy. However, may I suggest that we hold our hand for two weeks to give you time to reflect, after which this board will meet again to hear your decision?'

'Two weeks?' Jonathan looked round. 'One condition of my own. I'll not resign without my board votes I go.'

A glance exchanged between the Pokerfaces and Holdsby before Jones answered smoothly: 'Agreed. And at the same meeting, we might perhaps give further thought to Mrs Gadsby's proposal of extending our

354

market to a wider class of customer.

Jonathan Gadsby stood up. He said not one word but marched stiffly out of the first board meeting he'd failed to control in over thirty years.

'I'm going and that's all there is to it.'

'But you can't,' said Nell, almost shouting at Tom. 'It's vital for Gadsby's you be at the meeting.'

'And it's vital for me that I go,' he said, glaring. 'Do you hear me? What's Gadsby's ever done for me, eh, except stand in the way of what I wanted to do? I could really have been something if it wasn't for the damned store and it's not going to prevent me now. I'm going next week. And I'm going to beat the record. *And* by flying the west coast route.'

Her heart sank. That route was quicker as the crow flies, but had far less aerodromes than the eastern route, besides being far more dangerous terrain. None of her arguments swayed him. He was adamant and on 18 July, one week before the meeting, climbed into his Puss Moth at Croydon Airport and with a casual wave was gone.

Why should she feel so betrayed? thought Nell, as she returned to London to battle over what was to come. It hardly needed Jones's final overt bribe to convince her this was a carefully laid plan of which Holdsby was the instigator. The reason he wished to retain her – if he did – was obvious. With her voting with them, they would outnumber Tom, Lorimer and Charles. A vote wasn't legally binding here, but the bank would need to be seen doing things by the book. And now Tom was going, and there wasn't time to register a proxy vote. Holdsby, for all his faults, represented a future of sorts; Jonathan Gadsby was the past. He may still be the major shareholder, but without his iron grip as governing director, Gadsby's would be free to meet the challenges that lay ahead. This was what she wanted – and Holdsby knew she did.

★ ★ ★

Across the desk she met Holdsby's eyes, already triumphant. They were the first to arrive. He nodded at her pleasantly. 'We can work together, you'll see,' he told her complacently. She said nothing, except:

'I'm sure we can, Gordon, whatever happens.'

Jonathan Gadsby arrived last, not one inch of his magnificent craggy face betraying any emotion. How on earth did he react to the fact that his own grandson and heir had for all intents and purposes abandoned him? Nell wondered, her thoughts still chaotic.

His voice boomed out.

'The motion before this board is that, confidence in my chairmanship having waned, I be requested to resign from this board, that the office of governing director be abolished and a managing director be appointed in my stead. I have no comments to make, so I propose to take the vote right now. Proxy votes being ruled ineligible in this instance, my grandson Thomas Gadsby has no vote.' No trace of emotion. 'Mr Lorrimer?'

'Against the motion, sir.' Stoutly in view of the fact that he would be signing his own dismissal warrant in effect, Nell realised. No hope of his pulling through this one. He was an old man and Holdsby would get the better of him because he left his rear unguarded. Tom should have been defending it. And he wasn't, she thought bitterly.

'Mr Jones?' 'In favour.' Tonelessly.

'Mr Charles?' 'Against.'

'Mr Holdsby?' 'In favour with regret.'

Jonathan ignored the regret. 'Mr Palgrove?'

'In favour.'

'Mrs Gadsby?'

She looked at the man who had stone-walled her throughout her career. There had been no real battle, for there was only one choice. 'I've never hidden the fact I'm against your policy for the store, Mr Gadsby, and that I

356

feel broadening our appeal is the way to survive. Mr Holdsby agrees with me.' Jonathan was hardly listening, clutching his papers as if ready to depart already. 'But I don't agree with Mr Holdsby's methods. Gadsby's has always stood for quality, and it must continue to do so. There's only one person who symbolises quality, and that is Jonathan Gadsby.' He raised his head curiously, staring at her, as were the rest of the board, uneasiness creeping in to what had only been a formality. 'Reform yes, but only under the original banner or we are lost. And the person who carries the banner here is Jonathan Gadsby. I say call their bluff, sir,' direct to him. 'They won't sue. Let them withdraw their loans. There are other banks. And you, sir, are still Gadsby's. Against, I vote against.'

'You bloody fool,' snarled Holdsby, seeing what would happen immediately, just as Jonathan whooped in delight, shouting as if he were still a boy: 'You see? That's it. I'm governing director. Normal rules about abstaining from voting in motions against yourself don't apply to me. Not me. I'm Jonathan Gadsby,' he roared. 'The old dog lives on! By God, he does!'

'Why did you do it?' Jonathan demanded, after an invitation, nay, command, to attend Merrifield at the weekend, where he broke his strict rule of not discussing business when he took Nell into the study after Saturday luncheon.

'For the reasons I gave,' she said, surprised he had to ask.

He sighed. 'You're a bright girl,' he told her, 'a fighter. But you know you can't win against the Holdsbys of this world. I was a stupid old fool, I know it, to take him on in the first place and then keep him on just to spite Tom.' His voice quavered. 'But I've cut his claws now. No need to sack him. He's done some good things,' he added with a trace of his old defiance.

'I know,' said Nell. 'Yet he'll not give up his fight for

power. He wants it. Needs it.'

'And you don't.'

She considered. 'I want power to help Gadsby's,' she said at last.

'Then why didn't you seize it?' he snorted. 'If you'd supported him, you would have got your mass market, film dresses and anything else you wanted.'

'Yes,' said Nell bleakly. 'I know.'

'Now,' said Jonathan with great satisfaction, 'you're stuck with me until I die. And I'll fight you inch by inch, young woman!'

'Ah, but I can see a lion in the open more clearly than a snake in the grass,' she said bravely, trying hard to smile, and fully aware that the battle was only just beginning.

Chapter Eleven

'A is for Apple,' Nell patiently began once more, as in a rare fit of tranquillity David agreed to give his attention to intellectual pursuits after an afternoon of tearing round the gardens at Merrifield, chasing birds, balls and grasshoppers as the mood took him. Tiring of this energetic occupation, devoted though they were to the child, Mrs Emmeline and Miss Gertrude had long since retreated indoors for an afternoon sleep, leaving Nell to watch David from the apple orchard, thick with luxuriant Kent pippins, already ready for harvesting. David was two and a half now and there were times when she could almost forget that he was Lucien's son. He was hers and – she made herself believe, because of the bond between them – Tom's.

At Merrifield, however, Jonathan took him over almost completely. Fond though he was of Rose's three children, he did not wear the same look of pride when they visited, as he did with David. It was almost, Nell thought with amusement, as though David too was a prime achievement of Jonathan Gadsby's, to rank alongside the great store itself with which, at the moment at least, his future was irrevocably linked.

When the immediate jubilation of victory had subsided, Jonathan spent three days at Merrifield. Then he returned to his beloved store and went into action. He had only eleven days left before the bank pulled out, and full of anxiety Nell hovered in her office, expecting hourly summons to the Fourth Floor for crisis meetings. None came. A short memo informed her that Mr Jones and Mr Palgrove were no longer members of the board. So Gordon Holdsby was. Ah, well, at least they knew the measure of the man. Perhaps, she told herself, now that he'd made his bid for power and lost, he would appreciate where his best interests lay. Perhaps!

But what of the loan? She fretted, wondering whether to beard Jonathan and ask what was going on. If only Tom were here, she thought wretchedly. Still nothing from Jonathan.

Then another memo from the Fourth Floor. In his capacity as governing director, Mr Jonathan Gadsby had appointed Sir Bertram Bertrand to the board. For a moment Nell blinked in disbelief. Bertrand? Bobsy's son? Surely not. She'd always known Bobsy had a son, but he had been up at Oxford when she'd first met her; thereafter her visits had never coincided, and Bobsy had rarely mentioned him. Nell had almost forgotten she had a son, until at a club one evening with Melissa and Tom, a tall gangly young man had climbed on a table, lank straw-coloured hair tumbling over his face, and clad in sober dinner jacket over a bright purple silk waistcoat and blue shirt, augmented by a long matching purple cravat, proceeded to entertain the company with 'The Man who Broke the Bank at Monte Carlo' while performing a Highland Fling and juggling six glasses. His rather vacant-looking face spoke more of Wodehouse's Bertie Wooster than the serious businessman required in this crisis at Gadsby's.

Nerving herself, she marched upstairs to the Fourth Floor.

Jonathan was highly pleased with himself, chuckling as he saw the memo in her hand.

'Why?' she asked bluntly.

'Good chap, young Bertie.'

'Good stooge, you mean,' she retorted.

'Now, now,' he said indulgently, in high good humour. 'Young Bertrand's fixed the loan problem and he's in banking, you know.'

'No, I didn't know,' she replied. 'The last time I saw him he was juggling glasses.'

'High spirits,' Jonathan dismissed this airily.

'It's wonderful news about the loan anyway,' said Nell. 'I suppose we have to pay a price. At least he won't be Holdsby's ally.'

'Don't underestimate young Bertie, Nell.'

She tried hard, but if the board meetings he had so far attended were anything to judge by, his contribution would be hard to underestimate. He spent most of them smiling vacuously, nodding his head wisely, winking occasionally at Nell if he caught her eye, and doodling with some competence on the large sheets of Gadsby's writing paper provided for notes. Occasionally she saw him ambling through the store, mostly in the Sporting and Men's Wear departments, but otherwise, to her relief, he seemed to prefer his banking life. Duties did not strike her as the correct word to use in connection with Bertie Bertrand – as he was apparently known to the whole of the younger part of London society.

There had been other, more personal, consequences of the fateful board meeting too. One weekend at Merrifield Mrs Emmeline had asked her to pop into Jonathan's study. Unsuspectingly she had done so.

As she entered the door, she was suspicious. Although Jonathan at Merrifield was always a far different person to the Jonathan who ruled Gadsby's, today he was positively jovial. Always a bad sign, Nell thought uneasily, for in this mood he was intractable. And so it had proved on this occasion.

'I'm leaving it all to David,' he declared without preamble. 'I told Tom I'd cut him out if he went. He still did it.

Doesn't care a damn for Gadsby's. Or me,' he added darkly. 'That's it. Tom can be trustee if he likes till David comes of age. Not that I don't intend to be here till then. I do,' he shot at her, and looking at the vigorous face and bright eyes under their bushy grey eyebrows, Nell could well believe it. Her heart sank, as hesitantly she raised the question of Rose's children.

Jonathan snorted. Triumphant in his victory over Holdsby, he had no intention of being magnanimous with it. Holdsby should pay, and one of the ways he would do so was to see his children cut out from any major share in Gadsby's. He'd see Rose was looked after personally, but Gadsby's was going to be protected from Holdsby for good.

Rose had pleaded, cajoled in vain, he told Nell. 'You're a fool, Rose, I told her,' Jonathan recalled complacently. 'You dote too much on that snake of yours. You'll land up where I might have done, if I hadn't saved myself. But you can't fool an old fool, you know,' he concluded smugly, ignoring the fact that it was largely thanks to Nell and not his own powers of self-survival that he had not been ousted from his own company.

'What is D for, David?' Nell brought herself back to the present, aware of her son's wandering attention.

'Daddy,' cried the boy, wriggling on the hard seat.

'Or donkey,' said Nell wrily.

'Daddy home soon.'

'Yes, very soon,' Nell answered. Tom, to her pleasure and relief, had achieved his ambition and beaten the solo record flight time to the Cape. Since the eastern mail route was now established, and there was no challenge left there, he had used the western route he had explored earlier, and took four days, ten hours and twenty-three minutes for the journey of about 6,200 miles, thus beating Jim Mollison's record of last March by six hours fifty-nine minutes. He had been jubilant.

Pictures appeared in the press of him caught at the moment of triumph as he climbed down from the Puss Moth. Despite the weariness he must have been feeling, he had a brightness about him that she had not seen for a long time. He looked, yes, happy, and she rejoiced for him. A letter arrived for her via the newly opened mail route in which he told her, almost as a postscript, that he planned to fly across to Cairo, across part of the Sahara and the Egyptian desert. So the desert was still calling him. Vaguely worried, though not knowing why, she mentally put back the date of his arrival home by at least a month. Just at the time when she needed his support to fight Jonathan's ever-growing obsession with David.

'I'm going to look after that boy, missy. You'll see. After he's been to Harrow—'

'Harrow?' she asked cautiously. David's schooling was something she had to discuss with Tom.

'I put him down for it. Didn't Tom tell you?' Jonathan asked innocently.

'No,' said Nell, through gritted teeth. 'He must have forgotten to mention it.'

'Times are changing, missy, that's what you keep telling me,' Jonathan explained cunningly. 'Old codgers like me didn't need education to build a business up. Now it's different. If he's going to run the business properly, he's got to have the right background.'

'G is for Goat,' David cried, interrupting her thoughts and slapping a finger down in the middle of a belligerent-looking white nanny goat.

'And G is for Gadsby's, David.' She had had no choice after Jonathan announced his plans for David. She had once more contemplating resigning from Gadsby's after the board meeting, having no stomach for the fight ahead, but how could she abandon Gadsby's future, if David were to be part of it? She had to safeguard his inheritance until he was of an age to decide for himself what his future should be. Yet what of her? What of David's real father who didn't even know he had the son he wanted and which Melissa could not give to him? The sharp agony was too painful, and she realised her only way of everyday living must be to think of David as Tom's son, betrayal though that seemed. Lucien was the past. The present was David – and the ever-present daily worries of Gadsby's.

Angela Field now ran the Lingerie Department and Sporting Wear was in the hands of Peter Pride. Peter was a twenty-six-year-old Cockney she'd met on the never to be forgotten day when David got lost in Gamages while with his nurse. What Gamages' staff and the nurse failed to do, Peter achieved. Finding a small toddler nonchalantly helping himself to strawberries from his barrow in Gray's Inn Road, he patiently elicited the child's name with the help of more of his precious stock of fruit, put two and two together that 'aspey' might just mean Gadsby, and turned up with him at Nell's office before she knew he was missing.

Overwhelming him with thanks as she accompanied him to the Sporting Wear Department where he had declared, in response to her insistence, that he'd always fancied a fishing rod, she was so impressed with his pertinent comments on Gadsby's methods of attracting custom – compared, he implied, with his own prowess on the barrow – that she offered him a job as an assistant in the department. Within three weeks turnover had increased, within six she was asking his advice on stock, within two months he was assistant buyer. Now he was buyer, leaving her free to concentrate on Fashion.

Tiring of the alphabet, David decided to attempt a tree-climb in the orchard. She watched as he clambered up the small tree with a suitably gnarled and knotty trunk providing footholds for novice climbers. Thin and wiry, he had Lucien's build. Everyone told her David took after her, since he bore no resemblance to sturdy round-faced fair Tom, but every time she looked at him she saw not herself, but Lucien. Even the freckles beginning to appear on his face with the intelligent brown eyes darting from one thing to another reminded her . . . No, she would not think that way. This was Merrifield, Gadsby territory, and here lay his future; she was glad that Tom would be home shortly to provide another dimension to David's present largely female-dominated life.

She went to rescue David who, having clambered on to a low branch of the small tree and harvested an apple, had now discovered descent was not so easy. Nell returned to her deck-chair, and leaned back in the September sunshine, trying to resist the temptation to close her eyes. In the distance she heard the telephone ring in the house, wondering who would be inconsiderate enough to ring Merrifield on a sunny Sunday afternoon. She saw Mrs Emmeline coming out of the house, leaning on her stick which she depended on more and more. Nell cleared the deck-chair by her side, sweeping the pile of newspapers and David's picture books on to the grass.

Mrs Emmeline sat down carefully, but Nell knew immediately that it was not just sun that had brought her out.

'What is it?' Nell asked sharply.

'My dear, I am afraid our dear Tom is four days overdue at Cairo. It probably means nothing, of course, but the French aeroplanes are searching the desert, they tell us.'

'The desert?' All her earlier forebodings came back in a rush. Many of Tom's fellow fliers at his club had confided to her that they could not understand his obsession with the desert which they regarded as a great yellow stretch of dangerous territory that spelled disaster, and probably death, if one were forced to land. Yet Tom was actually seeking it out. Did he, she shivered, have a subconscious, or even conscious, desire for death? Or having achieved his ambition to break a record, did he now treat fate so lightly that he would challenge it? The Sahara held more fears for most airmen than any other desert, yet it was this he sought. And now perhaps it was claiming him. Then she told herself she was being ridiculous. He had been a week overdue before, and all had been well.

'We may not hear for some time, Nell,' Mrs Emmeline said gravely. 'If he has been found by Bedouins, as before, it could be weeks before he is returned to us, longer if he has to be ransomed. I am afraid, dear Nell, we must make up our minds to be very brave.'

Nell stared at her, her emotions numb. 'I think he's dead this time,' she said flatly, determined to face reality. 'You think so too, don't you?'

'It is possible,' said Mrs Emmeline, slightly shocked at Nell's reaction.

Slowly Nell got up. 'Grandfather?' she asked Mrs Emmeline.

'I have told him,' Mrs Emmeline replied.

Nell's bright red linen frock made a splash of incongruous colour as she made her way across the lawn, grateful that she did not have to break the news. It was hard enough, without that. She found Jonathan Gadsby in the library, slumped in his chair. Unaware of her entrance, he looked every one of his eighty-odd years.

'Well?' he said, looking up as she approached, as if daring her to offer a platitude. But there was no fire in his challenge. She knelt down and put her arms round him. He was very still, but after a minute he managed to say: 'A fine pickle, missy.'

'There is hope,' she said inanely, but meaning it. After all, last time he was found safely. With water, airmen who had force-landed could last until rescue arrived.

'Hope?' he repeated thickly. 'No, missy, hope is young David.'

★ ★ ★

366

They did not have to wait long. Twenty-four hours later they received a telegraph, then a telephone call from Croydon. A French mail plane en route to Dakar had reported seeing a crashed aircraft. A subsequent investigation found the remains of a Puss Moth. Tom was dead. 'Killed outright in the crash,' they were told.

For that Nell was grateful, having tortured herself with the idea of Tom having sought the desert purposely, then finding only a slow death through thirst. Even so, she found it hard to accept the finality of what had happened, still half believing that Tom would return as so many times before. Perhaps this was a help, for it made the terrible ordeal of making arrangements the easier.

'Were there hills nearby?' Nell asked the club authorities, as she organised the return of the body. They looked at her awkwardly, but two days later the answer came back yes. How could she explain that having hills nearby might make a difference, that the colours of the desert might have drawn him? Surely, oh surely, if he had intended to seek death he would have left some letter for her? Wildly she searched but could find nothing. Yet she could not get the thought out of her mind. She wished she could leave him buried in the desert where he had longed to be. Then she would be free to think of the man she had known at first, the man she had loved – or thought she did. The man who had shown her such kindness and generosity. Before Melissa had closed her magic circle around him, entrapping him for ever.

Instead there was a formal funeral at Merrifield. Nell was too stunned, too tired to resist Jonathan's almost beseeching request that Tom be buried there. It was a funeral for everybody, with little to do with Tom, it seemed to her. The press came to report on the death of the man who had achieved the new Cape record, on his grieving widow, and on the owner of Gadsby's. There was the added attraction of Melissa Hargreaves' presence, the famous star of stage and screen. How could Nell not have invited her? And how could she not have foreseen what would inevitably happen?

Melissa in London was something she could contend with; Nell met her for occasional dinners and luncheons, falling back naturally into the old ways of acting as Melissa's adviser on everything from leading men to nail polish. Only two subjects were taboo. Melissa's marriage and any mention of what Melissa did after the theatre on evenings she did not see Nell. 'I go to bed early,' was her virtuous answer. 'Alone,' Nell was firmly assured. If she doubted that, it was not something she wished to dwell on.

Now, hardly surprisingly, Melissa, in a large hat and sombre black suit, looked as beautiful and stricken as a grieving widow on a stage. All through the service in the church and at the graveside, Nell was conscious of no one save Jonathan and Mrs Emmeline. But afterwards, at Merrifield, she had strength enough to look around, to greet the guests. To her horror she saw Jonathan talking to the Comte and Comtesse de la Ferté. Her wits had dulled with grief and mourning. And wasn't that Maria? Slowly she turned her head. Inevitably there was Philippe, even handsomer now that he was in his thirties, talking to Melissa. And where Melissa was, Lucien must be also, on occasions such as this.

It was unreal. She was unable to believe that at any moment Tom would not come striding in through the door. But he did not. The person who threw herself sobbingly into Nell's arms was Melissa, and at her side, Lucien. He uttered conventional words of sympathy, words she answered – somehow – before turning away to see how Jonathan was.

If I keep going for another hour, Nell told herself, I can steal away and collapse. Only an hour. Only an hour . . . But how to survive it? In the end it was not so bad as she feared. Distanced, as though at the wrong end of a

368

telescope, she held herself together. It might have been anyone with Melissa. Anyone. Certainly not the Lucien she knew. It didn't hurt any more. And it wouldn't, if only she could remain in this cold, calm box she had built round herself.

He came without warning one evening. It had been a bad day at Gadsby's. She had even been unjustifiably disapproving of Peter's choice of cycling jackets, as a direct result of a wrangle with Holdsby over accounts. Sporting Wear was none of her business now and she knew it. Yet she'd still felt herself Peter's patron and found it hard to face the fact that she had no say in what he stocked. He'd even branched out into men's sporting wear, a brilliant idea she wished she'd thought of long ago. Now home, she kicked off her shoes. Even home was no refuge at the moment though. Life was full of solicitors, accountants, and letter-writing. She poured a drink for herself and sat down to tackle the day's post.

Then Lucien arrived.

'Shall I go?' he asked quietly, after Hornton had closed the door behind him.

Thankful they were in the impersonality of the large drawing room, her domain, she managed to shake her head, incapable of speech or movement.

Understanding, Lucien went to pour himself a drink with apparent calm.

It was that which broke down her defences. The same attitude, half-turned away from her, pouring the drinks, his hands on the glass. Just so had he looked four years ago, when in such righteous rage and indignation she had gone to his rooms in Conduit Street. But then . . . then . . . She hiccupped, and for the first time since Tom had died let out an involuntary cry. And as he turned to see what was wrong she cried in earnest with grief, with shock, with guilt. He sat down quietly, let her cry for a while, and then came to her, holding her not as a lover but as a rock.

'Why?' she asked, shaking, after a while.

'Why have I come?'

'No,' she blurted out.

He understood. 'Why did I marry Melissa?' His mouth twisted, and he held her closer. 'You would not have left Tom. You preferred him to me – or so I saw it then. I was very angry, Nell. I did not understand. Now perhaps I do. Melissa claimed she was destitute, she needed me as Tom needed you. Philippe did all he could to dissuade me.'

'Philippe did?' she echoed in disbelief. Had Philippe told him about Melissa's secret life, told him about her not being able to have children? If so, why on earth did he marry her, for all her claims of being destitute?

'I did not listen to him, for I thought that he tried to dissuade me from marrying so that I would not have children. But how right he was when he told me that although Melissa seemed so poised and assured, she was fragile, that she needed protection because she had been so badly treated by men, and that was why she needed someone to protect her.'

'He told you that to make you the more determined,' she said flatly. Philippe. The snake! He had told his brother nothing of the real truth about Melissa. How much had Lucien found out since? she agonised. That she was unable to have children, yes, but about her nymphomania?

'Philippe is not quite so underhand,' Lucien told her gently.

'You protect him? Despite what you know of him?'

'He is my brother. Even he—' Lucien broke off. 'Why do we talk of Philippe?' he went on impatiently. 'You asked of Melissa. She was almost penniless, Nell, her career was over. She was frightened, ill with worry. She needed someone.'

'Do you love her?' Nell did not look at him.

'Not as I love you,' the answer came straight back. 'But I told myself you did not love Tom and you stayed. She still needs my protection. I cannot leave her completely. Although she has a new career, she is still fragile.' He paused. 'You are her friend. You know it is true.'

'Yes.'

He paused then said gently, 'Now is not the time, Nell. I shall come again.' A pause. 'Do you grieve for Tom very much?'

'I – I am haunted,' she said abruptly.

'You, after all you did for him?'

'No. Because I fear he might have done it on purpose.' Fool that she was to say it. For there was David. Lucien must know she had a son. What possible reason would Tom have to kill himself after that? he might argue.

He looked at her in compassion. 'It is natural, Nell, to think that way. But I am sure it was not so in Tom's case. Do you know of the desert?'

'Only what Tom has told me.'

'It has a strange force,' he told her. 'I have talked to those who fly over it often. There is something in the Sahara that flyers call the *cafard*. It is a madness, an irresistible force that sends them temporarily out of their minds, and dooms them to destruction. It is perhaps because of the never-ending combination of sun and wind. Battling with it causes the pilot to lose all sense of where he is. Rather like staring into the wake of a ship, it can cause the dizziness, a fascination, an insane desire to leap into it. So, the *cafard* in the Sahara can draw the airman inexorably towards the sand, to land – or to crash – impelled by a force stronger than he.'

'The colours,' she could hear Tom saying. 'They seem to be calling to you somehow.'

'The *cafard*,' Lucien emphasised, 'deprives a man of reason.'

371

'Yes,' she said gratefully. 'Yes. I think it was that.' He had wiped out in a few words the misery of weeks. Now she could truly grieve for Tom and then begin to live again. For David. Only David, for Lucien was Melissa's.

'Ah, yes,' he said gently. 'I will come again when you are strong enough, and then you must introduce me to your son.'

David, everything centred on David. Lucien had spoken casually, only afterwards was she sufficiently composed to realise that he could not believe David to be his son, even if he had wondered about it. A sudden doubt was firmly dispelled. Even if Melissa guessed, then she would be the last person to plant her suspicions in his mind. Far more likely that in his bitterness at her rejection of him, Lucien would think that miraculously Nell's relationship with Tom had become that of a normal married couple. His anger and jealousy then had probably given way to emotional indifference, for all he said he still loved her. She tried to convince herself that this was for the best, yet everything in her cried out to tell him the truth about David. And if she did? She put the thought, temptation, away. Before even Lucien, there was a matter more pressing and one which could not be put off any longer.

She had to raise the question of Gadsby's inheritance, no longer bound by Tom's views on the matter. There had been seemingly endless discussions on Tom's estate with solicitors and Jonathan, who threw himself vigorously into the question of money as an antidote to grief. It was a surprise to her to discover that Tom had been wealthy in his own right, as a result of money left by both his parents and of trusts from Jonathan established on his birth, not to mention 98,000 10s 0d ordinary shares and 40,000 £5 preference shares in Gadsby's. It was a less welcome surprise to find that though the bulk came to her and David, a substantial amount of cash (not shares) went to 'my first wife Melissa, so that she shall never be in need'. She didn't begrudge Melissa the money, but it was a reminder in black and white that Melissa was ever-present. In his past, in her past, and throughout their marriage. In need? Melissa would always be in need, and if money could assuage it then Nell would willingly give her all she had.

'I'll still be leaving everything to young David, of course,' Jonathan told her casually after one such meeting, sending shivers of apprehension through Nell over what she must face.

Of course. It was only natural if David were Tom's son. But he wasn't. He was the son of Lucien de la Ferté. How could she give this additional blow to Jonathan Gadsby now? In David he saw the continuation of his hopes for Tom, a reason to continue fighting at Gadsby's, a reason for life. Yet now Tom was no longer here, how could she live with herself, knowing he was building hopes on false pretences?

'What's the matter, Nell?' Jonathan asked almost kindly. 'You look like a month of wet Sundays.'

'I can't let you,' she began.

'Can't let me do what?' he asked testily.

'I loved Tom,' Nell said awkwardly, conscious she hadn't the slightest idea of how best to put it, 'but ours was not the usual kind of marriage. He was fond of me, but—'

'Loved that woman, did he?' Jonathan asked sharply. 'Made a fool of himself over her. But what of it?'

'Because of that, he couldn't treat me as a wife,' she managed to say, then seeing his ire growing because of this apparent irrelevancy, 'our marriage was never consummated,' she blurted out.

Complete silence. Then, 'You refused?'

'No.'

'You trying to tell me my grandson wasn't a man?' His

373

face grew red with suppressed anger.

'No. Only with me it wasn't possible,' she said steadily, now the worst was over.

His face grew grey as he realised what this meant. 'David?'

'Tom adored him. To all intents and purposes he was his father, and David loved him. But he's not his real son,' said Nell flatly.

'Whose?' Then as she said nothing, Jonathan roared again: '*Whose*?'

'I can't tell you that, for the father himself doesn't know. But David – and you – would have everything to be proud of.'

'Proud?' he muttered disgustedly, the fire seeming to drain from his face before her eyes. 'By God, young woman, you've led my grandson a dance.'

'No,' she retorted sharply. 'On the contrary.'

Jonathan gazed at her grimly. 'You're twice a fool then. I was going to leave everything to that boy, you know.'

'I know. That's why, as Tom wouldn't, I had to tell you.' As Nell quietly left the room, Jonathan did not even look up.

Gadsby's seemed suddenly as gloomy as the world outside it. All department stores were putting on a brave front to pretend that the depression and general uneasiness about the world situation had not reached out their grimy fingers and touched them. It was an appearance harder and harder to maintain, however. Even Gordon Holdsby seemed affected by the general air of malaise, producing no new initiatives on costs. A passive acceptance of submission to adversity pervaded the store, not helped by the death of Tom Gadsby who had been universally popular. It was another reminder that the old days had gone and the future was uncertain.

Jonathan kept his own counsel for two weeks after their

last meeting and when at last he summoned Nell it was to the Fourth Floor and not to Merrifield. There could be only one reason for such a summons, she concluded, the same as there had been in 1925.

'You want me to resign from the board?' she asked non-committally.

'No,' Jonathan replied.

'You want me to surrender Tom's shares to you?'

'No.'

Nell looked at him in surprise.

'You may be a fool, missy, but you're an honest fool.' Jonathan managed something like his old grin. 'And I need honest fools around me.'

'You need more than that,' retorted Nell, a flash of spirit returning.

The eyebrows shot up in satisfaction. He'd drawn the reaction he wanted.

'You need a strong ally,' continued Nell slowly. 'And Sir Bertram isn't exactly that! That's why you want me. Otherwise, how are you going to keep Holdsby in check now that his children will inherit? You might as well hand the whole lot over to him now rather than lose it bit by bit.'

'You should know me better than that, missy. I know what I'm doing. We've both got problems, you and I.'

'We?' echoed Nell. 'But you haven't yet asked me what *I* want to do. And I want to resign.'

'Nonsense. Of course you don't,' he dismissed this impatiently. 'I've thought it through now. You gave me a shock over young David, I don't deny that. I wanted to get rid of you, lock, stock and barrel, but Mrs Emmeline put me right. Should have seen it myself. You're right. I want you on my side. You're objective, even with Tom's shares you're no threat to my control – and I'd rather have you where I can see you,' he concluded disarmingly.

'But,' said Nell slowly, 'you forget that there's nothing

to hold me here now, unless I choose. While there was Tom, David and his future, it was different. Now whom do I have to consider?'

'There's you,' he told her matter-of-factly. 'You've given a lot of your life to this firm.'

She smiled faintly. He'd noticed! 'That's why I don't want to stay to see Holdsby ruin it. Or you,' she added deliberately.

Jonathan chuckled. 'That's more like it. You're going to stay and help put things right. Look at the situation, Nell. There's me, there's young Bertie, there's you, there's old Lorrimer and Charles, both doddering on the brink of retirement. I'm not going to let them go until I've got things as I want them. I need your support.' He paused. 'Life's a funny thing. Here am I having to plead with you to support me on my own damned board of my own damned company! Trouble is, you might vote against me. All right, as governing director, that don't mean a thing. I can do as I damn' well please. But it doesn't do to do that too often. Not if the board is going to have a genuine interest in running Gadsby's properly. So I can't bully you too often,' he grumbled regretfully.

Nell was amazed to hear him speak so, and she repressed any suspicion that he was deliberately setting out to woo her. 'You'll have to get a replacement director for Tom,' she pointed out. 'Especially if Mr Lorrimer and Mr Charles leave. Sir Bertram's interests don't seem to leave much time for Gadsby's.' Nell tried to keep sarcasm from her voice.

'He's coming in full-time,' Jonathan told her complacently. 'As secretary.'

Nell groaned. 'That will be a big help,' she said ironically.

'You're right. It will,' Jonathan almost crowed in triumph. 'You wait till you know the boy better before you go thinking I'm in my dotage, missy.'

Nell shrugged. If Jonathan was right about Bertie, he'd

be an asset to fight Holdsby. If he was, then at the very least they would have someone else on their side to vote. There was only one problem. 'Suppose he's another Holdsby, out for power for himself?'

Jonathan shouted with glee. 'Then the sharks can tear each other to pieces, while we get on with running Gadsby's. What do you say, Nell?'

'We?' she enquired, astounded. 'But I don't agree with your policy. I never did and nothing's changed.'

He looked cunning again. 'I know what's best for Gadsby's – you'll agree with me in the end.'

Nell thought rapidly. 'I won't, but I'll stay on. I want something in exchange though,' she declared.

His eyes gleamed. 'What is it this time? Want to open a bargain basement, do you? Cracked cups at a penny a throw?'

'No. Well, in a way, yes. I want to open a new department.'

'Do you, by gad? Holdsby won't like that. We're already behind on the interest on the new debentures.'

'He'll like it even less if Gadsby's closes.'

'There I'm not so sure,' said Jonathan slowly.

At first she did not grasp his meaning. Then she did. 'You mean, the worse Gadsby's fares, the more it falls behind on its commitments, the more likely it is that you'll have to hand over to him – despite all that's happened?'

He nodded. 'Something like that,' he admitted grudgingly.

'Then we have to consider ways of increasing turnover.'

'And expenditure,' he pointed out.

'Not if we're careful and plan in time for the spring. I want to open a Picture-Goers Corner with Maria Maniosta. She'd give me very favourable rates for,' she rushed on over the dreaded word, 'mass reproduction rights in her dresses for Melissa's films for Falconwood, and I've got a factory ready to take on machine production. It won't affect our workroom.' Much as they could do with the work in fact, economics would not lend themselves to so much handwork. 'And they'll be good quality of course. Selling at about two guineas – to catch a wide market.'

'A few pretty frocks aren't going to save Gadsby's,' he snorted.

'Not by themselves. But if other departments, like Scarves, Jewellery and so on, back it up by ordering the accessories used in the films, to sell in the Corner too, it would help enormously. And if Melissa agrees to have her portrait everywhere, perhaps on china, jewellery, that sort of thing.'

He snorted. 'She ain't the queen, you know.'

'No, but she's a star, and her films are going to make her a bigger one. In times of bad economic conditions, people like escape, and that's what her films will provide. We'll start with Melissa, then broaden it to other stars.'

'No.'

'Then I resign.'

'Compromise. If your frocks sell, you can finance the china and fall-la-lahs out of its profits.'

'But that won't be—'

'My last word.'

'Very well.' Nell rapidly ran through costs in her mind. She'd manage somehow.

'And you stay on the board.'

'Yes.'

'Darling.'

'Good morning, Sir Bertram,' Nell greeted him demurely as they arrived at the Fourth Floor boardroom together. Her spirits rose as Bertie strode in to take his seat, complete with monocle, long wispy golden hair, bright pink shirt and mauve waistcoat. Not to mention the royal blue cravat tied with artistic carelessness round his neck. If he'd had a highwayman's hat she wouldn't have been surprised. This would be easy, with Jonathan on her side.

He beamed at her. 'Such a nice surprise of Uncle Jonathan's to call the meeting for today. Fits in nicely between my hair appointment and luncheon at the club.'

'Provided it doesn't tire you too much,' she said solemnly, seeing him suppress a yawn. Uncle Jonathan indeed. Old friends the Gadsbys and Bertrands might be, but there was no room for such informality at Gadsby's. But she was used to it by now.

'I can catnap anywhere,' he assured her. 'You're not to worry about me one little bit. I'll just nod off.'

He did too. To her horror he was peacefully asleep with his eyes shut when it was time to read the minutes. She kicked him under the table and he jerked awake. Gordon almost purred with satisfaction at seeing such an easy enemy. Lorrimer and Charles, in their old-fashioned morning suits, were united in disapproval

As she expected, Holdsby leapt into instant opposition to Picture-Goers Corner, despite Jonathan Gadsby's endorsement of it.

'And the money, Mrs Gadsby?'

'It will certainly need capital,' she agreed, ready for this. 'I estimate pricing the dresses at around £2—'

'Guineas,' put in Holdsby.

'No. Pounds for this market,' she said firmly having thought about this. 'Capital outlay for an initial stock of seven hundred would be in the region of £850.'

'Why so large an initial order?' snapped Holdsby. 'Rash, isn't it?'

'Because capitalisation of other products is going to come from the profits of the frocks. Besides, that's for three different styles.'

'Quite ridiculous to expand in time of slump,' declared Holdsby. 'The obvious answer is to put a few of these frocks in your Leisure Wear department and see how they sell.'

'No,' said Nell. 'We must go into it wholeheartedly, or it won't work.'

'As store director,' said Holdsby, 'I oppose it absolutely. And so, I'm sure, will Mr Charles.'

'It does seem rash, Mrs Gadsby,' he said apologetically.

'I don't agree,' said Mr Lorrimer stoutly. 'We must move with the times. Speaking for Supplies, I feel sure that, with care, an attractive addition to Gadsby's could attract custom.' He sat back happily, conscious he had both pleased Mr Gadsby and given his true opinion. It didn't always happen that way.

'Sir Bertram?' Jonathan asked smugly. Then louder. 'Bertie!'

Bertie, slumped casually in his chair, tore himself from a doodle of what looked like Daedelus' labyrinth.

'Me?' He looked delighted to be asked. 'Far too risky. That's my view,' and returned to his doodle.

'How?' demanded Nell, trying to keep impatience from her voice. 'Any new venture is naturally risky. But then standing still on a downward slope is risky too.'

'I was up at Newmarket once,' Bertie informed the company. 'Put my shirt on the favourite and it didn't come in. That's why I have to wear these things now.' He looked apologetically at his bright pink effusion.

'And what does Newmarket have to do with it?'

'Taught me a lesson. Eggs in baskets – that sort of thing.'

Nell stared at him. Fool or seer – whichever, he was having a disastrous effect. She'd warned Jonathan and he'd taken no notice.

'It looks as if the board's split, Nell,' Holdsby told her complacently. 'That means you don't have a mandate I'm afraid – not unless Mr Gadsby overrides us, as is his right.

However, he does not usually exercise it on matters such as this.'

Jonathan Gadsby glared but said nothing. Checkmated.

'On the other hand,' Mr Charles' thin voice broke in, 'now I consider Mrs Gadsby's figures more carefully from the Counting House viewpoint, I can see a merit in her argument.' He did not like pink shirts, he did not like Bertie Bertrand, and most definitely he did not like his powers as Counting House director impinged upon by upstart Secretaries.

Nell tried to restrain a laugh. 'I'm so glad that's settled. I'll let you have detailed costings and budgets shortly. I'm so sorry you don't approve, Sir Bertram. I think you'll find it will work,' she said to him as she passed him on the way out. 'Even if it doesn't at Newmarket.'

He yawned. 'Of course. If you get as far as that, Little Red Riding Hood.'

What on earth did he mean? she wondered crossly for a moment, then dismissed it from her mind.

Why hadn't the signed contract come back from Maria? Nell fretted. The factory was ready to go, with all the materials supplied. Yet here they were in January with no signed contract. Every time she telephoned she was told Maria was away, that the contract would be posted. Then finally the operator reported the line discontinued. All Nell's fears, hitherto subdued, flooded together. She must get to Paris – and quickly. From Croydon she took the first Imperial Airways flight she could get, in the *Hengist*.

It was not her first flight, but she still enjoyed the thrill of the huge four-engined machine rushing, then lifting into the air and soaring upwards leaving airport, spectators and fields far below. Then as luncheon was served, her worries took over once more. Why hadn't she heard? What had gone wrong with Maria? Even if the worst had happened and she'd had to sell the company, *someone* should have been in touch. Instead of that, silence.

Two and a half hours later she was in the Avenue Montaigne to find her fears justified. The House of Maniosta was unoccupied, its windows shuttered. Summoning her courage, Nell walked back to the Maison la Ferté. '*Est-ce que Madame Maniosta travaille ici maintenant?*' she enquired painstakingly of the doorman, who recognised her with pleasure.

'I will look after Mrs Gadsby.'

Intent on making herself understood by the commissionaire, she hadn't noticed someone else in the entrance hall. As Lucien came towards her, her heart sank. Here of all places. And now of all times!

'Please follow me, Madame Gadsby.' She followed him, for she had no choice.

Here in the familiar office she felt more at ease, as though she could pretend nothing had happened.

'I regret I have bad news for you, Nell,' Lucien said sincerely, but his voice remained that of the businessman, not the lover. 'You are waiting for the contract for Maniosta's film dresses. I do not think you will receive it.'

'But it was all agreed.' She had no fight in her, half-suspecting the truth. 'Where is she? Does she work here?' Was Lucien involved in this labyrinth of mystery? Then she understood what must have happened. 'You've bought her fashion house, haven't you? Philippe persuaded her to work for you, and now you've persuaded her to sell the company.'

'No persuasion was necessary.' His voice was cool. 'She had no choice. Her business went bankrupt. It has happened to many houses in the slump.'

'I have seen no signs of fashion being badly hit since I've been here,' she challenged him, and looking pointedly at the huge bunches of early flowers in his office, remembering similar ones in the entrance hall. 'In fact, rather the contrary.'

382

'It is true that we are making an effort to *appear* optimistic in our styles and colours. But, let us say, it is a case of the French stiff upper lip.'

'Even if what you say is true,' she continued, 'it needn't affect Maria of all people. She was successful, in demand. Like Chanel. What *happened*?' Nell heard her voice rising. 'She had an efficient manager.' She heard Maria's voice saying, 'I do not understand money.'

'Efficient, but perhaps she chose unwisely.'

'He was good with money, so Maria told me.'

'He was *very* good at money,' echoed Lucien grimly.

'He defrauded her?' Nell realised belatedly with shock. So that was it. Of course. She would not marry Jacques, so he took his road to power another way.

When he did not answer her, she leapt to the heart of it. 'He always worked for you, didn't he?' she whispered. 'You planned this, and he was your agent.'

'I worked at Cannes, Nell. I knew nothing of Jacques, nothing of Maria. I swear it.' Emotion appeared on his face at last.

'Philippe, of course,' she guessed bitterly. 'But he is part of the Maison la Ferté, and so are you.'

'I have persuaded my father to part with Jacques' services.'

'Too late for Maria,' she said shortly. 'Have you persuaded your father to part with her services too?'

'Unfortunately that is not possible.'

'Because she has the genius that Philippe lacks.'

'You are wrong, Nell. Philippe is very talented, though not in the same way Maria is. Together they are a good team.'

'Will he let her design in the way she wants to?' said Nell vehemently. 'Or will he hold her back? Use her gifts to further his own career?'

He flushed. 'Nell, you must realise I am a director of the Maison la Ferté—'

383

'So you cannot speak freely. Even to me,' she flashed. 'I want to see her – *now*. She'll tell me, if you won't.'

'She is not here,' he said flatly.

'So you're scared to let me see her,' she said scornfully. 'So much for Maison la Ferté integrity.'

'*She is not here*,' he emphasised, holding back anger with difficulty. 'Nell, you do not yet know the worst.'

'The *worst*?' she echoed disbelievingly. 'What worse could there be, for Maria, for the future of *haute couture* come to that?'

'Philippe has married Maria. She will bear his child in the spring. She is resting at home.'

Maria? That beautiful vibrant woman married to Philippe. At first, she could not take it in. Then, when she did, she burst out, 'Why?' How on earth could Maria be in love with Philippe? Or had that been part of the bargain? Had she found herself in a position when she had no choice – small wonder Nell had not heard from her.

'Philippe is a very eligible and charming man. He will be the next Comte de la Ferté after me. Her sons will follow in the line,' he said unemotionally.

'Maria is not so worldly, so materialistic. She's –' Nell choked '– one of life's flames. It was your brother brought this about. Took Maria's talent for himself, then her body, and talked you into marrying Melissa.'

'*Nell*! You are wrong. Philippe is bad but he would not do that.' Hearing the anguish in his voice, she wished with all her heart she had not spoken. Now that she had, however, she must go on.

'He would do anything to thwart you. He had to marry to beget a child quickly, knowing that—'

'Knowing what, Nell?' he said relentlessly.

'That you would not have any,' she finished, looking away from him.

'*Ça suffit*,' he said abruptly. 'Enough of this. Let us return to your contract, Madame Gadsby. I regret the

384

Maison la Ferté will not be able to support Madame Maniosta's verbal offer. We will not sign.'

'Because you—' She stopped. If he wanted to revert to business rivalry, then she must match him. No matter how great her own unhappiness. One by one all those whom she treasured most were being taken from her.

'And will *you* be utilising Maria's film designs?' she asked coolly.

'Naturally I cannot discuss our forthcoming collections,' he countered smoothly.

'I'm sorry,' she told him casually. 'Nevertheless, suspecting something was wrong, I have now made other plans.'

A glimmer of a smile came to his face. 'So it is as it used to be, Perfidious Albion.'

Her head came up. 'Yes,' she said proudly.

'So be it. You must act on these doubtless exciting "other plans".'

Panic set in on the homeward journey. What to do? Of course she had no other plans. She had material ordered, arrangements made for Melissa Hargreaves' face eventually to appear on everything from doormats to dirndls. Melissa— An idea began to form in the back of her mind.

'And here,' Nell concluded, flourishing a lordly hand, 'we'll have pictures of Madeleine Carroll, Jessie Matthews, Maria Corda – and I expect you've heard of these exciting new Gainsborough Films. You should see the costumes.'

Melissa, clad in dress and coat of fashionable checks with ermine trimmings (no depression for Melissa), stared at the dramatic display in Picture-Goers Corner indignantly. 'But where's my picture?' she wailed. 'I thought this was going to be all about *me*.'

'Oh,' said Nell, startled. 'I thought you must have heard by now . . .'

'You think you have won, my fair Shulamite. But you have not and this you will see.' The familiar voice on the telephone. Just that. No more and then the receiver was gently replaced at the French end.

Bluff. All bluff. She had won.

Triumphantly, Nell walked along Conduit Street past the Maison la Ferté. She glanced in the window – to see Maria's film dresses already displayed.

After one horrified lurch of the stomach, she turned round, went back to her office and rang firstly Falcon-wood to explain exclusive British rights meant just that and would they kindly tell Maison la Ferté to remove the dresses from their London branch forthwith; then the factory, desperate for work, but which had not been expecting to start production for two weeks; and finally Bertie Bertrand, who to her surprise had, despite his opposition, undertaken to be temporary buyer for the new department as a whole while Nell organised the first dresses for it. He hadn't needed to do much yet, since until dresses were sold, there would be no profits to spend on china, as per her agreement with Jonathan. Though Jonathan, she felt, might bend his rules if the dresses did well. She asked Bertie if he could spare a few minutes and he arrived in her office looking startlingly smart – though hardly with the old-fashioned correctitude that Gadsby's was used to.

'Rightio,' Bertie said cheerily, not taking in what she said. Then, cautiously checking, 'I say, I did hear you say Thursday morning, did I? Day after tomorrow?'

'You did,' Nell informed him succinctly. 'Take as many staff as you want – I've squared it with the other buyers – but Thursday it is. The first consignment arrives tomorrow evening.'

'Rightio,' he said, obviously still unconvinced, then seeing the look in Nell's eye, squared his shoulders in their elegant but incongruous pearl grey suit, said: 'Rightio then,' rather vaguely once again, and marched firmly out. Then he marched somewhat less firmly back. 'I say – your friend Melissa,' he opened awkwardly. 'Friendly word and all that. The Pink and Blue Club – not a good thing.'

'She's no longer going there,' said Nell, alarmed. That was one of the clubs she'd frequented with Robert and was notorious for more than bottle parties and high living. She herself had warned Melissa about it only two months ago after overhearing gossip in the store.

'Oh, darling,' Melissa had said impatiently, 'you are a fussy old thing. You used to enjoy clubs yourself. This is no worse than Ma Meyrick's. Better in fact.'

'Is that what she told you?' Bertie looked surprisingly concerned. 'Sorry to say it, but not like that at all. She's there regularly.'

'Drugs? Cocaine?' asked Nell, dreading the answer.

'Ah – yes – but it's the company, my dear. Dear Melissa isn't the most selective person in the world. Better to keep away. So they're saying.'

Nell felt sick, remembering suddenly that among Bertie's many friends were several in the police force. 'I collect them,' he told her once plaintively, 'by mistake. I only go after their helmets, dammit.'

She had taken the statement at face value at the time, deeming it part of his scatterbrained social life. Now she knew him a little better, she was beginning to wonder if he was quite as scatterbrained as she'd thought. She passed the warning on to Melissa once again, and to her surprise her friend listened. 'Very well, darling,' she sighed, 'if it makes you happy, I'll stay away. Sometimes,' she added crossly, 'I don't think you want me to have *any* fun.'

Sick with excitement, Nell arrived at Gadsby's at seven on Thursday morning to find Bertie there before her dressed in workmen's overalls – albeit in bright red – marshalling a small army. Worker bees scurried for the next hour and a half until at last a new window proclaimed Picture-Goers Corner open on the first floor, a trail of plaster models bearing a startling resemblance to Melissa Hargreaves pointed the way through the ground floor, and on the first Lingerie had disappeared into the background while in its place . . . Nell gulped. Perhaps a *little* overdone?

Bertie had not exactly skimped on eye-catching photographs and colours. Melissa's face stared out of exotic scarlet surrounds in huge photographs from the films where she was seen wearing the dresses shown on the models beneath. Miniature sets in the corner reminded the shopper of those irresistible moments in her pictures, took them in to view at closer range, right next to the shimmering film dresses. If only shoes, scarves, fans, gloves, could join them. Soon they would and with them would be replicas of cigarette boxes, cigarette holders, china – anything to make the shopper identify with those magic moments in which anything seemed possible.

Nell drew a breath. Indeed, anything *was* possible now.

For three months she tasted the sweet delights of victory. The dresses sold swiftly and continuously and when sales of those from *Dancing in the Dew* began to slacken, those from Melissa's new film, *Candlelight*, more than redressed the balance.

'Wasn't I right?' she said to Bertie smugly. He just smiled.

Emboldened, Jonathan authorised her to go ahead on the accessories. Then in June she received a call from Melissa at 1.30 in the morning. Not the Melissa she was used to, but an incoherent, screaming Melissa.

'You've got to come. Now!' were the only words she could make out.

'Why? Where are you?' she managed to get through the torrent of words.

A hail of sobs, gasps, then: 'Vine Street.'

'*Vine* Street? The police station?' Nell asked sharply.

'Yes!' A wail of defiance.

'I'll come.'

Nell hung up the receiver, wondering what on earth to do. A solicitor. Melissa might need one. But she could hardly ring up the stately Mr Bellow of Porter & Bellow, Jonathan's solicitor, at this time of night, even if she knew his private number. She needed help, advice, and there was no one to turn to. Or was there? She hesitated, but there was nothing to lose. Even a scatterbrained Bertie Wooster was better than no help at all. Taking a deep breath, she took up the telephone and spoke to the operator. Two minutes later a slightly less than cheery Bertie was on the line.

'Dear Melissa,' came his resigned voice after Nell had hesitantly explained. After all, it had been he who'd warned her, so he was involved to some extent. 'Nell darling, call a taxi – *not* a time for the Rolls, darling – and come round here *immediately*.'

'But—'

'No buts for Bertie, darling.'

They reached Vine Street thirty minutes later, now miraculously accompanied by a slightly dishevelled young solicitor, with a distinct slur in his voice, picked up en route from Ma Meyrick's.

Nell didn't immediately recognise Melissa, until someone she took to be a man in clown's make-up rushed at her shrieking in a now familiar tone. Others, ranging from drunks and prostitutes to society women, looking decidedly the worse for wear, watched without interest. The clown's top hat fell off to reveal Melissa's blonde head. Her lipstick was smeared all over her clown's make-up, together with mascara that had run down her cheeks.

With some difficulty Bertie's tame solicitor arranged

bail until the morning, and Nell pushed Melissa speedily into the taxi.

'Forgive me,' said Melissa brightly to Bertie, 'it's awfully nice of you to arrange bail for me, but who *are* you exactly?'

'Don't you know him?' asked Nell, confused.

'We never met,' said Bertie vaguely. 'How d'yer do?' He solemnly shook hands with her huge clown gloves and Melissa giggled.

Nell slumped despairingly back in her seat. Yet another fine mess Melissa had got her into. Assuming him to be a friend of Melissa's, she'd asked someone with whom she was on uneasy terms to arrange bail for a drunken wreck who was a virtual stranger to him and who, unless they were all very lucky, would be hitting the headlines in the newspapers in roughly twelve hours' time.

'What on earth were you *doing*?' she demanded of Melissa crossly as she made up a bed for her at Eaton Square. No letting Melissa out of her control this time.

'Nothing,' she wailed. 'Just drinking.'

'Like that?' Nell asked scathingly, looking at the discarded clown's costume.

'Oh, Nell, I'm so *tired*.' And the golden head hit the pillow in peaceful slumber.

The 'nothing' was enough to get Melissa six months in Holloway. The nothing had been offending public order by importuning gentlemen in Piccadilly while drunk and disorderly. Despite their success in getting Melissa charged under her original maiden name and in one of Nell's frocks hastily lent to her, the newspapers, quick on the scent, were there to greet the departure of the public's Number One innocent dewy-eyed heroine for Holloway.

Nell visited Melissa once a week, appalled at the thinness and bright red unhealthy flush on her face. Visiting times Melissa regarded as her personal appearance show and her febrile conversations were carried on at top pitch.

'Just think of the experience I'll have, darling, when I come out. Half those darling gentlemen thought I was a man in that costume. I could play Oscar Wilde.'

If she ever played anything again, Nell thought wrily.

Melissa had been replaced in *Morning Glory* by her understudy at the Princess Beatrice, though the play was shortly to close. Her new Falconwood film had closed after a week. There was no escape from everyday problems in watching a film about pure young love when its actress was in jail for soliciting. Its effects on Picture-Goers Corner had been disastrous. A special board meeting had been called when sales immediately slumped, with Gordon Holdsby openly triumphant, Jonathan challenging – and Bertie apparently asleep.

'What now, missy, eh?' Jonathan roared, a Methuselah presiding in judgement.

'I've stopped production till we have a new concept thought out,' she said more positively than she felt.

'Meanwhile, we have a department with no customers in a prominent place, which is having its effect on the whole of the first floor. What *is* your present stock?' purred Holdsby. 'Let me see,' he shuffled ostentatiously through his papers, 'three hundred in stock and a further four hundred at the factory. Nearly £1,000 tied up.'

'My design staff is working on an idea,' replied Nell grandly. Polly and Miss Gertrude were indeed busily employed at Eaton Square, adding trimming or scarves here, basques and godets there, changing full to slim Bishop sleeves with cuffs, anything to disguise the original. 'I'll report to you again in three days.'

But she was not to escape so easily. The question she dreaded from dear Mr Lorrimer, who belatedly remembered something they'd discussed at the meeting before last.

'And the china, Mrs Gadsby?'

The china. Crate after crate of mugs, cups, saucers and plates, with Melissa Hargreaves' face smiling out happily from each item and due into the warehouse in a week's time.

'What are we to do, Bertie?' Nell asked despondently afterwards in her office. Why on earth she was asking him, goodness only knew. He was hardly an ideas man, yet somehow since the Melissa drama she had fallen into the habit of discussing things with him. It occurred to her that he seemed to be a good catalyst. And how she needed one. There was nothing like being faced with the actual results of your foolhardiness in the shape of twenty-four crates of unusable bone china, the first consignment that would inevitably be delivered to Gadsby's stockrooms, although she could cancel future orders.

'I have the teensiest little idea, Nell. Just the teensiest.' He bent towards her and whispered in her ear, in a stage whisper though there was no one to hear save the Gadsby cat.

Her mouth opened wide with astonishment.

'So unbecoming, Nell darling,' Bertie complained. 'And I'd run it. So economical and such fun. All those lovely ladies.'

'And as they come out—' Nell grasped the possibilities and her eyes lit up.

'Precisely, darling.'

'And Bertie, what was that word you used – economical. Oh, that gives *me* an idea. What do you think of *this*?' Imitating him, she leant across and whispered in his ear . . .

'Over my dead body,' roared Jonathan Gadsby, bringing his large hand down with a crash on the table.

'Just a moment,' said Mr Charles, interested. 'I'd like to hear more.'

Jonathan glared as if remembering Charles was overdue for retirement.

'Naughty but nice,' said Bertie brightly. 'Cream cakes, Earl Grey tea, scones and cream, all served on naughty Melissa Hargreaves' china.'

Nell took up the baton. 'We'll move the Fashion Showroom up to the east end of the second floor, where the model and fitting rooms now are.'

'You won't,' said Jonathan. Silence.

'Then there'll be room for the tea-room at the west end of the second floor, with some reorganisation, and when they come out refreshed from tea, they'll walk through our new "Just for You, Three Pounds" department. Nothing to cost above three pounds. And in it, we can sell the film dresses, individually altered to justify the higher price – among others, of course.' She smiled brightly. 'And the first floor can display Fashion models and have an expanded Leisure and Sporting Wear department.'

They wouldn't have stood a chance had it not been unexpected support from Messrs Lorrimer and Charles, perhaps seeing a chance for revenge for the slights heaped upon them by Holdsby, or perhaps seeing it as a swansong to their Gadsby years to support such a dramatic change. Holdsby was supporting Jonathan through thick and thin these days, Nell noticed.

For a moment, Nell thought Jonathan was going to exercise his governing director's veto. Then he seemed to think better of it.

'Well, young woman,' he grunted. 'You've won. I'm out-voted. You've got your cheap-jacks' department. But only because we've got to shed that stock you've let us in for. Three guineas though, not pounds. This is Gadsby's, girl. You've one last chance, so make it work,' he told her meaningfully, 'or I'll have your guts for garters.'

★ ★ ★

'Nell, darling.' Melissa's tremulous voice on the telephone. 'I'm out.'

'But you—'

'I'm not very well. I'm at Bobsy's.'

Nell's mind whirled. Bobsy's? How on earth? Leaving her notes on the latest Paris trends, she went in search of Bertie whom she found deep in conversation with Peter Pride over the amount of cake that one lady could be expected to consume on average. With the closure of Picture-Goers' Corner, he had taken to tea-rooms with enthusiasm.

'Ah,' he said resignedly. 'So you know. Happened all in a rush this weekend, Nell. Take you down there tonight, shall I?'

She agreed, albeit with the thought that matters were getting beyond her control. So far it was to the good, she was forced to concede, although Bertie remained as much of an enigma as ever.

She found Melissa swathed in shawls with all the windows flung open in her bedroom at Missinden. She flung her thin arms wide open when she saw Nell, all the shawls promptly falling off.

'Go away, Bertie,' she commanded, coughing slightly. 'I want to talk to Nell alone.'

'Rightio,' he said amicably, obediently disappearing.

'What *is* all this, Melissa? Why are you here with Bobsy – and where's Lucien?' Nell added with an effort.

'Lucien's left me.' Tears poured down her cheeks. 'He really has this time. He never knew the extent of my – my weakness, until all this horrid prison business cropped up. We're officially separated. He says he'll support me, won't divorce me, but he won't ever live with me any more.' A pause. Then the racked small voice again: 'I think he'll come to you, Nell.'

'I don't know,' was all she managed to stammer, torn between delirious happiness and pain.

'He will,' Melissa burst out, clutching her, as she sat on the bed. 'Oh Nell, you won't take him from me, will you? Promise. I need him so. I've nobody. Nothing now. No career, no future. Nothing. I need to know he's still mine and not yours. You've got so much. You took Tommy from me, you've got David, and if you take Lucien too—'

'Melissa, it's not true that I *took* Tom,' Nell was outraged.

'They all leave me. Want me, and then leave me. Please don't take Lucien – ever, not even after I'm dead. Promise me. I need to know something's still mine while I'm dying.'

'Dying? What nonsense is this, Melissa?' Nell asked stiffly through dry lips.

Tears poured down Melissa's cheeks. 'I've got TB,' she said painfully. 'That's why they let me out of that place early. That's why the windows are all open. They say fresh air will cure it. Cure! There is no cure. It's in the last stages. Six months they say. Silly, isn't it?'

Nell was dumb, appalled, trying to disentangle fact from Melissa's fantasy. No, this was no fantasy. She was ill, she was scared. Nell put her arms round her.

'Oh, Nell, don't take him away. You promised once you'd always be my friend. Promise it again, Nell.'

She had to say what was in her mind or she would never be free of doubt. 'You married him knowing he loved me.'

'No, no, I didn't. I never knew till afterwards. I swear I didn't.'

Looking at her then, Nell could almost believe her. And what did it matter? It was past, it was done. It was the present that yawned as an abyss before her.

'Think how bad it would look for him to be living with you while I was dying,' the insistent plaintive voice went on.

How could Melissa use such outrageous arguments, and how could she, Nell, ignore them? Life without Melissa.

For a moment she forgot the betrayals, the weaknesses and remembered only the woman who had befriended her when she needed a friend, the loving, generous, life-giving Melissa – who had six months to live.

'Promise me, Nell?'

'I promise.'

'I said I would come,' Lucien said, 'but then I did not know what would make me come. And now I do.' He looked round the Eaton Square drawing room, which still spoke partly of Melissa. Her portrait adorned one wall, smiling out in all her confident beauty.

'Why didn't you tell me about her?' he burst out bitterly. 'Why not? Have you known all along?'

'Yes,' she replied. Useless to pretend she did not know to what he referred. 'How *could* I have told you? I didn't know you were planning to marry her. Philippe should have told you. He knew about her – *and* he knew she couldn't have children.' It was childish, a cry for anger, for all that had happened.

'Nymphomania,' Lucien said bitterly. 'That's the word they call it. I've talked to so many doctors and psychiatrists in the last months, I know more jargon than they do. It's a disease. She can't be blamed, I'm told. But *I* blame her, Nell. For ruining both our lives.'

'She can't help it, Lucien,' Nell said defensively. 'And she changed after she married you. She needed the security you gave her. She was almost cured until this latest slip.' She didn't believe it, but somehow she had to break his bitterness.

'Cured?' he said angrily. 'She had lovers from the first month after we were married. Why do you think I let her come to London alone? Because I could stand it no more. When you came round to Charles Street, do you know why I was so abrupt?' She looked at him, suddenly fearful of what he might say. 'Because I'd walked in and found her in bed with another man. And do you know who it was? It was *Tom*,' he threw at her. 'How do you feel about her loyalty now? Her friendship?'

'Don't!' Nell said numbly at this terrible confirmation of what her darkest imaginings had suspected. 'Please don't.'

'I'm sorry, Nell,' he said quietly. 'Did you love Tom finally? Did things come right for you? Tell me. *Tell me*!' There was insistence, not emotion, in his voice.

'No,' she replied instantly. 'No,' realising too late what her denial would mean, and adding quickly, 'not altogether.'

He stared at her in silence for a moment, then said: 'I want you, Nell, and I've come for you.'

'Lucien, I can't, she said quietly. 'Melissa's dying. She needs you, on whatever terms. I've promised her I won't—'

His face grew white. 'Promised – dying? You believe her?'

'She's got TB,' Nell said wearily. 'Six months.'

'I did not know. I am sad, deeply sad for her.' He paused, choosing his words carefully. 'But it changes nothing. One way and another she has ruined our lives. At some point we must say, no more. And that point is now – or it will never happen.'

'But I live here, work here, while you are in France. I promised her – while she's alive. I have a son.' Any argument she could use. Surely there were logical reasons to support her promise, even before Lucien's cool perceptive eyes?

'Yes.' He paused. 'What was it you came to tell me when you arrived in Cannes so unexpectedly?' he asked devastatingly.

'I came to tell you Tom was going to let me go,' she replied quickly, too quickly.

'Just after you had borne his child?'

She had no answer.

He swallowed. 'I will not, cannot, ask again, Nell. If you say no this time, our lives part for ever. I do not wish to see you – or your son.'

She had but to reach out and she would be in his arms. Was it fear that held her back? Was it love for him, so much she thought she would burst of it? Was it a promise given to a dying woman, a woman to whom she already committed her loyalty and friendship before she'd even met this man she loved with all her heart?

She was proud. And like Jonathan Gadsby, she was obstinate in her pride. She would not break a promise. 'Melissa is dying,' Nell said at last. 'She needs you.'

Like Jonathan, too, she was a fighter.

No proud music, no clash of cymbals as he walked away. So ordinary, so everyday a leaving, as though he would return in an hour. But he would not. Never again.

Chapter Twelve

Perhaps the sun would never come out again, Nell thought bleakly, watching as the rain beat down relentlessly on the windows of her office. True, now spring had come the massively high unemployment figure had dropped slightly from the peak of three and a half million in mid-1932. But in those twenty-two months there had been few signs of permanent improvement. And on top of the economic problems at home, a definite unease over what was happening abroad – and showed signs of spreading to England – was blotting out the memory of the optimistic '20s. Since Herr Hitler had become Chancellor, and announced his preposterous plan of drawing all those of Germanic origin wherever they might be in the world into one state, and then peremptorily withdrew his delegation from the League of Nations, the shadow of conflict which had receded since the Armistice of 1918 had once more been creeping over the international stage. And last year the Oxford Union, when debating the issue of whether if called upon to fight for King and Country they would do so, had jolted morale by passing the motion to refuse.

Amid all this Gadsby's staggered on, under the ever-decreasing impetus of its past. Nell's bespoke model trade in the Fashion Department was steadily draining away, although it had received two crutches in the tea-room and the Three-Guinea department. The latter had been an immediate draw, especially with its new attraction of personality frocks, according to whether customers deemed themselves (or wished to appear) distinguished, artistic, romantic, businesslike and so on. Now the tea-room too was proving a positive attraction, not merely an afterthought for those visiting the showroom.

It was noticeable that the number of orders for Gadsby's models had fallen since the mid-twenties by over two thirds. Moreover, the number of orders per customer had been slashed, as well as customers decreasing in number. The most significant statistic was that of the present customers for the models, nearly five sixths were new and nearly all of them had purchased either a ready-made Gadsby leisure dress or a garment from the Three-Guinea Department. How long before *all* their purchases were from the Three-Guinea Department? Add to that the fact that the latter's sales were increasing, and to Nell the writing was not only on the wall, it was shouting from the ceiling.

Bertie had now handed over the running of the tea-room to a Mrs Jolly, the thinnest and most morose-looking person Nell had ever seen. She had had severe doubts over the wisdom of Bertie's choice, but was proved wrong. Fortunately Mrs Jolly's cakes were as light and succulent as their maker was mournful, and even more fortunately, her very eccentricity attracted a fascinated and loyal clientèle. Tea at Gadsby's was rapidly acquiring as much a reputation as tea at Fuller's.

Jonathan Gadsby remained loftily aloof from all innovations. Despite his increasing age and gout (the existence of which he vigorously denied), he still took the morning walk around the store, though now it took longer and the eye was not so keenly observant. He had taken to leaving at Friday lunchtime for the journey to Merrifield, rarely coming in on Saturday, and often not on Monday either.

Mrs Emmeline and Miss Gertrude were becoming increasingly frail, and spent most of their time now at Merrifield. Nell took David there as often as she could, feeling that this was becoming her home. In London she felt isolated in a world she thought of as increasingly crazy. Despite the terrifying problems around them, and even greater ones menacingly looming, or perhaps because of them, society seemed to be going mad. Standing on the fringes, as Tom's widow, she saw and was utterly amazed by the careless abandon with which those who still had money were prepared to spend it. (Except in Gadsby's, alas!) The parties were more exotic than ever – she had an array of cards on her desk at home, inviting her to everything from a Cowboys and Indians to a Hawaian party. The less monied among the population found their own means of escape. Cinemas and dancing thrived. The more exotic the picture, the more wildly romantic, the more it pleased. Musicals, romances, adventures were lapped up eagerly by a wide and appreciative audience. Cinema was becoming a drug.

Curiously the depression seemed to be aiding British haute couture. The import controls had proved a boost to the good couturiers, and gifted newcomers like Hardy Amies were rapidly establishing themselves. For those lower down the tree, like Gadsby's, it was a different story, caught between the exclusivity of the haute couture houses from above and the mass marketing departmental stores from below. Nell felt she was forced to watch the exciting complete change in silhouette from the shapeless boyish twenties to the sophisticated tall slim elegance of the thirties with one hand tied behind her back.

Paris, too, had varying factions with many smaller couture houses going to the wall. Maison la Ferté, however, if not thriving, was surviving – chiefly due to its designs, the press reported, which had taken a new direction away from its former conservative and opulent image. Yet still there was not a word publicly or privately of Maniosta – and it seemed to Nell that the designs, even if a new direction for Maison la Ferté, were distinctly less

401

innovative than Maria's former flamboyant style.

Poor Maria, she thought compassionately, wondering whether Maria had forgotten her, having adapted herself to the Maison la Ferté, or whether she was so unhappy she could not bear to get in touch. She would be having her baby any time now if it was not already born. Nell had tried telephoning, she had tried writing. Neither avenue had been successful. The Comtesse Philippe was unreachable. Nor had Nell heard from or of Lucien. Not that she had expected to. It was as if the de la Ferté chapter of her life were completely closed. The only door that remained open was Gadsby's, and the problems of her life here in London.

One of which was Melissa.

It was now eight months from the day Melissa had told her she had only six months to live, and not only was she still alive, she was very much kicking. 'They say it's a miracle,' she announced proudly, having summoned Nell to Charles Street. 'I'm a wonder, my doctor says. He's such a dear.'

'St Peter probably sent you back,' laughed Nell, relieved.

'Bertie helped him,' Melissa told her brightly. 'The doctor said I was well enough to come back home, and Bertie said he'd look after me. So here I am,' she said. A pause. 'With nothing to do. Extinct as a dodo, darling.'

'You'll—' The words died on Nell's lips. How could she honestly say Melissa would easily get another job? It was as if Melissa Hargreaves, the sweetheart of London stage and screen, had never existed. Her films had disappeared from the cinemas, her stage career was never referred to in magazines and newspapers, almost as if they were ashamed of their former praise of her talents. No hero so ignored as a fallen hero, Nell thought sadly. It was as if Melissa had died along with the twenties. Only if she *had* died, just think how fulsome the press would have been then, she reflected.

Yet how glad she was that Melissa had not died. In some surprising way Nell could manage now to divorce her feelings from Melissa her friend from those she had for Melissa, wife to Lucien. Lucien was past, and past through her own doing, not just because of Melissa's actions now. Even had Melissa died, Lucien would never return to Nell. She had rejected him twice, and he would not come again. Meanwhile Melissa still lived, and with all her problems was still a bright ornament to life.

Today she did not look a bright ornament however. Or if she were, she was a jewel on a junk stall. She was lounging in an old-fashioned pyjama suit that had seen not only better but cleaner days. Charles Street, too, was untidy, uncared for, and in places dirty.

'Where's Gwen?' Nell asked, surprised. 'How could she let it get like this?'

'Like what?' asked Melissa, looking vaguely round.

'Untidy,' answered Nell diplomatically.

Melissa shrugged. 'Gwen left.'

'*Left*?' Nell repeated in astonishment. Gwen had endured Melissa's foibles through thick and thin for fifteen years.

'She told me my entertaining was too much for her,' said Melissa sullenly.

'You haven't been giving parties, have you, Melissa?' Nell asked, puzzled.

Melissa glanced at her, saying nothing.

'You don't mean you've been bringing lovers back here again?' Nell's heart sank as she realised what Melissa had meant.

Melissa laughed. 'Lovers? What a sweet word, Nell. All my many, many sweethearts. True love, every one. Even the plumber. Poor Gwen was so horrified by his buttocks.'

'Melissa!'

'I know, I know, don't nag me, Nell,' she continued pettishly. 'I can't stand it. I'm still ill, you know, even if I'm not dead. I expect you wish I was, don't you?' She began to cry hysterically. 'You wish I was dead. Then you'd go and live happily ever after with Lucien. Well, I'm not going to die, *and* I'm not infectious, so there.'

Nell's patience snapped. 'You're putting this on,' she told her forthrightly. 'You know very well no one wants you dead. On the other hand, no one wants you living like this, either.' She looked scathingly round. 'Why haven't you got another housekeeper?'

'I haven't really tried,' said Melissa casually. 'Anyway, I can't afford it on what Tom left me. You got most of it.'

'Nonsense,' said Nell through clenched teeth. 'You've plenty of money.'

'Oh, very well. I'll ring the agency. If I get them to come for interview this evening, you can see them too,' Melissa ordered brightly. 'Then we'll go out to dinner at the Ivy. That would be fun, wouldn't it? Noël and Gertie Lawrence might be there. They might give me a job.'

'Melissa, I have a child to look after.'

'Phooey. You have a nanny for him.'

'He likes to see his mother once in a while,' retorted Nell firmly. 'I'll come to interview your ladies with you, but not to the Ivy just to play stooge and tell everyone how marvellous you are.'

'Oh, very well,' sulked Melissa. 'If you want me to be out of work all my life . . .'

When Nell returned in the evening, Melissa was dressed ready for dining out, a flush on her cheeks that denoted more than excitement at the thought of the evening to come.

'Only one teeny little cocktail, that's all,' Melissa assured her, but Nell did not believe her.

From the three candidates, Nell plumped for Mary

Youngstaff, a self-composed widow in her forties, old enough to keep Melissa in her place and not be overawed, young enough to be a companion, if that's what Melissa wanted – and perhaps, thought Nell realistically, able to endure the occasional lover.

'Melissa, *do* take care, won't you? Don't get into any more night club games. You don't want to go to jail again, do you?'

'No,' said Melissa. 'No, I won't, I *promise*.'

If it hadn't been for Bertie, she would feel utterly hopeless about Gadsby's, Nell thought. With some surprise, she realised how dependent both she and Melissa seemed to have become on him, she for companionship, Melissa for emotional support. Bertie was always there, in devoted attendance, Nell thought gratefully. Was he in love with Melissa? She had no idea, and for a moment contemplated this idea. She hoped not. Bertie was far too nice to be sucked completely under Melissa's spell. Yet if he weren't in love with her, why was he always there, picking up the pieces?

At Gadsby's she could always rely on Bertie's sympathetic ear whenever she moaned about the store's ostrich approach to business. Nell was beginning to look at the showroom with positive dislike. From being the hub of a thriving wheel, it was more of a brake nowadays, and the slower its momentum, the greater the effects on the other departments still virtually subservient to it. Jonathan's – and now Holdsby's – answer was to increase profit margins on model orders, confident that once the slump was over sales would pick up. Paris couture was beginning to thrive again, so the de la Fertés had apparently assured him, and therefore so also would Gadsby's Fashion Department. It was all a matter of time.

It was all too clear to Nell, however, that although the worst of the depression was passing, overall store sales were *not* picking up. But if it was plain to her, why not to Jonathan Gadsby and Holdsby? Had everyone but she blinkered their eyes? Holdsby's answer seemed to be, use cheaper materials, and accessories. Nell firmly believed Jonathan was essentially right. Quality above everything, and that was what Gadsby's was known for – although quality should travel hand in hand with the times. Surely Holdsby could see his policy wasn't working? She puzzled over this and came to realise that his target had changed. Baulked at removing Jonathan from power, he had changed tack and decided to remain with him, in the expectation either of his imminent death or retirement through old age. Who else, he would argue, would have the experience to take on the reins at short notice, especially since his son would inherit? Bertie was no contender, nor Lorrimer nor Charles. So there was only one obstacle: Nell.

Was she in fact a threat, in charge of a dying department, once proud and opulent, now tired and old-fashioned? Opulence was out of place in this streamlined world where wealth was under, not overstated, in dress at any rate. There were fewer rich society women and they went to couturiers. Why should they waste money on exclusive copies of models?

Nell decided she was tired of irresolution, at seeing Gadsby's die before her eyes. She had nothing to lose, so she would lay all cards on the boardroom table. She did not care if she lost, for if she stayed to watch Gadsby's end, she was lost anyway. The Fashion Department would fail, and drag down Fabrics, Umbrellas and Scarves, Jewellery, Shoes and Millinery with it, since their buying had to be almost entirely geared to her own department. A department that this year had so far made slightly less than two hundred sales.

'Mrs Gadsby?' rumbled Jonathan at the board meeting. 'You have something to put forward?' He knew very well she had. She had warned him at Merrifield the previous weekend.

'Yes. In view of the falling turnover figures, I propose that the Fashion Department be scaled down to a size more in scale with its orders, that it caters for a minor trade with a few Paris or British models, and that the rest of the department be devoted to top quality ready-made garments to our own designs, just as we have successfully been doing with dance and sports dresses. This would mean laying off a few workroom staff, but this could be done slowly to avoid hardship, and retraining offered as sales staff if desired. I've prepared some estimates of sample costs, including factory production and additional finance, which could be repaid in three years.'

From the lack of surprise with which this radical statement was greeted, it had clearly been expected – Jonathan had lined up his legions already. She passed round the folders to the board members. Holdsby did not bother to open his.

'As simple as that, eh?' said Jonathan gently. 'What about the other departments?'

'They will be free to be fully independent for the first time. It can only help their futures.'

'Jolly good!' put in Bertie approvingly, earning a glare from Holdsby.

'And if it fails, Mrs Gadsby?' asked Lorrimer anxiously.

'It can't be worse than it is at present.'

'I believe it can,' declared Holdsby. 'I believe – and I think Mr Gadsby would agree with me – that it is disastrous to turn round in the middle of a depressed time and change one's image. It smacks of desperation.'

'We *are* desperate,' Nell pointed out bluntly.

'To appear so is worse.'

'Additional finance, Mrs Gadsby, is impossible at such a time,' said Mr Charles grandly.

'I'm sure on reflection you will recall that the Three-

Guinea Department and tea-room have repaid the expenditure many times over.'

'They were additional departments, Nell,' Holdsby pointed out kindly. 'Hardly the same as axing the heart of the business.'

And so the arguments began. No more than she had expected. And so was the result of the vote she demanded. She and Bertie voted in favour, the others, for their varying reasons, against.

'Howzat, missy!' Jonathan shouted triumphantly. 'My round, eh?'

'Not just a round, your victory, Mr Gadsby,' Nell said evenly. 'If you can call it victory. I believe you've just signed the death warrant for Gadsby's, and I don't want to be a witness to the final stages. I ask the board to accept my resignation.' She rose to her feet, calmly gathered her papers and left, to the sound of Holdsby's self-satisfied comments about women in business.

Jonathan Gadsby had said not a word, she thought, beginning to feel sick at the enormity of the step she had taken. Perhaps he thought she didn't mean it, that she'd retract it as she had before. But this time it was different.

She was walking away from Gadsby's for ever, yet her only regret seemed to be leaving Bertie marooned. He came cannoning down the stairs after her, and she stopped to reassure him.

'I don't blame you,' he told her earnestly. 'Gadsby's is all long knickers and plus-fours. Bit like entering Tutankhamen's tomb here nowadays. Without the curse.'

'It's even got that with Holdsby around,' Nell sighed. 'It was a bad day for Gadsby's when Rose married him.'

'What will you— Oh *golly*!' Bertie announced, alarmed, as they came down the flight to the first floor. There weaving unsteadily across the carpet was Melissa in what would have been a smart blue outfit had not the coat gaped unbecomingly open and her hat been knocked sideways on her head over untidy hair. Yet she had a sublime smile on her face. She was carrying a tennis racket, obviously just acquired in the sports department, and was busy swiping every potted plant in sight.

'Come to cut you some flowers, Bertie,' she announced. 'You've cut enough for me. Here's some in return. Whoops.' A vigorous swipe at one too tough to be felled brought both her and the plant off their feet; the plant cannoned into a plaster model which fell on to its backside with a crash, its head splintering to fragments. Melissa scrambled up, rushing to it and cradling it in her arms.

'Ambulance! Ambulance!' she cried gaily.

Nell and Bertie reached her together, endeavouring to shield her from the curious gaze of the shoppers, among whom a muffled whisper was already circulating. 'Melissa Hargreaves!'

A high-pitched giggle dispelled fears that Melissa herself had been hurt, and she resisted Nell's attempts to get her on her feet. Whereupon Bertie bent down and picked her up bodily with surprising strength for his thin frame and carted her off to Nell's office; or former office, she remembered wrily. There they brought Melissa coffee and cold water, the latter administered none too gently by Bertie directly on her face.

'Careful,' she complained, giggling inanely. 'I'll drown.'

Half an hour later she was restored to something like sobriety.

'I couldn't help it,' she told Nell crossly and shakily. 'Haven't you *ever* had a few drinks too many?'

'Not by lunchtime,' Nell replied tartly. 'However did you come—'

'Nell darling,' interrupted Bertie patiently. 'Not the first time.'

'Oh.' She realised what he was implying.

'I didn't get the part,' Melissa explained airily. 'And

they'd *promised* I should be Lady Jane Grey. I do so want to have my head cut off.'

Nell exchanged looks with Bertie. It was all too familiar a story by now. Rejected by the film world, Melissa was now bent on recapturing London theatreland.

'They told me I was too old. I'm thirty-four, can you imagine?'

Yes, Nell could, looking at her. All too easily.

'They said,' Melissa went on indignantly, 'they'd give me a character part if I'd stop—'

'Stop what?' Nell asked cautiously.

'Drinking. I told them,' she enunciated with dignity, 'I told them what they could do with a character part for a non-drinking mimsy-pimsy old spinster. A character part! *Me*! I'm a *star*, and they offer me a five-line part as an old woman.'

'It would be *work*,' said Nell firmly.

'I don't need work. I've got plenty of money,' Melissa retorted.

'There are other reasons to work.'

'*Not* in character parts,' said Melissa scornfully. 'I've got my pride, you know.' She rose unsteadily to her feet, and falling down again, was sick all over the floor.

After that, Nell heard little more about any further attempts on Melissa's part to find work. If she made any, she never referred to them, despite the fact that every time Nell visited her the golden head seemed to be bent studiously – and ostentatiously – over *Stage* or *Play Pictorial* or in her files of correspondence with her agent. Then after an interval of a month or two she seemed to enter a new phase in which her conversation was peppered with references to 'darling Ivor' or 'dearest Noël', usually accompanied by mention of parts that were hers for the asking. 'Not my type of role of course.' 'Hardly my metier, is it?'

410

It was some time before Nell realised that they were *all* figments of her imagination, and then only because Bertie faced her with incontrovertible evidence. In contrast, however, Melissa's social life increased. While her stage image might be tarnished, she was still considered an asset at smart parties, with her amusing tales of prison life. That is, Bertie told Nell, until drink got the upper hand and he was called upon to extract her with as much dignity as was possible in the circumstances and take her home.

And then? Nell tried not to speculate but it was increasingly difficult. She was coming to rely on Bertie's friendship, especially at Merrifield at weekends, where the sight of his lanky figure, usually outrageously dressed, with a battered trilby crammed over his ears for country wear, as though it were emulating a deerstalker, made David shriek with delight and her own spirits rise. For a trip with Bertie meant fun, whether they drove to the seaside or merely wandered through the meadows hunting for butterflies, frogs, wild flowers, or the fruits of the countryside. Bertie was surprisingly knowledgeable over foods produced free of charge by nature and for the first time Nell became interested in cooking. Mrs Emmeline and Miss Gertrude raised faint cries of protest at nettle soups and sloe gin, but Bertie was too much a general favourite for them not to eat every mouthful – which was (usually) delicious.

Of his other life, with Melissa, Nell was determined not to think. Did he love her, sleep with her? If so, did he know about the other men in her life, did he mind? But as these were all imponderables, and Nell could hardly enquire, it was easier simply to ignore them. Sometimes however this was not possible. Such as the day Bobsy came to see her on one of her rare London visits, and found Nell at home, bored, irritable and fidgety, wondering what was going on at Gadsby's without her.

'You look like a soggy cake, Nell,' she told her

critically. 'I heard you'd retired.' She unwound herself from her long scarves like a latter-day Salome. 'I've got a job for you. About time you rescued that son of mine.'

'What?' Nell said startled.

'Spends all his nights with that Melissa, I'll be bound. Flighty young madam. Sorry for her, but not at Bertie's expense. Do something about it, will you, Nell?' she commanded, sinking into a chair and pulling the bell-rope. 'Don't mind if Hornton gets me coffee, do you?'

'No,' said Nell, amused. 'Then you can tell me exactly how you think I can dictate Bertie's love life to him.'

'You'll think of something,' Bobsy blithely informed her.

But Nell didn't. Painfully she stumbled through a prepared speech about the worries of friends and the hidden dangers of Melissa. Bertie listened gravely, then commented, 'Rightio.'

'Rightio what?' said Nell crossly.

'Rightio. Heard what you said, old thing.'

'I'm not so much of an old thing, Bertie.' Nell was exasperated. 'I'm thirty-two, only three years older than you. And please do more than *listen*. Do something. If it's appropriate,' she added belatedly.

'Someone's got to look after her,' he remarked. 'No one but you and me. Her husband ain't interested.'

At this unexpected reference Nell's heart lurched. 'Do you know what he went through for Melissa?' she asked angrily, unguardedly, so much so that he looked at her in surprise.

'I can guess,' he told her.

'Do you—' Nell stopped. She could hardly ask Bertie if he went to bed with Melissa. 'Do you love her?' she asked awkwardly.

'Oh, Nell, old thing,' he said reproachfully. 'What a daft question.'

She was no nearer an answer, and on reflection had no

412

right to be, she thought ruefully.

How she missed Gadsby's. A dozen times a day she had to stop herself ringing Angela, who was now buyer for the Fashion Department, or Bertie, to ask how things were going. The temptation was sometimes irresistible. Often they rang her, which saved her dignity. She told a harried Angela what to do about calculating requirements per model, answered questions from the Counting House, as it was still called, on invoicing procedures, tried to tell herself that her slavish following of the fashion magazines was purely out of idle interest, but eagerly answered queries from Polly on design when Angela faltered. And on each occasion she bit back the one question she wanted to ask: How is Gadsby's faring? At Merrifield she managed, albeit with difficulty, to divorce her personal relationship with Jonathan from that at the store and despite the goading grin when he met her, refrained from asking him what was happening there.

In August 1935, when Nell had been away from the store for over a year, Jonathan Gadsby celebrated his eighty-fifth birthday much as he had his eightieth. A business party in London followed by a family celebration at Merrifield. 'I'm going to make my century, missy,' he chortled as she arrived with David. 'Don't you worry about me!'

He took her arm, a rare gesture, and led her to the lawn where the family was waiting. 'I miss you, young woman. Worries me having people around who agree with me all the time,' he said surprisingly.

'Then you should have listened more to those who didn't,' said Nell, amiably and without rancour.

'Miss the store, do you?'

'Yes,' she replied simply.

'Come back then.'

'Not while it's as it is. You know my terms.'

'*Terms*,' he muttered disgustedly. 'I'll not give way.'

'Nor will I,' she said. 'But that doesn't stop me wishing you a very happy birthday.' She kissed him on the cheek.

Remembering the last party she looked round at the company anxiously. No, thank goodness, there were no de la Fertés here, only a small party of intimate friends and family. Fortunately the former included Bobsy and Bertie, to offset the presence of Gordon Holdsby – though even he was disposed to charm today.

'Now he's got what he wants,' Nell thought sadly. Sad for Gadsby's.

Late that evening, when the guests had departed, they sat on the terrace quietly, she, Jonathan, Mrs Emmeline and Miss Gertrude. It was a rare evening when the warmth of the day still lingered late into darkness, the air still and heavy. There was little need to say anything for their contentment was mutual. Jonathan puffed on his pipe, regarding Mrs Emmeline affectionately.

'I've got an announcement to make,' he broke the silence unexpectedly. 'Then I'm off to bed. I'm tired.' Something Nell had never heard him admit to before. 'Emmeline, I'm going to tell Nell about The Hat.'

'Oh, *Jonathan*!' said Mrs Emmeline, highly amused. 'Do you really want to?'

'She's a right to know. Anyway,' he glared at his wife, 'it's high time. Nell's part of the family, and so she'll have to pass the story on to young David one day.' He held Nell's eye challengingly.

'I courted this girl,' Jonathan began fondly, patting Mrs Emmeline's hand, 'from the day I arrived in Welling. She was as lovely then as she is now,' he said proudly. 'You ought to have seen her in that white muslin dress with the blue bow on the bustle and cornflowers all over. I hadn't a penny to bless myself with, but Emmeline didn't mind that. I vowed that as soon as I'd made my way up, I'd ask her to be mine, and I was going to tell her that one Sunday

414

afternoon. It was a special occasion. A big party at Danson, which was privately owned then of course. I was Emmeline's escort. Proud as punch I was. She was the daughter of Welling's richest outfitter and hatter and I was just an apprentice. Very upright man, Emmeline's father, pillar of the church and all that.

'It was a hot day and all the girls decided to play tennis, while we lads went swimming in the lake. Well, we never bothered about things like costumes in those days, and I came out of the lake to find the other lads had pinched my clothes as a lark. All they'd left was my top hat. I could see the girls still playing so I ran for the manor house kitchens to bribe one of the staff for help. I ran like a hare with the hounds on his tail to the garden entrance to the house, to run down the cellar steps. Ran slap into Danson's owner and his wife, Emmeline's parents and Emmeline herself coming out of a garden entrance, and me wearing nothing but a top hat and my birthday suit. So I whipped the hat over the jolly John Thomas, turned and rushed down into the kitchens where I terrified the cook so much she gave notice.

'Next day I was summoned by Emmeline's father. I'd disgraced the family name, he told me. And do you know why? Not because of waving my dick in public, but because I'd used a Parks' hat to try to hide it with. He could never forgive the disgrace to The Hat. And that was that. Emmeline was sent away for a long holiday, and I was told she was getting married to a cousin. I moved on, and by the time I discovered she wasn't, I was. But I told her later, if it took me as long as I lived, I'd make up for the disgrace of that hat. Didn't I, Emmy?'

She unfolded her hands where they had primly rested in her lap, and struggled to kneel beside his chair. 'You did, Jonathan, and you have,' she said fondly, taking his hands. 'You were such a proud boy. Always were and still are.'

That night Jonathan Gadsby died peacefully in his sleep. A week after his birthday, Merrifield marked his passing and over five hundred people gathered at his funeral. Mrs Emmeline bore it stoically, with Nell at her side throughout. Old enemies joined with old friends, business rivals with colleagues, in respect and admiration for the life of Jonathan Gadsby. After he was laid to rest in the village churchyard, followed the ordeal Nell had been dreading of the funeral party at Merrifield. She managed to get through it as in a trance. Between looking after Mrs Emmeline, mopping up Miss Gertrude's tears, and supervising catering there was little time left to ponder whether at any moment she might run into Lucien. His parents were here as she'd expected, and meeting them had proved no more difficult than meeting other guests, for that gauche and eager Nell Watkins who had once long ago spent a weekend with them seemed a different person, and no part of what she was now.

Lucien was not there, but tension and strain made her tired beyond belief and when at last all had gone, she welcomed the quiet of the evening with just herself and her two oldest friends.

'What shall you do?' she asked Mrs Emmeline gently. 'Shall you return to Welling?'

'I fear dear Jonathan would not like that. I think,' she paused, looking at her sister who nodded, 'I think we shall remain at Merrifield, if you would be so kind as to visit us from time to time,' she added formally. 'We shall do very nicely here with Mr and Mrs Hopkins to look after us. And the motor vehicle will be useful. Shall we be able to afford a chauffeur, Nell?'

Nell smiled. 'I think you will find that Jonathan has provided enough for a chauffeur.'

★ ★ ★

The reading of the will took place with great formality on the following day. Gordon Holdsby arrived with a pink-faced Rose, greeted Nell pleasantly as victor to vanquished and took a prominent place in the library next to Jonathan's solicitor, Mr Bellow. Rose with great daring beckoned Nell to sit on her other side, but she smilingly demurred. Her place was next to Mrs Emmeline as support. She herself was a spectator.

Jonathan, it transpired, had left the whole of his personal fortune to Mrs Emmeline, with provision for Rose and her children having been made some time ago in trusts. There followed various bequests to staff and friends. With some amusement Nell watched Holdsby preparing to look modestly surprised as Bellow approached the matter of Jonathan's stake in Gadsby shares, especially the vital Founders' shares.

The solicitor cleared his throat, then read:
' "I bequeath all my shares in Gadsby's Ltd, comprising Founders' shares and ordinary shares, to my granddaughter-in-law Mrs Nell Gadsby, and hereby appoint her as my successor as Governing Director to the board of Gadsby's." '

A second or two before it registered, then Gordon gave an audible choke of rage and an incoherent fluster of oaths directed at Nell, his face purple with anger and venom. 'I'll contest it,' he promised, to a dazed and stunned Nell. 'You've played your cards very well. I under-estimated you. You knew about this, didn't you? He's been out of his mind the last few months. The board will support me on this.'

'The will was drawn up nearly three years ago, Mr Holdsby,' said Bellow coldly. 'In January 1933. Further-more, the necessary documents regarding Mrs Gadsby's appointment to the board have been placed with me to forward to the registrar.'

'He'd have changed the will if he'd lived. She left the

store. Resigned. He was going to change it,' Gordon shouted incoherently.

'Since he did not, I cannot comment. If there are no further questions?' William Bellow quickly gathered his papers and hurried away. He was thinking with some pleasure of the day Jonathan Gadsby had signed the will.

'There'll be a fine old rumpus,' Mr Gadsby had said with glee. 'Take no notice. Nell will survive it, you'll see. A few more fees for you, too, eh?'

Nell sat through it all without speaking. It was an effort to stay calm, but she desperately needed to think. Jonathan had changed his will after she had told him about David. *After*, not before. That must mean something. Later she would think about it carefully. Meanwhile she had to cope with the appalling scene here.

Rose was sobbing. Holdsby, livid, was shaking with rage, shouting at Mrs Emmeline who looked smug. The servants were undecided between flight and satisfying curiosity. Gradually all attention focused on Nell. For once she entirely ceased 'to cope'. Ceased to be rational and diplomatic. Oblivious of her surroundings, she threw back her head and laughed. Jonathan had left the store not to David, but to *her*, Nell Watkins. 'Thank you,' she said shakily to Jonathan's portrait. 'Thank you,' she shouted, laughing hysterically. 'I'll make it your store still. I'll pull through. Why? I'm the Girl from Gadsby's, that's why!'

'Really, Nell,' said Mrs Emmeline disapprovingly. 'Such intemperance.' But she was almost laughing too.

'I suppose you could say,' Miss Gertrude beamed innocently, 'that dear Jonathan has pulled something wonderful out of The Hat!'

Four weeks later Nell walked up the main stairs of Gadsby's bound for her first board meeting as Governing Director. No longer was she the young understudy who hurried up them illegally under the floorwalker's outraged eye. No longer an ignominious arrival as buyer of the Fashion Department. Now she was Nell Gadsby, major shareholder in Gadsby's, Governing Director of the board. She had been chosen by Jonathan Gadsby to carry on his store, and without restriction. He knew what she believed; he knew she would not change course for his sake. *And he did not want her to*. She could follow her instincts to do what was right for Gadsby's. It was not because she had been Tom's wife, not because she was David's mother, but because she was herself, albeit with the Gadsby name. How much longer would it be important in the modern world to keep family businesses family-run? Not much longer, she guessed, such was the capital needed. And perhaps Jonathan himself realised this in choosing her – a Gadsby, but not a Gadsby.

The news had even caused excitement in the closeted world of Watkins' Outfitters, when she visited her parents and brother to tell them the news. She could almost see her brother calculating how this might reflect favourably on his own plans for expansion, but her parents were simply pleased for her alone. It was a far cry from her mother's original ambition for her to take over the Misses Parks' business. Even so, she gathered from a letter from her mother two weeks later, the full impact of their daughter's change in status did not sink in until the Bexleyheath Chamber of Commerce sent an invitation to her father for a luncheon in his honour as father of Mrs Nell Gadsby.

Nell smiled at her fellow directors, as she opened the meeting, but ever sensitive to atmosphere was surprised to sense uneasiness – stemming, surely, from more than just Holdsby's equivocal stand. Only Bertie remained his usual apparently lackadaisical self, his hair tumbling over his forehead while he doodled caricatures of what appeared to be the Prince of Wales on the agenda sheet.

Perhaps it was her imagination, Nell told herself firmly. True, there had been some 'spirited' discussion at the earlier meeting after Jonathan's death, since an Extraordinary General Meeting had to be called to pass a special resolution to approve Jonathan's appointment of her as his successor. A farce since she was major shareholder with a vast majority of voting rights, but nevertheless it had to be done, with Mrs Emmeline, Gordon and Rose coming to London last week. Holdsby had tried in vain to put a spoke in the wheel by pointing out Nell could not vote with the shares Jonathan had left her since the will was not proven and no letter of administration had been granted, but it was a vain protest since he knew and she knew that the shares Tom had bequeathed her carried by far the majority of votes anyway. True, Mr Lorrimer and Mr Charles had been silent then, but they had seemed happy enough. Why were they now sitting here looking terrified out of their wits?

Holdsby flung down his gauntlet almost immediately. She had intended this to be a brief introductory meeting to set forth her plan for the reorganisation of Gadsby's in general, and to call another in a month by which time she would have firm plans to present. Holdsby, after all, was in a difficult position. As governing director she could appoint and dismiss what directors she chose, so she was somewhat puzzled at his immediate challenge after she had finished.

'I take it you are aware, Mrs Gadsby –' no Nell now, she noted '– that we are falling behind on interest repayments to the bank? I trust your budget takes account of this?'

'I am preparing my forecast,' she told them grandly. She could hardly say she hadn't got the slightest idea about it yet.

'Rathbone's are as happy as sandpipers. Don't worry

about them, one little bit,' Bertie told Holdsby amicably, coming to her aid.

'As a director of Gadsby's, I am not as happy as a sandpiper,' Holdsby announced. 'It seems to me that this *plan*,' he emphasised the word with slight, but not over-done, sarcasm, 'demands considerable capital as well as disruption at a time when (a) we cannot afford our present commitments or (b) any distraction from our prime target of maintaining our costs versus turnover ratio.'

'It does seem radical, Mrs Gadsby,' Mr Lorrimer put in disapprovingly, Mr Charles nodding. 'Mr Jonathan would—'

'I must make it clear,' Nell interrupted firmly, 'that Jonathan Gadsby entrusted me with the future of Gads-by's and that I intend to ensure it has one. The torch is in my hands, gentlemen, and I must run with it at my speed.'

A sudden tense silence, more fraught than anything her words could have caused. Before the next meeting, she needed to get to the bottom of it.

Night after night she worked through a maze of paper, trying to achieve the impossible: reconcile present finan-cial commitments with her determination to push through the radical changes she knew to be necessary.

'Burning the midnight oil, Nell?'

Bertie was making a face at her through the distorting glass of the door to her office. She looked up with a stifled shriek. 'You startled me, Bertie.'

'You look like a wastepaper basket,' he told her in comradely fashion, coming in and flinging himself down in the armchair.

'I'm drowning in paper.'

'Money? My metier. Let me have a dekko.' He squinted over her shoulder.

'You seem to have quite a few metiers, one way and another,' she told him.

He gave her a lazy grin, but did not reply. Instead he

picked up her notes and began to read. His air of vacuousness disappeared as he perused them, and once again she found herself wondering about his relationship with Melissa. He looked up suddenly and she flushed slightly at being caught studying him. All he said was, 'I think you'll need to polish it up for Rathbone's – I don't think "let's say £125,000" will go down too well.'

'Add "and tuppence" on the end,' Nell told him, laughing, 'and cut out the "let's say".'

'I see you were brought up with the right approach to accountancy,' he told her approvingly.

In a trice she was back at Watkins' Outfitters, watching her father painstakingly write up his books in neat copper-plate handwriting. And here she was governing director of Gadsby's. Did she deserve to be? A moment's doubt was dismissed. She could do it, and she would, somehow.

'You're not looking at it the right way, Nell,' Bertie said at last, after carefully studying the plans. 'You're thinking how to reorganise cheaply. You're thinking like Holdsby. Don't, or it will show. Think in terms of what you can do without completely, but don't pare down. It's a risk; you may lose your old faithful customers, but you have to take it. Why not abolish the showroom and bespoke trade altogether, and have a ready-made department? Not ready-mades bought in from wholesalers, but our own designs made up in limited quantities and high quality workmanship in our own workshops.'

'Outside,' she contradicted absently, an idea already forming in her mind.

'And lose all the workroom staff their jobs when the slump isn't yet over?' Bertie asked in surprise. That wasn't like Nell.

'No. We won't replace any that leave voluntarily or retire, and so pare it down gradually.' The idea was there, it had come, and now spilled out from her. 'Gadsby's *needs* its exclusive models. It's too radical just to amputate it. So why don't we switch the workroom to some real Gadsby originals? No more copies of Paris or London couturier models, but one hundred per cent Gadsby designs, ready-made up in our workrooms, with exquisite handwork. *Really* exclusive. The departments that supply chiefly to them, trimmings, hats, shoes, etc, can then sell to the public as well at full retail cost. Use the profit to capitalise further ready-made production.'

'Top-hole,' he said enthusiastically. 'I knew you'd come up with something.'

Her face glowed, then fell despondently. 'But who could design? I would need Polly for the ready-mades, and find another solution for Sporting Wear. And I'd need someone *good*.'

'Sleep on it,' he said. 'And remember, when the dogs of war are after you, there's nothing like producing your own dog,' he said mysteriously.

'It's a big gamble. Suppose—'

'So's life, Nell darling. So's love. But it never seems to stop us, does it?'

She grinned. 'All right. I'll put my shirt on it – or rather Rathbone's shirt,' she added, coming down to earth with a bang.

'I'll look after Rathbone's,' Bertie assured her. 'It'll be such a change, someone approaching them with expansion plans at the moment, they'll think you're the cat's whiskers.'

'Unlike my board – apart from you, of course.'

He shot a look at her. 'You know what I think, Nell? I'm pretty sure our chum Holdsby is pouring some poison in their ear – probably that your new plans mean no roles for them.'

'But that's ridiculous,' she exploded.

'Is it?'

'Of course. I'd never sack them.' She was amazed he could think that of her.

423

'I don't mean you'll be sweeping in like the Queen of Hearts shouting "Off with their heads", but you might find your progress leaves them behind. Old ways die hard.'

'Then they'll adapt.' She stared at him. 'I'll find other jobs in the store for them. I'll—'

'Precisely,' he said, and she fell silent.

Melissa no longer demanded Nell's frequent company in the evenings, for which Nell was relieved – until news reached her of Melissa's doings in one club after another, causing outrageous scenes, escorted by younger and younger and less and less savoury men.

'Thank heavens you keep an eye on her, Bertie,' Nell said thankfully. 'I hate to think what could happen otherwise. But what does she get up to during the day?'

'I expect she's busy tackling one studio after another, and getting drunk when they don't offer her ingénue parts as the vicar's daughter.'

Nell's heart sank, and nerving herself up, she had tackled Melissa, only to hear Bertie's guess confirmed.

'I'm only twenty-nine,' Melissa assured her unblinkingly, 'and horrid Jack Fisher said I could play this crone of forty-five. Imagine! Naturally I turned it down.'

Naturally, thought Nell wrily. But forty-five was an age Melissa could easily pass for instead of her true thirty-five, judging by the puffy redness of her face nowadays.

Nell looked at the photograph of Melissa on her office wall, happy, young and London's idol. Where was that Melissa now? Far away from the woman she met nowadays. 'Come in,' she called absently, as there was a knock on the door. In walked a stranger. Or so Nell thought at first, but it was not. It was Maria Maniosta. Gone was the confident stride. This was a conventional-looking woman of beauty, elegantly dressed in a slim-lined, wine-coloured dress with fashionable basques at the hips – and that was all. Where was the fiery challenge to life Nell remembered so well? Not in those dull eyes, nor in the uninspired if fashionable ensemble.

'Maria,' Nell began warmly, uncertainly, as the dark eyes flicked away from her.

Maria shrugged. 'Is all right, Nell. I have no right – not after the way I behave to you.' Nervously she took out a cigarette and lit it.

'What are you doing in London?' Nell fell back on conversation, worried lest her shock at Maria's appearance be too noticeable. 'Is Philippe—?'

'*Non*. I am allowed on my own! Philippe is busy,' Maria announced matter-of-factly.

'At Maison de la Ferté?'

'That, and perhaps trying to get an heir.'

'An heir?' Nell stared at her aghast. 'But you have—'

'I have two babies now. I have to work fast, *hein*? Two *girls*, Nell. Two lovely beautiful girls whom Philippe hardly looks at because they are not boys.' She flashed a grim echo of her former wide smile. 'I should not have said this, but you are an old friend. Still, I hope, if you can forgive me. It is ironic, is it not, that Philippe married me for my designs and for an heir? He thinks he is so clever. I have to try again. If it is not a boy, he says he will beget a bastard and adopt him. Not pleasant, huh?'

'No,' said Nell slowly, sick at heart for Maria, for Lucien. Philippe, so desperate to get the title, if not for himself then for his children. 'And what of your designs?'

'It does not work, Nell, being locked in a cage.' Maria bit her lip and looked close to tears. 'Jacques betrayed me. Made me bankrupt, because he was working for Philippe. I had little choice, and Philippe is not all bad. He can be so charming, so gentle. He is all those things – when matters go his way. But when they do not, he is not cruel, not unkind, he is simply ruthless. He puts one aside and walks on. I am allowed to produce ideas for la Ferté,

425

but they are not good designs because they do not come from the heart, and even then they are modified to suit the house. To suit Philippe.'

'And your something beautiful? That beautiful thing for which you will be remembered? What of that?'

'A butterfly is beautiful, Nell, but it is like a sunbeam, it is hard to catch.'

Nell rose to her feet, a great hope, a great excitement flooding through her. 'Come with me,' she commanded.

Obediently, Maria followed Nell down to the Fashion Floor and was given a tour round it.

'This is Gadsby's *today*,' Nell told her flatly.

Maria looked at the models critically. 'I find it hard to say this, Nell, but I think there will be no Gadsby's tomorrow.'

'Oh yes there will be,' said Nell firmly. 'Now you've come.'

Maria looked at her, a smile beginning to light up her face, her eyes. Then it disappeared. 'I told Bertie—'

'Bertie?' Nell picked up sharply. 'What did *he* say?'

'He said you would want to see me,' said Maria. 'That is all.'

Nell grinned. 'So you are my dog of war?'

'Your—?' Maria was indignant. 'You think I look like a dog? It is not good, this, but it is not bad either.' She glanced down at her dress.

'No, no. It's only a phrase, Maria. He meant you're a soldier in our war for Gadsby's future.'

'But I cannot design for anyone but la Ferté,' Maria wailed. 'You must realise that.'

'How would they know if they were Gadsby originals? If you were willing not to be identified with them by name? Are you *employed* by la Ferté? Do you receive money for your services?'

'No,' said Maria. 'No longer. I am just Philippe's wife.'

'It is foolish of the Maison la Ferté not to guard its

426

assets more securely,' said Nell demurely.

Maria stared at her, then in one glorious burst of her old laughter threw back her head. She slapped the Governing Director of Gadsby's on the back. 'We make those stuffed Ferté lions roar with a different song, eh, Nell?'

'*Magnifico, Maria! Magnifico.*'

'Suppose this plan does not succeed, Mrs Gadsby?' Mr Charles stared nervously at his copy of Nell's twenty-four-page plan for the transformation of Gadsby's, which she had distributed on her arrival at the meeting.

'We should be no worse off from the point of view of sales than we are at present. This method offers us a chance of keeping our old clients while attracting new, with virtually no additional finance and quality maintained.'

'How can you offer your old customers the same standard of design, Mrs Gadsby?' Mr Lorrimer joined in querulously.

'I'm not yet at liberty to go into that fully. I think, however, looking at my record, you can be assured that my instincts for good design have not diminished.'

A glance between Gordon Holdsby and Mr Charles which did not go unnoticed by Nell. 'No doubt,' Mr Charles said, surprisingly firmly for him, 'but there remains the matter of the interest outstanding on existing finance, let alone investing new capital.'

'Sir Bertram will take this question,' Nell told him, hoping her voice did not sound as tremulous as she felt. Bertie had assured her all would be well and she believed him. Nevertheless . . .

'Question of finance,' he said cheerily. 'All arranged. Went to see Rathbone's. Only too pleased to underwrite the risk. Good for prestige to be linked to expansion. Here are the details.' He pushed a folder towards Messrs Holdsby, Lorrimer and Charles.

Holdsby hardly glanced at it. 'Congratulations, Sir Bertram. However, it hardly tackles the underlying problem of the advisability of undertaking this risky and ill-advised plan of Mrs Gadsby's.'

Nell flushed. 'Your reasons?'

'Simple. In times of depression one nurtures one's remaining credibility; a leap into the unknown is suicidal and I for one do not intend to be a Gadarene swine.'

'Nor I,' declared Mr Charles.

Lorrimer hesitated, then clearly acceded to a prearranged plan. 'Nor I.'

'I see. Is there any point in taking a vote?' Nell asked slowly, her mind racing. A silence. 'So it is three against two. But I, as Governing Director, can overrule the decision.' A sharp intake of breath from Bertie made her realise she'd fallen into Holdsby's trap. Unavoidably perhaps, and now inextricably.

'I rather thought you might, Mrs Gadsby. The late Mr Jonathan had a "policy", if one might so term it, of allowing majority decisions of the board to go unchallenged. Save when he objected strongly. Which was frequently. I had hoped – indeed, I believe you had intended – to change this policy. It seems not. A poor look-out for Gadsby's future, Mrs Gadsby, which does not augur well for this plan –' he flicked at it contemptuously '– or any other. In the circumstances, I would like to offer the board my resignation.'

Bertie's face registered obvious delight, Lorrimer's and Charles' no surprise at all, Nell noted, dispassionately. Her own first reaction was overwhelming relief, the second was caution. It was all too easy. He'd lost at Gadsby's, but that didn't mean he'd give up altogether. She watched him go with some interest. Would his supporters follow suit? She couldn't believe they would do so, and they didn't. But they didn't vote for the plan either. They abstained, slightly pink at their own daring.

'Does this mean you won't put your heart into implementing it?' she asked them boldly.

'No, Mrs Gadsby, it does not,' Mr Lorrimer told her firmly. 'We may have lost, but we still have the interests of Gadsby's at heart.'

Not entirely satisfactory, somehow, but relieved it was over, Nell dismissed it from her list of problems.

'Thank you, Bertie,' she said afterwards in gratitude for his support. 'Onwards.'

'Upwards,' he said. 'But don't forget to look behind you.'

'Why?'

'There's a porpoise close behind you. Holdsby's walked off with your plan.'

It didn't take long for news to emerge that Holdsby had joined the board of the ailing Oxford Street store Malting's, which had, like Gadsby's, obstinately refused to change its ways in face of the slump. It was rumoured to be near bankruptcy and now Holdsby was going in as Managing Director.

With her plan.

Preoccupied with a myriad problems, involved in reorganisation from the colour of the carpet in her new ready-made department (now dubbed just the Fashion Department, as opposed to the Model Department) to the opening budgets for the newly independent accessory departments, Nell saw little of Melissa in the run up to Christmas. Telephone calls elicited the fact that she was perfectly wonderful, darling, and there was positively no need to worry about her. It was some time before Nell found out she had been misinformed on this point. Sitting at home one evening, having just persuaded David that bed on the whole was preferable to yet another sleepy game of Snakes and Ladders, she had a telephone call from Bertie.

'Trouble, Nell,' he said briefly, far from his usual flippant self. 'Melissa. Can you get up here quickly?'

'Where's here?'

'Charles Street.'

At least it wasn't a police station this time, Nell thought thankfully, seizing coat and scarf, her mind racing through endless possibilities of what trouble Melissa might be in this time. Deciding not to call for her chauffeur, she took a taxi to Charles Street. The door was on the latch and she rushed in. There was no one downstairs so Nell ran up to the bedroom where she found Bertie bending over a prostrate Melissa, lying on the bed. It was also a virtually unrecognisable Melissa: her face was swollen and bruised, blood streamed from a cut above her nose and she had a broken tooth. Bertie was expertly administering first aid.

'She refuses to go to a hospital,' he said anxiously. 'I think there's no real danger.'

'What happened?' demanded Nell, slipping into a role of nurse's assistant.

'It wasn't me, your honour,' said Bertie.

'I never thought it was,' she sighed crossly.

Melissa lay still, her eyes closed.

'Beaten up by one of her young men because she didn't pay him enough is my guess,' said Bertie brutally.

Melissa's eyes shot open. 'I didn't – I never have to pay,' she croaked. 'It's all a lie.'

'Come along, darling,' said Bertie patiently. 'Let's be honest for once, shall we?'

Nell swallowed hard, to prevent tears forming. Melissa forced now to pay for love? How could she have failed in her friendship and allowed such a thing to happen, and, worse, not even realised? She made an effort to overcome her revulsion, reminding herself that this was still the Melissa she had loved. She helped Bertie undress and put her into bed, unable to avoid noting that both Bertie and Melissa were clearly well used to this procedure.

'I want you to stay,' said Melissa childishly, clinging to Nell's hand.

'I'll come tomorrow – but I can't stay tonight, Melissa. You know that. You've got Mrs Youngstaff. Bertie will stay too.'

'No, I won't,' he said simply.

Tears welled up in the still lovely eyes.

'Don't open up the water-works, Melissa,' said Bertie, more severely than Nell had ever heard him speak before. 'I've got to see Nell home. It's time someone gave her some thought.'

She began to protest, then belatedly realised that perhaps Bertie wanted to avoid the possibility of being dragged into bed with Melissa. She was quite capable of it even in her present state.

'Yes,' she said, grateful enough not to have to embark on a search for a taxi.

Half-an-hour later, after Mary Youngstaff had returned from her evening off, to take up the reins again, Nell climbed into Bertie's comfortable old Wolseley, which he drove erratically. Bertie had no interest in matters mechanical. Or in anything else on the road, it seemed to Nell, hiding her eyes as he swerved to avoid another car that had rashly decided to dispute precedence at Hyde Park Corner.

She almost staggered as she climbed down when they reached Eaton Square, and Bertie's hand, surprisingly strong, gripped hers. 'I'll see you inside,' he told her. 'I could do with a drink.'

It was the last thing Nell felt like but she could hardly refuse him, she supposed wearily.

'I'm sorry if I dragged you away,' she said awkwardly. 'I always thought you and Melissa—'

'Shared a bed?' he supplied cheerfully, though erroneously. She would never have dared suggest it to his face. 'Makes a change. Most people think my tastes lie in

431

my own sex. Like to keep people guessing, you see,' he explained.

Nell blushed, for the same thought had occasionally occurred to her. 'You're very good to Melissa,' she said sincerely.

'So I would be to a wounded puppy. Especially if he belonged to you.'

'Isn't that love of a sort?' Nell commented, knowing she was speaking inanely and not knowing quite why.

'No.'

'Couldn't you love her? She needs it.'

'No,' he replied again simply. 'I love you, old thing.'

Nell dropped the brandy glass she was holding out to him. 'I'm sorry,' she said, staring at the liquid seeping on to the carpet, and apparently unable to move to pick the glass up. 'They always do that in stories, don't they? Drop glasses at such moments. I never believed it actually happened.'

'It's the shock,' he told her kindly. 'I just thought I'd mention it. You've been on your own long enough, haven't you?'

'Oh, Bertie,' she said miserably, 'you don't understand. You really don't.'

'Don't I?'

Chapter Thirteen

'Peace for our time,' repeated Bertie non-committally, turning off the wireless.

'You don't believe it?' asked Nell. Her first reaction was relief that Prime Minister Chamberlain had brought back such a message of hope from Munich it must surely shatter the pessimism that had set in during the last few years as the shadow of war once more lengthened. No sooner had the depression begun to ease than European security again seemed under threat; Italy invaded Abyssinia, bitter Civil War broke out in Spain, in which ominously Adolf Hitler had weighed in firmly with his material support in aid of the Fascist side. Nor was the threat only in Europe, for Japan was at acrimonious odds with America over Japanese depredations in China. And now in 1938 Hitler's threat to Czechoslovakia had made the outbreak of war an imminent probability. Until this meeting in Munich.

'I believe our chum Hitler has achieved the peace he needs, but whether it's for our time or his remains to be seen.' Bertie's normally pleasant face was troubled. 'At least it gives us time to prepare.'

'You think war's unavoidable? Surely now he's united Germany and Austria, and regained the Rhineland, that's all he wants. Especially if the dispute over the Sudetenland is settled.'

'If you believe that, Nell, you're a woolly-headed optimist,' he told her bluntly. 'As well believe Melissa has forgotten what it's like to share a bed.'

'But—'

'There are no buts this time, Nell. I'm sure of it. Mussolini in Italy, Franco in Spain, Hitler in Germany – Fascism is uniting. What do you think the International Brigade is trying to do out in Spain in this Civil War? Just what we'll all be trying to do shortly: stop Fascism in its tracks. The Civil War is a trial battleground for the Luftwaffe. We may live to regret we're not involving ourselves more deeply but leaving it to the few who feel strongly enough about democracy to fight its enemies wherever they are. Herr Hitler will be on the march again, you can be sure of that. *Ein Reich, ein Volk, ein Führer*. There are Germanic peoples the world over, and he'll reach out for them one by one. Or that will be his excuse anyway. We'll be left sitting like hedgehogs with our backs to the oncoming steamroller, optimistically hoping that if we don't see him, he's not really there.'

'I've never heard you talk like this,' Nell said, as much bewildered by this new Bertie as sobered by his prophecies. 'If what you say is true, how long will it take?'

He shrugged. 'However long it takes Adolf to do something so outrageous that even Chamberlain has to open his blind eye.'

'Will it affect us?' Nell asked after a moment, aware that it was an inadequate response.

'Us?' Bertie stared at her, about to say something, and changed his mind. He reached out his large comforting hands and clasped hers within them. 'It might make you want to marry me,' he said lightly. 'Wars can have a funny effect on people.'

She and Bertie had been lovers now for two and a half years. No, more than that, she realised with some surprise, so quickly had time passed, so pleasantly, giving her the personal stability she needed in order to throw her energies into Gadsby's. When he had made his first amazing declaration she had shied away from him, physically and emotionally, simply because no one had stormed the defences of her inner self since Lucien.

Then, a few days later, she plucked up the courage to visit him and face the problem head on. Using the constant underlying ache of Lucien as an iron shield against assault, she had explained, hesitantly, and then firmly, just why there could be no one else in her life.

Bertie let her ramble on, until at last the outpouring of explanation, excuses, doubts, petered to a halt. Then he said: 'But my dear old duck, I've known all about Lucien de la Ferté for simply years. Eons.'

She stared at him. 'You *knew*?'

'He's Melissa's husband, duckie, and Melissa ain't the soul of discretion.'

Nell wrestled with this, and then cut the Gordian Knot: 'Then you know why I don't want—'

Bertie sighed. 'Nell, come to bed,' he said firmly, and taking her hand had led her to the spartan bedroom in his flat, so taken by surprise that she hardly protested. Terrified that the spectre of the past would loom before her, she was first puzzled, then overwhelmingly grateful that it did not, so different was Bertie's love from what she had known before. His gentleness and tenderness filled her with a humility and content which made her responsive without need for passion, that inner self was not invaded but comforted. And then, after he had withdrawn, he asked her to marry him.

Stricken, she could say nothing.

'Don't worry about it.' A quick anxious smile from Bertie. If he did, as the months wore on, he had given no outward sign. Every quarter day he promised he would renew the offer, and each time she refused. Why? Bertie never asked, but she asked it of herself. She suspected he believed it was because she secretly hoped Lucien and she might one day be together again, but that was not the reason. There was no chance that that could happen. Not because of Melissa, but because of what lay between Lucien and herself. Twice she had turned from him because of other commitments, and the heart could cease to love under such battery. Twice she had failed him, and he would not risk her doing so again, no matter what might occur.

Bertie never stayed at Eaton Square but their weekends were spent at Merrifield with David, who adored Bertie, under the tolerant if somewhat disapproving eye of Mrs Emmeline. Fortunately Bertie always managed to make her laugh, so disapproval did not last long. She was alone now for Miss Gertrude, whose valiant spirit failed at last to keep pace with her elder sister, had developed pneumonia following a fall in the garden in the autumn of 1937, and died as uncomplainingly as she had travelled through life.

'I wonder why she never married?' Nell commented sadly to Bertie on their way back from the church. 'To keep Mrs Emmeline company, I suppose.'

'Didn't she ever tell you?' Bertie replied casually. 'She was in love with the son of the local chemist. He was a soldier, much to Mr Parks' disapproval. Nevertheless, they saved up for seven years to get married, and then he was killed in the Zulu War just as they were about to publish the banns. He was a piper.'

'Is that why Mrs Emmeline requested "The Minstrel Boy" should be played at the service?' asked Nell, pondering the oddity that she, who had known Miss Gertrude all these years, had not had the slightest idea of her romance, whereas Bertie seemed to have a surprising knack of prising information from even the tightest oyster shell. She had even commented on it once. 'You're wasted as Gadsby's Secretary,' she laughed, when he produced some amazing facts and figures on Holdsby's latest exploits. 'You ought to be Our Man in Berlin.'

'Perhaps,' he said, shooting her a charming smile.

Mrs Emmeline had resolutely refused to come to live with Nell but asked that she should spent her weekends at Merrifield, though she conceded the occasional one to Nell's parents or to Bobsy. She continued to live there happily, cosseted by Mr and Mrs Hopkins, with a lad to do the strong work.

David was thinning down slightly now that he was nearly nine, losing an early childish chubbiness he had developed when he was about six. He was a quick thinker, and had a way of looking at her that was disconcertingly reminiscent of his father. Nell had never told Bertie of his parentage, nor of her relationship with Tom; if he guessed David's true father, he never referred to it, and she certainly had no intention of bringing the subject up.

Merrifield had become a place of joyous escape from the business worries. Striding over the fields with an adoring David in tow, or sitting by the fire, long legs stretched out before him recounting ghoulish ghost stories, Bertie became a veritable Pied Piper in weaving enchantment around the weekends. So used was she to his presence by now that it was with some surprise that she listened to his announcement that he wouldn't be coming for the annual blackberrying hunt. It couldn't be that he had to visit his mother, for Bobsy often dropped in to Merrifield or they motored up to see her. Had he another woman in his life? Nell examined this thought and asked herself if she would mind. Honesty made her admit that she would mind very much.

Bertie still saw much of Melissa and Nell relied on him for reports when she herself could not visit as often as before because of home commitments. She had never told Melissa about the changed relationship between herself and Bertie, but had a distinct feeling that Melissa was well informed on the subject. Finally it became an open secret as Melissa, clearly curious, announced she'd like to visit Merrifield.

'It would do me good,' she told Nell innocently not long before Miss Gertrude died, 'to get some country air. I'll come this weekend.'

Nell had thought wildly even as she mechanically replied: 'That would be lovely. Do come.' Should she live a lie and order Bertie not to appear? Pretend she had invited Bertie as a friend? Or behave naturally? The latter won.

Melissa had remained in the house with Mrs Emmeline and Miss Gertrude as Bertie and David set off on a walk. 'You go too, Nell. I'll just sit and watch you catch butterflies. Bertie butterflies, I call them,' she giggled. 'What did I tell you, Nell? They all leave me for you.'

Red in the face, Nell stalked off, obscurely feeling guilty. Not that Bertie was any the less assiduous in his care of Melissa; he was always there for her when she needed help. Yet something, it was becoming apparent, was changing in Melissa's life.

'I think she's keeping something secret,' Bertie had told Nell thoughtfully not long after that weekend. 'There's a sort of smile she puts on when there's something she doesn't want us to know.'

'I know the one,' said Nell resignedly. 'Has she started drinking again?' Melissa's 'cures' were becoming increasingly frequent.

'Did she ever stop?' asked Bertie a trifle acidly.

Melissa chose her own moment to reveal her secret. She arrived at Gadsby's Fourth Floor one day, dressed in a square-shouldered coat with an absurdly tiny hat perched on the golden curls. After the narrow shoulders and large brimmed hats of recent times, she was an eye-catching sight – the sort that instantly made everyone else feel out of date. Apparently oblivious to her own dramatic appearance – which had been much neglected of recent times –

she was flourishing an envelope. 'Tickets for my first night,' she announced airily. 'For you and darling Bertie. David too if he wants to come.'

'First night?' Nell almost choked. What new fantasy was this?

'I've done what you said I should. I've taken a character part. Only because the management begged me to do it,' she hastened to explain.

The latter wasn't quite true, Nell later discovered. An old friend had given her this last chance, provided she stopped drinking. And how suitable a part. An ageing actress who still believed she was eighteen. Was it deliberate cruelty on the part of the theatre? No, Nell decided, when she saw *Fallen Leaves*. It was brilliant casting, all the more brilliant because Melissa was clearly unconscious of any parallels at all. She displayed all her earlier gift for comedy, enhanced by the lack of any need to seduce. Probably the producer had knocked that out of her, Nell thought grimly. She was feeling distinctly uncharitable since before the performance she and Bertie had visited Melissa's dressing room and found her taking a swift nip from a small silver flask.

Caught out, Melissa gave a bright smile. 'Just for courage, darling.'

'Give it to me,' Nell demanded, alarmed and furious.

'I'm not a child. You mustn't upset me, Nell. Not just before I'm due to go on. After all, I'm meant to be drunk in the part. I'll be fine, you'll see.'

And she was.

In the dressing room afterwards, Nell threw her arms round Melissa and hugged her. 'I'm so pleased for you. You were marvellous,' she told her genuinely, holding back further discussion of alcohol till a more suitable time.

'Yes, I was, wasn't I?' said Melissa complacently. 'I told you it would be all right. You see, I can do it after all. And now,' she added happily, 'let's all go for a teensy weensy drink.' She glanced at their faces. 'No?'

'*No!*'

About two months later, Nell read with sinking heart but without surprise that the role of Jennie Potter in the popular hit *Fallen Leaves*, which Melissa Hargreaves had created to such effect, had been taken over by its understudy as Miss Hargreaves had been forced to resign for health reasons. Scarcely able to restrain her anxiety, she hurried round to Charles Street as soon as Gadsby's closed. Melissa was sitting in the drawing room, her feet up on a chair, a glass by her side, happily reading *Vogue*.

'What's wrong, Melissa?' Nell demanded.

'Wrong? Nothing, darling.' Melissa's eyes ostentatiously slid back to *Vogue*. 'Aren't these new romantic full skirts just ducky?'

'The papers say you've left the play for health reasons,' Nell ploughed doggedly on.

She shrugged. 'A lot of fuss about nothing. They said I wasn't strong enough. Foolish, isn't it? Just for a little drink or two.'

As usual this proved to be an understatement. Relentless questioning drew the sulky admission that it had been more than just one drink or two, and that on the last occasion it had been touch and go if she could find her way round the stage, let alone remember lines accurately. Rumours about nude dances at nightclubs and increasingly bizarre behaviour at restaurants had further fuelled the theatre management's decision that enough was enough.

'Oh, Melissa!' Nell said despairingly.

She hurled the magazine across the room. 'Don't keep saying "Oh, Melissa" in that way. You know I never wanted to do character parts. It's all your fault, Nell.'

'Naturally,' she hissed through gritted teeth. 'So what now?' She knew she was taking the wrong tack, that belligerence would produce at best hysterics and at worst obstinate reticence. Once again, however, Melissa surprised her.

'I shall go for a holiday,' she announced with dignity.

'Where?' demanded Nell suspiciously.

'A cruise,' answered Melissa brightly. 'I might bump into the Duke and Duchess of Windsor. Or a millionaire in search of a beautiful wife. Or a nice burly sailor. Who knows?'

'Are you going alone?' This didn't bode well.

'Perhaps,' said Melissa offhandedly, bending down to pick up *Vogue* again. 'You know, I think I'll go to Hartnell myself – he seems to cater for my personality. Romantic and innocent.'

Nell looked at her suspiciously, but she appeared perfectly serious. She said no more about holidays, and Nell thought she had forgotten the idea, until a telegram summoned her to see Melissa off at Tilbury, and bring a supply of caviar from darling Fortnum's. Battling crossly through the crowds, Nell arrived to see Melissa followed by twenty or so suitcases apparently jogging along in pyramids all by themselves; only some pairs of feet beneath suggested staggering porters in their midst. Melissa was not alone. She was with Gadsby's designer, Sebastian Fowler . . .

Gadsby's, despite the routine everyday problems, had become Nell's pride and pleasure. From the days when she had burned so fiercely to be able to help run it and could not, now everything was under her control for good or ill. By 1937 the store was showing every sign of emerging from its doldrums into a brighter future. Unless that future contained war. But there was no point worrying about imponderables, she supposed.

She took a daily morning walk around the store, as had Jonathan Gadsby, and no doubt, she told herself in amusement, she was blinding herself to its defects as had he. Nevertheless she took the same pride in it as he, gloating when checking the returns from the various departments, which one by one had begun to show profits under the new arrangements.

Joe had been reinstated as buyer of Fabrics in early 1936 though his private life remained gloomy – Polly and he had separated once more – but obstinate to the last Joe was insisting on a separation order only, and not divorce. He threw everything into his work now. He had rapidly discovered that even the wealthiest of customers occasionally had need for rayons, shantungs and machine embroidered washable cottons, and that wool mixtures could safely be sold side by side with pure wool. Hosiery found that sales of lisle and artificial silk stockings flourished and did not detract from, but increased, turnover in pure silk; millinery now sported berets and tam o' shanters. Gloves offered serviceable as well as decorative wear.

Their increased profits were partly due to the determined but subtle influence of Sebastian Fowler.

Sebastian had been produced by Bertie in 1936 like a rabbit out of a hat at a time when Nell was still floundering in her vast scheme of reorganisation. Mr Fowler, he had said quietly, might be responsible for some rather jolly window designs to lift this daily task from the departmental buyers' shoulders. Nell shot a sharp look at him. Bertie might sound casual, but she realised there was nothing casual about his suggestions. In a flash she weighed up the pros and cons. 'Does he have interior decorating skills?' she asked cautiously.

'His father is a magician, and trained him to be one too.'

Wasn't that what might be needed? she realised with excitement. Someone trained in the art of illusion? 'We'll try,' she told Bertie enthusiastically. 'Provided he doesn't carry out a Vanishing Ladies trick!' she added cautiously.

'No. He's only an expert in sawing them in half,' he assured her solemnly.

'I wonder,' she said thoughtfully, her mind racing on through possibilities, 'if he could create a sort of Gadsby image?'

Sebastian was no Bertie. Sebastian was very tall, rather plump, rather serious, in his early thirties and extremely conventional. Until, that is, you looked more closely and observed that blandness hid determination, and convention was a magician's cloak he donned at will to hide behind. It was some time before Nell decided she liked him very much.

Change came not dramatically but little by little, so that no sweeping alteration caused uneasiness in old customers, yet somehow new ones were attracted. There was no more emptying windows at night; instead they were lit to act as magnets to passers-by, each one creating its own illusion. A crocodile of shoes walked in green fields under a golden sun; a wood seemingly created from hats, with one model wandering through; ladies in diaphanous dresses posed by silver streams; columned palaces complementing tall elegant models in slim evening dresses. A cunning stage effect provided a ghost model in full-ornamented Edwardian evening toilette, standing behind her 1930s slim, elegant counterpart.

From windows Sebastian progressed tactfully to internal design, so that customers were subtly distracted from an intended journey to the Coats and Costumes Department (at last renamed from Mantles) to view at closer quarters the delightful dress glimpsed through an intriguing arch. Miraculously he achieved most effects from stock, so that little extra finance was involved, and junior assistants found themselves eagerly cooperating in slack moments with the fashioning of paper arches and mock sunbeams. At first wary, buyers ceased hostilities when it was apparent that profits reflected to their own glory, not

Mr Fowler's. He remained in the background, apparently unambitious.

By 1937 Gadsby's board showed little resemblance to the one Nell had inherited. Mr Lorrimer and Mr Charles had remained only a few months before leaving to join Holdsby at Malting's, in pursuance, she discovered via Bertie, of his promise of lucrative positions before their retirement. No such jobs existed, they discovered too late, and it had been left to Nell to ensure that their retirement was not the financial nightmare that their actions had inexorably led them to. But their leaving had been a blessing. Bertie took over Charles' responsibilities, Peter Pride joined the board as Stock and Supplies director, the bank had insisted on being represented on the board and Robert Galt had joined them without fuss, selected by Bertie from his erstwhile colleagues. Gadsby's, Nell had thought happily a few months ago, could have done no better. There were still conflicts, of course. No sooner had the profits shown an increase in the first half of '37 than Peter Pride, the most enthusiastically aggressive of the board, proposed expansion into provincial stores.

'Why stop at the stock? We could buy the whole lot.' Peter looked round his co-directors and grinned at their startled expressions. 'What a lark, eh?'

Robert Galt blinked. Larks were not the bank's usual approach to business. Nor were casual mentions of extra finance of £2½ million to buy two ailing provincial stores in Birmingham and Bristol respectively.

'It makes sense, Nell,' Peter urged. 'Why have your first class designs exclusive to Gadsby's when you could sell them to subsidiaries?'

'Because a profit of £120,000 hardly justifies additional expenditure of £2½ million,' she retorted, pushing away a glorious vision of Gadsby stores all round the country in favour of prudence. 'I'm sure Mr Galt would be the first to agree.'

Robert Galt opened his mouth, but Bertie got in first. 'You're being a dinosaur, Nell,' he informed her kindly. 'Bit of a Jonathan Gadsby yourself in your way. It's the way of the future. Peter's right.'

'My bank—' said Galt, clearing his throat nervously.

'We'd have to float,' declared Peter, eyes lighting up.

Nell took a deep breath. 'Suppose we make sure we can swim before we float,' she said. 'Let Gadsby's make a decent profit several years running, *then* we'll talk about expansion. Unless—' She stopped, then turned to Robert Galt. 'Suppose we edged into provincial stores, by running fashion departments with our models, and taking the financial risk?'

'It's an idea,' said Galt cautiously. 'A toe in the water, certainly.'

'All for five toes myself,' said Bertie.

Nell laughed excitedly. 'Shall we look into it?'

The franchising of Gadsby's models to five selected provincial stores was put under the management of Peter Pride and took much of the rest of 1937. During the course of it Gordon Holdsby had reappeared, like the demon king in a pantomime. He had disappeared the same way down a trap of his own making at the beginning of that year. The accession of the Prince of Wales to the throne in January 1936 had inspired many stores to see in the pending coronation an easy solution to lack of trade. Holdsby, at the still ailing Malting's, like many other stores, placed enormous orders for commemorative china and other such items for the forthcoming coronation. Only memories of the disaster of Picture-Goers Corner had stopped Nell from following suit. She firmly forbade any department to order commemorative ware of any sort. Sebastian could pay due tribute in window displays at a fraction of the cost.

The abdication of Edward VIII late in 1936 and the

cancellation of his coronation caused enormous repercussions within stores committed to thousands of pounds' worth of stock. More than one went bankrupt – including Malting's to which this was the last straw. Holdsby's reputation, however, survived. He presented himself as the innocent victim of circumstances, trying valiantly to save a dying giant. Somehow too he came out enriched financially as well as in prestige, although he deemed it prudent to lie low for a while. Then he popped up once more like a rubber duck upon the sea of commerce, as managing director of Matthews Ltd. Matthews had two small fashion stores for middle-aged women in Oxford Street, but more importantly had a chain of such stores around the country. Holdsby's first move was hardly unexpected, but it was swift.

'He wants me to join him, Mrs Gadsby,' Polly Simpkins told her in the spring of 1938. 'Says he wants to raise the level of design in all his shops.'

'And do you want to go?' Nell asked evenly, trying to keep back the strength of her feelings.

Polly fiddled with the fringe on her corded belt. 'Not really, but—'

'You don't like our using Maria Maniosta's designs for the Paris model department,' supplied Nell kindly. It had been obvious enough.

'I've been through this once before with Maison la Ferté, you see,' Polly burst out. 'Mr Holdsby says you'll drop me if you can persuade Maria to do more for you. She's more important to you than me, he says. Just as she became at la Ferté,' she added bitterly.

'I rely on you for all ready-made Gadsby models and some of the Leisure models,' Nell said steadily. 'That's about fifty per cent of the Fashion Department as a whole, and over ninety per cent of Gadsby's in-house design.'

'If it were anyone but *her*—' cried Polly desperately. 'As soon as she came to la Ferté, it was all different.

446

Philippe never had a chance. She just gobbled him up.' She stopped. 'I'm sorry, Mrs Gadsby, I shouldn't have said that.'

'That's all right, Polly. I understand,' Nell told her compassionately. She'd never enquired about Polly's relationship with Philippe, but it was clear enough. She sighed. Now what to do? There was nothing she *could* do, was the answer. 'I must leave the decision to you, Polly. But I only want people to work here if they're as committed to Gadsby's as I am.'

A long pause. 'I'll stay, Mrs Gadsby,' Polly replied at last. 'If only I could use my own name.'

'You know that isn't possible, Polly, and why,' Nell told her. 'It must be Gadsby's design.' An idea suddenly struck her, however. 'But there's no reason in your case why you shouldn't get more personal credit. Suppose we arrange for the magazines to do articles about you? Introduce you personally to *Vogue* and the other fashion magazines as Gadsby's main designer?'

Polly's face brightened. She'd said *main* designer.

Holdsby was obviously not waiting on Polly's decision, however, thought Nell amusedly. His spring advertisements had proclaimed top Paris designs, and by now, the early autumn of 1938, were suggesting a distinctly new image. For one thing, he introduced a hair-dressing department into the Oxford Street store, a startling innovation that annoyed Nell the more because she had not thought of it first. She was convinced that outside hairstyling was going to become a much more widespread habit than was the case at present, and where better to have one's hair styled than in a fashion store? In other fields, he seemed to take a positive line in mocking Gadsby's.

During the summer, Gadsby's Ascot Week had been followed by Matthews' Henley Week. Matthews' Summer Days display had therefore promptly been echoed by Gadsby's Lazy Daisies show, at Nell's urging, but to

Sebastian Fowler's patent disapproval. Caught one day by Bertie walking past one of Matthews' Oxford Street stores to see what new plan Holdsby might have, Nell shame-facedly laughed at herself.

'It's you ought to join the Secret Service, Nell,' he told her reproachfully. 'All you need is dark glasses to make the perfect Ashenden. It isn't like you, Nell. You're becoming negative. Whatever Holdsby does, you must do. Don't. Have the courage to lead and not look behind you.'

Nell sulked crossly for a few days, then admitted he was right.

As 1938 had progressed, however, the threat of war began to cloud the horizon, advancing nearer and nearer with German mobilisation in August until the hopes for peace had seemed entirely crystallised in Chamberlain's mission first to Berchtesgaden and then to Munich. Now, the reality that despite Chamberlain's reassurances the threat of war had not gone away, was beginning to sink in.

'How would war affect the store, do you think, Bertie?' she asked, slightly ashamed at such parochial concerns.

'As it would affect everything, duckie,' he told her. 'Remember what that fellow said in the Parliament a few years ago: "The bomber always gets through"?'

'Bombs?' she repeated, startled, a new dragon rearing up in front of her. She had been thinking in terms of food and supplies shortages and loss of menfolk, strains on family life, loss of trade. 'Bombs. Like Guernica!' she thought dizzily. 'Here in London? Surely it couldn't happen? Not now Chamberlain has agreed the secession of the Sudetenland?'

'Remember the Gothas and the Zeps?' asked Bertie succinctly.

Nell did. She'd been at school during that war and remembered running out to see the huge airship, a dark shape in the late afternoon sky, hearing stories told in hushed voices about the damage they wreaked. And the Gothas. Formidable black shapes in the skies of Kent, making their way steadily towards London.

Since then, the Luftwaffe had become far more deadly – the stories of Guernica proved that – and Britain had been dragging its heels over increased armaments expenditure. Suddenly the arguments she'd read about in Parliament over naval and air force expenditure ceased to be boring exchanges on unreal issues, and became frighteningly relevant.

'I was just a darling golden-haired little boy in black velvet knickerbockers then of course,' Bertie told her serenely.

'You were at least twelve,' she pointed out.

'Young for my age,' he assured her. A pause, then: 'They'll come again, Nell. The Luftwaffe was the first service Hitler re-armed. If war comes, that is,' he added. But he no longer sounded cheerful.

'Now he's finished helping Franco, Hitler's walked into Czechoslovakia! Dear old chap,' Bertie announced in March the following year.

By now Nell had come round completely to Bertie's way of thinking on German intentions, so this was scarcely a surprise. Italy's invasion of Albania a month later was. If Mussolini was going to ape his fellow Fascists' moves one by one, it did not bode well for Europe. Germany, Italy and Spain against Britain, France, the Low Countries and the Balkans, with Scandinavia and Russia unknown quantities. She almost wished she could be as head in the sand as Melissa, who seemed to have embarked on a further round of recklessness. Sebastian had moved into Charles Street, and Mary Youngstaff was still staunchly presiding there, so she dismissed Melissa temporarily from her list of problems. Until late April when Sebastian, who had now joined the board, casually revealed he had moved out again.

'We don't share the same tastes, Nell,' he informed her. 'Or rather, we do.' A grin. 'Which is why I'm leaving. Melissa isn't too pleased, since Rufus was a gentleman friend of her own. She brought him home, poor Rufus, and ate him alive. He fled to me, which is why I'm leaving. She needs a nurse, though, Nell.'

A *nurse*? What on earth did Sebastian mean?

She picked up the telephone as soon as Sebastian had left her office and asked for Melissa's number. The familiar voice was a little less radiant than usual, but still vibrant. Still Melissa. 'Oh good,' she said, 'we can all meet for a celebration. You, me, and darling Bertie. The Troubadour at nine.' And the receiver was replaced.

'What are we celebrating?' asked Bertie when he arrived in a taxi to pick Nell up. Even he admitted now his driving was hardly suitable for London traffic. 'It's not her birthday, is it?'

'I've no idea. Some mad idea of Melissa's,' said Nell gloomily, carefully smoothing the green satin dress as she sat down in the taxi. She had planned a quiet night listening to the wireless.

Whatever the celebration was, it was clearly going to be Melissa's evening. Dressed in a slinky black satin short evening dress, she was hopping happily round the dance floor doing the strangest quickstep Nell had ever seen – and Sebastian was with her, though not enjoying himself, judging by the agonised expression on his face. She waved happily when she saw them and came back to the table alone. Sebastian had departed thankfully to rejoin Rufus. Melissa was painfully thin, Nell noticed with some alarm, and there was an unhealthy flush on her face. Perhaps it was just the black of the evening dress?

'Champagne!' ordered Melissa munificently. 'Gallons of it.'

The candlelight flickered on the table throwing weird shadows on their faces. Melissa's was definitely not only pale but gaunt. No longer beautiful, thought Nell with a pang.

'What are we celebrating?' asked Bertie idly. 'Not that it matters.' He eyed the Veuve Clicquot label appreciatively. 'What glorious aspect of life meets your favour today, Melissa?'

'Death, darling.'

'What on earth do you mean?' asked Nell sharply, after a short silence. 'Whose death?'

'Mine,' replied Melissa lightly, drinking rapidly from her glass. Bertie put his hand out to cover hers. She drew on a cigarette. 'I shouldn't be doing this,' she told them brightly, as they watched her, unable to speak, waiting for her to explain. 'Should I?'

'Tell us, Melissa.' Nell spoke through painfully dry lips, dreading what she'd hear.

'Darling, that silly old consumption has come back. To think I always wanted to play La Dame aux Camélias, and now I'm going to get the chance. Including the last scene, the doctors tell me.'

'Melissa, old thing,' said Bertie heavily. 'You're not having us on, are you?'

'No.'

Bertie took hold of her hand and kissed it. 'Not possible,' he assured her anxiously. 'Got it wrong. Haven't looked better for years,' but the words stuck on his lips, so patently false were they.

'They were wrong last time, Melissa,' said Nell, trying desperately to be rational. 'You told me years ago you only had six months to live. And see, here you are, all these years later. Not dead at all.'

'You still remember that, don't you, Nell?' Melissa looked at her oddly. 'I haven't changed, you know. I still mean it.'

No need to ask what she meant. Nell knew only too well. Powerless to reply, she stayed silent as Melissa continued brightly: 'I think I'll come back and haunt you all, wailing and wobbling in white, just to make sure you're not doing anything I disapprove of. You wouldn't like that, would you, Nell?'

'Melissa,' Nell replied more steadily than she felt, 'you're talking nonsense. There's no chance of that.'

Did Melissa relax slightly? Bertie looked from one to the other, puzzled.

'I'm quite sure they mean it this time,' Melissa told them brightly. 'That silly doctor kept talking about a cure not being far off, but it's not near enough to catch me. I'm too far gone. So what does one little cigarette more or less matter, eh? Let's celebrate in grand style.' She took out another, and looking round defiantly, tapped it on the table, lit it and burst into tears, the cigarette falling from her mouth.

Quietly, Bertie put an arm round her shoulders. 'Let's go home, Melissa.'

There was no news from Bertie all next day. He did not come to the store – nothing new recently, Nell realised for some reason – and there was no answer from Melissa's telephone. The following day Bertie came to her office and threw himself down in the armchair.

'You look as if you could do with a stiff coffee,' she said critically.

'Not coffee, my love. I've had enough stimulation for the last thirty-six hours, getting Melissa settled.'

'Settled?' Nell asked, with a feeling she was not going to like this. 'Where?'

'Brace yourself. Merrifield House.'

'Merrifield?' she shrieked. 'But she can't – not with Mrs Emmeline there.'

'Melissa just happened to be talking to Mrs E,' said Bertie carelessly, as Nell looked at him suspiciously,

452

'and Mrs E offered. Truly. Nay, she *insisted*. I pointed out the risks, and then she pointed out that she was eighty-seven and so far as she was concerned the risk wasn't too great, and moreover where else could Melissa get the air that she needed? Added to which the Kent and Canterbury Hospital had expert advice to hand, added to which the Lenham Chest Sanatorium is not too far away if things get too much for her, and it makes sense, Nell. Nor –' seeing she was about to erupt '– would Mrs E let me tell you first. Said she knew you'd object but that you just fussed over her like an ancient Rhode Island Red.'

'I don't,' said Nell indignantly. 'But you know what Melissa's like. Look at the dance she led you and your mother last time.'

'It's different this time, Nell,' said Bertie seriously. 'It really is.'

'Yes,' she said bleakly, staring at the suddenly irrelevant paperwork on her desk and wondering why the writing suddenly looked blurred. 'I suppose I was just hoping it wouldn't happen – or that if it did she'd just dance off stage singing. And come back for her bow.'

'Not this time, I think,' he said gently.

'Come in,' Nell called out automatically to a knock outside. She could never get used to the fact that she now had a secretary to answer such demands. On this occasion she wished she had waited for to her horror in walked Philippe de la Ferté. Bertie, seeing the look on Nell's face, got up quickly to divert attention from her. Philippe's sharp eyes flashed quickly between the two of them. Bertie's obvious casual familiarity as he lounged in the chair had not been lost on him.

'Philippe, how nice to see you,' Nell managed to say with a reasonable appearance of sincerity. 'I'm not sure if you've met. Bertie, may I introduce Comte Philippe de la Ferté. Philippe, Sir Bertram Bertrand.'

'Howdyerdo?' Bertie accentuated the lazy superciliousness of the stage Englishman, making Nell want to giggle.

Philippe bowed. 'We met at Mr Gadsby's funeral, I believe.' He summed Bertie up, dismissed him as a nonentity, and turned deliberately to Nell again. 'A spur of the moment visit, my dear. I came to visit our London store, and having heard so much about the transformed Gadsby's I decided to take a tour. My congratulations. Certainly a change since dear Jonathan's day.'

'What a pity you've been round already so that I'm deprived of the pleasure of taking you round myself,' Nell said in an excess of politeness, hating this social fencing.

'A personal tour of the Fashion Department would be most enjoyable,' suggested Philippe lazily. 'I glimpsed some most interesting designs. In some I detect the hand of *la belle* Polly. In others—' He paused. 'Something reminiscent of – *non*, I cannot yet grasp it.'

'Come and have a closer look now,' invited Bertie cordially. 'We'll show you round.'

Nell looked at him gratefully for the 'we'. So Bertie didn't take to Philippe – his often stated policy to her was always 'grasp nettles firmly, snakes tighter, and out-and-out bastards like a ruddy boa constrictor'.

'So long since we've met, Nell,' Philippe said regretfully as they rode down in the lift. 'Maria will be so sorry she was unable to accompany me on this trip. She is *enceinte* once more.'

'You have two daughters, I believe?'

'Louise and Maria. I am a devoted papa.' I bet, thought Nell cynically. 'And your son?' Philippe added oh-so-casually.

Bertie intervened, obviously aware of the tension though not knowing the cause.

'David's a splendid little fellow,' he said proprietorially. 'I look forward to meeting him again. Perhaps you will bring him to France, Nell, to introduce Tom's son to the family.'

'If circumstances permit that would be delightful,' replied Nell, wondering just how long she could keep this polite badinage up. Or was it just badinage? Was there not a hint of emphasis on the *Tom's* son?

The 1939 autumn dresses were mingling with the last of the August holiday stock, the short-sleeved muslins and linens contrasting oddly with the subdued colourings of the long-sleeved woollen dresses. There was nothing subdued about Polly's evening dresses, however, hastily rushed through after Paris trends had become apparent. Long, slim, luxurious (but inexpensive), velvet, with a daring long slit up the side, one style with draping, another belted.

'And the exclusive models?' murmured Philippe, making no comment on these. 'They do not seem to be on show, save for this.' He gestured to one of Sebastian's displays in the small alcove department devoted to exclusive models, sheltered from the eyes of the piratical by a cunningly constructed partition decorated with pictures of twentieth-century fashions. At the entrance was a plain black velvet tunic afternoon dress, beautifully cut. Over it was an apparently ordinary little jacket, in purple, with thickly padded pockets, gold trimming, and dramatic Renaissance sleeves.

'There is something about its shape,' commented Philippe thoughtfully as he studied the jacket, 'that almost reminds me of – no, that is not possible.'

He was taunting her, she was now convinced. He must know of Maria's involvement, Nell feared, or at least guess. 'We have talented designers at Gadsby's despite the fact we no longer purchase from Paris,' she assured him. Indeed she didn't purchase from Paris. Maria sent rough sketches which were worked on by the now small

455

but highly skilled workroom staff who turned them into toiles. One of the staff was excellent at cutting, and the combination worked well. Provided Philippe did not pursue any suspicions he might have.

'My father,' he told her earnestly, 'will be delighted to hear that Gadsby's fares so well. He always had a high opinion of you, Nell – as did all our family.' He smiled charmingly. 'So nice that our two families have kept so close, both privately and in business.' He picked up the purple jacket. 'Do bill my London store for this. I believe it will be some compensation for Maria for her missing this delightful reunion.'

'I take it that snake is brother to the Comte Lucien?' observed Bertie when Philippe had left.

'Yes,' said Nell shortly. 'Melissa's brother-in-law, and *very* unlike his brother.'

'Ah.'

Nell said no more. It was unfair on Bertie perhaps, but this was her private past and she did not want to involve him in that. Bertie was the present and the past was no more.

Nell's unease over Maria remained as the threat of war increased. Suppose Mussolini and Hitler joined forces? That would make Maria's position in Paris difficult should war break out. Suppose Philippe did not protect her as his wife and she were interned? Nell pulled herself together impatiently. Not even Philippe would go that far. There were far more pressing worries for her to deal with.

Black-out exercises, calls to join the ARP, first aid courses, now gas masks had made their way into everyday life. Some of it could be turned into fun, albeit fun with a jarring edge. David was her biggest problem. Should she put his name on his day school list for evacuation from London? For if war came everyone seemed to think that Hitler's first aim would be to try to bomb the capital out of existence. Yet David pleaded not to be sent away. As so often, Bertie came up with the answer.

'Send him to Mater,' he declared.

'Bobsy?' Nell looked hopeful. 'Would she want him?' True, David was very fond of her.

'Adores him,' Bertie assured her. 'She can get him into a local school if we work quickly. Missinden is being requisitioned if war breaks out so she'll be living in the Lodge or the stables. Doesn't seem to mind which.'

Gadsby's seemed to acquire a momentum of its own as the summer passed. Black-out material was displayed prominently in Fabrics, black-out drills were practised. The basement hastily ceased to be solely store-rooms and became an emergency staff air-raid shelter, and in August a new small department sprang up and flourished by the main door: The 'If War Comes' counter sold helpful guides and displayed free government literature. On 23 August the 'if' changed to 'when' as the non-aggression pact between Russia and Germany was signed. As soon as it was announced, Nell drove David down to Bobsy's, foreseeing that the following day the roads might be jammed with people on similar missions.

So there was no hope now. Ever since the invasion of Czechoslovakia no rational person could have doubted that war would come. In April conscription had been announced for twenty-year-old men. In August the reservists began to leave their homes, recalled to serve. A feverish excitement gripped London, intensified on Friday 1 September when Hitler invaded Poland and the Anglo-French ultimatum was issued to Germany to withdraw. That day the official evacuation of schoolchildren began.

Nell decided not to leave London that weekend. She felt she had to remain near the store, even though Eaton Square seemed unnaturally quiet without David and the cheerful whistle of Frederick, the man who'd acted as part footman, part waiter and part odd-job man, but who had now been sucked back into the army. She asked Bertie to come round to dinner that evening, and he did so.

'I've got to go, Nell,' he told her gravely afterwards.

'It's early yet.'

'No, I mean I've got to leave Gadsby's. I've been called up. I'm going tomorrow.'

'You?' Nell stared at him, a sick feeling creeping over her. 'But, Bertie, aren't you over age? Surely, you must be.'

'My brain isn't,' he told her. 'Anyway, I'm a youngster by Army standards, at thirty-four. I'm still on reserve. I should have told you earlier, but I thought I'd wait till war seemed certain.'

'Your brain,' she repeated. 'You mean—'

'Maps and things like that,' he interrupted quickly. 'I've been doing a bit of cartography for Whitehall recently.'

'You're not telling me the truth, are you?' said Nell slowly. 'You've been working for the Army on and off for some time, haven't you?'

'Oh, *Nell*,' he said disarmingly, grinning. 'With luck it won't make much difference as far as you and I are concerned. I'll be in London to begin with. Depends how things go. Pity. Khaki never was my colour.' He pulled a face.

Nell didn't laugh.

'I might even be able to keep a brief eye on Gadsby's,' he added consolingly.

'Gadsby's!' she said in dismay. 'I'd forgotten about Gadsby's!'

'Now I know you love me,' he said. A pause. 'Shall it be yes?'

'No, Bertie,' she replied sadly, after a pause, sorely tempted this time with the future so uncertain. Yet, however bleak the future, marriage just wasn't possible. Even now, and even to Bertie.

He sighed. 'The lamps are going out again, Nell. All over Europe. And the world too probably. You need all the torches you can get. However dimmed for black-out regulations.'

Melissa's condition worsened in September, as if in protest that the veil of lightheartedness and happiness she had flung over her public had now been ripped to shreds by Adolf Hitler. Not that Hitler's tanks were blasting into England as they had into Poland. After the first panic on declaration of war, the public was settling down to wait. Naval action had taken place, the atrocities of the sinking of the *Athenia* and of the loss of the *Courageous*, but of the threatened air raids, the massive strike against London or Paris – nothing.

Melissa had been growing visibly weaker before Nell's eyes on each successive visit. Lucien had been to see her twice, she told Nell with an attempt at humour, so she knew she must be dying. Nell held her hand and said nothing, for there was nothing to say.

So far Merrifield had not been requisitioned, but it was probably only a matter of time and Mrs Emmeline had made emergency plans. When she telephoned one Wednesday night, Nell thought she had rung to say she was moving, but she had not. She had telephoned to say that the doctor had declared Melissa was unlikely to live until the weekend. Perhaps she had been hoping against hope that this was yet another false alarm, but the news came as an almost physical blow to Nell, panic suddenly seizing her as a yawning hole of a world without Melissa, for good or ill, stretched before her. She telephoned Bertie and with some difficulty he arranged to accompany her the following day.

Melissa was lying in a glass conservatory that Mrs Emmeline had insisted on constructing over the terrace so that she could be sheltered yet enjoy the light. Even since she had last seen Melissa, five days earlier, there had been a change. She was almost emaciated now, and her face greyish. She turned her head slightly as they came in.

'Nell, Bertie,' she cried in a weak travesty of her old voice.

They tried hard to talk to her of London, of all the hundred and one tiny funny incidents of war, and none of the serious side. Melissa hardly listened. Then she cut across them: 'Do you know,' she said excitedly, 'I feel strong enough to go for a walk. Do let's.' She swung her feet to the ground, staggering slightly as she got up. Nell was about to dissuade her but Bertie signalled her to stop as the nurse came rushing in to fuss around with heavy wraps.

Melissa dismissed both nurse and wraps impatiently. 'Let's go out in the sun,' she said happily. 'I feel so much better just seeing you both. Just fancy, perhaps that silly doctor was wrong when he said I wouldn't live till the spring.'

So she did not know yet how serious it was, Nell realised, trying desperately to conceal her anxiety.

'Is there anyone else you want to see?' she asked casually, naming a few friends. 'Or Lucien again?'

'No.' Melissa linked her arms in Nell's and Bertie's. 'You are my two best friends. Who needs husbands?' Her grip tightened. 'Do you think there might be conkers?' she asked as they walked slowly across the lawn, her eyes on the wood at the end of the gardens. 'Or chestnuts? It's harvest time.' She swung free of them and turned to face them, saying apologetically, 'I don't like to think of the year dying, you see. If it does, I just might go with it. But I won't, I *won't*. Not now.'

She ran a few steps towards the wood, stumbled and collapsed. At the sight of the frothy bright red blood spurting from her mouth Bertie ran without a word for the house, while Nell threw herself down beside her, supporting Melissa's head so that she would not choke. Unable to take her eyes from that blood. She couldn't die, not Melissa.

The blue eyes opened, and looked up at Nell. 'Darling,' she whispered painfully, between gasps for breath as the flow slackened, 'I did know, all the time. About Lucien. I'll make it up to you – I—'

Unable to say anything, emotion choking her, Nell kissed her forehead, held her hand.

Only a whisper now. 'It has been fun, hasn't it?'

'Yes, Melissa.' Tears blurred her eyes. Not Melissa. Please, not Melissa.

In the distance she was aware of the nurse and Bertie rushing towards them with a wheelchair. Why did they hurry? Nell wondered. Didn't they know they would be too late? She put her head close to Melissa's lips which were struggling to move again. 'I don't want to go alone, Nell. It's dark. Come with me. Please.'

'They're waiting for you, Melissa, all those whom you made so happy.'

'You're sure?'

'Quite sure.'

Chapter Fourteen

The sun shone on the day of Melissa's funeral. Since none of her family was traceable, Mrs Emmeline and Nell had decided she should lie at Tom's side. A quiet funeral had been their original intention, but wartime or no, this was clearly not going to be possible. Friends who had forgotten Melissa while she was alive telephoned Nell insisting on attending; fellow players and management remembered only the bright star and not the dark night. Uncomplainingly, Mrs Emmeline put Merrifield at the disposal of any who wished to stay. On the reserved list for requisition by the Army, at the moment the house was still hers alone, where she lived looked after by the faithful Hopkinses. The 'lad' had, like his contemporaries, been called up, as had the gardener, and the grounds already bore testament to the fact. Today, however, the mellow sun shone on leaves beginning to turn colour with the year, as Nell put on her black suit, preparing for the ordeal ahead. As ordeal it would be.

During the last few weeks she had picked her way through life almost hour by hour, dealing with what had to be done, or planned, methodically and dazedly. She missed David terribly during the week, her only chance to see him had been during the one weekend she went to Missinden. As well as the problems wartime had brought to Gadsby's, travel itself was hard as days grew shorter and blackout became an increasing deterrent to motoring with no street lights and only masked headlights. She had hardly seen Bertie since war broke out, owing to his commitments at the War Office, whatever they were. He had managed to take time for the funeral today, however, driving down by some miraculous means in the pitch dark in the middle of the night. His cheery face had popped round her door early this morning, much to her relief. To go through today's ordeal without him would have made it impossible. Completely unbearable.

She shivered as she adjusted her hat, remembering what lay ahead for her, remembering that cold and distant voice on the telephone when she had to telephone Lucien to tell him of Melissa's death.

'*Je vous remercie*, Nell. I am grateful to you for telling me.'

Vous? She stared at the telephone, as she replaced it on the hook. *Vous*? Had it descended to that? That was the worst of telephones. How could you tell what emotions, what meaning, lay behind the words it relayed? Today Lucien would be here. She fought to come to terms with it. Philippe and Maria also. At first Lucien had informed Mrs Emmeline, not her, Nell, she noted, that he would not attend, but arrange a Catholic service in Paris. Then with sinking heart she heard that he had changed his mind.

Why should it matter? Their love affair had been over for many years, and what had once been shared had died in the time that had passed. If her love belonged to anyone now, it was to Bertie, she told herself. Yet the very sound of Lucien's voice, and the dull ache that still lay deep within, flared into painful sharp life. That didn't mean Lucien felt the same as she did, she told herself. How could he? She had rejected him too often, no matter what the reason. There would be other women; perhaps *one* other woman. Nell stared at her reflection in the mirror. Onwards, she told herself. Onwards. It didn't mean much, but it made her feel slightly better as she picked up her handbag and joined Bertie and Mrs Emmeline downstairs to wait for the cortège.

The grey Norman church was full. She saw through the open doors that people were even standing at the back. How pleased Melissa would have been, she thought, overwhelmed by unexpected tears pricking at her eyes. She smiled up gratefully at Bertie, who had Mrs Emmeline on his arm, as they stood aside to let the coffin pass into the church. Then Lucien stepped out of the shadows of the porch. Why had she not seen him earlier? Lucien, pale in black, older, more lined. Lucien who took his place beside her to follow the coffin. Automatically she went to move back, to give him precedence as Melissa's husband, but swiftly he reached out and took her arm to prevent her. Melissa had united them in death as she had divided them in life.

Maria's voice soared out over the muted gathering at Merrifield where about two hundred people had arrived and were now talking in low voices, those from the stage and screen trying to subdue their natural extrovert instincts, those from other areas of Melissa's life looking somewhat lost.

'Hey,' shouted Maria, her tall elegant figure striding to the piano. 'This is no good. Not for Melissa, eh? We enjoy ourselves, yes?' She began to pound out, with scant regard for the Steinway, the theme song from Melissa's last film, *Love in Paris*, and in a trice the gathering was transformed, one song following another, and when inspiration was exhausted conversation turned from hushed whispers to stories of Melissa, everyone trying to outdo his or her neighbour with the more salubrious anecdotes of Melissa's path through London and French life. Slightly shocked at first, Mrs Emmeline listened with some amusement to the unusual funeral party.

'*Madame Nell, chère Nell, je suis enchanté.*' Philippe,

the years having only added to his good looks, was kissing her hand. 'First Tom, now Melissa. She will be greatly missed,' he said gravely, kissing Nell's hand. Was there irony in his voice? No, she decided, she was becoming obsessed with thoughts of his duplicity. It must be because of Maria, she decided, staring at her friend, and her annoyance that the generous, vibrant Maria had been thrown into Philippe's shadow. Professionally and privately too, it seemed.

Nell had received a brief note from her shortly after Philippe's visit regretting that her commitments meant she could no longer design for Gadsby's. The very briefness showed who was behind it.

Maria's sudden exuberance at the piano seemed to have petered out; she looked drawn and wan in her neat black costume. Perhaps she was still tired after the birth of the baby – with some uneasiness Nell remembered her concern that there had been no word of the new baby. Wrapped up in worry for Melissa and preparations for war, she had lost track of the passing months, and Maria's letters had been strictly business only. Certainly there was no sign that she was pregnant now. As if reading her thoughts, Philippe said lightly, 'Maria is not well. She told you, naturally, of her miscarriage?'

'No,' said Nell, horrified. 'Maria, I'm so sorry.'

She flushed and said nothing.

'A son,' said Philippe lightly. 'It would have been a boy.'

A look passed between them which Nell could not interpret, but which filled her with uneasiness. Abruptly Maria turned away, just as Bertie, unruly fair hair conscientiously smoothed down today, came ambling up and put an affectionate – or protective – arm round Nell.

'Ah, Sir Bertram. What a pleasure to see you again.' Philippe's sharp eyes flickered inquisitively over the proprietorial arm. 'We see too little of our friends, do we not,

Lucien?' His eyes looked over Nell's shoulder.

'Yes,' replied Lucien shortly, forced, obviously unwillingly, to join them. Did Bertie's arm tighten round her or was it her imagination? Lucien hesitated. 'Forgive me, Nell.' He stumbled over the word as if for the moment he had been going to say 'Madame Gadsby'.

'You have met Bertie, Sir Bertram Bertrand – Bobsie's son?' she cut in.

'*Non*.' He greeted Bertie politely, but turned as soon as he decently could to Nell once more. 'The solicitors tell me you are an executor of Melissa's will. Forgive my mentioning this so soon, but I must depart very shortly.'

So cold, so businesslike – what had she expected? He was correct, polite, as always. And she must be the same.

'Yes,' she replied briskly. 'I am.'

It was a complicated will, as might be expected from Melissa, and further complicated by her having a French husband, although her will was made under English law. Tom's allowance stopped with her death. The capital reverted to David. Her remaining money she had divided between Nell and Bertie, after many small bequests had been made. The latter were going to cause the problems. Generously she had left small mementoes to people long since disappeared from her life – if they had ever existed. Tracing them could prove a nightmare. To Lucien she had left only the jewellery he had given her on their wedding.

'If you require assistance,' Lucien proposed, 'my solicitors are at your disposal. There will have to be consultations between them and Melissa's, of course, because of the complications of French marriage law.'

'Johnson – Melissa's solicitor – can manage,' said Bertie shortly.

Nell looked at him in surprise. It was unlike Bertie to be so curt, even in these circumstances.

Lucien flushed, bowed slightly, made his goodbyes as quickly as possible and was gone. Gone for ever now, realised Nell, numb with spent emotion. She had expected no more, so why the nagging, irrational anti-climax?

'Why were you so dismissive to him?' she asked Bertie that evening. 'Because of me?'

'No,' he said, considering the question carefully. 'Because of Melissa. He took her on and abandoned her,' he said disapprovingly.

Nell was silent, considering the validity of this over in her mind. She thought of Tom who adored Melissa, yet had been driven to leave her because he could stand the strain no longer. She remembered that Lucien had taken her in when she was destitute in France, only to find himself betrayed from the outset. So much to explain, so impossible to do it, for Bertie had seen Melissa at her worst and remained her friend. But if he had been her lover, might it then have been a different story?

'You don't understand,' she said at last, and inadequately.

'Perhaps not,' he replied, gently enough. 'And perhaps I don't want to.'

That night he came to her, sitting on the edge of her bed, a dim figure in the heavy blackout until she put a bedside light on. 'Shall I stay, Nell?' he asked her bluntly.

She reached out her arms to him in answer and drew him to her. Did she want Bertie or did she want to dispel the memory of Lucien? she wondered for a moment. Then her gratitude to Bertie, her need for comfort, her love for him, took over, and an old ghost slipped from her mind. For the moment.

By the beginning of November the reality of war was casting a longer shadow. The bright days were gone indeed, vanished with Melissa, with Lucien, and had left only grey behind. Or rather black. Even with the Government's slight relaxation of regulations, the blackout was a major stumbling block – quite literally – in daily life. Nell

stood one day at her office window, looking out dispiritedly over the rain-washed rooftops. Then she shook
herself impatiently. If there was anything Melissa had
taught her, it was that to survive one must laugh on,
outwardly if not inwardly. She had David and Bertie and
Gadsby's, and that was enough for any woman.

Gadsby's had taken on a different look in the two
months of war, as if it too had been called to the colours.
It had taken much planning, much hard work from the
board and the staff. On the ground floor, turnover in the
Wartime Emergency Department that had sprung into
being in earnest on 4 September was slipping, not because
of decreased demand – far from it – but from slowness of
new deliveries, and, worse than slowness, ominous short-
falls in orders when they did arrive. Demand had been
heaviest for blackout material, selling rapidly in August
and accelerating in September, and then for torches and
candles. Now it was impossible to get any of them. Angela
had set up a uniforms department on the first floor, not
for the services but for the WVS, Red Cross and ARP
workers. The whole Fashion Department, particularly the
Economy Department, as the Three-Guinea Department
had been renamed, had a distinctly military feel to it, as
Polly added epaulettes and square shoulders and pockets
to simple, straight-cut dresses, and was doing well. Sales
of millinery on the other hand were slumping, perhaps
because of an underlying feeling that such frivolous occu-
pations as buying new hats were unpatriotic in wartime.

When she noticed this on the monthly returns, Nell
discussed it with Peter Pride, missing Bertie's affable,
all-round percipience. Peter tended to think straight
ahead in pound sterling lanes. Excellent – provided you
threw in a pinch of caution. 'Do you think this is chance or
do you think it's a trend?'

Peter looked at her sharply. 'Might be a short trend,
Mrs G, if it's all over by Christmas, as they say. Looks as if

we've called Hitler's bluff after all.'

'All over,' echoed Nell. 'Bertie doesn't think it's started yet. And *I* think . . .' She stopped, following her train of thought.

'Yes, Mrs G?'

'Trousers,' she said simply, then laughed as she saw his startled face. 'For women. Let's pay a call on Angela.'

'Slacks for air-raid shelters,' Nell said succinctly, knowing Angela could follow her shorthand through long familiarity.

'But there haven't been any raids,' she pointed out dubiously.

'There might well be. We have to be ready, at least with plans. And more than that. With men away, more and more women will be doing men's work. We have to prepare. Less hats and frivolities. More practical wear.'

'And if nothing happens—'

'If we wait, it will be too late,' said Nell firmly. 'We gamble on fashion trends and take it for granted. Now we'll gamble on a fashion *necessity*.'

It was true nothing had happened yet. The air-raid shelter and sandbags in the cellars were left in peace, save for the women who faithfully dusted and cleaned them each day. Apart from a false alarm a few minutes after the declaration of war, nothing had happened at all – except at sea. Confident in the Navy's powers, London returned to relative normality very quickly. Cinemas and theatres reopened, sports began again, and blackout restrictions were very slightly alleviated to allow dimmed headlights and white paint on cars' running boards and to mark some road edges, since blackout was killing more people in accidents than the Germans. Servicemen swarmed everywhere, with the self-conscious look of those in waiting; travel was increasingly difficult, with troops crowding interminably slow trains. Why they had to run slower was a mystery to Nell, as for the second time she arrived at

Merrifield well after dark instead of mid-afternoon.

Many of the younger sales assistants had been called up now, and their places taken by young married women without children, with little to do now their husbands were in the forces. The changeover happened quietly and without fuss. There was too much else going on. Turnover was up, but analysing it Nell noticed that more and more was being spent on accessories than on new dresses, and in the Fashion Department, a rise in the sale of economy and other ready-made dresses was counter-balanced by the fall in the sale of dance frocks, evening dresses, sporting wear and leisure. And where cheaper dresses were concerned, another familiar problem reared its head as Christmas approached.

Gordon Holdsby appeared once more. He had been at the funeral and Nell had exchanged a few polite words with him – so polite, she was reminded of deadly duellers saluting each other with their swords before they got down to business. Matthews was sprouting stores in city centres like molehills, but its Oxford Street property remained its centrepieces. It was no rival to Gadsby's, despite its annoying habits, for Oxford Street was not Regent Street, and Matthews remained essentially a Lilliputian dancing round a Gulliver. Until now.

'The bid's been turned down.'

Peter came into her office to give Nell the bad news without preamble.

'*What*?' Nell stared at him, staggered. For some time she had had her eye on premises adjacent to Gadsby's, positioned just across one of the side streets off Regent Street that created the island of Gadsby's property. It would, the board had agreed, make an excellent addition for expansion of departments, probably into men's wear.

'You've been pipped at the post. The lease is going to Matthews and they're moving out of one of their Oxford Street stores.'

Holdsby, always Holdsby, she thought savagely. She didn't have to ask why he'd chosen this particular site. He would do anything to spite her. Would he raise the tone of Matthews or try to lower that of Gadsby's? she wondered gloomily. Anything might happen. She knew she was being irrational, that Gadsby's reputation was good enough at the moment to withstand twenty Holdsbys, yet the thought of his working there, next to them, a mosquito ready to sting, was worrying.

Afterwards she was to remember the Christmas of 1939 with great affection, a last snook cocked at the horrors of war to come. Mrs Emmeline, Bobsy, Bertie and David, those she loved best, she told herself, in festive mood over a huge turkey that with unaccustomed extrovert daring Mrs Emmeline had acquired from a local farmer. 'Just in case food rationing comes in next year,' she explained, lest this extravagant gesture be thought unpatriotic.

Bertie dressed up as a pie-man with an incongruous stove hat above his overalls, thus making him look rather like a black and white tree trunk. As he advanced with the flaming pudding, to David's delight he proceeded to execute a dance with it, long legs flying wildly, until finally he placed it on the table, still mercifully intact and right way up.

Managing to subdue David's boisterousness long enough, they listened to the King's Speech at the fireside, then embarked on a series of games that sent an exhausted David to bed at nine.

'What will 1940 hold, do you think?' said Nell. 'For you, for us, for everyone?' Everyone here – and those she could not be with.

Mrs Emmeline took their hands in hers. 'Dear Nell, dear Bertie, when tomorrow comes, let us remember today.'

★ ★ ★

Le Reveillon. The eve of the New Year. And what would 1940 bring? Lucien stood in his father's study at the Château de la Ferté alone with his own private thoughts for a moment, glad to be away from his mother's party and the guests' blind optimism. Only fools could think that Hitler had changed his mind. He was biding his time over this harsh winter, that was all. Sooner or later he would strike. And just as in 1870, just as in the First World War, France would be over-confident and under-prepared, underestimating her enemy. It would all happen again, this game, this farce of war. And what part could he, Lucien de la Ferté, play in it? He was forty-one, too old for active service, and the Maison de la Ferté depended on him now his father had all but retired. It was up to him to safeguard its interests. One day, he was fully aware, that might have to be against his own brother. Perhaps war might change things, by bringing about the conflict he dreaded, a conflict so deadly between himself and Philippe that it could not be solved without disaster to the family and the fashion house.

The past was past; too late to avenge himself for the wasted years of unhappiness into which Philippe had precipitated him; a marriage that was a mockery, the child that could never be his . . . not to share, at least. Nell was happy now with someone else, and whatever suspicions he had about David must remain buried. Love was past, and only the future remained. And that, he must ensure, he and not Philippe would control.

On the night of 8/9 April 1940 Hitler struck. He had not missed the bus after all, as Prime Minister Chamberlain had boasted only a few days earlier. He invaded Denmark and struck at Norway. The unknown took shape and flared into the tangible fact of war. Uneasily the rest of Europe waited, especially in the west. Diehard optimists claimed Hitler had invaded Scandinavia as protection for himself against attack; defeatists predicted a German-occupied London within months, and realists saw that chiefly Hitler was after oil. On 10 May Hitler's panzers thrust into the Low Countries and the British Expeditionary Force, at last allowed over Belgium's borders, advanced to meet them; they were soon in retreat as the panzers, troops and Luftwaffe stormed on, pushing the BEF back and striking through the Ardennes into France, then across it, in order to trap the BEF between its pincers.

And it was at this critical time that Nell was forced to cope with the daunting task of clearing out the contents of Melissa's home. Probate had at last been granted, and the contents of the house had been left to her, apart from a few specific items willed elsewhere. It was a job Nell had been dreading, and one that could not wait for the lease on the house had been sold. Her periodic visits to Charles Street to check it was all right had been brief, and now to get rid of piles of clothes and personal effects at such a time was a daunting task.

It took her three days to sort everything out, choosing what to keep and what to sell or give away. Some things she could not bear to part with, for they shouted to her of Melissa. Her aura was so strong here that Nell was glad she was on her own and had not accepted offers of help, as if the Melissa of old could thus be remembered the more easily.

Almost at the last she opened the desk, which she had decided to sell; the contents would be burned. As she opened it, Melissa herself seemed almost to tumble out in the untidy profusion of letters, postcards and photographs. Resisting the temptation to read them, Nell burned them pile by pile in the grate. Tom's bold writing on some made her catch her breath, but she steadfastly continued her task. Lastly was a pile of bills. Glancing quickly through them in case any remained unpaid, Nell was about to throw them on the fire when an envelope heavier than the rest fell on to the floor. There, marked quite clearly in Melissa's handwriting in the distinctive mauve ink she always used, were the words: For Nell.

She picked the envelope up from the carpet with a sudden shiver despite the fire. It must be something quite old, she reasoned, something Melissa had meant to give her years ago, and forgotten about. Reviews of her plays, probably. She used to do that. Yes, reviews.

For Nell – and it wasn't reviews. As she opened the envelope, a key fell out. A huge iron key that would fit nothing here. Nell stared at it, wondering what on earth it was. Something important? A key to a box or chest? To an outhouse? But she had come across nothing that would need such a huge key.

And then she remembered.

It was a key she'd once used.

Nell began to laugh weakly, her laughter mixed with tears that began to roll down her cheeks. How like Melissa. She had said she would make it up to her, and Nell had not known what she meant. Now a great joyousness filled her. Oh, how like Melissa not to do it up in a box, or to leave a message or a bequest. Not even neatly labelled in the desk. For Nell, and that was all. Nell would find it, Nell would manage as she always had. How like Melissa to leave her most generous gift, the gift of her heart so casually, sure it would find its way, that it would convey its message of absolution from an old promise so unerringly.

It was the key to Lucien's villa.

So it was coming. The British forces were fighting like rats in a trap, forced back on Boulogne, Calais and Dunkirk. First the wounded, now the fighting troops themselves were being evacuated from Dunkirk and with them those of the French who chose to continue the fight from

England. For France was doomed now, of that Lucien was sure. He was no defeatist, but even he could see his countrymen had no will to fight this war, as they had the first.

Panic was seizing hold of Paris, insidiously creeping up over its population as the first streams of refugees from the north began to crowd through the city, making for safety in the south. Next came the noise of bombardments not far away from the city itself – and last night Paris itself was bombed. Ever since the Germans had blasted their way into Denmark and Norway it had been clear to him what must soon happen, and yet the 10 May had taken France and Britain by surprise as the panzers streamrollered their way through Belgium and then across France itself. So much for the vaunted Maginot Line. Never finished, assumed impregnable, and in the event bypassed. The Germans had simply lifted the latch of the gate to France and walked through.

Lucien had hurried back to Paris from Cannes when the news reached him and ever since had been locked in consultation both with his family and the Chambre Syndicale de la Haute Couture. There was a plan that if Paris fell, the best of its couturiers should work together in Biarritz where Molyneux had offered accommodation to his business rivals. Lucien himself wanted to supplement the plan by offering to share the Cannes premises of the Maison la Ferté, which were large enough to accommodate at least one other firm, in addition to moving the Paris branch down there. For in no circumstances could he work in an occupied Paris. He could work with Schiaparelli perhaps, or even Lucien Lelong himself, the head of the Chambre Syndicale. But his plan was rejected by his own family – under Philippe's influence.

'*Non*,' said Philippe, shrugging. 'I am desolate, Lucien, but I do not agree. How much better that we should all remain in Paris and keep the flame of couture alive.

Sooner or later this war will end, and Paris must therefore retain her position. We want to be here, not bypassed in Cannes where we would become a minor house.'

'Over? By the time Hitler has finished there may *be* no Paris,' Lucien retorted. 'His heart will be set on Berlin being the centre of the Reich, not Paris. Paris will be destroyed at worst, at best be a subsidiary; perhaps our Maison would even be moved to Berlin. This is what you want?'

Philippe laughed. 'Ah, *mon frère*, you lack courage.' An easy smile at his father. 'You do not love France as I do, if you foresee her defeat so easily. You are no hero,' Philippe murmured, a quick provocative glance at his father's Legion of Honneur photograph above his desk.

The count frowned.

Lucien stared at his brother contemptuously. He was puzzled, battling with anger. He needed to think clearly, for it was unlike Philippe willingly to place himself in danger.

'What have you to say, my son?' the count asked heavily. 'Philippe is right, I think. No true Frenchman should desert the capital. We are not peasants like those poor folk outside, deprived of all they possess. We must set an example, to show France has a future. And that couture has a future.'

'A future? *Mais oui, mon père*, a future supplying dresses to German officers' wives. Who else would be able to afford them?' Lucien said bitterly.

'Italian officers' wives,' Maria entered the conversation, her throaty voice bitter. 'Il Duce would doubtless wish to lick Hitler's boots and join the war if France capitulates. After the fighting is over, naturally.'

Maria. Of course Philippe would have little to fear from an occupied Paris, calculating that Germany and Italy would soon be allies.

This was not a Maria Nell would have recognised, for in

the presence of the de la Fertés she was usually withdrawn, unsmiling, wary. Except for now. She threw back
her head in what was almost her old guffaw.

'*Si*, Lucien, I am Italian. So it would be natural, would
it not, if the great Mussolini joins this war, that I, an
Italian designer, would be so, so popular with the German
and Italian officers' wives? At last I will be famous again.
Mon mari may even allow me to put my name to some of
my designs.'

'*Tais-toi!*' Philippe's face was suddenly ugly.

'And suppose I do not wish to design for fat *signore*,
hein? I am not Fascist, me,' Maria continued fiercely.

'In a few days,' the count interrupted coolly, 'we will all
be Fascist or die.' And as Lucien angrily began to
interrupt, he held up his hand. '*Non*, I am old, maybe, but
I am still the head of the Maison la Ferté. Philippe is
partly right, *mon fils*, Paris must remain Paris as long as
we can keep her so – even if this means we must appear to
welcome our conquerors.'

Lucien rose to his feet. '*Entendu, mon père.*' His mouth
set in a hard line.

'There are other ways, *mon fils*,' his father murmured
quietly as Lucien walked past him, in a low voice that, as
Maria and Philippe began to argue, only he could catch.

The key to Lucien's villa. Nell held it aloft in triumph as a
host of memories swept her back to the sunny Provence
where David had been conceived, where she and Lucien
had loved, to the villa to which she had returned only to
discover that he had married Melissa, the villa whose gate
now might stand wide open in welcome. This key . . . But
too late, surely? This was mere fantasy. Whatever Melissa's gift, the remote stranger who had greeted her at the
funeral implied that the past was buried together with her
friend, his wife, who would forever lie between them. Yet
Melissa herself was surely urging her on with this key,

absolving her from any lingering doubt over a promise foolishly, irrationally given. The path to Lucien's villa was before her, if only she chose to take that first confident step upon it.

Her love for Lucien, though buried, rose to the surface like a tidal wave. Her love for Bertie was gently, firmly swept aside. She thought bitterly of the wasted years, then looking once more at the key, dismissed them. Yet suppose he had really changed? Did he still remember? Still love her? They were different people now, changed by the experiences of the years. Perhaps he too had a new love who had displaced the old, not hidden it, as Bertie had hers. How could she presume that he remembered, as did she? That his love too could be resurrected?

Nell stared at the key, as though in itself it might be an answer. Suppose it was? she thought crazily. She would go, she must go, and go *now*. The fantastical impulse seized hold of her, and settled into a certainty so strong that it would not let her go. Yet how? War stood in the way, as it divided lovers everywhere. She could telephone perhaps to Cannes or to Paris? No, how could she tell him on the telephone? What to say? She must use the key, show him it and explain its significance.

But how to get to France in this mayhem? With the Germans advancing on Paris, there was no civilian travel possible. The evacuations from Dunkirk were over now and the English were streaming out of Paris to Bordeaux or further south to return to Britain. And that was where she too would go. South to Cannes. Lucien must be there to keep the business going in the south, with Paris in so much danger. But suppose like last time she found another woman there? Suppose . . .

No more supposes, she told herself firmly. She would go anyway, though aware she was behaving like a lovesick girl and not a responsible mother and businesswoman. She argued that if she went to the south – if she could only get there – she'd be in no danger save of discouragement or rejection. Now the evacuations had finished from Dunkirk, perhaps there might be ships going south. Certainly there must be some to Bordeaux, maybe further. After all, there must be residents on the south coast who would want to return? Yet how was she to get a passage? Desolately she realised there was only one way.

'I have to go, Bertie, I'm sorry,' she blurted out finally, after she had haltingly explained what she needed. She could not bear to look at his face.

'Nell,' he said at last, after a long silence, his voice flat, 'you're quite mad, you know that?'

'Yes.'

'And irresponsible.'

She thought about that. 'Perhaps,' she admitted grudgingly, 'but too much time has passed. David is his son, you see. I want him to know he has one.'

'Telephone him,' said Bertie, unemotionally. If this was news to him, he did not react to it at all.

'Would you do that, if it were you?'

He winced. 'But it's never likely to be me, is it?' he said bitterly. 'Suppose you don't get back? You'd like me to be responsible for David, I suppose. Anything else?'

'You're not making it easy,' Nell retorted angrily.

'That's a damn' stupid thing to say.'

'The answer's yes, but there's no danger, how can there be? I want to go straight there and straight back. Even the Germans can't occupy the south of France as quickly as that.'

'The Italians can, if they enter the war.'

'Then I won't leave the blasted ship,' she shouted in tears. 'I'll just shout. Will that satisfy you?'

'Me? I've served my purpose. What have I to do with it?'

480

Her anger evaporated, and she stared at him aghast, then came to him, putting her arms round him, as he stood stiffly before her. 'We've been happy, haven't we, Bertie?'

'I thought so.' Unmoving.

Bertie: long legs flying over the grass in pursuit of a rabbit, capering with a butterfly net, climbing the old oak tree to rescue a cat, who promptly ran down of his own accord. Bertie, who laughed with her by day and held her safe by night. 'You *know* so,' she said gently. 'Because it was so. *Is* so. I'll be back. Lucien's place is in France, mine in England. With you.'

Bertie telephoned her the next day, 7 June. 'Things are getting bad, Nell. The Wehrmacht are over the Somme and the Luftwaffe are bombing Paris to blazes. You must leave today, to stand any chance at all. There's a ship leaving Portsmouth this evening to pick up British residents in the south of France. I've got you on it, with a whole lot of arm-squeezing, told them you were a dab hand at first aid and about to join the Red Cross.'

'Bertie,' her voice cracked with emotion. 'Thank you.'

'Don't mention it. Report to the harbourmaster to pick up your permit and brush up your bandaging. It's not going to be comfortable, and it's not going to Cannes. Only Marseille. And Nell,' he added, 'come back safe, you crazy woman.'

Uncomfortable was an understatement. The *Primrose* was an ancient coaling vessel, whose weatherbeaten crew eyed Nell with a respect that puzzled her immensely since she was only too conscious she was in the way. Her offers of assistance were turned down, a bunk was made available by the captain volunteering to share with his Number Two and the captain's head (a term that puzzled her till she realised it meant the lavatory) was thus hers alone, a privilege she only appreciated to the full when she glimpsed the officers' sanitary arrangements. Only after they'd been at sea for two days did she realise with some amusement that they probably thought that since no woman would voluntarily stick her head into the chaos of France, she must be a secret agent. Especially since her bandaging of one cut finger had not proved very efficient.

It took four incredibly slow days to reach Marseille early one morning; no one wanted to check passports or permits, clearly thinking no one would be mad enough to want to stay here longer than they needed. The hordes of people thronging the harbour were evidence of that. All nationalities, shouting in unknown languages, packed the harbour, possessions ranging from tidy suitcases to parcels untidily bulging, inefficiently tied with rope or string. Children, women, men, young, old. No one was immune from war. Refugees from the Low Countries and the North of France, foreign nationals struggling through this bottleneck to regain their homeland, bargaining with boat owners, crowding any gangplank in sight in the hope of an escape. Forlorn groups of what could only be English nationals, residents of the Riviera, trying belatedly to return to England as the impossible loomed ever nearer the possible.

'Tomorrow night, Mrs Gadsby,' the captain told her. 'If we're not forced out before then,' he added grimly, looking at the crowds. He'd already set an armed guard on the gangway.

'I'll be here,' she said stoutly, trying to subdue her terrors at seeing the mob ahead. How, she hadn't the slightest idea. No use hoping for a boat. A brief conversation with one of the harbour officials convinced her of that, even if the sight of the crowds did not. The railway station then. There must be trains. By now, the strain of the last few days combined with the alien frightening scene at the harbour, was catching up with her, and she was fighting tiredness, as well as nausea as she fought her way through even thicker crowds at the station.

'A ticket to Cannes?'

Not so simple, she was told with many shrugs. There ought to be one in an hour, maybe three. Or six? Who knew these days? They must wait for the express from Paris. Express, did he say? From what he'd heard . . . But Nell had had enough. Thanking him, she picked up her bag and left. Remembering she'd had no breakfast, she managed to buy a stale-looking baguette with a lump of unappetising sausage inside it – just as a train belching smoke and smuts pulled in. The noise intensified. Was it stopping here or going on? Towards the Pyrenees – or towards Nice?

'Cannes,' she yelled at an uninterested porter. 'Cannes', pushing her bag towards him. Tempted he hesitated, then enthused by the sight of the francs Nell was waving at him, grabbed her arm.

'*Oui, oui.*' He dived through the crowds pushing their way from the train to the exit. More refugees. Who could doubt it? Suitcases, fur coats, the look of fear in the eyes, the abandoning of normal courtesies, pushing, trampling, the survival of the fittest. Marseille, gateway to freedom. Surely the train must have completely emptied? thought Nell, still clinging desperately to her porter. But when he finally climbed aboard with her bag, the train was still packed to overflowing. With the solid determination of those in possession, the seated gazed without interest at the newcomers. The porter plonked her bag down in the corridor, already lined with people. No point asking for a seat. Clearly there was none. And she'd even stupidly asked the ticket office for a first class ticket. In this bedlam! But at least she was in a train going somewhere, and with luck, Cannes.

She paid the porter and sank gratefully down to sit on her bag, remembering too late to pull out the now squashed baguette. She felt sick, but she must eat, she told herself. Eat . . .

Interminably slowly the train chugged along the south coast, glimpses of the blue Mediterranean, a strange contrast to this horror of a journey, nauseated by tiredness, the smell of Gauloises, and unwashed people. One of whom was her. The captain's shower had failed to work after the first day and she was faced with the choice of sharing the officers' shower or a handbowl of water. She chose the latter, but it was inadequate. Coal dust seemed ingrained in her skin, and the smokey dirt of the train had done nothing to improve the situation. There were smudges of dirt on her clothes and her hands. Probably her face too. She had stupidly brought nothing to drink, and the sausage had been vile.

Suddenly it was all too much. She felt the nausea rising. Stumbling, not even apologising, she pushed her way along the corridor towards the one primitive lavatory. It was occupied, and a queue of people guarded the door. She must take her turn, their indignant shouts told her. Her stomach refused point-blank to take its turn, and despite the clicks of disapproval, not so much at her obvious condition as of the enormity of opening a window in a French train, she thrust her head outside and was ignominiously sick. White-faced, weak and trembling, but feeling much better, she drew her head back in, just as a voice in polite concern said: '*Vous êtes malade, madame*?' A handkerchief proffered by a hand, none too clean. That voice, that hand. She must be ill indeed. Illusion. Fancy. Dreams. She had only to turn her head to dispel them. So she turned.

Lucien stared at her, immobile for a second, then almost fell against the side of the jolting train. 'Nell?' Nothing else. Just 'Nell?'

'Why—?' she tried, and stopped. 'What are you doing here?'

Even Lucien failed to look impeccable now. '*Et toi?* What—' he whispered.

'I was looking for you.' The tears poured down her face.

'For me. *Here?*' Lucien began to laugh weakly, pressed up against her by people impatient to pass. 'Madame Gadsby of Gadsby's, my Nell, seeks me here. Like this?' He drew his finger tenderly across the dirty smudge on the breast of her jacket, laid it on her cheek, across her mouth. He drew her into his first class carriage, where he sat her firmly down after a sharp altercation with a usurper. 'For now, Nell, you sleep. Then you shall tell me. You shall tell me all. When we reach Cannes.'

Cannes seemed untouched by war, save for servicemen milling around apparently without purpose. Even some holidaymakers still disported themselves on the beach. Monsieur Dufy had taken their baggage but Nell elected to walk.

'Let's go along by the sea and then up the hillside,' she begged.

He looked at her gently. 'If you wish.'

She could not explain that somehow, if she walked that route again, it might expunge the memory of her other visit.

'Paris is falling,' Lucien told her quietly, as they walked along the Croisette. 'Two nights ago, the will to resist collapsed. People had been leaving in their thousands for the last week, because of the bombs. The night before last the government left, and yesterday Paris was declared an open city by our army. *By our army*!' He clenched his fist, banging it on a palm tree in disgust. 'I was lucky to get on that train. I had to fight my way on like an animal. So perhaps you, too, think I desert my city, my country?' he said to her suddenly, almost accusingly. 'Philippe stays. I go. This is what you expect, *hein*?' His eyes flashed.

'You must have a reason.' How strange that the sun

should be dancing on the sea, shining down on them in such incongruous contrast to what they discussed. 'Philippe has stayed because of Maria, hasn't he?' she guessed immediately.

'Yes. Two days ago Italy entered the war. Suddenly Maria is oh-so-important again to my brother.'

'And she?'

'What choice does she have?'

'Everyone has choices of some sort,' said Nell. 'The Maria I know won't conform to what the Germans want. You'll see.'

'Most do. Even Frenchmen. Shops are already preparing display notices to boast of "German spoken". Any moment now the Germans will arrive. But I – I refuse to bow the knee.'

'So that's why you're here?'

'Yes. I will continue the Maison la Ferté in Cannes. So long as the Germans let me. What else can I do?' he said lightly. 'I do not wish to grow fat on profits from selling to German army wives and mistresses. France will go on, the true France will *always* survive. Somehow. Somewhere. But I worry for you, Nell. If France falls now, then England must surely be next, in order that Hitler can turn his attention to conquering Russia – and after that the world is his.'

'Napoleon didn't manage it, neither Britain nor Russia.'

'Napoleon did not have a Luftwaffe or tanks.'

'England won't fall,' Nell said stoutly. 'Not with Churchill in charge. You could—' she choked at the enormity of the idea that suddenly came to her. 'You could come to England and help France from there. So many Frenchmen have. You could go into Intelligence.'

'*Non*. I am a Frenchman, and at such a time I must be in France. Here I *know* I can do something. *Le bon Seigneur* will show me how.' He took her hands gently. 'He has sent me you, after all, and that was far more difficult for Him.

486

How long will He spare you for me, Nell?'

'I can't stay here,' she cried quickly, lest temptation make her yield.

'I would not let you. We do not know what lies ahead for English people here yet. Besides, you have a son,' he added unemotionally. 'And Gadsby's.'

'But for one day I have you,' she said quietly. 'And that is more than all the world.' Then she looked at him in wonder. 'Do you know, I thought perhaps you did not love me any more?'

'And how, my Nell, could you think anything so foolish?'

The hillside was a blaze of colour as they turned to walk up La Californie.

'It is over ten years since we parted. We are older, we are changed.'

'You speak of yourself, perhaps?' he observed quietly. 'You love another?'

'No.'

'Ah.'

'And you?'

'*Jamais*.'

She must explain. 'I have great affection, a kind of love, for someone, but—'

He would not let her finish. 'All I know is that you are here again, my Nell, and that when we have walked through the gates of the Villa Fleurie those ten years will vanish – and our love will not.'

'No, let me do it,' she cried, as they reached the gates, and he stretched out his hand. She pulled the key from her pocket and showed it to him.

'These gates are not locked.'

'They were to me,' she said sadly. 'I could not come to you before. Melissa made me promise, and now, with this key, she has relieved me of it.'

487

'You let Melissa stand between us?'

'Yes. As did you.'

He sighed. 'So much time wasted . . .'

The late afternoon sun beat warm on her back, her suit was heavy and stifling in the heat and uncomfortable now, as he took the key from her hand and put it in his pocket, then opened the iron gates. 'You see, they were never locked,' he repeated. 'Never against you. Come, Nell.' He took her hand, as Madame Dufy bustled towards them with cries of delight, interspersed with much throwing of hands in the air and cries of, '*Les Italiens, ils arrivent. Ils arrivent. Demain, demain.*'

Lucien talked to her swiftly in French, his face grim, then turned to Nell. 'Rumour says the Italians have occupied Monte Carlo and Nice. They will soon be here. Perhaps—'

'No. I won't go till tomorrow,' she said firmly, gripped with fear. 'Not now. No matter what.'

He gave a small exclamation and led her into the house, up to the bedroom they had occupied so many years before.

'What will Madame Dufy—'

'Madame Dufy will think nothing. Especially since it is obvious, *ma truffe*, that you are in need of something quickly.'

Mistaking his meaning, she came towards him, but he grasped her by her arm. 'A shower,' he continued politely, removing her jacket and propelling her into the bathroom with its old-fashioned bath and shower attachment.

'This is like the first time we met,' she laughed, dropping her skirt, relieved at being out of those terrible clothes. 'You stripping off my clothes.'

'There is one difference, *chérie*,' he replied, undoing her brassière and unknotting his own tie. 'This time I strip myself as well.'

No sense of strangeness, his naked body next to hers standing in the bath, directing the shower as she lathered and washed herself. No sense of strangeness as she soaped his body for him, as his hands slid over her body, as he towelled her dry. Only immense happiness as he stood still for her to dry him, until at last she finished and let the towel fall.

'You see, Nell, men and women do not change,' he said gravely, then his face broke into a smile, the worry lines disappearing as with a shout of joy she flung her arms around him. Immediately he swung her into his arms and carried her into the bedroom.

'I am wrong. You do change,' he hissed in her ear.

'How?'

'You are heavier.'

'I am as light as my heart,' she retorted gaily.

'Then show me it is still mine,' he said passionately, covering her body with his own till she cried aloud in desire and delight.

And afterwards, when they lay on the bed – 'I cannot leave you again, Lucien. I cannot.'

'You must, Nell,' he said gravely. 'We have a son.'

She was very still. 'You knew?'

'Not at first, but then I guessed. Only that would explain Philippe's increasing hostility – then I saw him. David is a little like me, is he not?' he said wistfully.

'Yes.' Her heart must surely break. 'Could you not come to England?' she pleaded. 'We could be together. He should know you.'

'No. Not while there is war. I cannot leave, Nell, any more than you can stay. It is a dream to think otherwise.'

One evening, one night together, and then came the hell of getting back to Marseille. No more trains, Lucien decreed, but the roads here were as cluttered as out of Paris, as the Italians encroached further in the expectation of Axis control of the whole of France, and English residents, belatedly realising the danger, made their way east.

It took ten hours to reach the chaos of Marseille harbour once more, and Nell saw the *Primrose* was still there. Was she glad or sorry that the question was decided for her? The ship was packed, far worse than the train, with women, men and children fighting for space even on deck. Crying, shouting, insisting, demanding, a way out of a way of life that had not yet left them. Nell reached the gangplank only with Lucien's and Monsieur Dufy's help, just as it was about to be pulled up. At first the permit made no difference and she was pushed back – then a sailor recognised her and changed his mind.

Tears filled her eyes as parting became a reality.

'When we find a way, Nell. When God wills it.' Lucien kissed her and turned away, blinded by tears. Then turned back, trying to laugh. 'You forgot this.'

'What?'

He pressed the key to the Villa Fleurie into her hand. 'You will never need it. Always, Nell, always unlocked.' Then he was gone and the gangplank lay ahead. Slowly the ship began to pull away as she fought her way to the rail on deck. At first she thought he was not there. Then she saw him. Smaller and smaller his slight figure on the quayside, greater and greater the width of sea between them. He raised his hands to cup his mouth, shouting out in an exuberant last cry over the distance that divided them:

'*I love you, Nelly Watkins.*'

Chapter Fifteen

'Wales?' cried Nell in despair. 'But it's so far away. How will I ever see him? The war might go on for years.'

Bertie gave this his earnest consideration, uncurling his long legs from a chair as if to give emphasis to the seriousness of his thinking. 'We'll manage it,' he assured her finally. 'Ma's right though. David can't stay in London and now he most certainly can't stay in Kent. Whether the Germans invade or not there's going to be a fight, and it's going to start soon.'

She knew Bertie was right. David's school had been fortunate to find another in Wales willing to take them in at a time when every large house in the country was already requisitioned, and every school in the west expanded to double its normal size. Nevertheless Wales had a distant sound to it that the rest of England did not. Suppose the invasion happened and the country was occupied . . . No, there was no point in thinking like that. If it did happen, they would win. 'Won't we?' she asked Bertie uncertainly.

'Yes,' he replied laconically. Not that logic told him so. Logic said that all the vast preparations for invasion in Kent, all the secret War Office measures for guerilla warfare, all the civilian measures in erecting barbed wire and concrete road blocks as tank traps and taking down signposts to confuse the enemy, all the training by Local Defence volunteers, would go for nothing against the German steamrolling war machine.

And yet instinct told him that somehow Britain would survive. Who was it said that in the end it was the spirit of a nation won wars not its armaments? Whoever it was, was right with Bertie. Nevertheless, he acknowledged ruefully, a few weapons wouldn't come amiss. All very well for Churchill to deliver aggressive speeches about fighting on the beaches, in the fields and on the streets, but even Churchill was rumoured to have added under his breath: 'What with? Broomhandles, I suppose.'

There was his mother to consider also. Bobsy Bertrand resolutely refused to leave Kent. She was too old, and Hitler would have a hard job subduing *her* if he got as far as Missinden, she'd told him cheerfully. Equally obstinate, Mrs Emmeline refused to leave Merrifield. It had now been requisitioned by the Army, who allowed her one wing, but after a week of this she elected to move into the old Dower House with the Hopkinses. From there she had the pleasure of company on the estate without the inconvenience of 'Run, Rabbit, Run' blaring out from the gramophone. Thanks to some gentle arm-twisting by Bertie, Merrifield was chosen as an Army HQ, and not for lower echelons; every Sunday evening Mrs Emmeline was formally invited to dinner, an occasion she much enjoyed, dressing up in her black lace to complement their dress uniforms.

This mid-July weekend, however, Nell and Bertie were spending with Bobsy in a strangely quiet Missinden without David tearing about. Bertie had not questioned her, to Nell's relief, on what had happened in France, apparently merely glad to see her safely back again; he had made a brief enquiry as to whether her mission had been successful. 'Yes,' she had replied gratefully, and that had been that.

Since then she had seen him very little, busy as he was at the War Office. Two weeks ago, Hitler had bombarded Britain with pamphlets demanding the country's surrender. These had become curiosities, or had been put to baser purposes, but not taken seriously. It had evidently been Hitler's last warning for now the Luftwaffe were taking up the offensive in the Channel against shipping. Already the dull boom of warfare could be heard from the Channel as the RAF fighters flew to intercept, and they switched on the wireless to hear Charles Gardner's excited commentary.

Later that night, with only the call of a late bird disturbing the warm silence, Nell and Bertie walked in the gardens. Impossible to believe on such an evening that all this was under threat.

'When do you think it will begin in earnest, Bertie?'

'Not long now. Once they've got air superiority over the Channel, they'll have to fight for air superiority over Kent to provide cover for the invasion troops.'

'Unless they use paratroopers,' he might have added, had he been alarmist. 'Dropping down like a plague of locusts as in Rotterdam.'

But Nell followed his thoughts precisely. Rotterdam had been bombed with heavy casualties while the city was surrendering. When Paris was surrounded in June, everyone had feared it would happen there too. But the bombing had been lighter than expected for beautiful Paris had offered no resistance, but had laid herself open to the invader. Nell had seen the photographs of a smug Hitler victorious in Paris in the *Illustrated London News*, and wept for the city she had known – a Paris where Lucien might still be. In an agreement signed in the same railway coach as the humiliating treaty that denoted German defeat in the First World War, Marshal Pétain had agreed with the Germans to split his country in two, a demarcation line running across it, the north to be occupied by the Germans and the south run by the Marshal and his government from Vichy. So the south remained free yet not free – for who could doubt where its allegiance must lie? Monte Carlo was apparently unofficially under Italian occupation, which was being vigorously resisted, but of the rest of the Riviera there was no official word, only the frantic stories of English residents returning to their homeland.

'It might be a long war, Nell,' said Bertie, breaking the silence at last.

'But we'll win.'

'I'm thirty-five,' he continued. 'If Britain holds firm then Hitler won't just give up. The war will be fought in other theatres, Africa, the Middle East – God knows where. And Russia is what he's really after, of course. So that means I might have to go abroad . . . You do realise that?' he asked matter-of-factly.

'No, I hadn't,' Nell replied bleakly. Life without Bertie? With some dismay she realised how much she depended on him for advice on Gadsby's, for companionship – for love.

'Mind you, this is hardly the time to contemplate long distance travel. There's plenty to do here at the moment. Maybe I'll end up living in Chislehurst caves. You could come and cook me meals over a fire like a Stone Age wife.'

'What on earth are you talking about?' she asked blankly.

'Rubbish, I expect,' he replied hastily. 'But we all have to make plans just in case. I expect you have at Gadsby's.'

In fact Nell had not discussed the possible consequences of occupation with her board. 'Like Hitler, we can move fast if we have to,' she had reasoned, 'and why make plans for something that might never happen?' She began to wonder now if she'd been right.

'I'd like,' Bertie was saying, 'to think I had more of a family if I have to go abroad. I want you to marry me, Nell.'

The night air was very soft around them. She might

never see Lucien again, and now she would be divided by war from Bertie too. How easy it would be to say yes – and how impossible.

'I can't, Bertie,' she said gently.

'Would you have done so if you hadn't gone to France?' he said after a moment, obviously unsurprised.

'Perhaps,' she answered miserably. Perhaps – if there had been no Melissa, no key.

'Between us, we've made a mess of things.'

'No,' she said stoutly, rejecting this. How could it be a mess when Bertie had given her so much, and she had given all she could?

That night he did not come to her room. In the early hours of the morning she rose and went to him. He held out his arms for her, and held her close.

'Je regrette, Signora. Mais merci, comme même.' Lucien, tight-faced, showed the woman out. She might have proved a good customer. Refusing her orders would reflect badly on the Maison la Ferté. The plan for Parisian couturiers to work together had come to nothing, with Molyneux and Creed forced to return to England. Paris haute couture was fearful, for it was rumoured that it was to be moved to Berlin. Much depended on the Cannes branch. Yet how could he serve an enemy of his country? Cannes was swarming with many nationalities nowadays. The richest of the English had now left, on two ancient overcrowded ships sent by the British Government. Those with nowhere to go still remained in their villas, preparing to brave it out.

Down to Cannes to fill the gap flocked the rich of Paris, particularly the Jewish, confident no ill could befall them here. German and Italian officers on leave eyed the town proprietorially, their wives eagerly patronising the stores. But he was not forced to serve them, Lucien reasoned. For the sake of the house, he tried not to refuse outright.

'*Je regrette. Signora, Meine Frau*, it is impossible to obtain the material, sufficient models, buttons . . .' Anything to avoid selling to them. He knew it was merely a foolish and futile gesture, which would achieve nothing and be noted by no one save the enemy. He should do something constructive to help his country throw off the yoke.

Vichy France – was it victory or a defeat worse than that of Norway? The French still ruled themselves here, nominally. Yet the Vichy police, the Milice, were already beginning to be feared. Ever since Dunkirk, stray servicemen from the fighting in the north had been making their way south in the hope of reaching safety. They were usually easy to spot, he'd heard, some still in uniform, some distinguished by build, or language. Those of their countrymen still in the south were apparently doing their best to help shelter them from the Milice, for they risked internment at the least. In Marseille, the former pastor of the Scottish church, Donald Caskie, had reopened the seamen's mission in Marseille – and helped more than seamen, it was rumoured, in rooms not so visible to the public eye. Two Scotswomen continued to run their tea-room, and they too were rumoured to be advising and sheltering servicemen. And he, a Frenchman, there must be something he could do? Something more than refusing to sell pretty frocks to Italian women.

'Velvet, *madame*, for the winter. With this hat, perhaps.' He watched a sales assistant persuasively talking a customer into an expensive and frivolous evening dress. With war and death all over Europe, was it not obscene for a man to be so employed?

No. Perhaps not. If the Trenchard sisters ran their tea-room, Caskie his mission, then he too should continue his calling. And when the opportunity came, as come it must, then he too could act. Was it not after all in the spirit of resistance for women to cock a snook at fate, to dress elegantly, to offer a defiance to the world. As good a

French heart could beat beneath velvet as beneath sack-cloth and ashes.

What of Nell far away in England? Would they ever meet again? Surely the British could not prevail against Hitler, with only her distant commonwealth to support her? Perhaps he would meet Nell again under the common umbrella of the Third Reich, subjects to Adolf Hitler. No. That must never happen. He stared stark truth in the face. Sooner or later he must face the fight head-on himself. And in that fight, what was one life, one love?

His decision made, he took the telephone off the hook, and telephoned the Italian woman. '*Signora*,' he purred, when her voice came on the line, 'a happy chance. We can obtain the model you require after all.' In September, the fear of invasion receded, whether because of the valiant Few of the RAF, or the Day of National Prayer, or the wrong weather conditions for the invasion to set sail. During August, with the air battle raging over the Kent skies, Nell had rushed down to Merrifield to be with Mrs Emmeline as often as she could at weekends. Not that Mrs Emmeline seemed much in need of companionship. With the whole of the British army now apparently her devoted servants, not to mention the Hopkinses, she seemed to take everything in her stride; she was as at home in the Anderson shelter, as when she had presided over formal dinners at Merrifield House. She took as great an interest in what was happening overhead, as David himself would have done. He was furious to be missing the excitement of dogfights, Messerschmitts and Spitfires. Had he been there, he wrote indignantly in his round childish hand, he could have been helping the war effort tracing crashed Mezzies and Heinkels, instead of missing it all stuck in boring old Wales. Boring but *safe* old Wales, Nell amended gratefully.

Since the glorious day of 15 August, when the RAF had apparently shot down 182 planes, the Germans had sent fewer planes, but still they were relentlessly keeping up the onslaught. And then came the bombers, no longer targeting Kentish airfields but London itself. On 7 September they had bombed London in earnest for the first time, when the docks were pounded heavily in a late afternoon raid. Four hundred and thirty people had been killed and 1,600 injured. Three days after that Buckingham Palace itself was bombed, and since then they'd come every day. And their activities were no longer confined to military targets. Listening to the proximity of the explosions, from the Gadsby air-raid shelter in the basement, Nell tried to convince herself that they were farther away than they sounded. So far the store had escaped. But today the noise thundered ominously close, and was getting closer. She tried to concentrate on the chatter all around her. So much for thinking all the work they had put in on planning the shelter had been unnecessary. The sirens had sounded every day this week, and staff, management and customers had packed in together until the all-clear came.

A particularly loud explosion was undoubtedly nearby, and there was a moment's silence in the shelter before bright conversation was forced out once more. Then louder and closer, until the building shook rather than trembled.

It was the helplessness, the feeling that above her Gadsby's might be burning and she could do nothing but wait. Frustration not fear gripped her, until right overhead there was the undoubted thunderous crump of falling bombs. Above them, around them. They were caught by the fear of being stifled, trapped like rats. Nell stilled herself. She picked up her book again and signalled to one of her staff to put on the gramophone. Loud. Very loud. To drown all noise from outside except the eerie continuous wail of the all-clear of the siren.

When at last it came, Nell was first out of the door,

heart in mouth, scrambling up the stairs to the fresh, or rather acrid, smoke-laden air of Regent Street.

At her first horrified glance the whole of Regent Street seemed in ruins or burning. Then she saw it was not so, but the Quadrant had certainly been damaged. The stores opposite had been hit. Gadsby's? Fearfully she turned her eyes upwards. Not burning, thank heavens, for next door Matthews most certainly was. As customers hurried to return to their homes, staff ran in to the store to check for incendiaries. Nell and the board had made arrangements for this, and she and Peter Pride went to the Raid Review desk on the ground floor to await reports. One by one departmental staff reported in, and Nell breathed again, hardly able to believe their luck. An incendiary through the roof had brought down the ceiling of the directors' dining room, and the staff were dealing with the small fire now, Angela reported.

Leaving Peter in charge, Nell went out to see how Matthews had fared. The far end of the store was ablaze, a small crater in the roof had blown in glass from the middle of the building and there was apparently further damage at the back, judging from the fire engine speeding round there. Another fire engine was tackling the main blaze in front. Well, there was nothing she could do till the blaze was out. Or was there? she thought suddenly. At the near end of the building, Holdsby's voice could be heard shouting directions at staff and going to the door she could see him organising a chain of sand buckets. There seemed pitifully few, either buckets or staff – Holdsby's cost-cutting measures again no doubt, she thought caustically.

'Can I help?' she shouted.

He paused momentarily. 'Yes,' he replied. 'Sand buckets and people to form another chain.'

Ignoring his offhanded tone, she hurried back to Gadsby's organisation desk, quickly detailing twenty staff to go to Matthews and returning with them. Incendiaries had started several small fires which the fire service had not the resources to cope with, though they were threatening stock. It took two hours of exhausting dirty work before everything was clear, and damage patched up for safety.

'I'll send over our carpenters tomorrow morning,' Nell told Holdsby. 'That way you may manage to open in the afternoon.'

'Gracious Gadsby's, eh?' Holdsby said superciliously, giving nothing, obviously angry that he had suffered where she had not.

'Certainly,' replied Nell coolly. 'No store is an island, especially at the moment.'

Lucien dreaded his visits to Paris. It was not the city he had known. It was peopled by strangers, the Parisians sullen, resentful, and worst of all quiescent. If any of these citizens illicitly listened to Churchill's stirring broadcast speeches, their faces showed no signs of it. Day to day existence appeared their sole aim, battling with strict rationing while their visitors ate and drank their fill. It had become a silent city. Few Parisians had motor cars now. Bicycles were the accepted way of individual transport. The Maison la Ferté was, as Lucien knew, still waiting to know its fate. The count had insisted all staff should remain, to avoid the dreaded *Service de Travail Obligatoire* introduced by the occupying forces, but they were patronised less and less by Frenchwomen, and more and more by German or Italian women – the latter attracted by Maria's designs.

'You will visit the château, *mon fils*,' his father had said on his arrival, more as a statement than a question. 'Your mother wishes to see you.'

Lucien hesitated. 'I have little time—'

'Come,' commanded the count.

The château grounds were unkempt through lack of gardeners. '*Service de travail*,' explained his father. 'All our able-bodied men are sent to Germany. We have no gardeners now, save Jean-Pierre. He is eighty, and the German factories decided they could spare him,' he added ironically.

Lucien glanced at his father but said nothing. Already he had learned that in war if one said nothing, one risked less. He had no doubt of his father's allegiance, but today Philippe also would be here. Philippe with an Italian wife. Who could tell where his loyalties lay?

Maria and Philippe were present at luncheon; she looked magnificent in a deep red wool costume and yet Philippe, Lucien noticed, scarcely glanced at her.

'So, you are doing well, Philippe?' Lucien probed.

'We wait, *mon frère* – we design and we plan. We couturiers have decided it is our duty to do all we can to continue to operate here, in the interests of haute couture.'

'A profitable decision,' remarked Lucien drily.

'And dangerous, in my view,' commented the count. 'Hitler will never let us prosper. He will not allow Paris to outstrip Berlin. He will order the couture houses to move there if too many German ladies patronise Paris houses.'

'He will not move ours, Papa,' said Philippe smugly, unwisely.

'You have a special understanding?' asked Lucien coolly.

'Maria naturally—' Philippe began speedily.

'No, Philippe, do not drag me in,' his wife interrupted. 'I work because we must live. If it were not for that, I would not design a *shroud* for those fat slugs.'

Philippe's enigmatic eyes rested on her briefly as Lucien laughed. 'Maria is so extreme, *mon père*. Not a business-woman.'

Lucien expected his father to come to her defence, but surprisingly he did not. Instead he picked up his glass and regarded the claret. Wine at least was not rationed provided you could guard your cellars against requisition.

'Paris is not dead, my children. What you see now is not the true Paris, but a bandage put on to heal its wounds. The true Paris will rise again, when it is ready. To France, my sons.' He rose to his feet and raised his glass. '*La patrie.*'

Obediently his family followed suit, yet Lucien felt it was to him his father spoke. To him alone.

'*Mon père,*' Philippe said quietly, 'have you given further thought to my suggestion?' as they resumed their seats.

'Suggestion?' Lucien looked at him sharply.

'It seems to me that you disapprove of the way we run our business here, *mon frère,*' Philippe explained apologetically. 'I wonder if it would not be better to divide the two houses completely. You employ your own designer and workrooms, at least while France is divided. Then there would be no need for you to visit Paris.'

The idea was attractive, Lucien admitted. One he had often considered. Yet if Philippe suggested it, he reflected, it must be in his personal interests, not those of the Maison.

'*Non,*' said the count angrily. 'I run this company still. And I say no.'

Philippe shrugged. 'As you wish, Papa. As you wish.' He smiled deprecatingly at his brother.

If the two houses *were* separated financially, how much more easily the control of the Paris house would slip into Philippe's eager hands, Lucien reasoned. But how could he *know* the house would remain open? Was he gambling? No, Philippe had plans – that was clear. Their father was ageing visibly now, tiring of the struggle, overwhelmed by the catastrophe of German occupation. In theory, Philippe could run Maison la Ferté as well as he, Lucien, but Philippe was no businessman, quite apart from the questionmark over his motives.

Lucien took a walk in the grounds after luncheon to clear his head and was surprised when Maria joined him, ostensibly to play with the girls but in fact with other matters in mind.

'What do you really think of Philippe's plan, Lucien?' she enquired.

'It might suit me,' he replied lightly. Maria was an enigma. Philippe's wife, yet Nell's friend. An Italian who claimed to be anti-German.

'Do not let it,' she said. 'Ah, Lucien, you must remain part of the same firm, for your father's sake. If you break with Paris, there is nothing you can do to help France.'

'To help France? That is a very sweeping statement. Especially since you are Italian, Maria,' he said gently. He was curious, very curious now. What did she mean, help France?

'We are all dupes, pawns in others' plans,' she said fiercely. 'You believe I think this is good, eh?' She waved her arms excitedly. 'You think I believe killing Communists and Jews is good, just because I was born Italian?'

He said nothing. Trust no one.

She gave an exclamation of disgust. 'You are like Philippe, Lucien, I see now. You are all show, all outside. And inside you are soft *pudding*!' Her eyes flashed and she stormed off, leaving him looking after her thoughtfully.

On the Sunday, Lucien decided not to attend mass but to make his departure, only to find somewhat to his surprise his father elected at the last moment to remain behind also.

'Before you go, my son, I wish to show you something,' he explained.

There was suppressed tension in his voice. Puzzled, Lucien followed him through the grounds to the gardener's house. The old man, Jean-Pierre, was nervous, though Lucien could see no reason for it. He followed as his father walked upstairs and into one of the two small bedrooms. It was empty, but the beds had been occupied.

Mystified, he watched as the count knocked three times on the ceiling with his stick, and cautiously the loft door opened.

'*Descendez, messieurs*,' the count ordered.

Sheepishly, furtively, two overall-clad peasants swung themselves down.

Peasants? thought Lucien, staring. Not with that build. Not that fresh complexion. They looked – then he knew. 'You are British?' he asked simply.

Neither said anything.

'This is my son,' said the count. 'Comte Lucien. You can trust him.'

'Private Jenkins, Harry,' said the more forthcoming of the two.

'Private Peters.' The other, of wirier build, was still wary.

Lucien shook their hands, and turned enquiringly to his father.

'They are survivors from St Valéry, *mon fils*. If the Germans find them, they will be imprisoned. They came here a month ago, brought by a local farmer who could no longer care for them. What shall we do with them, *mon fils*?'

His father, asking him? Lucien battled with emotions. His father was a Chevalier of the Légion d'Honneur; ten years ago he would not have dreamed of consulting anyone. Now he grew tired, old, and with this question was passing the baton on to Lucien. The roles were reversed. Without a word spoken, he found himself now to be the thinker, the planner, the holder of the family honour.

'Give me two weeks,' he replied. 'They cannot stay here longer. It is too dangerous. I will return next week on some excuse, and something will be arranged.' He shook the men's hands. 'Courage, *mes amis*. You will be home soon.'

Easier said than done, however. Lucien pondered the problem as he returned to Cannes. There was no escape across the Channel now. Perhaps from Brittany . . . He thought about this for a moment, then discounted it. He knew no one well enough in Brittany to consult. No, it must be the south. If he could get them across the Pyrenees – but how? Then he remembered the Seamen's Mission in Marseille. If he could contact Donald Caskie . . . Yes, that was what he could do. How to get them there? Train was the obvious answer, but they would need false papers. And they did not appear to speak French. He brooded for a moment. It was impossible. Then he pulled himself together. It was far from impossible. And what's more, there might be others in need of the same help . . .

'We would need safe places of refuge,' Lucien explained. 'A whole system, with a collection point in Paris to take the men down to Marseille. And we must contact the British government to arrange for boats to pick them up.'

'You are mad, Lucien,' Maria said cheerfully, with some resemblance to her old self, 'but I too am mad. You do not think of me as the enemy any more, huh?' She had observed his earlier reticence.

'I don't think you are an admirer of Signor Mussolini.'

She spat inelegantly in answer. 'Or of Signor Hitler. And why you tell me all this?' she asked curiously.

Lucien paused. This was the difficult part. 'I know that it is not fair of me to ask you to help. You are married to Philippe, whom I would not trust with this knowledge, and you are the mother of two little girls. It would be dangerous for you, *especially* for you, being an Italian. Do you understand?'

'*Si. What* will be dangerous?'

'I want to centre the operation on the Maison la Ferté!' said Lucien slowly, as she goggled at him, then exploded into laughter.

'You *are* mad, *mon ami*.'

'*Non*. The Germans are least suspicious where they are most welcomed.'

She shot a look at him. 'This is true.'

'The men could travel as designers of Maison la Ferté travelling to the Cannes office.'

'You think English Tommies can pass as dress designers?' she cried incredulously.

'In the right clothes, Maria. Which you can provide. Those who do not speak French could be foreign workers employed as couriers for the dresses to be sent to the Cannes branch. There is someone you can trust in the stockroom?'

She thought for a moment. 'François.'

'Then they will see only him. Not you. And I will speak to François. You must remain above suspicion. Especially to Philippe.'

She hesitated. 'He is not all bad, Lucien.'

'He is my brother, I know that.'

'It is the inheritance. The title. I do not know why it means so much to him, but it does.'

'If France does not win this war, there will be no titles,' Lucien reminded her.

'I will have no more children now,' said Maria matter-of-factly. 'I am thirty-six, and they said when I lost my son, my *bébé*, that it would be unlikely I could have more. So there will be no heir for Philippe. Not from me.' Her face clouded, then brightened. 'So I will sit in the centre of this web of yours in Paris, and organise these houses, *hein*? Somehow I will do it, never fear. Though for

506

whom?' she asked. 'The British do not fly over France, and there cannot be many British servicemen still on the run.'

'We must make our plans now. It takes time. We need, for instance, to find a forger. I have managed to get some papers for the two in my father's house, but we need someone in Paris. Sooner or later the RAF will start retaliating for these bombing raids on their homeland, and then we shall see. And there are many prisoner-of-war camps too. Men will escape, and have no way of reaching home, unless there are those to help. With you in Paris and me in Cannes to organise their journey, it will all be possible, you will see.'

'You sound very confident, Lucien. Of what?'

He had incautiously raised his voice, and Philippe passing the office had entered.

'Of surviving these new measures imposed on couturiers, Philippe. Maria was just telling me about them,' Lucien said smoothly. 'It seems Papa was right. The Germans are jealous of the attractions of Paris fashion houses for German women, and so we have been rationed to seventy-five new models per season. Not to mention these restrictions on the width and length of skirts. If I were you—' He hesitated.

'Yes, *mon frère*, what would you then do? To me the answer is simple. We raise our prices.'

'Impossible,' said Maria.

'Possible, but short-sighted,' Lucien commented. 'If frocks must be dull, then where shall fashion look but to hats?'

'*Si*, Lucien,' Maria shouted, clapping him on the back exuberantly. 'Hats. Big hats. Little hats. Unrationed hats. Feathered hats. My animal hats. Silly hats. Bow hats. Me, me – I design them.'

'If I agree, darling,' Philippe said smoothly. 'I believe I run the Maison?'

'Your father runs the Maison,' said Maria tactlessly. 'He will see sense. Huh?'

The look Philippe gave her was not pleasant, but it was speedily replaced by a smooth smile. 'As I do. Naturally, for anything in La Ferté's interests. I will put it to him tomorrow.'

As his own suggestion, no doubt, Lucien thought wrily. He glanced at Maria, who shrugged.

The board presented a strange aspect in wartime. No Bertie, who had had to resign, Robert Galt, who hardly ever attended, Peter Pride who was busy with the provincial stores, Sebastian, who had first been called up, then rejected again as medically unfit, Angela and Polly Simpkins, whom she had appointed when Bertie bowed out – and Joe, delighted at his elevation, and apparently no longer at daggers drawn with his estranged wife. So far neither he nor Peter had been called up. On a bad day, attendance was down to the three women and Joe, but today both Peter and Sebastian were present. Almost a full house.

'It can't be long now,' Peter offered brightly. The dreaded spectre of clothes rationing had hung over their heads for a year. Food obviously had been the first commodity to be rationed, but clothes were now clearly on the agenda. With more factories being turned over to producing war material, less and less were engaged on fabric manufacture, and so hard were supplies to obtain that rationing might almost prove a relief – if they could find a different source of revenue, Nell reasoned.

'It might not work against us,' Polly said doubtfully. 'After all, even if a dress is to be so many coupons, that doesn't regulate the price it's sold at, does it? We could sell a frock for a hundred guineas, and it would still take the same number of coupons.'

'I don't think we'll be selling many at a hundred

guineas,' said Nell drily. 'Even at ten, come to that.' It was beginning to be considered unpatriotic to buy new clothes and more fashionable, even in the most affluent circles, to boast of making do. 'We're stuck, in my view, with the choice we've had all along. Either we bring our prices down to Matthews' to gain turnover, or we maintain quality and price and face losses.'

'Selfridges are still making a profit – and they don't sell rubbish,' drawled Sebastian.

'No, but we're more dependent on fashion than they are. We'll have to lay more emphasis on accessories.'

'Clothes rationing would apply to them too, wouldn't it?' Joe asked hesitantly, this being his first board meeting. He remembered nowadays, with some surprise that he had once sweet-talked the fearsome Nell Gadsby in Bexley Woods. 'Scarves and that sort of thing are sure to be rationed.'

'Then we'll have to find things which don't demand coupons. Like coats made out of blankets. Dresses of curtain materials and so on,' Nell said determinedly.

'I don't think that's very patriotic,' said Joe, slightly reprovingly.

'Apart from that,' added Polly more practically, 'the authorities would jump on it.'

Nell laughed. 'True. Then how about putting blankets and curtain nets rather ostentatiously on sale in the Fabric Department, and a few pictures of suitable coats and dresses around? That way customers can have the idea themselves.'

'Right,' said Joe enthusiastically. 'And how about an Economy Show?' He looked round nervously at their blank faces. 'You have shows for the nobs in the Fashion Department, why not the Economy? Fifty-five ways with a scarf—' He broke off, losing his nerve.

'I say,' Sebastian commented first. 'Not bad. A model parade, showing what's on coupons, and how many, and how much. And we can slip in some models showing what can be done with old blankets.'

Only Polly remained silent in the general chorus of approval. Nell glanced at her, wondering why, then forgot it as she raised her own brainwave.

'A repair department – what do you think of that? New lamps for old, like *Aladdin*. Bring in your old clothes and let Gadsby re-design them into new ones.'

'Yes,' said Angela enthusiastically. 'Not cheap, but it would help make up for lack of revenue in Fashion.'

'It's not Gadsby's, is it? Anyway, I wouldn't have the time,' said Polly obstinately, to Nell's surprise. She was usually more enthusiastic.

'Then your assistant could do it, or else we'll take on a new designer,' Nell said firmly.

'I think Polly's right,' Sebastian said. 'It'll lower the tone of the store.'

There were nods of agreement.

'Nonsense,' said Nell, irritated. 'This is wartime.' She sighed. 'We'd better vote.'

The vote was four to two against.

'I'm sorry,' said Nell unhappily. 'On this occasion I'm going to overrule the vote again. I'm sure you're wrong here and I'm right. I'm sorry.'

With set faces they left, leaving Nell to ponder the wisdom of her decision. It had been a psychologically bad move – yet for Gadsby's she knew it was right. Above her, the portrait of Jonathan Gadsby seemed to be staring down with great amusement.

Nell saw little of Bertie nowadays; somehow with daily work, plus setting up the new department, plus protecting the store during the Blitz, plus lack of sleep through nightly raids which sent her stumbling into work next day, the weeks slipped by. His leave never seemed to correspond to her days off, and she realised with surprise that she had not seen him for three weeks. By chance that evening he came to Eaton Square.

'I've got something to tell you,' he began without preamble, looking decidedly out of sorts for Bertie.

'You're going overseas?' she asked in trepidation.

'Not that I know of, though I don't doubt it will happen some time or other,' he told her wrily. 'No, it's – I've decided to get married, Nell. To someone else.'

She went cold, thoughts whirling, the prospect hitting her like a hammer. She had taken him for granted, assumed his devotion, no matter what, even when she turned down his proposal of marriage.

'That's – surprising,' she managed to blurt out, aware of her selfishness in not reacting more positively.

'I'm quite surprised myself. It's this Blitz, you know, and what might come after it. I decided if I have to quit this country for overseas, I wanted to leave some sort of stake here. Selfish of me, I suppose, but there it is. I love you, you know that, but there's no future. You're living in the past or in the future, I don't know which, and I don't want to spend the rest of my life being second best. I'd like a wife, even children maybe. Of my own,' he added unemotionally and devastatingly.

Children. Nell realised now how selfish she had been that she'd never even thought of this aspect. By clinging to Bertie, assuming David to be family enough for him, she was stopping him from enjoying a fuller life.

'I'll miss you, Bertie,' she said sadly. 'I love you – as much as I can, you know that.'

'Yes. But sometimes it's not quite enough. Marriage seems a good idea, in wartime at least.' He smiled at her warmly, relieved to have got it over with.

'Who— You'll be careful who you choose, won't you, Bertie?'

'Always careful, old thing. You'll like her. She's an

ATS girl who works in my office. She isn't going to faint if I go overseas.'

Nell wanted to ask if they were lovers. If— She stopped herself. She had no right to ask anything. She had lost that right the day she left for France to see Lucien again.

'Come to the wedding?' he asked anxiously.

'Will she mind?' Nell asked hesitantly. 'Does she know about me?'

'Yes. But she's a sensible lass. She'll like you.'

Nell had severe doubts on this, but swallowed them. 'I have only one condition, Bertie,' she told him. He looked slightly worried, and she laughed. 'Let Gadsby's provide the wedding dress.'

'*Bonjour*, Lucien.' Maria's dark head popped out of her office at the sound of his voice. 'I have some ideas to discuss for the autumn. I know it is early but I should like a preliminary talk.' She led the way into her office.

'You have the consignment ready for Cannes?' he asked her coolly. It was the third such journey, and they were beginning to acquire a routine.

'Today, you will pick them up at the Gare de Lyon.'

'Why?'

'Because Philippe visits the warehouse today.'

'*Entendu*.' If either of them thought it strange that they should thus avoid any involvement by Maria's husband, neither commented. '*Famille, patrie, travail*', the slogan the Nazis had demanded replace '*Liberté, egalité, fraternité*', was hardly applicable here. 'The men are correctly clothed?'

'Yes, I took the clothes to Choufleur' (their code-name for the owner of the Paris safe house in Ville d'Avray) 'last night.'

He exclaimed. '*You*? But it is dangerous. Please, not again. Is there no one else?'

'There is an assistant here I might perhaps trust.'

512

'Very well. If you are sure Philippe—'

'He does not notice her existence. Too lowly. You have no difficulty travelling?'

He shook his head silently as he passed over to her the money for funding the safe houses and expenses. 'No, but I feel I need a woman to travel with me. Three men from a fashion house looks odd and will in time attract suspicion. I intend to ask Marguerite, my assistant in Cannes. You have no objection? She will not know of you, only of Betterave.' (This was François's code-name.)

'You think I am afraid to go?'

'No. But if we are discovered, then it is worse for you than for a Frenchwoman.'

She sighed. 'Never fear, Lucien. The Gestapo would not hold me.'

The conductor on the Marseille train was almost a friend by now. A silent one, however. As were many in Paris. No one knew. Many suspected. Lucien had even heard rumours that other lines such as his were opening up. Captain Ian Garrow, he suspected, was organising a line from the north to the Seamen's Mission in Marseille. After much thought, he decided to set up his own arrangements for returning his 'consignments' to Britain, rather than overburden the Seamen's Mission or risk the Pyrenees route into a supposedly neutral Spain. About as neutral as Vichy, he thought savagely. Accordingly he had made cautious enquiries in Toulon, where the French fleet were immobilised under the Vichy agreement with the Germans. Here he contacted the captain of the *Lumière*, a sister ship of the *Fresnel*, lightships run by the Public Works Department and which regularly travelled along the coastal ports and over to Algiers. The *Lumière* made regular trips to Algiers from its home port of Marseille. His 'consignments' would be taken from Cannes by the *Lumière* to Marseille, then on to Algiers, where his courier would easily enough find another ship willing to take them on to Gibraltar – at a price. What happened then he didn't know, but since it was British, he presumed all would be well. He suspected Ian Garrow must be in touch with London perhaps by radio, but on reflection preferred to keep his efforts separate.

He summed up his new charges critically. Elegant, with the beautifully tailored suits, till one looked at their aggressive jaws and faces, undoubtedly not French. Too tall, too stocky, too scared, too belligerent. Suits could not entirely make the man. He glanced at their papers, signalling to the porter to put the consignment of dresses in their compartment, not in the guards van. He glanced at their papers.

'Yves Picard, Belgique – you speak French, Monsieur Picard?'

'*Un peu.*'

'Enough to deceive the Germans even with that accent?' he asked ruefully.

The man nodded confidently.

'Monsieur Picard, you are the courier for the fashion house of Maison la Ferté. You carry packages of dresses. You are a mute. You do not speak, *hein*?' Lucien told him firmly.

The other one did speak French, but had problems of a different sort. 'I didn't know I was going to have to be a bloody pansy dress designer,' he announced.

'Not all of us are pansies, my friend,' Lucien told him grimly. 'And which do you prefer: to be a dress designer, or a POW for the rest of the war? We all risk our lives to help you, *mon ami*. All you risk is POW camp. You should be proud to wear this suit.'

The man laughed shamefacedly. 'Something to tell the Rose and Crown, I suppose.'

They were left in peace for an hour before the Control came round. The sound he had learned to dread. '*Papieren, bitte.*'

The guard was with them when the door was thrust open, phlegmatic but watchful. The Germans riffled through their papers as Lucien handed them all over with a bored, '*Maison la Ferté, Paris et Cannes*', pointing to the baggage. '*Mon colleague Dupin, et un courier.*' Just the right touch of disdain.

All would have been well had not 'Dupin' sneezed.

'Bless you,' said his companion automatically.

'*Gesundheit*,' grunted the German at the same time.

'*Une blessure*,' said Lucien hastily. 'You are right, Picard. He is indeed sick.'

'*Blessure, c'est Krankheit*,' explained the guard speedily, officiously and erroneously. '*Très serieuse*,' and shut the door hastily.

The fourth occupant of the carriage, a thick-set farmer, gazed stolidly out of the window as though the presence of two impostors in the carriage interested him not a whit.

It was a year since Blitzkrieg had broken out across western Europe, 10 May 1940. Nell wondered idly if the Germans had remembered it too, as she switched off the wireless. They had been quieter recently. Perhaps at long last they were giving up the attempt to flatten London completely. Perhaps the RAF were winning their offensive against them. Perhaps Hitler would suddenly decide one small island wasn't worth bothering about when Russia beckoned so temptingly from the east.

It was on evenings like this that she most missed Bertie. Travel was so difficult that she only went to Merrifield once a fortnight. On the others, she made a despairing attempt to concentrate on Gadsby's future and make sense of conflicting departmental returns. It wasn't easy and tonight was going to offer no improvement as uneasily once more she heard the eerie wail of the siren. It seemed to reverberate in the pit of her stomach. Just when she was telling herself it was over.

She wearily gathered her belongings together to hurry to the shelter. Perhaps it would just be one quick token anniversary raid. It was not. It was too relentless to sleep, too concentrated to wonder if she might risk dashing to Gadsby's. She wished she'd done as she often did and slept at the store herself. At least then she'd know what was happening to it. True, her fire-watch was efficient. The few small incendiaries that had come their way since last September had been dealt with efficiently and swiftly. But still she worried. Other stores had suffered far more.

Tonight the bombers were coming in strength, that was clear. She was alone in the shelter she usually shared with her neighbours and the Horntons, who were out for the evening. She didn't envy them the task of fighting their way into a public shelter of the Underground. Unable to bear the suspense, she peered out. The sky was red all over London, the thunder of aircraft still continuing. It had told her nothing save that this was a major raid and she could do nothing but curb her impatience. The all-clear did not go until well into the small hours. Grabbing a jacket to throw over her shelter suit, she ran into the street, which seemed as full as if it were day – and as light from the flickering skies.

'Everyone got it tonight,' someone told her with relish. 'Westminster's hit hard.' Seeing an ARP badge she grasped the man's arm. 'Regent Street?' she asked anxiously. A shake of the head. She tried to tell herself that to the north-west the sky was not lit up, but it was. No need for masked torches tonight, but she had grabbed one anyway. No point in taking a car. She managed to get a lift to Park Lane, then ran through devastated Mayfair where every other house seemed to have been ripped apart by some giant hand in the last seven months. The acrid smell of fire grew stronger in her nostrils all the time. Gadsby's was still there when she arrived, but it was not the Gadsby's she had known. She saw it stand tall and proud among flames, which were being opposed by what seemed a woefully inadequate fire force.

The whole of the southern end of the building was well alight. Fighting her way through the watching crowd, she found Joe, face streaked with dirt and perspiration.

'Why are there so few engines?' she shouted at him in agony. 'And where's the water? Why aren't they doing something?'

He put his arm round her, half in comfort, half restrainingly, as if fearing she might rush into the flames. 'The pressure's low, Nell. They can't do anything. It's the Thames – the level's right down – and they're having to draw on it because central water mains have been hit in South London.'

She heard him but it meant nothing faced with Gadsby's imminent destruction.

'But the watch?' she cried. 'Why didn't they see the incendiaries and put them out before the fire took hold?'

He stared at her, his face suffused with anger. 'They tried to, Nell, though there were a hell of a lot of them. They might have managed it though – if it hadn't been for Holdsby.'

'Holdsby?' she whispered.

'He was here. He told the watch he'd alert the ARP to get the fire engines.'

'Well?'

'The fire people didn't get the message for half an hour – and then were told it wasn't urgent. It could have been the ARP at fault, but—' He broke off, seeing her face.

'It wasn't,' she said bleakly. I should have been here, I should have been here, drummed in her head ceaselessly.

It was another two hours before the fire was out, and by that time over a quarter of Gadsby's was a blackened mess.

'Open for business on Monday, Nell?' Gordon Holdsby strolled up to her as she turned away from thanking the firemen and surveyed the horror in front of her, darkened now that the fires were dying down.

'Why did you do it?' she asked dully, all strength ebbing from her.

He didn't even bother to ask her what she meant. She had too much pride to hurl at him, 'I helped you when you needed help.' It would merely go to feed his 'victory'.

'Because I've always hated you, Nell,' he told her pleasantly. 'And Gadsby's, too. I wish the damned lot had burned down.'

She stared at him as anger began to creep back into her, strengthening her. He should not get away with it. Gadsby's would not only survive, but flourish in its adversity. They'd show the world what Gadsby's could do, what London could do. She held her head proudly.

'Gadsby's will be open for business on Monday morning.'

Chapter Sixteen

The smell of smoke was everywhere; what hadn't been destroyed in the fire was permeated with it, and speckles of ash could be found even at the end of the store farthest from the blaze. Nell marched round Gadsby's with as many directors as could be gathered, like a general inspecting yesterday's battlefield. Only in this instance the real battle would begin today, Sunday. With no transport south or east, most of the staff would be unable to reach London, even if they were willing to try. Of those living west and north, who possessed a telephone, they had managed to contact about two hundred. They were unhesitatingly attempting the journey in, sacrificing their Sunday. Nell had arrived at first light, after two hours' sleep, to maximise salvage time. By eleven o'clock Peter and Joe had by a miracle organised damage assessors and demolition squads, and by even more of a miracle, winkled out builders prepared to devote the day to dividing the fifty per cent habitable part of Gadsby's from the totally destroyed and unsafe sections. Sebastian took a solitary tour of inspection, returned to a corner of the ground floor tucked behind Umbrellas and Scarves, and promptly began a departmental reorganisation plan.

Peter, in his element, ran his central organisation desk as efficiently as once he'd run his stall in Gray's Inn Road. Once the demarcation line of safe and unsafe had been declared, and partitions erected, he held court on the ground floor as one by one departmental assistants reported on smoke damage. Those with no departments left to go to – Coats, Shoes, Jewellery, Lingerie and Men's Wear – rummaged for salvageable goods through the mountain tossed unceremoniously by workmen into the middle of the floor affected. Worst hit were Coats, Men's Wear and Shoes, whose stockrooms had also been affected; the stock of the Coat Department had been totally destroyed.

Thank heavens it was May and windows could be flung open, thought Nell, leaning out from the Fashion Department window and gulping deeply. Not that the air outside was much better. Smoke still seemed to hang everywhere. In Westminster, the Houses of Parliament and Victoria Street had been badly hit. South of the river there was said to be terrible devastation, and roads out of the city were impassable. She turned back and went to help Angela with the sorting of their prized model dresses. She made a face as she smelt them.

'Perhaps it will wear off,' said Angela hopefully.

'Would you fancy it?' asked Nell, holding up a black tunic dress, and holding her nose delicately.

'No.'

'Then there's no help for it. We'll have to hold a smoke damage sale. Starting tomorrow. Let's get Sebastian up here.'

'But the replacements,' wailed Angela. 'There's virtually nothing left here worth selling, and the summer's coming on.'

'Then I'll have a word with Polly too,' said Nell cheerfully. 'Perhaps even Mrs E.'

'Smoke damage sale,' repeated Sebastian five minutes later, sipping a cup of so-called coffee. 'What would old Jonathan Gadsby have made of that?' Even for those who had never worked under him, Jonathan had become a legend. A legend that, had she but known it, his granddaughter-in-law was fast emulating.

'I reckon the old chap might have been in his element,' said Peter stoutly.

'Quality,' barked Nell, in affectionate imitation. 'We've got to maintain *quality*.'

'So we will,' said Polly, hurrying in to join them after having made arrangements for someone to look after her son. 'Nothing but the best smoke-damage.'

They had to laugh – there was precious little else to do save cry, thought Nell, contemplating their antlike efforts to repair their Everest of a mountain.

Gradually, however, some kind of order was established. The barricading wall to the unsafe part was tastefully decorated with anti-Hitler cartoons and posters. 'After all, we can't make it look anything other than it is,' Nell argued when doubts were raised. 'Why not make it even more obvious?'

The Smoke Damage counter was positioned ostentatiously by the front entrance, in order to reassure customers that inferior goods would not be sold in regular departments. Advertisements proclaimed a visit to the tea-room might be worthwhile with special attractions on the menu such as ginger cake and raisin bread. An enormous map tastefully executed by Sebastian and placed on a prominent board by the front and side entrances explained the new lay-out of the store. The Coats and Men's Wear Departments were temporarily abandoned, but Jewellery, Shoes and Lingerie were relocated to spare corners elsewhere. It all *looked* good and that was the main thing, she thought happily. Thank heavens for Sebastian's inventiveness in display. Such was the apparent wealth of goods on show, that few would guess the present barrenness of the stockrooms, and the horrors that faced the store in filling them up again. But that, Nell decided, weak with exhaustion and lack of sleep, was tomorrow's problem. For the moment, one last task remained.

At nine o'clock, as dusk fell, Sebastian and Peter clambered up builders' ladders outside to hang a huge banner over the main portico: 'Gadsby's Goes On'.

Nell walked slowly home an hour later, resolutely putting off all thought of the problems that would face them in the weeks to come, and luxuriating in their achievements of the day. Gadsby's would go on, Holdsby or no Holdsby, Hitler or no Hitler. And so would London. Despite all the horrors of the last winter, its spirit had not been broken, though many of its houses, churches, docks and shops lay in ruins. At least Paris had not had to face that. What had occupation brought for its people? Were they still resilient, or were they cowed into submission? she wondered.

And what of Lucien? Not a word of the Paris fashion scene – if indeed there still was one – ever reached London. Was he in Paris? In Cannes? In this silence, this battle, there was both death and hope. And she must choose the latter.

Lucien arrived at the Château de la Ferté, puzzled as to the reason for this fresh summons. True, it fitted in well with his plans. Since the spring the escape line des Truffes, as he had code-named it (since their cargo, like Nell herself, was precious) had carried out a further eight 'collections', on each journey accompanied by a new designer or courier. So far travel permits had proved no problem, no doubt because of the la Ferté name. Only when Philippe remarked, jokingly, of Lucien's new-found affection for Paris, did he finally decide to take his assistant Marguérite into his confidence. Eagerly she had successfully carried out the next 'collection', and two since then. Out of the blue, however, his father had summoned him to attend a family meeting at the château.

Immediately he reached Paris he had sensed a difference in the city, indefinable but there. The former air of sullen acceptance and resentment had changed. Now people looked you in the eye, even as they queued for the meagre and uncertain rations, controlled by the new Nutrition Service. On his journey to Paris he was always laden with suitcases full of food, often eyed greedily by others on the train. He felt like one of the many blackmarketeers; the food was not for his family – Philippe's good relationship with the occupying forces saw to that – but for the employees at the Maison. As he handed it out, he would feel guilty because for him in the south there were no such things as ration cards and rationing.

'*Mon fils.*' His mother was looking older now, for all her brave attempt to remain elegant, the perfect hostess. And yet because that was obvious he felt a rush of affection for her that he had not known before. He kissed her gently three times.

'*Lucien.*' His father appeared at the door of his room and they embraced, all the more warmly for what had passed at his visit to the château last autumn, nearly a year ago now. His father had not enquired what had happened to his charges, and for that Lucien was grateful. The fewer people who knew of his work the better.

'There is a change in Paris it seems, *mon père*,' he said tentatively. 'More confidence among our citizens.'

His father inclined his head. 'It was Colonel Fabien, my son. You heard?'

'He shot a German officer at a metro station,' Lucien said. 'Yes. And in retaliation, the Nazis shot seven innocent Frenchmen. An example *pour encourager les autres*,' he quoted wrily.

'Ah, yes, but not as the Germans intended,' said his father. 'They shot Communists, thinking that the execution of such people would prove an example to the people but not outrage them. But they were wrong. It has in truth encouraged the others. It has encouraged resistance. A way of fighting back has been found.' He glanced at his son. 'This is not a war as my war was. This war will only be won in France by individual commitment, the spirit of resistance. And now at last it has been born.' His face glowed with its old fire.

Lucien's face remained impassive as he fought the impulse to confide in his father. It seemed that what he was doing was not a small gesture by an isolated group of people, but if his father was right, part of a new movement that would grow and grow, and in the end prove unstoppable. A movement of which he was part.

At dinner his father, presiding over a more meagre table than hitherto, lovingly produced three bottles of Châteauneuf du Pape. His cellars had been emptied and its precious contents stored in a specially constructed cellar under the stables lest the Germans call at the château. So far they had been allowed to remain here undisturbed by the occupying forces, but one false move in Philippe's good working relationship with the Germans and this might be at an end.

'A toast, *mes enfants*.' He nodded towards his wife, then Philippe, Maria and Lucien. 'The Maison la Ferté and its future.'

A strange toast at this moment, thought Lucien as the velvet liquid slid down his throat, conjuring up memories of other happier meals here, of days gone by. The reason for it did not become apparent until after dinner.

'I have come to a decision,' the count announced sombrely. 'I am told by my doctor that my health will not improve and therefore I am retiring from *la Maison*.'

A sudden stillness from Philippe. Watchful, calculating. Obviously this was as new to him, as to himself, Lucien realised. Why hadn't he been told his father's health was giving cause for concern?

'*Mon père*,' he asked, troubled. 'You are ill? What is wrong?'

'My doctor informs me that my heart does not appreciate working in Paris at the moment. He tells me that curiously many people feel the same. I am luckier than most, however. I have two sons.'

'We cannot run the Maison la Ferté together, Papa,' said Philippe, smiling. 'One alone can have power, and as I—'

'*Oui, mon fils. Tu as raison.* And this is why I have called you together to announce my plans. I understand this will be hard for you, Philippe, but –' Philippe's face turned stony '– I wish you, Lucien, to come to Paris to run the Maison la Ferté.'

'*Quoi*? Impossible. Why do you so insult me, *mon père*?' Philippe was on his feet. '*I* am here in Paris already. Have I not done well?'

'Yes. But you, Philippe, are no businessman. You are an excellent designer and salesman, and your gift with customers is unsurpassed, but now a house such as the Maison la Ferté needs more than all these. It needs a businessman to steer it. You, my sons, will work together as you always have, for the good of the firm,' he finished firmly.

'I will not,' declared Philippe passionately. 'I have carried on working in difficult conditions in occupied Paris while my brother takes his ease on the Côte d'Azur. *I* have built this new clientèle for which my brother sees no need. And you call *him* a businessman? Expect me to work under him in Paris? For it is not possible for *me* to leave for a land of comfort,' he sneered. 'It would not be permitted by the authorities.'

Lucien fought for control, his mind whirling. To be head of Maison la Ferté was what he had always wanted – yet how could he do it? To him now his most important work was the escape line he had so carefully established, which was beginning to grow as its links became more widely known. The Ligne des Truffes too was a business, the business of winning the war. That should surely come before running a fashion house. How could he continue to run the line from Paris? He had thought his father half guessed what he did, but he must have been wrong. If he, Lucien, came to Paris, who would arrange the despatch of his 'parcels' in Cannes? Who look after them?

Yet to leave Philippe in charge at the Maison would not only be letting his father down, but also perhaps risking the safety of the line by increasing the risk of discovery. Already it was dangerous. With Philippe in complete control, the use to which the stockrooms were often put might be discovered. 'Parcels' now arrived there in blue overalls, and changed into beautifully cut suits for the journey south. Only François knew what was happening; if his staff noticed anything unusual, they ignored it. But under Philippe it might well prove a different story. Yet on balance, perhaps, that risk should be taken, for there was no one to take his place in the vital organisation of the onward despatch of his 'parcels' once they reached the south.

'Perhaps Philippe is right, *mon père*,' he began hesitantly.

'You are not brave enough to come to occupied Paris?' His father was deliberately taunting him, Lucien realised. He flushed angrily as Philippe gave a short angry laugh of triumph. 'My brave brother! See into whose hands you would have entrusted the Maison la Ferté.'

'Lucien,' said Maria stoutly, 'is by far the best suited to run the House. Perhaps he can run the whole business from Cannes?'

'What a devoted wife,' murmured Philippe.

'I work for Maison la Ferté,' retorted Maria, 'and I speak in its interests.'

'As an assistant designer,' Philippe reminded her, 'who has lost the flair that once she had.'

'And whose fault is that?' she rejoined.

'Perhaps because you exhausted it working behind my

back for other companies. Gadsby's – and perhaps others. Hardly in the best interests of la Ferté, would you say?'

Maria had never told Lucien that Philippe had guessed her connection with Gadsby's. There was a sharper rift than he imagined between the two then. No wonder she was so willing to help the line. But open conflict was not in anyone's interests. He opened his mouth to intervene, but his father forestalled him.

'Ça suffit,' the comte said sharply. 'I would remind you all that we are in the middle of a war. No matter what our private feelings, we must do the best for the future of couture, for the future of Maison la Ferté, for both reflect the future of la France. The House will continue to be run from Paris, and Philippe continue to work here. Lucien will move here and his assistant can run the Cannes branch perhaps with more frequent visits to Paris.'

'Very well, *mon père*, if this is your desire,' Lucien said stiffly, his mind racing. Not with thoughts of Philippe, whom he could handle, but of the future of the Ligne des Truffes. 'But I do so on one condition – my job at Cannes is close to my heart. Though its day to day direction may safely be left to Marguérite, I wish to oversee it personally. I would like you to arrange with the authorities for me to have permission to leave Paris when I wish, in order to ensure all is in order in Cannes. You may tell them, if you wish, that their wives would not thank them for not permitting my presence in Cannes from time to time. I have a certain popularity with them that Marguérite cannot hope to assume.' He tried to give this a distinctly sexual innuendo. After all, his father could not know his true monastic life-style. Monastic at least since the line began. Casual amours were too risky for him, any longer *affaire* too dangerous for the woman as well as himself. Not that there had been any of the latter since Nell's visit. Always at the back of his mind was a hope that one day they might be together again. A futile hope perhaps. But nevertheless it lived on.

'An affair of the heart, my brother?' Philippe asked casually afterwards, when their father had retired to bed. There seemed no hint of the earlier venom in his voice.

'As you say, Philippe, an affair of the heart.'

'You need not fear, Lucien,' he said after a moment. 'It is true I disapprove of Papa's decision, but I regret my outburst this evening. Naturally I will work closely with you to ensure the future of the firm. After all, it is in all our interests that we do so, is it not?'

He did not seem to require an answer. Relieved, Lucien was left to ponder the problems of the line and how it would be affected. At the moment he was at hand to make *ad hoc* arrangements with the *Lumière* as and when evaders were ready to leave Cannes. From now on, they would have to wait and be shipped in larger groups. Wait where, though? The Villa Fleurie was the only place, but was it fair to ask Madame Dufy to look after groups of men at a time? It needed thought, and if Marguérite no longer travelled to Paris so frequently, whom would he use?

'It is simple for me to travel south,' Maria told him eagerly on the morrow as, apparently by chance, she bumped into Lucien in the château gardens.

'No, Maria, you take too many risks already. I will not allow it.'

'But I will,' she said firmly. 'If my Cerberus allows it,' she said lightly, glancing up to a window in the château where Philippe looked down on them. Maria was his wife, his property – and a useful one at present with her Italian nationality. Even her flirtation with disloyalty over the Gadsby affair had been turned to his advantage. She would not dare do anything of the sort again. There was only the matter of an heir that remained to be settled.

'Why do you stay with him if you dislike him so?' Lucien enquired, hearing the note of disdain in her voice.

'Dislike? I do not *dislike* Philippe,' said Maria, surprised. 'but I take care his interests lie in keeping me with him. Take care that yours do also, Lucien. Even more, yours.'

'But still you stay with him?'

She could have told him of nights when Philippe loved her so passionately that all doubt was dispelled – until the morning light. But she did not. Philippe was her husband and the father of her children. She was a true Catholic, and what was done was done for ever.

War wasn't like a game of toy soldiers, with its line of cavalry pitched against line of glorious cavalry; war was battling with rations, queueing for food and endless, endless coupon counting. Clothes rationing had been brought in on 1 June, carefully announced so that staff could forgo their Whitsun bank holiday for two frantic days of preparing for the Tuesday. Every item from stockings to coats had to be labelled, at least initially, with the correct amount of coupons – the old unused margarine coupons at the moment, which caused added confusion. The Tuesday and Wednesday had been the busiest days Nell could remember, as, convinced that rationing would mean a shortage of clothes, women – and men – hurled themselves into a shopping orgy and confusion was the worse confounded through unfamiliarity with the number of coupons required. In fact, did they but realise it, clothes rationing had been brought in partly because there were too many clothes available. Cutting down supplies would mean the closure of factories. And closure of factories would mean more workers for munitions. Inevitable, but what was it going to mean for the factory owners? And, more urgently for Nell, what was it going to mean for Gadsby's? The board had held an emergency meeting after a week of rationing. Coming on top of their already improvised departmental system, it had been emergency indeed.

'And so farewell Sporting Wear Department,' Nell said finally. 'I'm really sorry, Jonathan –' doffing an imaginary hat to the portrait '– but people are only going to spend coupons on essentials.'

'How about hello, bigger department for "New Dresses for Old", with a section on converting old clothes to sportswear?' said Angela brightly. Her Fashion Department was well down on turnover because of the fire, despite the workroom's best efforts. Even the attraction of the Economy Department had not compensated sufficiently for the shortfall.

'It's going to be a struggle. We need some quick turnover,' said Joe, stating the obvious, flushing when everyone looked at him ironically.

'What do you suggest, Joe?' asked Polly, only a hint of impatience in her voice.

'Well, a . . .' Joe looked wildly round for inspiration '. . . a sort of Improvisation Department.'

'That applies to the whole of Gadsby's at the moment,' Polly pointed out scornfully.

'Wait,' Nell intervened. 'What do you mean, Joe?'

'I don't know,' he muttered, abashed.

Sebastian suddenly got interested, seeing an opportunity for his own talents. 'With a slogan, you mean? To tie in with "Gadsby's goes on". We could have a cartoon type figure – hey, like the opposite to Mr Chad. Instead of his peering over the wall saying "Wot, no . . .!" we'll have another one scampering about saying "Gadsby's Got the Answer".'

'Yes,' said Nell thoughtfully. Then more positively, '*Yes.*'

'But we won't always have the answer,' said Joe, puzzled.

'Then we'll tell them the answer is to do without,' Polly told him blithely.

'What about elastic for knickers?' Joe said doggedly, wondering why everyone collapsed with laughter.

'Kirby grips,' said Angela hastily. 'We could supply a suggestions sheet on how to make them. Sell the piano wire at the side.'

'Sugar and water for setting lotion,' said Nell, inspired, then laughed again as they turned on her, pointing out all they could sell would be the water!

'Then we'll publish a booklet of Grandma Gadsby's Helpful Hints there too,' she recovered quickly. 'We'll have a suggestion box by the front desk, for the public to contribute to it.'

Now, in the autumn of 1941, the scheme was in full flood, helped out by the purchase, wherever possible, of surplus service blankets, with the suggestion that these would make excellent swagger coats or dressing gowns. Quantities of curtain nets and muslins – coupon free – for underwear were going well. But the hard work was taking its toll and Nell found she was grateful for the earlier closing hours that had come in last week. They might cut down turnover but it gave more breathing time for hard-worked staff.

'I've got good news, Nell.' Polly popped her head round the door.

'It'll be the first this year,' she retorted. 'What is it? Are you and Joe getting back together again?' It was a constant wonder to Nell that they had managed to work together after Polly's return from Paris, even though their marriage had broken down.

'No, you romantic old thing.' Polly laughed. 'In fact, the contrary. Joe's finally agreed we might as well get divorced. We've been separated five years now.'

Nell pulled a face. 'I'm sorry, Polly.'

'Why?' she asked, surprised. 'I'm pleased.'

'Yes, but if I hadn't suggested you designed for us in the first place—'

'It's nothing to do with you, Nell. It would have happened one way or another anyway. Now, the good news is this. You know that collection by outstanding British designers that's been sent to South America to help exports? Well, some of them are hoping to get together under Hartnell to form a society of designers, and have approached me. And what's even better is that now I've also been approached to help design for a hush-hush government scheme for providing excellent designs at cheap prices, all of which will get a government approved label for good value.'

'Is this anything to do with the rumour that they'll soon bring in some kind of restriction on clothes – how much material can be used in skirts, narrower trousers and so on?' asked Nell with foreboding, seeing more problems ahead.

'I expect so. It's a sort of compensation for it, is my guess. Anyway, it will be fun for me. All the top designers have been asked. The really *top*!' she said, laughing. 'Hartnell, Amies, Digby Morton, Molyneux, Bianca Mosca – and Polly Simpkins. So I shall be doing my bit for the war effort after all,' she crowed.

'That's wonderful, Polly. I'm so pleased,' said Nell warmly.

'It will be good for Gadsby's too,' she said anxiously, lest Nell should think she was deserting the ship. 'Especially the New for Old Department. Oh, you should see some of the awful things they bring in. Do you know, Lady Lenham brought in a dreadful old mauve-coloured thing covered in bows, frills, black buttons and ribbons.'

'Not Number 21?' interrupted Nell delightedly.

'Pardon?'

'An old joke,' Nell giggled.

'Oh. Well, I re-designed it. It was so long it reached the

cellars, so I cut it to knee-length, used the material for drapery and ripped off the frills and furbelows. It really looks quite nice now.'

'I think we should put our prices up for a Polly Simpkins re-design,' said Nell, frowning. 'It doesn't seem right for you to do a whole design for thirty shillings.'

'The workrooms usually get the work, so Gadsby's earns extra there,' Polly pointed out. 'Anyway, I enjoy it. Mind you, I could do with some more help there than just my one assistant. How about we use another junior designer as well, and I oversee them?'

'Excellent.' And so it would continue, Nell thought. Endless adaptation, change, economies, making do. And now the winter was coming – but pray heaven not bringing the bombers again.

Spring shows at Maison la Ferté were not the excitement they had once been. Then they had been at the centre of the fashion world. Now the only people who would see the new dresses were the ones who could afford them: collaborators or Germans. Yet they had to continue as if nothing was different. It had not been as hard as Lucien had expected to work with Philippe – or to accustom himself to an odious clientèle. Philippe had been as good as his word – too good, Lucien sometimes thought uneasily. He devoted himself to design and customer relations, while Lucien took care of the business side. No problems getting hold of supplies. Wheels were oiled, restrictions waved aside – and for that he must thank Philippe. Nevertheless there was a fundamental difference between them. Philippe believed when this war finished they would be part of the Reich; Lucien believed that France would once more be free. So long as their beliefs did not directly clash, they would work together. After a few initial hiccups his escape and evasion line was operating well under the new regime. Perhaps even better, he told himself cautiously. Had his father known about his involvement with the Resistance? Sometimes Lucien suspected he had, but if so the Comte had said nothing – and that was the wisest way.

Although the Ligne des Truffes was operating smoothly now, there were dangers. One supposed evader had proved to be a German infiltrator, only spotted by the quick-wittedness of the safe house owner's son. They'd had to steel themselves to shoot him, but there was no alternative. Not in war. Since then Lucien had ordered vigorous interrogations of every 'parcel', and so far the line remained unbetrayed. But it was a warning sign that the Gestapo was aware of their activities, even if not of the details. Maria remained responsible for the running of the safe houses as far as Paris, and he for the onward transmission. Once or twice a month he made the journey to the south, and once a month Marguérite came to Paris. The Dufys looked after the 'parcels' in his villa, until the *Lumière* collected them once a month. They would gather on a beach outside Cannes, and be picked up by a local fishing boat to be taken out to where the *Lumière* was waiting. Then they would go first to Marseille, where they remained hidden, and then on to Algiers, under the couriership of a volunteer Cannes fisherman. So far the arrangement had continued to work perfectly, save for one occasion when through a misunderstanding the 'parcels' were waiting on the wrong beach. All was well for the moment, and that was as much as he could hope for. The future was a dark questionmark.

'*Bonjour*, François. The consignment is ready?'

'*Oui, monsieur.*' Uninterested grunt. The consignment of dresses was carried out to the van by a stalwart courier, in an ill-fitting suit, and an elegantly attired 'designer'. It was almost routine now.

But this particular journey was not. The train was packed and to his horror Lucien found they were sharing the carriage with two German officers, accompanied by their wives. One was instantly recognisable as one of their clients. No escaping the problem. He leaned forward: 'Frau Müller. *Enchanté*!'

A pleased smile. 'You recognised me. I told you, Fritz, about the Comte Lucien.'

The officer was genial. 'After more sales, are you?' he rumbled.

'Travelling to my Cannes branch with the consignment for the summer. My assistant,' he casually introduced his companions. 'Forgive him, he is Norwegian, speaking little French.' The other 'parcel', given time to think, promptly went to sleep. The 'Norwegian' spontaneously let fly a spate of guttural gibberish which should earn him a place on the comedy stage after the war, thought Lucien, heart pounding, hoping that neither officer had taken part in the Norwegian invasion.

The effort of keeping up a two-sided conversation with the Germans all the way to St Raphael where they left the train, and with his 'Norwegian designer', left him exhausted and the 'parcels' white-faced with fear. Thank heavens this was the night for the pick-up, and they would soon be as safe as possible in the circumstances. Safe of course, he thought ironically, save for treachery, mines and U-boats, or *Schnellboote* that decided to get suspicious.

He watched from the shore that night as the fishing boat picked up his six 'parcels' and moved silently out into the blackness of the Mediterranean. In a month or two they would be home in England once again. In London perhaps. Where Nell was. He turned back towards his homeland. How much longer?

Every day there seemed more bad news. Every commodity seemed in 'short supply' now, and that could only mean merchant ships weren't getting through, because they were being sunk. That and the need for more and more factory space for war material. In the Western Desert, the only place where anything seemed to be happening, it was happening for the worse. Tobruk had fallen, and although Auchinleck was making some kind of stand at a place called El Alamein, nothing seemed to be coming of it. It was at best stalemate.

'Bother,' Nell remarked crossly and inadequately, throwing aside the paper and going to the kitchens to inspect the progress of the Woolton Pie she had patriotically put together on Mr and Mrs Hornton's day off. She sat down in the kitchen to eat it, just as the doorbell rang. It was Bertie.

She had missed him since his marriage. Oh, how she missed his easy companionship – and his love. Sometimes he would drop round or take her out for lunch, sometimes he and Maureen would come over. But naturally it was not the same, though she had come to like the frank, rather rough and ready Maureen more and more.

'I'm eating in the kitchen,' she told him. 'Come and join me. I can find a glass of something to wash it down, but it's pretty revolting.'

He came in with alacrity, but wrinkled up his nose when he saw what it was. 'I'll stick to the wine, thanks, Nelly. That to me looks like a disaster cooked into a catastrophe.'

'I never claimed to be a cook,' she said crossly.

'You were always good at survival before. Your gifts seem to have deserted you.'

'Is this just a polite social call?' she enquired sweetly.

'No, I came to tell you Maureen's pregnant,' he said directly. 'Do you think that's irresponsible of me?'

'Oh, Bertie, I'm delighted,' she said spontaneously. 'And no, it's not irresponsible. Life goes on, war or no war. Even more important to have children.'

'That's what Maureen said. But I'm going abroad, Nell.

You'll read about it soon enough in the newspapers, so I might as well tell you now. Usual conditions?'

She nodded.

'Auchinleck is being removed as C-in-C in the Desert, and the plane that was carrying his successor, "Strafer" Gott, has been shot down. Anyway, he's dead. So they've appointed General Montgomery. Name mean anything to you?'

'He was a commander in France, wasn't he?'

'Yes. Not everyone's cup of tea, but different to Auchinleck, that's for sure. And the Army can do with a shake-up out there. Things are getting critical.'

That was an understatement. He knew just how disastrous the shipping losses were in the Atlantic. Singapore had fallen, together with Malaya, Hong Kong, Burma, and the Japs were threatening India. In Russia Hitler was sweeping on as yet unchecked. Even with the Americans in the war now, it looked bad. GIs and air force personnel were beginning to come in to Britain, but most US eyes were focused east, not yet west.

'Oh, Bertie, won't that be dangerous?' she asked fatuously, and then apologised.

'Yes. Not very, though. It's the chaps in the front line suffer – as a result of our decisions. That's the tough part.'

'What will Maureen do?' Nell asked, focusing on the practical.

He twiddled with a spoon. 'Her parents have been bombed out and are living with relatives; she doesn't see eye to eye with Bobsy and refuses to go to live with her, and I don't want her living alone, so—'

'You're asking if she can come and live here?' Nell asked, startled. She liked Maureen, but as for sharing a house . . . Then she was annoyed with herself for even hesitating for a moment. 'Of course she can, Bertie. It'll be nice to have a baby around the place again,' she said bravely. In fact she couldn't think of anything worse than a baby to cope with, especially if the Germans took up their bombing campaign again.

'Good.' He was pleased. 'I'll make sure it has my beauty and Maureen's brains.'

'I'll get an outsize cot.'

Maureen moved in the following week, and Hornton nearly moved out. Maureen was far too bouncy for his liking. Beaming and clumsy, she found it hard to adjust to the routine of the household, such as it was in wartime, and Nell had tactfully to explain that the Horntons' quarters were sacrosanct even in wartime. She was not to pop her head round the door and ask where they kept the coffee. Gradually a compromise was reached whereby Maureen had her own rooms in the house, with a stove installed and her own limited cooking equipment. She was still inclined to giggle when dining with Nell at Hornton waiting on them, thus upsetting his feelings. These occasions were rare, however, since she and Nell kept such different hours that they lived almost separate lives. In this way, they got on well throughout the winter. Maureen insisted on working up to Christmas, but in the end became so tired that she gave up in mid-November, to wait for the birth in February, spending much of her time reading newspaper reports of the progress of the war in the desert.

They had celebrated the news of El Alamein, Montgomery's victory in early November, by dinner at the Dorchester, since in the now unlikely event of an air-raid customers were allowed to sleep on the premises on mattresses supplied by management.

'I tell you what, Nell,' announced Maureen cheerfully, 'I reckon I could get used to this way of life after all. Never thought I would. I suppose I'll have to if I've got to live at Missinden some day.'

'Don't you want to?' asked Nell curiously, thinking of all the fun she'd had at Bobsy's house.

Maureen shrugged. 'I'm from Catford, not the country. It's a bit different to how Bertie was brought up.'

'*I* like Missinden and I'm from Bexleyheath,' Nell told her.

'Are you really?' Maureen asked in surprise.

'My father had a draper's shop there. Has, in fact. My brother runs it.'

'I always thought you were born with a silver mansion in your mouth.'

'Not me.' How long ago it seemed, thought Nell. She rarely saw her parents now. Try as she might, she could establish no real contact with them. It was almost as if she were a stranger. She had taken David to see them before he left for Wales, and they talked to him as politely as if he were fifty years old and the local mayor. Her brother had expanded the business to the upstairs rooms when their parents moved, and her parents now seemed prouder of this achievement than of Nell running Gadsby's, a fact in which they could never quite believe.

'Bertie's mum frightens me, I suppose. She's so different to mine.'

'So's Bertie,' Nell pointed out. 'They're much alike.'

'But Bertie's kind.'

'So's Bobsy in her way,' said Nell, nostalgically remembering their first meeting, and preparing to deal with the pain memory would bring in its wake.

'Bertie loved *you* once, didn't he?' Maureen said suddenly. She had never mentioned it before.

'Once,' said Nell steadily. 'But it's long over. You do believe that?'

'Yes,' said Maureen. 'I do now. I was never sure. But when I told him I was pregnant, *then* I knew he loved me. Gosh, look, there's cream on this pudding.'

It was also in the November of 1942 that the Allies landed on the coast of North Africa, and the Germans promptly marched in to occupy the south of France. For Lucien everything changed. In the previous six months the activities of the line had expanded at Maria's urgent insistence. He had wanted to be more cautious. By their present methods they could now escort a maximum of eight evaders a month to comparative safety. It was not enough. They could take more – if the 'parcels' travelled independently on the trains as foreign workmen. Then Maria pointed out they need not even travel through the premises of the Maison la Ferté. With workmen's outfits they could travel straight from the safe house with a courier to the Gare de Lyon and meet Lucien or another courier there. They would travel separately, and meet at Cannes or Marseille.

Lucien didn't like the idea for some reason. The running of the safe houses was becoming twice as dangerous, with the whole of France now occupied. It was even more tempting for neighbours to report suspicious movements. Sometimes as many as twelve servicemen gathered at the Villa Fleurie. It was too many and too dangerous, however careful the instructions he gave about the amount of refuse that left the house, the number of times the toilet was flushed, the amount of food Madame Dufy bought at the market.

The occupation provided another major problem too. The Toulon Naval Fleet scuttled itself rather than become German, and with Toulon port under German control Lucien could no longer contact the *Lumière* lightship; in any case the *Lumière*'s visits to Algiers were now abruptly halted. In this sudden emergency he had been forced to pass his last collection of parcels on to the O'Leary line in Marseille who used the Pyrenean escape route and was in touch with London. It had been difficult, for naturally they were suspicious, and for one moment he thought he would get a bullet in his back for his pains. Checks with London had established the bone fides of his parcels and of himself and all had been well, but he did not wish to continue using this route. He was urgently waiting now to hear what London might propose for the future. He gathered they had an agent in Gibraltar to look after evaders and his hopes were high, much as he disliked control being removed from his hands.

He still wondered occasionally whether he was right to have stayed in France, whether he should have gone to London and worked for the Free French. But it was the temptation of Nell that beckoned there not reason. He knew he was more valuable here. Each returned airman told Britain that there were still good patriots in France, that she was worth saving. It was little, but it was something, and worth the risks. Though how much longer he could maintain the disguise of junior designers and couriers accompanying him, he did not know. True, the Maison la Ferté employed junior designers and couriers, but so many different faces? And did they constantly need to be on the move? Luckily the guards on the train were mostly true Frenchmen. Not by a blink of an eyelid did they reveal that anything was out of the ordinary.

Spring at last and with it more good news. Hitler had met his match at Stalingrad this last winter, and now, in May 1943 it seemed the Battle of the Atlantic might be nearing its end.

'Good,' said Maureen practically, when Nell read out the headlines. 'We might get some decent orange juice at last. Or at least by the time Bernadette's grown up.' Despairingly, she put the bottle in the baby's mouth once more, and the usual tantrum followed.

'What do you do with a baby who doesn't like milk?' Maureen wailed.

Nell laughed. 'Give it to me. I'll have a go.'

Bernadette, as Maureen insisted on calling her, had been born in February. She was anything but a saint, however. The birth had been easy but to make up for it she had made life hell for them both ever since. Maureen was not a natural mother, over-anxious and over-panicky. Nell was therefore often awakened in the middle of the night by an exhausted Maureen shaking her violently, crying, 'What do I do now? She won't stop screaming.'

She was beginning to feel like screaming herself, but obediently hauled herself from bed to try to help.

David had come home for Easter and was far from impressed to find a baby installed. Africa was much more exciting.

'When this war's over, Mum,' he cried excitedly, 'can we go to Africa? I'd like to see El Alamein.'

'When this war's over, David, we'll go to Timbuctoo, if you like,' laughed Nell. 'Anywhere, just to get away from London.' Especially France . . . The end of the war was not even remotely in sight, but it was something to hope for.

Bertie had not managed to get home for the birth, which was a great disappointment.

'They've kicked Rommel out of Africa now,' said Maureen mutinously. '*Why* can't he come home?'

'I expect they're planning the next stage,' said Nell.

'Italy, I suppose,' said Maureen gloomily. 'That's what the buzz was would come after Africa when I was in the War Office.'

'Not Greece?'

'Nope. Italy. You know, Nell, it's all the worse now they're winning, in a way,' she burst out. 'It's not so easy to be patient.'

As if in complete agreement, Bernadette began to scream again. With a sigh, Nell picked her up, while Maureen studied the newspaper.

'*Tu pars aujourd'hui*, Lucien?' Philippe came into his brother's office with a concerned look on his face.

542

'*Oui.*'

'It is most unfortunate,' frowned Philippe, 'for today *le ministre* comes to approve our autumn designs for quality of fabric and price. Naturally he has to see you. I am not able to take responsibility for this. I could ask him to postpone his visit, but it will not look well.'

Lucien looked at him sharply. It could not be postponed, and Philippe knew it. One did not postpone *le ministre*, but why had it been arranged for today? He could not enquire and draw Philippe's attention to his annoyance. If Lucien refused to stay, Philippe could rightly claim Lucien was prejudicing the interests of the Maison by putting Cannes first. There had been several such small tricks recently; always in the past he had foreseen them and managed to avoid them. This time there was no escape. He had to think and act quickly. He had been a fool to think Philippe had ever given up his ambition to run the business; sooner or later he would make a major move to do so. Meanwhile he could only try to continue forestalling it.

'Naturally I can travel tomorrow,' he told Philippe smoothly. 'I will make arrangements. Cannes can wait a day for me.' It couldn't, but he wasn't going to tell Philippe that. By now, a new routine had been established. The gallant *Lumière* had left its base at Marseille to defect to the Free French in Algiers, and its captain had arranged with a less well-known ship to make a monthly pick-up from the Bay of Cannes.

'I thought you mentioned that the dresses had to be there by tomorrow, however?' Philippe asked him. 'This concerns me. I wonder if we can find a courier in the stockroom to take them for you. Shall I enquire?'

'It is urgent, true,' Lucien was forced to admit. 'But I will talk to Cannes. I am sure they can wait a day.' Anything to get Philippe out of the way so that he could think.

As soon as he had gone, Lucien hurried to find Maria, praying there would be time to stop the 'parcels' leaving their safe house. He found her at last in the warehouse, checking the inventory of models to leave for Cannes.

'Lucien, it is not possible,' she cried, alarmed. 'They will already have left.'

'They must go back,' he said peremptorily.

'*Impossible*,' Maria said. 'It is far too dangerous, and their travel papers are for today.'

'But who can accompany them, Maria? They cannot go alone. Can you find someone?'

She considered, and a wide grin came to her lips. 'Yes,' she said, 'I will go myself.'

'*Non!*' Lucien's face darkened. '*Absolument pas*! What would Philippe say?'

'He will say nothing,' she said coolly. 'I will leave a note for him to say, honestly, that I have always wished to see the Cannes office, and so I am going instead of you, so you can stay with the minister. I have often told him that I wish to go to Cannes. The children have a splendid nurse and there is no problem. I will return tomorrow.'

'I do not like it. You must not go.'

'You cannot stop me, Lucien,' she told him, amused. 'I make my own decisions. I am a big girl. Also, I am Italian. I can travel freely. Remember?'

Locked in discussions with the minister, Lucien heard no more from either Maria or Philippe. After all, he tried to reassure himself, she would sail through the controls more easily than he did himself. And yet . . . and yet . . .

It was three o'clock when the minister departed and almost at once Philippe burst into his office. 'I have terrible news,' he told Lucien, sitting down heavily on a chair, his face sombre.

'*C'est notre père? Maman?*' Lucien asked sharply.

'Maria.' Philippe's voice broke and he hid his head in his hands.

Lucien fought to control his panic, his worst fears confirmed. 'She is ill?' he asked with alarm. There's something wrong, she should not have gone, hammered at him.

'It is some terrible mistake, of course. I shall go to the Avenue Foch immediately. Tell them who she is. Who I am.'

Lucien leapt up. Avenue Foch? The Gestapo HQ? 'Tell me.' He shook Philippe like a terrier until he pulled himself free, a glint of satisfaction on his face – or was he imagining things?

'Please, brother. I know you are worried about Maria, how fond you are of her, but such concern! Let me explain. It seems she has been arrested for helping two Allied servicemen to escape on the Cannes express. Such an extraordinary thing. Such a terrible mistake. It will naturally be sorted out. But you will forgive me if I leave the Maison early – I must do my best for Maria right away.'

Lucien choked back his words. He must think logically. He watched Philippe go out, apparently a man distraught. But was he? This seemed no accident – Lucien himself kept here at the last moment, Maria going on a dangerous journey in his place. It was a trap. Yet how could it have been? Philippe could not have planned that she would travel instead of his brother, even if he suspected both their involvement in Resistance activities. He would not know until he read her note written just before she left. Did he take advantage of the moment? No, this was a plan – to keep Lucien here. A double trap. But how did Philippe know of Maria's involvement? A terrible thought occurred to him. He picked up the telephone, and asked to be connected to the warehouse. 'François Lepard, *s'il vous plaît*,' he barked.

'*Pas ici, Monsieur le comte.*'

'Where is he?'

A pause. 'We do not know, monsieur.'

Slowly Lucien hung up. A small thing, he might quite naturally be out of the stockroom. But it was strange. Perhaps this was indeed a terrible accident for Philippe. Perhaps he had found out about his brother's involvement in the line, but how could he have planned that Maria would go in his place? Because he knew the consignment was urgent and he knew his wife, came the answer. Naturally she would tell him she was going, and he would have informed the Gestapo. Even if someone other than Maria went as courier, the betrayal of the line would be accomplished. With François' help. But why? Why endanger his own wife?

A thought so terrible came to Lucien that he first banished it, then reluctantly recalled and reconsidered it. Yes, Philippe's wife, the mother of his children, but a wife who had produced only daughters. Not the son Philippe so craved. If there were no more Maria, he could marry again. Yet surely no man, least of all his younger brother, would do such a thing? Or would he? Lucien began to feel sick as he reasoned further. Philippe craved to run the business, he craved to inherit their father's title. He would get it if Lucien had no son. No one knew about David, even if he could be legitimised, and Philippe would get the title sooner if he, Lucien, were removed . . .

No, this was craziness, craziness . . . even to imagine that Philippe would send his wife to what might be imprisonment – no, certain death. But was it so crazy? Maria would never divorce him . . . he would not try to save her . . . and as an Italian she would be shot for treason. And if you accepted Philippe could do that to Maria, then to what lengths would he not go to rid himself of a brother?

Lucien moved swiftly to the window and glanced down into the street . . . a Citroën outside, and not the one Philippe was so proud of having arranged with the Germans to continue to run. This one had all the familiar trappings of the Gestapo. Even now a second car was arriving, and the occupants of the first must be approaching . . .

He swallowed, trying to separate reality from fantasy. Then he knew: *this* was truth. In a flash he ran from his office, along the corridor, up a flight of steps to the end of the building. Here a fire escape led to the roof across the roofs of the adjoining houses in the Avenue Montaigne. He ran like a hunted animal, keeping well back from the road side of the roof. Reynard the fox – he was hunted, but he had the cleverness of the fox itself. He knew Paris, as his pursuers did not. But where to go? He could make for the château, ask the same sanctuary as the servicemen – no, that would involve his parents, tell them of Philippe's treachery, and that he would never do. Besides, there were others to think of. Suppose torture had forced Maria to talk? He shuddered, but it had to be thought of. If he could get to the safe house in Ville d'Avray, he might be able to warn Monsieur and Madame Chabrais before the Gestapo reached them. But first he must make sure he had shaken off his pursuers.

He ran down the fire escape of what he calculated must be the Maison Matigne, the premises of a rival couturier at the far end of the Avenue and almost at the Place Alma Marceau by the river. Coolly dusting himself down, he walked in and marched down the stairs like a visitor just leaving, strolling past the commissionaire who stared at him incuriously. Lucien de la Ferté was well known in the Avenue. Glancing briefly left, he was aware of activity further up the street outside Maison la Ferté. He'd been missed.

He turned briskly right towards the *quai*. Across the Pont d'Alma? No, any pursuing car would see him. He turned upriver, crossing to well below road level by the river itself. The throb of an engine roared past him across the Pont d'Alma. He hurried on, across the beautiful Pont Alexandre III, just an elegantly suited man, like so many others in Paris this spring day.

Once across the river, where wealth was not so apparent, he felt conspicuous. He doubled back along the Quai d'Orsay, anxious to leave this exposed road. He turned into the Rue Soucouf in order to feel safer with tall houses on both sides, then right into the Rue St Dominique and then left again. He was in the Rue Amelie; in the *quartier de gros cailloux* as they called it, after the church built with unusually large stones, he remembered inconsequentially. Church? Sanctuary? No, the sound of a car engine made him dive into a small café full of blue-overalled workmen who stared at him curiously. He strolled to the bar and calmly ordered a broth, rough and unappetising but better than what was served as coffee nowadays. He felt curious eyes boring into his back and began to chat with the woman behind the bar. Through a curtain he could see a thin blue-overalled man sitting at a table in the owners' private rooms. An idea came to him. He leaned across, confidentially to the woman behind the bar and whispered. He must take a risk. A gleam came into her eye.

She went through to talk to her husband and returned after a few moments. He found his heart was pounding. Whom to trust? Whom to fear? 'Go out,' she told him. 'Round to the back entrance. Take care you're not seen.' He finished his soup and strolled out again.

Five minutes later two men left the rear of the café, wheeling a barrowload of coal. Both wore rough trousers, overalls and caps. 'The Boche take all our coal,' grunted one, spitting elegantly into the gutter. 'Before they came, this café had a good business delivering coal. Now, this is the first load for three months. I am glad to help you, monsieur, suit or no suit. But I am grateful to you for the gift. I will wear it when the Boche goes.'

Lucien, his face bedaubed in coal grime, nodded his thanks and dived off into the metro. So far so good. Heart in his mouth he boarded the Billancourt metro squashed up with hundreds of his compatriots. No first class for Frenchmen. He exited at the terminus and began to breathe more easily as he began the walk through recently bombed streets to Ville d'Avray. With luck he might warn the Chabrais and disappear with them into the unknown labyrinth of secret France.

But luck was not with him. When he got to the neat villa, it was the Gestapo, not the plump, friendly Madame Chabrais who welcomed him in.

'Come, Comte Lucien,' the Germans were always formal, 'let us test your memory once more . . . If it remains as feeble, you will be of no use to the Reich. You might as well be shot. Like your colleague.'

Colleague? François? Madame Chabrais?

His head sagged. The Gestapo's actions were not so polite as their words. Finally they lost patience as he fainted in pain, and dragged him back to his cell.

'Tomorrow morning they will shoot François,' a voice shouted above his head through the mists of pain. 'You may watch him leave if you wish and call out a parting message. It may refresh your memory.'

When morning came he would not look as they wanted him to. Then he heard François calling to him: '*Monsieur le comte*!' How could he refuse a last message? Painfully Lucien dragged himself to the tiny window of his cell overlooking the yard, lying on the floor, the only way he could see out of the tiny aperture. François did indeed stand there, but unshackled, unbound. It was Maria who marched proudly to her death at Fort Mont-Valérian.

'Maria!' Lucien let out a long drawn-out cry of pain and horror as she turned, seeing his face twisted in agony behind the bars. She managed a semblance of a smile, and he pleaded, 'Forgive me.'

'No,' she called. 'Hey, Lucien, this is *mine*. Wouldn't Nell be proud –' they dragged her away, but she still managed to shout '– that I've made my beautiful thing, eh?' She threw back her head and laughed. She was still laughing as they bundled her into the van.

They did not shoot Lucien. They had no wish to create a martyr by shooting a member of France's aristocracy, they told him. The Italian, now, she was different. She was a traitor to her country, Germany's good friend. As for Comte Lucien, it was convenient there was transport leaving today. He could join a party of Jews who would be leaving for light work in Germany, so that he could have the honour of carrying out his *Service de Travail Obligatoire*, which he had hitherto been excused, in the Fatherland itself. He was fortunate, was he not?

Chapter Seventeen

Austerity Britain indeed, Nell grimaced. Poor old Danzy, Beesknees and Ample would have had a fit if they could have seen Gadsby's Fashion Department today, in the early-autumn of 1943. Every tenet held immutable in their day had been turned on its head by war. Simplicity was now patriotic and fashionable, ostentation downright vulgar. Making do was patriotic – buying new clothes was not. In the old days, quality not quantity had reigned supreme at Gadsby's and here it could still triumph over its neighbours, with the aid of coupon rationing. A fair system but in the end it proved to work in favour of the better-off and against those who struggled for a living. If one was spending eleven coupons for a dress, why not spend in money as much as one could afford? A well-made, top quality garment would last, whereas further down the economic scale, one would still hand over eleven coupons, but cheaper dresses might only last months instead of years.

It was just as well, from Gadsby's point of view. They were still working with only half their former floor space; some of the minor bomb damage was being slowly repaired but most was abandoned till rebuilding should be possible. There was little spare space for an abundance of stock, even if the latter had been easy to obtain.

The Fashion Department with its Gadsby-designed ready-made dresses, coupled with the Utility Department (as War Economy had been renamed when the

Government-inspired Utility designs came on to the market), were still the centre of Gadsby's, albeit the racks of dresses and cramped quarters in no way resembled the store that Jonathan Gadsby had first created. Only the exclusive model department was allowed the luxury of space, and even that was scaled down drastically in proportion to its turnover. Polly's beautifully cut tailored dresses were displayed to full advantage, together with matching hats (again for the better-off, since most women had forsaken hats for headscarves) and in the middle a wedding dress. Most weddings now were hurried affairs, often in register offices, and those who were set upon the traditional approach often hired or borrowed dresses from friends. Thus it had come about that in addition to several dresses for sale, Gadsby's also ran a discreet wedding dress hire service.

'Poor, poor Jonathan.' Mrs Emmeline had shaken her head in sad disapproval of this, to her, extraordinary step. But then, at Merrifield, she did not know how London struggled. And how long would that struggle continue? Forever it seemed to Nell, as winter approached once more.

Despite the shortages, despite the neverending battle of daily life, no one really doubted now that in the end the war would be won by the Allies. But then what would happen? she wondered, The Government could hardly wave a wand like a fairy godmother, and declare that everything would immediately revert to pre-war conditions. The turmoil might be worse than after the First War. Rationing would surely continue but expectations would grow.

Maureen popped her head inside Nell's office door. Now that Bernadette had attained the venerable age of seven months, Maureen decided it was time to do her bit for the war effort. At Gadsby's for preference. Mrs Jolly had declared that her legs were playing her up and it was time she took things easy, and so, with Bernadette in a cot, Maureen now ran the tea-room, running a fine line in chocolate fancies and ginger parkin.

'Letter from Bertie today,' she announced. 'Somewhere in Europe, of course. As if we don't know. Italy, of course.' The moment the Allied landings on Sicily had been announced in July, they had guessed where he was, and now General Alexander had pushed across the Straits of Messina to the toe of Italy.

'I've always wanted to go to Italy,' Maureen said lightly. 'I bet, knowing Bertie, he'll be wandering round Pompeii, forgetting all about the war.'

Nell tried to laugh. 'Probably that's exactly what he's doing. The Italians have asked for an armistice.'

Maureen brightened. 'That's good, isn't it?'

'Yes, if the Germans . . .' Nell bit back the thought that promptly entered her head – that if she were Hitler she'd be ordering the panzers to start their engines right away and head down into Italy to take over where the Italians had bowed out.

Maureen glanced behind her as someone approached. 'Well,' she said brightly, 'I'll be going.'

Somewhat surprised at her hasty departure, Nell rapidly realised the reason when Gordon Holdsby entered. Speechless, she gazed at him in amazement. She had to endure him still at the occasional family gathering, but an invasion of her office was too much.

'Not a social visit, Nell,' he told her, blandly aware of her reaction and sitting down uninvited. 'Business.'

Her eyebrows shot up. 'Between Gadsby's and Matthews?' she asked pointedly.

'Yes. We've decided to concentrate on our Oxford Street store. We're giving up in Regent Street.'

'And?' she asked quietly, her mind racing. So Matthews' business was faring badly. So much for taking Gadsby's trade away, she thought triumphantly, not bothering to utter hypocritical expressions of regret. Cheap clothes (shoddy would be a more accurate word) under wartime conditions had failed to attract a Regent Street trade.

'You might want the lease,' he told her. 'There are others who would, but I am a businessman first and foremost. Whether I like it or not personally, I have a duty to my board, and Gadsby's is the most likely to want it most now you're deprived of so much floor space.'

Thanks to you, she wanted to hurl at him, but did not. It sounded a wonderful opportunity, but – beware the Greek bearing gifts.

'You have the details? I will put it to my board, Mr Holdsby.' She could not bring herself to address him by his Christian name. As he had said, this was business.

'Rent on a five-year lease, plus a premium of £100,000 to us for taking it over.'

She laughed. 'Austerity, Gordon, and that applies to general business as much as it does to food shops.'

'We might be prepared to negotiate for a quick answer.'

Things really must be bad, she realised with quickening interest. She mulled it over that evening and called a board meeting for the following week.

'It would give us the room we need and stop us falling over each other, and on such a short lease, it might suit us well until we rebuild. But the premium is ridiculous on top of rent.'

'Offer sixty per cent,' Robert Galt told her, doing rapid sums on his pad, 'conditional on bank approval,' he added hastily.

'Very well.' She hesitated. 'I think, however, the negotiation might go more smoothly if someone other than I were to handle it.'

She was well aware that however brave a face he might put on it, Gordon Holdsby was not going to forget he'd been forced to kowtow once more to Nell Gadsby.

Was there another life? Had there ever been? A life in carefree Paris? A life with Nell? Too far away, too painful to think of now. All the mind could do here was try to plan how to get through each day. There were always ways of survival. The catch was how far to go and still remain a human being. At what point did one say: This I will not do?

Prisoner No. 102387 F did not expect to live. He realised that he could be said to be fortunate, for those over forty should automatically have been pushed into the death queue. At the time he had not realised that that was what it was, but now he knew only too well. Somehow he had been steered into the queue of those fit to work for the Third Reich. Perhaps when he entered Auschwitz he did not look his forty-odd years, perhaps the Gestapo or the French police in Paris had ordained something different for him, though why he could not imagine. One way or the other he had been sent here to end his days in this vast prison, forty separate camps within one enormous enclave. '*Arbeit macht frei*' was emblazoned over the huge gates of its entrance, the first thing he'd seen when the train at last juddered to a stop to discharge its cargo of dead, dying and those about to die. More shouting, rifle butts to push them into groups, queues, then into showers, a number on his arm, realising he must stay aware of what was happening or he too might join those others. He did not know their fates but subconsciously he noted that the elderly, women and children were automatically weeded out. For special care, they said, as the pathetic, crying, confused groups left for the neighbouring camp of Birkenau; those who couldn't be expected to endure the tougher conditions of the SS work commandos. But the thin black smoke trails and whispered comments told a different story. Only the youngest and fairest of the women were reprieved.

He had no name now, he was only a number. Those on hard labour got better rations than other inmates, if you could call two bowls of thin gruel a day good rations. At first fantasies of Parisian meals would fill his mind, but not now. Now gruel was as good as a *coq au vin* for it signified a means of survival. Through lack of food and hard labour he had lost weight to the point where he was sometimes too weak to hold a pick. Today his neighbour had seized his and broken stones for him, pushing it back into his feeble hands as the SS came by. Soon they would notice and he would die. Now he no longer had the strength to talk. You worked, you ate, you slept, and somewhere deep inside this deteriorating body you lived, buried, stifled, alone. You tried not to notice thinning ranks, missing faces of which all too soon you would be one. Somewhere in this camp, he told himself at first when he still had strength, there must be a resistance movement. Those on heavy labour, however, had not the strength to seek it out. Besides, what could it achieve? There was no escape from Auschwitz, save by death.

The prisoner was aware his number was being shouted at the door of the hut that was 'home' – just in time, for lack of immediate response could mean a flogging, or hanging by the hands for an hour. He concentrated on staying on his feet and walking unaided to the door. If this was the path to the gas chamber then he would walk it upright. If not, he needed to prove that he still had strength. His dulled eyes registered, as he walked between the two SS guards, that it was the Political Office to which he was being brought – the euphemistic term for the building used by the Gestapo.

Again his number was hurled at him like a question. '*Oui.*' '*Verstehen Sie Deutsch?*' '*Oui.*' 'De la Ferté, L.' '*Oui.*' Strange how his own name sounded less familiar than his number now. Why was he here? For death? Had Philippe discovered he was still alive? So be it.

'*Ja, mein Herr.*' Automatic answer.

'*Franzosisch?*'

'*Ja.*'

So it was not to do with Philippe, this summons. Nor was it to death. A grunt and he was jerked aside to make way for the next number, and into the Political Office's general workroom.

Forty pairs of eyes looked up as he entered, prisoners' eyes, mostly dulled but some curious – the first sign of life he had seen in a prisoner's eyes since he entered Auschwitz. Even in his weak state he wondered why, and then realised he could find out. If he were to remain here, it would mean no more hard labour. Here he would work in an office – the Gestapo office. There might be something he could do to help other prisoners, however small.

He had been in the office two weeks, working on hospital records, when he became aware that there was more going on in this office than the Gestapo knew about. Here there were Communists working, homosexuals, Czechs, Poles, even Jews. And he was gradually conscious that some of them were watching him, almost it seemed summing him up. He too was more able to think, now his body, though weak, was not broken by hard physical labour day by day.

He was thinking about the strange Nazi mentality, of keeping meticulous records of every operation, of their even having a *Revier*, a hospital at all, when life was so cheap. True, anybody in it longer than six weeks was automatically sent to the gas chambers, but for others, a clean sickroom was provided, with doctors, nursing staff and limited supplies. It was noticeable, however, there were few Jewish patients. Apart from in the notorious Block 10, of course, over which a veil of secrecy was drawn, and where patients – apparently healthy patients – seemed to live for weeks on end. Only the hospital records before him gave some kind of clue: *casus explorativus;*

castratio, or sometimes *sterilisatio*. What this might mean, he refused to allow his mind to speculate. He was not yet able to contemplate its implications. For the moment he needed energy to concentrate. For the first time, it occurred to him that his own survival might be possible. Not survival just for the day, but survival, somehow, until this camp was liberated by the Allies. As someday surely it must be. If one had a brain, it might be possible to go on living – and try to help others do so too.

Kent still seemed one vast fortified war camp. For months before 6 June, fields had been crowded with tanks, and specially built air fields had sprouted all over the county. Civilians naturally were not allowed near – which was fortunate because many of them were dummies. Despite the fact that the invasion when it took place was launched from the South Coast, and did not touch Kent, everything still remained in place. Curious, thought Nell, struggling against the odds to reach Merrifield. Now that the Allies had broken out from Normandy, perhaps troops would start moving from Kent, she thought, and so it proved. Dummies disappeared and the county crawled with servicemen, troop trains and RAF. Especially the RAF, which had a more immediate task than giving cover to the advancing forces. Once again its prime object in Kent was home defence, with the advent of the first of Hitler's Revenge weapons, the flying bomb, of which he had despatched the first one week after D-Day and never stopped. Kent and London were the worst sufferers, but this weekend, come what may, Nell was determined to be with Mrs Emmeline on the anniversary of Jonathan's birthday, an event she insisted on celebrating with a gathering of his family.

It meant she'd have to converse politely with Gordon, Nell realised gloomily. Fortunately she still got on well with Rose, albeit somewhat guardedly on both sides. It was all the more important for her to go since David, who with ill-conceived timing had come back to London for the summer, was anxious to see Merrifield again. 'After all, Ma,' he pointed out with logic, 'it's no worse in Kent than here, is it? So we might as well go.'

Merrifield House was by no means the hive of army activity it had been. Most of the battalion was in France, and only a few officers were still in residence at Merrifield. Mrs Emmeline had settled down in the lodge, however, and was sitting in its small garden when Nell arrived. Thanks to Mr Hopkins, the garden was tidier than those of Merrifield, and in this peaceful setting it was almost possible to forget the war.

'How I wish dear Jonathan was here. He would have loved this,' Mrs Emmeline pronounced to Nell, watching David manfully suggesting to his cousins, with whom he did not get on, that the four of them try a game of rounders.

Rose's ingenuous face clouded at the mention of her grandfather's name, but her husband glanced quizzically at Nell.

'Perhaps Nell would not share your wish,' he murmured.

A moment's shocked silence, then before she could reply they heard the sound of aircraft engines – and not Spitfire Merlins. That distinctive, not to be mistaken, sound. 'Shelter!' shouted Holdsby, leaping up and grabbing Rose. 'No. The children,' she screamed at him.

Almost in a dream, knowing that that noise might stop directly above them, as the Doodlebug engine cut out and that then they would only have eleven seconds before the explosion, Nell rushed to where David had last been seen. He was gazing up at the sky with every appearance of interest as she grabbed his arm.

'See that?' he panted, as she rushed him towards the

house, deeming the Morrison shelter inside to be the safest place.

As they reached the back door of the lodge, the noise stopped as an engine cut out above them. Almost as soon as she realised this, Nell took in that Mrs Emmeline was not with them. Agonised, she had no choice. She pushed David under the shelter, then heard it in the silence, the sound of the lavatory cistern above, and groaned. Mrs Emmeline was not going to be inconvenienced by a mere doodlebug, that was clear. Eleven seconds, eleven seconds. If she could reach Mrs E . . . But David was suddenly at her side again, taking matters into his own hands, dragging her under the heavy metal shelter as the world caved in around them in a rumbling of noise, rubble and dust showering around them, imprisoning them. A singing in her ears, a roaring, then nothing until she heard David's voice at her side, terrified, tentative.

'Mummy?' He hadn't called her that since he was eight. 'Mummy?'

'I'm all right, David. You?'

'Yes. It's black.'

He was right. She could hardly see him and yet it was only five o'clock. They were cocooned in a heap of brick and stone. Heartened, David regained his initiative. 'I think,' he told her importantly, 'I can see light through here.' And began to push.

'Careful,' she said automatically before realising how stupid that was. They had to get out. Yet suppose the roof caved in? Was there still a roof, in fact? Sudden claustrophobia seized her and she crawled to David's side to help him scrabble and claw at the pile.

'See?' He began to poke at a small hole. Dust filled her nostrils and mouth.

'Here,' she gasped, 'tear off a bit of this pillowcase –' for this bottom layer of the shelter was an improvised bed '– tie it round your mouth and nostrils.'

It didn't take long to clear a hole large enough for David to scramble through. 'I say,' he told her soberly, 'there's no ceiling, no roof.'

Heart in her mouth Nell enlarged the hole and scrambled through, clambering over rubble that had once been part of the lodge's roof. The eastern wall appeared still intact with part of the drawing room ceiling and roof. It was the western side that had suffered most – where Mrs Emmeline had been. She felt sick, trying to control her fear.

She glanced at David whose face was white. 'Get into the grounds and away from this,' she told him firmly. 'I'll—'

'No, I'm jolly well coming!'

Outside they saw Gordon and Rose and their children, emerging from the Anderson shelter in the garden. Rose immediately burst into tears and threw her arms round Nell.

She gently dislodged them. 'Mrs Emmeline,' she shouted urgently at Holdsby. 'She's in there somewhere.' She pointed to the enormous pile of rubble that had once been the west side of the lodge.

'Not a hope,' he said succinctly.

She cast an indignant look at him and ran to the rubble. Dismayed, sickened, she knew Gordon was right. How could anyone have survived in this? Smashed furniture, bricks, tiles, wood, stone, plaster – once a home, now a pile of useless rubble.

'If she was in the bathroom,' David said, his voice trembling a little, 'she'd be about there.' He pointed. True enough, there was something like a piece of smashed wash-basin there.

By now there were several army officers from the house rushing towards them.

'Mrs E,' Nell shouted. 'There!'

They wasted no time in words, but threw themselves

into clearance with their bare hands. 'We'll have to wait for the squad, ma'am,' one told her after a moment. 'No shifting this lot without it.'

'There,' shouted Holdsby. 'There's the bath, at any rate.' One of its iron feet could clearly be seen sticking out of rubble perilously poised on one side of the mound.

'She might be underneath, and I could get in there,' cried David excitedly. 'I'm small enough.'

'No!' shouted Nell.

'Let him do it, Nell,' Holdsby said slowly. Rose had taken their children away, Nell saw. Only David was left.

'It's too dangerous,' she retorted.

'She's right, sir,' one of the Army officers said gruffly. 'He could pull the lot down on himself if he's not careful.'

'No, he wouldn't,' said Holdsby easily. 'It's sense. Surely it's worth it for Mrs Emmeline, Nell?'

He was mocking her. If David died – if David died, Nell might feel honour bound to leave the Gadsby shares to his family. No – the thought was too terrible. Surely he did not care that much for the inheritance of Gadsby's? Or hate her so much?

David had torn free of her restraining grasp and was already wriggling through, beyond their reach. She gave a low moan, burying her head in her hands, unable to watch, yet unwilling to leave Holdsby by the hole. Just in case, just in case. A muffled sound – a tremulous shout. 'I think she's here. The bath—' Then the sound of collapsing rubble.

'David!' Nell screamed.

Nothing for interminable seconds. Then wriggling feet, and at last a bleeding, grimy, but grinning David. 'She's alive. Hurt. She said hallo.'

It took the rescue squad and ambulance another twenty minutes to arrive, and then a further half-hour as bit by bit the rubble was lifted off. And eventually Mrs Emmeline,

with a broken leg and arm, was carried out, now unconscious, on a stretcher.

'Nell, you and Gadsby's have the luck of the devil,'
Gordon Holdsby told her, watching dispassionately.

He could have pretended it was like any other office job –
if he could forget he was dealing with who should live and
who should die. There were disadvantages to working
here. In the office you were observed, you were known,
you were more than a number, you were a face, and this
made Lucien uneasy. His instincts were still to remain
anonymous, so that at any sign of danger he could simply
disappear. But it was becoming harder.

He had learned that in his position it was indeed
possible to help others. He now accompanied the SS when
they went through the hospital to decide who had been
there too long, who should die and who should work. He
had seen that it was possible surreptitiously to change the
cards of those who were picked to die for those of men
already dead. Not too often, not too many. That way it
was simple and effective. Tattoo numbers could even be
faked, though that had meant working with another
prisoner in the office. He had been careful and it had
worked. He had done it twelve times, but after the last
occasion someone had spoken to him in the office.

'You would like to see our newspaper? The camp
newspaper?'

He thought speedily. An underground newspaper – he
could be involved in the Resistance movement here. But
no. Not here. It was safer to work alone. He would join no
groups, for he trusted no leadership other than his own.

'*Non*,' he said at last, 'but do not fear. I prefer to work
alone.'

The man shrugged, and Lucien became aware in the
next few days that he was carefully watched. If there was
trouble in the office, any suspicion he might give them

563

away to the Gestapo, he would be killed, he knew – and not by the Gestapo. Or he might be betrayed by the other prisoners in order to allay suspicion from themselves. Unlikely, but possible. And Lucien de la Ferté, leader of the Ligne des Truffes escape and evasion line, would be high on the list for execution if his name came to the notice of the top ranks of the camp authorities, or if the Resistance movement grew so strong in France that Hitler ordered extreme reprisals as a warning.

Surely the war could not go on much longer? But when it ended perhaps they would all be slaughtered rather than the Germans reveal what had happened in Auschwitz. It was more than a work camp, it was a death camp; death by gas chambers, death by shooting in the yard between the notorious Block 10 and Block 11, death by injections of phenol, so rumour went. And death in the cause of experimental operations. Of what significance was his one life in this hell? He must do his best to save who he could – and if that included himself, so much the better.

Even so he would have to 'disappear' well before the war's end for Philippe would never let him live to return to France to tell his story, if he found out he was alive. He could check through the French police and Gestapo at any time, and thus soon Lucien must make sure that any such check was unsuccessful.

Just one more visit to the hospital. Walking behind the beautifully polished boots, blocking one's ears to the shouted orders, closing one's nostrils to the smell of fear, and one's mind to what was to happen to many of these men. The hospital and doctors were incongruously spotless. They had few supplies it was true, but otherwise the hospital could have been in Paris for its efficiency and maintenance. And this in a death-camp, where thousands upon thousands were expendable because they were Jews, or because they were old or sick, or young.

None of this showed in his face, as he nodded to one of

the doctors. Many were prisoners themselves and active or passive collaborators with the Nazis. This one he was not sure about. He had a habit of avoiding looking him in the face, especially today. Had his activities with the cards been noticed? When he returned to the office, he discovered that some of his fellow workers had been arrested. Nothing happened to him, but nevertheless he took precautions.

It was only when he returned to the bunkhouse that he knew he had been betrayed. The doors were flung open, two young SS officers stood in the doorway, blocking what light could enter.

'*Nummer* 102387 F. *Heraus*!'

Death, so long eluded, had come to claim its due.

Paris was free once more. The newspapers were full of pictures of General de Gaulle and French and US troops driving through the streets of the city. Paris sprang once more into joyous life, and shook herself free of oppression.

Even in war-torn England life seemed hopeful again, Nell thought thankfully. The assault of the doodlebugs was slackening now the Allies had reached the Pas de Calais where many of the flying bombs' launching sites were; Mrs Emmeline was out of danger, though still in hospital; now Paris was free, and so was the south of France. There had been a little shelling in Cannes, she had read, but nothing very serious. Soon, soon, she must be able to contact Lucien. Not yet, but telephone links must shortly be restored now surely? And letters. Anything to end the silence of four years. These last weeks were unbearable, worse than the waiting of all those years of war.

Full of excitement, she ordered special displays at Gadsby's to celebrate the liberation of Paris – which in a way was London's also for nothing now could seriously affect the city, she reasoned, not with Hitler in retreat. She was wrong. On 8 September the first rocket fell in Chiswick, the first of the terrible V-2s that were to cause such devastation in London over the next six months, a weapon not preceded by any warning as the doodlebugs had been; only a bright flash in the sky to herald the destruction it would cause. The battle of London was far from over.

Nell schooled herself to wait patiently. Lucien would telephone as soon as he could. When he did not, she reasoned out that they were busy with autumn collections, then knew with the first twinge of worry this could not be so. Had he met someone else during these four years? Sense told her no. Fear told her yes. Eventually in early October she placed a call to the Cannes office of Maison la Ferté. A stranger's voice. Why did that make her feel so uneasy?

'Comte Lucien, *s'il vous plaît*.' The words so long unspoken that meant so much.

'*Monsieur le comte ne travail plus ici, madame. Je—*' She hung up the receiver, a sudden inexplicable nausea welling inside her. He would be in Paris then, if he no longer worked in Cannes. Of course, she realised, relief flooding through her, perhaps he now ran the Maison. Perhaps his father had retired. Reassured, she telephoned Paris.

'*Monsieur le comte Lucien, s'il vous plaît.*'

'*C'est de la part de qui, madame?*'

What innate caution made her reply 'Gadsby's *de Londres*.'

It was not Lucien who came on the line, but Philippe's unmistakable voice that replied, protesting his delight at hearing from her.

'Where is Lucien?' she blurted out, ignoring his pleasantries.

'Darling Nell, I am so glad you are well. I have heard

such terrible things about Gadsby's and the bombs.'

'*Where is Lucien*?' she demanded again.

'Nell, how can I tell you? I wanted to see you in person, to save you grief. We do not know. Lucien was unwise – the Gestapo took him and we fear he is dead. There has been no news now for well over a year. And Maria, my wife—' He stopped, grief in his voice.

'What of her?' she whispered, her hands clammy on the telephone.

'Lucien was not only foolhardy himself, but encouraged her to be also. And, as an Italian—'

'Where is she?' Nell cut through, terrified now.

'Dead,' he answered in a low voice.

'I will come to Paris,' she said in a voice she hardly recognised.

'There is no point – we know nothing. *Can* know nothing until we know what has happened. Lucien was taken to a German camp in Poland, we believe. As soon as we hear, Nell, then you too shall know. You are part of our family, Nell. Maria would have wished—'

She hardly heard what he was saying as, murmuring hurried words of conventional sympathy, she hung up. Lucien missing. Maria dead? Why? What had happened? Had he been part of the underground movement? Yes, that must be it, and for that the penalty was death. Yet Philippe had said he had been taken to Poland. There was still hope. There must be. Perhaps he was imprisoned there and would be released when the war was over? So wait, wait – until Germany was conquered. Yet another winter of waiting, another winter of austerity.

It was many months before the whole terrible truth of Germany's concentration camps was known, as the Russians and Allies advanced from different directions and liberated the camps one by one. Majdanek was the first of the death camps to reach the headlines in the British newspapers in October. If Lucien were in Poland, then his camp would be liberated by the Russians. She might not even hear about it. But she did. At the beginning of February she read, with mounting horror, of the liberation of a Polish camp called Oswiecim.

Nell grew cold. If Lucien had been in the Resistance, then he would have been sent to no ordinary PoW camp. They were for servicemen. It would be one of *these* nightmares – she stared aghast at the terrible pictures and Pathé newsreels. Was one of those walking skeletons Lucien? Or was he merely one of the thousands of dead as Philippe had told her? She besieged Philippe by telephone, but always the answer was the same. No news.

By April the newspapers were full of how refugees were streaming back to Paris and she could stand the agony no longer. She must go herself and find out if there was the slightest chance of Lucien's being alive. Philippe was hardly going to bother, she reasoned. He had too much to lose. Only by determining the truth for herself could she be sure – and try to come to terms with what had happened. She even had business reasons to visit Paris. Gadsby's had to find out what was happening to fashion in France, after all.

Almost as soon as Paris had been liberated last autumn, some of the popular press had rushed to report on how fashion had fared there during the war. It had not proved a good move on their part, and a distinct anti-Paris feeling had grown not only in the trade but amongst British women. After all, during the war British designers had come to the fore, achieving a good reputation for tailored wear. In addition clothes rationing and restrictions were very much still part of the British woman's life. There was little desire to read about how well Parisian women were dressed. *They* might be liberated, but British women were not. By this time, the spring of 1945, attitudes had softened slightly. True, the feeling (whether justified or not) remained that Britain had been slogging it out while

Paris danced on its merry way during the Occupation, but nevertheless Nell sensed there was a distinct curiosity as to what might be happening to fashion in Paris couture houses. After all, sooner or later clothes rationing would end, went the reasoning, and British designers had to know the current trends – whether or not they could yet follow them.

Yes, she would go to Paris herself. Making the decision, however, proved much easier than carrying it out. Civilian rail travel to and within France was still being re-organised in Paris by British and French rail officers working together. It was hardly comfortable but it was possible. An old Southern Railway ferry took her from Newhaven to Dieppe; there she had to wait twenty-four hours for the next train to Paris, and when this arrived, she nearly missed it – taking it for a goods train. The waggons had been converted with seats, but by the time it jolted and bumped its way into an old railway station near the Bastille, Nell was heartily sick of railways, trains, and fellow passengers.

Paris wore her freedom with bravado and bitterness. At first sight little had changed: shops and cafés flourished as always, the women were as elegant as ever. Nell remembered reading an article by a French milliner in which she had declared that women had felt it a duty to remain elegant during the Occupation. But then, Nell thought defensively, French women hadn't had to work in munitions factories, hadn't been bombed by day and night. There were many signs, however, that Paris had its scars, however bravely worn. There were hardly any cars, crosses and flowers marked places where Frenchmen had fallen during the Liberation, and now interspersed with tailored coats and well-cut suits could be seen gaunt defiant figures still in what must surely be prison – or concentration camp – garb, almost flaunted before their fellow citizens. Suppose Lucien . . . No, Nell decided. She needed at least a day to acclimatise herself to Paris again, a day before she faced Philippe. A day she would spend pretending that Paris fashion was all that brought her here.

It took very little of that time, however, for her to see that haute couture was on the march again in Paris – if indeed it had ever stopped. But what use would these exciting tiered skirts be in London, or all this side drapery and cascade skirts? British regulations forbade any excess use of material. Imitation bustles, fullness at the back – she sighed. Impossible. Or was it? She had a sudden idea that perhaps ribbon sashes could be used for the same effect and they would pass regulations. She made a quick note on her pad, as she prepared to face the Maison la Ferté. Not Philippe yet, just the models on show. She wanted to see, to *feel*, what was happening there.

The commissionaire had changed. This was the first minor shock. So had the whole style of the entrance. It was still formal, but somehow it looked cheaper, less impressive. Perhaps she was prejudiced, she told herself, as she asked to see the model gowns. Model gowns – while outside concentration camp victims were milling around. Incongruous indeed.

'You like this, Nell? It is our new line. The diabolo line, we call it.' Philippe, approaching as silent and unobtrusive as a snake, suddenly spoke by her side. She whirled round.

She saw Philippe who was almost plump, more lined, and definitely prosperous. 'How good to see you, Nell.' He kissed her hands. 'Our collection will interest you, I hope.'

She looked at him coolly. So he had not changed. He knew perfectly well she was not here to see the collections. Well, she could play that game too.

'It is interesting, Philippe. A novelty. Those wide shoulders take the eye to the nipped-in waist, then the pleating carries it on to the wide hem – which gives it balance.'

'Precisely,' he purred. 'I see you still have your good eye for the future.'

'Oh no,' she said swiftly. '*This* isn't the future. This is just what I said – a novelty to amuse for a season, but then what? It is not a trend, but a kink.'

His face darkened. 'Still lost nothing of your forthrightness, Nell. I will tell my wife your opinion of her design technique.'

'Your wife?' she whispered, pale, 'but you told me Maria—'

'Not Maria. Dear Maria is dead. After the worst of my grief was over, I married again. Did I not tell you? Michelle is also my designer, as well as my wife – and mother to my baby son.'

'And to Maria's children?' Nell said through dry lips.

'Naturally.' He smiled, clearly pleased with the effect of his announcement.

'I want to know what happened to Lucien, Philippe,' she said abruptly.

He sighed. 'I understand. It is not convenient, but yes, we must talk. Pray come.' He led the way to his office and began to tell her of the past four years.

'You see,' he finished at last, 'I believed Maria loved me – instead it seems that Lucien and she had a rapport I did not appreciate. More than just an emotional rapport, perhaps? She was under his spell. He has – had – that gift. She was Italian, and therefore naturally she suffered most when the Gestapo discovered the line and their work for it. For her it was treason, and she, not Lucien, paid the immediate price.'

'How did they find out?' she asked sharply, trying to

keep her thoughts logical, to suppress her instant repulsion at his suggestion that Lucien and Maria had been lovers.

'A man in the stockroom whom they foolishly trusted. He too was shot when the Gestapo had obtained their information.'

Nell shuddered.

'Maria is revered here in Paris since the Liberation. The Comtesse Philippe is a name that will live.' He seemed proud, Nell thought, filled with unreasoning fury. Philippe – who had married again as soon as he could, and still hypocritically talked of his love for Maria.

'We all worked for the Resistance, Nell,' he continued. 'My parents, myself, Lucien and Maria, though in different areas. Lucien was the unlucky one. He was captured and dragged down Maria with him. I fear he talked. My task was to pretend to collaborate with the Germans, and to pass on information to my father who had contacts in London. This is the trouble in war. One must work in the dark. My father asked me for help and I gave it. How could I know that Lucien was endangering the whole operation by using the house for Allied servicemen evading the Germans – and dragging my beloved wife into it too?'

'I take it you have heard nothing more of him?' she asked dully. So plausible, so possible. Yet she could not believe Lucien would willingly endanger Maria, or that he would have given way under pressure and betrayed her. Yet how could she be sure? Under torture, not knowing what he was saying . . . No. This was *Lucien* they were talking about. Lucien would never do that. Never. Philippe was lying, as he always had.

'Yes. The news is bad, Nell,' he told her compassionately. 'I have discovered through my contacts that Lucien was sent to Oswiecim, a concentration death camp in Poland. The Germans call it Auschwitz. It was liberated in

January by the Russians. Lucien was not among the survivors.'

Nell's face was ashen. She licked dry lips. 'I see.' How did Philippe know and how could he be relied on?

He took her hands in his. 'We must grieve together, Nell. I have lost many of my family. My first wife, my father who died of a broken heart, and my brother. I have made every enquiry I can from survivors who are now returning from the camps. I have interrogated all I meet. I have asked the Red Cross, I have enquired through the police department. I have asked Resistance workers. No one speaks of Lucien. Someone would know by now if he had survived. Alas, he is not listed on the Red Cross survival sheets.'

She scraped back her chair and shakily stood up. He came round the desk to her, and held her briefly in his arms. She remained rigid and he gently released her. 'When you have recovered from this shock, dearest Nell, it would give me pleasure to welcome you back as a customer – and as a friend. I will never forget Maria, but I have married Michelle to give my daughters a mother once more. We would be delighted to welcome you to dinner. We, who share so much of our past, must share our future too.'

Murmuring hypocritical words of thanks she escaped, and in shock wandered aimlessly down to the Seine. Married again? Yes, of course. But to have an heir. Trying to sort out emotion from fact, she turned along the *quai* and walked over the Pont Alexandre Trois. It was spring and all Paris seemed to be making love. All the world was making love now the end of the war was in sight. Except for her. For Lucien must surely be dead. As she struggled to come to terms with this, a picture of Melissa dancing over this bridge once came into her mind. Melissa – the past rose up before her, and with it more memories of the past. Fact, not emotion. Philippe had

573

caused trouble in the past, Philippe had always been jealous of Lucien. He wanted him dead. Perhaps he knew he was dead. Knew he was dead, because he had engineered that death. This was too terrible a thought and she tried to banish it. After all, Philippe, too, had worked for the Resistance. Or had he? She only had his word for it.

She looked up at the trees breaking into leaf. A new life. Unbearable beauty, when Lucien was dead. *If* he was dead. She would not trust Philippe, but make separate enquiries, however painful.

The Red Cross was inundated both with never-ending lines of refugees and with families desperate for information. This was the other side of liberated Paris from the cafés and trees of the Champs Elysées. Horrified by the lines of patient, gaunt skeletons, Nell had to wait two days before she could reach someone who could spare the time to answer her query.

'*Non*.' The name of Lucien de la Ferté meant nothing to this Swiss woman. 'He isn't on our list.' She glanced at Nell compassionately. 'It isn't conclusive, but it's not a good sign. The Germans evacuated some of the Auschwitz prisoners before the Russians arrived and sent them to other camps. But he isn't on their lists either. They've liberated another camp this week, Belsen, but there doesn't seem to be a record of his being sent there.'

'He was in the Resistance. I believe he helped escaped servicemen.' Wasn't that what Philippe had mentioned?

'Oh!' The woman brightened, glad to give hope, however little. 'Then try the British Awards Bureau, at the Grand Hotel, Palais Royale. Rue de Valois.'

Without having a clue what on earth an Awards Bureau might be, Nell set off to find the hotel, which turned out to be considerably less grand than its name. Without great hope, she entered and was directed to the first floor, which was almost as crowded as the Red Cross headquarters. To her surprise the office was staffed by the British

Army, who offered no explanation of their presence as some hours later she had a chance to explain her mission.

'Lucien de la Ferté? Comte Lucien?' the officer asked with interest.

A quickening of hope. They knew his name.

'Ran an evasion line from Pas de Calais through Paris to the south,' the officer continued. 'We didn't have much to do with him because he funded it himself. Sent to Auschwitz in 1943, I'm afraid.' He looked at her, then away, fiddling with his pen. 'We kept as strict a trace as we could on what happened to those chaps.'

'But Auschwitz was liberated in January,' she said desperately. 'Isn't there any news of him?'

The officer, forced to look her in the eye, became human, compassionate. 'I'm sorry. Very sorry. He was executed last August.'

'How can you *know*?' she whispered, ashen-faced. 'There are so many camps. How can you be so certain without checking?'

'It's my job to find out about the Resistance leaders first,' he explained apologetically. 'Look.' He picked up a file from the desk and pushed it in front of her. 'No. 102387 F Ferté, L. de la. Shot 27 August 1944.' The words swam before her eyes.

'But—'

'The Germans kept careful records, you see, of all executions, and we got copies from the Russians. Not the gas chambers, of course—' He broke off. 'Are you all right?' he asked, concerned.

'Yes,' she managed to say. She must be sure, absolutely sure. 'They could be wrong, these records.'

'He hasn't yet returned to Paris. And—' he hesitated.

'And?' she asked in agony.

'We had confirmation from someone who worked with him.'

'What confirmation?' she continued inexorably.

'He was betrayed by one of the prisoner doctors in the hospital.'

It made no sense. Doctor? Hospital? In a death camp? Nevertheless, she could blind herself no longer. Philippe had for once been telling the truth. Lucien was dead. Dead for the Resistance, like so many others. She had survived the war and he had not. Melissa's last gift to her had been in vain. Dumbly she thanked the officer and turned away. 'There's no mistake, I suppose?' she asked hopelessly.

He shook his head kindly. 'He's dead, Mrs Gadsby.'

She stood by the Seine as she had with Lucien so many years ago. She heard his voice again, when stupidly, all for the sake of a promise, she had turned him from her. 'For what will you live? What else is there?'

She had told him there was only one way she could live without him. And the same way lay open still, a heritage for his son: Gadsby's.

Chapter Eighteen

Nell looked down from Gadsby's window on to a sea of heads, aimlessly milling about in frustration waiting to celebrate. Gadsby's had just closed for the day, its staff like everyone else despairing of hearing the news which so obviously must be about to break – that the war had ended. Flags were already flying from many shops, but Nell decided that until news was confirmed, Gadsby's flagpole should carry no flag, nor should the Victory banner be displayed, although plenty of bunting was already in place. It was a kind of superstition, she supposed, they should not display too much confidence. No V-2 rockets had fallen since March, but even now in early May the fear remained that the Reich, although in its death throes, might still have an ace card in its hand as when Hitler had hurled his troops against the Americans in the Ardennes only a few months earlier.

A few minutes ago every wireless set in Gadsby's – and there had been many plugged in today – had informed the nation that the Prime Minister would not be speaking that evening. The day had ended not with the bang of victory but with the whimper of anticlimax. Nell had ordered the news to be given over loudspeakers to the people flocking in the street outside, and a ripple of disappointment had run through the crowd, which nevertheless was reluctant to disperse.

'Have you heard the news?' Angela popped her head round the door.

'The war appears to be over, but *they* don't want us to know,' said Nell crossly.

'No. Really important news from the Board of Trade. Bunting is going to be coupon-free for the next few weeks,' Angela laughed. 'Provided it's in patriotic colours of course!'

'Make some dresses of it,' Nell said promptly.

'Rather skimpy.'

'Frills.'

'I'll put some in Haberdashery, New Clothes for Old – and on the Gadsby's Got the Answer counter,' declared Angela brightly. 'Tomorrow,' she added firmly, closing the door behind her. Nell's addiction to work could be fanatical at times.

'I wish we had Got the Answer,' muttered Nell, roving round the empty store restlessly. There was nothing to call her home. David was still in Wales, though his school had already made plans to return to Kent as soon as hostilities came to a formal end. Eaton Square seemed cheerless now that Maureen had moved back into her own home with Bertie, who had returned to the War Office after the crossing of the Rhine. Even Hornton now that the days of bombing seemed behind them was making it clear that camaraderie was at an end; convivial suppers in the staff quarters would no longer be tolerated.

Yet the true emptiness was in herself, Nell acknowledged ruefully, switching on the wireless as if to provide the stimulus she could no longer give herself. Lucien was dead and the rest of her life stretched bleakly before her. A few more golden years with David, and then again emptiness.

The wireless crackled as the programme was interrupted for yet another news announcement. And at last, belatedly, unbelievably, it came: the news they had awaited all day. Tomorrow would be Victory in Europe Day, a national holiday, as would be the day after. The war was over, at least in Europe.

The war was over! Nell stared at the wireless as though doubting the news could really be true. Then it sank in. *It really was over*. She leapt up, out of her office, down the stairs into the darkened store, switching on lights in ecstatic abandon, and shouting to whoever might still be there: '*It's over! It's over!*'

On the ground floor the night watchmen gathered to see their governing director flying down the stairs.

'It's over,' she told them joyfully. 'They've just announced it. Victory in Europe Day tomorrow.'

Then she found she was being swung unceremoniously off her feet, whirled round by one pair of brawny arms after another. A bottle of Scotch and some glasses appeared, and hot fiery liquid warmed her as tears and laughter combined.

'The flag!' she announced, hiccuping.

A cheer went up as they raced up the stairs. Twelve victory banners were unfurled on poles over Regent Street beneath the second-floor windows, and finally on the roof the Union Jack was proudly raised on the flagstaff. More Scotch. And more. After an hour, she left the men to it and wandered through the mighty store of Gadsby's.

An empty life? When she had all this? she thought proudly.

Fired by impulse, she pretended she was twenty-three again, running up the stairs trying to evade old Harbottle's eye. She minced up the last steps on to the first floor, ignoring the barricaded part of the store to her left. She could almost imagine Miss Copsy was standing there once more, clad in one of her old-fashioned chiffon teagowns. Ghosts from the past rose to meet her, The Dragon, Old Ample and Beesknees, an accusing jury to meet their new buyer. But I showed them, she told herself. And most of all, the ghost of Jonathan Gadsby himself on the Fourth Floor. How had she fared in his eyes? She had presided over the years of the greatest and speediest changes in fashion that there had ever been. She had changed Gadsby's into a competitive store before the Second World War broke out. Now what would happen? it suddenly occurred to her to wonder. The First World War had insidiously changed women's outlook after its conclusion. So might the Second. But how? Impatiently she dismissed this thought. This was a time of victory, not doubt.

'Jonathan,' she told him solemnly, 'I've done my best. It might not have been how you'd have done it, but the days of bustles and bows are over, the women you knew vanished more than twenty years ago. No store could have survived in these years the way you wanted. It had to change.' Why did she sound defensive? she wondered. She knew she was right, and had proved she was. She had fought and won, and as a result Gadsby's was still here. That was *her* victory. Yet what of the other Nell? The one who had run so lightheartedly up the stairs all those years ago. No victory here. Death had taken Tom, taken Melissa – and now taken Lucien.

But left her David, she reminded herself firmly. David for whom she worked so hard. Gadsby's would be preserved for him. She recalled an article in *The Lady* some time ago about what women would require of shops after the war. The day of the big store was over, it informed its readers, because of greedy over-expansion in the thirties. The big store was now so over-departmentalised that it was confusing for the customer, it argued. Perhaps British stores should start little shops within the larger parent as was happening in New York, it suggested. Nell had dismissed the idea with amusement. The answer was surely to streamline departments. Simplify and amalgamate, and not bewilder with trying to offer too many different types of goods to the customer. And this she had done at Gadsby's. Each department was independent, responsible for its own profit, and her refusal to allow diversions into goods other than those pertaining to fashion (save for wartime emergency goods) had been right.

Yes, Gadsby's had come through the challenge successfully. It would survive. Nothing was going to change for a long time anyway. Clothes rationing would obviously continue for a while. Time enough to think of haute couture again after that. Meanwhile, the way ahead was still hemmed in by austerity and utility. Nothing needed to be done yet, and Gadsby's was flying its flag proudly.

A massive tribal dance of celebration wove its way across St James' Park towards Buckingham Palace, thousands of people who tomorrow would mostly be strangers again.

Bertie, one arm round Nell, the other round Maureen, jigged them along in a *Wizard of Oz* dance, shouting incomprehensibly in the din. It didn't matter, because Maureen appeared to be singing 'Roll Out the Barrel' and Nell was trying to recover from a stitch in her side caused by dancing and yelling at the same time. The Palace balcony was draped in crimson and yellow. They were so far back in the crush that when the Royal Family eventually came out they looked mere dots from where they were standing. It didn't matter. Nothing mattered tonight as lovers embraced, and strangers were lovers for the night.

Late in the evening of VE Day they made their way back to Bertie and Maureen's flat in Queen Anne's Gate where Maureen had laid on a victory supper for them, their two staff and an over-tired toddler, with Bertie producing like a magician a bottle of champagne.

'One of the privileges of travelling on business to liberated France,' he laughed.

Nell caught her breath.

He glanced at her, belatedly aware of his tactlessness,

and put an arm round her. 'VE Day, Nell. Sadness is for tomorrow.'

'Yes,' she said, smiling again and holding out her glass.

'I give you a toast,' he shouted. 'Britain and her future. A brave new world. May she thrive for ever.'

'And Gadsby's with her,' Nell added gaily as they drank, and did not notice Bertie's slight hesitation before warmly he raised his glass. 'And Gadsby's.'

The summer was a hard one. After euphoria came reality and the reality was that austerity's grip was tightening, not loosening. Only the fact that it was summer made it bearable. Supplies were more and more difficult to obtain, and the prospect of changeover of workforce from predominantly female to male sometime in the future, with the upheaval, resentment and financial hardship it would cause, meant few risked celebrating with new clothes. And matters could only get worse when demobilisation eventually started.

Goodness knows when that will be, thought Nell glumly. It was all too easy to forget – save for those with loved ones in the forces – that the war was *not* over. That it was still very much on against Japan. Until that war too had ended, many servicemen faced the prospect of being sent to the Far East. Then early in August the dropping of two atomic bombs brought Japanese surrender and VJ Day. Certainty, at terrible cost, had been achieved.

'When do you think you'll be demobbed, Bertie?' she asked him idly one day, when he came to the store to take her out to lunch.

He shrugged. 'No telling, Nell. Next year maybe. Perhaps in a month or two.'

She brightened. 'Oh, good. So I'll be able to tell the board you're coming back. We must plan how we reorganise board responsibilities.'

He did not look at her as, lunch ordered, he studied his

582

glass of wine intently. 'I'm not sure I am, Nell.'

'You are what?' she asked blankly.

'Coming back to the board. Even if they elect me,' he said a little pointedly.

'That's a foregone conclusion. Of course they will. I have complete control over who's appointed to the board anyway. They're only rubber-stamping my decision,' she said, surprised and alarmed. 'And what on earth do you mean – not coming back?'

'You look at things differently during war,' he told her slowly. 'It changes you.'

'You seem the same old Bertie to me,' she said gaily.

But he took no notice, continuing as if she had not spoken. 'Out in the desert, you see life more clearly. I've got a family—'

'But it's a secure job, and well paid,' she interrupted. The desert, always the desert. She felt as if she were with Tom again, facing a challenge from a force she did not know and could not reckon with.

'I need to go forward, Nell,' he told her bluntly. 'Is Gadsby's going forward?'

'Of course,' she answered, astounded.

'What are your plans? I've heard about the fashion shortages there are going to be this autumn now all the manufacturers have to concentrate on exports, but I haven't heard your plans to get round them.'

'We're concentrating on building up other departments,' she replied spiritedly. 'And making up more of our own exclusive models.'

He sighed. 'It's going to be a whole new world, Nell, and a tough one. Women are being demobbed from the services now. Selfridges are giving fashion parades specifically aimed at them, because obviously they see them as a whole new market – and more than that, a whole new way of life. What are you doing and what do you see?'

'We can't copy Selfridges' idea. We're having our usual

autumn parades,' she said, irritated. 'And there'll be utility clothes amongst them naturally. But servicewomen are no problem,' she told him, switching attack. 'They'll buy utility stuff. It's the wealthier women we've got to woo back.'

'Lifestyles are going to change, Nell. *All* women will want to work. Fewer and fewer are going to be the "idle rich" – especially now we've a Labour government.'

'There'll always be wealthy women,' she told him defiantly, wearying of this discussion. A nagging voice was saying: What did it matter?

'Certainly, but the wealthy too will change their way of life. They'll be more active, they'll need tougher, cheaper clothes, as well as a few more expensive models. Jonathan thought in terms of pleasing women devoted to pleasure, or rather who worked at pleasure; you have thought in terms of a society in which pleasure and work were given equal weight. Now it's going to be a society in which work predominates. Haven't you realised that?'

An angry flush came to her cheeks. 'With clothes rationing utility clothes will continue, but after that—'

'Yes. What are you planning for after that?'

'There's no use planning now,' she snapped. 'We don't know when it will end. And when it does we can adapt little by little.'

'Only in accordance with a long-term plan. And you haven't one. The Nell I used to know would have had.'

'Are you accusing me of neglecting Gadsby's?' She was more shocked than angry.

'I'm accusing you of shutting your eyes in self-satisfaction.'

'That's not true!' she burst out, raising her voice and then flushing as neighbouring tables stared. 'I have a board,' she hissed. 'I consult them.'

'They are subordinate to your wishes. As you said, in effect they rubber-stamp your wishes.'

'I meant only as far as directors are concerned, and I *always* take note of their views in *everything*. It just *isn't* true.'

'Of course it is. It always will be because of Jonathan Gadsby's bequest. Because of your Founders' shares which give you overpowering voting rights and because of Jonathan's mantle as Governing Director which, whatever you say, keeps real power in your hands.'

'I've got David's interests to think of. He's nearly sixteen, it won't be long before he comes of age and he'll be taking over—' she blurted out, faltering as she saw Bertie's expression.

'Precisely.'

Merrifield was slowly coming to life again. The army were still in occupation, but were in their last weeks there. Mrs Emmeline was comfortably re-installed in one wing, recovered from the effects of her injuries, and though frailer, walking again. At ninety-four, her back as upright as ever, with her walking stick only adding to a regal appearance. Like the dear Queen, she announced proudly, by whom she meant the Queen Mother, Queen Mary, of whom she was a fervent and loyal admirer. This weekend she quickly divined that Nell had something on her mind other than an enjoyable stay at Merrifield with David.

Needing little coaxing, she poured out her anger and indignation over Bertie's strange attitude. 'How dare he imply that I'm ruining Gadsby's by over-control? He just doesn't understand how much Gadsby's means to me.'

'He may understand only too well,' Mrs Emmeline observed.

'But how could he accuse me of not thinking about Gadsby's future?'

'Is it true?'

'No,' she exploded.

'Then you have nothing to fear.'

'But he even implied,' Nell was still indignant, 'that I was past my usefulness to Gadsby's but hanging on because of David.'

'Are you?'

'I *have* to think of David,' she burst out, aghast at this attack from such an unexpected quarter. 'The governorship is to be passed to him together with the shares. That's what Jonathan wanted, and surely you of all people would want to see done what he wanted?'

'It is so very easy for the living to understand what the dead want – interpreted according to what they want themselves.'

Nell grew red. 'But Jonathan wanted a Gadsby to run the store. You *know* he did.'

'I believe what Jonathan would have wanted more is for Gadsby's to continue, and continue successfully. That may be the case with David at the helm, or may not.'

'Of course he'd be successful,' Nell said angrily.

'Does David want to run Gadsby's?'

'Of *course*.' This was getting ridiculous. Even Mrs E was turning things topsy-turvy. 'He loves Gadsby's. He always has, even from a small boy.'

'He's sixteen now and what can be a passion at eight years old might not necessarily be so to a young man.'

'But he's got to do it – I mean, he's my heir,' she stammered.

Mrs Emmeline smiled sadly. 'Got to?' she repeated. 'Have you thought to ask him, Nell?'

Leaving Mrs Emmeline to have a sleep, Nell walked round the gardens to try to calm down and to sift emotions from facts. The flower borders were higgledy piggledy with late self-sown nasturtiums, antirrhinums and montbretia fighting for existence. Soon the young gardener would be back to help. Unless he too decided he wanted a new life. After the First World War many staff had decided they wanted different, 'better' lives than in service, though whether they had found them to be so in practice was questionable. Winning the peace after the Second World War still lay ahead. Uneasily she thought that this could be true of Gadsby's also. Her indignation returned. Ask David? There was no *need* to ask David. Of course he would want to go into Gadsby's. He had been expecting to go into it all his life. She loved Gadsby's, so would he.

David arrived home an hour later, after playing cricket with the village team. Seeing him on the terrace, slumped down with a glass of Tizer, Nell went to join him, nerving herself up to tackle him head-on.

'Have you given any thought to what you want to do after you leave school?' she asked, trying to sound casual. 'I take it you'll stay on till you're eighteen anyway and take advanced matric?'

'Yes. A bit,' he said carelessly, taking a deliberately noisy sip of Tizer through the straw and draining the glass.

Nell's heart sank. He was on the defensive.

'Yes?'

'I'll stay on all right.' A pause. 'I want to be a doctor.'

Nell went very still. 'I naturally thought you would want to come into the store as your grandfather intended.' She tried to keep her voice even.

'I don't think I'd be very good at that,' David told her simply. 'It bores me.'

'Bores you?' she repeated, horrified, then forced herself to say: 'When you're older, you won't find it so. You see—' She stopped, she must listen and not lecture. She had asked and now she must be told. 'Why do you want to be a doctor?'

'I think I'll be good at it.'

'You'd be good at Gadsby's. Why have you never told me this before?' Try as she might, she could not keep reproach from her voice.

'I thought you'd never listen. You always assumed I wanted to run the store – well, I *don't*,' he finished defiantly.

'When you're older—' she repeated weakly.

'I'll feel just the same. Besides,' he added awkwardly, 'what fun is there in going into the family firm? I want to do something of my own. Something *I've* done, not what's handed to me on a plate.'

She could not reply, so taken aback was she.

'Anyway,' he muttered, 'it isn't as if it's *my* family, is it?'

Out of the blue. No question of not understanding what he meant. Nell was too horrified to answer.

'I'm not a Gadsby, am I?' he continued truculently.

'How did you find out?' she asked through stiff lips.

'Uncle Gordon told me a year ago.'

Of course. Holdsby. That momentary impulse she had seen in his eyes to push David to his death had not been imagination on her part. Baulked of that, he had chosen this route to thwart her, to make sure that Gadsby's, even if it continued, should not be under Gadsby chairmanship.

'I'm not really a Gadsby, am I?' David continued quickly. 'That's why the will was changed, after Father – Tom Gadsby – died.'

'It made no difference,' she told him firmly. 'Jonathan *knew* you weren't Tom's son, but still wanted you as his ultimate heir. I know he did. That's why he left it to me to look after for you. You must believe that, David. He loved you, and so did Tom. Very much.'

'More than my own father?' David said sulkily, emotion beginning to surface after being bottled up.

'Oh, David.' How to answer that? To tell him his father had had no chance to love him? 'Why did you never talk to me about it?'

He shrugged in a show of bravado. 'I haven't seen much of you. When I was here you were always so busy.'

'That was the war,' she told him. And Gadsby's, the truth nagged at her. 'I sent you away because I loved you. You must believe that.'

He flushed in embarrassment. 'Yeah, but . . .'

'But?'

'But I want to know who my father is,' he told her belligerently. 'If you know, that is.'

She gasped in outrage, and his eyes fell. 'I'm sorry,' he muttered.

'I'm the one who should be sorry,' anger was evaporating, 'for not guessing you might find out from that ghastly man. After all, I know just what he's capable of. He didn't tell you who your father was? He guessed, I'm sure.' Whether rightly or wrongly, she did not know. On the verge of telling David about Lucien, Nell stopped. Not yet. Not quite yet. But soon. 'His name is not important. He died. He was French. He died during the war, helping the Resistance.'

There was a flicker of interest. 'Like George Millar?'

'Who?' Then she remembered the man the newspapers had been full of who had fought with the Maquis. 'Something like him. I don't know all the facts. But when I go to to France to find out, you shall come with me.'

David stared into his glass. 'But Father – Tom – was still alive when I was born. That makes you—'

'I can't tell you about it, David, without hurting a lot of people,' she cried, agonised.

'Yes, you can,' he burst out. 'You've got to. I want to know *now*.'

She thought for a moment. What to say, how to explain? 'Do you remember your Aunt Melissa?' she asked eventually.

'Yes. She died years ago.'

'Do you remember what it was like to be with her?'

'It was fun.'

'More than that. It was like being swept into an

enchanted world, sometimes a horrific one. But magic, exciting – until you were dumped back. You'd forget all about it – until the next time.'

'Like when she took me to the pantomime and told me stories? But that was kids' stuff.'

'No, it was everyone's stuff. She did the same to adults too, in a different way. She caught us all in her spell, Tom, me, your real father . . . others too. She never meant to hurt anyone, but she flew along through life, faster and faster, unable to stop. It wasn't Tom's fault he couldn't have children, it wasn't mine or your father's that we couldn't marry. And then war swept us apart.'

'And now he's dead, so I'll never see him,' David said mutinously. 'He's dead, like Daddy, like Grandfather.'

'Yes. I'm sorry, David.'

'What sort of chap was he?' he asked, trying to appear unconcerned.

Nell considered, ignoring the emotions that tore at her. How to describe Lucien to a sixteen year old? 'I don't think I can describe him,' she said at last. 'Someday I'll take you to his France, and introduce you to his family.' Philippe would not mind now, she was sure. Philippe after all had achieved his dearest wish, the title of Comte de la Ferté. 'Tell me,' she asked finally, 'did knowing about your father influence your decision about Gadsby's?'

'No. I always wanted to be a doctor. In fact,' a grin crossed his face, 'it almost made me decide to go into Gadsby's after all, just to spite those Holdsby types.' David disliked his cousins immensely, particularly the two girls. 'Oh, I say,' he added delightedly, 'I never thought of that. If Daddy wasn't my father, then those awful girls aren't my cousins.'

Nell laughed. 'Absolutely not. You're free, David, unencumbered – though I do have to confess one awful truth. Your French uncle has a son but he also has two girls.'

'Doesn't anyone want boys any more?' David muttered disgustedly.

The old summerhouse – she could sit there and think. What better place than where Jonathan Gadsby himself used to sit, puffing on his pipe looking over the gardens of his beloved Merrifield. Late honeysuckle and the smell of tobacco plants filled the air as Nell tried to wrestle with the truth. David did not want to run Gadsby's. So were all her years of effort in vain? No, only if she had done it for his sake alone, surely? And that wasn't the case. Gadsby's was *her* life, her love, some might say her obsession. So this terrible feeling of waste, of anti-climax, did not stem entirely from David's decision. From where then?

She sat there a long time, thought of Jonathan in his old Panama hat which still hung from a hook inside the door. How had he felt, having planned all his life to hand his life's work on to his son, then his grandson, only to find that fate in the end betrayed him. Jonathan, striding through the store fearful of change – no, not fearful, *impatient* of change. A single vision unhindered by what anyone else might think, a vision that in the end had hurt his beloved store, not protected it.

A single vision that had driven him on. But wasn't that what she'd pursued? Achieved – and now saw threatened? A vision that had become an obsession.

Just like Jonathan Gadsby's.

Slowly she rose from her chair and saluted the old Panama.

'Ask him to tell you about The Hat,' echoed in her ears.

Now The Hat had told *her* all she needed to know about its owner – and about herself. Above all, about herself.

Nell looked round at the people assembled in the large formal boardroom. Her colleagues and her friends: Peter, who'd marched into her life when David was only a

591

toddler, Robert Galt, who'd proved an undemanding, loyal supporter for ten years, Sebastian, who'd taken her ideas and transformed the store with them, Angela, Polly – and dear Joe. 'I've called this meeting for one reason only. I want to propose a radical reorganisation of this company, beginning with a complete restructuring of the shares. Of course, this means an extraordinary general meeting of shareholders must be held too, but as you know I hold the majority voting rights so this presents no problem. However, I need your support, even if strictly and theoretically I don't need your consent—' she paused '– as things are constituted at present.'

Startled, enquiring faces were turned to her.

'It means a major change to the Memorandum of Association, of course, and we may have to take the matter to the courts.' She hesitated, then plunged on: 'But Gadsby's future is the most important consideration, and for that the most effective form of management is essential, whether it remains a private company Gadsby-controlled, or is eventually floated as a public company.'

She certainly had their attention now. To those who remembered the days of Jonathan Gadsby this was heresy.

'Initially,' she continued steadily, 'I propose that my Founders' shares be converted into ordinary and preferential shares. I propose to offer many for sale at good rates if any of you wish to acquire any. A majority holding will remain in my control temporarily, but in compensation I propose also that the Articles of Association be amended to abolish the position of Governing Director, and for the board to be reconstituted under a Chairman and Managing Director with normal voting rights.' She stopped and there was a moment's pause. Then they all burst out talking at once. Sebastian's was the loudest voice.

'Have you considered what this means for you, Nell?' he asked anxiously.

'Yes,' she replied steadily. 'It means I'm giving up Jonathan Gadsby's stranglehold on power, which he passed on to me believing he was acting in Gadsby's best interests. Now,' she smiled, 'I'm not so sure it is any longer. Not with colleagues like you. I want the board to run the company in future and not me.'

'But it means, Nell,' Robert Galt pointed out, 'that the board would have the power to elect whom it wishes as Managing Director – theoretically,' he added diplomatically. 'Of course, your managing directorship could be stipulated in the Articles.'

'No. The board will have more than theoretical power,' she answered coolly. 'It will have real power. You see, I don't want to be Managing Director. I would like to remain on the board, if you agree. I would even be Chairman, if so voted. But not Managing Director.'

They stared at her, stunned. It was Polly who managed to speak first. 'Why, Nell, *why*?'

'I suppose because I began by knowing Gadsby's was the best store in London; but when I was in a position to keep it so, I gradually lost sight of the fact that it isn't standing still that is in Gadsby's best interests, it's moving. During the war, we've had to adapt, not move. Now it's over we've got to march forward. So I believe it's time for someone else to take over. Not even Montgomery can march at the head of an army for ever.'

Three months later the legalities had been settled. Her pen moved over the paper as if held by someone else. Surely this couldn't be her, Nell Gadsby, signing away her life's work? She took firm hold of herself. Watching her were friends and colleagues, and they would continue to be so. They could change, might turn to enemies with power in their hands, but wasn't that just what Jonathan Gadsby had feared, and as a consequence let Gadsby's die little by little? By severing the cord, she risked the end of

Gadsby's, true, but she gave it more – the chance of living on into the second half of the twentieth century.

'As by agreement I remain in the chair for the purpose of this meeting, we now have to discuss the election of a Managing Director.'

'I think we're all agreed, Nell,' Sebastian spoke for his fellow directors, 'that you should reconsider and that it should be you.'

She gulped. 'I'm grateful,' she said slowly, 'more grateful than I can ever convey, for all the confidence you have in me. But I can't accept. If Gadsby's is going forward, then it must go forward in a new direction. And I don't think I'm the best person to march at the head.'

So it was agreed. Peter was elected as Managing Director, with herself remaining Chairman, and a resolution had been passed that Sir Bertram Bertrand be asked to rejoin the board. Gadsby's would effectively be in new hands. Nell felt flat as they left the board room, aware that already a new current of excitement had been engendered by the board meeting. She knew she had been right to resign from absolute power. Nevertheless, as she watched her friends crowding down the stairs together, eagerly talking, she felt deflated; it was only right that she walked down the stairs alone, she told herself. She was the past, they the future. But wasn't that just what she wanted?

She was walking away from Gadsby's in its own best interests. Like the girl herself, Gadsby's had grown up.

The coming of spring made Nell even more restless. She had regretted her decision as regards Gadsby's very little. Far from it. Being Chairman was a far easier task than her former one, she discovered. She had regained her old enthusiasm, had learned restraint when decisions went against her and not to interfere in departmental issues. Most difficult had been relinquishing her daily walk round

594

the store; she found the only solution was not to attend more than once a week. A Chairman should be rarely heard and never seen, Bertie hinted gently.

Time had hardly hung on her hands with David home during winter evenings, but now the days were lengthening and the reign of blackout lay far behind them, he spent more time with his friends, and often she found herself visiting Merrifield alone at weekends – a fact Mrs Emmeline took more philosophically than did she.

On impulse one early April evening she took herself to the cinema to see one of Melissa's old films. How dated it seemed nowadays compared with Hollywood's colourful best. Yet Melissa herself rose above it, her golden voice and charm still casting their spell. It added to Nell's restlessness as she walked home to Eaton Square. How ridiculous to live in such an enormous house now, she thought. Perhaps she should move. Go back to Mayfair? No, not back. Those days had ended, though the future stretched she knew not where.

Melissa still accompanied her, the music still with her as Nell let herself in quietly to avoid disturbing Hornton. The fire was glowing warmly, and she dozed off in the armchair, having made herself a huge mug of cocoa. A mundane everyday scene, but Melissa still danced around her dreams.

'Oh, darling, what's the matter?'

Nell woke up with a start. In the dimly lit room, the voice was so clear she could have sworn Melissa herself had spoken in her ear. Shaken, she poured a brandy, seeing the cocoa already cold and undrunk. What on earth was the matter with her? For once Nell felt sorry for herself, wondering if she had been right to give up control of Gadsby's so completely. Already things were moving swiftly, with talk of public flotation, buying up provincial stores, even selling franchises for Gadsby models. No, she had been right. It was someone else's turn. She no longer had the objectiveness to direct it. Her energies seemed to have deserted her. Perhaps she should be like Melissa and dance through life?

'Oh, yes, darling, do,' Melissa agreed with enthusiasm.

Nell giggled. She, practical Nell, seeing ghosts again after only a few sips of brandy.

'I'm not a dancer,' she said defensively.

'*Everyone*'s a dancer at heart,' replied Melissa gaily. 'It's just not everyone has a chance to do it. But you have, Nell, don't you? Go on, dance. Oh, do, darling.'

'Where do you expect me to dance to, Melissa?' Nell asked wrily. 'Fly round the world?'

'Why not? Such fun.'

'Don't be silly, Melissa,' Nell told her tartly.

'Oh, darling, don't be beastly. Remember what fun we had. We did have fun, didn't we?'

With a cry, Nell buried her face in her hands as an old memory caught her by the heart. The sudden jerk of her elbow knocked flying the lamp insecurely lodged on the flap of her writing desk to her side, and in her ineffectual plunge to catch it, Melissa's photograph and her own leather pen box toppled after it.

The lamp, pulled out of its socket, plunged the room into darkness and Nell knelt down in the darkness trying to put it back in, cursing and bumping into the fireplace and furniture. With light once more in the room she swivelled round on her knees to pick up the results of her carelessness. The photograph had been thrown from its frame and the contents from the pen box. Melissa's face smiled up at Nell from the carpet, and on top of it lay a rusty iron key.

'Boats? Can I go fishing?'

'There will be all the boats you could possibly wish for, and yes, you can go fishing.'

Nell had beaten David to it in pulling up the blinds of

their compartment on the Blue Train to see the Mediterranean beyond. Cocooned in what was comparative luxury after the converted goods waggons of the previous year, away from the bomb damage of the Channel coastal towns and faced with the familiar six-course meal, it was possible to imagine the war had never happened, that she was the old Nell, hastening to Cannes with Lucien. Only a momentary twinge of sadness gripped her that that was past, and that it was her son who accompanied her, the son Lucien would never know.

On the way back they would stop in Paris and she would introduce David to Philippe. Perhaps he would have returned then. She had been surprised on telephoning the Maison la Ferté to be told that Philippe was not there, only his assistant, and it was not sure when he would be back. But in any case she could still show David the Maison la Ferté on the pretext of carrying out commissions for Angela and Polly in studying Parisian fashions, for all that they were of little use to British designers still bound by wartime restrictions. Nevertheless they needed to keep abreast of developments, Nell told herself firmly.

But first she would take David to Cannes.

Within weeks of liberation in August 1944 the hotels of the Riviera had been open to tourists again. Caught in the viciousness of the V1 and V2 campaign, the south of France was still a far-off dream for most Britons, though. Even now, in the spring of 1946, most of the British to be met with in Cannes were those who had doggedly remained throughout the war, often pensioned off servants who had nowhere else to go, and who would have starved without the help of the Red Cross. Now a few villa owners were coming back to reclaim their properties, and houses that had been German-occupied were being put back in order.

Nell booked in at the Carlton, almost with bravado, to face the pain of memory head on. The Croisette seemed unchanged; only when later they went for a walk towards the summer casino did they see any signs of war damage. The town had escaped lightly, though she was told some villas towards the back of the town had been destroyed by shelling.

The spring sunshine had brought the Cannoises out in force, in all their former elegance. Boleros, peg-top skirts, beautiful soft colours – Nell looked at them objectively, not with her old critical regard for fashion. Beside them, even her new blue costume, which had taken all her remaining coupons, looked dowdy, and she resented that this should be so. Cannes may have escaped lightly from the war but London had not.

Lightly? She was overcome with guilt. How could she say that when perhaps it was here Lucien had worked to save Allied servicemen, a task for which he had given his life; when loyal Frenchmen had grouped together in resistance, and when forced by the government to move to the interior of France had formed the Maquis?

'Is this where my father lived?' David strode at her side as she walked along the Croisette the following morning, trying to appear nonchalant, a man about town. Now, *now*, she was strong again.

'Yes, on that hillside.'

'Where?' he demanded, unable to suppress his excitement.

'I'm going to show you.'

'Now?'

'Yes.'

'Good.'

What would she find? Would the villa be derelict? Owned by strangers? Did Philippe perhaps own it now? Nell put her hand in her pocket and felt the reassuring iron key.

This was not going to be a sad occasion, she determined, but a happy one. She had David by her side, and

Lucien in her heart. The sun was shining and the villas of La Californie were awakening into their former glory after years of neglect. She greeted them as old friends. The air was perfumed with the smell of flowers from the hillsides of Grasse, mixed with the smell of pines.

'What's that birdcage monstrosity?' David pointed, as they turned a corner of the road.

'It's not a birdcage, you idiot, it's a belvedere. Those are the grounds of the Villa Kasbek where the Grand Duke Michael of Russia lived.'

'He wasn't my father, was he?' asked David with interest.

''Fraid not,' she laughed. 'Were you thinking of taking on Uncle Joe Stalin and making a bid for the Imperial throne?'

'Better than school,' he rejoined.

'I don't see it as much of a life for a doctor.'

He glared at her. 'That's not fair.'

'Perfectly fair.'

'What's that?' he asked, as they got further up the hillside.

'A fountain in memory of Prince Leopold, Queen Victoria's son. He lived at that villa up there. And no, you're not related to Queen Victoria either.'

'I hope he enjoyed the climb,' David announced cheerfully.

'Round here,' Nell said casually, branching off the road, 'is the house where your father lived. I expect his family still own it, but I doubt if anyone lives there, though there's probably a—'

She broke off. How could it look so unchanged? These paths, the trees and cypresses flanking the old gates, seemed not to have altered in fifteen years. Hesitantly, she drew the key from her pocket.

'I don't think they're locked, Ma,' said David, surprised she had not tried the gates first.

Never against you, Come, Nell. Old echoes, old ghosts.

They weren't and David entered eagerly, almost running up the drive.

'Wait,' Nell tried to call. After the chasm of war and the pain of loss, she expected the villa at least to look different. But its shabby pink-washed walls and worn green shutters spoke only of passing time, not of change. Welcoming them in the spring sunshine, surrounded by palms and spring flowers spilling from terracotta pots on the balconies, was a mirage that surely could not be. It must have altered, it *must*.

'Wait,' she called again. Why? Wait for what? There was no one here. Nothing but a bird singing in the orange tree, and a lizard scuttling past on the marble steps that led up to the front door.

But the door opened into the past. Or the present? For surely it was Madame Dufy who stood there, puzzled then slowly recognising her? Nell could not speak as she walked up to the entrance. She tried to frame the words, but none came.

'Madame Nell! Oh, Madame Nell!' A stream of *provençale* French followed.

'David—' Nell turned, but he seemed to have disappeared; then she saw him deep in conversation with Monsieur Dufy. What was Madame saying as she pulled her inside the villa?

'*Monsieur le comte a télephoné déjà?*' was all Nell understood.

'I did not stop in Paris to see the *comte*, madame,' she explained in halting French.

'He is not there. He is here.' Another stream of French.

Here? Philippe? It did not seem right that Philippe should be in this house.

'*Il était malade, très malade.*'

'I'm very sorry. He won't want to see me,' said Nell, beginning to shiver, trying to escape. She did not want to see Philippe. Not here, not in this house of happiness.

Madame Dufy grasped her by the shoulders. '*Mais oui, oui.*' She would not let her go. More French. 'He arrived only last week. *Il était un prisonnier*—'

'*Prisonnier*? Philippe?'

'*Oui*, he also now, but *le comte* . . .'

'But the Comte de la Ferté is dead.' Guy had died of a broken heart, surely? Wasn't that what Philippe had said?

'That was a trick to deceive the Gestapo.'

Nell felt dizzy. Philippe here? His father alive?

She hurried after Madame Dufy who was disappearing through the rear door into the garden of the villa. 'Madame, I will leave,' Nell called, hurrying through on to the shaded terrace. 'I just wanted to see the house once more. Just once, although Comte Lucien is dead. I wanted his son to see it,' she said simply. 'But now we will go.'

'*Mais il est encore en vie*,' Madame Dufy said with tears in her eyes.

'*Oui, madame*, he lives again in his son who is talking with your husband.'

'I see your French has not improved, *ma truffe.*'

That voice. She spun around. Somewhere a bird sang in triumph, somewhere in the house she could hear David, airing schoolboy French to Monsieur Dufy, somewhere Madame Dufy's footsteps could be heard as, duty done, she left to busy herself with the kitchen chores, somewhere a cricket chirped. She was aware of all these things, and none of them. Lying on a bed at one end of the terrace, struggling to sit up, looking at her with the glory of love in his eyes, was a man – a man so dear, so familiar to her, he seemed her own self.

It was Lucien.